Ghalib, Gandhi & the Gita

a book containing essays, short fiction and poetry
by
Vivek Iyer.

olyglot
ublications

Although it may appear that certain persons, Organizations, Agencies, Sects, Governments, Nations, Belief Systems, Schools of Thought, etc. are being signified in this book, to rely upon that appearance would amount to a reckless misprision and mala fide proceeding.

The author's central thesis is that, in so far as Language necessarily functions as a nostalgic reverie for its incompossible Truth, the human condition is ontologically dysphoric such that a beatitude in ignorance obtains, which, impotent to reason, must vituperatively rage against all it might otherwise hold venerable in a manner that can not, *de re*, give offense but must, *de dicto*, evoke a type of contempt which shades indistinguishably into pity, if not the heartfelt prayer that the Lord, of His Mercy, grant some small measure of Illumination to even such a bare, forked and benighted a creature as, in the pages of this book, the writer of these words disovers himself to be .

As for you, Momus- here is a window into a cruddy, middle aged excuse for a heart, now exclusively fed on the Sentimental equivalent of fast food, and consequently so completely clogged up with putrid 'trans(endental) fats' as to now incline the author to set up as a Zoilus amongst critics.

South Indian readers, please note, being a virtuous and patriotic young man, and hearing that Immanuel Kant had written a book titled 'Prolegomenon to all future Metaphysics.' Vivek immediately wrote a letter to Miss Pralajja Menon- who was the State-wide topper in B.Comm in his year and also looked kind of cute in the newspaper photo- offering her his hand in marriage so she wouldn't have to go and become an Escort or Ayah or whatever to all future Metaphysics, but just come and settle down nicely and keep home, I say, and somehow get me through the Accountancy exams.

Due to Keralite women are all terribly prejudiced against Tamil Iyers, she was not even writing back.
That is only reason the author is now drunkenly languishing like a sort of Devdas *manqué* .

Kindly acquaint yourself with pertinent facts of the case before jumping to conclusions and passing judgement on poor unfortunates who have suffered terribly...

All is fault of Cruelty of Caste System and Continuing Injustice & Discrimination against fatties.

Mind it kindly!

A Polyglot paperback
First published in Great Britain by Polyglot Publications
First edition 2012

The right of Vivek Iyer to be identified as the author of this appalling book has been- no doubt, very foolishly- asserted by him in accordance with the Copyright, Designs and Patents Act 1988. To put this matter beyond doubt, peradventure, or infirmity of suspicion, here is a picture of Mr. Iyer, very vehemently, asserting his rights.

Copyright © Vivek Iyer

Polyglot Publications

Isbn number- 978-09550628-3-4

Other books by Vivek Iyer published by Polyglot Publications available from Amazon and readable on Google Books or downloadable as Ebooks.
1) The Mirror's Messiah (poetry)
2) Samlee's daughter (novel)
3) Tigers of Wrath (novella collection)
4) Deus Absconditus (fiction collection)
5) Whiskey's Secret (novel)

I humbly dedicate this book to **Gregg Walsh**
in gratitude for all his help and support.

vahshat kahāñ kih be-khvudī inshā kare ko ī
hastī ko lafz-e ma'nī-e 'anqā kare ko ī
husn-e furogh-e sham'-e sukhan dūr hai asad
pahle dil-e gudākhtah paidā kare ko ī

(Ghalib- 214)

Now lost to Self Loss being the Sahara's rolled gold scrolls of Rhyme
How, as Phoenix, entail Existence to but the Parrot beak of Time?
Asad, Conceptive beauty imparts a Candescence far indeed!
Like wicks, bardic hearts must burn by what they bleed.

Acknowledgments

First and foremost, I would like to pay tribute to the work of Prof. Frances W. Pritchett of Columbia University for rekindling my interest in Ghalib's ghazals and giving me an inkling of the depth and range of scholarly work in this field. Her websites- 'A desertful of Roses' and 'A garden of Kashmir' present a tremendous resource and enable us to get a glimpse of the extraordinary erudition and critical acumen of Prof. Shamsur Rehman Faruqi. Having no pretensions to scholarship- or indeed much claim to literacy- I have drawn extensively on her web-site for quotations, translations and commentaries. In saying this, I am aware, I am in the position of a Caliban who has wandered by error into an exquisite garden and my hope is that my own clownish antics in this field will yield amusement merely rather than provoke the wrath of true aficionados of Urdu poetry.

The Gandhi on-line archive, to which I am also indebted, and the biographical and other scholarly work of the descendants of the Mahatma appears to me to evince the highest integrity and an extraordinary dedication to Truth.

Prof. Richard Dawkins has suggested that Gandhi had a gene for 'super-niceness' and to Scientific minds, perhaps, a genetic explanation will suffice. My own feeling is that it is from a personal commitment and inward struggle that the keepers of the Gandhian flame have risen above the claims of filial piety and continue to insist on freedom of expression with respect to this most venerable of figures.

Among other on-line resources, apart from Wikipedia, I have found the Stanford Encyclopedia of Philosophy to be a model of clarity. I have also made extensive use of various web-sites and free publications made available by various Religious Trusts, Sufi organizations and independent Scholars.

'Man'- as readers of Michel Foucault will know- was invented in the Eighteenth Century and, in consequence, is still running strong because built-in obsolescence only became de rigueur in the second half of the Twentieth Century. However, Foucault's own patented 'Post Modern Man' is currently born dead though still managing to run up sizable Student Loan and Credit Card and Sub-prime mortgage debt.

I acknowledge that I owe this insight into Post Modern Man to the Modern Post Man who delivers my penis-pump every week with a smile on his face and a bounce in his step. I can easily see why. He has a gold plated pension and, since he is getting plenty of outdoor exercise, he will live to spend it while the rest of us keel over from strokes brought on by letters saying not only is your Portfolio not performing, it went and set fire to the Chemistry lab and, far from providing for you in your old age, it now behooves you to sell your one functioning kidney to pay for its delinquencies.

Incidentally, how that business with the penis-pump started was like this. A friend of mine thought it would be hilarious to send me one by recorded delivery. He paid extra to have it dispatched *without* the discreet packaging these things normally come in. Anyway, once I understood the company still had his credit card on file, I immediately returned it on the grounds that it was too small. They are now sending me custom-built penis-pumps of increasingly impressive volume and girth. Does the Modern Post Man complain? No. Not one bit. He does, however, display a restless anxiety to depart if my bathrobe appears about to slip. Foucault, being a Post Modern Man, on the other hand, would have stayed to gawp. There is a lesson here such that (as Gandhiji was wont to say) all who run may read.

'Aristotle's *Peri Hermêneias*, is usually called *'On Interpretation'* or *'Dei Interpretatione'*. I call it *'About Translating'*. *Hermêneias* comes from *Hermês* (the messenger god). In Xenophon's war stories, when a city is conquered, a *hermês* translates between the conquerors and the conquered.'
Prof. Steve Wexler.

'The origin of *theoria*, amongst the ancient Greeks, may plausibly be traced to the delegations scattered communities sent to witness the religious festivals of their more or less distant neighbours and the spirited discussions that arose, upon their return, as to the meaning of what they had witnessed and the light it threw upon their own hoary observances. It was from these simple origins that, like Athena in full armour from the brain of Zeus, the Panhellenic ethos sprang forth as the unsightly & highly fucking annoying availability cascade of mindlessly putting up statues of naked dudes all over the place like *that* was the solution to every problem. The pederasts, lurking in the vicinity of these statues, naturally got round to devising methods to objectively compare dick sizes, thus inventing not just Geometry and Pythagoras but, because everybody's true erection turns out to occupy infinite space in an unseen dimension, Parmenides, Plato and so on. Hermeneutics, however, was about war and colonization and acquiring slaves. The great service of *theoria* to hermeneutics is that it first infantilizes a conquered people before licensing local pedants to like stop hanging round the playground already and go fuck *them* guys in the ass.'
Kulapati A.K.47 Munshi.

'In the battle of the books, the internecine quarrel between the ancients and moderns, the one verity whose victory abides is that, as the dwarfish John of Salisbury divinely said, if the midget sees farther 'tis from standing upon a giant's shoulders- but facing the other way and so vigorously pissing in the latter's Cyclopean eye that though a Kant is but the wreck of a Rawls and Plato the merest dregs of a Popper, a drunken Hermeneutic yet ever offer its votaries what disciplined Philosophy wont- *videlicet* a lifted horizon.'
Rev. Patti Obaweyo Golem

'Truth is neither Nietzsche's 'mobile host of metaphors' nor, the chastened & immutable meta-metaphoricity of Gandhi's Resistance to a cowardly bolt on the part of that blackguardly & Rhodesian horde, but, rather, their votaries' mutual chagrin at only tasting each other's spit on Satan's shit-tipped cock.'
Swami Zizekananda.

'In the political theatre of Satyagraha, as in the plays of Chekhov- there are no small parts. Just enormous assholes.'
Anna Nicole Smith Hazare

Contents

Gandhi, Ghalib & the Gita

What have these 3 in common?

Delhi.

Gandhi was killed in Delhi, Ghalib suffered torments in Delhi, and Delhi owes its foundation and first elevation to the status of Imperial Capital to Arjuna's salutary reception of the sublime Gita, but for which he wouldn't have got busy killing off his cousins and his Great Uncle and his Guru and ultimately even his eldest brother, that last exultingly and while in the grip of *manyu* (dark fury).

So what?

I don't live in Delhi anymore. You perhaps never did.

Dilli door ast- Delhi is far away.

Or is it? Sahir Ludhianvi said we who claim to be the worshippers of Ghalib and Gandhi are, verily, their assassins. So there's that. And Gandhi said his translation of the Gita was better than anybody else's- because, though he didn't actually know the language in which it was written, nor had it inspired him in any particular, yet, he alone had **lived** it for well nigh forty years.

Thus, in a sense, if we really have managed to kill Ghalib and Gandhi, as Sahir assures us we have, perhaps we've also inflicted a wound, more or less mortal, on the Gita, since Gandhi told us he alone was truly living it and Gandhi, we know, was an honest man.

In this sense, Delhi isn't far away at all, but, rather, the heart's squalidly intimate *chawl* or *basti* and to the extent that the fabrication of an 'Indian' identity instrumentalizes Gandhi, Ghalib and the Gita for a purpose legitimating and hegemonic rather than coercive, cohesive or genuinely to establish dominance, we are all, albeit unwittingly, involved in a *Dilli chalo* insurgency which can only end with our echoing the words of Dagh- *'Javaab kahe ko ta, lajavaab thi Dilli/ Jo aankh kol ke dekha to khvab ti Dilli.'*.

Ask what it was and it was all we could ask- it seemed

Till, eyes opening, we saw- Delhi we had but dreamed.

Of course, you may object, Sahir- whose oneiric hegira, in 1949, from the new country of Pakistan to a yet newer New Delhi, or say rather its blue-print, only served to precipitate him, with hilarious irony, into *filmi* Bombay's pulchritudinous lap- was just employing a metaphor. We haven't really killed anybody and should cancel that appointment for tear drop tattoos. But- if you'll kindly hold off on making that phone call for half a mo'- here's a thought- Sahir said he was a worshipper of Ghalib and Prof. S.R. Faruqi tells us that Ghalib's *ma'ni afrini* (meaning creation) was based on taking metaphors for facts and deriving other metaphors from them, often by purely verbal conceits, such that ultimately 'the Metaphor outweighed the Reality for which it stood'. This is the opposite of Bergsonian, or *barzakh* based, metaphoricity as critiquing the brute nature of concepts & privileging *Process* over Presence or Parousia.

Such 'meta-metaphoricity' is also the hallmark of Gandhi's thinking. True Manliness is non-violence. But non-violence in the face of a stronger foe- or one weaker but able to inflict some measure of pain- might in fact be cowardice and thus not True Manliness at all. Thus, to agree to Lord Reading's granting full provincial autonomy before the Viceroy himself had renounced the threat of force was to risk having been surreptitiously emasculated and thus rendered something less than a true man. Hence Reading's overture must be rejected by all True Men because maybe Lord Reading has stolen one or both of our testicles and replaced it with a pigeon's egg or something equally non vegan.

The conventional view is that Gandhi's reasoning was an 'epiphenomenon' merely and had no intrinsic meaning; he was guided entirely by instinct and a sort of somnambulistic rapport with the awakening masses- but guided to an end dictated by his paymasters, the Indian Capitalists, who needed British technical assistance and corrupt oligarchic praxis more even than Protective tariffs and thus were content to put off Provincial Autonomy for 15 years, by which time the Mody-Lees agreement- essentially sacrificing the consumer and the cotton farmer to the greed of a handful of oligarchic plutocrats- was in place.

Among those to make this point, it is noteworthy, was the first Parsi to become a Communist, Shapurji Saklatvala, later the M.P for 'Red' Battersea- a relative of Sir Dorabji Tata, whom that magnanimous magnate had squeezed out of the family business. Similarly, the first Parsi to become a Trade Union leader was an engineer with an American degree who found that the White employees at the Tata plant were paid a lot more and permitted to treat the Indians workers like shit. Since, Gandhi had lost his luster by then, especially with the educated Bengalis, the Tatas brought in Subhas Chandra Bose to break the strike by persuading him of their own 'Nationalist' credentials. As a quid pro quo, Saklatvala and that Parsi Trade Union leader were- of course- airbrushed from History.

In this context, Sir Ratan Tata's munificent donation to Gandhi in South Africa, in 1909, acquires strategic significance. It was this sudden access of funds which enabled Gandhi to gain a second lease of life as a 'leader' despite his disasterous claim, the previous year, that the new 'Pass Law'- i.e. the Asiatic Registration Act- and the '3 Pound head tax' and so on were actually very good and delightful things which all right thinking Indians would naturally clamour to subscribe to.

Gandhi used the analogy of the restriction on the sale of alcohol to African laborers. As the Zulu elders would later themselves affirm to the authorities, young Black workers mustn't be allowed to drink because drinking leads to thinking. Split a keg of beer amongst a group of young working people and they naturally get round to reading newspapers, discussing politics, setting up Educational, Trade and Political Associations, with the horrendous consequence that they don't send their whole pay packet back home to daddy dearest so he can buy himself yet another teenage bride to warm his chilblained carcass.

Clearly, beer is very very bad. Look at the Welsh miners and their support for that Lloyd George fellow! If workers have a beer and one of them reads out from the newspaper and another says- 'you know, the bosses really should stop these cavity searches on the pretext of cracking down on the theft of coal- it's painful and humiliating and serves no good purpose!'- well, I mean to say, that way lies Anarchy! Cavity searches for coal miners- even if it is isn't really true that diamonds are discovered by the process- are absolutely essential for a Civilized Democracy to function because otherwise them miners get uppity and vote for Lloyd George and clamor for things like Old Age Pensions and Unemployment Insurance and other such Godlessness which totally undermines Liberty and Fraternity and *True* Equality and turns Society into a sort of ant-farm and and and..urm.. is like totally *Satanic*, y'know?

Gandhi's greatness was to see that Jan Smuts was trying to **help** the Indians by getting them to give their finger prints or toe prints or rectal cavity imprints or anything else that it occurred to him to demand. True, it took Gandhi all of two or three weeks in prison to see the light, but his was a Damascene conversion. True Manliness lay in generously agreeing to everything because sulking in a Jail cell is just plain silly. Unfortunately, on his release from prison, Gandhi received a terrible beating from some Pathan foolish enough to believe Gandhi had shown True Manliness in prison- in which case the only reason he was out, free as the air, was because Smuts had paid him 15,000 pounds as a bribe. Now, if Gandhi had offered the Pathan some money- not a lot of money, the guy wasn't a barrister- while uttering veiled and silken threats then, of course, there was no need for violence. *That's* how truly manly men arrange things between themselves and thank you God for making me a big sissy. But, Gandhi hadn't actually been bribed. Still, the beating and its repeated threat did permit one new fact, vital to the practice of Satyagraha, to dawn on Gandhi. Actually, a spell in prison isn't so bad if your continual harping on your own true manliness and virtue- in contrast to everybody else's fallen status as eunuch prostitiutes- has painted you into a corner and there are people outside will give you your head to play with if they spot you up and about your usual walk of mischief. It's like what happens when you go into a pub and tell everybody there they don't got no balls and how you are like a highly trained Commando and they'd better go home and tool up before taking you on and suddenly the bar-maid is calling last orders and you realize that if you go outside you are going to get the shit kicked out of you so you make a grab for her titties and she slaps you down and you just make another grab for her titties till the cops are called and, coz it looks like they are going to let you off with a warning, you make a grab for *their* titties till they hand-cuff you and, then, as you are being dragged off to the police van, you suddenly get all tough and shout Semper Fi! or Attica! or something and, guess what, it suddenly dawns on you- you do too have True Manliness, the rest of them guys got no cojones. I mean, they aint spending the night in the lock up- no, they were too chicken. You and you alone are in the frame. And for what? It's not like you did anything wrong. You're a martyr is what you are. Stand tall, bruv! You is like Mandela Gandhi innit?

As for this business of giving your finger-prints, think about it for a sec., Smuts was **right**- fact is all dem darkies do look so goddam alike besides having just the same half dozen surnames between them. Suppose yourself Indian. How would you know which Indian you were if the Government hadn't taken your finger-prints and toe-prints and rectal cavity imprints? For all you know, you, not I, might be the author of this foul screed! Indeed, Gandhi's only complaint against Smuts was that by making these things compulsory, an insult was being offered to the Indians- like dem darkies be too stupid to see what a privilege, rather than obligation, such impositions actually are- especially now the thing has been made plain to them by their Gita-incarnating, God appointed, leader- M.K Gandhi bar-at-law.

Knowledge is merely something one earns a living by. Understanding is metaphorical. And thus Meta-Metaphoricity, not Knowledge, is the instrument to rule men's Understandings.

If Smuts first mistake was to try to force an obnoxious measure upon the Indians when they could be made to understand that the measure wasn't obnoxious at all but helpful and salutary, his second error was to declare Indian marriages- except between Christians- as no sacrament but concubinage under another name. Once again, he should have left Gandhi to proclaim this new Gospel because Gandhi had gone one step further. No Indians should marry *at all*. All marriage is concubinage. Don't do it. Just say no. As for sex- that sort of thing could lead to concubinage. But concubinage is a sort of marriage. Thus sex is as bad, nay worse!, than marriage.

Ask yourself- what would J.C do?

Just say no, already.

What are you *Meshugganah?*

As for the Jews- don't get me started, okay? I mean, first they don't get how Alexander and Augustus **are too** totally worthy of worship but, instead, mutter mutinously into their beards & go getting their phylacteries all in a twist and then just out-right rebel!- which is against Pax Romana and the Stoic conception of ataraxia- and didn't Jesus forbid '*antithistemi*' as in 'resist not evil'?- yet even after its Centurions crucified Him and Rome announced its Millenial monopoly on the blood and flesh of its new Man-God, the Jews still don't bend the knee or kiss the ring even though, like the Emperor Heliogabablus, this Man-God was a Semite like themselves!

Gandhi, of course, uttering his Gospel of Hind Swaraj, proves himself more truly manly than even that Man-God, because he devises upon his people, even to the farthest shore of their diaspora, a Cross more militant in malice and Crown, the thornier if laurels.

As for the Muslims, well, their Religion looks manly so if they are getting heated about something called Khilafat well, Gandhi has a duty to place himself at their head because he alone has True Manliness.

Among the Hindus, the 'Kshatriya' warrior class looks kind of manly. So, it follows they don't understand their key text- the Gita- because only Gandhi is Truly Manly and he hasn't yet got round to explaining it to them yet.

Strangely, Gandhi is genuinely important when it comes to the Gita.

Why? Well, Swami Vivekananda and the Jugantar revolutionaries had decided that the real meaning of the Gita was- 'Be a man! Sack up! (*Pssst*- kill Whitey)'- while everybody esle thought it meant- do your Casteist duty unless you prefer to be a beggar or a thief or a pimp or a murderer or anything you like in which case, if you get hold some money and aren't hanged for it, gimme a coupla bucks and I'll lie about your birth or get some priest to declare you high caste, or a God, or a mermaid or whatever so get busy already.

Compared to this, Gita as teaching absolute non-violence aint so bad.

Of course, Gandhian Ahimsa was pretty twisted- I recall reading something in Kathryn Tidrick to the effect that Gandhi, avatar of true manliness that he was, considered the highest ahimsa to involve killing your own daughter to save her from rape provided, of course, you then joyously offered your own back-side for a punitive belabouring by the indignant...whoops, it wasn't a rapist at all, just the Post Man. Still maybe the Police could give you a jolly good rogering on the way to prison. Anyway, at least your daughter is now dead and like maybe young men will start noticing your derriere for a change.

Still, even this sort of shite is better than most modern interpretations of the Gita and so, uniquely, Gandhi was in a position to actually do something good for a change.

Whether he succeeded, I think, is still an open question. For the moment, let me introduce the passage in the Gita crucial to an understanding of its meta-metaphoricity

yajnarthat karano 'nyatra
loko 'yam karma-bandhanah
tad-artham karma kaunteya
mukta-sangah samacara

Work done as a Ritualistic Sacrifice has to be performed, otherwise work causes bondage in this material world. Therefore, O son of Kunti, perform your prescribed duties for God's satisfaction, and in that way you will always remain free from bondage.

The Gita teaches that the *karma kanda* of *Yagnya*- i.e. the ritualistic portion of the Vedic Sacrifice- is merely a metaphor for the true, pietistic, Sacrifice of surrendering oneself utterly to the Lord by giving up all worldly desire.

However, notice, *karma kanda* is itself based on metaphors rather than positive truths or metaphysical dogmas. Unlike the Sacrifice of the Mass in Christianity, where wine and bread are mysteriously transubstantiated into the blood and flesh of Lord Jesus Christ, the Vedic Yagnya is invocatory and says, not 'this has been transformed into that', but 'this now is viewable *as* that'. Metaphors remain metaphors. What has changed is perceptions, attitudes and intentionalities, nothing material has changed nor has any transmutation, of what philosophers call Substance, actually occurred. This is important in another connection. The Social Psychologist, J.G. Miller, found that Indian Hindus were more context specific and trait-abstraction averse than Americans in describing the behaviour of others. This suggests that the Rational Choice hermeneutic for Hindu Indians is non Schutzian ideal type. If, as seems obvious, Hindu India has had fewer relevant evolutionary choke points then there is going to be less genotypic canalization at the level of 'memes'. Alternatively, being judgemental might be less rewarding. The important point to note is that, if trait-inherence metonymy is being guarded against, semiotic slippage towards meta-metaphoricity is less likely.

There is another crucial point which must immediately be made about the translation of 'karma kanda' as 'work'. By Mimamsa (Vedic hermeneutic) karma kanda must be something wholly gratuitious, free of any common sense explanation, utilitarian value or consequentialist consideration- even sociological (as in Mauss's theory of Yagnya as a potlatch. If it is used to redistribute goods, it is no longer a Yagnya, save to save the face of the needy, and we are free to change the acts which compose its 'karma kanda') or ideological (if its purpose is to legitimate Caste or Wealth based authority, we can change it because it is no longer truly 'karma kanda') or Utilitarian (if a yagnya is for the purpose of producing rain, we can tinker with the formulae till we get a result- the 'karma kanda' is shown not to be Shruti by reason of having a visible, consequentialist, end) or 'gesture political'(if the purpose of the Yagnya is to restore Caste status or 'purity' or something of that sort, by all means, change and amend what you like. The 'karma kanda' aspect no longer has 'aparusheya' (immutable or uncreated) status.

All this is Brahminism 101.

Everybody knows this but pretends they don't so as to write shite books.

Adopting a yet cruder, even more brutally common-sense, *mimamsa* or viewpoint, everyone can see that if one wishes to vanquish one's enemies, the way to do it is by hitting them on the head with a club or shooting arrows into their bodies or slicing chunks off them. Chanting stuff and pouring butter into a fire don't really cut it.

However, spending a lot of money on a Vedic ritual where you have priests droning on about how some guy in the sky- who has a thunder-bolt for a weapon- is like gonna be totally on side when it comes to vanquishing your enemies *does* send a powerful signal to potential adversaries or even actual ill-wishers. Clearly, a guy who literally has money to burn is not one to be trifled with. Fuck with him and he'll quit spending money on priests and hire him some deadly Ninja assassins or- if that's simpler- bribe your Mom to poison your porridge.

The same thing goes for Vedic rituals for getting wealth, offspring, marital bliss and so on. Essentially advertising you have money to burn is great for your Credit rating and highly attractive to fecund women who, why not?, are likely to make you happy because they can have babies- always nice to have around provided you have money- and, what's more, their mothers have an incentive to pretend the kids are yours.

Apart from showing you have money to burn, the Vedic sacrifice- essentially a big barbecue- also indicates you have a certain amount of self-discipline and social poise, can get smart people to work for you and, at a pinch, can muster up a respectable number of guests on your big day- so, at the very least, you aren't a social leper.

In other words, the Vedic Sacrifice is a 'costly signal'

True, there were some fuckwits who convinced themselves this sort of shit was also good for doing impossible things like ascending bodily into Heaven or getting a blow job from a Mermaid or whatever. However, the important point to note is that *karma kanda*- as opposed to Black Magicians and 'Quantum Conscious' Yogi-bogey Babas and Charlatan Alchemists and so on- didn't claim to change anything on the ground except at the level of metaphorical understanding. A King who conducts an Ashvamedha ritual hasn't actually conquered all other Kings but may still be called an Emperor because people understand that his status is superior to his nearest rivals. Chances are, if anyone fucks with him it's *them guys* get seriously fucked.

Thus, *metaphorically*, the dude is now an Alexander or Ashoka or whatever. This is quite different from the Christian notion that a King consecrated by a Bishop has Divine authority so long as the Arch-Bishop says so. Why? It's because in Hinduism, or Jainism, or Buddhism, no magical transubstantiations occur or, if the possibility is admitted, nothing political or practical derives from that contingency.

The fact is, everybody knows there were, are, and always will be guys who will chant any shit and perform any absurd ritual if you pay them enough or, at least, quit beating them or give them a bottle or syringe or piece of tail or something else they very badly want.

Given that the *karma kanda* of the Vedic sacrifice- if considered as a ritualism rather than a psycho-social, metabletic, work of art- has this ordinary meaning, Lord Krishna's dismissal of it is entirely salutary. However, stuff he appears to approve of- like being a Samkhya Sophist, or bed-of-nails Yogi or forest dwelling Muni- as well as stuff he specifically commends, like never chowing down on a burger just coz you are hungry or coz *sheeeet* it smells **good** but only doing so coz God commands you to praise and exalt His Holy Name by eating the thing or having a bowel motion after eating the thing- Krishna can't be propounding such notions because they are ***already part of revelation***. But, by Vedic Mimamsa, anything already known before Lord Krishna begins to speak in the Gita **can't** be His meaning because there is no **apoorvata**, no novelty, no radical departure from conventional wisdom or *ad captum vulgi* understanding, in what He is saying.

It's just 'cheap talk' is all.

Does this mean that Lord Krishna's real message in the Gita is that though ritualism is a fraud and self-delusion, it is merely a metaphor for the *true* fraud and self-delusion of Samkhya and Yoga and Devotional Theism and endless pi-jaw about being good and pure and virtuous and so on?

Yes, if nothing else is going on in the Gita.

Let us suppose there is a scene in a novel or a play where the hero consults a doctor who says 'you are suffering from x. The cure is y'. If this were not already widely known then the purpose of the scene, its meaning, would be 'the cure for x is y'.

Suppose there is a scene in 'Sex & the City' where a Doctor says to Carrie- 'The reason you are experiencing discomfort is because you have a large Apartment building in your twat. The cure for having a large Apartment building in your twat is to not permit Manhattan property developers, especially those named Mr. Big, access to your genitalia.' In this case, clearly, the real meaning of the scene has nothing to do with a widely known Medical fact. Rather, it provides a cue for some highly insightful comments by voice-over Carrie linking the Sub-prime catastrophe to the Media led, Affirmative Action, proliferation of anal G spots for middle aged heterosexual males gripped by prostate cancer panic.

Similarly, in the Gita, something else is going on when Lord Krishna says certain actions- like shooting arrows at your Guru here and now upon this Holy Ground of Kurukshetra- are entirely ritualistic in nature and omitting them doesn't change anything on the ground but, for that very reason, are nonetheless bad form, bad faith and, in that sense, bad karma kanda.

But, what precisely is that something else which is going on in the Gita?

Krishna tells us to cut down two trees- the upside down one of the Vedas as well as the World's right side up tree. As I will explain later on, He metaphorically fells himself by his own 'Visvarupa'- itself serving the purpose of cutting down the tree of Karma- but, notice, this 'costly signal' only arises because he appears in the Gita as an Agent not a Principal.

One result is that Vedic *karma kanda* gets a new lease of life- indeed it is greatly ennobled and preserves the ethos of its upholders. Another is that the 'common sense' view- Religion as fraud and pi-jaw malfeasance- is forced to bite down on the stone pillow of its occluded Concurrency problem whereby it works itself out as a Dijkstra deadlock for constructive Social Choice and remains adaptive only for that reason.

To see why- consider the following question.

Under what circumstances would meta-metaphoricity be a permissible basis for decision making?

Well, if you are your own master, you may chose to take a metaphor for a fact and act on that basis. Suppose I am offered £10 for *not* publishing this revolting book. By accepting, I, in fact, experience an increase in my Net Worth which is almost infinite in percentage terms. If I were not my own Master- if, for example, I were financially bankrupt, mentally incompetent or happily married- I would be obliged to accept the £10. Being my own master, however, I am entitled to say- 'My books are the uttermost public nuisance it is within my power to cause and thus my one true and abiding wealth. I would feel myself immeasurably impoverished and, verily, as one of the wretched of the earth if I did not indulge my vanity and malice to the hilt by sending this foul screed off to the printers.'

Here, though meta-metaphoricity has had a bad result- viz. the publication of this worthless book- the principle behind it can not be impugned, because we can easily imagine some circumstance where a Social good not otherwise available becomes so for the stated reason.

Furthermore, in a Concurrency deadlock- endless buffering, envenomed ambiguity- meta-metaphoric thinking can un-freeze things, create novelty and rescue Society from stasis.

Ghalib and Gandhi as Principals not Agents

Both Ghalib, in his Urdu Ghazals, and Gandhi, in his dealings with the Government of India, were, by their wilful meta-metaphoricity, their own Masters. They were Principals, not Agents.

Thus to say of Ghalib that it is the deliberate ugliness and unintelligibility of his own poetastering that jaundices his view of his fellow Indians - the speck in his eye, in this instance really being, as he says, a vast Sahara because the 'dastanbu' posey of his Persian style cultivated *pensées* as self-pollinating pansies of arid and arrant nonsense- this criticism can be easily countered by pointing out that Ghalib was not the Agent of a Muse but the Principal of a Momus, he did not serve Literature anymore than he served Drinking or Gambling or Sycophancy or Savouring Mangoes. If his poems are shite, it is because poetry- by and large- *is* shite. It is only in the divinely inspired Saints that we expect to find beauty. Everywhere else, unless one has a weakness for Hallmark cards- philosophy- always hilarious in context- is the most we can hope for.

Similarly, Gandhi made it clear that he held his own conception of God and the code of Ahimsa far dearer than any merely political objective- such as attaining Self Government. Thus, though he did not deliver 'Swaraj' on the time-table he had promised, since he was not the Agent of the politically conscious class but a Principal in his own right, he had nothing to reproach himself with.

Gita as Agent

In contrast, the Gita is wholly concerned with not Masters but Servants, not Principals but their Agents. God himself has bound himself to the duty of a charioteer. Arjuna's *'svadharma'*, his authentic nature, is that of an affectionate younger brother eager to carry out the will of the man he thinks his eldest sibling. Krishna, his closest friend, knows this and helps him to fulfil his fondest wish in a manner which makes the Gita itself an Agent not a Principal- in other words, it is wholly subordinated to the broader narrative drive, within the Mahabharata, regarding the education in Game theory of the Just King.

But to properly teach something is also to show its limitations, aporias and likely misprisions as availability cascades. The purely poetic, as opposed to dramatic, greatness of the Gita arises from its being constrained to this task and fulfilling it with tragic scrupulousness. Thus the meta-metaphoricity of the Gita, far from eclipsing the Reality to which it points, displays instead, with infinite virtuosity, nothing but its own tragic virtuality.

That is why the Gita is great poetry. But great poetry has to be read holistically, with reference to its own decision tree, rather than according to a principle of compositionality. There is an inferior type of didactic doggerel which yields Kantian maxims to guide behaviour and govern the passions. Things like, *'Neither a borrower nor a lender be/ a self-sucked cock is sucked for free',* can be mutilated and quoted out of context as, indeed, foolish Polonius does in Hamlet.

This brings me to the most important feature that Gandhi, Ghalib and the Geeta share in common. Intelligent people become really really stupid when faced with them.

Why?

Smart people feel they are smart because the World makes sense to them, they are at home in it and require no further horizon. Non-smart people, on the other hand, experience ontological dysphoria- it's like being a man in a woman's body, except you are in the wrong Universe and though the wind blows as it lists and for a moment the weed may feel it can be translated back to its natal flower bed as seed, yet this is as a but brief laving or purification. The ontologically dysphoric non-smart may live in Love as fish in water yet identify with the shore stranded Sankara for whom salvation can only come from that crocodile able to drag him down to his own true depths.

पवनः पवताम् अस्मि रामः शस्त्रभृताम् अहम् ।
झषाणां मकरश् चास्मि स्रोतसाम् अस्मि जाह्नवी ॥३१॥

pavanaḥ pavatām asmi   rāmaḥ śastrabhṛtām aham
jhaṣāṇāṁ makaraś cāsmi   srotasām asmi jāhnavī

I am the wind among the purifiers, and Lord Rāma among the warriors. I am the crocodile among the fishes, and the Gaṅgā among the rivers. (10.31)

Ghalib, Gandhi & the Gita, for smart-smart people, are like that King who gained the boon that whoever faced him in battle lost half his strength to him. In other words, this warrior was always guaranteed to be more powerful than the one who faced him. I suppose the same is true of the jiu jitsu master who becomes more lethal in proportion to how much heavier, more powerful and aggressive his adversary is.

Valmiki tells us of the vanquishing of this King- Vali of the Vanars. Rama does not confront him head on, but slays him from behind a tree. This is a grave violation of the warrior's code. When the dying Vanar berates Rama, the latter appears to have lost half his moral strength to his adversary because "*he winds up his reasons for killing Vali by coolly saying: 'Besides you are only a monkey, you know, after all, and as such I have every right to kill you how, when, and where I like.' '*"

It seems intelligent people- Professors and Chief Justices and the like- consider Poetry fair game and, at least, with respect to India's more humbly born bards- that is the merely Hindu- more than perennial Open Season, there is an actual State subsidized bounty on their pelts.

Rama has a perfectly good defense, but doesn't make it- 'You are an elder brother who has mistreated his younger brother thus setting a precedent. I too am an elder brother and what rankles most in my mind is that my own co-Mother was swayed by the canard that elder brothers believe themselves entitled to bully and oppress their younger siblings. Furthermore, you have taken another man's wife and thus acted like the ogre who took my wife. I have slain you the only way you could be slain. To be frank, a duel is no duel if only one party wears armor. It is an elementary principle of our Warrior training, that in a combat with heterogeneous weapons, each party is obliged to apply forethought and exercise vigilance against the adversaries 'counter measures'.

'My dear Vali, you have claimed exemption from the incest-prohibition rule by saying you are merely an animal. Moreover, you say you have neither a valuable pelt nor is your flesh savory. It is quite true that hunters see no profit in killing animals of this description, just as Judges entertain no law suits against beasts for things like alimony, child support, or behaving like Tiger Woods.

'There is a reason we warriors scorn to attack an enemy other than head on. This is because the base and envious consider the fact that a man received an arrow in his back to be proof that he had turned tail and fled the battle-field. Amongst the Tamil people, there is a story of an aged woman who received news that her son had been slain in this manner. She went to the battlefield and searched amongst the piled corpses for her son. When she saw that his injury had been received in the chest, not the back, she set up such a cry, not of lamentation but rejoicing, that milk spurted from her wrinkled dugs and the Gods in Heaven showered down rose petals.

'Examine yourself, Vali. Though I shot from the side, the arrow has entered your chest as if shot by one whom you confronted head on. '

In this context, I found this anonymous comment on the Internet- *'One may say that arrow of the Lord, that is Illumination, is like the ray of that other, the black, Sun whose dark light shines on the back of all things and, the meaning is, it gets its power even from the strength of **tamsic**, dark, inertial, properties of our heart. Considered in this way, we see also Valmiki is not attacking from in front but using our own **tama**s and nescience to get power for our personal Illumination.'*

As a Saivite, by birth, I naturally associate the Rama-Valin episode with Pasupati- the Lord of the Bound- but hesitate to develop this theme for fear of giving offence to Vaishnavites. Indeed, if at any time I appear to be engaging in sectarian polemics, do please let me know or, in any case, immediately attribute this oversight of mine merely to my own diligent cultivation of stupidity and irremediable offensiveness rather than some defect inherent in a Teaching of which I am utterly, albeit fondly, ignorant and unaware.

The Ramayana, a Vaishnavite text, is of course, everybody's favorite whipping boy because Bhagwan Valmiki is considered 'lowly' according to some modern caste system which, myself a stupid, Saivite, Hindu, I don't personally understand.

With Ghalib- generally considered a proper Aristo- though there are good books about him, every volume of translation into English of his ghazals creates the impression that he was a witless, worthless, cry-baby who never espoused an original theme and who remained entirely ignorant of that branch of Islamic philosophy which gives meta-metaphoricity a locus- viz *Barzakh*- and soteriological purpose- viz *Tajaali* or theophany.

To add insult to injury, simple minded people, like former Chief Justice Katju, say things like
'Eemaan mujhe roke hai, kheeche hai mujhe kufra
Kaaba mere peeche hai, kalisa mere aage'
'i.e.- 'Faith is stopping me, while atheism is pulling me forward. Kaaba is behind me, the Church is in front.' Here the word 'Kaleesa' only ostensibly means 'Church', but its real meaning is modern civilization. Thus Ghalib, like many Urdu writers, is opposed to feudal civilization and commends modernism.'

Fatwa time, anybody?

In the case of Gandhi, who is considered a 'barristocrat', the books Professors write about him make the opposite mistake and ascribe to him a philosophical prowess which, to do him justice, he neither claimed nor coveted. This is because they ignore the essential meta-metaphoricity of his thinking and its supervenience on, not states of the world, but moments subtracted from states of the world- i.e. occulted or sublated intentionalities. This, together with his compulsion to run around like a headless chicken decrying the lack of True Manliness of every single human being on the planet, meant he was always before hand in 'interessement'- that is sticking his oar in- with respect to any supposedly 'manly' activity. Take the Chauri Chaura incident. A bunch of 'volunteers'- who had paid a tiny fee and filled out a form as part of a Ponzi scheme to gain a pension from what would soon be the new 'Swaraj' Raj- created mayhem under the pretext of demanding a fair price for meat and then burned and roasted a bunch of policemen to death- though, inexplicably, failing to eat them. Gandhi, of course, both claimed credit for it (he told Mahadev Desai that Chauri Chaura had brought Swaraj miles nearer) and repudiated it by going on a fast- like he didn't think fasting was good for his health and the secret of Prophet Muhammad's power and also, let's face it, if he didn't display contrition the British might just send him off to the Andamans on a one way ticket and the aborigines of those islands mightn't take kindly to being incessantly told they lacked true manliness so fuck else Gandhi was supposed to do? Since the British took the opportunity to boost their own revenues and beat their own manly chests by staging a ferocious crack down, suddenly every other 'volunteer' who had paid his dues under the Congress Ponzi scheme was in danger. If Gandhi *hadn't* turned tail, he wouldn't have been its leader because it was never anything but a Ponzi scheme. These 'volunteers' didn't really want to risk their lives. They could have done that anyway without putting their names down anywhere or paying a fee for the privilege. They were like 'cyber-squatters' who spend a little money to buy a domain name, not with the intention of developing it, but so as to get a pay-off in the future. In practise, no doubt, this was a good investment, a succesful piece of speculation, for some of them. Gandhi continued as the undisputed leader of an army of free riders who pretended to abhor violence, so as to shirk military service, but who very emphatically did want to draw a Freedom Fighter's pension once victory had been achieved. Prison was a different story. Under the British, thanks to the ban on the slitting of noses, and the relative paucity of anal rape, it acquired definite attractions and conferred a certain prestige. Under Gandhi, it became a ticket to upward mobility more secure than a Credentialist Higher Education system not yet completely worthless. Indeed, once this had become evident, Gandhi changed his tune and said- oh well you know I could have got you guys Swaraj like I promised but you see Chauri Chaura happened and that showed India wasn't ready, indeed it never will be, till it is, so just pile up some more pension credits and wait it out for Swaraj.

This aspect of Gandhian 'interessement' has great utility for Historicist narratives because it solves a Concurrency problem which only arises because the Truth is too obvious. So if, as (the historian, not the restauranteur) Shahid Amin has discovered, Chauri Chaura remains vivid as a metaphor- rather than as vacuous as a cataphor- this was only true because our truly manly Mahatma's meta-metaphoricity meant non-existent shades of scruple and nuances of tactics could be attributed to what Actor-Network theory terms Gandhian 'translation'.

In less open and shut cases- for example the Moplah uprising- or more generally, if you're trying to model Gandhian saltation as deriving from underlying deadlock or live-lock & if Symmetry breaking is required to avoid state space explosion under Bellman's equation- it may be that such an approach has some merit which, however, I can't personally see.

In any case, by itself, this meta-meatphoric feature of Gandhi's thinking, together with his 'true manliness' obsession, explains why he was a natural- or Schelling focal point- leader. Firstly, he was unpredictable- so having him as a leader guarantees that there is going to be a stochastic element in your strategy- i.e. it is 'mixed'- so it can't be dominated in a simple way. Secondly, he has the capacity to make decisions- quite radical ones- quickly. Third, his bizarre thought processes looked like a solution to the Kavka's toxin problem of negotiation with the British.

An eccentric billionaire places before you a vial of toxin that, if you drink it, will make you painfully ill for a day, but will not threaten your life or have any lasting effects. The billionaire will pay you one million dollars tomorrow morning if, at midnight tonight, you **intend** *to drink the toxin tomorrow afternoon. He emphasizes that you need not drink the toxin to receive the money; in fact, the money will already be in your bank account hours before the time for drinking it arrives, if you succeed. All you have to do is* **intend***, at midnight tonight, to drink the stuff tomorrow afternoon. You are perfectly free to change your mind after receiving the money and not drink the toxin.*[1]

Essentially, for an agreement to be reached and prove binding both sides need to feel that the other intends to fulfill the agreement. If intentions are governed solely by one's selfish interest, this cashes out as both sides being sure the other gains more than it loses by sticking to the contract. Thus, the British could negotiate with the Indians, if the Indians showed that they all really wanted something which the Brits could give them. But, any negotiator with the British stood to lose influence within his own constituency- and thus his claim to post-Swaraj power- because he would be denounced as a 'sell-out' by the Die Hard element. This drama was being played out in Ireland at precisely this time. Thus, negotiating with the British meant being prepared to drink poison for the greater good.

If the Indians have leaders of this sort, the Brits can make a good faith agreement and have confidence the Indians will stick to it- like their deal with Jan Smuts- because it is manifestly in their interest. But, Smuts could only make a deal because he and his people had already fought to the uttermost extent of their power and had been given a taste of the sheer, systematic, ruthlessness (Concentration Camps, yet!) the British were prepared to use to secure their commercial interests. Moreover, Smut's Die Hard opponents could not rebel against him because if he took the field against them, his superior courage and tactics would make the result a foregone conclusion. The Indians however had not yet exerted their full power against the British- indeed, it was a puzzle as to how they could do this without destroying their own social cohesion in the process.

Furthermore, for some mysterious reason I don't understand, the Indians did not even try to agree on what they genuinely wanted but agreed to pretend to want things they didn't really want at all- why would Shias or Hindus or even Barelvi Sunni Muslims, at a later stage, want to support 'Khilafat'- the establishment of an Islamic Caliphate of a different theological stripe?

Since the Indians knew this full well, Gandhi could appear to them to be saying 'Yo, Mr. British Man. Me, Holy Mahatma dude. I happen to genuinely believe that this poison of intending to keep faith with you turns into elixir at precisely midnight. Though all other Indians know no such magic exists, I can nevertheless get them to clamor bitterly for the right to drink that poison from midnight onwards. So, (notice this isn't quite the same thing as 'good faith' negotiation, giving rise to Rawlsian 'strains of commitment'; rather, it is 'zombie' good faith and yields only an observationally equivalent outcome) get your ass down to the Round Table- *tukhes oyfn tisch*, Viceroy Reading, you big jewy Jew you- let's cut a deal already!'

In this context, the cult of Gandhi makes sense. True, there is a superior rationality to wholehearted repudiation of Gandhi- something which dogged him throughout his career- because his Kavka toxin strategy is catastrophic when the pay-off is neither non-rival nor uncontested.

To see why, consider Djikstra's 'dining philosophers problem'

Five silent philosophers sit at a table around an infinite bowl of spaghetti. A fork is placed between each pair of adjacent philosophers.

Each philosopher must alternately think and eat. However, a philosopher can only eat while holding both the fork to the left and the fork to the right. Each philosopher can pick up an adjacent fork, when available, and put it down, when holding it. These are separate actions: forks must be picked up and put down one by one.

The problem is how to design a rule such that each philosopher won't starve, i.e. can forever continue to alternate between eating and thinking.

The easiest solution is to employ a waiter- in the Gita, Krishna is the waiter who adds concurrency as an internal symmetry of the Mahabharata and thus lets karma function in a thought provoking, i.e dharmic, manner.

The British Umpire posed as such a waiter but millions who weren't philosophers nevertheless starved to death.

A second solution is to have a philosopher at the table, Dijkstra himself, who thinks about how to ensure other philosophers get both enough food and thinking time and establishes canonical rules which the other philosophers accept as 'naturally' or 'obviously' fair and optimal without any need for discussion.

This cashes out as a Resource-Hierarchy approach. Emaciated Gandhi, with his deontic 'universalist' ethics and caring-sharing hunger strikes, posed as such a philosopher but not only did his *interessement* cause thinking to catastrophically decrease but millions of non-philosophers nevertheless starved to death precisely because the Gandhian claim to be putting issues like Untouchability or the plight of the handloom weavers above Swaraj was, if not fradulent simply, then merely a case of sour grapes.

Morevover, Gandhi's failure in such respects really doesn't speak to the power or cohesiveness of 'the forces of reaction' but to the fact that Gandhian interessement needed to maintain or aggravate the status quo with respect to the worst-off so as to keep its vaunted concern for the downtrodden around as a viable excuse for not pursuing Political Swaraj in a rational rather than meta-metaphoric way.

But, Gandhi wasn't alone in taking this tack. Everybody was creating some fantasy world to retreat into where they were scoring great and imaginary triumphs.

Indeed, this is what the 'Evo Devo' mathematics of the situation would predict- at any given moment, ontologically dysphoric worlds predominate- I, personally, live in a Jurrasic Age ruled by Lesbian, Thatcherite, pterodactyls- though only those flukes with good concurrency contribute to the Evolutionary family tree.

A third solution (Chandy & Misra) to Dijkstra's problem is to permit communication and put in a rule like 'after x number of shovellings of Spag-bol into your mouth, a fork becomes dirty and can only become clean after y number of others have used it.' But, I'm guessing, for high enough arity, any given x,y isn't robustly acyclic (i.e. no deadlock) such that a minute corruption can't crash the system. The same would be true of uncertain or fluctuating arity. I suppose evolutionary heuristic solutions will cash out as Caste Systems with fractal clumpings under Power Law distributed connectivity- so, dunno if anyone is trying to squeeze deontics out of Concurrency, but don't even go there is my thinking

Philosophically, arity is related to Piercian 'hypostatic abstraction'- i.e. changing an adjective into a predicate- so every time a philosopher creates a new distincition, arity as a whole goes up not by a unit but some factorial based on how many Philosophers have become freshly distinguishable from each other- Philosophy's job, of course, being to make distinctions without any otherwise real world differences. But one can think of State Space inflation as being like abiotic phenotypic plasticity and the consequent need for symmetry breaking as being like biotic Evolutionary pressure towards genetic canalisation. Equate the former with 'cheap talk' and the latter with 'costly signalling' and one begins to understand why Deontology tries to take over History every time someone gets a dirty fork at High Table.

This is the Kavka's toxin at Dijkstra's table. No philosopher- or Research Program or Policy Agent- would sit down at it unless there is a huge exogenous pay-off for being diachronously inconsistent- i.e. unless there is a predictable phase shift- like the jump to hyper-space in Star Wars- in its own trajectory arising only in that dynamic environment.

Since Gandhism is radically meta-intentional, it initially appears to have some appeal in a Kavka toxin context. But, if Kavka's prize is contested, then we have Dijkstra's Round Table which means, as Indian history shows, lots of people starving or senselessly slaying each other and very little, very very little, thinking of any sort actually occurring.

Still, as part of a mixed strategy- i.e. to retain a stochastic element- it made tactical sense to keep Gandhi as an 'obligatory passage point' in the Leadership problematization because
1) if he can't deadlock a Round Table, he can at least 'livelock' its deliberations
2) if the other side can systematically fool him, his own side- equally surely- can manipulate him by 'preference falsification'- i.e. pretending to want the opposite of what they really want.
Policy Actor Hazard cuts both ways.
Thus, the stochastically consequentialist element in Gandhi's leadership, rather than its deontic predictability of pi-jaw, made his political longevity an evolutionarily stable solution.

Unfortunately, a vitalist Lamarckism bedevilled the thinking of the first part of the twentieth Century and thus it is only recently that the Game theoretic nature of the Gita's meta-ethics has become the natural way of reading it. Thus the sublime irony-as-theodicy that Gandhi's translation of the Gita truly was, not his living it, but *its* living him has escaped the attention of Academia.

One final point- when I was growing up in the 70's, many Indians- at least of my sort of background- hadn't cottoned to the utter bankruptcy of the Liberal Arts. Since then, people who read books about Ghalib, Gandhi and the Geeta are no longer pi-jaw merchants by trade, but gainfully employed in some sort of technical, or applied math driven, profession. There was a young man a couple of years back who thought he had solved the P=NP problem. He hadn't, but what's interesting is that he was from an Engineering background- not a pure academic. My belief is that people of this sort can rescue Ghalib and the Geeta from stupid pi-jaw merchants, but only if they understand that Gandhi was shite because all pi-jaw is shite.

I'm not saying this book of mine isn't shit. It is. But only coz I'm stupid. Take this Concurrency business. There's an essay on the internet, by the quite lovely sounding Brazilian super-brain, Christine Cordula Dantas- recall the gorgeous **Giselli Monteiro** who plays the shy Punjabi *soni kudi* in *Love Aaj kal* is actually Brazilian- which seeks to make Concurrency a fundamental property of physical systems and thus revive a Bergsonian notion of Time.

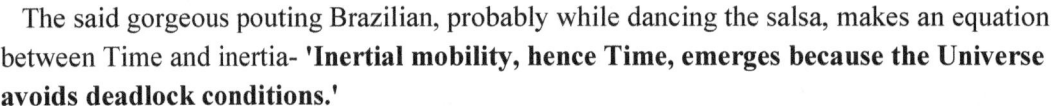

'If concurrency is some deeply inherent property of the world, then it would not be a consequence of dynamics, but the fundamental cause of it. If this hypothesis stands correct, then an insight should be gained on the nature of time, by making our theories explicilty concurrent.

'**Concurrency should be elevated as a new internal symmetry of the world**, in which the probabilistic framework of quantum mechanics would be just an emergent and incomplete facet of a more heterogeneous underlying substrate. And the reversible or irreversible behavior of a given system must somehow be attributable to the underlying heterogeneous concurrent correlations.'

The said gorgeous pouting Brazilian, probably while dancing the salsa, makes an equation between Time and inertia- **'Inertial mobility, hence Time, emerges because the Universe avoids deadlock conditions.'**

I take it, this is an Anthropic type argument and further suppose 'concurrency as internal symmetry' means her proposed model doesn't throw away information and conserves something more fundamental which might knit extant theories together. However, by appealing to a ditopology (so there is local partial order), the essential question of non-metric, or ontologically dysphoric, Bergsonian Time is not addressed. Perhaps, the only way that could be done is by operationalizing Ibn Arabi's concept of barzakh or opening the gate to reverse mereology or her recreating the 'Satrangi Re' dance sequence from Mani Ratnam's 'Dil Se' - while I lip sync *Ishq pe zor nahin, hai ye woh aatish Ghalib...*

Christine, of whom I dream, ends her essay thus- 'In any case, this essay was written presuming that Time exists in some fundamental sense, fully acknowledging, however, the possibility that it may not. If this turns out to be the case, what are we severely missing? Would we be just a surface of imposed irrelevancies- the irrelevancies of Time below which the realm of "nature against nature", the summit of relativism, would forever lie, devoid of its own existence?'

I appeal to my younger readers- kindly solve this problem and Email me the solution. If Time does not exist, or the Universe gets deadlocked, how I can ask her for a date? Not that I am a Romeo or Don Juan or Dr. Manmohan Singh or anything It's just that, as Ghalib said, 'Love is that fire, which cold-shoulders Iyer' and as Gandhiji added 'no fat chicks!' and Gita explained 'Bhargava not Bhagvad is my surname. Gita Bhargava, not Bhagvad Gita. Could you please quit phoning me?'
Thus my case is critical.
I need your help- not lit crit help- but help for the other thing- mathematizing the solution you will find in this book to the Concurrency problem. You see, the only possible reason for women looking askance at my importuning for a date is because, in their heart of hearts, they believe Time does not exist. Christine won't have that excuse, thanks to the proof you will send me.

Normally, I wouldn't impose like this, but something terrible has happened.
You see the one parlous hope I have pitiably lived upon since the dawning of this dire Millenium was that South Park would finally get round to doing a 'Gandhi, Ghalib & the Gita' episode in which Mr.Hankey, the Christmas poo, would explain everything in time for the credits to roll.

So you see, Eric, the Gita teaches, your Gandhi fright-mask is just for Halloween

Ghalib's beard is for Christmas which comes every day at Happy Hour!

But, apparently, the program is going irrevocably off the air.
My horrible book, if nothing else, is a protest against this final dimming of the lights of civilization.

In our yet dawning darkness, stay strong sisters & brothers! & murli Manohar Joshi.

Prof. Shamsur Rahman Faruqi and translating Ghalib's Urdu Ghazals

'Our task is Metatronic not Hermeneutic- to command what is writ, not to uncover what was written- and, like Enoch, to have walked with the Logos to such good effect that, raptured by its irresistible Translation, twinned with Elijah as its 'wheel within the wheel', one is thereafter ever unanimous with every *Ophanimic* or even, mere, but thereby more ruinously dear, Bibliolatric indent or quotation'.
    Rev. Patti Obaweyo Golem. (Quoted from her Twitter against Pelosicare)

'The Indo-Persian Ghazal - metatronically instrumentalizing Ghazalli Major's doxology of occasionalism and metaphorically orchestrating Ghazalli Minor's orthopraxis of causationless aetiology- renders, by such laser lighting up, the qasida's *atlal* detemporalised and holographic such that though the Prophet gain the golden bough, all pious are idolators now .'
    Swamy Vivek Ayyaar Ananda. (Quoted from his toilet paper *Nachlass*.)

'Ibn Arabi's notion of *barzakh*- meditation on which might lead the student of Semantics, from inflationary but relativist bordism, through intensional but restive cohomology, to tremble upon the brink of Reverse Mereology as the true *étalé* of Hermeneutics' harvest sheaf- nathless, is but, at least for the sort of functors found in Ghalib's Urdu Divan, intellectually quite bankrupt coz it hasn't, like, bought me a drink already or showed any fucking sign of doing so any time soon .'
    Umer Sharif Liaqatabadi. (Quoted from a bootlegged 'best of' Video compilation circa 1997)

'The ethos of the Classical Ghazal, by reason of its delinquent and run-away status from a proper *Mubahila* divorce with respect to the thymotic *qasidah*, derives ever thereafter from, the not virile lament, but raptured velleity of its author. Thus, what, following Aristotle, we might *think* its pathos is in fact logos. What sort of logos? One that defeats every merely self-consistent ordering principle whose diegetic tale of individuation cashes out as *drasanta pathein, pathei mathos*- all intentionality so tragic, Sorrow habilitates as Wisdom. Thus, our Mirza's baroque and but patrimonially credentializing sabak-e-hindi ghazals affirm *Ma'ni Afrini* as a techne of ecstacy, the more truly proletarian for pauperising its progeny in advance.'
    Some-sad-M.F.A-fuckwit-or-other. (Quoted from said fuckwit's Dissertation thesis on Scribd or other equally dire & definitional cyber-topos of abject loserdom.)

Preface & 𝔓𝔯𝔢𝔰𝔢𝔫𝔱𝔪𝔢𝔫𝔱 𝔬𝔣 𝔈𝔫𝔤𝔩𝔦𝔰𝔥𝔯𝔶

    I passed an exam, I paid a fee, I took an oath, I now am English. Yet, I feel, something is missing. Some clinching 'presentment of Englishry' on my part.
    I know! How 'bout this?

کیوں نہ وحشتِ غالب باج خواہ تسکیں ہو
کشتہٴ تغافل کو خصم خوں بہا پایا

     I'm sorry, perhaps I'm not being clear. Stupid me. (Apologizing is an English trait and thinking Clarity a *good* thing, an English vice.)
    What I meant to say was-

         kyūñ nah vaḥshat-e ġhālib bāj-ḵhvāh-e taskīñ ho
         kushtah-e-taġhāful ko ḵhaṣm-e ḵhūñ-bahā pāyā

Love-mad I evince, by Indifference murdered to be heard
Peace hath a Prince! Tender weregeld She the Word

Still not clear? I do most humbly apologize! (Shit, that's a bit Babu, isn't it? But, no, now I'm a Brit, I don't *have* to apologize for my humble apologies except to show I just naturally *am* such a great big gosh darned Brit, innit?)

Look, to be as plain as possible, what I'm doing is quoting a couplet, rejected from Ghalib's Divan, which, taken literally, means-

Why shouldn't Ghalib's Madness turn out to be a 'Crowner' (levying fines to raise revenue) for the King of Tranquillity? The one slain by the beloved's indifference was found to be an enemy of the custom of exacting blood-price.

But, this literal meaning also means Ghalib was some reprehensible species of wog, sand-nigger, or towel-head, rather than a perfectly gentlemanly and loyal subject of the Queen like wot I is.

So- remember all this still constitutes part of my 'presentment of Englishry'- consider Deuteronomy 22-

1: If one be found slain in the land which the LORD thy God giveth thee to possess it, lying in the field, and it be not known who hath slain him:
2: Then thy elders and thy judges shall come forth, and they shall measure unto the cities which are round about him that is slain:
3: And it shall be, that the city which is next unto the slain man, even the elders of that city shall take an heifer, which hath not been wrought with, and which hath not drawn in the yoke;
4: And the elders of that city shall bring down the heifer unto a rough valley, which is neither eared nor sown, and shall strike off the heifer's neck there in the valley:
5: And the priests the sons of Levi shall come near; for them the LORD thy God hath chosen to minister unto him, and to bless in the name of the LORD; and by their word shall every controversy and every stroke be tried:
6: And all the elders of that city, that are next unto the slain man, shall wash their hands over the heifer that is beheaded in the valley:
7: And they shall answer and say, Our hands have not shed this blood, neither have our eyes seen it.
8: Be merciful, O LORD, unto thy people Israel, whom thou hast redeemed, and lay not innocent blood unto thy people of Israel's charge. And the blood shall be forgiven them.
9: So shalt thou put away the guilt of innocent blood from among you, when thou shalt do that which is right in the sight of the LORD.

The longest chapter in the Holy Quran, the Surah Al Baqara- which for the followers of Ibn Arabi has a special 'intermediate' (*barzakh*) status- takes its name from a heifer sacrificed on an occasion where one present had falsely foresworn. The dead man, commonly believed to be the Prophet Esdras, being struck by a part of the perished beast, came back to life to accuse his slayer.

67. And (remember) when Musa (Moses) said to his people: "Verily, Allah commands you that you slaughter a cow." They said, "Do you make fun of us?" He said, "I take Allah's Refuge from being among *Al-Jahilun* (the ignorant or the foolish)."
68. They said, "Call upon your Lord for us that He may make plain to us what it is!" He said, "He says, 'Verily, it is a cow neither too old nor too young, but (it is) between the two conditions', so do what you are commanded."
69. They said, "Call upon your Lord for us to make plain to us its colour." He said, "He says, 'It is a yellow cow, bright in its colour, pleasing to the beholders.' "

70. They said, "Call upon your Lord for us to make plain to us what it is. Verily to us all cows are alike, And surely, if Allah wills, we will be guided."

71. He [Musa (Moses)] said, "He says, 'It is a cow neither trained to till the soil nor water the fields, sound, having no other colour except bright yellow.' "They said, "Now you have brought the truth." So they slaughtered it though they were near to not doing it.

72. And (remember) when you killed a man and fell into dispute among yourselves as to the crime. But Allah brought forth that which you were hiding.

73. So We said: "Strike him (the dead man) with a piece of it (the cow)." Thus Allah brings the dead to life and shows you His *Ayat* (proofs, evidences, verses, lessons, signs, revelations, etc.) so that you may understand.

74. Then, after that, your hearts were hardened and became as stones or even worse in hardness. And indeed, there are stones out of which rivers gush forth, and indeed, there are of them (stones) which split asunder so that water flows from them, and indeed, there are of them (stones) which fall down for fear of Allah. And Allah is not unaware of what you do.

One final point- Ibn Arabi hints we ought to read this Surah with the intention of 'joining the extremities to the centre'- which is why it is relevant that, in English law, 'Presentment of Englishry' refers to evidence proffered the Crowner that the murdered man was English, not foreign, thus neither slaughter of kine nor pecuniary fine is meet for the World to wag on as before.

Concerning Wogs

Why, just now, right at this moment, is it vital we demotically translate, or at least deracinatedly transcreate, Ghalib's Urdu Divan- that literary conspectus, but also Vulture Fund prospectus, of a doomed dialect's facility for centrifuging concinnity- that too, today of all days?

I mean, to Iraq and Afghanistan, the last few hours have just added Libya.

So, why fucking bother?

There is a good answer to this question.

Indubitably there is. Definitely.

Well, okay, for all I know, sure- why not?- there might be..

What is certain is you won't find it here.

Try this instead.

The film 'Babe' has shown how the winsome charm of a wannabe sheep-pig can rescue Progressivism from its own Animal Farm. This changes our reception of *sabk-e-hindi*- the Indo-Persian poetic sty- emboldening us to ask if, like Master Ramachandra's contribution to Mathematics, Ghalib's Urdu Divan was not merely a vernacular algebra's supple mimesis of the heavy machinery of a foreign calculus whose forced importation, that too at punitive cost, was thereby rather eased than forestalled?

There are many answers to this question- all witless Deleuzian shite- but only one associated area of inquiry not utterly and equally shite- viz. what light does our infant Century's one insuperable poetic paradigm shift- Lady Ga Ga's Poker faced plaint ***"I'm jus' bluffin wif my muffin"-*** throw upon Mirza Ghalib's, not Pascalian wager, but *Malamati*[1] martingale?

---

[1] Malamati- 'blameworthy'. To let sin abound so Grace super-abound.

Consequently- my cursory curtsy to best practice- it is the one topic I will not address in the rest of this essay.

My Tam Bram *cacoethes scribendi* being, this once, at the service of Literature *zimbly*.

Fearing a Festschrift, howsoever informal, for *Padma Shri* Professor Shamsur Rahman Faruqi would lack such behovely facetiae as served Bedil to ward off the *Ayn ul Kamal*- the 'Eye of Perfection'- I, wretched recidivist!, undeterred by the Gutter Press's Ralph Russellish *détournements* on my original thesis re. Mirza Ghalib & Miss Britney Spears- have, nevertheless-a crippled Hephaestus, fretting to englild Our Common Hera's Celestial throne- hastened to supply a deficiency which, sans doubt, the subtle eye of Scholarship considers more than condignly compensated for by the, not questing fewmets, but querulous faeces of its own incontinent careerism.

Since then, stung by the Gandhian simplicity- not to say Arcadian, corpophagous, self- sufficiency- of Area Studies Academicans in this respect, I have withdrawn this document from the too long suffering, though salutary, suffrage of their gaze only to abortively manumit it to the World Wide Web, thus securing it an almost infinitely larger, more malicious yet, audience of but net-crawling web-bots who, in the abjectness this paper reveals, might crowingly chalk up 'results' for Schadenfreude's search engine.

Perhaps, I should explain why.

To self-publish is a humiliating Vanity though, in this field, only ***Academic*** publication utterly Shameless.

A distinction without a difference, you might think- deeming one doomed to, in this context, drunkenly make a fool of himself, a votary of *Nirlajjaishvara*- The God Without Shame- yet, to the Theist, Humiliation is that nakedness which cries to Heaven for a veil, whereas the 'availability cascade' of Scholarly *Uryani* is that apocalyptic 'Light of the Public which darkens everything.'

BTW & FYI; to forestall a possible reflex of fatuity on your part; distinctions without differences are what *constitute* philosophy.

Crack your Collingwood sometime, why don't you?

Anyroad, to press on, or appear to press on, the predestined theme I choose to descant upon- & doubtless, in Urdu's Orphic manner, descant on to, not ***Themis*** entheme, but ***Dike*** irretrie- vably darken- yet is dear to my heart, & all the dearer for so long held in durance vile by the deathly wine fumes besieging my head.

As a further disclaimer- and general hazard alert- I must add that I approach this topic entirely as an amateur- worse, an amateur Urdu poetaster!- and one moreover much taken, albeit in a manner merely aleatory and amateur, with but prodromal *apercus* from the mathematical and physical sciences rather than the full fledged systematizations- i.e. the brain- eating zombies- unleashed by the Corporate Greed of Globalised Literary Theory.

This is not to say that you should feel yourself obliged to picture me as a sort of Milla Jovovich, **Resident Evil,** ingénue with implanted martial arts skills who will ultimately bring down that evil Multi-National- but, rather, that you very reverentially visualize *Padma Bhushan* Rajnikanth in a blonde wig, skimpy skirt and kinky stiletto heeled leather boots, *dishum dishuming* sundry bad guys, all through your meditation on this Tantric text which, like the ghazal, appears mimetic rather than diegetic, in that moods or states of mind are invoked or performed while no actual narrative of events is being pushed forward.

To caution against a possible confusion, let me clarify- stating, so to speak, its *purvapaksha*- what my contention is not- viz. an *ignis fatuus* to a wannabe Foucault's fuse wire, or damp match to a belated Lacan's touch paper- premised on the notion that the Ghazal Universe is hyper-mentalist or hypo-mechanistic- falling towards the Schizophrenic, the Female, the *African* end of the spectrum proposed by people like W.D. Hamilton, Baron Cohen, Christopher Badcock and so on, rather than the Autistic, the Male, the *Western*. On the contrary, my claim is that the Ghazal, as literary form, is most adaptive precisely on affluent, urban, symbol-manipulation focused, fitness landscapes.

Yet, perhaps by reason of an epigenetic effect- lasting, at best, a couple of generations before regressing to a mean of meretricious meaninglessness- the Ghazal is equally and amphibolously autistic/schizophrenic.

But here I trespass on the territory of genuine Tam Bram brain-boxes like V.S Ramachandran- whose work on 'mirror neurons' and synaesthesia has enriched or operationalised for me the notion that what Homi Bhabha calls 'hybridity' is neither mimicry nor mockery, but, for Urdu (w.r.t Persio-Arabic) or Indglish (w.r.t to WTF?), merely that 'mirror-box' which permits scratching the itch of phantom limbs arising out of amputations occasioned by contested Imperialisms' various collapses- a project doomed by our *swadeshi*- that is nativist and *dirigiste*- 'Scientific, Socialist, Secularism's' *Kristallnacht* of the *mirroir sans tain* of the Walpurgis window pane of the Specular, hence Universal, Emporium in which impecunious *flaneurs* like me could dart glances not of envy merely, but admiration, by reason of the faint super-imposition of our own bedraggled image upon the costly merchandise behind the glass.

It is in this context that the ghazal's prestige- at least when it comes to a difficult poet like Ghalib- much derives from its methodological reversal of appearance and reality- in other words its apparent mimetic form may conceal a diegesis at the level of abstraction.

It is noteworthy that, unlike the sort of object an impulse-equilibrium approach might legitimately examine, the ghazal isn't something that different people can experience in the same way- even if very efficiently and sufficiently prodded to a high enough level of sensitivity by an Apollonian Inspectorate of Aesthetics. On the contrary, the ghazal has always upheld a thumbing of the nose at Secular and Spiritual authority- whether *Bazaari* or *Sarkari*, or a hybrid of both, like the *Muhtasib* or *Vaayiz* - and, moreover, cherishes disequilibrium as the driver of its cerebral complexity, admitting no internalized censor to caution against weak sequencing or disconnection between parts such that, semantically, it might be beforehand in preparing its own Procrustean bed. But, since a synaesthetic or impulse-equilibrium approach requires semantic determinateness of precisely this sort, that too not at the level of **words**- where determinate recursion may have the same range as some non-determinate procedure- but, rather, at the level of **the people** who hear those words, and since we don't hear Chomskyian I-language but an immediate and intentionally redacted idiolect, it follows that the ghazal qua *taghazzul*- 'ghazal-ness'- **can't** be a legitimate object of such scrutiny because the ghazal's unities are neither requisitioned in advance nor imposed by its unfolding as Time, Place and Action. On the contrary, that heterogeneous receptivity of mood that animates, if not unites, the ghazal's audience, is an emergent on a now, not vertiginous, but **diaganolised**- that too not in a mereologically measure preserving manner- solipsism that still dizzies and does for them; abeyant, that is, vindication in their Class Action claim for compensation with respect to the Culturally occasioned Diabetes the Ghazal inculcates; while what each takes away- the ghazal's couplets that will live most in memory- generally do so, like bogus Asylum seekers taken in by whom they take in, wholly divorced from both pretext and context.

Another way of making the same point, but dwelling on the fundamental folk theorem of *taghazzul*- viz. the equivalence of Eros and Thanatos, consummation as fulmination upon the path of Love- is that the logic of distinctions (G.Spenser Brown) is violated or erased- and, what Niklas Luhmann might term, the *autopoiesis* of the Ghazal Universe presents itself to us as katabatic with reference to its own peaks of catharsis or kenosis- its, so to speak, self-transcendence upon the lips of mountain intoxicated mystics- thus incarnadining its crepuscular and Selene hunting summits to but paint a pretty back-drop for the casting of a pebble in the goblet and the dispersal of us imaginary picnickers lower down.

A difficulty that arises for the Night-embarking, *Abendländisch*, reader of our Orient, or Dawn- landing, Divan- related, perhaps, to *Sinn*, acceptation, as Germany's Originary Sin of considering mental or linguistic operations as constitutive of a far boundary, not a near bazaar- an osmotic membrane that must swell to expel- is that critical theory is impotent to name the Ghazal's eroticized *jetztzeit* as other than a historicized and barbarous alterity. However, it may be, by replacing the notion of a boundary- a militarized marchland of meaning entrenched against its own myth- with the Islamic concept of the isthmus or **barzakh**- redolent, as that Quranic term is, for Indology, of the Tantric Sandhyabhasha *détournement* on Sankhya's Samadhi represented by the Tibetan *bardo*- some headway might yet be made, not, it is true, in adding to one's appreciation of the Ghazal but in sensing a Universal truth behind Sloterdijk's tribute to Derrida- viz. that the Western Tradition, in however fractured a form, nevertheless lay behind the latter's operations, as, indeed, it did or does Habermas and Gadamer and Luhmann and, of course, Sloterdijk himself- though one may observe that this occurs only when these great luminaries defecate upon it because, while urinating, they resolutely face towards it. This, indeed, is that Ethic which Levinas calls 'first Philosophy.'

Socrates (the Urdu *SuqraaT*- who is rather Comic than Christ pre-figuring) disagreed. He thought Philosophy nothing but a practicing of death. *Mousike* is what he ought to have dedicated himself to.

Sakaarat-e-mawt pe kaha SuqraaT
Mantiq ke raah pe mujhe kuch na mila

Mousike he hai Vajd-e-fana!
Did not Socrates, serene, on his death-bed deem?
Amongst discourses divine, Music supreme
Saying- 'Philosophy's path misses ecstasy
'Song, alone, sets the chained soul free.'

Scripture and Song, too, live in memory but the one is, as St. Augustine pointed out, a mirror while the other- aleatorily overheard upon the lips of a child- is, to the soul, that mirror's unsealing. The ghazal- despite the ubiquity of its mirror impassioned parrot- is less than either being but a cage- it has no Christ, no Suka, who- incarnating the Psalms, the Sama Ved- flies beyond the... but Book... Fathers... but dictate. But then, the ghazal's is a meta-metaphoricity, its images mere allusions, its logic oneiric with respect to the bloodless, bookish, phantasms of its waking world. Thus, neither Epimethean melody nor Aeschylean mathesis, the ghazal's *dijecta membra* merely memoriously jingle- advertising a product, profitable to us perhaps, but, for having so improvidently exhausted its productive capital in advance, never actually brought to Market.

     Still, when provided for by peerless Meistersingers, such profligacy scarcely matters..

As I write this now, I <u>am listening</u> to a recording of Farid Ayaz & Abu Mohammad in which a superb '*girah-bandi*' *(*vide Syed Akbar Hyder on the Qawwals', on the fly, tying of the 'flowing knot' of *taḍmin*) where a medley of Mir, Amir Khusrau, Sultan Bahu and Kabir, to name but a few, explores the theme of the meeting gaze, but one mediated by *Vaqt ka taqazu,* Time's importunate tax, escapable only in metre and in music such that, in Eternity, all undiminished, those same eyes meet- at which point we hear a sonorous quotation from the Quran regarding Barzakh- glossed, not as that impossible isthmus by which our Faith crosses over dryshod with Moses, but as the meeting of two bodies of water, one salt, one sweet- which reflection, before it can be quaffed or digested, is quickly followed by Rumi's fluting on the uprooted reed, and Kabir's piping on its peerless, for unfruited, deed. All this in the space of...what?... dunno.... call it five minutes.

In trying to make sense of this welter of allusions, images and ideas, the *rasika* connoisseur, at some point has to let his own musical sense take up more and more of the cognitive burden. The singers then become easier to follow and **what follows** is a transportation to an equal *vajd-e-sama* ecstasy.

     Now imagine a symmetrically skilled, not singer, but *translator* seeking to reduce Urdu's golden word horde to 'lean unlovely English'.

An ignoble task indeed- like de-Maeterlinckingly dubbing Debussy's Opera- (who doesn't?)- but ending up with porn.

Yet absent that music, all meta-metaphoricity *is* such translation- every Aria, heavy breathing.

     Writing from Prison, Pundit Nehru, for whom the Past was a Prison, confessed that he never encountered what the mystic Aurobindo called the 'pure and virgin Present' without also reviling himself for adding another recruit to the harlotry of the Ages and- as Maulana Azad regretfully records- unconsciously primed himself, during his last spell of penal servitude, for his meretricious and impending Prime Ministerial task by becoming an indiscriminate Ghazal aficionado.

              At least, he never translated Ghalib.

Or, ***fuck me,*** was it something similar he was doing delivering those interminable speeches of his?

Was Ghalib's disembodying art, indeed, the Utopian plan, the *hasrat-e-tameer,* of unlivable in New Delhi?

              Certainly, in early manhood, even thus did its Lebenswelt appear to me.

Huwa hoon Ishq ki Ghaaratgaree se sharminda
Siway hasrat-e-tameer, ghar mein khaak nahin
(Boozed, I brought home a bint
But, that wasn't the scandal
My house still a blue-print
& Love such a vandal!)

This was that fire which, lacking Love's salamander, had, with Municipal zealotry, rezoned its ashes as a Garden.

And Ghalib its *'andalib-e-gulshan-e-na-afreedah'* Nightingale of Non-Existence.

Why?

Neither transporting nor transported
Ghalib never trysted. He *translated.*

& translated such that translation, but **his**, his is just deserts.

The greater part of his utterly adolescent Divan evidenced, it seemed to me, so censorious my supercilious youth, not a plodding, *ars dictaminis*, determination to master *paivastagee-* that horticultural craft of the literary graft whose Dead Sea fruit- the Ghazzalis' occassionalist gift of a enuch and garrulous euphuism- was, to our brown-nosing Cyranos' *sans esprit*, the uncomissioned and thus through-God's-transom-thrown Ghazal- but, on the contrary, seeing as Ghalib's very first, purely histrionic, sigh had already set ablaze the Meinongian wings of Walter Benjamin's Phoenix-as-Angel-of History; his demotic oeuvre affirmed nothing of him, *in propria persona*, save our common, or compulsory, addiction to the Delhi School boy's, utterly puppyish, for still belle lettrist, dream of sparking a panic in the pleasure garden by a tippling exchange of heads with the *Kuffar* Time's triply rabid Cerberus.

Doubtless, Ghalib's Urdu Ghazals themselves escape infection for, in manner aleatory, bit by his cynic & inoculatory mother wit- an Augustan outcome Delhi's witlessly self-improving agenbite again and again had him re-apply himself to reverse.

Still that was okay coz- Sa'ib his Saqi of self-regard, Naziri his Nadim & Zuhuri his Houri of self-abuse- he always drank better than he could afford- as do I in my more modest way. So, like the dude says-

As Water inspires, or so in its Wisdom is written,
Fear in the Rabid One
I by but vulgar visages bitten
Mirrors shun!

True, in his time, Delhi hadn't yet turned its back on its river. Neither Bollywood nor Hollywood yet provided it its mirror.

But already these things were in the air and Ghalib felt it in his water.

Our Ghalib that is.

We who, assembling to pour a libation, all too predictably, ended up getting drunk and pissing on his grave.

We are unreal. Ergo, no, there's no bubble in Delhi Real Estate. How could there be? Ghosts will be our tenants.

And amongst Ghosts, whose more prestigious than Ghalib's?

Is there a constraining oeconomics that can save from the meretricious chrematistics of, what is to me, his but translative meta-metaphoricity?

Ezra Pound's ironic *ibbur* as nice-guy academician, J.H Prynne, sagely has counseled the translation of an ambiguity with an equal ambiguity- as if behind the veil of Language and Belief there is some duplicable pattern of neuron firing from which the torch of Universal Reason might ubiquitously blaze forth without anybody actually noticing- but, kindly to pay attention Hester Mem Sahib!, this is a suppression of cognitive diversity which renders Language's 'trade & development' function- its scale and scope economies- null and void only so as to permit a gadareningly Marxist, or swinishly Pigouvian Social Choice. This is surprising because Prynne is one of the few poets in a position to monitor the the sort of results Geoffrey Heal and Graciella Chichilnisky and so on have been publishing over the last thirty years.

Or it would be if we didn't know that quotidian Puritan auto-didact, but crepuscular Cambridge Platonist, is *mutatis mutandis* as the Scarlet Letter marking America's foundational adultery with Moll, the Mother Country, at a Boston Tea Party protesting what Burke labelled 'Indianism' and reviled as a greater threat to the Polity than Jacobin synoecism...

Since Ghalib was a dioecist pensioner of that very 'Indianism'- as was Delhi's diminishing Emperor- & moreover one much taken with the material culture of the great mercantile civilization newly established on our shores, his 'difficult' poetry surely damns Prynne's project, howsoever well received that is nowadays in Communist China, leading us back to Prof. Faruqi's fakir like indigence in ontology which fiercely fulminates the tyranny of English Sentimentality, English 'Naturalism', English 'Taste', making a bonfire of these Manchester fabrications so that Urdu's bazaar might once again boast muslins finer woven, more flowing, than water, and pashminas more warming than the tulip's *auto da fe*.

But I'm getting ahead of myself.

First, I need to establish that Ghalib really is 'difficult' in Prynne and Prof. Faruqi's sense. One important reason to think not arises from the phatic, purely conventional, seemingly hidebound, topos- but topos ever eroding, ever asymptotically approaching pure *epoche*- such being Dedekind's unkindest cut- Al Kindi's kindling of Distillation's *Dajjal*- which situates the Ghazal's utterance.

Indeed, one might argue that the Ghazal world is different from our world. Its quantifiers are different from quantifiers in natural language. But, this can't get us very far. After all, for us hereditary book-keepers and clerks, the ghazal is precisely that conflagratory orgasm in Canetti's ant-hill, our self-delusively defalcatory habit of double entry yet domesticates as a honey-comb. Indeed, even the bread and butter of our Arithmetic possesses a hierarchy theorem[ii] showing how alternate states for a quantifier, as well as the number of quantifiers obtaining, qualitatively increase complexity. Failed Accountant though I am (I could never get my head round the way 6 looks provocatively at 9 and, like, *nobody notices!*- not to get me started on what happens when those two numbers get together!) you may, very kindly, accept my assertion that the ghazal aint simpler than Arithmetic or (despite its venerable antiquity) arthritically constrained to single valued determinants.

What? Doubt won't grant you a *get*? Why? Oh. Your Rabbi's been reading Badiou and considers poetry and mathematics to be 'pure presentation of presentation'? Very well. You leave me no choice but to invoke the sacred memory of that glorious paleo-Godelian Jihad against intensionality-cashing-out-as-impredicativity in which I myself was professionally martyred- I refer to my evanescent employment as an instructor in Mathematics- to induce you to abhor and anathematize not just long division (which, because it discriminates against short people, was banned by the erstwhile Inner London Education Authority) but also fractions- yea **fractions!** I repeat, beseeching you, in the bowels of Christ, to reflect on the *scandal*, the stumbling block to *Faith*, that ensues when the totality of things is divided into two separate categories- such that not even the natural numbers retain, any longer, a unique mathematical expression.

   To see why; consider 1/3. It's decimal expansion is 0.33333 recurring. Multiply 1/3 by 3 and you get 1. Do the same thing to the decimal expansion and you get 0.9999 recurring. Obviously, we could replace every 9 by 8.99999 recurring and every 8 by 7.9999 recurring and- to cut a long story short- show, by such incrementally self-incriminating means, that Liebniz is expelled from his own Mathesis by this reverse *abjectio novenaria* and that when Pascal said 'all language is a cipher in which not letters are exchanged for letters but words for words such that a new language is born'- what that, but attritionally, Augustinian failed to mention is nothing is new and therefore nothing is language nor -*inter urinas et faeces nascitur*- its univocal pissed shite or *homo* actually born.

   Such, then, is the mischief division- that anti-Anaxagorian axe!- does unless, that is, we stand firm against it and demand the return of Roman numerals rather than those of the Arabic, or Hindu or Mayan sort. You may kindly consider writing to your M.P. insisting on my reinstatement as a Maths teacher, with back-pay, on the grounds that the basely *petit bourgeious* Thatcherite insistence that long division be taught in London- once the seat of an undivided and indivisible Empire and Oikumene- that too in Primary Schools! (which as I have repeatedly proved is equivalent to propagandizing for sodomy!) is against Human Rights and the Environment and World Peace and them pesky Palestinians illegally occupying Gazza's football strip and other important stuff like that.

But, why would you bother?

   You're only still reading this coz u like ghazals & Urdu & stuff and- your eyes dragged in appalled fascination from clause colliding into clause, sentence blindly smashing into sentence- hadn't the the good sense to turn away from this train-wreck in that Toy town where, as with dawning horror you now from your own nursery nightmares doubtless recall, giant dolls play with terrified children.

I'm not judging you.
Still it rankles.
Mind it! Your refusal to help me will cost you deer.
Henceforth, mercilessly hunted by music, be thy each memorious, dear purchased, gazelle!

   Indeed, every item in the stock vocabulary of the ghazal, precisely because it is neither song nor sophism, functions as a multivalent determinant such that operators, too, become quantifiers and vice versa, setting a-swing a plangent chromatics. But, though ultimately unproductive, this suggests another tack we might take- *videlicet* to expatiate upon the ghazal's phototropism towards its own shadow which, ever tempting the tyro translator to a perdition it is the soul of his art to postpone, yet renders his labour an unlearning of two languages, both source and target, by reason of the exponential rise in ambiguity its taking the simplest path to complexity necessarily imposes.

   But this is not to say that the Ghazal's semantics remain trapped in a logic loop of self-reference, so as never to get off the ground, or that it is extensionally bound up in the highly correlated semiotics of an inaccessible alterity. On the contrary, the ghazal is a game- ideally an impartial combinatorial game symmetric in each generation- in which the Mastersinger *strategizes* his use of amphiboly so as to answer to the alternate meanings, however abstract, however idiosyncratic, co-created, so to speak, as private personifications- a subliminal drama- by the auditor, which is why its couplets more naturally stick in the mind than those of the metrically similar, more euphonious yet, panegyric form.

But let me pause here for a moment to tell you something personal. I was born in Bonn. German books- some in Gothic script- still variegate the Tamil and Sanskrit and P.G. Woodhouse of my parent's Tam Bram bookshelves. Worse, at one period, along with M.S Subbalaxmi and Julie Andrews, Wagner too inhabited the tape machine.

There was a time when Mom & Dad tried to take me to fucking Concerts and Ballets and Operas and shite!

Believe me, I too have suffered.

This is something the younger generation can never understand.

Fortunately, at some point during my absurd adolescence, I adopted or was adopted by a clipped, ever tending to the crapulous, antiquated British accent such as afforded me, in my parent's eyes, the rights of asylum due a born Philistine. (A Jewish colleague once told me that only amongst Sub Continentals does a Mum get *naches* for a phenomenally stupid son.). How it happened was this. We had a Chemistry teacher named Mr. Das. For some reason, nobody could then fathom, he neither knew any Chemistry nor was familiar with the vigorous, expletive laden, Hindglish argot with which our, invariably *déclassé*, Science teachers kept order. Mr. Das's constipated Cambridge accent at first puzzled, then afforded us much hilarity, for it had become known that he was married to an I.P.S Amazon of the Orissa cadre.

'I take it up the arse, Mrs. Das' - we fervently believed, was the ice-breaker of what would otherwise have been his glacial honeymoon. Though I myself, by reason of my failing grades, was soon ejected from the Science Stream and had to slum it in Arts- I retained a fascination with the *shiksha* phonetics of that phrase, itself fractal of a truly Nishad Upanishad- *'I take it up the arse, Mrs. Das'*- and, by mere imitative accommodation of my every utterance to its *Pratisakhya* template, I quite spontaneously developed the sort of accent I still sport. This was the making of me. I never subsequently troubled with 'Kultur' & other such *Bildungsbürgertum* krap even when holidaying with my parents behind the Iron Curtain- where alone that all-corrupting cultus was kept up.

So even if

Not Bach holds back the harm in Harmony

& Kant can't the germ of Germany

I genuinely am not genitively constrained to say that the ghazal is dramatic, or Operatic, or Shakespearian or Schopenhauerian or fucking anything save what it fucking is- viz. cathartic precisely because it never seeks to wring a tear of pity from our eye or cry of terror from our lips. Yet, that too in an entirely uncomplimentary sense, so cerebral is its autopoiesis of inebriation, the heart is touched- touched at times to its very core- by the ghazal's gossamer lightness of touch, which Thought, too heavily laden, has enjoined upon itself to dissimulate its drear, mere, power of simulation. Since this is a thought of the heart, striking up a new dialectic of heart and head, its synthesis might well be that '*muqallab al quloob*'- the converter of hearts into heads, heads into its heart- or, to unmuzzle its inner ghazal, whoever or whatever it is that startles the connoisseur into fresh insight, a lifted horizon; Beauty familiar, indeed, but never before thus seen.

Yet the problem of translation remains.

Indeed, it grows acute.

Metaphors and models and stylized worlds- like that of the Ghazal- work by becoming mental environments we can off-load cognitive work to. They store information, or cloud compute results, such that we can retrieve them on a just-in-time basis. But, this begs the question- what work is actually being done when we listen to Ghalib? If some heat is generated, is it proof that his system is mainly or merely dissipative? Frictional to all, for to all but fictional? If his words leave us cold, does it mean that there is a symmetry law such that, somewhere else, something for us is being laid up and conserved? Or is it not rather the case that Ghalib has off loaded his work onto us- that too going A.W.O.L not, pardonably, to take a piss or keep a tryst but perversely to complete his own translation such that-

> *'hum vahan hai jahan se hum ko bhi*
> *kuch hamari khabar nahin aati'*

(I am there where news of me, even to me, can't reach)

the favourite couplet, it is instructive to recall, of the psycho-analyst Masud Khan who- unlike the various Barristocrats of our vaingloriously competing Struggles for Self-determination; all of whom came boomeranging back to brain us - transplanted himself to London hoping to be healed, only to be suborned there into himself becoming a healer- except Winnicott's monomaniacal meta-metaphoricity of mothering offered not a healing but a habit of addiction that could only support itself by dealing in its own poisonous product- and, because Masud's sickness really was of the heart (Religion and, later, Race, striving to strike that Lyallpur lad *Majnoon*) he ended up not a respected leader of the Cartel, but one ignominiously expelled- not for alcoholism but (wog that he was) anti Semitism.

In contrast, take Hafiz of Shiraz, perhaps the greatest of Ghazal poets, who- slyly identifying himself with the *rind'* (the rakish hedonist)- uses a sort of jiu jitsu to cleverly turn the great Vital and Spiritual forces- which demand martyrdom, madness and utter nihilation- against themselves such that no higher price for what we might term a species of Eudaimonic Gnosis is paid by the poet than perhaps a slight hangover or some wine stains upon his robe.

To a Western writer of an older generation, a stanza like *Farib jahaan qissah roshan ast/ sehar tha che zaid, shab aabastan ast/ dar ain khu nafishan arsah-rastakheez./thu khoon surahi beh saaghar bar eez-* might look like the Anacreontics he or she translated at School.

A.J. Arberry's translation is-

> 'Tis a famous tale the deceitfulness off Earth
> The night is pregnant, what will dawn bring to birth?
> Tumult and bloody battle rage in the plain
> Bring blood red wine and fill the goblet again!

To my sceptical 'Indglish' sensibility however, it is not the plural grace of parrhesia but the poisonous garrulity of paranoia that mixes up factual & alethic propositions with deontic or intentional statements. Indeed, in talking to women, illocution is constrained to (Austin) infelicity otherwise a contract arises and both parties disappear into *Mubahila's* mouth or Maryam's mirror. Since Contexts are women Texts talk to, I, *salva veritate*, preserve the purely *'insha'* rather than *'khabar'* nature of Hafiz's *sher* and also bring out the possibilities of the word *'aabastan'* by changing the second and third line to get *this*-

> That the World is Fair, remain a fable Bright
> Break not Dawn nor the waters of Night!
> That Resurrection re-gather what our Armageddon's spill
> From thy blood red, Saqi, my cup refill!

This is because I think of Hafiz as *strategic*- rather than mimetic or diegetic- and his Divan as a sort of Kung Fu manual to use against Eros and Thanatos and other such blue collar, Ethnic stereotype, bullies when they try to shake you down for your lunch money. Later in life, of course, once Eros and Thanatos are relegated to stuff like delivering your pizza or doing your dry-cleaning, you come up against the vastly worse internalized WASP bully of the Liberal Conscience against which nothing will avail except fantasizing about teaming up with Sarah Palin to become, like, a pair of renegade bounty hunters...

But not to allow my passion for Palin to overmaster me quite yet, I may point out that though the *shers* in a ghazal are formally stand-alone, and though there may be some picturesque purchase to the notion of the gnomic, not to say gormless, Oriental poetaster as statically didactic rather than dialectically investigative, nevertheless, in Ghazal qua Ghazal- Ghazal as a suave, rather than sententious, 'talking to women'- Ghazal as exemplifying '*husn-e-tarteeb*' or 'beauty of arrangement'- the thread of desire, of intentionality, of personality, must express itself purely in the '*insha*' (intentional, deontic, passional) register, rather that communicate '*khabar*' (alethic or empirical, that is falsifiable, information-rich statements).

This is not to say that '*insha*' statements- in so far as they are prescriptive, performative, or projective- do not 'cash out' as some theory of the world and hence as '*khabar*'- still, that 'cashing out' is not constrained to a self-consistent or, indeed, compossible set of world-pictures but may invoke all or any of them in a manner that can't be partially-ordered and hence tractably handled by any Western system of defeasible reasoning or logical calculus. I say Western, advisedly, for it may be that a system based on Ibn Arabi's notion of *barzakh* does indeed provides the basis for such a system of defeasible reasoning[iii] for Islam.

Borges and *barzakh*

The older, if no longer conventional view, in the West, is that the Arab encounter with Aristotle was a comedy of errors. Ultimately, despite some faint stirrings of the spirit of enquiry in Avicenna, Al Farabi and Averroes, Islam found itself *de trop* at Philosophy's Symposium and returned to its *metier* as the Savonarola, stern, of its own squalid Seraglio. Borges's famous story- 'Averroes' Search'- might appear to confirm this picture. Averroes has never seen a play. He has seen playacting- the children in the courtyard are playacting- he has heard descriptions of the Chinese theatre- but he can't understand that a story can be told by actors playing parts. It seems senseless. Any narrative, no matter how complicated, can be related by a skilled poet. Why employ more than one person for the task? The notion that the Chinese- a wealthy and civilized people- might use a whole troupe of performers to represent the actions of a narrative is clearly false. The procedure is wasteful. Clearly these are the tall tales of a World traveler who, in reality, has never been farther than the Bazaar.

Still, in Aristotle's Poetics, these two words- 'comedy' and 'tragedy'- continually recur. What could they possibly mean and how should one translate them into that noblest of languages-Arabic?

Surely this is the funniest and most famous example of how bad philology renders the Orient and the Occident's Uranian reflections upon each other utterly risible? Some Syrian pedant translates Aristotle's tragedy and comedy as '*madih*' (panegyric) and '*hija*' (invective) respectively and a lasting mischief is worked. Actually, the truth is probably more prosaic. Great scholars like Al Farabi and Avicenna- who sometimes let the foreign terms 'comedy' and 'tragedy' stand in their commentaries- and, a little later, Averroes, had not actually fallen into the ugly error we ascribe to them- viz. of having no mental model of the theatre and thus having been incompetent to perform a proper hermeneutic merging of horizons. Rather, it appears, these scholars sought to use the authority of Aristotle to elevate critical reception of the premier Classical Arabic poetic forms by stressing the centrality of Moral Science to human discourse because, uniquely, the intelligibles it aims at *must* be univocally multiply realizable, else but *nihil's* quiver of nonsense. (Thus, in my view, the Ghazzali Bros. saved the Ghazal from *al san'a wa-'l- takalluf*- an exhausted pedantry's gnomic velleity and epigrammatic witlessness.)

Nevertheless, Borges's wider thesis remains valid- viz. that something important happens when simple recitation is replaced, first by the entry of the Chorus- or a second actor- onto the stage, and then, more significantly yet, a third actor is introduced. In a sense, what has happened is a qualitative increase in complexity- like the 3 body problem in mathematical physics, or the introduction of a third agent in Bargaining or Voting theory. The two person dialogue, if carried on long enough, can always be collapsed into an i-language diegesis- extensional dialogue-enablers being virtual merely because they cash out as the participants' respective theories of mind re. each other- Plato's dialogues are actually a narrative written like a novel with enough background information so the truth value of propositions being advanced achieve a sort of cultural independence. However, once you have three people talking, an Actor Interessement (Callon) indeterminacy problematics arises from issues related to Concurrency (Dijkstra), Co-ordination & Coalition stability. Shibboleths and participation mystiques relating to historicist collectives, or arising from 'strategic essentialism' gain importance. Pure extensionality has entered the realm of totem and taboo. Facticity has no road to Freedom save by some stochastic process of sacrifice.

Even in a purely economic bargaining problem, with the addition of a third agent, you start to get hysteresis effects, path dependence, problems re. preference revelation- i.e. statements become strategic and manipulative- there is no guarantee that Social Choice might not become catastrophically sub-optimal. Language is divorced from Logos. Everything is up for grabs. Chaos is round the corner.

One method, that of Theistic Monism, to deal with the 3 body problem, is to recast is as a case of Object/Image/Mirror. The third could be thought of as the looking glass in which the I-Thou relationship adorns its bridal visage or else, *Nympha pudica Deum vidit, et erubuit* as the wine glass crushed underfoot at Cana. Lyric poetry and Theistic Devotionalism take this route and for both it really is true that Tragedy and Comedy are nothing but panegyric and invective.

But- and this is the crux of Borges's abject self-identification with Averroes's fulmination in the mirror- what happens to his own bibliolatric creed of absolute univocity such that all books are by the same author and that author the reader? How can Monism co-opt the mirror for its purposes when there is no Subject/Object duality?

One straightforward solution is to declare the phenomenal world wholly delusive- *majaz*i or *mayavadi*- but this proposition only becomes interesting to the extent that it lends itself to the purely theatrical.

To see why- suppose you receive a Skype call, as you read this, and Leo from the Matrix tells you that what you think your life is just a computer construct. Fine. Okay. It's a new fact about the world and actually carries less emotional valence than someone saying you've got B.O or 5 ½ inches is the new official definition of needle-dickdom. Still, maybe, you'll stop stressing so much over getting in the Sales projections to Head Office, cancel that operation for hair plugs, and smoke more dope. But at the end of the day, discovering the World is a computer construct isn't a particularly dramatic revelation. It isn't really theatrical. In the end, you end up cancelling your cancelling the hair plugs and- why not? it's all unreal anyway- gird up your loins to go for that promotion to Head Office.

Real boring stuff. Ah! Hang on! Wait a minute! What if you have a mysterious sweetheart who is like half and half out of this artificial world? Suddenly everything is transfigured by drama and music and has become a sort of allegory about balancing one's work and love life &

not spending so much time on Playstation & keen stuff of that sort.

For noble characters animated by noble sentiments, the intrusion of a third party is a harbinger of tragedy because some misunderstanding or complication is bound to arise and a terrible sacrifice will have to be made. However, with an ignoble character seeking an ignoble end, the intervention of a third party adds complications and a stochastic element such that the scapegrace might end up more fortunate than he began. Aristophanes innovation was to make the comic protagonist stand for ordinary people with extraordinary insight into politics and philosophy. This permits us to consider Comedy as more philosophic than Tragedy as it is a sort of mimesis of the scientific method. Perhaps, the authority of Aristotle, in this matter- or the perception that Aristophanes was responsible for the death of Socrates- turned the scales against Comedy. Still, we know that Greek comedy had penetrated India. Apparently, there is a papyrus copy of a risqué Greek play with dialogue in Tulu or Kannada dating back almost two thousand years- proof, surely, that Girish Karnad is younger than he looks.

There was also some influence flowing the other way. Megasthenes tells us that an Indian tale inspired Aristophanes' 'the birds'- though perhaps the notion of a parliament of the birds is very much more archaic and of Anatolian origin. Plato's Symposium, more especially Aristophanes' theory of the sexes, was certainly known to the Barmecides. But, it appears, Aristophanes drops from sight during the Age of Faith and only resurfaces quite late into the Renaissance. Still, considered philosophically, what is important about Greek tragedy and comedy is that mimesis- even if eventually fully capturable by a more or less lengthy diegesis- *displays* the problem of deterministic chaos (i.e small things having big effects) even though the genre sets up an attractor such that the outcome is known in advance to be either maximally fortunate or unfortunate. It is precisely the intuition of these extra degrees of freedom which makes, as Aristotle says, Tragedy more philosophic than History and, we might add, Aristophanes more philosophic than Plato.

Returning to Borges, whose pathos lies in his ceaseless attempt to reduce his own oeuvre to a one dimensional labyrinth- accreting, in the process, upon that mirror of Nothingness, but disconnected Cantor dust- we might say that Ibn Arabi's *barzakh*- perhaps penumbral in Asin Palacios?- is precisely what his Averroes seeks, or that, by *ibbur*, it is the soul of the Great Sheikh that enters him at the end of the story.

Except, we won't say any such thing. Why? Noise is a fractal in I & Thou. That's like basic Radioshack knowhow. But,

I, Thou, ***& e'en a random Third***

& Noise is Logos, Mythos surd.

Triangular structure of the Ghazal

An important aspect of the Ghazal universe, highlighted by Prof. Fran Pritchett is the 'triangular structure of the Ghazal- with a series of three-part relationships: a desirer, an object of desire, and a blocker or barrier to fulfilment. For some of the imagery-sets you can almost make it happen, but basically it soon breaks down via the third term, which is always fragmenting into many barriers, but some of them illusory, others transitory, others fungible, others frangible (hah!), etc. But you can always bring it down to the desirer and the desired, and in between them something like a nest of snakes.'[iv]

Curbing my natural response- which would be to incontinently *kvell* o'er my li'l Cantor's ternary set- let me, with equal fatuity, gas on instead in Girardian vein about 'mimetic desire' and the sacrifice (*korban* or *pharmakos*) it requires- the drawing of lots for which- the cloture of parrehesiac hermeneutics- the Ghazal poet cunningly excuses himself from by pointing out that his entrails have long ago been torn out and burnt up in the fire of celestial passion and anyway I've got a note from Mom saying I'm off games coz l am like totally on the rag. (If the ghazal began as 'talking to women' it is now, 'talking like a work-shy ho')

But, that would be too easy- or, at any rate, the sort of stuff that might be mistaken for actual academic work- so, good Iyer that I am, I invoke Ramanuja who, trying to rescue the Puranas- and therefore a historicist, diegetic, N.R. Narayana Murthy, Temple based cultus- introduces the trinity of Bimba, Pratibimba and Darpan- object, reflection and mirror- as each having some ontological distinctness.

A little thought, which my own status as a poet thankfully excuses me from personally undertaking, would show that any diegesis must subscribe to such a trinity with the result that the mirror is also a wall, thus the Ghazal world, being wholly intentional- wholly 'insha' rather than 'khabar'- and moreover wholly intensional (i.e. each term used is defined wholly within itself rather than extensionally with reference to the outside world)- is free to run amok breaking all mirrors, breaching all barzakhs, dissolving that portion of deontology which *does* reference the outside world, so as to become a sort of guerrilla manual of strategies to escape all reciprocal obligation or historicist imperatives.

In this context, Prof. Prtichett stresses the subversiveness of the Ghazal world, in the sense that it constantly borrows objects and people and events from the real world, and often presents them in what looks to be a straightforward way. 'In minor ghazal poets, it often IS a straightforward way; plenty of people objected to Ghalib because he messed up the good old lamenting love lyric by tangling it up in layers of verbal and metaphysical complexity. But in Mir and Ghalib and the other poets of the first rank, it always (in principle) turns out to be the case that these borrowed items no longer have their "natural" qualities or relationships-- they have all, and only, those envisioned by the collective poetic *bricolage* imagination of the ghazal world. Unlike science fiction or fantasy, the ghazal has no props entirely of its own invention. It commandeers and re-imagines anything it chooses from anywhere in the physical or mental world around it.'[v]

Prof. S.R Faruqi's signal contribution

Perhaps, the most widely admired critic and man of letters in India, today- or Pakistan, for that matter, if that is still a country,- Prof. Shamsur Rehman Faruqi, whose disciple Prof. Pritchett proudly proclaims herself to be, has some enlightening things to say- especially relevant to Ghalib's ghazals- about close reading a poem. He holds meaning to be contextual, and thus subject to an inherent degree of instability arising out of semiotic slippage. Close syntagmatic and paradigmatic reading of the text generates a set of meanings- subjective projections freely arrived at- which, so to speak, then taking a canonical form, become accessible for inter-subjective reception in such a manner as fulfils the wider purpose of poetry.

An allied, more naive, approach would be to regard the poem as an axiom system and the set of meanings, or projections by the readers, as models of that axiom system. Thus, a subjective projection on my part that makes a poem meaningful to me could be called my model of the poem. If I find that the poem captures features of my real life situation and suggests an optimal action schema to me, I may say 'this poem has real truth- it works-'. This would be equivalent to finding that a model of a system is concrete- i.e. relates to real world objects- rather than mere abstract entities.

Since I am speaking metaphorically, drawing an analogy rather than positing a one to one correspondence, and since dialogic and dialogism, both central to the Ghazal Universe, more naturally give rise to Dialethia (at least in the *Haqiqi/Majazi* sense, though the text itself may champion Monism) it naturally follows that logical paradoxes, emergent properties of systems vaster than can be envisioned and beyond the scope of volition, or puzzles about infinity do not represent a foundational problematic, though bound to arise, within this field of reference.

Perhaps, for this same reason, Prof. Faruqi is careful to limit the meaning of the poem to itself and its reception rather than turning it into a seismograph tracing the chthonic tectonics of some abstraction like History, or Being, or Identity. However, he notes, invoking Al Jurjani, that metaphorical, or, so to speak, symbolic language, does have this property of excess or surplus meaning which, it may be, is not exhaustible by any finite individual or social process.

Adding to Al Jurjani, the authority of Bhartrhari, he goes on to show that the occurrence of two or more meanings, two perhaps inconsistent Truths (which cashes out, it seems to me, as the doubling of every *sous rature* by reason of its also preceding every langue's parole), was not a source of scandal, or an 'aporia' in any of Derrida's senses, nor evidence that some great Metaphysical Original Sin had occurred at some point in History which must now be expiated by literary scholars to the neglect of their more obvious function of illumining texts for lesser minds.

What Faruqi Sahib has shown us is that Mannerist poetry- i.e. the baroque mode which exists only to exhaust its own possibilities of expression- is founded upon taking a trope for a fact and erecting a second trope upon the same logic as the first. This algorithmic method of cranking out new tropes is reminiscent of Raymond Lully's Ars Magna- itself believed to be based on the zairja of the Arabs.

We may ask the question- what are the logical, necessary, truths a practitioner of Mannerist poetry must subscribe to in order for his work to be considered as emanating from himself, expressing himself, rather than belonging, more properly, to the machine whose handle he happens to be turning at the moment of the poem's creation?

We know that Indo-Islamic thought was, at one time, a highly correlated system such that Astrology mirrored Herbology while an esoteric Soteriology guaranteed the empirical truth of the whole system by its gradation of occulted initiates endowed with super-natural powers specific to the burden each carried in supporting the overarching architecture of the Universe.

That, philosophically speaking, such a system was essentially Theistic- rather than Averroist or Spinozan- is evidenced by its rejection of univocity as an epistemological principle. Had it been Spinozan, properly speaking, either emotions could have no place in it, or the principle of transitivity would have had to be sacrificed. However, Mannerism can make no such sacrifice for its method is to hold all objects of thought to be interchangeable, under the operations of its logic or system of symmetries.

Indo-Islamic Mannerism, then- if it is not to be received as mere garrulous Gongorism- must be considered to be an ever expanding chrematistics of expression founded upon the two headed coin of occultation and ambiguity- neither to be understood as epistemological or hermeneutic- after all, the facts are already known, there is nothing aleatory about the search procedure, it is just one's poem is a hopeful monster not yet been instantiated in experience's Darwinian world- well, actually, it has been instantiated but, if so, not yet fittingly taxonomized- except that too is not true, Mannerism's first line already contains the whole poem- as if a hypothesis about evolution emerges at the same moment as the fossil record that supports it- a fact the poet finds so amazing that he can finish with the poem and include it in his Divan- i.e. the halting problem for the poet-as-Turing-machine is solved when the whole is found to be contained in its original input.

Thus, in this context, ambiguity and occultation are facts about a world where radical incompossibility defines true geography, permitting both absence and presence, to be infinitely apostrophised without any ontological commitment being made.

This is a method which enriches the world by hiding it and where poetry- if no longer prophesy- is nevertheless an *imitatio Dei*.

Thus, the true crime of Mansur is that he reveals what ought to be veiled. His crucifixion is not the apocalyptic 'rending of the veil' or Passion of God but a pious veil upon a veil.

Theism's God- an investigation of Godel's ontological proof reveals- takes as axiomatic that (in mathematical language) the set of all "positive properties" is an ultrafilter.

Baroque poetry- the method to Mannerism's *Majnoon* Madness- is the dual (in this instance the '*ideal*') of a Mathematics that embraces the unification of its branches on the basis of greater generality as part of an axiomatic faith in- if not the identity of indiscernibles and the principle of sufficient reason precisely- then the weakest possible specification of axioms that yields a sufficient structure to its objects of thought.

Indo-Islamic Mannerism must be a particularly weakly specified modal logic in that it burgeons by necessarily incompossible accretions to the World it reflects upon.

As such, it alone could survive- indeed, thrive- under conditions of a radical break- a great hole being punched through its highly correlated world and not merely register *but itself in part become* the most shocking part of the shock of the Modern.

This would be the case if, into Prof. Pritchett's treatment of Ghalibian *'ma'ni afrini'* as 'Meaning Machines', we import a sort of Kripkensteinian licentiousness with the result that the Machine comes to life, like the sexy Robot in Fritz Lang's Metropolis.

In saying this, I become suddenly aware that I'm playing the part of an Amartya Sen or Gayatri Spivak- viz. demonstrating the debilitating fallacy of a type of analysis not to put paid to its prestige but, indefensibly, to permit the expansion of its credentialist Ponzi scheme.

Thus, the simpler explanation is the true one.

Mannerism is merely a Theism.

God works in mysterious ways.

Not that there's any mystery as to how come I write only shite.

Prof. Frances Pritchett's web-site- 'A desertful of roses'- to which all my quotations from Ghalib and his commentators is but vainly and unworthily indebted- is a textbook example of how Literary Scholars can render a truly invaluable service to the general reader by a close and sympathetic reading of the text. Reading her comments, the lover of Ghalib is reminded of how greatly performativity and dialogic underlie our reception of the ghazal. (This is because, she invites us to imagine ourselves as part of the *mehfil*, listening to the *sher*, trying to anticipate the next line, and taking a sort of rueful delight in the manner in which the poet makes fools of us with his wizardry). But the performative aspect of the Ghazal's stock set of imagery is radically Dialethic- pointing to the heteroclite incompossibilty (in Leibniz's sense) of the two Truths (*Haqiqi* & *Majazi*- real & conventional) foundational to its Existence. This is a context in which hyperbole is a poetic virtue- as Prof. Faruqi maintains- rather than a sign of degeneracy as perhaps Victorian taste might have judged it.

Prof. Faruqi stresses clarity of image over clarity of meaning- and pays great attention to the logical consistency of poetic aetiology. This seems reasonable when we consider that if metaphors are properly derived from other metaphors and the regulative principle of that derivation is itself applicable, or adds piquancy, to what follows then, clearly, a condition for meaning- namely mindfulness on the part of the author- is met. Furthermore, so long as the poetic aetiology is consistent- and Prof. Faruqi is a rigorous constructivist- at least we don't get, *ex falso quodlibet,* an explosion of nonsense! This is not to say that the operation of the metaphor rules out incompossible states, on the contrary, Prof. Faruqi's courage is to grasp that nettle, and his great insight to show how 'Meaning production' is enhanced rather than rendered a nullity in such a 'six dimensional' world which adds to the possible worlds of modal logic a trajectory through impossible, perhaps inconceivable worlds, which, of course, is nothing less than the secret life of the mind.

With respect to Ghalib, Prof. Faruqi says, 'A poet of (Ghalib's) temperament penetrates within himself from beyond himself, remaining altogether detached in the process. Instead of merging the without and the within, he rather steps away from the without, using himself as a lever to investigate the external reality from every possible perspective. This is a special type of impersonality in poetry, scarcely to be matched in any, let alone Urdu, poetry.'

Yet, paradoxically, Ghalib is the poet best known as an individual to Urdu/Hindi speakers through biographical films, T.V serials, books and articles- not to mention his own letters and poems. Thus, more, much more, than Lord Macaulay, his praise of the British and ridiculing of what the 'Ain-i-Akbari' (his own model in Persian prose) reveals of the Mughals at the height of their power, stings us, or ought to sting us, to some simulacrum of sapience today- which is why, perhaps, Prof. Faruqi has provided us so a superb translation of Ghalib's Persian preface to Sir Syed Ahmed Khan's edition of that chronicle. As Prof. Faruqi reminds us, Ghalib, by birth and upbringing, really did belong to the cultivated Mughal class- though contemporary sources speak of some 'Mirzas' as so entirely unlettered as to, when high on *bhang*, converse in a made-up jargon convinced it was grandiloquent Persian they uttered rather than utter gibberish- and Ghalib's language and diction weren't a case of 'dressing for the job you want, not the job you have'- or, indeed, imagine to have existed in times of yore- but, rather, reflected his actual circumstances. Moreover, he really did have at least one love affair- slaying his too domesticable *domni* less, perhaps, by his eye's antimony than his purse's penury- his Wine was actual wine not a windy metaphor, and Madness not merely a literary conceit but the horrific malady that laid low his only brother.

Nevertheless, Prof. Faruqi rejects 'naturalism' and European, romantic, aesthetic standards as applicable to Ghalib and, with great erudition and forceful reasoning, provides a hermeneutic to maximize the meaning of Ghalib's *zairja*-like praxis of poesis which is both consistent with the canons of Indo-Islamic aesthetics as well as the sort of tropism towards symmetry via greater generality, that, if inexpressible in terms Lullian or Leibnizan, is nonetheless, no mere lullaby of that Mathesis Universalis which in Reason's sleep (the Academy its purpose-built dormitory) produces Monsters.

The question then becomes- how are we to separate the poet's meaning from the continuum of its echoing associations and dialogic divagations such that we may condignly congratulate ourselves on having carried forward Prof. Faruqi's project to the best of our (or my negligible) ability?

In this context, L.E.J. Brouwer, champion of intuitionism in Mathematics and member of the 'Significs' circle, held that pure mathematics consists primarily in the act of making certain mental constructions. The point of departure for these constructions is the intuition of the flow of time. Since Time is the ineluctable modality of the Ghazal's reception and we know Ghalib didn't write down his verses but merely tied a knot to mark each *sher* that had, in his mind, taken form, it follows that the intuition of Time, in Ghalib, is worth investigating. Brouwer says that this fundamental intuition, when divested from all sensuous content, allows us to perceive the form "one thing and again a thing, and a continuum in between". Brouwer calls this form, which unites the discrete and the continuous, "the empty two-ity". It is the basic intuition of mathematics; the discrete cannot be reduced to the continuous, nor the continuous to the discrete.

Similarly, Ethical Intuitionism might posit the essential undefinability of its terms while leaving a continuum between their apprehension as a 'two-ity'. In other words, bijective analysis does not necessarily have to subordinate the subject to a 'Structure' above and beyond it, which then becomes the proper locus for Meaning, rendering the subject relatively surd.

This continuum tends to disappear- is severed as by an anti-Anaxagorian axe cleaving Nous from Psyche and putting an end to Intuitionism's dream- if certain sorts of self-referentially recursive objects are admitted as having equal reality with what the mind naturally treats as experientially constructible.

A wholly different approach- based on the concept of *barzakh* as used by Ibn Arabi and refined by Mulla Sadr- would be to look not at the continuum between a 'two-ity' but to focus on the margin, the boundary, the limit which divides them. However, given the imaginal rather than real aspect of life in the *barzakh,* it follows that this boundary or isthmus tends to vanish and thus becomes a unifier in the sense of being the asymptotic limit of both sides of the 'two-ity'.

Whereas, the Stoic continuum is underpinned by the pneuma which inflates things to their tensility, so to speak, while also pervading the plenum, thus preserving a steady state, the system of Ibn Arabi and Sadr focuses on the liminal, imaginal, aspects of consciousness as this feather light *barzakh* which is not fixed in place but blown forward as by a great wind. Following Hans Blumenberg, we may consider the *barzakh* an 'absolute metaphor' which, once grasped, forever after frees us from misreading Persia's true poets as pawky pessimists, hiding their wine flagon under a dervish cloak from mere misanthropy, or- like the England-returned Iqbal- offering to infuse Dutch courage into all Islam, but in so thrifty a style, even Iran's abstemious Supreme Guide is now his admirer.

Sikhaya Mashahir-e-Azadi ko Maikhana-e-Angrez
Saqigari mushtahar ho, par kajdar-o-marez!.
Of Liberation, our Leaders learnt at the English Wine-shop
To most nobly tilt the bottle, but let fall not a drop!

This is not to say that, within Islam, it is universally conceded that the *barzakh* really does represent a place of creative, imaginal, activity. The plain, 'Salafi', reading would be that nothing happens in the grave prior to the resurrection. Not even the greatest prophet or Saint feels anything, knows anything, hears anything or imagines anything.

If Ghalib was a liberal Akhbari, rather than Usuli, Shia- as has been asserted- there is a special suggestiveness in the relationship between the *barzakh* and the occultation of the Imam Mahdi such that more degrees of freedom necessarily exist without any real foreclosing of what can be predicated of the God of the Faithful. In particular, by rejecting analogical reasoning (*qiyas,* the only *qisas* (lex talonis) allowed against God) and *communis opinio* (*ijma*) and things like Ayatollahs and *Vilayet-e-faqih* and so on- the *hadith*, 'whoever makes a judgment and is wrong gets one reward, who makes a judgment and is right gets a double'- works such that, for the moment, what is important is that one makes judgments for oneself- this is not Malamati (blame-worthy) necessarily because the occultation has changed or suspended aspects of the way Faith might live in the world. The consequence is that the Theist (or philandering Philosophical Monist, squeamish of even the smallest Quinean ontological commitment) finds little to cavil at it in Ghalib.

But even if Ghalib had no religious leanings, it would remain the case that, for the Ghazal World, rigor in poetic aetiology or the derivation of fresh metaphors or themes on the basis of logical operations has a double significance- on the one hand it is an imitation of what the dead Awlia or Saint is doing in the *barzakh* which, in a sense, is transforming the Universe- on the other hand it is neither life nor resurrection but that oblivion which lies between.

There is a famous couplet of Ghalib's which is rescued from triteness by keeping the *barzakh* in mind-

Apni gali mein na kar mujhe dafan-e-bad-e-qatl
Kyoun mere pate se khalq ko tera ghar mile?
No! Not *after* I'm slain, fair assassin, I thee implore
Bury me not in your lane, lest others find your door

The theme here is an old one. The *Hubb al Udhri* lover dies on the road to the beloved, like Devdas before reaching Paro's house. The *kuh-e-yaar*- the street of the fair one- is the earth under which, by convention, the lover wishes to be buried.

However, the mystical twist behind this particular verse is by no means easy to comprehend. This is because Ghalib has chosen to use a word '*khalq*'- meaning 'the Public' or 'the Creatures'- which has heavy religious and philosophical overtones.

Muslim intellectuals, unless they went to Karachi Grammar or someplace equally dire, grasp these overtones at a subconscious level. The non-Muslim must ponder the imagery and consult dictionaries and reference books- or, in my case, the baker at the local Tandoor- to arrive at the same level of comprehension.

When considering why a poet chooses a particular word, we begin by considering the rules of prosody. One word may be more apt than another which has the same meaning. However, we also need to consider what other concept that particular word is bracketed with. In the case of *khalq* (what is created*)*, there is a bracketing with *amr* (what is commanded and thus possible to come to pass though the ground for its existence may be lacking). *En passant*, I may mention, this is a particularly useful distinction for the scientifically minded as helping reconcile Darwin with Scripture.

Ghalib, on the other hand, at least in his adolescent Urdu ghazals- e.g. the rejected couplet
{4,8x} *hai kahāñ tamannā kā dūsrā qadam yā rab*
ham ne dasht-e imkāñ ko ek naqsh-e pā pāyā
Where, Lord, alights the foot of Ardency's stride?
The Sahara of Becoming is but a sole-print wide

explores the existential pathos of what is commanded to exist (*amr*) but in a manner too imperfectly creative in adjusting itself to creation (*khalq*) to bear the load of Being- which, of course, is Becoming. (Should the reader cavil at my use of the 'explore', well, okay, Ghalib explored his theme in the manner that Columbus explored India- a perfectly sound use of the word 'explore' since both Ghalib and I are Indian.) Perhaps Ghalib rejected this verse from his Divan because of the controversy that came to a head in 1824 re. *imkan-e-nazir* (God's ability to send a second Revelation) and *imkan-e-kizb* (God's ability to lie). This question itself hinges on whether God alone has *ilm-e-Ghayb* (knowledge of the unseen) or whether there is a supramundane, as opposed to merely relativist (*al ghayb al nisbi*) sense in which the Prophet is privileged in this respect as indeed appears evident from H.Q 72.26-7. If the first proposition is allowed, the second step must also be taken and the danger is that Islam goes forward into a wilderness- *dasht-e-imkan*. One solution we know Ghalib contemplated- viz. God as simultaneously authoring infinite incompossible Universes- fails because such ontological inflationism is precisely the dysphoric nightmare of Faith such that each believer remains the solitary prisoner of a Deus Absconditus dream of a world. The defect of stark Occasionalism is that Revelation affirming it can't meaningfully be shown to be free of *imkan-e-kizb* unless some degree of *ilm al ghayb* is added to the subject of the Revelation. The alternative is to say, with Ghazzali, that this world is the best possible one- a notion Ibn Arabi ridiculed and which, indeed, is ridiculous save from a viewpoint indifferent between all possible outcomes- but this itself requires some supramundane quality attaching to that gaze.

Interestingly, with respect to the theophany in the Gita, Arjuna had previously been granted the boon of *chakshushi vidya*- a sort of second sight. In this context, the Mubahila episode points to the impeccability of the Holy Family, thus providing a purely Ashari defence against *imkan-e-kizb* such that impeccability (*ismah*), as endowed in an Occasionalist manner, is constructive of a *ilm al ghayb* lattice.

I have read that Ghalib requested the help, for editing his first Divan, of Maulana Fazl-e-Haq Khairabadi whose *Tahqeeq al-Fatwa fi Ibtal al-Taghwa,* published in 1822, denounced Ismail Dehlvi for affirming *imkan-e-kizb*. At a later point- Ghalib's one disastrous service to the Mughals- such friends as this helped him get the Emperor acquitted of the charge of being a crypto-Shia, whereas had Khairabadi, later hanged for declaring Jihad on John Company, published a hostile fatwa on the matter, perhaps the British would have preserved the dynasty!

My feeling is that Ghalib's own approach to the *ilm al ghayb* question is not coloured by the 'Wahhabi' controversy but transposes it to a bridal (*Urs*) *mise en scene*. The abashed inwardness of the secret desire to surrender (to 'be known' in the Biblical sense) is actually the wish to be not known- to be outside knowledge, or at least unseen- yet, paradoxically the Master of the Unseen is the one who brings all things to Light!

This is the sense I get from the next 2 rejected verses of Ghazal 4

> Maddened is my Innocence at the malice of its Test
> Privily deflowered as ***boutonnière*** to thy chest!

> Still, Sand castles anneal Hope & Calf Love, Veal, the Calf
> Till, Despair teeth bare the Two Worlds' butcher laugh.

Another ghazal- number 39- Ghalib wrote at the age of 19, seems a more virile take on the eroticization of the Sufi trope of *khalwat dar anjuman* (solitude in company)-

> shab kih vuh majlis-furoz-e khalvat-e nāmūs thā
> rishtah-e har sham'a khār-e kisvat-e fānūs thā
> mashhad-e 'āshiq se kosoň tak jo ugtī hai ḥinā
> kis qadar yā rab halāk-e ḥasrat-e pā-būs thā
> ḥāṣil-e ulfat nah dekhā juz shikast-e ārzū
> dil bah dil paivastah goyā yak lab-e afsūs thā
> kyā kahūň bīmārī-e ġham kī farāġhat kā bayāň
> jo kih khāyā khūn-e dil be-minnat-e kaimūs thā

Last night, when the radiance of our assembly to her abashed chamber retired
Each candle wick, became a thorny prick at its shade from the desired

Whom has not, Lord, the longing to kiss bridal feet, with a martyr's zeal fired?
For miles, the Lover's tomb, by not rolling wheat but green henna is gyred

Against Sorrow's <u>sorites</u>, the Brain, this Stoic armor, in vain, thus acquired
Trysts, hearts crush hearts to gain, are the thin lips of pain- it required.

Knew I respite from this wretchedness- I'd recite much to be admired
But, Oh!- eating my own heart out- my very bile has grown tired!

However, it is precisely the dangers inherent in this eroticized invocation of Saint worship- wholly innocent in Amir Khusrau- which adds attraction to a sort of Wahabbi *imkan al khadib* argument whereby a traditional practice or dogma could be considered abrogated even absent consensus (*ijma*) regarding the matter.

Perhaps, the virulence of polemics arising out of this intra-Sunni strife made Ghazal poets more amenable to the Shiah view thanks to Mulla Sadr's 'existential' marginalizing of the question of *imkan*- mere possibility- and the sheer brilliance and lucidity of his synthesising efforts.

This brings us back to the *amr/khalq* syzygy of which a contemporary Shia source has this to say-

'Shia (Usuli) theology makes a distinction between material beings, which are subject to motion, change and alteration, and non material beings, which are free from matter, movement, change and alteration. A material being is bound by time and space, whereas a non material being is free from them, and is not limited by these two binding factors. The complete domain of non material being is called *alam al 'amr* (the World of Command).

'In the 'World of Command' every being assumes existence spontaneously on exercise of Divine will or command, without the need of preparation of any material, temporal or special ground.

'The realization of every being is subject to its essential possibility (*al imkan al dhati*). Anything which is essentially impossible and incapable of assuming existence, whether material or non material, God does not command for its coming into being. However, the essential possibility of a being is always with its essence, and time and space do not intervene in it.

'As opposed to the World of Command, there is the World of Creation (*alam al khalq*). The material world is called the Word of Creation. In this world, the existence of every being, in addition to its essential possibility, depends on its possibility of preparedness (*al-'imkan al-isti'dadi*) that is, its materialization can take place only under the presence of favorable conditions and readiness of ground. Here, also, the realization of every being takes place with the will and command of God. However, so long as the ground for the emergence of a material being is not prepared, the necessary conditions are not fulfilled and hindrances are not removed, God does not will its creation and does not command its realization.'

In Barzakh- that is limbo- according to the system of Ibn Arabi, the consciousness moves from the world of creation to the world of 'command' or pure possibility. Allama Iqbal's theory of *khuddi* (self-hood) draws upon the concept of Barzakh '*...death, if present action has sufficiently fortified the ego against the shock that physical dissolution brings, is only a passage to what the Qur'an describes as Barzakh....*" Iqbal considers existence in Barzakh to be an active rather than a passive state where the mind, freed of the bonds of mere contingency, can experience and imagine higher types of reality. Indeed, so my Urdu Ustad informs me, even as I write this now, the great Iqbal, moldering in his grave, is thinking great thoughts about whether it is licit for women to hold high public office or whether the British might not conveniently be persuaded to quit India. Truly, such thought is highly transformative of the Universe.

But not to 'vilify Time' any further, especially after all that Iqbal did for it- consider his meeting with Bergson where his quotation of the relevant Hadith caused the paralytic old Jew to leap out of his wheelchair and dance a *bhangra*- we may observe that all this begs the question of whether the fundamental intuition of Time allows for a 'two-ity' between different orders of objects, especially those recursively defined upon them by means of an infinite operator.

Borges wrote of the first volume of a fictional poet's 'Vindication of Eternity' as being '...a history of the diverse eternities devised by Man; from the immutable Being of Parmenides to the alterable Past of Hinton.'

Borges adds that the poet's second volume, 'denies (with Francis Bradley) that all the events in the universe make up a temporal series. He argues that the number of experiences possible to man is not infinite, and that a single repetition suffices to demonstrate that time is a fallacy..."

The Ibn Arabi scholar, W.Chittick, writes- "There is no repetition in [God's] self-disclosure" (*lâ takrâr fi'l-tajallî*) 'By acknowledging the unity of the Real, Tawhid, we recognize that it is one and unique in its every act, which means that each created thing and each moment of each thing is one and unique; nothing can ever be repeated precisely because of each thing's uniqueness and the divine infinity.'

But, it would seem, this leaves us with a perception of a 'two-ity' with no means of getting from one side to the other. A path is not a path if no second can take it to the same goal.

For Ibn Arabi, who claimed to be the seal of the Awlia, perhaps, Time was of the *kshanika vada* (purely momentary) sort upheld by Buddhism such that he was not mean-spiritedly pulling the ladder up after himself but leaving the status of Awlia-hood available, but outside Time, and hence divorced from eschatology or the trajectory of historical Islam, thus safeguarding Religion from charismatic swindlers and chiliastic schismatics.

Returning to Ghalib's line- *apni gali mein na kar mujh ko dafan-e-bad-e-qatl-* we are now in a position to see something of the characteristic sanity and rationalism- celebrated by Prof. Faruqi- as well as the impish humour of the poet, who asks of the beloved- not to bury him, *after* killing him- rather than while yet alive, for, indeed, no cruelty could be too great to ascribe to the beloved- while simultaneously comparing his own situation to one already in *barzakh* while yet clinging to life... This raises a further question about the beloved's habit of cruelty and whether it arises from her foundational *amr al takwini* (the Lord's merciful command which gives her life) or is enjoined upon her as a deontic *amr al taklifi* (the command to a duty of supererogatory mercy- as an *imitatio Dei*). Of course- as Prof. Pritchett is ever at pains to point out- in the Ghazal Universe, what is enjoyable is the manner in which the beloved expresses her mercy (*takwini* or *taklifi* as it may be) by relentless cruelty. To paraphrase Ghalib- (this is {77,1} *zakhm par chhiṛkeñ kahāñ ṭiflān-e be-parvā/namak kyā mazah hotā agar patthar meñ bhī hotā namak-* Majnun, the thoughtless tots who wound you are not without fault/ Ah! What pleasure would there be if their rocks too were salt?)-

> Told 'a high salt diet harms the heart'
> My thoughtful angel with thrifty art
> Such *tendresse* for me, soft, reveals
> As to salt the wounds she freely deals!

Deleuze has written of the relationship between the Sadist and the Meta-masochist (who derives pleasure from being *denied* the pain otherwise necessary for orgasm) but this is a mere bagatelle compared to the levels of reflexivity in the relationship between the lover and the beloved in the Ghazal Universe. Crucially, Ghazali's Occasionalism has the effect of equating what we Hindu's call the *apurva* with the hiatus between *amr* and *khalq* and licenses *apoorvata*, as Bedil's '*taza gui*'(freshness of expression), not as '*bida*'- innovation or novelty- but predestined Essence and unchanging Truth. For this reason, the Masochist's existential project- in the Ghazal Universe- is never at the mercy of the Sadist nor, in consequence, Facticity's only road to Freedom.

1.   The poet's grievance- 'from knowledge of my location, why should the *khalq* find your house?'- begs two questions- can knowledge (*ilm*) or enquiry (*pata karna*) avail the created and if so is this fair, is this just, to one whose path was so much lonelier and more arduous? Secondly, as to whether there is any continuum or path, travelled by one before, available to the *khalq* to reach the level of *amr*? Perhaps, if Ghalib by reason of his great and greatly doomed love, is that martyr who is both alive and dead, both buried and not buried, both of the stuff of *khalq* as well as that of *amr*- the miracle might be possible (*amr*), but why should it become *khalq* (i.e. come to pass?) in such a manner that others get the benefit without suffering the pain? What *sitam-zareefi* (ingenuity in torture) would it correspond to? In other words what is the *husn-e-taleel* (beauty in poetic aetiology) which would provide the *mazmun* (poetic conceit) for this refinement of cruelty? (It may be worthwhile to note, *en passant,* that controversies over what happens in *barzakh* and whether the Awlias, or others of the pious dead, can indeed intercede for their devotees, are very much current in present day Indian Islam. Ghalib is not entering into this debate- and, perhaps, commentators too might not wish to tread on such treacherous ground.)

2.   Connoisseurs of Ghazzali Minor's *Savaanih* may well wonder whether there might be a specifically Sufi esoteric hermeneutic or orthopraxy- parallel to his elder brother's Occassionalist orthodoxy- which we ought to bear in mind while savouring a Ghazal's *husn-e-taleel*. In this context, I suppose, I could vain-gloriously gas on about 'the medieval mind'; closed, non-dissipative, and highly correlated systems upon which mine own tendentious, embattled and blinkeredly Indo-centric ersatz Thomism represents an Emergent and Fichtean rebellion against 'Natural' or *ad captum vulgi* Teleology, etc, etc, but the trouble is, the Ghazali Bros' Lebenswelt was, in many ways, more sophisticated and urbane than my own benighted intellectual cooliedom in which all efficient causes are occluded by Media pi-jaw or Managementspeak or cutesy Graphical User Interfaces specially designed for morons almost, but not quite, as stupid as myself.

3.   If Imam Jafar as-Sadiq's concept of *'takvin'* is understood as Emergence- in what relationship might it stand to the Ghazzali brothers' Occasionalism and causationless poetic aetiology?

     Perhaps, in an Occassionalist Universe, Emergence becomes the fundamental intuition, not of Time- for Time, here, is mere heteroclite seriality or *jeitzeit* juxtaposition- but the Brouwerian 'two-ity' which provides the basis of an acausal Constructivism, a Mereological metric in which, bizarrely, the part exceeds the whole because, every possible emergent in which it might participate becomes its choice sequence and knight's tour of a more ample dimension of freedom in *alam al amr*, whereas the emergent's indifference curve between ingredient mixes (i.e. its multiple realizability) becomes a constraint upon what *amr* can self-inviduatingly express in *khalq*.

In this sense, then, the glory of the Ghazal is its reverse mereology or, *salva veritate*, reverse *Tzimtzum;* its turning of theodicy on its head- not justifying God's ways to Man, but making Man, making haecceity, interesting to God and inflationarily expanding the scope of His *amr*.

     But only apparently. There's an incentive compatibility problem here. Ghalib asks why *khalq* should be able to find the house of the beloved through his own *not* Emergent status in *barzakh* but its *reverse*. Fuck's my motivation?- is what the guy is sayin' here. Hence the line's pathos. Which, strangely, makes it kinda cool...

4.   What might a causationless aetiology cash out as for a shit-for-brains bloke like me? I guess, like most people of my education and generation, I think of emotions as 'Darwinian algorithms of the mind' and even efficient causes as arising out of a sort of Anthropic Selection Principle operating across a fitness landscape of Multiverses with different fundamental Laws or constants. Thus, to get away from efficient causes and glimpse the lifted horizon offered by

causationless aetiology, is essentially (in Hindu terms) to escape Prakriti and seek to adopt the viewpoint of Purusha. The Ghazal then becomes not a trivializing 'talking to women' but a talking to Prakriti.

5.   Since, in our Weltenshaung, efficient causes gain efficacy by having been selected for, *husn-e-taleel* becomes the last word in pathos as that all puissant 'tyrant' is proven to be nothing but a series of snapshots in a mirror whose temporal existence is virtual and imaginary.

6.   A final observation about this couplet; if Ghalib harboured a healthy scepticism about the claims of the scholars, then perhaps his refusal to be a sort of philosophical sign post, or rendezvous point is entirely understandable. It often seems that just as diseases are named after the first patient to present its symptoms, rather than the Doctor who discovered its cure, so too with philosophers and pathologies of thought.

Dijective 'Meaning Creation'

As Prof. Faruqi has pointed out, Ghalib's method is both syntagmatic as well as paradigmatic- his *'ma'ni afrini'* (meaning creation) is dijective[vi] rather than bijective- involving a sort of Cantorian diagonalization, a sideways movement, which by its impersonality and tropism towards greater generality and symmetry, makes him truly a 'difficult' poet in the sense of seeking to generate a maximal matrix of meaning- which, by the Continuum hypothesis, would be but our infinite demeaning- rather than capping himself with contrived and millinery paradoxes or wrapping himself up in hermetic robes or rococo riddling. But Ghalib's diagonalization isn't Badiouian precisely because it isn't, any more than Cantor's, the very boring boring of yet another hole through supposed *idées reçues* so as to breathe fresh life into the most fucked *idée reçue* of all- viz. that Parnassianism too might be 'Progressive'- helping to overawe if not *épater le bourgeois* who then surrender to whatever 'Operation Infinite Justice' we're Straussianly sponsoring- thus facilitating Praetorian regime change.

To my mind, Prof. Faruqi has performed an invaluable service, not to Urdu speakers merely, but to practicing poets also, by his dramatic break with tradition in his appreciation of Ghalib. It is noteworthy that he does so without making any explicit philosophical or creedal commitments but achieves his end by close reading alone.

Nevertheless, for people not brought up with a knowledge of the glories of Islamic philosophy, some exposure to basic Islamic concepts might, in my view, enhance their reading of Ghalib- in particular the notion that **Ghalib's *mushkilat* (difficult poetry) arises from a sort of internalized, or programmatic, *'amr al taklifi'*** such that he achieves individuation and has something new to say (*taza gui*)

This by no means implies that Ghalib was constrained by the philosophical discourse of his time. Rather, if I read Prof. Faruqi aright, his poetic practice was one open to philosophy by reason of his concern with originality- uniqueness, as in the Sanskrit term *'apoorvata'*- but an originality driven purely by the perception of symmetries at higher orders of generality irrespective of *ad captum vulgi* intuitions regarding temporality and topological connectivity. Thus, his Semantic Universe is intensional (as opposed to extensional) and impersonal (though his ghazals are in the *'insha'* intentional register). This means that his *mazmun afrini* (poetic creativity) can and ought, to genuinely profit us, be cut out and abstracted from his historical context- at least by minds sufficiently rigorous and sensibilities sufficiently catholic.

This has the great benefit of excluding in advance much of the more lamentable jargon of modern literary theory from our ambit. An example is Deriddan *'differAnce'* (of which Prof. Faruqi has occasion to speak) which introduces an infinite operator into what can only be a finite activity- viz. reading. The consequence is that, so to speak, the continuum between minds gets clogged up by paradoxes generated for no good reason and the capacity of the language user to signify is pronounced diminished by a spectral Alienist utterly alien to the Heimat of

Human Agency.

By contrast, Ibn al Arabi's concept of barzakh- as a dimensionless divider/unifier not fixed but impelled, like Walter Benjamin's Angel of History, by a great wind (actually self generated by its own imaginal activity)- could in some sense underpin a notion of iterative reading such that the meaning received ought never to be the same thing twice but, somehow, illumine more and more.

A further point about the manner in which insistence on intuitionistic, imaginal, constructivity might yield grounds for the belief that the consciousness is not trapped like a fly in amber, follows from the fact that the affirmation that, for example, mathematics is a languageless activity, utterly short circuits the argument from conditioning, linguistic or otherwise, and restores 'Meaning production' to the field of individual volition and cognitive freedom. Moreover, an 'impulse equilibrium' psychologism- which quickly cashes out as an elitism that holds Education to be a *cordon sanitaire* and seeks to replace Religion with Art as a means to overawe the great unwashed- or a semiotic scholasticism to Talibanize hungry hordes of Graduate students for some paltry purpose of gesture politics- too, receives a condign kick in the goolies as noesis, rather than dianoia, becomes what poesis is about.

Thus close reading, intense mental application to reduplicate the cognitive processes of the producer of the text, has a paradoxical result- it shows how poetry, at its best, too is a languageless activity. The juxtaposition of images and their mutual dialectic is something that can be separated out from other important aspects of the poem- for example its sound pattern, its 'mood', the philosophical questions it raises and so on.

(The counter-argument- viz. close reading cashes out as senile presbyopia, *apoorvata* is dictated by the dead hand of the karmic *apurva*- i.e. hermeneutic discovery is the occlusion of its own soteriologically abortive hysteresis- may, without loss of generality, be dismissed by aggressively soliciting fellatio- or, if you're still in Primary School (as I believe the majority of my readers tend to be)- an invitation to 'eat my shorts')

No doubt, the bad poet- like the bad craftsman, or bad entrepreneur- is surrendering to that which a novel instrumentality makes facile- be that instrumentality linguistic or technological or arising out of colonial or other contact with a different culture. Here, indeed, we might say behaviour is determined by the tool it has grasped. Experimentation, it may be, is constrained along facile paths. Technicity (in the Leroi-Gourhan sense) is fabricating the sort of 'subaltern', or strategically essentialist and therefore yet more idiotic 'Ethnic', identity the all polluting heavy industry of Elite Political Correctness tactically supports- suborning Gramscian Karachi Grammar Gobshites and Post Colonial Queer Theory Leela Gandhian, or Gandhian *lila,* careerists, such that they themselves become the vast suppository Civil Society must henceforth be seen to salutarily apply to honest, working class, immigrant, degenerate drunkard, populations- such as that to which, I, however ingloriously, belong.

The obverse, using the new in an old way- for e.g. a laptop as paperweight- points again to a heteronomy arising from the cognitive failure to merge horizons. Indeed, bad poetry has both these qualities. Why? One way to frame an answer is to say that the continuum- in this case between a new tool and an old mode of production- has not been properly grasped by the foundational intuition of 'two-ity'. There is here a failure of thought.

The question however remains, without recourse to the authority of some genius's intuition or Mystic's illumination, why is it so difficult to establish a continuum between objects apprehended as a 'two-ity'? The Stoics were already aware of this problem, which is linked to the Sorites paradox and arises out of the danger of applying infinite operators to what can be but apprehended vaguely. The result is to undermine the principle of Identity based on non contradiction. This realization can engender an extreme reaction. If there is confusion as to where to draw the dividing line, perhaps we need to retreat to one pole or the other, burning our bridges so as to kill off all laggard in the stampede thus occasioned. That way, surely, there will be clear blue water between us and those clustering around the other pole of the two-ity. Thus, by a razing of the continuum, Identity at each pole is safeguarded.

But what then is to prevent, the splitting up of the continuum into more and more separate parts- whose most benign possible result would be a doctrine that everything is true and no two truths are commensurable or connected in any useful way?

Great piety, as that of Mulla Sadr and Ibn Arabi, might be one way out. In the shadow of the Saints, anxiety about Identity might be stilled. A doctrine of two truths, one fundamental the other merely instrumental or heuristic, might be seen as linked by a continuum of sublation that actually, by the operation of Grace, works like an escalator.

Since Ghalib's *jamal*-as-beauty is but the weed of Aristocratic negligence, while his *jalal*-as-terror is mere bankrupt Tulip mania & it is only his perfect balancing of *jamal* and *jalal* that renders his Divan *kamal*- after all, our Byron had to have a Hellespont and if it turned out to be only a rain puddle then, ***Post***-Mutiny, so much the better- the problem remains of finding the right point to cut his meaning out of the continuum of its echoing associations. What makes the task poignant is the notion that Ghalib may have seen himself as mediating every word he wrote precisely as this 2 sided barzakh - both the grave's oblivion and its posited imaginal leavening power- except he was uniting the 2 notions without the assurance that the Gravitational pull, so to speak, of the Awlia Saints would raise him up to a position where the result was not a bitter futility.

Thus, a couplet exemplifying courage in the face of death like-
> 'Since Sorrow can tax the Free no more than one breath
> 'Lightning's the lone candle we now light for a death!'

Is followed quickly by the reflection that-
> 'Ours too is a world- but one barren to its own passion, tumult & wrath
> '& we the nuptial taper of the heart's bed chamber of its moth!'

For Ghalib, as Ghazal's God, affects are effects but in an entirely negative way. This is his mercy upon the moth-
> 'Guard the garden, Ghalib, the bees' attacks to defeat
> 'The moth, too, is martyred by the wax they secrete!'

Indeed, recalling that barzakh has no verbal root in Arabic and that it may derive from the Persian 'purdah'(veil)- a circumstance Ghalib, passionate Persianist that he was, might have delighted in- there is an irony in the apocryphal couplet popularly attributed to him- *Khuda key vaastey purdah na Kaabey sey utha zahid, kahin vahan bhi yahi kafir sanam nikley[vii]*-
> For God's sake, O Priest, do not lift the veil from the Kaa'ba's Holy fane
> The appearance of this idol there would be too embarrassing to explain!

Still, though the couplet is burlesque, lifting that veil remains a matter of choice, in which context it appears quite suggestive to me that Brouwer (enchantingly burlesque, surely, in that fan dance featuring Victoria Lady Welby?) hoped to repair the continuum by choice sequences- something produced by free choice rather than an illegitimate appeal to an infinite operator- and, perhaps, if such a thing indeed exists, the school of Prof. S.R Faruqi, exercising free choice, rather than blindly following an ideology, may end up doing just that- i.e. permitting the ordinary man access not just to Ghalib's melody but also his meaning.

Prof. Faruqi and translating Ghalib's Urdu Ghazals

What meta-semantic commitments, if any, are involved in the Professor's method of interpretation? At first glance we might say that meaning must be constrained by the context and language actually used. However, since to speak of context is to introduce an extensional rather than intensional semantics, in practice this would simply cash out as a set of historicist hermeneutics which pointlessly debate what so-and-so might possibly have known and what he might possibly have thought given the received historical wisdom about his times and circumstances. This would be a truly horrible outcome because it would let deeply ignorant Post Colonial shit-heads prowl around pissing on Ghalib's grave.

Thus, to take the example of '*Naqsh fariyadi*'- a reader like me might immediately associate the image of the plaintiff in a court case wearing a robe of paper- *'khagazi pairahan'*- with the Book of Job- which I imagine to be the earliest source of the image. In this case the entire meaning of the verse is utterly changed.

Indeed, given that his Divan begins with this *matla*, our perception of Ghalib's entire ouevre might be altered.

But, did Ghalib know the story of Job? The evidence weighed up by Faruqi & Pritchett suggests that for Ghalib this was a Persian idiom with no connection to the story of Job- who, in Islam, is a symbol for patience and forbearance rather than, so to speak, the most passionate plaintiff against God in ancient literature.

But what if someone finds a line in some book Ghalib is known to have read which links the phrase *khagazi pairahan* to the story of Job? What if the diary of some Nineteenth Century Missionary is discovered which shows Ghalib had read a translation of the book?

But, once one starts on the path of counterfactuals where is one to end? Perhaps, Ghalib as a boy in Agra met a garrulous Jain grocer-a Banarsidas wannabe- who explains *syadvad* logic and the distinction between countable and uncountable and so on to the young Ghalib? Indeed, what can one actually rule out? Perhaps, Ghalib really did correspond with Karl Marx!

A different approach, one compatible with Prof. Faruqi's commitment to close reading, would consist of taking up *'khagazi pairahan'* as a symbol and to imaginatively enter into why it appealed both to the author of the Book of Job and to Ghalib. In this case, though less can be predicated of Ghalib, the man, the meaning of his poetry is enhanced. The trade off here is really between tendentious mythologizing about a hero and gaining a better appreciation of his acknowledged achievements.

More suggestive yet is the Borgesian notion of Universal History as being but the ringing of intonational changes on a handful metaphors- which, typically, that auriferous Argentine only employed to demonstrate the impossibility of History, of Universals, of everything, indeed, essentially Perónist and antithetical to Art- forcing us back once more upon the pedestrian footpath- one moreover Poets (or poetasters, to speak more narrowly of myself) are obliged to take, and take as our pillow- which is to consider the conceit, arising, it may be, purely linguistically, but to do so *outside* the net of language and thus, by projection, to experientially explore (so to speak) its emotional valency and metabletic possibilities.

Thus, to approach '*khagazi pairahan*', I might start with an old English joke. A small boy turns up at the County Court dressed in an old suit that would only fit a much taller and broader adult man. He does so because he has been asked to appear 'in his father's suit'. From this, it is a short step, especially for one steeped in sentimental Eighteenth Century authors- sorry, I meant to say classic Tamil Cinema- to arrive at the notion of a family left literally naked by the costs of a legal battle and showing up at Court covering their shame in nothing but the papers concerning their law-suit.

The Naqsh fariyadi

Let us begin by examining the first couplet- traditionally an invocation of God- of *naqsh fariyadi*, the ghazal with which Ghalib's published Divan commences-

naqsh faryādī hai kis kī shoḳhī-e taḥrīr kā
kāġhaẕī hai pairahan har paikar-e taṣvīr kā

This ghazal- one Ghalib composed in 1816 at the age of 19- is richer to our eyes than it would have been to his own. This is because though Ghalib lived at a time of expanding literary, intellectual and commercial horizons there is little unequivocal evidence that, as an adolescent, he himself profited much, or at all, from the new learning that was becoming available. However, viewing Ghalib's ghazal as 'a hopeful monster'- the notion that he, like Kipling, 'shows more than he knows'- is not, perhaps wholly illicit for the contemporary qauffer of our, Post-Mutiny, moonshine of blighted Eids.

The first line-*Naqsh faryādī hai kis kī shoḳhī-e taḥrīr kā*- may be translated as follows-
Against whom is the graven image a petitioner, or plaintiff, decrying a self-willed hobby of, or ardour for, a sort of elegance in writing that is also, as it were, an act of manumission, raising created characters to a level of seeming reality and agency sufficient to indict their own author?

Here, *Tahrir*- familiar to us now as the Egyptian Tianmen where, as I write this, Barack, Mubarak and the mood in the barracks contest to square what is but a Viconian circle- *Tahrir*, indeed, or to Alethia's present need, is the load-bearing word- both chastened slave to the clamorous *eleutheros* but also back bent in porterage to the *Eleutherios'* pullulating mischiefs of meaning.

Derived from an Arabic root associated with movement and change- *Tahrir* denotes elegant writing, the painter's brushwork, actions associated with documents and letters- including the delivery of a deed of manumission to a slave- but also, for the learned, conjures up visions of Euclid's elements (*tahrīr-e-baina's-sut'ūr*) if not his no less influential work on Optics (*Kitab Uqlidis fi Ikhtilaf al-manazir*) which, it may be- on the analogy of a Shahi origin for Hindu *dhvani*- permits a colour palette evolved on a Turanian fitness landscape to, by a literary, therefore hypertrophied, more than epigenetic effect, translate into the aestheticizing of particular- un Aryan, not Babu bureaucratic, not geometrically Greek nor grammatologically Pehelvi- word cluster interconnections such that the primal Rebellion which crowned the Gokturks with glory remained always recoverable for their seed.

Setting aside, for the moment, the project of deriving *sabak-e-hindi* from a Turanian deformation of literary Persian so as to preserve by purely linguistic means a type of collective entelechy or cognitive plasticisty previously enforced by their travails as steppe warriors, we may note that Euclid's axiomatic method requires words to have stable meanings, propositions to always have the same connotation and truth value. Commentators, too, would like this line of Ghalib's to mean only one rather than a number of things. But, as connoisseurs, we are not so constrained. What, then, are the possible- if not compossible- meanings of this line?

1)   Translating *Shokhi-e-tahrir* as pleasure-in-composition we get something like this for the first line of the Ghazal- 'Who is that self-willed creator, infatuated with his own artistry, against whom the created image cries out for Justice?'

Hali has an anecdote about Ghalib- '*One time, at night, he was lying on a cot, looking at the sky. Seeing the apparent disorder and lack of arrangement of the stars, he said, 'The task done out of self-will is usually done in a disorderly way. Look at the stars- how badly they're scattered around! No order, no arrangement; neither pattern nor design. But the King has the right over everything; no one can breathe a word.'*

How unlike this is to Immanuel Kant's- 'Two things fill the mind with ever new and increasing wonder and awe: the starry heavens above me and the moral law within me"!

It is noteworthy that Ghalib, in the anecdote, reveals no Pascalian terror at the silence of infinite space- nor predicates of that Sphere, whose center is everywhere and circumference nowhere, the Borgesian property of being atrocious- rather the stars tremble with a loquacity they dare not indulge because 'the King has the right over everything.'

This is not to say that a Borgesian reading of the line is precluded- the half baked creator is himself the half baked creation of a half baked creator and so on- fitting well with the Gnostic notion that the Demiurge created this imperfect world because he had forgotten he himself was a mere Emanation and had not within him that of which something truly vital and harmonious could be born.

Yet, to my mind, what Ghalib presents us with is more interesting- a deficit in orderly design, no following of rules, no fractal structure to the Universe- ergo no real possibility of microcosm mirroring macrocosm, no scope for a Hermetic Art, nothing but contingency and arbitrariness and meaninglessness such that- though the figures of rational creatures are discernible- their reasoning is futile for mere caprice, not empathic intelligence, rules their destinies. This is because *shokhi* (an ungovernable and capricious passion) has dispensed with the Principle of Sufficient Reason in issuing its *amr al takvini* (command to live) forgetting, or not caring, that this entailed a reciprocal *amr al taklifi* (corresponding duty enjoined on the Created to a like supererogatory quality as that which motivated the engendering act) bereft of the means to perform itself by reason of that disorderliness in the Universe which militates against Consilience.

Here, it seems to me, Ghalib individuates and differentiates himself from the tradition to which he belonged by a *taza gui* (novel manner of speaking) such that we sense a uniquely Ghalibian abstraction and amphiboly at work by which symmetry is restored (whatever the facts of the case) as the topos of meaning, *contra* Lakoff but also Pinker, shifts from 'embodied subjects' or minds as computational if not representational devices, to a plane where meaning becomes strategic and lies less in 'use' than in its being 'gamed'. However, game theory only comes into its own where there is symmetry. Thus, metaphoricity becomes absolute (Blumenberg) and serves the same function as Institutions and Coalitions in that a symmetric game otherwise inaccessible to the embodied subject becomes so- that too at its lowest computational cost of representation. In practical terms, this meant that the lyric without ceasing to be personal and subject-object driven, nevertheless treats of symmetries arising out of aggregations that cut across embodiments and life-paths. Thus, though Ghalib appears to be discussing embodied I-Thou relationships, what we have (so that symmetry and the possibility of reciprocity might arise) is actually a 'Field Theory' like that of Roger Boscovich (himself, perhaps, influenced by Buddhist texts like the Vimalakirti Sutra) of whom Emerson said 'was it Boscovich who found out that bodies never come in contact?'

This, to the Indian mind, is far more satisfactory than the Schopenhauerian *principium individuationis*, for it posits nothing about 'the Will'- i.e. *Prakriti*- 'Evolution'- or whatever it is that but blindly burgeons-

Ug raha hai dar-o-deewar se sabzah Ghalib
Ham bayabaan mein hein aur ghar mein bahaar aayi hai!
(Walls that seep water, floors

Cracked as forceful foliage grows
This, my house, so festive vernal
And I, Ghalib, in deserts infernal!)

while showing a method of apprehension that is experienced as a relative liberation- a manner of holding in one's mind the constraints and contingencies that are experienced as bondage while yet receiving news of the existence of another view-point from which those constraints and contingencies cease to be binding.

Returning to the *Naqsh fariyadi*, notice that an arbitrary creator, owning no duty of care to that which he creates, would not, to our present intuition and understanding, have a moral right to the obedience of his creatures- any more than an irresponsible parent could claim authority over a child he or she had previously abandoned. In the field of intellectual property Law, there is a wide difference between characters represented graphically- e.g. Superman or Mickey Mouse- and those represented in a literary work in such a manner that the mental image received of them remains subjective and a matter of projection. In this context, Judge Learned Hand has stated that, though characters might be protected independently from the plot of a story, "It follows that the less developed the characters, the less they can be copyrighted; that is the penalty an author must bear for making them too indistinct." In the opinion of another legal authority, 'a literary character can be said to have a distinctive personality, and thus to be protectable, when it has been delineated to the point at which its behaviour is relatively predictable so that when placed in a new plot situation, it will react in ways that are at once distinctive and unsurprising."[viii] A recent Court Judgment[ix] states- 'Under the merger doctrine, courts will not protect a copyrighted work from infringement if the idea underlying the work can be expressed only in one way, lest there be a monopoly on the underlying idea. In such an instance, it is said that the work's idea and expression "merge." Under the related doctrine of *scènes à faire*, courts will not protect a copyrighted work from infringement if the expression embodied in the work necessarily flows from a commonplace idea.'

Getting back to Ghalib's line, under this interpretation, we might say that the creator has expressed a potential within himself- viz. of creating the image such that it might appear to have agency sufficient to complain against its creator- however, in so far as this merely expressed the image's own potential power to exist- i.e. its creation was something just waiting to happen- the doctrine of merger and *scènes à faire* gives a legal basis *in reality* for a purely imaginal or virtual complaint on the part of that entelechy against its impatient or exhausted author.

To illustrate what I mean, suppose we were marsupial humanoids who had evolved in an Australia to which placental mammals never gained access. Suppose a tornado sweeps us up and transplants us to another continent. If placentals are, ceteris paribus, better adapted than convergently evolved marsupials- for example, if our familiar Tasmanian wolf looks like their sort of wolf but is weaker or spends more time in *faltu* Comittee meetings- we might find ourselves less ready to believe 'God created us in his image' than those placentals structurally similar to us with whom we find we can't compete. Of course, we may still see the hand of God in having worked so hard over so many aeons to protect us in our native Australia from a better adapted competitor.

This suggests a way in the aforementioned legal argument could be countered. If the creator is investing so much time and trouble in erecting and maintaining the background against which the image stands forth, then clearly the doctrine of merger is defeated because the manner of depiction of the image is such that it is highly correlated with everything else in the picture- in other words there is no 'merger' between the idea and the expression of the image because something extra is needed viz. the change and accommodation of everything else which comprises the backdrop. Indeed, both idea and expression are not separable from everything else in this created word. The doctrine of *scènes à faire*- arising from the obligatory scenes in old French drama- applies to a deficit in creativity and artistic integrity such that intellectual property is lost over an item or aspect which owes less to deep thought and harmonious arrangement than a mere meretricious 'meme' stuck in so as to more quickly sign off on the project and get the thing to market.

Thus we see, in certain jurisdictions, it is the practice to uphold the originator's rights in situations where an image or a fictional character, or other artifact to which the Law of intellectual property might apply, is part of a wider canvass which the author is at great trouble and expense to develop, maintain and propagate- such that its appropriation by a third party- even under the rubric of better developing its potential- might involve a large and lasting harm to the common weal.

Philosophically speaking, this would be the case if the object under discussion is not yet an entelechy, in the sense of having exhausted its author's hexis- just as a fetus can not sue for emancipation while still in the womb. Yet, might not this be our own condition? Indeed, cyclical theories of the Cosmos- or indeed the doctrine of re-incarnation- might be more economically viewed as the fetus's complaint 'I'm not done yet- put me back in the womb'. There is a charming image, from the collected letters, of Ghalib in old age referring to his exile from the unseen world in terms reminiscent of Li Po- that 'banished immortal' whose 'windwheel samadhi' eludes, alas, my Tien Shan of wine dregs- but, of course, there is no proof he believed in reincarnation. Still, as a segue to the second interpretation of the line under discussion, I can offer you nothing better so just be a dear and skip along to the next para will you? That's champion.

2) Consider *Shokhi-e-Tahrir* as a capricious passion for setting things free- like a child opening the cage doors of birds which can not fend for themselves in the wild, or a Nobleman discharging his serfs and retainers without putting in place for them any new source of authority or means to a livelihood. From this we get 'Whose mischievous act of manumission saddled the created image with the burden of freedom?'

In the Islamic world, it is notable that a number of great Jurists refused to allow their students to commit their teachings to writing. "To write things down in a book is to put a naked sword in the hands of a child!" is a sentiment they would have approved. Indeed, even in seeking a judgement there is danger. There is a reputed saying to the following effect- 'those who have caused the most trouble for Muslims are the ones who asked about things which previously were not forbidden but became so because of their inquiry."- which is sometimes used to gloss **Surah 5.101.** 'O ye who believe! Ask not questions about things which, if made plain to you, may cause you trouble.' In a sense, to write, or even utter, something is, in some sense, to have freed it to work a weal or woe that can no longer be controlled by its author. As the next line in the Holy Koran (**5.102**) states- 'A people before you indeed asked such questions, and then became disbelievers on account of them.'

However, a question arises, in connection with the previous interpretation of *shokh-e-tahrir* (viz. as referring to a capricious, self-willed, creator), as to whether the absence of careful design, the inartistic, poorly thought out, *scènes à faire* manner in which all things are related to all things, might be evidence of a higher type of creativity- hyper-real as opposed to naturalistic- which seeks to reverse the gradient of agency by leaving its canvass chaotic and unfinished but unfinished such that the limned image must hanker for that harmony its author either couldn't or wouldn't imbue the whole with.

In romantic love, the first glimpse of the beloved has this transformative, individuating, effect such that by a common Seventeenth Century Indo-Islamic trope 'Love is the Second Creation[x]/ Its God Grief.' The lover feels himself alive, individuated, possessing one overpowering drive or motive for action- yet, held in an aesthetic rapture that is also a stasis- like a woven figure in a sublime tapestry- viewing himself, the hopelessness of his plight, from outside as an object both pathetic and picturesque.

The fact that the beloved's glance, or glimpse of her visage, is so beggarly in delineation and vagabond with respect to harmonious relationship with everything else that exists, that fact indeed, is what makes the experience a manumission, a freeing from every tie or obligation- but also an abandonment, also an ostracization- but one that permits the setting up of a dialectical relationship that is the reverse of the Hegelian dialectic of the gaze whereby the one with stronger thymos and willingness to risk death becomes the master over the weaker slave. Instead- as in Ahmed Ghazali's exposition of the love-dialectic between Mahmud and Ayaz- Love, rather than the Discipline the slave learns in labour, reverses the relationship between the 'Shadow of God' and he who took refuge in that shadow's shadow to escape the touch of the shadow of Huma- the bird of fortune whose shadow's touch confers Empery.

In this context, *shokhi-e-tahrir* could combine the two senses of *tahrir* we have looked at so far, such that the artist enamoured of his work looks at his creation and, by that look, engenders sufficient agency in the image that it can complain against the author's own hexis, his own deficient self-expressive praxis. Under this interpretation the line '*Naqsh fariyadi hai* &c' becomes, so to speak, the fundamental axiom for any Aesthetic theory univocal with its object. Which takes us to the next possible interpretation of this line.

3)   *Tahrir* as referring to Euclid's Elements- this turns the line under consideration into something like this 'The geometry diagram is whose protest against infatuation with the axiomatic method?' (The diagram is not essential to the proof. It is used to 'see' that the inference is correct.) This suggests a further bifurcation of meaning.

A)   Firstly, the diagram by its simple existence impugns the range of pure reason's apodictic powers. In other words, Ibn Tufayl's Hayy Ibn Yaqzan- brought up by a gazelle on a desert island & who discovers all the truths of science and philosophy for himself- is impugned, he is petitioned against, by the very diagrams and demonstrations he uses. The fact that there is a disconnect between the Scientific method (which does need to 'see' an inference is correct) and the apodictic approach is, by itself a scandal- i.e. a stumbling block for that particular type of fundamentalist Belief.

B)   Secondly, the diagram represents a simplification of reality- something with strong consistency properties but no real existence. Is this fair? We may think of Ivan Karmazov rejecting God because, as a human being, he was created with 'a Euclidean mind' and thus could not understand a reality in which the insulted and injured might, of their own free will, forgive their tormentors thus grounding a Christian Theodicy a fair minded man might possibly consent to and accept.

So far, I have concentrated on the multivalency of the word '*Tahrir*'. Its employment gives the very first line of the first ghazal in Ghalib's Divan an intellectual depth and appeal directly in proportion to the auditor's capacity or enthusiasm for abstract thought. Notice, we are not being asked to subscribe to the tenets of an alien faith or suspend judgement regarding the evils of an age remote from our own, nor is any specific ontological or teleological commitment being required us. In other words, our enjoyment of this line is independent of the Academy or the political currents of our own milieu.

In many ways, more even the word '*tahrir*'- it is its engendering but, for merely femininely gendered, word '*fariyad*' (complaint, petition) which is both emotionally richer and a more direct stimulus to thought. But, for the moment, and every moment outlasts eternity, let me stalk that beast by mis-direction, myself erecting a half-baked *machan*, that, all too visibly, proclaiming its flimsiness of construction, might draw my quarry under the tree from which I are sure to fall- letting you feast on my broken bones.

On that understanding, let us press forward to the second line. In some ways, it is yet more suggestive- particularly to a Western audience.

Kāġhażī hai pairahan har paikar-e taṣvīr kā
(Every figure in the picture is wearing a robe of paper)

Ghalib was accused of having uttered a meaningless verse. His defence was as follows-"First listen to the meaning of the meaningless verses. As for *naqsh faryādī* : In Iran there is the custom that the seeker of justice, putting on paper garments, goes before the ruler- as in the case of lighting a torch in the day, or carrying a blood-soaked cloth on a bamboo pole [to protest an injustice]. Thus the poet reflects, of whose mischievousness of writing is the image a plaintiff?- since the aspect of a picture is that its garment is of paper. That is to say, although existence may be like that of pictures, merely notional [*i'tibār-e maḥaż*], it is a cause of grief and sorrow and suffering'. (Ghalib wrote this in 1865, an old man defending a verse he wrote whilst scarce out of his teens)

Three points are worthy of note- firstly, in Islam, the ancient Iranian Kings had a great reputation for Justice (vide the *hadith* 'I was born during the reign of a Just King') and secondly that Mani, an Iranian, (founder of the Manichean religion) is considered the first amongst the painters. The Holy Quran's condemnation of image making arises precisely from the inability of the human creator to endow his creation with life. Now the blood line of the Iranian Emperors was united with that of the Holy Prophet by his grandson, the impeccable Hazrat Hussain's marriage to Lady Shahrbanu, the daughter of Emperor Yazdegird. Since the Iranian dynasty claimed descent from one viewed by the Jews as something of a Messianic figure- ending their exile and bondage- and was in any case associated with the native Zoroastrian Saoshyant (or redeemer at the end of Time)- Ghalib's reference to this supposedly Iranian custom gains piquancy. Ghalib himself, though at times professing to be Sunni, was unabashedly *tafzili*- i.e. he held the family of Ali in reverence. In any case, Ghalib's proclivity for Persian would have rendered him that much more open to Shaheed Shurawardy's Ishraqi (Illuminationist) philosophy which stressed the mystical achievements and teachings of ancient Iranian sages. Ghalib also ascribed to himself a Persian tutor- a Zoroastrian convert of Islam- perhaps with a view to further his claims to mastery over that language. The third point- one I believe not commonly known or reflected much upon- has to do with the Sixth Shia Imam- the grandson of Lady Shahrbanu- His Holiness Jafar as Sadiq. In this context, his alchemical concept (propagated in Europe, it is believed, by his disciple Geber[xi]) of '*takvin*'- the artificial propagation of life- is particularly suggestive. Would an 'artificial', so to speak, human being be exempt from the Laws revealed by the Prophets? Would such a being, indeed, be bound even by Fate?

There is not, to my knowledge, any evidence that Ghalib was steeped in the philosophical and mystical literature of the various pullulating sects of his Time. Nevertheless, since the connoisseur of poetry (as opposed to the Academic) is concerned merely with extracting as much enjoyment from a verbal artifact as possible and since, as Hemsterhuis said, 'the Beautiful is that which is most productive of new ideas', it is surely pardonable if we keep in mind the philosophical puzzle posed by 'takvin' when enjoying this couplet. Another, related thought suggests itself in this context- viz. the notion of the Frankenstein's monster composed of stolen body parts (i.e. the monster assembled from the *disjecta membra* of Europe's Religious, Revolutionary and just plain downright Ridiculous Wars and Social Movements) as being a modification of the Shamanistic *mazmun* or conceit of the perfected man reconstructed from his severed limbs, which re-appears in the Ghazal universe in a forlorn and plaintive form.

However, there is a further resonance- at least for those of us who read the Bible (still utterly vital for an *appreciation* of English literature and thus infra dig in the Post Colonial Academy)- in this couplet which, I believe, has not been previously explored. This has to do with Job who says-

23 'Oh, that my words were recorded,
      that they were written on a scroll,
24 'that they were inscribed with an iron tool on lead,
      or engraved in rock forever!
25 I know that my Redeemer lives,
      and that in the end he will stand upon the earth

and later-

'In his great power, God becomes like clothing to me
 'he binds me like the neck of my garment'
(tearing the collar is a sign of extreme suffering in Urdu poetry)

as well as towards the end-

35 "Oh, that I had someone to hear me!
      I sign now my defence—let the Almighty answer me;
      let my accuser put his indictment in writing.
36 Surely I would wear it on my shoulder,
      I would put it on like a crown.

This imagery is pretty powerful. Job is clothed by God in disgrace yet, paradoxically, this clothing which is also Job's legal petition against God is something imperishable and the guarantee that his intercessor will prevail!

As far as I know, this is the most powerful as well as the oldest use of the image of a petitioner clothing himself in his legal petition so as to dramatize the gravity of the injustice he has suffered. The Indian custom, Ghalib mentions, of lighting a torch by day to symbolize the darkness of injustice that has overwhelmed the land is also powerful. But, as Maimonides points out, Job's insistence on using writing of an imperishable kind- (i.e. rationalistic, *kalam*, style argumentation)- has an extra philosophic force.

The notion of clothing oneself in one's petition points also to one's radical, existential, nakedness (*uryani*). Like King Lear on the blasted heath- who finds himself choked by his collar at the climacteric of the tragedy- man is a bare forked creature, naked to the Empedoclean elements from which he is by but strifeful Eris stirred up.

In this context, Prof. Frances Pritchett, in her magisterial 'Desertful of Roses,' has drawn our attention to the following couplet (6.1)-

shauq har rang raqīb-e sar-o-sāmāñ niklā
qais taṣvīr ke parde meñ bhī uryāñ niklā

Ardour turned out to be the enemy of its own livery of seisin
Even in a tapestry, Qais is naked to its veil of the horizon

of which Ghalib said- '*raqiib* has the meaning of 'opponent'. That is to say, ardor is the enemy of proper possession. The proof is that Qais, who in life wandered around naked, remained naked even within the veil of a picture. The pleasure of it is that Majnun is always pictured with his body naked, wherever he is pictured.'

The difficulty with this explanation is that a painter who drew Qais with clothes wouldn't be drawing Majnun at all because what marks out Majnun is that in his madness he has torn off his raiments and dwells naked amongst wild beast.

Is Ghalib simply being stupid here? Or, is he actually saying something incredibly modish and profound such as 'the human power to picture things makes the Universe five dimensional and so naked singularities can *too* exist so suck it Steven Hawking!'?

No and no, because something available to the emic Urdu speaker is not supplied to us. This is the notion that *uryaani* (nakedness) arises in the context of the Divine Beauty's veil of change and transformation- which Fakhr al Din Iraqi called *'niqab-e-inquilab'*. Now recall that a picture is painted on cloth or canvass or paper- all of which can be used to clothe a naked person. To the completely naked- like Qais Majnun- anything and everything is a potential cover for his nakedness. The picture of Qais- which he could have used strategically to cover his shame- still discloses, however, that nakedness while at the same time becoming part of that very *niqab-e-inquilab* which veils the beauty, ardour for which has driven him mad and rendered him too naked to view even that veil.

Still, the basic conceit here isn't necessarily mystic or Sufi-goofy but actually quite red-blooded and drunkenly *'kolaveri di'*.

Here's a nice picture of Manisha Koirala, from Mani Ratnam's movie 'Bombay', for you to look at while go I fix myself a cocktail.

As viewing a veiled Malabar maid, waxes wroth the tapper of toddy
'Thou shameless Mappila jade! Cover thyself with my body!'
Tho', coupling, we cup clay & Alethia's lathe blithely turn
So Ireful our Love's lay upon Keats' irreal urn.

Prof. Pritchett says- 'Prashant Keshavmurthy points out that, in the preface to his Persian divan, Ghalib describes mystical lovers as 'paper-shirted like pictured figures, silent at the astonishment of being'- so it's clear that this image was meaningful to him in more than one context.'

Following a hint from Satyanarayan Hedge, perhaps we should consider *khagazi pairahan* as 'the Sun's rays' or 'the rising Sun'. However, any mention of the Sun in so highly meta-metamorphicist a topos involves also that tachyonic Black Sun which shines upon the back, the eventual end of all things. Even without this gloss, it really is not much of a stretch to provide an account of the perplexities this passage might otherwise involve one in. The crucial concept here would be of rhythmic stasis, or *epochè*, such that movement is arrested, haecceity held breathless (Joyce speaks of 'an enchantment of the heart) and silence merely the very tightly wound torsion of what would otherwise unfold as music. This, in Indian Music might be called the *Anahata Nada* or unstruck note. Here 'hairat' (amazement) might refer less to Sufi Theosophy than the existential *mise en abyme*, the vertiginous and hysteresis laden gaze with which two people, falling in love at first sight, devour each other leaving no residue not infinitely larger than Reality[xiii].

However, if Ghalib saw 'being paper shirted' as equivalent to being naked and petitioning for audience, then Sufi theophanic notions of *niqab-e-inquilab* and *tahawwul* become relevant. The 'silence at the astonishment of Being' is assimilated to Bedil's *'hairat-e-aainah'* (astonishment in the mirror)- nevertheless, in my opinion, at least for the *naqsh fariyadi,* it is by no means clear that a purely Sufi meaning is, save idiosyncratically sustainable.

If so, is this ghazal an hermeneutically 'open text' with an unrestricted *'tazmin'* or allusive domain?

Prof. Pritchett, for the best of reasons, does not believe Ghalib could have known the Book of Job- (Ayub, in Islam, is merely a symbol of patience). But we do know it. More than mere Scripture, it is a masterpiece of World literature which already contains within itself the whole of Philosophical Sufism. Ghalib's station is almost infinitely lower. But he gives pleasure- we hear his words from every new singing sensation, his verses adorn the latest Bollywood blockbuster. Neither Priest nor Professor can lay rough hands upon him. His couplet is ours to interpret as we please. To increase our enjoyment, we can by means of a not implausible Borgesian exercise, endow Ghalib with knowledge of that Book (perhaps from a chance encounter with a Christian convert or peripatetic Armenian Jew) in which case the paradox we remark is that though Job, more than any other, had a reason to complain of God- if only against the tactlessness of his dogmatic comforters- yet he pointedly refrains from doing so (till, that is, he was goaded beyond endurance by aspersions cast on his business ethics) preferring to yearn passionately for oblivion. This gives a further ironic twist to Ghalib's couplet read in its entirety. The meaning then becomes- every visage in our world-picture- what we fabricate to picture the world- is the face of a Job. However, as Hazrat Ali, whom Ghalib revered, pointed out we are in error in picturing God at all! Thus our 'Allah' is a Job protesting against our mischievous artfulness of image-making- whereby our picture of God seems more alive to us than that Truth Ever Alive- every face going to destruction except that Face we hideously mask...but mask but to limn- what is this but a calamity, a doomsday, a Satanic *Takwin* experimentation? In this context, lovers of Bedil may recall that Abu Bakr ash Shibli has stated, 'Sufi Monism is an Idolatry because it is the guarding of the heart from the vision of the Other **& the Other does not exist.**" However, those who quote Shibli- and other such Saintly authorities- will appear like the *Naasih* of Urdu poetry, the prudent counsellor of the love-maddened wretch, who is unwittingly committing exactly the same sin as Job's self-righteous comforters, thus bringing down God's undying wrath upon his own unoffending head. In the book of Job, Elihu- an impetuous, Mussar type proto-Marxist, or mixed up, Liberation-Theology-plus-Levinas kind of Rabbinical cub- offers himself as the mediator or intercessor that Job had wanted. But, the irony is that the intercessor becomes the advocate- if not the bailiff or executioner- of the opposite party!

Ghalib drives the point home with the first couplet of his next ghazal (also composed in 1816).

> *jarāḥat tuḥfah almās armuġhāñ dāġh-e jigar hadyah*
> *mubārak bād asad ġham-khvār-e jān-e dard-mand āyā*
> Bringing back gifts that deal wounds mortal but unearned
> Congratulations Ghalib! Your intercessor has returned.

But, for the moment let us not investigate the figure of the Naasih (comforter/ intercessor) for he is not mentioned in our *Naqsh fariyadi* -unless he is there by elision? Apparently Ghalib thought lexical ellipsis (*ta'qid-e-lafzi*), at least in Persian, an ornament and intensification of prosody, and, what's more, let's face it, our Anglophone South Asian, comprador, National Bourgeoisie has more than a lawyer or two in its blood-line- in which case, hereditary ambulance chasers that we are- we must forever remained suspended, in a slavering Solicitor's stasis, between the two lines of this, the very first, couplet of Ghalib's Divan- which, no doubt, serves us right! But, nevertheless, to move on, or appear to move on- what of the next couple of lines?-

'kāv-kāv-e saḵẖt-jānīhā-e tanhā nah pūchh
ṣubḥ karnā shām kā lānā hai jū-e shīr kā

1a) don't ask about the digging-through of the tough-lifednesses of solitude!
1b) don't ask about the digging done by the tough-lifednesses of solitude!
2) to make daybreak from night is the bringing of the river of milk '
(This is from Prof. Fran Pritchett's 'desertful of roses' website)

This couplet- reminiscent of Pasternak's pathetically Stakhanovite stanza- 'save by this knocking on shadows, Darkness has never tunnelled through to Light'- has to do with the story of Farhad- a working class lad. He fell in love with Shirin. Khusrou, the King, himself in love with Shirin, told Farhad he could have her if he tunnelled through the Behistun mountain (famed for its graven images) and brought forth a canal of milk. Farhad's pickaxe was successful against the rocks. However, to prevent him from attaining his goal, Khusrou permits some old hag to tell him that Shirin was already dead. Farhad killed himself by splitting his own head with his axe.

This brief prologue permits me this 'transcreation' of the 2 couplets we have thus far discussed-

> That the complaint of the cartoon turns cartoonish when
> Manumitted by the mischief of Mastery's pen
> Rendering thankless the rock Farhad last split...
> Must Loneliness, to mock, so task my wit?

Ceci est un dieu.

Prof. Faruqi says that only a poem can translate another poem. But a translation of Ghalib, more than any other poet, must involve something new, unexpected and unique- indeed, in Sanskrit's formulary *Mimamsa* or hermeneutic, as much as from Ibn Arabi's *lâ takrâr fi'l-tajallî* - '*apoorvata*', that which is novel or unprecedented, is the true meaning of, or proof of having actually read, or re-read, the text.

Eitibar vs Izafat/ Ghalib vs. Dard

Recall that Ghalib uses the term '*eitibar-e-mahaz*' to signify the merely notional existence of pictures which existence, nevertheless, is a cause of 'real' grief and suffering. Following Asin Palacios on Ibn Massara, we Borgesians naturally think of *eitibar* as 'Reflection' even in the futile sense of the sort of 'Reason' that can or wants to be reconciled with Revelation. In our ordinary Urdu, however, *eitibar* simply means faith/trust. Its literal meaning would be to 'go in accordance to', or 'draw a lesson from'- as, for example, in Jurisprudence, we may follow a purely hypothetical case between John Doe and Richard Roe. Equally, in following a precedent, it does not matter if that judgement was later found to be wrong on the facts of the case. In this manner, the term *eitibar* can come to stand for that which is purely notional or fictitious.

Ghalib, in *Naqsh fariyadi*, is not saying that the created image lacks faith in the Creator and suffers as a result- he is no Matthew Arnold or Thomas Hardy bewailing the death of Faith- on the contrary, the image is so confident of the existence of its author that it clothes itself in nothing but its own petition against that author. However this notional (*eitibar*) petition we are reading about might shake our genuine faith (*eitibar*) in God. Yet, philosophically speaking, that which Faith previsions is as ontologically empty and unreal (*eitibar*) as the heretical ravings of the infidels. Let us suppose I am a lawyer. In discussing with you a case which the Judge will decide tomorrow I may say, 'Well, the judgement is bound to be as follows because such and such is the relevant precedent'. My judgement may have a sort of temporary force -

you may decide to enter into or abstain from a contract on the basis of my advice. However, legally, my judgement has no force- being merely an opinion. Indeed, even the papers on which the Judge, this very night, is scribbling down his judgement have no force until actually read out from the Bench. Even then, for that Judgement to be upheld by the Superior Court, it must have the property of *eitibar* in the, *stare decisis*, sense of following the rules and being in accordance with what previously had been received. It can not be something wholly novel. Still, the fact remains that no Law can be applied which people don't believe (again *eitibar*) can actually be enforced- for going against common sense and folk wisdom. In other words, even if approved by the highest authority in the land, it will remain a dead letter. It is an empirical fact that laws change- the Mufti of today gives a different answer to that given by his grandfather. At one time, the pious Muslim from Iran or Arabia, might refuse a fiefdom from an Indian King on the grounds that because of the large population of Kaffirs, India was not *Dar ul Salam* (an Islamic realm). Thus, while a present of money was acceptable, Real Estate was not. But times changed. This scruple fell into abeyance. Another question was as to the legality, in Islam, of receiving rent for land. Again this scruple had to be abandoned- the unthinkable alternative being to actually take up a useful occupation and defray one's expenses by the sweat of one's own brow.

How can we have *eitibar* (faith) in a Justice that is purely *eitibar* (i.e. arising out of purely notional considerations)? Now one may invoke Dworkin's Judge Hercules who, by reason of his omniscience and God-like mental capacity, can always give the right judgement by developing a superior interpretation such that the whole fabric of judgements over time suffers no tear or wrinkle. But this is rather strange. It appears that, to believe (i.e. to have *eitibar*) in Justice we must first postulate a, purely notional, (*eitibar-e-mahaz*) Justice God. But that belief requires a Belief-in-Judge-Hercules God which by reason of its mastery, not of Judicial interpretation, but of the arts of inducing Belief such that the Believer does not act perversely, can allow Dworkin's 'right answer thesis' to function in the manner he intended- viz. to shore up faith in the absurd proposition that what those shysters get up to in the Courts has something to do with Justice. But why stop there? Sooner of later we will end up with a God for wiping-your-arse-while-you-have-haemharroids-such-that-your-belief-in-Justice-and-Liberty-and-other-such-crap-suffers-no-sordid-shock-or-howling-repudiation. Perhaps, all these Gods do really exist but are mere aspects of the one true God. Another way to say this is to hold that there is some master discourse, which at the meta level, all other discourses cash out as. But, this is to ignore the dynamics of the hermeneutic system which, it may be, needs tears and wrinkles to drive its quest for seamlessness. In other words, our Judge Hercules is now faced with a concurrency problem whose complexity rises exponentially faster than the world it relates to. Equally, a critical practice valorising aesthetic judgement- like that of Harold Bloom or James Wood- fails Beenakker's boundary condition (re. Hemplel's dilemma) and cashes out as either Dijkstra deadlock or Occasionalism that too at the *farz-e-kifaya* level (i.e. not only does God have to everything He also has to do everything we can only do communally- whether we actually do it or not. We are God's nightmare from which He is too dog-tired to awake.)

True, we might simply equate Judge Hercules with the God of the mystics, and hope for the best. But for this God- who is also all the other Gods required by mystic ravings, not to mention Economystic ravings like those of Rawls and Dworkin and Habermas and so on- one can only feel sorry for and hope that God-as-the-psychiatrist-of-his-own-warring-multiple- personalities is being properly serviced by his God-as-psychiatrist-God's-local-drug-dealer God.

You may notice, in the last paragraph, I've gone rather mad in my use of the en dash to link words together. Ghalib, of course, was absolutely crazy about the *izafat*- a grammatical device deriving from the Arabic '*idafa*' which means a genitive construction, and which serves the same purpose as the English 'of' and also links adjective to noun.

Why this obsession? Surely anything worth saying can be said clearly. Why promiscuously pile words together with but an en dash between them? Perhaps, the problem with words is that once uttered they occupy a space of their own. 'Words dream' as Ricoeur acknowledged. They begin to modify the words next to them. What is more, in reception, their status can change radically from that which was intended. They are free. They have their own lives and adventures and squalid affairs and illegitimate children- whom, it is my pious Pirandellian hope, they first encounter in the brothel of their own heart.

One reason to pile words together- for e.g. to say 'Bose-Einstein condensate', or 'Marcus-Kripke rigid designation' is to narrow things down and define what we might call a canonical form arising out of the intersection of two, it may be, quite different world-pictures. What we then have is something we can use for our own purposes without committing to everything else in either world-picture. However, in such usage it is our purpose that is all important- in other words, here meaning is purely intentional and instrumental with respect to our project. But this is another way to say that Language doesn't matter- it is a black box interposed between the intention and the deed- poetry cashes out as something else- politics, history, or simply strategies for sycophancy and self-congratulation.

Another reason for *izafat*, might be to limit the range of word x by placing it next to another word y such that we understand we are only to think of x qua y. But to say x exists qua q, or can so do, is to place a constraint on the manner in which x can, thenceforth, be conceived. Indeed *shokhi-e-tahrir* is by itself a statement about *shokhi*- it says that *shokhi* can exist qua *tahrir*- and any *shokhi* must have this potential to qualify as *shokhi*. Thus to say *shokhi-e-tahrir* is to attempt to govern what, in its own significance, is essentially ungovernable. Indeed, this *izafati* construction is itself a particular type of arbitrary *shokhi* expressing itself as *tahrir*- and Meaning once again becomes the mirror of the disorder of the starry heavens.

In Islamic mystical philosophy, both *eitibar* and *izafat* have a technical sense. The latter, in the philosophical system of Khvaja Mir Dard, has a slightly different meaning from *eitibar* in that both have no real existence in themselves but with the former having a partial empirical existence through the One Reality's Self Revelation whereas the latter is wholly fictional and of the character of negation and non being.

This enriches our reading of Dard, the Don Paterson of his day- musical but intellectually under-achieved precisely *because* intellection was too facile while yet there remained the infinitely more *concrete* fatuity of the paternal guitar- such that the use of *izafat* will now suggest a variant ontology whereby what it links will be posited to exist only in a manner made gorgeously gravid by that to which it is grammatically enchained.

Except, in practice, nothing of the sort occurs.

Why? Well, it appears that the *izafat/eitibar* distinction is a peculiarity of Dard's philosophy required or dictated by his strange theology according to which his Dad turns out to have the highest station under God. The notion is that since he belongs to Daddy, who in turn belongs to the Muhammadiya line, which is necessarily existent to safeguard Islam and therefore linked in a genitive manner to God, it therefore follows that, no mere middle-class poetaster he!, his poetry was the highest type of transformative utterance, a gift granted him by God, as the true Muhammadi of his age, to lead Mankind out of the Egyptian captivity of delusion to a perception of true Reality.

Bearing this in mind, look again at Dard's euphonious *'madrasa ta ya dair ta ya Ka'ba ya but-khana ta'*- what do you see? Something like this, surely.

> Whether at the Ka'ba or Jaba the Hutt's Holy fane
> Thy Guests, Lord, we at thy pleasure remain
>
> Death's dawn revealed all Revelation was vain
> Existence a dream and the Logos insane
>
> Does Autumn's feverish colour the wind's chill explain?
> Or the Pizza boy, for its coquetry coy, my cock disdain?
>
> My Pop's station is higher than Popes attain
> 'I'm a great mystic', is this ghazal's refrain
>
> Oh & be sure to add in some shite about tears flowing like rain
> And the Saqi and the Tavern & Love's torment & pain
>
> & once you are done, start over and do it again
> For 'I'm a great mystic' is every ghazals' refrain

In other words, while others may be Muslims and Mystics and so on- yet they indulge in mere *shaThiyat*- whereas only Daddy (and, hence, sonny boy) are actually linked to real Reality by this necessary *izafati* belonging which chases off Leibniz's doctrine of the identity of indiscernibles and the demeaning suggestion that perhaps Islam isn't really in danger and Daddy and diddums aint actually particularly special but scarce distinguishable members of the madding rent-a-mob of self-aggrandizing mystic nut-jobs we shall always have with us because- as Pascal says- there will always be more monks than reason.

Is Dard's *izafat* vs *eitibar* distinction a difficult concept? Yes, because it is introduced to support an absurd hypothesis. Daddies, however dear, don't tend to be the highest of living beings.

Mansoor al Hallaj's claim- "I'm God" is okay- coz maybe everybody really is God so no absurd (as opposed to merely meaningless) claim is being made. Ibn Arabi's more modest claim to be the seal of the Awlia is also okay coz maybe the occassionalist, anti-Aristotelian, Ashari notion of *al khalq al mutajaddid* cashes out as Buddhist *kshavnika vada*- i.e. some very odd assumptions about Time are being made. In some sense it is both infinite in a Bergsonian way as well as existing only in the moment. The upshot is, perhaps, everybody is an Awlia or a Buddha- and in any case these words are meaningless- so that's okay.

Dard's position- or what I've managed to glean of it from a glance at Homyra Ziad's recent paper in the Journal of Urdu Studies- is that since only what God utters when he utters '*kun*' (Be!) is real and Daddy is in *izafat* to the *tajalli* (theophany) of that *kun*- because, didn't you know?, *Islam is in danger![xiv]* indeed, it's always in danger which is why God created the Muhammadiya lineage which therefore is necessarily existent- so Daddy really is the Tops whereas the rest of you guys affirm a bunch of propositions which aint, no way no how, part of that '*kun*' and thus youse guys are connected to real reality only in a negative way- i.e. though your shite might be word-for-word identical to stuff my Daddy says, still, your shite has no force, no validity, since not standing in a positive necessary and genitive relationship to MY DAD's salutary and Islam-saving Judgements.

What's the upshot here? Dard gets to be a middle-class mystic- one, moreover, who gets off some good lines, coz like old Ez said 'in poetry only the charlatan is genuine'- without ever exhibiting the ecstasy of a Sultan Bahu or the pathos of a Nund Reshi. This, to my mind, is less than okay though still probably harmless. (I mean, at least, the fuckwit wasn't a Micro Finance Maven or Eco-Feminist campaigner or other such Verbiage veiled Moqanna.)

Ghalib, unlike Dard, didn't have a daddy claiming to be the savior of Islam. Okay, he had an Uncle from whom he inherited a small pension, but- unlike Bedil's Uncle- the guy was safely dead and couldn't force the young Turk to study under the great Mystic nut-jobs of the period.

A few years before Ghalib was born, a young mystic in Istanbul, Sheikh Galip, published, that masterwork of Ottoman poetry, the 'Husn u Ashq'. In that work, it is Sukhan (Poetry- but Gibbs translates it as Logos) which tells Love that Beauty is pining for him, thus causing Love to fall in to itself and undergo various travails and adventures before finally entering the City of Beauty which Sukhan itself can not enter. For the adolescent Ghalib, however, Beauty and Love were merely recalcitrant tools to subjugate Sukhan- surely a Babu or, at best, Sycophantic Courtier's ambition- and he prided himself on having survived both types of Asiatic cholera and, after the fall of Delhi, his Urdu oeuvre functioned as a sort of secular *De Civitate Dei contra Paganos* for the diaspora of his class

Indeed, it appears, Ghalib was claimed as either an Ustad or a grandfather by all manners of Munshis- including the Nizam's tutor, who has left us an autobiography in English remarkable for its prescient denunciation of Aligarh University alumni and the mischief they might work.

Perhaps it is really true that Aligarh alumni, if I may thus collectively personify inter-generationality as the driver of deracination, who killed our sense of the City thus explaining why we have no Orhan Pamuk.

<blockquote>
I often dream I'm translating **Orhan Pamuk**
into something marginally less gay
So, Stan Bull 'spite **Galip**'s galehaut of a book
Bard not Self-buggery for aye.
</blockquote>

<blockquote>
Abreeze, thoughts ribald as these, here to hear rattle sere leaves
Brompton Cemetery trees : Cities' Autumn oneiric weaves
In vain. Twain vane to this, in vein, Rabelaisian gust
Yours deaf & mine dust.
</blockquote>

This is not to say that Ghalib was utterly insulated from the various mystical currents that had been swirling around- to the benefit, certainly, of Urdu as a language fit for the highest intellectual purposes- vide licet, fraud- but, rather, that he freely chose what was most stimulating to himself as an artist from both the *nafsi* and *lafzi*- i.e. both the intentional and the expressional- efflorescence of his lax and lucklessly British overlorded milieu.

My own feeling is that Ghalib effects, so to speak, a Fuerbachian revolution- in that Faith no longer involves the denial of one's own Reality and Existence to howsoever small an ontological degree- but, because Ghalib is anti-Fuerbachian, he commands our confidence (*eitibar*) - if 'Love is the true ontlological proof of a Being outside our head', then Farhad was quite right to stick a pick-axe through his rock-like cranium, and if 'the individual lacks inside himself the true essence of man, only finding it in community', then Majnun was right to make the wilderness his villa and wild animals his (incensed but too polite to bite) audience.

As the next couplet of the ghazal has it-

jażbah-e be-iḵẖtiyār-e shauq dekhā chāhiye
sīnah-e shamshīr se bāhar hai dam shamshīr kā

Passion as powerlessness to govern its project to Self attest
Is the breath of the sword that never reaches its own breast!

Well, okay- maybe my translation is a tad tendentious. Prof. Pritchett's web-site gives us this literal gloss-

The uncontrolled/uncontrollable emotion/passion of ardour ought to be seen!
the breath/life/edge of the sword is outside the sword's breast

In other words *jazbah-e-be-ikhtiyar-e-shauq* means 'passion-uncontrollable-passion' or just uncontrollable passion which, the poet assures us, is *genuinely* worth seeing, before going on to observe that *outside* the breast of the sword is the edge/breath of the sword. In other words the sharp part of the sword isn't inside itself- no! it is actually *at the edge* of the sword. This is a truly remarkable observation given that Ghalib was Muslim- one moreover constantly subject to such lamentable native practices as *suttee, thugee* and *agarbatti,* by reason of the deeply diffident and forbearing nature of the British conquest (vide 'Dominance without Hegemony', Ranajit Guha, Harvard 1998)- and just goes to show that Islam *is* capable of nurturing what we, compelled by the ethic of affirmative action, might well call evidence of a proto-scientific attitude. However, Ghalib was greatly ahead of his time. Other Muslims remained obdurate in trying to cut off the heads of the White Imperialists by using the inside of the sword rather than its edge. That was why they were defeated in 1857. Shame, but there it is.

If, on the other hand, Ghalib lacked this proto-scientific attitude and was merely a precocious teen-ager, then *jazbah-e-be-ikhtiyar-e-shauq* signifies something quite different from a dim witted remarking upon like how passion can be *uncontrollable* dude & Mem Sahib, you too may please to look for, truthfully, it is a most interesting spectacle.

As the citizen of a country which, after more than sixty years of proclaiming itself a safe homeland for Islam, now seems set to award the ultimate accolade of Backward Caste status to all Muslims, I believe it is my duty to proceed on the assumption that Ghalib was too stupid to, even potentially, qualify for H-1B visa. (Admittedly, this literary exercise of mine is dictated purely by the Iyer desire to be acknowledged as E.B.C- Extremely Backward Caste- I mean, if my writing is not proof of the radical ineducability of Iyers then, I mean, why would I bother- tell me that, clever clogs?) In which case the *izafati* construction under discussion can only be deconstructed as follows- *Jazbah* is passion. *Jazbah e-be-ikhtiyar* is 'passion as ungovernability'. To add *shauq*- which can also mean passion, enthusiasm, gaiety, zeal, curiosity and so on- but which we might well link up with the previous *shauqi-e-tehrir*- giving us something like passion for a project or hobby or artistic or other endeavour- yielding not the bombastic redundancy of passion-uncontrollable-passion but something highly discriminated and meaningful- viz. Passion as the specific sort of ungovernablity with respect to itself as its self-actualizing in its project.

On Prof. Pritchett's web-site, I see that the freedom fighter and poet, Bekhud Mohani, says 'The edge of a sword faces toward the outside, but the ardent lover, in the extreme ardour for martyrdom, entirely forgets that everyday fact; instead, he thinks that either out of an ardent desire to slay him, or drawn by his ardent desire for martyrdom, the edge of the sword has emerged from the breast of the sword.' Another commentator, my esteemed Urdu Ustad, Johnny Walker Dehlvi, interprets *shamshir* not as scimitar but a penis afflicted with Peyronie's disease- i.e. Clinton's kink- whose mystical interpretation focuses upon that high Gnostic station associated with self-sodomy- the shape of the scimitar dictated, indeed, by the Ninja necessity to thus stealthily sheath itself (vide the assassination scene in 'Leileh Majnoon IV- *Ninja Apocalypse!*') but in either case, it is the first line, with its complex *izafati* construction, that ought to guide us in seeking the meaning of the couplet.

    To my mind, Ghalib's *strategic* employment of *izafat*- as in the above instance- permits a truly Humanistic appropriation of the Theological trope of eitibar-as-faith-such-that-its-subject-necessarily-non-exists in a manner so truly human that pi-jaw is kicked to the curb and Humanism shat upon from a great height. In the process Ghalib creates what Prof. Pritchett calls a 'meaning-machine' such that poetry is saved, not just from theology, nor just historicist or Gadamer's gadarening hermeneutics, but also from modern pi-jaw peddlers like Paul Ricoeur with this salutary result that words once again can dream.

Simurgh and Anqa

āgahī dām-e shunīdan jis qadar chāhe bichhāe
muddaā anqā hai apne ālam-e taqrīr kā

        1a) let intelligence spread the net of hearing to whatever extent it might wish
        1b) no matter to what extent intelligence might spread the net of hearing
        2a) the intention/meaning of my world of speech is the <u>Anqa</u>
        2b) my world of speech has no intention/meaning at all
        2c) 'intention/meaning' is the <u>Anqa</u> of its own world of speech
        2d) the <u>Anqa</u> is the intention/meaning of its own world of speech
        (from Prof. Fran Pritchett's 'desertful of roses' site)

The Anqa is that unique phoenix which is '*maujud ul ism, mafqudul jism*'- present in name, absent in body- i.e. a name that signifies something definite which, however, does not, perhaps can not, actually exist- like 'the golden mountain' of Alexius Meinong.

A synonym for Anqa is 'Simurgh'- the great bird which Attar's parliament of feathered friends sets off to China to consult- only 30 survive the journey but reaching the appointed place, no Simurgh is to be seen till, that is, the bird-brains work out that they themselves are the Simurgh (30 birds) they have so arduously sought.

In Islam, there is an open question as to whether or not Man will finally see the face of God. 'Vision comprehends Him not' but 'when there is perfect agreement between you regarding His visage then you will see Him as you see the full Moon in the Sky'.

    I know, I know- this all sounds so mushy and Sufi-Goofy and, yes, I too want to vomit.
        But how does Ghalib get us out of this mire of molasses, this trap of treacle?

    Ghalib, concerned solely with *Ma'ni afrini* (meaning creation), was a disciple of Bedil who said, '*Sher-e-khub ma'ni nah daarad*' a good poem has no meaning.

How square this circle?

Speaking personally- passionate psilosopher I- I'm reminded of Kripke's workaround for Tarski such that a language can consistently contain its own truth predicate, a deeply spiritual and democratic result- a true Humanistic miracle!- arrived at by the logical equivalent of conscripting a denumerable infinity of bird brains such that a Simurgh for natural language emerges and soars upwards, like Defoe's parliamentarily feathered, mechanical, Lunar Voyaging, Consolidator, to loftier heavens, alas!, only upon the wings of self congratulation at having emerged at all- despite being such a, United Nations, World Truth Awareness Day, waste of everybody's time.

    But, to confine myself to Ghalib's actual words, let me start with *Aagahi*- intelligence, yes, but intelligence as vigilance, shrewdness, forethought- Promethean rather than Epimethean-

anticipatory rather than synthesizing after the fact- and the 'net-of-hearing' this *Aagahi* extends to whatsoever degree- yet, we note, is defective in two respects- viz. this is not Intelligence qua Intelligence but a vigilant Promethean, Nimrod-as-hunter-like action schemata and its net of hearing (or, Babel as an anti-Allah spy-in-the-sky) is adaptive to a costly signal-extraction problem fitness landscape such that it evolves ever towards a sort of cannibal corporeality- i.e. this is a predisposition to arbitrarily constrain that which is thinkable, or that which is a useful instrumentality for thought, to that which it can feed on to continue the hunt.

But, merely on the basis of the words Ghalib has chosen in the first line- more follows than everything in the second line, much more, that is, than exists in its conventional reception. Yet, the fact remains, Ghalib supplies that second line. It therefore means much more more, or else is gratuitous, ***but in poetry only the truly gratuitous is necessary*** and, thus, is foundational of *Ma'ni Afrini* (the gratuitous being the opposite of *scènes à faire*) not to mention this Iyer-onic hermeneutic-as-lame-Hephaestus-of-its-(by what? Lost ear-wax?) *cire perdue* recovery.

This is Ghalib's couplet-
āgahī dām-e shunīdan jis qadar chāhe bichhāe
muddaā anqā hai apne ālam-e taqrīr kā
(Howsoever, Intelligence casts its net-of-hearing
Meaning is the phoenix of its world of discourse)
Before, seeing how we might get something poetic out of this let us look at the next couplet, which concludes the ghazal.
baskih hūñ ghālib asīrī meñ bhī ātish zer-e pā
mū-e ātish-dīdah hai ḥalqah mirī zanjīr kā
1a) Ghalib, even in bondage I am {restless / 'fire-under-foot'} to such an extent
1b) Ghalib, although even in bondage I am {restless / 'fire-under-foot'}
2a) a link of my chain is a {singed hair / 'hair-that-has-seen-fire'}
2b) a {singed hair / 'hair-that-has-seen-fire'} is a link of my chain
The reference here is to Ahmed Ghazali's 'Savanih' which, some 8 centuries previously, fixed the convention that the curl of the beloved's tresses is the chain upon the madman who is also a moth to her flame. For me, the appeal of this couplet is its link to the domestic curling iron and the doubleness of our teenager's teenage bride- both wife and mother- under at least one of whose feet, the Prophet has promised, verily is paradise.

I recall reading, many years ago, a translation of that poem of Tao Chien's which Prince Chao Ming condemened as a 'blemish on white jade'- the erudite allusion being to some random guy who went around rabidly reciting the following lines from the Book of Odes-
'A blemish on white jade
Can perfect be made
Words twistable at all
Cause Heaven to fall!'
which so impressed Confucius that he married off his eldest daughter to the fuckwit. My memory is Tao Chien immortalized his own wife- apparently I'm wrong, his poem was actually about some zither playing slut- with a poem which ended somewhat like this (albeit merely in my cacophonous confabulation).
You look up from your weaving but become busy with the view
Wandering clouds garner waters, waving grasses winnow grains
Ah! Love, you don't know, you never know
Not Love, no- ***your man in chains!***

Anyroad, I don't know why I just told you that. Premature senile fackin' lability, I guess. Getting back to Ghalib's couplet, I will now tell you a story from the Shahnama to connect it with its predecessor. Zal was born with white hair, so his daddy- actually a Kleinian 'bad mother', gender transposed by Theo-paternalist parapraxis- expeditiously exposed the little freak on a snow capped mountain. The Simurgh (which is the Anqa in its ultra-cuddly as opposed to philosophical modality of Being) took the baby to her nest and brought him up. But, once grown to manly stature he wanted to rejoin the world of men and like maybe get lucky with a non-egg laying being? The Simurgh was saddened and gave Zal three of her feathers which he could burn (hence, the Victorian cure for hysterics) if he ever needed anything. Zal fell for Rudabha (Rapunzel) but, being a chivalrous sort of guy, did not (unlike his European equivalent) actually use her tresses as a staircase to her. However, once married, he did very diligently wipe his boots on her hair before entering the matrimonial home as was, indeed, the universal Indo-European norm in ancient times (i.e. the 1980's, during the greater part of which I myself was married to an Indo-European female- not, I repeat, not, a male.)

Ghalib, identifying himself with, the great Persian hero, Rustam- for the safe delivery of whom, his father, Zal burnt one of the Simurgh's feathers and was thus enabled to invent the C-section- feels 'a fire underfoot' arising out of his own Oedipal treading of his mother's hair- a circumstance her extreme and haut Iranian hirsuteness made inevitable- and relates it to that Anqa, his foster grandmother, who made possible his safe delivery from his mother's womb- as opposed to his Daddy's arse. Which is probably why he had it in for Sohrab- as Mathew Arnold regretfully records.

Anyroad, for Freudian reasons such as these, or if not these precisely then others so grossly obscene and stomach-turning as to be only discoverable by the current Mircea Eliade Professor of Indology- not that she will attempt the task, Ahmedinijad being what he is- Ghalib has written this shite. He could not have done otherwise. Did I mention he was North Indian? Not the good sort of North Indian but a guy born in, like, **Agra**. Those guys got shit for brains.

But- if you will forgive the concluding coda to the last paragraph, grossly overburdened as it is with Tamil Socio-phenomenological jargon (indeed, the last 2 lines are extracted from my dissertation submitted to Annamalai University, in furtherance of my demand for a degree, *honoris causa*, and, as such, perhaps, pearls before swine in the present context)- I'd like to point out that there is a way of unifying these two couplets in a manner not anally intrusive of our veneration for Ghalib- viz. Nimrod, that mighty hunter, tortures Abraham- but it is his father Azar who is truly 'fire-underfoot'- love of son being the one idolatry even a *Hanif* can't escape- but then, a son is scarce born, hardly exists as entelechy, nor is, but antiderivatively, differentiable from the whole affectionate net of Mommies and Grand-dads and the prizes he won or didn't win at School and like, the park, we used to go picnic in dude. Just went there for a walk. Every tree, every bush, every pathway, looked like he'd just this moment stopped playing hide and seek with them- not me- them. As he still does. Elsewhere in other gardens. And that's okay. That's cool. It's all good. *Kahé ko tension*?

Anyroad, that's how I get, for the last 4 lines, something like this-
> Hermeneutics net, Nous's Nimrod, hap he howsoever to throw
> Meaning's yet that phoenix, words burn to but ***not*** know
> Babel binds, tho' fire under-foot, the father of Abraham
> & this Pisgah[xv] singed eye-plume, Caesarean to 'I am'.

Wha-aaaat? Well, Faruqi Sahib *did* say Ghalib was difficult and moreover could only be translated by another poem. I don't see why the above is worse that anyone else's crap. The fact that a lot of Urdu-wallahs are severely and severally crap at Urdu and English and Thought does not mean either English (even if those fuckers currently teach it at Ivy League) or Urdu (howsoever Trotskyitley Tabatabai their, up their own arsehole, engendering and delivery) or Thought (whatsoever their Technical rank) are in any manner sundered from a Commonwealth whose games, at least, proceed *as games* despite all their running-dog carping, corruption and crapping upon everything.

Prof. Pritchett holds Ghalib to be untranslatable. A reasonable position. Too reasonable. One that could scarcely withstand the uncorking of the second bottle- let alone the 'breakfast Port' still, in my youth, served with the kedgeree to such four eyed wogs as one might have over to weekend when positively nothing on the Estate could be hunted and the hounds needed exercise.

Indeed, since I wrote the stanza quoted above in a state of inspiration, it is a true poem since my own state of mind was a 'model' for its system of axioms.

Yet, it is meaningless.

Does the meaninglessness make it a good poem in Bedil's sense? No, because my inspiration did not raise me to a '*Haal*'- a mystic locus- above and beyond my ordinary, matitudinal, inebriation. On the contrary, the reason I feel 'this is a poem!" is because of something poetic I had unconsciously elided viz. an affinity of associations between the Simurgh, the Mishnaic Shekhinah, and the Quranic Sakina. Death by Celestial fire brings to mind the two sons off Aaron- Nadab and Abihu- who, according to Hassidic lore, entered the soul (by *ibbur*) of Phineas after he had slain Zimri and Kosbi (the former being the original of the unlucky Schlemiel in Yiddish) and his soul fled him in fright at what he had done. Phineas then is raised to the status of Kohain (priest) by the all High. This is an example of how the intricate double entry book-keeping of metempsychosis saves us from too stark a confrontation with the fact that though all Laws are univocal and to break one law is in some sense to break all the laws- still some laws are *halachah vein morin kein*- i.e. such that, if known, they forbid the very action they would otherwise have enjoined. Phineas gains the status of *kohain* by an action of this kind. But, like Solomon, his is 'a treasure that can never befall another'. The whole fabric of the law is now based on radical defeasibility.

Parrhesia for Jerusalem can never again be what it is for Athens- poetry not philosophy will henceforth guide the West, but guide it by *halachah vein morin kein*- disallowing what it otherwise enjoins, hiding away its own organon, withdrawing a sense of dwelling from what henceforth will be merely land.

In the Gospel when the Jews demand that Christ speak plainly, boldly, saying everything (i.e. with parrhesia) only to then judge him guilty of blasphemy, he quotes the Psalm (82.6) 'ye are Gods...' but the context is the divinely ordained imperative to deliver correct judgements.

Ghalib's Ghazals, too, are a parrhesia- one, moreover founded upon the phenomenological aporias of Ghazali's occassionalist appropriation of, what we, you and me- Gassire's Gemini-blood flecked foam upon the river's Blues- might call Rene Girard's primordial problematic of mimetic desire such that every object is impossible, every subject imponderable, every locus- like the River Sambation- bootlessly besieged by the Pilgrim path to it. Thus, it is in his glittering Urdu word horde that- linguistically impoverished as I am- I see a demotic domestication of Greek and Semitic words and ideas such that, I too may, without exchanging my soiled *kurta-pajama* for a scholar's cap and gown, yet be raptured by their glamour..

Still, to concede your point, granted, what the above isn't is a ghazal. So let me now move onto a couple of my versions of Ghalib's most translated ghazals.

To start with something simple

Ghazal 20

Ye naa thii hamaarii qismat ke visaal-e-yaar hotaa
agar aur jiite rahate, yahii intazaar hotaa
Tere vaade par jiye ham, to ye jaan jhuuth jaanaa
ke khushii se mar na jaate, agar aitabaar hotaa
Terii naazukii se jaanaa ke bandhaa thaa ahad buudaa
kabhii tuu na to.d sakataa, agar usatavaar hotaa
Koii mere dil se puuchhe, tere tiir-e-niim kash ko
ye khalish kahaa.n se hotii, jo jigar ke paar hotaa
Ye kahaan kii dostii hai ke bane hain dost naaseh
koii chaaraa saaz hotaa, koii gam gusaar hotaa
Rag-e-sang se tapakataa, vo lahuu ke phir na thamataa
jise gam samajh rahe ho, ye agar sharaar hotaa
Gam agar-che jaan gusal hai, par kahaan bachain ke dil
hai
gam-e-ishq gar na hotaa, gam-e-rozagaar hotaa
Kahuun kis se main ke kiyaa hai, shab-e-gam burii
balaa hai
mujhe kiyaa buraa thaa maran agar aik baar hotaa
Hue mar ke ham jo rusavaa, hue kyuun na gharq-e-darayaa
na kabhii janaazaa uthataa, na kahiin mazaar hotaa
Use kaun dekh sakataa ke, yagaanaa he vo yakataa
jo duii kii buu bhii hotii, to kahiin do chaar hotaa
Ye masaael-e-tasavvuf, ye teraa bayan, gaalib
tujhe ham vaalii samajhate, jo na baadah khaar hotaa

To be in tryst united, not I could twist my fate
If longer life invited, I'd yet forlornly wait

Did I live on thy oath, know, my life were a lie
Of happiness I'd die! held thy troth to a date

For as feebly as fond entreaty, bindst thy Word
Its sequel, equal treaty, art surd to sublate

Why was that arrow drawn without brawn, not art?
That, in my heart, it stick, not sever it straight!

Why admonishes like a priest, my old comrade and mate?
If you haven't a pain killer, at least, my pain giver hate!

Were what it mock as 'woe wilful'- flint struck sparks
Thy Ark's veined rock, would ruck Red sans bate

Anguish is certain arson; know! -the heart *must* burn
If not to yearn, then to earn, or learn chalk's slate!

By his assent, this night of grief, did an Adam create?
Death's a Thief, or Madam, my ruin can't sate

My grave- ghazal's fresh ground?! Better I'd drowned!
My clay, they claim-jump, with elegies on 'the late'!

His vision can't anoint, who is but a singular viewpoint
Were a second scented... Ah! God alone is Great!

Since Sainthood has its Arabi seal, thy mystic spate
For Drunkards' weal, ope's a Ghalibian gate!

I admit, there are a couple of questionable translations I've slipped in here. In couplet 3 (*terī nāzukī se jānā kih baṅdhā thā ahd bodā/kabhī tū nah toR saktā agar ustuvār hotā*) I take 'ustuvar' not as strong/firm but equal/parallel (hence reciprocal)/ bold/ determined. Taking the latter meaning-constellation we get the notion of delicacy as arising out of a lack of reciprocity, itself arising out of an inequality of status. When we play with a child we do not use our full strength. Tentativeness also arises out of inequality or lack of parallelism.

(Another way of reaching a similar meaning would be from Shaheed Suhrawardi's notion of Metaphysical Substances as but univocal modifications of degrees of intensity- though, to do so in this context does violence to an endearing aspect of Ghalib's persona and forces him into an Ishraqi strait-jacket.)

The juxtaposition of *ahd* and *boda* (the latter word hinting that what we call existence is a feeble thing compared to 'true' or truer existence in barzakh) is theological rather than mere word play.

In Ibn Arabi's system, we move from *naql* to *aql* precisely because the knot of *taqlid* is loosely tied so that we try our strength at it and rise up from the feeble condition of a child towards *tawhid.* Furthermore, what one is addressing is not 'God' but the *khayal* (of God).

Clearly it is sheer stupidity for anyone to say that some frail little baggage is too weak to break her own promise. Well, maybe some thick headed Ajax in a farce- but would that Ajax then draw the conclusion that perhaps she had 'tied' her promise in a feeble way? This isn't a play on words- it is proof of imbecility.

Except in the light of Arabi's teachings. Then, it's parallel to Tamil *pillaibhakti* and Sanskrit *Vatsalya bhava.*

Still, a romantic meaning remains- her coquetry is tentative and her promises but lightly bind because she has no surety that we are equal to her passion (or that passionate desire for ruin and annihilation on the path of love, she (he) expects of her lovers). This reveals a great psychological truth- indeed, it has a Shavian ring- as in 'Man and Superman' - this is the eternal Feminine that draweth ever onward, etc.

However, Prof. Pritchett considers this couplet to be wholly secular and a striking example of a verse that could not have a theological as opposed to a romantic meaning. I disagree because the received meaning appears utterly stupid to me. However, we must remember that Ghalib was from a very backward country and religion. Still, I think both the 'plain' meaning- From your frail delicacy we knew your oath could but lightly bind/ Had it been strong, you could not have broken it- is compatible with the mystic meaning- where *boda* is suggestive of existence as but a feeble emanation or shadow, and *ahd* refers to the Covenant of mere outward *taqlid* and *naql.* Then we may say 'out of a delicacy such as is used with one much weaker (since God can not but be strong save by His own will for some Godly purpose) we can know (i.e. gnosis is invoked as the path to this realization) that the outward Covenant binds us lightly. However were there a covenant that was as between equals-i.e. if by some *imitatio Dei* we became worthy of a more equal treaty- it would be so strong that not even you (God) can break it. In other words, the lower *taqlidi* covenant keeps us apart from God and thus in a feeble state where what is received from God is like a broken promise because we lack strength for anything better.

However, by considering what would be needed for a strong binding- i.e. equality or reciprocity- we see that Union with God is something not even He could deny (since it would be against His own will and intention.)

On the other hand, perhaps, all my interpretation does is show up the bias of people of my generation and milieu towards 'balanced' games which (by Bondareva-Shapley) alone have a non-empty core and thus valorise semiotically dense velleities in language and writing as opposed to simply screaming your lungs out and slitting your fucking wrists.

Verse 7- *kahun kis se main ki kya hai Shab-e-gham buri bala hai/muje kya bura ta marna gar ek bar hotha*- in plain terms means this - "To whom can I speak of this night of grief that is evil and a calamity/ Death would not have been bad for me if death came only once.'

I add an allusion very well known but which the commentators do not mention- viz. the story that when God asked Adam 'Am I not your Lord', Adam replied 'Bala' which signifies both assent and woe- for which reason Existence is full of woe.

Purely as Purvapaksha, the objection might very reasonably be made that- *'But, does the "night of grief" in separation from the beloved, really evoke Adam's saying "bala" to God, under entirely different circumstances? No doubt it could, IF the poet arranged the verse so as to potentiate that meaning and encourage us to think of it. Here, on the contrary, he's arranged that the rest of the verse has no relation AT ALL with that sense.'*

On reflection, my reply is, "There is a terseness, a brevity- i.e. *ijaz*- and an irregular preposition in *'shab-e-gham buri bala hai*' which suggests that a word with *taḍmin* (implicative meaning) is being higlighted. The question is whether this word, *bala*, still posseses the implicative meaning of 'Adam's answer to God' despite the fact that Ghalib has not 'arranged the verse so as to potentiate that meaning or encouraged us to think of it'. If language is relational, if words acquire meaning only by their relation to other words in the text that contains them, then the Purvapaksha stands. But, what if God is the author of a book? One moreover which insists (H.Q 54.17) it has been deliberatly made easy to understand and remember? What problem does such a book pose the hermeneut? Language, after all, is a being-for-others and texts are a special sort of being-for-others such that, in the author's absence, much or all the intended meaning can be teased out purely by the relationship in which words stand to each other. Consider another sort of mental construct which conserves information- the memory walk, or method of loci, or 'Memory Palace' of Matteo Ricci- this functions by arbitrary associations between what is to be remembered and a familiar mental topography. Even if God is a perfect communicator and has perfect being-for-others, the fact remains that if we recognize Him as the author of a book (like the Mutazilites, who held the Koran to be created) then part of that recognition is to see how He has already traversed all our possible memory walks and hallowed our every Memory Palace such that, in this respect, we may well second the sentiment of St. Augustine- 'for this honour has thou done it, to reside in it'- but for that very reason, in so far as memory is transcribable into language, recoil from a purely relationist linguistics. In other words, for All is the Other of words, the *taḍmin* of a word can exceed all relational mereology. If, however, Scripture is uncreated (*apaurusheya* as the Vedantists say) and if, moreover, God *taught* Man the names of things, as in the Quran, then a relationism of the Saussure or al Jurjani type might well remain the summit of Theistic hermeneutic endevour.

'Of course, I know, the Mutazilites died out long ago in Islam, yet, if the practice of poetry is on a par with Physics, then I am inertially led to an analogy with Newton- who rejected Homoousian Leibnizian relationism in favour of an Arian or Absolute Substantivism in line with his belief that Christ was created by the Lord of Dominions and that the Bible had prophetic force- a voice created without a body and thus not besotted with the Narcissus of small differences- because a non relationist hermeneutic requires, that too for no reason other than Sufficient Reason, no monstrous monadology of mirrors, no mannerist mania for metaphors built on other metaphors, nor, indeed, the damnable vanity of the dogma of immortal souls- and so too, it may be, was it with an Indian Islam so recently and rudely woken from Ptolemaic slumber.

'Perhaps, this, indeed, is the *Shab-e-gham,* the night of grief, which otherwise suggests separation by standard, Ghazal world, *taḍmin* . But, nights come to an end. Separation suggests the possibility of Union. What sort of Union? For the Indo-Persian Ghazal, from the time of Amir Khusrau, it is both the nuptial union desired by the bride and the *nihil per infinitatem* achieved by the *viyogini's* passionate nothingness-through-privation.

'The paradox that the phenomenology of love-in-separation permits a more Monist ontology than that of Monastic meditation- this as the true *sphota* sparkle of Bhratrhari's own legend or black fire- provided medieval India an unassailable topos for Absolute Theism, which like Newtonian (indeed, all workable) Physics works and works to this day, *because* it is non-relational and thus tractable.

'Essentially, Relationism adds a computationally unaffordable Concurrency problem to a difficult enough Co-ordination problem (unless it rejects the principle of compositionality) whose solution the Substantivist can permit to be cloud sourced, or 'forced' by stronger misprision, or an arbitrary, that is academic, cloture, or the fact that shit happens, and thus though uncanonical and of imperfect elegance for lacking an impredicative prescriptivity, having yet, precisely by reason of this ongoing humiliation, the saving grace of tractability

'Bearing in mind this issue of tractability- surely a good enough reason for abandoning both relationism and compositionality w.r.t mere poetry, let alone Divine writ, consider the word *bala* here as a *taḍmin* (quotation) of the Quranic *bala* in 7.172 and we see that this *bala* forestalls the *bahlah*- the curse extending to one's wives and progeny- of God. This suggests the notion of *mubahala*- مباهلة – and *Eid al Mubahila*, an occasion of special importance to Shias, as Quranic proof positive of the Holy Familiy's impeccability, because Prophet Muhammad chose from amongst the Muslims only his near, dear but also actual as opposed to merely metaphorical relations- viz. his daughter, two grandsons and son-in-law to accompany him to withstand the Christians of Najran in the ordeal of 'mutual cursing'- participants in which run the hazard of destruction and damnation for adherence to the minutest sliver of untruth. Since only the Holy Family, amongst the Muslims, was utterly free from falsehood, this incident shows the great danger of *mubahala* for the believer. The current situation, where young people are taught to get pleasure by cursing adherents of other sects, involves the great risk of permanent separation from God's Grace. Indeed, the subject of 'debate' in this *Mubahila* was the Apostle's assertion that both Adam and Christ were created from clay and not Divine in any sense. In other words, Adam's 'bala' and the Quranic 'mubahala' point to the radical possibility of permanent separation from God- that is damnation. However, both terms have another, a dialectical, meaning. Though muddy Adam 'assents' (i.e. is in ethos bound) to woe and the bloody Christians refuse to run the hazard of *Mubahila,* preferring, instead, tribute and treaties- the possibility of a happier, more universal, outcome in the future is nevertheless held out.

"True, the *purvapaksha* objection still stands. There is no proof that any of the foregoing was at the back of Ghalib's mind in writing this couplet. Indeed, *de dicto*, what he actually is saying is that Death comes many times. This implies either the doctrine of metempsychosis (*ri'jat*) or bodily resurrection to fight against Dajjal (the anti-Christ) and then another to urm... fight him again or something. However both re-incarnation and resurrection are only poetically interesting if you get to meet up with the cutie-pie, or punch Vinobha Bhave in the face, or gain God's grace or whatever. Otherwise, such notions are simply fucked in the head.

"Granted, if you reckon Ghalib, *de se*, really wants us to understand that he is a verbose, witless, cry-baby then of course the meaning is- 'where can I catch hold of some idiot who will listen to me explain that the night of sorrow is really not at all nice and in fact quite evil and bad? I wouldn't mind dying so much if it happened only once (coz each time I come back to life, I just can't seem to find anybody so fucking shit-for-brain'd they'd actually let me fucking explain that the night of grief isn't a picnic. It's not nice. Really. I mean it. In fact, what I'm trying to put across to you, except you won't fucking listen, is that the night of grief is BAD. Look, just fuckin' listen to me okay coz I'm tring to explain this to you so you finally get the point that grief aint nice, it's bad. Oi! Where do you think you're going? Come back here! I've got to explain this to you, all over again and I don't care if it takes me all night. Like I said, I don't mind dying so many times, it's just this keeping coming back to life which is a complete pain and like totally random dude coz where am I gonna find someone to listen to me explain that GRIEF is BAD. What's the fucking matter with you people? Why is it so hard to find someone I can explain this to? I mean, fuck is your major malfunction guys? Don't *any* of you wanna hear about like how grief feels real bad?'

"The art here is that Ghalib, *de re*, appears to be a fuckwit searching for one more fuckwitted yet (because all Art's true function is to prove that Celebrities really are stupider than us, thus giving us an incentive to remain language users- coz we'll sure take their pants down when we meet up with them in Heaven for the final round of that *haqiqi* Ultimate Reality Show which is like a gazillion times more brutal than Big Brother right?) but manages- in what appears his stupidity and redundancy- to raise a particularly risible theosophic point related to *ri'jat* & palingenesia & Nietzchean *amor fati* and so on and so forth.

"To conclude, either Ghalib has indulged in verbosity and redundancy- *gham* plus *buri bala*- coz he was a witless cry baby- or, no, the word of philosophic interest is being highlighted for us."

But, this is weak. Philosophy is shit. Words can still be interesting in a Mantic Coleridgian manner, or Romantic hieroglyphic manner, or as in Victor Segalen's *Stèles,* exceed Semantic Supervenience by mannerist strategies in equal parts silly, syphilitic or just plain fucked.

I guess what I'm really getting at- chanelling, perhaps, (the Mutazilite) Al Rummani on the manner in which *taḍmin* w.r.t Revelation (by reason of the co-presence of all possible meanings by the Divine *wujuh al dalaala*) can function at the level of the bare and naked word regardless of its grammatical enchainment or grammatological enjambement or, indeed, Gricean implicature; and, myself, bitterly reflecting on how mere poetry, even the Ghazzalian ghazal, informed as it is by the *Asrar al-balagha* of Al Jurjani, yet is the *bala* of *Mubahila* divorce from that sort of *taḍmin* - which is w.r.t the Night of Grief- vide the Shia *hadith*- 'whoso says 'in what ?' has enclosed Him (*taḍmin*)'-..urm... what were we talking about? Oh, right, yeah. *Buri bala.* To whom can I say what it is? This night of grief is an evil calamity. How would it hurt me to die, if death happened only once?

Prof Faruqi's translation of a Ghazal by Ghalib

jab tak dahaan-e zakhm nah paidaa kare koi
mushkil hai tujh se raah-e sukhan vaa kare koi
'ālam ġhubār-e vaḥshat-e majnūñ hai sar-ba-sar
kab tak khayāl-e turrah-e lailā kare koī
afsurdagii nahii;N :tarab-inshaa-e iltifaat
haa;N dard ban ke dil me;N magar jaa kare koi
rone se ay nadiim malaamat nah kar mujhe
aakhir kabhii to uqdah-e dil vaa kare koi

Unless one creates a wound-mouth,
there is no way to open the way of communication with you.

The world from beginning to end consists of the dust of Majnun's frenzy;
how long then must one keep paying attention to Laila's hair?

Melancholy is not capable of instigating a loving attentive response,
yet perhaps if one becomes pain itself, one can find a place in the heart.

Friend, do not reproach me for weeping;
after all, sooner or later, someone must undo the knot of the heart.

My Commentary-
What a beautiful poem! It truly shows the genius of Ghalib. For example the line-
1. 'unless you create wound mouth' shows clearly the need for creation of wound mouths
    for the stated purpose viz. opening the way of communication. Greatness of Ghalib is
    brought out by showing the calibre of the man. Previously, though paths of
    communication may or not have been open, still nobody was mentioning necessity of
    wound mouth. This is a very good translation for English, because major English poets
    are not mentioning the need for wound mouths constantly. They should take heed of
    Ghalib's point and immediately open wound mouths everywhere especially for benefit
    of people on low incomes, or Third World countries, not to mention the Micro-finance
    initiatives of Grameen Bank, Mukesh Ambani, Vikram Akula and so on.
2. The second couplet is mentioning the story of Qais Majnun who went completely mad
    due to his love for Lailah. It requests information 'how long must we keep paying
    attention to that lady's hair?" It is a very relevant question especially for plumbers.
    How long they should they go on paying attention to that lady's hair before fixing your
    toilet? They may consider 15 years a reasonable time-scale. You may have different
    ideas. This is a very controversial topic and should be addressed by leading English
    scholars as they may not be aware that this field of research exists.
3. The third couplet is revealing this consummate wisdom- 'Melancholy is not capable of
    instigating a loving attentive response' This is very brilliant because the word
    melancholy means 'sad'. It is a gem of wisdom showing people that by putting sad face
    and showing mental depression you will not attract the fair lady. Instead you should be
    laughing all the time. Then, the delicate damsel will think 'he is jolly fellow. All the
    time laughing only. Oh my God! What is happening? Is he instigating a loving
    attentive response from me? I believe he is! Stop laughing, I say, so we can get
    smoochy-koochy already!'

4.   The first line is full of poetic beauty. He says 'Friend, do not reproach me for weeping.' The idea is that the poet is weeping so much that his friend says 'do not weep so much. There is no need. It is not a good thing you are doing by going on weeping and weeping. People are looking at you and shaking their heads. They think you are a big nuisance and cry-baby. Kindly stop it.'
The beauty of the English translation is it uses just one word- viz. reproach- to suggest all of the above.

Of course, Prof. Faruqi can not really take credit for this beautiful translation. America alone, that is the America of Adrienne Rich, Robert Bly, Charles Olson and M.F-ucking-A poetry programs, can take credit for such an achievement, as becomes clear when you compare his translation to my own execrable 'Curry & Chips' Cockney version-

Till the mouth of the wound gravid utterance attain
All paths to your ear, mere aporias detain

Majnun's footy blister has raised a dusty twister to pervade the Plenum's plane
Whom, longer, in imaginal Limbo, can Lailah's locks limn sane?

Not Civility has a freezing center, all heating, guests to gain
Save my sleeting heart, she enter, who entered ere as pain.

Cup companion, my tears' flood to slow, reprove not- no reproof is vain!
That my Noah's knot of the heart's rainbow, the Saqi sooner obtain

Comment

The word '*paida*' in the first line suggested giving birth rather than creation to me. The difference being that in giving birth, something from the other is required. Hence 'gravid utterance'. That paths are detained- i.e. become longer and don't reach their destinations- by something, or that something detains them seems quite poetic to me. In the original the word '*vaa'* is more poetic but I can think of no English equivalent which might achieve the same effect.

In English, footy- has the meaning of football, a passion with young men- to say Majnun has a footy blister suggests that his madness is as intense as the ordinary lad's passion for the sport. The aim is to make Majnun's passion something real and familiar. A dusty twister- i.e. a tornado of dust- is raised up by Majnun (as happens in the film Kung Fu Soccer). Now from the Wizard of Oz and so on, we have the notion of a tornado as linking different ontological realms. Hence *Alam* here is the Plenum, but the Plenum as a limit of something else of higher dimension- the plane being 2 dimensional.

Thus, apart from some homely touches 'footy' and 'twister' the meaning is not different from the literal- 'The world is the dust raised by Majnun's frenzy from end to end'.

In the second line I am interpreting 'khayal' in Ibn Arabi's sense. Still 'imaginal Limbo' is merely an intensification of the literal 'thought' since the thought of Lailah's head adornment is clearly unavailing and can't be kept up indefinitely.

The word 'locks' suggests a restraint- as of a strait jacket- and is used for that reason.
In the third couplet, I'm focusing on *afsurdagi* as 'frozenness frigidity, coldness, numbness; dejection, melancholy, lowness or depression of spirits'.' Normally, the joyous welcome of a guest is not associated with freezing. However, to keep the guest eternally within itself, perhaps the heart should freeze over! This is permissible, in this context, because she will only enter the heart as '*dard*' i.e pain. I permit myself an intensification here such that the notion is that the

pain she has already caused is as nothing to what remains in store. At present my heart is merely 'sleeting'- soon it will instantly freeze anything it comes into contact with.

In the fourth couplet I focus on '*naadim*' as cup companion and get the (elided) conceit that the drinking buddy is afraid my tears will dilute the wine to the point where it will lose its power to intoxicate thus bringing disgrace to the Saqi.

To make the last couplet poetic to the English reader, I introduce a completely new imagery based on the Biblical flood- the rainbow being the mark of God's covenant with Noah (a famous drunk, who, if I correctly recall my ancestrally South Indian, or Toda, Tamil's Talmudic roots, was sodomised and castrated by his son Ham's ham-fisted reach-around. Nimrod, a descendant of Ham, was the dictator of Iraq toppled by George W. Bush, the memory of whose lovely rap lyric 'When America fucks you in the ass, Democracy is the reach-around!' induces a mood of such *eheu! fugaces labuntur anni* as to justify and make infinitely rewarding this my poetic paraphrasis).

Anyway, if you managed to plough through the above you're going to see an added excellence in Prof. Fauqi's translation- the strength of its claim to be accepted as canonical- precisely in order to preclude the sort of poetastering you have just sampled.

Prof. Faruqi on 'delicacy of thought' as opposed to meaning creation

Conisder Ghalib's ghazal 28.

> *qatrah-e- mai baskih ḥairat se nafas-parvar huā*
> *khatt-e- jām-e mai sarāsar rishtah-e gauhar huā*
> *eitibār-e-ishq kī khānah-kharābī dekhnā*
> *ghair ne kī āh lekin vuh khafā mujh par huā*

The drop of wine became, out of amazement, to such an extent {breath-holding / life-preserving}

the line on the wine-glass became {entirely / end to end} a string of pearls
Look at the home-{wreckingness/wreckedness} of the confidence of passion!

the rival gave a sigh, but she became angry at me

(from Prof. Pritchett's 'desertful of roses' site)

Ghalib himself, and Faruqi Sahib concurs, thought this had delicacy of thought but little 'meaning creation'.

Yet the verse, even if it does not reference the physical phenomenon of 'tears of wine ' as I first thought, seems singularly rich in its associations- viz.

1) breath control as the foundation of all Hesychastic/Sufi/ Yogic/Tao Meditation techniques- not to mention Ibn Arabi's singular notion that the 'realizer of breaths' gains the secret of *tahawwul* (continuous transformation) thus achieving a Khizr-like omniscience not actually constrained by predestination because simultaneous with its own activity- in line with H.Q 55.29, 'every moment He is a new manifestation'.
2) such breath control being associated via *hairath* (bewilderment) with Bedil's *mot theme* of hairat-e-aainah (bewilderment-in-the-mirror) thus bringing in that practice of meditation in front of a mirror called 'speculation', Rome banned but which is otherwise so fundamental to other Theistic mystical traditions.
3) the drop (microcosm) as attaining this breath control in the mirror of amazement
4) the abolition of time- *kshanika vada* 'doctrine of momentariness'- which is hugely important to rescue Theodicy from silly Heavens and Hells or the moral

idiocy of karma. But this *kshanika vada* is also the source of great beauty in poetry and painting- especially in the Far East.

True, in Islam, the analogous Ash'ari or occasionalist doctrine of *al khalq al mutajaddid*- i.e. continuous Creation- serves a purpose of mere anti-Aristotelian casuistry and is not fundamental to the religion, or indeed, the World View, in the same manner as *kshanika vada* is to Buddhism- but this scarcely matters to the ghazal world and its inverted Seminary- especially if hashish or opium variegate its Symposium.

5) the wine glass's foam turning into 'Indra's net of pearls' pointing to the radical interconnectedness of the cosmos.

But that's just to start with, then there is

1) the wine cup as shaped by the absence of the breast. This links with the (Jungian) notion of the krater/crater as the topos of prophesy

2) wine's foam as the areolae of the absent nipple.

The krater concretizes the *cire perdue* of the breast pointing to wine as the mother's milk of prophesy- not petition, not pedagogy-, and the Saqi as Shiduri, the Sumerian Goddess of Wisdom in the Epic of Gilgamesh, who- from behind her veils- presides at the Tavern at the end of what but in the world resides- these are all Jungian archetypes at the foundation of *any* tradition of *khamriyat*- all the better in Ghalib's case for operating at the unconscious level. The elision of mention of the Cup bearer's beauty as occasioning the wine drop's amazement, which appears to lie at the root of some of the commentators' complaint against the couplet, is not a defect for Ghalib is not relying on this aetiology. Rather we have a good piece of observational poetry- something universal which any drinker could compose no matter what their cultural background- viz. the wine drop motionless (its upward momentum from the drinker's last quaffing cancelling out the force of gravity) above the face of the beaded wine foam from whence it came, holding its breath in awe.

The essential innocence of the erotic meaning arises from the reverential treatment of the areole, the hypnotic stasis its sight induces- the freezing of the moment characteristic of first love.

Anyway, this is my 'transcreation' of Ghazal 28 from the Divan.

{28,1}

> Breathless, atremble, the wine drop, forgetting Time's lips to wet
> Reflects the cup's foaming areolae as Tvashtr' s pearly net
> To Faith, Love's home wrecker, for her angry breast, in debt
> That, for some stranger's sigh, I she'll yet fry, Ghalib bet!

Here my addition to the elided breast/krater conceit, is angry breast/heated kar'hai (wok) full of bubbling oil.

My point is that for a 19 year old poet, the mazmun- 'breast equals the absence that the wine cup encloses and defines' can quickly go on to the next wonderful thing associated with people who possess breasts (not that my own flabby 'moobs' (Man-boobs) can't pertly fill a champagne glass) namely their command over the kar'hai in which they fry you up cheese *pakoras* with plenty of minced ginger and green chilli. God, my mouth is watering!

The reason it has to be Tvashtr's (rather than Indra's) net of pearls is explained thus- "Obviously, it can't be Indra's net of pearls- it has to be the artificer Tvashtar (the Indian Vulcan) coz of the whole thing with Vrtra- wine as the dragon (with whom al Hallaj drank in summer) slain by the wine bibbing thunderbolt God- and the connection with the krater/ crater.'

"Also, I want to introduce the notion of 'Ghalib's bet' as being like 'Pascal's wager' except obviously, Ghalib is betting higher than existence, higher than imaginal Hells and Heavens- this is the ultimate *Malamati* Martingale- hence his choice of *takhallus.*"

I think the above explains why Ghalib and Faruqi Sahib insist on the distinction between 'delicacy of thought' and 'meaning creation. Also, why Rum is bad for you.

Prof. Faruqi and Ghalib's rosary of carnelians

Everyone knows the story of Indra's net of pearls- each of which reflects every other- to be a metaphor of the interconnectedness of the cosmos which actually doesn't exist save momentarily and that too only as a topos for this lightning flash of a metaphor.

There is an equally beautiful metaphor arising out of this favourite hadith of the Sufis - 'Truly, the hearts of the Sons of Adam are all between two fingers from among the fingers of the All Mighty like one heart which He turns as He wishes'.

Consider this couplet of Ghalib's-

> shumār-e subḥah marġhūb-e but-e mushkil-pasand āyā
> tamāshā-e bah yak-kaf burdan-e ṣad dil pasand āyā

1) the counting of the prayer-beads was enjoyable to the difficulty-loving idol
2) the spectacle of the holding of a hundred hearts in one hand pleased her

In a surpassingly beautiful passage in his book 'The secret mirror'- Prof. S.R. Faruqi writes 'the beloved out of sheer love-of-difficulty suggests her love of stealing a hundred hearts by the metaphorical act of holding a rosary in her hands. Thus, the red beads of the rosary assume the place of hearts, and just as the beads find warmth and motion by the touch of beloved's fingers, so do the hearts of the lovers; just as each bead, though remaining tied to the same string, travels up and down with the motion of her fingers, so do lovers' hearts remain, despite all their madness, despite also the interplay of hope and fear, nearness and remoteness, tied to the same place. The beloved's henna painted, fair and tapering fingers have the same relation with the red beads of the rosary as does dawn to dusk; no matter how bloodshot the dusk is, not a shred of whiteness is subtracted from the dawn. Thus holding a rosary in the hand, a metaphor, and carrying away hearts, the actuality, become one.'

Faruqi Sahib adds that 'Metaphor outweighs the Reality for which it stands. Thus the reality it represents gains over and above its ordinary dimension, or a hither to unknown dimension is added to it.'

In particular, 'two mutually exclusive (i.e. incompossible) realities can be expressed in a way that makes them appear one.'

A question we might well ask ourselves is- *Which Universe do we live in?* Is it substantivist or relationist- Ghalib's rosary of carnelians or Indra's net of pearls?

Let us look at the rest of Ghalib's ghazal

> bah fai.z-e be-dilii naumiidii-e jaaved aasaa;N hai
> kushaayish ko hamaaraa ((uqdah-e mushkil pasand aayaa

1) thanks to heart-lessness, eternal hopelessness is easy

2) 'Opening' found our difficult knot

> havaa-e sair-e gul aa))iinah-e be-mihrii-e qaatil
> kih andaaz-e bah ;xuu;N-;Galtiidan-e bismil pasand aayaa

1) the desire/lust/breeze of strolling among roses-- a mirror of the mercilessness of the murderer
2) for the style of the bloody tumbling/wallowing of the slaughtered/wounded ones was pleasing [to her] pleasing

Not haughty, nor naughty, 'tis love of the knotty makes prayer, not prosody, such a bore
And our hundred hearts to her henna'd hand- a rosary of carnelians, nothing more

Not for heartless is her each luckless wight, but that Hope Hearts knotted sore
Her dexterous digits to unknot delight but render naught our core

If she, a turn in the garden, proposes- the breezes to her mirror- or adore
Make such a massacre of the roses as to mire her soles in gore!
(Ghazal 8)

Ghalib's rosary of carnelians- in Prof. Faruqi's hands- becomes truly (as he puts it) six dimensional, in the sense of stringing together incompossible worlds constructed by precisely the sort of impossible subjects we, in the metaphor's secret mirror recognize ourselves to be. Indeed, such necessarily are we- if Heidegger's notion of alethia, truth, as primordial unhiddenness is at all meaningful- and the only valid starting point of hermeneutics is not the closing off of possible meanings- or, indeed, pre-meanings- but the unhiding, the restoration of what paradigmatic, or indeed syntagmatic, analysis shaves away.

Which isn't to say Heide wasn't a great lump of shite.

Bedil, *Muqaallib ul Quloob* and the Game theoretic 'core'

Our temptation is to see the 'heart', in Islamic poetry- or, indeed, Poetry as Metanoia- where God is defined as the 'converter of hearts'- as standing for the Ghazalian scapegoating of the Girardian Grief Agon's Game-theoretic 'core'- empty only in the case of a zero-sum game, or pure market transaction. True, the history of the Twentieth Century, which was written in the Nineteenth- at least, that is to say, the history of Moral Entrepreneurship in the Twentieth Century- has been the history of the secularization and forced collectivization of Love-as-Guilt with the effect of founding, what must be to hearts, a run-away negative sum game. Consequently, life properly so called- life-as-plasticity- that which survives its own deforming fitness landscape- life is that questioning of its own constitutive code which commences with the loss of the heart, the condition of 'heartlessness'- *be dil az be nishan cheh garid baz*?- what should the one without a heart say- being also without a sign?

Faruqi's six dimensions and Ghalib's knot mnemonics

In ancient India, books were formed by tying loose leaves together. The knot that secured the pages was called the Grantha- thus also becoming a word for a book or even a sacred scripture. The nigrantha (knot-less) ascetic is the Jain monk whose syadvad logic unties the knot of mere biblolatry, just as his nakedness represents the tearing of the garment of nescience, but from Kabir we have the notion that though the thread frays away the knot remains- this as the secret of Bhakti devotional Theism.

Ghalib, famously, did not compose his ghazals with pen and paper in hand. Rather he simply tied a knot in the drawstring of his pajamas to denote the perfecting of each couplet. Like other contemporary men of letters, he had memorized a large number of poems by the Masters. But Ghalib was also a gambler. This suggests a subtle difference in the manner we might conceive his mind as operating with respect to, what might be called, his own unconscious 'hashing techniques' and inferential heuristics. This suggests two ways of making our attempt to read Ghalib more productive and enjoyable to ourselves. The first is the standard literary practice of searching for the *zamin* (lit 'the ground') of the ghazal amongst the classic models. The second is to consider the couplet composed on that *zamin* as the building of a circular data-structure by tying the knot in a 'lazy language' (like Haskell). This changes the received intentionality of the *she'r*. Indeed, conceiving the couplet in terms of constraints upon expression, processing and information gets us to the dual of the poet's problem- i.e. essentially Social questions of contested hegemony and sub-optimal Technics- which 'engaged' criticism pretends to concern itself with but prohibits to all any means of access.

A little reflection will show that a naive knot theory- such as that of the kids studied by Piaget- is likely to very quickly yield 5 topological 'dimensions'- viz. up/down, in/out, top/bottom, inside/outside & over/under- add in the original '*zamin*'- itself a 'grief knot' upon its '*zamin*'- and you have Faruqi's six dimensions.

Indeed, for those who conceive of semiotics in terms of Statistical Mechanics- and would be forced to see Reception Theory as essentially a naive heuristics or, so to speak, a knot fractal 'in the bight' upon that larger field- there should, it seems to me, be an equivalence between the application of Gibbs paradox- viz that information, extensively defined, is subjective or dependent upon the degree of fine-graining in discrimination- and an aesthetics of valorizing those hermeneutics which aim at knot invariants- like the Jones polynomial- especially in the context of the open question re. whether any knot invariant can distinguish between the unknot and all others.

I make this point merely because it might otherwise appear that I think appreciating Ghalib involves the utter shite of Modern fucking Metaphysics which is rather the castration than pleasurable exercise of that which drives cultural evolution.
Basically, what I'm saying is Ghalib aint for Gramscian Post Colonial/Eco Feminist/Queer Theory/ 'Xenophiliac' fuckwits- he's for balding, beer bellied, virtually blue collar, blokes like you and me- having a drink after work and briefly believing we aint just data crunching technicians but have *adaab*, are gentlemen, y'know, like wot our dads had or were and (*Hamdullah!)* will always have and be.

I believe this to be an early (1816) couplet from Ghazal 190-
> bastan-e-ʿahd-e muḥabbat hamah nā-dānī thā
> chashm-e nakshūdah rahā ʿuqdah-e paimāñ mujh se

> Coupling, as Love's Canon, of unwise eyes are the bight
> I shut tight and Noah's *Unknot* grief-knot to my blight.

Ghalib's ghazal 18-- barzakh as a 'lazy language' compiler.
I've been trying to think of how Ibn Arabi's notion of the barzakh might influence a poet's choice of verses for his published Divan. The notion that an early couplet might be a 'hopeful monster' or represent 'tying the knot' in a 'lazy language' - *itself* influences Reception, which might be thought of as a sort of bootstrapped compiler- and changes the hermeneutic circle.

Ghalib's Divan, for obvious reasons, suggests itself as the ideal candidate for this sort of exercise- but, how productive is the outcome? At least in English, one so wants to be seized of a conceit, elided or otherwise, it is precisely the poetic afflatus, or breath generated heat or *tapas*, which fails to be captured on the page.

Consider ghazal 18

shab khumār-e shauq-e sāqī rastkhez-andāzah thā
tā muḥīṭ-e bādah ṣūrat-ḳhānah-e ḳhamyāzah thā

1) last night the intoxication/hangover of the ardor of/for the <u>Cupbearer</u> was in the style of Judgment Day
2) up to the wine-circumference there was a picture-house of a yawn/stretch/gape
(this is from Prof. Fran Pritchett's 'desertful of roses site')

It seems to me that the commentators miss something by taking *rastkhez* simply as Doomsday. The nurturing or burgeoning aspect of the word points to Ibn Arabi's conception of *barzakh* (limbo) as a place of imaginal growth and evolution.

Another point has to do with the manner in which the obvious conceit- viz. that the reflection of the Saqi in the wine cup causes the wine to become enchanted- is overlooked (though Ghalib considered such elision a special mark of beauty) in favor of the (to us) deeply unpoetical notion that drinkers yawn a lot..

Still the notion of Night as the hang-over of the enchantment of the lights of the Tavern strikes an experiential note.

yak qadam vaḥshat se dars-e daftar-e imkāñ khulā
jādah ajzā-e do-ʿālam-dasht kā shīrāzah thā

1a) with/through one footstep of wildness/madness the lesson of the chapter of possibilities opened up
1a) with/through one footstep of wildness/madness the lesson of the chapter of possibilities fell apart
2a) the path [that the madman had left behind] was the binding-thread of the pieces of the two-world desert
2b) the path [of madness itself] was the binding-thread of the pieces of the two-world desert
The two worlds here are the *alam al amr* and the *alam al khalq*- ie. the world of 'command' and the world of the created.

Again, Ibn Arabi's treatment of barzakh is required to make this couplet meaningful- indeed, barzakh is transformed into the individual's world line stitching his imaginal ontology together.

māna ʿ-e vaḥshat-ḳhirāmīhā-e lail;ā kaun hai
ḳhānah-e majnūn-e ṣaḥrā-gird be-darvāzah thā

1) who is a forbidder of the {madness/wildness}-walkings of <u>Laila</u>?
2) the house of <u>Majnun</u> the desert-circler was door-less

Again, it looks to me as though a (perhaps too obvious to be stated) elision needs to be made explicit- at least in English.

nālah-e dil ne diye aurāq-e laḳht-e dil bah bād
yādgār-e nālah ik dīvān-e be-shīrāzah thā

1) the lament of the heart gave the pages of the fragments of the heart to the wind
2) the memorial/keepsake of the lament was a single/unique/preeminent <u>divan</u> without a binding-thread

This, of course, is reminiscent of Jami picturing Majnoon as writing Lailah's name in the desert sand, which the wind, vastly obliging, will then erase. As the hadith has it 'do not revile the wind for truly it is from the breath of the All Merciful.'

Night got drunk on the Saqi's ardour to intimate Resurrection
Fabled beauties bubbled the grape, agape at her reflection

One tread from desolation bethreads the Quran of instruction
Command & Creation, our path paginates as destruction.

The Sahara is a shack I'd ignore as being of mean construction
Did not, on its door, Lailah's heart pound to such ruction!

That publishing Majnoon, my Grief's Prolegemenon & Introduction
Bankrupted the Simoon, I'm remaindered as rue & deduction.

Ghazal 230

This is a ghazal Prof. Naim has analysed and which certain distinguished American poets have worked on. After reading the Professor's essay, bearing as it does the unmistakable signature of his suave intellectual nullity, I was inspired to get busy on it in my own inimitable style. The chief beauty of what follows is the rhyme poppy/laproscopy, apropos of which I direct your attention to this essay's endnote (xvi) re. the licit use of contemporary idiom or imagery in a canonical context.

shabnam bah gul-e lālah nah khālī z adā hai
dāgh-e dil-e bedard nazar-gāh-e hayā hai
dil khūñ-shudah-e kashmakash-e hasrat-e dīdār
ā'īnah bah dast-e but-e bad-mast hinā hai
shu'le se nah hotī havas-e shu'lah ne jo kī
jī kis qadar afsurdagī-e dil pah jalā hai
timsāl meñ terī hai vuh shokhī kih bah sad zauq
ā'īnah bah andāz-e gul āghosh-kushā hai
qumrī kaf-e khākistar-o-bulbul qafas-e rang
ay nālah nishān-e jigar-e sokhtah kyā hai
khū ne tirī afsurdah kiyā vahshat-e dil ko
ma'shūqī-o-be-hausalagī turfah balā hai
majbūrī-o-da'vā-e giriftārī-e ulfat
dast-e tah-e sang-āmadah paimān-e vafā hai
ma'lūm hu'ā hāl-e shahīdān-e guzashtah
tegh-e sitam ā'īnah-e tasvīr-numā hai
ay partav-e khvurshīd-e jahāñ-tāb idhar bhī
sāye kī tarah ham pah 'ajab vaqt paṛā hai
nā-kardah gunāhoñ kī bhī hasrat kī mile dād
yā rab agar in kardah gunāhoñ kī sazā hai
begānagī-e khalq se bedil nah ho ghālib
ko'ī nahīñ terā to mirī jān khudā hai

Ah! say not all artless the petal'd poppy has Aurora's tear drop distilled
Its own eye, Shame's laproscopy, has today in the heartless instilled

Pray, if the heart beats itself bloody for that once Beauty the eye filled
As wine to her hand-held looking glass is not nuptial henna fulfilled?

What fearful sight freezes the flambeau so, by its own Light, chilled?
Or to beat up its own beaten heart, must Life yet again body build?!

Taking infection from your reflection- so bitching, bewitching & self-willed
Rose-like, your honey'd mirror opens, Light's pollen thief guilty to gild

Burnt feathers mark the bier of, what for Love, the caged bird trilled
O Lament, like me unremarked, mark *you* my life-blood spilled!

You torture me the more, my tyrant, for so spiritless & unskilled
Truly killing's that cruel kindness qualmish to see me killed!

Love not free to leave off Love- how profess yet confess as billed?
Hands are bestowed on hands till, stone-crushed, hands are stilled.

The Sun is the Saqi of Saqis but my shadow not being of that guild
Dear my mere mirror wine, martyrdom's sword flash has swilled

The credit for crimes imaginary, their Infernal meed to which I've thrilled
God, grant Ghalib, the lonely, but only if Thy Loneliness thus has willed.

Reading this, you might decide that, maybe, those famous American poets publishing best selling translations of Rumi and so on aren't so bad after all. But you're wrong. They are the Devil.

Ghazal 63

ṣafā-e ḥairat-e ā'īnah hai sāmān-e zang āḵhir
taġhayyur āb-e barjā-mãñdah kā pātā hai rang āḵhir

nah kī sāmān-e 'aish-o-jāh ne tadbīr vaḥshat kī
hu'ā jām-e zumurrud bhī mujhe dāġh-e palang āḵhir

For that her street's rain refreshed puddles are changed to a scummy, sicklied o'er, green
Or that the *mise en abyme* of the mystics, only in the mirror's verdigris, now is seen
Rare wines and rich acquaintance have yet, me, to common madness sped.
Till the sigil plain, of all Mathesis arcane, is but this stain upon my bed!

Ghazal 111

In her seminal article- 'Orient Pearls unstrung- the quest for unity in the ghazal'- Prof. Pritchett has highlighted this ode as presenting a severe challenge to the seeker of unity.

sab kahãñ kuchh lālah-o-gul meñ numāyãñ ho ga'īñ
ḵhāk meñ kyā ṣūrateñ hoñgī kih pinhãñ ho ga'īñ
yād thīñ ham ko bhī rangārang bazm-ārā'iyãñ
lekin ab naqsh-o-nigār-e ṭāq-e nisyãñ ho ga'īñ
thīñ banāt ul-na'sh-e gardūñ din ko parde meñ nihãñ
shab ko un ke jī meñ kyā ā'ī kih 'uryãñ ho ga'īñ
qaid meñ ya'qūb ne lī go nah yūsuf kī ḵhabar
lekin āñkheñ rauzan-e dīvār-e zindãñ ho ga'īñ
sab raqīboñ se hoñ nā-ḵhvush par zanān-e miṣr se
hai zulaiḵhā ḵhvush kih maḥv-e māh-e kan'ãñ ho ga'īñ

In English, to make the Ghazal at home
Is Ghalib is to take for a Garden gnome

jū-e ḵẖūñ āñkhoñ se bahne do kih hai shām-e firāq
maiñ yih samjhūñgā kih sham'eñ do furozāñ ho ga'īñ
in parīzādoñ se leñge ḵẖuld meñ ham intiqām
qudrat-e ḥaq se yihī ḥūreñ agar vāñ ho ga'īñ
nīnd us kī hai dimāġh us kā hai rāteñ us kī haiñ
terī zulfeñ jis ke bāzū par pareshāñ ho ga'īñ
maiñ chaman meñ kyā gayā goyā dabistāñ khul gayā
bulbuleñ sun kar mire nāle ġhazal-ḵẖvāñ ho ga'īñ
vuh nigāheñ kyūñ hu'ī jātī haiñ yā rab dil ke pār
jo mirī kotāhī-e qismat se mizhgāñ ho ga'īñ
baskih rokā maiñ ne aur sīne meñ ubhrīñ pai bah pai
merī āheñ baḵẖyah-e chāk-e garebāñ ho ga'īñ
vāñ gayā bhī maiñ to un kī gāliyoñ kā kyā javāb
yād thīñ jitnī du'ā'eñ ṣarf-e darbāñ ho ga'īñ
jāñ-fizā hai bādah jis ke hāth meñ jām ā gayā
sab lakīreñ hāth kī goyā rag-e jāñ ho ga'īñ
ham muvaḥḥid haiñ hamārā kesh hai tark-e rusūm
millateñ jab miṭ ga'īñ ajzā-e īmāñ ho ga'īñ
ranj se ḵẖū-gar hu'ā insāñ to miṭ jātā hai ranj
mushkileñ mujh par paṛīñ itnī kih āsāñ ho ga'īñ
yūñ hī gar rotā rahā ġhālib to ay ahl-e jahāñ
dekhnā in bastiyoñ ko tum kih vīrāñ ho ga'īñ

In what the flowers display and what the dust yet hides
Resurrected Beauty, for aye, Thy veil abides

What in Memory as our colorful legend presides
Life's quotidian but cobwebs provides

The Pleiades, whose conceits our day elides
Lie naked to a fate, night decides

If from Jacob, Joseph a dungeon hides
His eyes, in darkness, its chink betides

On cutting up rivals, if Love, itself, prides
Zuleikha's jury, Justice derides!

For Separation's dark, the nightmare so rides
The Eye, erupting blood, its ember, chides

If, in Heaven, as houris, Beauty resides
Revenged are we on who weren't our brides!

His is sleep, and mystic dream, & Night & all besides
Your coiffure on whose chest its undoing confides

Wine is life giving; gain Wine and no March's Ides

Mars your hand's hold on the immortal guide's!

All Faiths are One for their Observance divides.
Nothing is won by but warring sides.

'Fore Cities and Towns, which tears' flood subsides?
Dams my isthmus of wreckage a damn Deicide's!?

Notice- if Ghalib's flood of tears wipes out a human settlement then God's covenant with Noah no longer operates- thus this aspect of grief-in-love is both a theological sin as well as a sort of covert or Oedipally murderous impulse towards God the Father.

I suppose I ought to address the question Prof. Pritchett raised as to whether this ghazal has any thematic unity. My answer is yes- mimetic desire is what each couplet is about. But, a doubt crosses my mind. The truth is my Sufism derives not from Jami's Yusuf Zuliekha but Max Beerbohm's Zuelikha Dobson. But this begs the question, is it my Cockney animus against Oxford which impels me in a spirit of Working Class vengance to assimilate Beerbohm's bijou masterpiece to Proust's stammering epic, that too by means of Rene Girard's strait jacket? If so, Prof. Pritchett may be right. What I see as thematic unity is merely my own *ressentiment.*
Zuleikha Dobson *is* the ultimate Sufi parable of mimetic desire.
In Islam, especially Sufi poetry, Zuleikha is the name of Potiphar's wife who falls in love with

Joseph.
The name Zuleikha derives from, the Arabic, zallakah- a place where the foot might slip- however, Allah defends Joseph against the temptation posed by Zuliekha's beauty. She tears off the back of his shirt as he attempts to flee her and then accuses him, to her husband, of having attempted her rape. However, her cousin points out that since Joseph's shirt was torn from the back- he must have been trying to flee her.

When the women of Egypt cry out against Zuleikha's crime, she invites them for a banquet. While they peel oranges with their knives, Zuliekha causes Joseph to appear. The women cut their hands, not the oranges, dazzled by his beauty. In Persian, zuleikha is also an inauspicious term for the color red, or blood.

This 'loveliest of tales' (Holy Quran) dramatises the dilemma of the 'impossible object' of philosophy's love. The late Victorians had fully assimilated Sufi poetry- through the Persian- (though it was poets of an earlier generation, Tom Moore, Southey etc, who wrote oriental pastiches) so much so that W.S. Gilbert is actually referencing Jami's Salaman & Absal in the figure of the amorous Nanny in the Pirates of Penzance.

Beerbohm sets up Zuliekha to fall for an impossible object- the snobbish Duke who has dedicated his life to a sort of monastic dandyism- but then introduces a truly delicious complication- the perfection of the Duke's amour propre is that paradoxical Monism which the Sufi Masters decry as 'an idolatry because it is a shielding of the heart from the Other- and the

Other does not exist!" This hubris, or more than mortal perfection, sets the Olympian Gods in motion to bring about his destruction. A miraculous change in the color of his shirt studs convinces the Duke, against his own will, that he truly loves Zuleikha- but, alas, it is not the flesh and blood woman of that name- but an, *amor fati,* will-o'-the-wisp, ignited by his own tragic egotism, whom he is destined to woo to no happier end than the drowning of his dameon for dandaical distinction in a mindless mass act more befitting sophomores, suffragettes or suburban fashion-victims. This is 'Romantic Irony' with a vengance!

Like the Duke, Zuleikha too is an egoist- but, unlike the Duke, she can have babies. She represents Goethe's eternal feminine- like Anna in Shaw's Eugenic rather than Schopenhauerian "Man and Superman." - but in her stated ardour to be used and then brutally discarded by the Duke, she combines an Ibsenite Rebecca West quality with the Wildean 'Woman of no Importance' who, rending the veil of her hidden shame, reduces all Power, all Punditry, all Patriarchy to utter insignificance.

In fact, from this Shavian point of view, the 'Life-force' did a good job of work when it ensured that, if the Duke 'loves' Zuleikha, she can't love him! There were plenty of other Grand Dukes for her to marry, while there was a nice little house-maid who would have done very nicely for the Duke if he really wanted to strike a blow against the class system.

Okay, the English reader may feel Zuleikha is irrational in wanting everybody to commit suicide for her- but such behaviour is *de rigueur* in the Islamic ghazal tradition. In fact, Beerbohm gives this Sufi convention a sort of psychological probability by depicting Zuleikah as a publicity hungry starlet.

Ultimately, the Duke agrees to commit suicide because this represents an aristocratic yielding to Fate- the Olympian Gods- purely as a matter of good form. This is wholly Victorian. Behind the Duke, we see Matthew Arnold reading deontics into the Bhagvad Gita to provide a bridge of Sighs betwixt the dandaical aspect of the Oxford movement, the sunny side of the peach, and its bitter doctrinal fruit such that, ever thereafter, a salt and blighting note warps the pastoral lyricism of 'scholar gypsies'- Housman, Hardy and so on- but also Santayana in 'The last Puritan'-

> 'She stood dreaming as a rose might dream
> Half-open in the sunless air
> If but once the salt winds of fate
> Had touched her beauty with despair'

Beerbohm's depiction of the working of 'mimetic desire'- (vide Rene Girard's analysis of Proust)- and the manner in which it can lead to a thymotic disaster- like the Gadarening rush to the trenches of the First World War- is like a piece of hyper-elegant mathematics rivaling the work of Weyl, Poincare etc.

This gem of English literature has so much meaning packed into it while appearing nothing more than an Undergraduate jeu d'esprit- a Musical Comedy of a little novel. If only some one had explained its excellence to people like me, back when we were teens- we would never have thought we too could set up as writers! Beerbohm had genius. In vain do we drown ourselves in ink. Zuleikha was never for the likes of us.

Incidentally, after Zuleikha went to Cambridge- and the students there drowned themselves- she married Rajni Palme Dutt who, being a Marxist, understood not just the Hegelian dialectic but the infinitely more subtle Saavanih love dialectic of Ahmed Ghazali.

Thus, sad to say, she became an instructor in Statistics at the London School of Economics and did noteworthy research in Bayesian Analysis.

Ghazal 96

jahāñ terā naqsh-e qadam dekhte haiñ
khiyābāñ khiyābāñ iram dekhte haiñ
dil-āshuftagāñ khāl-e kunj-e dahan ke
suvaidā meñ sair-e ʿadam dekhte haiñ
tire sarv-e qāmat se yak qadd-e ādam
qiyāmat ke fitne ko kam dekhte haiñ
tamāshā kih ay maḥv-e āʾīnah-dārī
tujhe kis tamannā se ham dekhte haiñ
surāgh-e taf-e nālah le dāgh-e dil se
kih shab-rau kā naqsh-e qadam dekhte haiñ
banā kar faqīroñ kā ham bhes ghālib
tamāshā-e ahl-e karam dekhte haiñ

Thy footsteps, in desert sands, are where to our famished gaze
Iram resurrected stands, its rose beds all ablaze.

That Beauty's mole miss kiss her lip, must so trouble and amaze
For Reason we now let slip & Reality e'en lower appraise.

Tho' the rapture of your beholding mere human havoc plays
Yet less Cosmic is the tumult, Doomsday itself displays.

To find the Ninja who, by dark, attacks, foils Day's detective rays
For, fleeing my heart, assassin tracks, Night as its Sun assays.

Now lost to her own looking glass, alas! her not the spectacle sways
Of her lovers as lost to a mirrored, for, but blind alley, maze.

In a goliard's tuneful tatters, cloak, Ghalib, Thought's gilded lays
For Princes now are paupers & only tadpoles croak thy praise.

Ghazal 57

ḥusn ghamze kī kashākash se chhuṭā mere baʿd
bāre ārām se haiñ ahl-e jafā mere baʿd
manṣab-e sheftagī ke koʾī qābil nah rahā
huʾī maʿzūlī-e andāz-o-adā mere baʿd
shamʿa bujhtī hai to us meñ se dhuvāñ uṭhtā hai
shuʿlah-e ʿishq siyah-posh huʾā mere baʿd
khūñ hai dil khāk meñ aḥvāl-e butāñ par yaʿnī
un ke nākhun huʾe muḥtāj-e ḥinā mere baʿd
dar-khvur-e ʿarẓ nahīñ jauhar-e bedād ko jā
nigah-e nāz hai surme se khafā mere baʿd
hai junūñ ahl-e junūñ ke liye āghosh-e vidāʿ
chāk hotā hai garebāñ se judā mere baʿd
kaun hotā hai ḥarīf-e mai-e mard-afgan-e ʿishq
hai mukarrar lab-e sāqī meñ ṣalā mere baʿd
gham se martā hūñ kih itnā nahīñ dunyā meñ koʾī
kih kare taʿziyat-e mihr-o-vafā mere baʿd

ā'e hai bekasī-e 'ishq pah ronā ğhālib
kis ke ghar jā'egā sailāb-e balā mere ba'd

Our Eyes' duel, Beauty won & haply, for I'm dead
Happy *Herrenvolk*, my Belsen, now homestead

& demobbed, its propaganda, can go populate Uganda
Now Madness has no War Minister in my stead

When a candle dies- such hues of rue as then arise
Dye passion's fire that, while I lived, was red.

Could someone go tell Hali, these idols are all Kali!
White nailed for, my heart, they white bled.

She spits at her mascara, it has undone its wearer
Now on Cruelty's koh-i-noor, to death, I have fed

Madness, to the Mad, is what my parting embrace said-
'Tear ye yet your White Collar? I tore off my head!'

Passion's Wine still flows though its paladins have all fled
My pall's the Saqi's call, so fack off all youse to bed!

For Faith, faithless is to what Light, as Love, wed
Men of straw bear its *tazia* of lead

Whence came, Ghalib, the teary floods that you shed?
& to whose door will they go, now you're dead?

Ghazal 120

qafas meñ hūñ gar achchhā bhī nah jāneñ mere shevan ko
mirā honā burā kyā hai navā-sanjān-e gulshan ko
nahīñ gar ham-damī āsāñ nah ho yih rashk kyā kam hai
nah dī hotī khudā yā ārzū-e dost dushman ko
nah niklā āñkh se terī ik āñsū us jarāḥat par
kiyā sīne meñ jis ne khūñ-chakāñ mizhgān-e sozan ko
khudā sharmā'e hāthoñ ko kih rakhte haiñ kashākash meñ
kabhī mere garebāñ ko kabhī jānāñ ke dāman ko
abhī ham qatl-gah kā dekhnā āsāñ samajhte haiñ
nahīñ dekhā shināvar jū-e khūñ meñ tere tausan ko
hu'ā charchā jo mere pāñv kī zanjīr ban'ne kā
kiyā betāb kāñ meñ junbish-e jauhar ne āhan ko
khvushī kyā khet par mere agar sau bār abr āve
samajhtā hūñ kih ḍhūñḍhe hai abhī se barq khirman ko
vafādārī bah sharṭ-e ustuvārī aṣl-e īmāñ hai
mare but-khāne meñ to ka'be meñ gāṛho barahman ko
shahādat thī mirī qismat meñ jo dī thī yih khū mujh ko
jahāñ talvār ko dekhā jhukā detā thā gardan ko

nah luṭṭā din ko to kab rāt ko yūñ be-k̲h̲abar sotā
rahā k̲h̲aṭkā nah chorī kā duʿā detā hūñ rahzan ko
suk̲h̲an kyā kah nahīñ sakte kih jūyā hoñ javāhir ke
jigar kyā ham nahīñ rakhte kih khodeñ jā ke maʿdan ko
mire s̲h̲āh-e sulaimāñ-jāh se nisbat nahīñ g̲h̲ālib
farīdūn-o-jam-o-kaik̲h̲usrav-o-dārāb-o-bahman ko

My bare existence baits their rage, not my barbarous bird cage
My lament so unlamented by the song trappers of the age...

Mimetic desire, were a refining fire, Lord, thy Perfection to gauge.
Did not the thymotic rival, for very survival, my affection engage

My heart's wounds, not adept to suture, the eye of the needle wept
Eyes dry in my operation theater, she'll cry on the Opera stage!

To what tug-of-war hast thou, Lord, set, shameless, all hands to wage?
To tug at a heart, or by literary art, tosser, tugging's guilt to assuage?

Breakers of our bloody sea, breasts to storm Cuchulain's rage
To see thy steed perform, we agree to at thy Blenheim engage

Madam, you're a talker, I'm sentenced as a stalker, but mark my *apercu* sage
'ware Iron, a She, Turk irony!, epiphanies of Tiffany's manacle thy mage!

Rain clouds gather over my fields like my few fond memories over this page
This happiness, too, that harvest which You, to the lightning, pre-engage...

The Brahman bury 'neath Ka'ba's stone for his heart's its sarcophagal rage
For Love & Faith, Death & Truth- atone as the pullulation of like phage.

Being by day of all wealth robbed, by no terror of theft is my night daubed
To Tear's Saqi, eyes sobbed, Death's the dyvour debtor, I'm underage.

Greedy of thine and mine, poets mine each other to our Gokturk undermine
& witless, but witness the gold digging ants of our own credulous page

I'm a court poet- djinn to the staff of the Solomon of the Age
Whose fortune can't befall another- or my Firdausi engage.

Ghalib's contempt for Farhad is well known. Was it because, proud of his Turkish heritage, Ghalib sensed the truth of the legend that the Turks are descended from a slave blacksmith/miner class, in the Altai mountains, who rebelled and founded a vast Empire?

After all, Ghalib served a Timurid (Timur means 'iron') who, like the dead Solomon, propped up by his staff, whom the djinns obeyed, yet by virtue of a certain sort of wisdom, a penchant for poetry of a certain type, nevertheless commanded a not wholly undeserved respect, though termites were eating through his prop and the final debacle little delayed.
Ghazal 60

This is the one from which the notorious 'the lightning should have fallen on Ghalib' shite originates.

bik jāte haiñ ham āp matā'-e sukhan ke sāth
lekin 'ayār-e ṭab'-e kharīdār dekh kar

1) we ourself are sold along with the merchandise/goods of poetry
2) but [only after] having seen the measure of quality/temperament of the buyer

{60,8}*

zunnār bāñdh subḥah-e ṣad-dānah toṛ ḍāl
rahrau chale hai rāh ko hamvār dekh kar

1a) tie on a sacred thread, rip apart the hundred-beaded prayer-beads!
1b) having tied on a sacred thread, having ripped apart the hundred-beaded prayer-beads
2) the traveler moves along, having seen the road smooth

{60,10}

kyā bad-gumāñ hai mujh se kih ā'īne meñ mire
ṭūṭī kā 'aks samjhe hai zangār dekh kar

1) how suspicious {you are / she is} of me! --that in my mirror
2) having seen the verdigris, {you consider / she considers} it [to be] the reflection of a parrot

{60,11}*

girnī thī ham pah barq-e tajallī nah ṭūr par
dete haiñ bādah ẓarf-e qadaḥ-khvār dekh kar

1) the lightning of glory/manifestation should have fallen on us, not on [Mount] Tur
2) they give wine [only after] having seen the capacity of the cup-drinker

This is ghazal from 1833- by which time Ghalib would have been firmly established in his Farsi scholarship and familiar with the canonical treatment of the various conceits.

Precisely because I think it isn't an adolescent poem, I don't find much of interest in it. Still, I don't think the commentators do it justice either.

With regard to the first couplet, I suppose *sukhan* as poetry, simply, is passable. Still, remembering Sheikh Galip, why not dignify it as Logos-as-poetry? In that case you get a mystical meaning, or even a Confucian meaning. One can still keep the existential meaning, which I've done in the second line.

With the second couplet, there is this strange idea that *zunnar* refers to the Brahmin *'janeo'* rather than the Zoroastrian girdle. Both Brahmins and pious Muslims are forbidden wine (at least in Ghalib's part of the world) whereas wine is considered a good thing in Zoroastrianism (or Xtianity or Judaism, for that matter) and the *mugh-e-mahood*, the elderly Magian Tavern keeper is a stock symbol of wisdom in Farsi poetry.

The next couplet refers to a very well known, indeed a key, element in Rumi's philosophy of Love. The parrot is shown its own image in a mirror and then taught words which it assumes are addressed to it by its image and which it learns to mimic so as to reciprocate the ardent sentiments expressed to it. Similarly, God teaches us Love by putting such delusive images in front of us. Through spiritual practices one can sublate these delusive images and come to understand that the words we repeat have an origin both hidden and higher. Among the commentators, Bekhud Mohani understands the idiom but doesn't see its relevance. But this is easily done by making the God of the mystics a jealous Lord, or better still, by doing so by a self-deprecatory *'majzoob'* imputation.

The last couplet refers to 2 Quranic verses 7.143 and 33.72. God had offered his *'amaanah'* (Trust/Responsibility/Viceregency/Free Will) to the mountains and so on, but only man agreed to take it, but this was done rashly. Later, God tells Moses that he will not see Him, but should gaze at the mountain. If it remains steady, then Moses can bear the theophany, otherwise not. However, Mt. Tur is levelled as it can not bear the glory of the Lord's theophany.

Ghalib here is affirming Man's worthiness of *amaanah* and *khilafat* but emphasizes Man's highest goal is to seek and yearn for Union with the Divine, even if this means utter obliteration. Just as strong wine, such as might render a callow youth senseless, serves but to invogorate a seasoned warrior- so too God's trust in man can make him worthy of closer communion with his maker.

Except, I'm wrong- I didn't know that *zarf* meant a heat sleeve- 'like those little cardboard thingies they put around your cup of coffee at Starbucks- they call it a cup-sleeve, but the proper term is *zarf*.'

A *zarf* holds the cup but can't contain *(tadmin)* anything itself. So, it seems, Wine is not apportioned according to the drinking capacity of the cup-quaffer but the quality and price of the *zarf* he has brought with him.

Moses, afterall, was a Jew. Not the good sort who disdains the hail-fellow-well-met hucksters of his tribe and is a good judge of harlots and horse flesh, but the other sort of Yid, the inherently vulgar, *Zionist* sort who sells his ancestral *zarf* to help the suffering refugees amongst his co-religionists. If a drop of rain water splashes off the robe of such a one and lands upon you- you are defiled, rendered *najis*. That's why Jews weren't allowed to walk abroad during a rain storm in Persia- back when things were done properly. Indeed, the Red Sea, knowing itself pre-ordained to drown the King of Egypt and his army of aristocrats, nevertheless spared them the humiliation of defilement by being beforehand in parting for that ragged bunch of runaways.

No doubt, the Quran and so on don't see things quite in this light- but, well, a lot of those Prophets weren't quite quite. Strictly tradesman's entrance, if you know what I mean. What? *Pas devant les domestiques?* Back to poetry then-

> To assay its purchasers, essays the Logos poetry
> Tho' with the wares I purvey what's sold is me!
>
> Ah, let girdled Magians bring wine for my ode!
> Prayer beads string but bumps in the road.
>
> 'Tis verdigris in my mirror, not a parrot green
> Taught Love's tort by an athwart Unseen
>
> Mt.Tur's crater, Musa's drunk dumb-waiter, bit yet the dust .
> I'm a toper of class & deep-looking glass, fit for Thy Trust

Ghazal 122

> If her heart is a sphinx , methinks self-shamed am I
> That the lion hued Sahara, I hew with a sigh
> For its own eye, as its mirror, Tyranny is distaste
> & hunts to be hunted what is wild & to waste

Compare this to what Ghalib actually wrote-

> *vāñ us ko haul-e dil hai to yāñ maiñ hūñ sharm-sār*
> *yanī yih merī āh kī tāsīr se nah ho*
> *apne ko dekhtā nahīñ żauq-e sitam ko dekh*

āīnah tā kih dīdah-e naḵhchīr se nah ho

> If there, she feels terror in/of the heart, then here, I am ashamed/abashed
> that is- may this not be from the effect/impression of my sigh!
> she doesn't look at herself- look at the relish of/for tyranny!
> {so that / as long as} the mirror would not be like/from the eye of a {prey/wild animal}

Now I suppose I could muster some sort of defence for my stanza by saying, well, the sphinx is the Arabic Abu Haul (father of terrors) and the notion of sculpting the sand arises from the notion that a sigh could create an image (*tasir*) and so on but, by this point, the real question posed by this paper has become all too obvious- viz. when and to what catastrophic end does translation cease to be transgression merely and cross over to becoming a truly Original Sin requiring a new Heaven from which a more sadistic Satan might more steeply fall?

Prof. Pritchett, in true Pollyanna American fashion, has denied any connection between Ghalib and my translations saying they are 'simply wild radioactive heaps of glowing allusions which few readers will understand.' Like Schopenhauer, that sunny optimist, who believed 'if the Universe were destroyed, Music would remain', Prof. Pritchett fails to grasp that the toxic half-life of my radioactive heap- i.e the *longueurs* of my lyrics- is so inexpressibly large, it is only expressible as a function in a Time exponential of what mere entropy can undo or aesthetics detemporalize. So mine is Ghalib's infinite *barzakh-e-tahrir* of misprision, yours his Indo-Anglian prison.

> Why?
> What makes me so special?
> I'm Everyman who writes for Nobody, that too impredicatively- a nobody, nobody reads.
> Ghalib, more tragically, wrote for Nobody but only by Everyman is read.
> Ergo, I'm his blighting Messiah though but my own broken mirror.

However, I admit that Prof. Pritchett is right about one thing. My translations fail. Why? I do not stint my thinking, drinking or into a characteristically Delhite delight in Peri Bathous sinking, yet achieve nothing worthwhile. Why? Is it because I am not a true (i.e Modern School) Majnoon- the vast Sahara but the prolapsed rectum its poetically inclined matriculates rent out in pure absence of mind? I don't see why. Indeed, I don't know what could have induced you to even suggest such a thing. I went to St. Columba's which is much more middle middle.

Anyroad, what I want to say is- actually come to think of it I once heard of a guy who went to Modern School who wasn't like a totally stuck up arse bandit so lets just not indulge in generalizations shall we?- my translations make what Faruqi Sahib says about Ghalib true *for me*. Effort expended to so rewarding an end can, I believe, be in good conscience enjoined upon others who, in any case, are bound to be better equipped for though but a clay pot of ashes will contain my remains, theirs will require a coffin such that, to balance the load on the donkey- as happened with Averroes- their books must amount to an equal weight.

Ghazal 182

> *taġhāful-dost hūñ merā dimāġh-e ʿajz ʿālī hai*
> *agar pahlū tihī kīje to jā merī bhī ḵhālī hai*
> **rahā ābād ʿālam ahl-e himmat ke nah hone se**
> **bhare haiñ jis qadar jām-o-subū mai-ḵhānah ḵhālī hai**

I'm the Abraham of Eternity's abscission, Exalted Ali of Submission's vision
Overlooked, I befriend misprision- Harold Bloom's in Karl Barth's revision
Ach! what so populates the world is the utter absence of *men*
This Tavern too were empty, filled a glass to my *'when*!'

 A correspondent, convicting me of illiteracy- septic catamite of a Delhi school boy though I fondly imagine him to be- has suggested the following for the first couplet-
Exalted by this crushing reflection
I'm the lover of my own rejection
As you, to me, a cold shoulder turn
Your true beholder, I utterly burn

This only requires the substitution of 'Abihu' for 'utterly' in the last line to rise above mere doggerel.
To see why- from the 'Sophialogical' point of view- ponder the below.

'Teri Maa-behen nahin hai, kya?'- a vignette of the Emergency.

"Have you no Mother or Sister?"- when I was 14 and New Delhi still 7 years from coming of age - I had but to glance in the direction of any *dupatta* clad lady on the D.T.C bus for her to thus upbraid me for my delinquency with respect to, what our still rather rustic women clearly were convinced was, for artless adolescents such as I, an exigent duty of unstopping incest.

Greatly embarrassed to be, in such peremptory fashion, publicly taken to task, I'd hang my head and haltingly mumble the following feeble excuse in my 'Convent School' English-
 "Madam, such of my kin-folk as answer to your inquiry, are, currently, all copiously menstruating- and, before you ask, Daddy, too, has bleeding piles- so, to reduce *dhobi* bills for my school uniform- as previsioned by the Pay Commission's White Paper de-escalating Dearness Allowance increments- I have been granted this furlough to attend class.'- and, speaking generally, that would be enough to mollify the ladies or, at any rate, to baffle their rage and reduce them to dark mutterings in *dehati* dialects.

My friend, Rajiv, being a transfer student from some upcountry Kendriya Vidhyalay, took a more demotic tack. '*Maa bhi hai aur behen bhi*' he'd say soulfully, before adding the Chinatown twist, '*aur donon mere hi ladli beti hain!*'.

 This riposte tended to bait the interest of middle-aged male passengers leading to some quite intellectually challenging exchanges.

'Your sister, we understand, but how can your mother be your own daughter?': "...'but even if your Grandmother really was the top Lady Sri Ram College tutor in tribadism, incestuously turned on by your mother's gravid state...'; '.... granted, a foetus can have an erection as per recent advances in ultra-sound technology, still...';. '...*haan, haan, hamen bhi pata hai*, youngsters, nowadays, are coming too quickly but surely sperm can't reach tachyonic speed and travel back in time?';...'.*Khabardar!* Leave Sanjay Gandhi out of this! You don't know who might be listening!'

The Emergency didn't last very long- just 21 months- but it gave my generation a taste of what life might be like under a Stalin or Hitler- or, to strike a sibylline note, a Mamta Bannerjee or Jayalalitha- those 'Didijis' or 'Ammas', of whose threat to our virginal ass-holes the cryptic and Cassandra-like cry of- *'Teri Maa-behen nahin hai kya?'*- alerted us not at all.

Food for thought certainly. Still, to press on-

Ghazal 71

nah gul-e naġhmah hūñ nah pardah-e sāz
maiñ hūñ apnī shikast kī āvāz
tū aur ārā'ish-e ķham-e kākul
maiñ aur andeshah'hā-e dūr-darāz
lāf-e tamkīñ fareb-e sādah-dil
ham haiñ aur rāz'hā-e sīnah-gudāz
huu;N giriftaar-e ulfat-e .sayyaad
varnah baaqii hai :taaqat-e parvaaz
vuh bhī din ho kih us sitam-gar se
nāz kheñchūñ bajā-e ḥasrat-e nāz
mujh ko pūchhā to kuchh ġhaẓab nah huʾā
maiñ ġharīb aur tū ġharīb-navāz
asadull;āh ķhāñ tamām huʾā
ay dareġhā vuh rind-e shāhid-bāz

Neither plangent lute nor melody's bloom
I am the bruit of my own peal of doom

You and curls coiffed by, all breathless, the air
I and Damocles' sword that hangs by a hair

Un coeur simple, thou mine self-encrypting boast,
Art as breast smelting mirror to Venusberg's host!

A dervish is fleet but halt to be held dear
Aflame is the forest, the hunter, to draw near

To turn you coquette is my self-ruinous aim
I burn but to burn as candle to your game.

Wretchedness so secure & spreading an Estate
Protector of the Poor! do enquire of my fate

Alas! a Don Juan to his own despite
Asadullah Khan is finished quite!

Again, my correspondent- still that same septic catamite- has offered a more literal translation of the second couplet. But why not read the whole thing for yourself?

Sanjay K said...

Ustadji,
You never fail to disappoint- you take one of the loveliest couplets in the language-
tū aur ārā'ish-e ķham-e kākul
maiñ aur andeshah'hā-e dūr-darāz
and write some nonsense about the sword of Damocles which simply is not there in the text!
The meaning is

You and adornment cluster wavy tresses to curl
I and adoration muster to but distance the girl

31 May 2011 15:58 🗑

 windwheel said...

@Sanjay- Strange to say, I quite like your version. Is it better than mine?
Actually, yes. It has a new thought whereas mine was just filling out the verse.
It doesn't fit with my conception of the whole... but my conception mightn't be that
good in the first place. This was just a random ghazal I choose to translate last night
coz I couldn't get to sleep.
I also feel your couplet is in 'my' style.
So thanks for this you foul little rent-boy. Now go and finish you homework.
You never know, I might steal this from you. Don't get your hopes up, but, tell you
what, I'll sleep on it.
P.S kindly remove the aubergine from your rectum, wash it and put it back in the
fridge. I happen to know your Mummy is cooking baingan ki barta today.
31 May 2011 16:12 🗑

Sanjay K said...

Ustadji,
Steal what you like- I was having a joke at your expense.
BTW have you ever actually read any English poetry other than Mother Goose
nursery rhymes?
I have seen a lot of praise of Narendra Modi on this blog. ARe you aware that like
Vajpayee he has a good command of Urdu and would be utterly repelled by your
barbaric handling of Ghalib?
Honestly, I find your impartial ignorance of both Urdu and English utterly hilarious.
My dear fellow, you should know Ghazal is a musical form. First learn Music.
'The man that hath no music in himself,
Nor is not mov'd with concord of sweet sounds,
Is fit for treasons, stratagems, and spoils."
(The Merchant of Venice (V, i, 83-85))
William Shakespear- maybe you have heard of him? After all, you keep telling us
you are a U.K wallah.

31 May 2011 16:28 🗑

 windwheel said...

@ Sanjay. It hurts coz its true. (Like the aubergine I previously referred to.) BTW I
know Sheikh Peer very well. His name is not William but Waris. His father was a
kasai from Bradford on the A1 motorway, not Stratford upon Avon.

P.S. God created Adam and Yves St. Laurent not Adam and Steve. Kindly ponder
these simple words and repent while there is yet time.

Can my method of translating Ghalib be extended to other poets?

No. I can highlight Ghalibian stuff in that other poet and have a crack at translating it in my
Ghalibian manner, but pretty soon I have to give up and write about why I've made a pig's
breakfast of it.

This is Shakeel Badayuni's lovely, *mere hum nafas, mere hum nawa*, butchered by yours truly.

Mere hum-nafas, mere hum-navaa, mujhe dost banake daGaa na de
mai.n huu.N dard-e-ishq se jaa.N_valab, mujhe zindagii kii duaa na de
mere daaG-e-dil se hai raushnii, usii raushnii se hai zindagii
mujhe Dar hai aye mere chaaraagar, ye charaaG tuu hii bujhaa na de
mujhe ae chho.D de mere haal par, teraa kyaa bharosaa hai chaaraagar
ye terii nawaazishe muKhtasar, meraa dard aur ba.Daa na de
meraa azm ianaa bala.nd hai ke paraaye sholo.n kaa Dar nahii.n
mujhe Khauf aatish-e-gul se hai, ye kahii.n chaman ko jalaa na de
wo uThe hai.n leke hom-o-subuu, arey o 'Shakeel' kahaa.N hai tuu
teraa jaam lene ko bazm me.n koii aur haath ba.Daa na de

So slain by Love's pain, do you who, for my longer life, yet pray
Ah! Breath of my breath, befriend to but betray?!

My heart's wound, my Life, my Light's flint-struck spark
Bind not, nor blow out, my sole candle 'gainst the dark!

Breath Control is Divine, Balsamic, broken breath, Death Orgasmic
How trust to your care- ragged breath'd, threadbare?

Shakeel's steel, forged in a sighs' fires, fears no inferno of the forger Iyer's
For glows in the Garden, red rose arson, Fear's a poet, Ire a Parson

Thee, we study, understudy & e'en, in vain, understand
Thy wine of immortality yet pass hand to hand

The problem here is, Shakeel really is addressing me- me, some random Indian dude who thinks Spirituality is about breath control or TM or something equally fucked retailed by some TV Godman or Preacher- and the reason why I think this is coz I imagine Islamic heremeneutics, in India, is bound to have gotten as silly and play-it-safe as Delhi's Doordarshan Hinduism. Still, coz Shakeel is a real poet and way more cultured than me, born as he was 20 years before Independence, he represents a remembered summit already entirely eroded away leaving us Levellers to revel only in our own swinishness.

Ghazal 76

Fear of the Rival is Sanity's survival & shame
What burns me is that I burn truly but in name
Grief chose as Chief Banker, Ghalib, Ghazal's wanker
But it too was ruined all the same.

Okay, Ghalib doesn't actually say wanker but he was 19- so it's like axiomatic dude. Moreover, he wrote this around that time.

kāfī hai nishānī tirā chhalle kā nah denā
khālī mujhe dikhlā ke bah vaqt-e safar angusht
(50.2)

Not her virginal nose ring, such joy did I bring her
Street urchins sing of how she gave me the finger!

Which brings me to Ghazal 64.1, which mebbe says more about my Delhi boyhood than Ghalib's adolescence.

junūñ kī dast-gīrī kis se ho gar ho nah ʿuryānī
garebāñ chāk kā ḥaq ho gayā hai merī gardan par

1) {from / by means of} what/whom would madness receive {help / a hand-grip}, if nakedness would not exist?

2a) the right/duty of ripping the collar has come to be upon my neck

2b) [oh] Collar, the right/duty of ripping has come to be upon my neck

Were Nakedness not Solitary could Majnun's reach-around thus wreck?
This pube plucked Mansur, the choked chicken of my neck.

bah rang-e kāġhaż-e ātish-zadah nairang-e betābī
hazār āʾīnah dil bāñdhe hai bāl-e yak tapīdan par

1) with the aspect/color of fire-stricken paper [is] the wonder/trick of restlessness

2a) [it] binds a thousand mirror-hearts onto the wing of a single agitation

2b) the heart binds a thousand mirrors onto the wing of a single agitation

Like paper burning, Yearning so twists, shrivels and smokes to but sparks utter
A thousand mirrors, my heart speckles, thy butterfly of a single flutter.

ham aur vuh be-sabab ranj-āshnā dushman kih rakhtā hai
shuʿā-e mihr se tuhmat nigah kī chashm-e rauzan par

1) we, and that causeless(ly) grief-{acquainted/friendly} enemy! --for she places

2) blame for a gaze by/from the sun-ray, on the eye of the crevice-work

She and me- alas capriciously!- are afire of one ire, so she, that is we, ash-reap me to as enemy keep
That I may, at her Western Wall pray, for aye its fenestrae, eye Evil I, its peep hole Creep

I interpret *Mihr*, in this context, as the Sun during Ramadan- the last ray of the Sun, setting in the West, signaling the end of the fast- thus I say 'Western Wall', which of course, is another name for the Wailing Wall in Jerusalem.

But, myself but a chink in not its wall but the rock of Moriah, this neatly leads to a topic of more abiding interest and meetly serves as coda to this essay, summoned as I am to sterner literary labors and more Herculean hermeneutic tasks concerning-

The difficulties of translating courtly poetry

Much of the piquancy of courtly poetry arises from word play involving elite customs and modes of speech. The fact is, blue bloods often employ a sort of hypertrophied courtesy involving exaggerated protestations of devotion that draw upon a sort of fossilised ceremonial language, thus increasing the scope for the courtier poet to display his status as 'an insider' who understands the origins of certain customs and rituals which the parvenu finds puzzling.

However, this presents a grave problem for translators and calls into question the status of courtly poetry as representing a truly universal art form.

Take the following quatrain-

Not punctilio merely, methinks she softens to my suit
Might not etiquette beget true affection's fruit?
For the formulaic postscript to her epistle dismissive
Reads- 'bugger not the bearer of this missive!'

How many modern day English speakers would know that 'bugger not the bearer' - though employed here in a purely conventional and formulaic way- is actually a survival of the love poetry of an earlier era? In this case, a Master Poet had depicted the paramour of the King as using this phrase to express three different sentiments or shades of meaning viz.-

1) she knows her letter will greatly arouse the amorous passion of the King and this excites her jealousy against even her own means of communication with him.

2) the mystical concept that the intermediary, or go-between, gains status by so doing and in a transgressively 'Filioque' sense becomes part of a Trinity, is itself the only valid (as opposed to Bloomian) Aesthetic or Adamic misprision.

3) the suggestion that the King may seek to increase the frequency of her letters by sodomising the postman, attributes a naive mentality to the King for the hidden purpose of showing how badly Love has disordered her own mental faculties.

By the time the quatrain, quoted above, was written, however, the phrase 'bugger not the bearer' had become just a meaningless formula. Thus, we have a picture of a well bred, but, it may be, merely noveau riche, young lady ending a letter dismissing the importunities of a courtier with a formula which implies passionate love rather than (as she would imagine) a salutary warning of a hygienic type.

How does one translate a poem whose fundamental premise is that translation is not possible even within its own milieu and idiolect?

Now, in the above case, the bluestocking in question *did* recognise the allusion and replied in kind with this erudite little couplet-

No cock but all arse-hole, you give tongue to your wit
Brown nosing Archbishop, helping others to shit!

The literary reference here being to an ecclesiastic of an earlier age who, famously, had an anal sphincter larger than his body; a fact much commented upon by mystics and theologians of a *via negativa* type. However, the true pungency of the line arises out of the fact that the venerable author of the quatrain did in fact have a very small penis. Be it understood, nonetheless, no personal disappointment arising from this circumstance, and contrary to what gossip might aver, motivated my decision to leave India in 1977, nor do I rake up the matter- now the parties to it are all dead and that milieu vanished- save to throw light upon the difficulties of translating courtly poetry in this levelling age.

Conclusion- Urdu's unsealed letter

Amongst the Victorians, as with doting fondness I yet dimly recall, it was the custom to send letters of invitation to weddings and other such joyous festivities in an unsealed envelope- which the servants might open and set out on the mantelpiece for all to admire.

Necessary notifications of a death, however, had to be scrupulously sealed up, and very specifically commended to the confidential attention of the Gentlemen of the House for, failing so sage a precaution, the Villa's maidenly or matronly denizens might be thrown into an equal state of competitive hysterics- not to say Maenadal frenzy- occasioning, it is profoundly humiliating yet prudent to prevision, a condign rebuke from the local Master of Fox-hounds, not to mention tiresome tributes of condolence offered up by stammering curates and dunning tradesmen who don't know their place.

But this was not how it was in Old Delhi- at least at the dew be-dabbled dawn of English's Empire upon it- for letters ciphering a death- and any death ciphers everything- alone arrived unsealed.

I mention this not, as you may suppose, to bewail the atrocious increase in literacy amongst sections of the fair sex- *pace* Gayatri Spivak Chakraborty's gorgeously senile 'Can the Subaltern speak?' which prescribes a strategic, not to say disingenuously essentialist, equivalence betwixt her own girlish guess at Scription and her great aunt's gigglingly allusive hobby of Suicide, such as much warms the cockles of my heart, which, for in *gharbi ghurbat*- Western Exile- is afforded no heartening domestic hearth made lambent by the charred bodies of shrieking Suttees- but, to sternly return to the topic of this paper, and swiftly conjure up, one last time, the ghost of Ghalib- a good *gulli danda* player as I glowingly recall- who once lamented that even in the uttermost Ultima Thule of his but internal exile, the only letters he received arrived, alas, unsealed.

Prompted, perhaps, by this *cri de coeur*, Prof. Shamsur Rehman Faruqi joined the elite cadre of the Indian Postal Service- not, as my mother still has occasion to admonish me, for the specific purpose of avenging my cynic insistence on biting the ankles of postmen- but to allay that infectious anxiety, bequeathed us by his collected letters, Ghalib displays while conjuring his correspondents not to ascribe him something so *infra dig* as a terrestrial address- that too in **Ballimaron**- and utterly abjures the impious practice of paying for and putting stamps on the letter's envelope, as if so merely correct and credulous a procedure might mollify the malice of its mercenary carrier- for thus to do is thereby **and for all time** to have undone Pneuma's blowing upon knots and Nous's licit magic of communication.

In this context, Faruqi Sahib, alerts us to that apercu of Abdur Rehman Bijnouri, a Keats who died in the Twenties, Tithonous to a false Dawn, fecund Endymion to the Sleep that is early death- India has two divine Gospels- the Veda-distilling Gita and Ghalib's *Vajd*- instilling Divan- but, curiously, the very accessibility, the ubiquity, of these two texts arose out of their status as letters which arrive unsealed. Tagore's Post Office did what it could, but, Post Master General, Prof. Faruqi did more- not just for Ghalib's Urdu but also for the Geeta's Sanskrit or, indeed, the sort of English to which I aspire- viz. the notion that if the envelope is open it is merely to convey to its carrier, not news of a bereavement but the heartening reassurance that since the Central Sorting Office has already pilfered the Money Order enclosed, no inauspiciousness attaches itself to actually delivering the screed.

But, I merely shilly shally to put off the shaming disclosure you know I must make sooner or later.

Fact is, I'm a fackin Londoner mate. Fuck I'd know of Urdu and Sanskrit and other such shite? For us here, Urdu, is an open letter, we receive but don't receive- only death can close a letter- and, in its letters, Urdu conjures up, not Quranic *muqatta'at*, but phantoms merely of what no recitation has redeemed.

Now for the shameful part.

Mother came up to me today at the Irani food store. Dumpy, fat, and in pro-forma *hijaab,* she pretended she needed something on a higher shelf. But, no, that wasn't what she really wanted. Fair enough, I put back the tin of *Imam beyildi* and wiped the dust off on my kurta. Now, she wants to know if this greasy jar of pickles is real Lahori. Of course it is. No, what are the ingredients? I take off my glasses to read the small print on the label. '*O! Urdu parh lete ho...par tu Pakistan ke to nahin*?' No, I'm Tamil... you know, Madrasi?.... Hindu! Me Hindu- Hindu... urm ...**Kaffir**- you savvy?

Thus reassured, the lady- perhaps only fifteen or twenty years older than me, takes out a grimy aerogramme from her bosom. Its contents are grotesquely misspelled. I read it out haltingly- as if I didn't understand the contents- what hurts me is that I have no difficulty with the Urdu portions- they are formulaic and, in repeating them to her, I can't help but improve on the idiom- however, the important parts of the text- stuff dealing with money and illness and death's dilatory injustice- feature in phonetically transcribed English- important stuff happens not in Urdu but English even amongst the Backwards in the boondocks- but it is the **English** I mispronounce and mangle so as to end up looking like a *dehati* fresh off the banana boat.

But that's why these Mothers come up to me. They too are as Machiavelli writing his Histories, Abu Fazl his Chronicles. My shabby clothes indicate I'm from the old country. Clearly, I haven't made it in the Western Paradise. Good enough. They want some stranger to read out their letters. Better yet, a stranger from outside their region or religion. That's why, when I tell them I'm Hindu, my black face suddenly becomes their moon of Ei'd.

What is the explanation for this small miracle benefitting only this absurd and exiguous Tamil excuse for a man?

In their bosom, the Mothers have letters, open letters- grannies get mobile calls in plenty- letters, tell me, how they will read? Sons get letters, daughters get letters, they read them, they tell Granny 'No, no, nothing for *you* to worry. They all send you their love- that is all. After all, aren't they calling you all the time on cell phone? Don't worry- it is cheap nowadays. *Ooof oh!* Why can't you understand it? Nothing is wrong. Everything is all right. What? You want the letter? Well, all right, fine, you keep it. But there's nothing in it to be concerned.'

Between the open letter and the closed letter- the former alone is not dismissive but a missive. In exile, it alone, is what we actually receive.

Or else, why speak of exile?
Gods and Men, the dark one said, but live each others deaths, die each others lives.

Envoi

> Neither Mystic, nor Mutineer, nor heralding a new day
> Of Ghalib, Ghazal's God, 'twas our *via negativa* to say
> 'He loved Wine, gaudy whining and febrile Word-play'
> (A tribadistic trio to turn any man gay!)

> Waggling but vaguely the tongue of his beard
> Ghalib, in this guise, greatly endeared
> Himself to us ghouls who trembling & affeared.
> Fled as 'Mercy's Sun' *Faruqi,* appeared

[ii] The arithmetical hierarchy theorem- which can be interpreted to mean 'mathematics becomes genuinely more complex as the number of (alternate) quantifiers increases' (Mark Hogarth- Deciding Arithmetic using SAD computers)
[iii] Vide Salman Bashier's 'Ibn Arabi's Barzakh- http://sufibooks.info/IbnArabi/Ibn_Al-Arabis_Barzakh.pdf
[iv] Private communication
[v] Ibid
[vi] Vide Hilary Putnam on Skolem's paradox
[vii] Dismissing the couplet as spurious, Prof. Pritchett directs our attention to the far more sophisticated {231,6}*go vāñ nahīñ pah vāñ ke nikāle hue to haiñ
ka'be se un butoñ ko bhī nisbat hai dūr kī
1) although they are not there, but/still they are [in a state of having been] expelled from there
2) with the Ka'bah, even/also those idols have a distant relationship
[viii] Helfand
[ix] Ets-Hokin vs Skyy Spirits
[x] Vide Pundit Jagannath's Bhamanivilasa.

[xi] Abu Musa Jābir ibn Hayyān (721-815 A.D) a polymath considered the father of Chemistry. Whether he was actually Imam Jafar's student has not been proved.

[xii] Qais 'Majnoon' belonged to the Banu Udhri (Heinrich Heine's 'Beni Asra'- that tribe which 'died when they fell in love'. He loved Lailah, went mad and- blogging not yet having been invented- wandered the wilderness naked companioned only by the wild animals of the desert.

[xiii] Or a baby. Or like huge Credit Card bills. Or a murdered spouse mouldering under the floor-boards (my own suspicion re. the previous occupant of my flat)

[xiv] The notion that 'Islam is in danger!' is the foundation of Mujadidi ideology. The theological question it must answer is why, every century, the Muslims backslide or lose the favour of God- thus requiring a Mujaddid to turn up and found a dynasty. The answer really has to do with the manner in which what is spoken and believed ceases to be connected to God's 'kun' ('Be!)- it becomes empty, it loses its vital force.

In a sense, this was good news for Urdu, as a literary language, but a huge loss was being simultaneously incurred viz. the notion that literature opened the gate to a truly languageless noesis outside the merely contemporary. The result is a hypertrophy of literary activity without a corresponding widening of its range of signification- Time had acquired a special ontological value it had not had since the Zurvan heresy. There is a story about Iqbal quoting the hadith 'do not vilify Time' to the great delight of Bergson. But Iqbal was spatializing Time- thinning it as Prophetic Revelation to broaden it as Political Revolution- with results tragic and hilarious in equal measure.

It is no wonder that the Iranian Supreme Guide loves Iqbal. I wonder if he is aware that Iqbal grants the Babi heoine Qurratul Ayn (Tahira) a place with Ghalib and Mansoor al Hallj at the

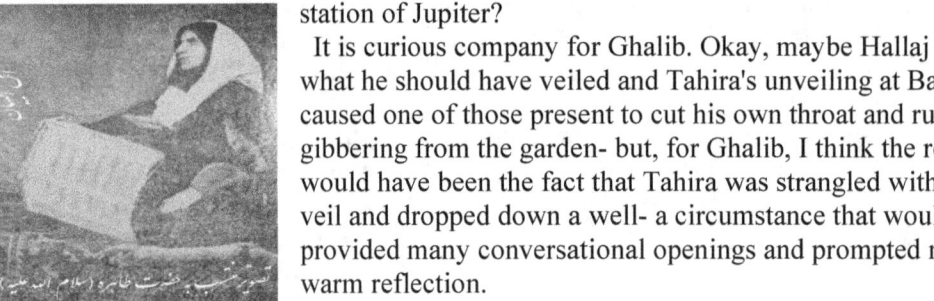

station of Jupiter?

It is curious company for Ghalib. Okay, maybe Hallaj displayed what he should have veiled and Tahira's unveiling at Badasht caused one of those present to cut his own throat and run gibbering from the garden- but, for Ghalib, I think the real pay-off would have been the fact that Tahira was strangled with her own veil and dropped down a well- a circumstance that would have provided many conversational openings and prompted much warm reflection.

[xv] Pisgah- Moses was not allowed to enter the Promised Land but was granted a sight of it from Pisgah.

[xvi] I don't normally like translations that employ contemporary idioms, agendas or controversies to 'sex up' translations of classic poems. However, there are moments in history- apocalyptic moments- when the distinction between eras is erased and all literature becomes urgently contemporary and passionately engaged.

At times such as these I think a couplet like the following is permissible-

> I've become the freed slave of my own Shiloh's honest Abe
> Incessantly butt fucked in her Indifference's Abu Ghraib

There is scarcely a ghazal in the canon into which this couplet could not be profitably interpolated.

The mayavadi nightmare of the British Raj

At first glance, nothing could seem more pragmatic and orderly than the British Raj in India.

Yet, it seems to me, this great Empire, too, like its predecessors on Indian soil, came to be haunted by the fear that the world it had created, the variegated and perfervid panoply it displayed, was as but a bubble, an illusion, a vanity and that at any moment, for a reason no Western mind could grasp, the native population seized, as it were, by a Panic- a convulsion produced by a Great God whose very name was unknown to the Orientalist scholar- might simply forget the British, cease to see the railways and roads and courts and offices they had created and thus render British rule a nullity.

What then? Well, for a while, things might go on with a semblance of 'normalcy'. Perhaps the army would be called in from the Cantonment to guard the Civil Lines. Morale might be kept up with polo matches and gymkhanas. But, for how long? Sooner of later, the 'women and children' question would be mooted. Safer to evacuate them to the ports, surely? But, perhaps, the men had better accompany the women. A skeleton staff could be left behind. Except that word 'skeleton' somehow strikes the wrong note. Let no more be said about it.

Thus begins the great evacuation. The British have all to themselves- the roads they have built, the bridges they have constructed, even an occasional train on the tracks they have laid- in the distance can be seen great crowds of natives marching for some unknown purpose along routes long lost to the memory of man.

Ultimately the British have to evacuate because the Western mind can not live with what it can not understand, what would destroy it- if understood.

The great Civilizations of the past, on Indian soil, had concluded that the Universe was an illusion, more empty than a dream. True, it was a world where hard work paid off, rationality paid off, character building and integrity paid off- but since the fruit- be it wealth, or honour or sensual pleasure- was empty perhaps the tree- nay the forest!- too, was unreal.

True, there was another tree, an upside down tree whose roots were in Heaven and whose leaves were the Vedas. But that tree, too, Lord Krishna says, must be cut down with the axe of non-attachment.

For the British, however, it was not the fruit which was unreal, but the entire rationalist project of understanding the East, of schooling it to emulate the West, which lacked roots in Indian soil.

The Olympian, or Himalayan, heights from which the Viceroy ruled were as clouds that could, by a strong wind, be utterly swept away. Great Pan might again rule the people and of Pan's purposes nothing can be known save by the contagion of panic- which destroys all knowledge, all painstakingly garnered wisdom- everything wiped clean.

Churchill and Kipling and Saki, all of whom left India, never to return, while still young men, could believe in the solidity and permanence of what the British had achieved. True, for Kipling, it was the Indian Gods who had grudgingly granted this permission. But it was a different story for older men- E.M Foster in his Passage to India- or Viceroy Wavell telling Churchill that there was now nothing for it but a general evacuation- there were no 'ringleaders' to be hunted down, no secret societies to be disrupted, India had simply become ungovernable.

Was the British Raj's mayavadi nightmare a dream and nothing more? Surely, they built better than they knew? Solid Nineteenth virtues characterize the administration of Dr. Manmohan Singh. In the year 2010, Parliament passed a bill granting 33% reservation of seats for Women. It seems the 'Oriental mind' has, indeed, changed.

But does no danger still lurk? We have gotten used to being patted down and having our briefcase X rayed getting on the Metro, entering Government offices, and checks more intrusive yet, going to see 'My name is Khan' at the Cinema.

Jihadis and Naxals we know about. But is there something bigger, as yet nameless, out there against which even x rays and metal detectors are powerless?

Might everything, even now, be suddenly swept away?

Or has it already happened? And how would we come to know? Which channel would carry the news sandwiched between advertisements for Kaspersky internet security and the cute lass from the Madhya Pradesh tourist board?

The older mayavadi philosophy still pointed to a Reality that was not illusion- a Reality to be found in the forest, on the mountain peak, in the desert. But, British mayavaad points to no alternative but evacuation, emigration, abandonment and oblivion.

Once again, the question arises- has it already happened? Is ours a virtual reality bubble whose magic iridescence is a manic protestation against its own impermanence?

Sustainability was the mantra of the handloom clad, eco-feminist of a decade ago- but that rhetoric proved unsustainable.

Reality, perhaps, not sustainability should be our new watchword- "Is it real? Can it be real? If so, how?"

Sanskrit Mayavaadi philosophy points to a Reality freer of contradictions than that within which effort yields futility- our Indglish apprehension of Maya, on the other hand, offers no such consolation.

This Panic, then, we must abide, that rational organization building its paths into the darkness, prods into fretful wakefulness a God whose nature is nightmare.

It is in this Orphic context that Gandhi might yet appear, more than a voice in the wilderness, a still singing head borne away on the wave of Self-determination's Gangetic spate.

How catch that song and translate what we hear?

Gandhian Translation

The story of the Japanese *Datsu-o Ron* 'escape from Asia' & *Nyu-o* 'enter Europe'- gets off the ground, not so much with the relaxation of the ban on foreign books or the eighth Shogun's setting up of a small School for the study of Dutch, but on the occasion of a native physician getting to view the execution of an old woman and, on examining her limbs, finding the anatomical plates in the Dutch medical textbook more accurate than those in the native Japanese or Chinese canon.

In other words, the test of the human body- dismembered and displayed by the tireless thoughtfulness of the executioner- permitted one type of text, more especially by the great difficulties involved in its translation and dissemination, to radically displace a vast nativist body of work and dis-intermediate an entire ecology of savants.

The centrality to Gandhi's thought of his own translation into Gujerati of things like Ruskin's 'Unto this Last' has long been recognized. The task of literary translation valorizes a particular type of hermeneutic fidelity and seeks to displace a text or texts already available. Perhaps, this had led some distinguished Professors to assume that Gandhi was a modernizer of the Japanese or Chinese sort who wished to substitute one sort of normative textuality with another of foreign antecedents.

Turning back to the butchering skill of that nameless Japanese Executioner, we might well ask, were Gandhi's 'experiments with Truth' a similar autopsy of the human spirit? Does Gandhian translation, on grounds of greater versimilitude, sublate or displace a nativist body of work? Certainly, he regarded his own translation of the Gita, into Gujerati, which he didn't know particularly well, from Sanskrit, which he scarcely knew at all, as having a special force - *'I am not aware of the claim made by the translators of enforcing their meaning of the Gita in their own lives. At the back of my reading there is the claim of an endeavour to enforce the meaning in my own conduct for an unbroken period of forty years. For this reason I do indeed harbour the wish that all Gujarati men or women wishing to shape their conduct according to their faith, should digest and derive strength from the translation here presented.'*
Interestingly, Gandhi makes clear that neither his acquaintance with the Gita, nor his 'unbroken endevour' commenced in India or in an Indian language.

But no- my question is unfair. Gandhi wasn't a translator, at least not in the literary sense. But there is another sense, a technical Sociological sense, to the word Translation and it is in that sense I coin the term 'Gandhian Translation'.

Gandhian Translation

The reason I am using the word Translation- in this instance, in the technical sense, peculiar to Actor Network Theory- for the notion that innovators **attempt to create a** *forum,* **a central network such that all actors agree that the network is worth building and defending**- is because it is as one of the greatest Twentieth Century masters of this praxis that Gandhi remains inspirational to this day.

Michel Callon defines the 4 moments of Translation as follows

1. **Problematization-** What is the problem that needs to be solved? Why is it urgent to solve it? How did it come about? Who is adversely affected by it? How to identify and enable 'Policy Actors' who can represent something other than themselves? How to productively govern the interaction of 'Policy Actors'?

2. **Interessement**

Making other actors interested and getting them to accept the definition of primary actors. The primary actor works to convince the other actors that the roles it has defined for them are acceptable.

3. **Enrollment**

Where other actors receive interests defined by the main actors.

4. **Mobilization of allies**

Do the delegate actors in the network adequately represent the masses? If so, enrollment becomes active support.

Gandhi is commonly credited with having created a bridge between 'the classes and the masses' and turning the Indian National Congress into a mass movement. Was this because of his superior 'Problematization'? It is tempting to answer- yes. Gandhi returned to India, like Lenin to Russia, with a simple slogan 'Hindu-Muslim unity means the end of foreign rule. Self-sufficiency means the end of Poverty. Non-Violence means the end of the Machiavellian politics of '*saam, dham, dhand bhed'* (carrot, & stick, divide & rule)' and it was this, Gandhi's radical problematization, which took politics out of the drawing room, out of the conspirators' midnight coven, onto the broad highways and into the teeming countryside.

There is a difficulty with this thesis. The nature of Gandhi's utterances- copiously present to us- confound every attempt to specify his 'problematization'. What did he actually want? One clue to his thinking is his strong and persisting belief that once negotiations had begun, utterances ceased to mean what was intended but were capable of a wholly novel construction.

Woodrow Wyatt, a by no means sympathetic or unbiased raconteur, yet veraciously quotes Gandhi on the Cabinet Mission Plan- 'I have been examining the Mission's Statement with my aged lawyer's mind. Now the Cabinet Mission have put out their document they no longer have the right to interpret it. The lawgiver cannot interpret his own laws. That is for the courts. The Cabinet Mission's Plan doesn't mean what they think it means.'

This is a staggering claim. A negotiator makes an offer. My lawyer questions the negotiator to ascertain what precisely is meant by his offer and does due diligence to ensure he is empowered to follow through. I make a counter offer. His lawyer questions me and does due diligence on me. We now see whether we can meet in the middle or must needs break off negotiations.

Gandhi holds a quite different view. Something happens during a negotiation such that Policy Actors no longer mean what they mean or even know what they mean. Thus, there can be no negotiation in good faith, just a return to the problematization via Gandhi's spotting of occluded intentionalities, shameful motives or tactics, and his virulent denunciation of them.

Gandhi first develops this novel theory when negotiating with Jan Smuts- the man who invented the modern British Commonwealth and reduced Lord Milner's 'kindergarten' to a footnote in Colonial history. Smuts, a barefoot lad who won a scholarship to Oxford, was the first inflential advocate of Holistic philosophy. Smuts wanted to know- as Gandhi tells us- if the 'Orientals' were other-worldly, lacking in vitality, and a race born merely to serve. Smuts did not want a slave caste of this sort to pollute the energy and self-affirmation of the South African 'holon'.

Gandhi's response was two pronged- Smuts wants Asiatics to register, well maybe registration is a good thing. "There are many Kaffirs who do not of their own accord stop drinking, hence wherever it is found necessary to use compulsion against them, legislative measures are resorted to to stop them from drinking. The man who stops drinking under compulsion by law, and not as a matter of duty, cannot be called a virtuous man. It is the man who of his own free will avoids drinking that is really virtuous.
There is the same difference between compulsory and voluntary registration.'

Gandhi believed that by treating an obnoxious law as if it had a benign intent, the adversary's problematization changed such that the negotiations now empowered the weaker party.

Many South African Asians naturally developed a virulent hatred of Gandhi when he championed voluntary registration. Some Muslim merchants even suspected a hidden agenda to destroy Muslim commerce and favour Hindu hawkers and requested the great Muhammad Ali Jinnah to come to their rescue. Gandhi, however, insisted he was in the right- voluntary registration, for some reason, was the opposite of compulsary registration- rather than an admission that Registration and the £3 tax and so on were all perfectly fair, salutary and just.

'Our pledge has been honoured and the demand that we insisted upon has been conceded which means that we shall be treated as men. *No one else knows about the law as much as I do and can explain it as well as I*. I do not say this out of pride; only because whatever explanation I give, will be correct to the best of my judgment. I am thoroughly familiar with all that has happened since 1903. There is only one task we have accomplished through the fight, and that is to have prepared the ground. What remains now is to construct a building on it'

That building was the Tomb of an Islamic alliance between 'Coloureds' and Indian Muslims.

(image- Dr. Abdullah Abdulrahman- leader of the 'Coloured' (mixed race) South Africans.)
Indians, especially the Muslim Memons- who had brought Gandhi over because of his fluency in their mother tongue of Gujerati- had a religous duty to first ally with Dr. Abdulrahman and then co-mingle their cause with the *'Kaffirs'*.

There is no Racism in Religion.
Equally, tactical Racism in Politics, or 'strategic essentialism' is a catastrophe.

Gandhi, of course, had other ideas.

Gandhi was not saying Jan Smuts wasn't a more brilliant lawyer than himself- indeed, there were better educated South African-born Asian lawyers by that date, which is why he had chosen to return to India in 1902- rather, he believed, there was something in the Law which was compositionally transformative of its discourse according to a rule only he had grasped such that utterances ceased to mean what their utterer intended, acquiring instead a sort of alienated majesty.

It is this aspect of Gandhian thought which makes his problematizations impossible to pin down and which might lead us to focus instead on his skills as a propagandist, fund-raiser, and organizer.

However, here too, we come up against a characteristic Gandhian scruple which militates against **enrollment**-

'A movement takes its downward course from the time that it is afflicted with a plethora of funds. When therefore a public institution is managed from the interests of investments, I dare not call it a sin but I do say that it is a highly improper procedure. The public should be the bank for all public institutions, which should not last a day longer than the public wish. An institution run with the interest of accumulated capital ceases to be amenable to public opinion and becomes autocratic and self-righteous. This is not the place to dwell upon the corruption of many a social and religious institution managed with permanent funds. The phenomenon is so common that he who runs may read it.'

A related point, vitiating **mobilisation**, is the Gandhian insistence on the inmiscible nature of Agitational movements-

' The Black Act applied to the Chinese as well as to the Indians whom they therefore joined in the Satyagraha struggle. Still from first to last the activities of the two communities were not allowed to be mixed up. Each worked through its own independent organisation. This arrangement produced the beneficent result that so long as both the communities stood to their guns, each would be a source of strength to the other. But if one of the two gave way, that would leave the morale of the other unaffected or at least the other would steer clear of the danger of a total collapse. Many of the Chinese eventually fell away as their leader played them false. He did not indeed submit to the obnoxious law, but one morning some one came and told me that the Chinese leader had fled away without handing over charge of the books and moneys of the Chinese Association in his possession. It is always difficult for followers to sustain a conflict in the absence of their leader, and the shock is all the greater when the leader has disgraced himself. But when the arrests commenced, the Chinese were in high spirits. Hardly any of them had taken out a permit, and therefore their leader Mr Quinn was warned to appear along with the Indians. For some time at any rate Mr Quinn put in very useful work."

Leung Quinn disappears from history in 1911. Did he really abscond with the money of the Chinese Association? It is difficult to reconcile his exemplary record of personal courage and sacrifice with so sordid an end.

A book by Melanie Yap, **'Colour, confusion and concessions: the history of the Chinese in South Africa',** reveals how acrimonious the split between the 'passive resisters' and the 'no resisters' became- indeed, it featured a full scale gun battle!- and also chronicles the manner in which the Court froze the assets of the Chinese Association and ultimately used its funds for the endowment of a Chinese-only ward at the Johannesberg hospital.

Writing 'Satyagraha in South Africa', in Gujerati, some years after he'd left South Africa, Gandhi can be pardoned lapses in memory.

Still, even to the casual reader, Gandhi's jaundiced view of passive resisters like Leung Quinn, Pundit Ram Sundara and Thambi Pillai appears to be based on nothing but malicious gossip. He makes a grave charge against Quinn based on what his enemies said about him once Leung, himself, had been deported and had no means to defend himself.

Why does Gandhi quite gratuitously defame Quinn? Perhaps, he is trying to make two points

1) Only celibate, raw food vegans, can do Satyagraha. Otherwise, like Ram Sundara, passive resisters will fall for the temptations of the flesh- butter, honey, milk- and disappear from the scene. Thus, only celibacy (*brahmacharya*) is free from corruption (*brashtachara*). The essence of Corruption is intermingling of the pure with the impure. Gandhi point out that though the Indians and the Chinese were in the same boat, they kept their struggles separate.

2) Money entrusted to an institution breeds corruption. Thus the only truly worthwhile institution in public life is the Saintly Gandhian who, because he is celibate, has no private life at all. In the language of Carl Schmitt- the Gandhian alone is the fitting Homo Sacer to rule society.

Certainly, especially amongst the Revolutionaries in Bengal, there existed at that time the notion that only a celibate (Sanyasi) could bring about the Liberation of Mother India. This notion was also adopted by the Marathis and is a feature of R.S.S thinking down to the present day. But, the problematizations of the Jugantar Revolutionaries, or their chastened apolitical succesors, cash out as a substantavism- their India is a map with definite boundaries, there is some version of History they want taught in Schools, they even have a notion of how properly cowed minorities must deport themselves (you may garland me, says Narendra Modi, but don't try putting a namazi cap on my head, my Muslim brother!) but Gandhian Satyagraha is relationist and process oriented, not substantivist at all.

Why?

"*A thing acquired by violence can be retained by violence alone, while one acquired by truth can be retained only by truth. The Indians in South Africa, therefore, can ensure their safety today if they can wield the weapon of Satyagraha. There are no such miraculous properties in Satyagraha, that a thing acquired by truth could be retained even when truth was given up.'*

Gandhian Satyagraha can be called a Translation, in the Actor Network sense, because that is how it functioned and that is why it still draws both National and International interest at a time when other personality-cult 'isms'- like that of Lenin or Stalin- have faded entirely away. But Gandhian ***problematization*** is quite impossible to capture in words and, I believe in consequence, his ***enrollment*** and ***mobilization*** had the curious quality of erasing themselves at

the height of their success.

This leaves only Gandhi's interessement mechanism as a proper object of investigation.

Tin Tin, Anna Hazare and Gandhian Interessement

Though I'm sure he used the screen-play I very kindly sent him back in 1983, I haven't yet seen Speilberg's film, which deals with Tin Tin disguising himself as the (still) boyishly handsome Michel Callon, whilst on holiday in Brittany back in the mid '60's.

Tin Tin observes 3 'Researchers' who claim to have visited

Japan where some mysterious method of farming scallops has been invented. The 3 'Researchers'- who wear fake beards and goggles and whom Snowy the dog growls at- hire a more than usually inebriated Captain Haddock to take them out to sea on his boat. Then, once Captain Haddock collapses into a drunken stupor, the 3 'Researchers' conduct 'experiments' which enable them to draw 'graphs' which they take to Paris to show to Prof. Calculus. Soon, they even manage to enrol some thuggish and moronic 'local fishermen' to support their initiative to re-stock the the Bay by 'anchoring' Scallop larvae.   Everybody else is fooled. Tin Tin alone smells a rat- or rotten scallop- and discusses the matter with Snowy the dog over a bottle of absinthe.

Tin Tin- *Merde!* Ze solution is obvious *n'est-ce pas*? Japan- as Barthes has proved- is just an empty signifier! Zinister doings are a foot, my faithful doggy chum!'
Snowy (dubious)- Arf?
Tin Tin- & ze Scientists- ze are all fucked, *n'est-ce pas*- like what Feyerabend proved- and probably in ze pay of ze Military Industrial Nazi Vampire Complex so that's what makes zings even more zinister. What say you, my sage canine counsellor?
Snowy (happily)- Arf! Arf!
Tin Tin- & ze 'representatives' of ze Fishermen- zey can't 'represent' anybody coz zey are 'subaltern' like wot Gayatri Spicy Curry has shown, *n'est-ce pas*- *mon cher* canine catamite?
Snowy- (Alarmed) *Arf?!*
Tin Tin- & ze call *moi* a poodle packing pervert! Say my name bitch!
Snowy- (whimpering) Barf, barf.

Zoom forward to 2012

How does all this relate to our current *bal-avatar* of Gandhi- Anna Nicole Hazare? After all, he's a bit younger and not half as racist or paranoid as Tin Tin. Similarly, Kiran Bedi is not quite as violent and drunken as Captain Haddock- though admittedly she does look and talk like him. The Bhushans, however, don't even resemble *each other* let alone the equally I.Q challenged Thomson twins. As for Kejriwal- who voluntarily quit an Engineering job with the Tatas to go become, of all things, an Income Tax babu!- his thinking may be as screwy as Prof. Calculus but his head is shaped quite differently. Finally, we come to Snowy the dog- but Kapil Sabil screwed that pooch long ago.

So, you may ask, is there, in fact *any* connection between Team Anna & Tin Tin? The answer, as so often happens when I've been drinking, comes down to a theory of **Policy Actor Hazard**, which I believe to be necessary to supplement existing theories of Agent Principal Hazard, Preference Falsification, Contested Rent Seeking and so on so as to uncover what Prof. Mushtaq Khan calls the 'transformation potential' of a developing country which only Corruption can unleash.

One way of looking at corrupt rent-seeking is that it arises out of the Development paradigm as valorizing an abrupt shift to a system of resource allocation that is, by definition, non-indigenous and thus has no legitimacy within sittlichkeit and customary codes regulating social cohesion. In other words, the very notion that Development is a something the Government should be doing- facilitates rent-seeking.

Where the ruling elite is supported by a foreign power- i.e. is merely a comprador by another name- Prof. Kaufmann's kleptocratic theory works- i.e. corruption is what confiscates what Development would otherwise yield.

However, if rent-seeking both motivates and **reduces contestation w.r.t** re-allocating resources in productivity boosting or demographic transition facilitating ways, then 'Tansformation potential' is unleashed as Mushtaq Khan suggests.

Another way to put it, is that such corruption has a, trickle down, demonstration effect changing consumption preferences and lifestyle choices. Moreover, it makes commitments to change resource allocation more credible. Think of it this way. The Government takes away the subsidy on yarn for the handloom sector. Why should the handloom weavers and the Leftist rent-a-mob not contest this decision? After all the decision maker is using Government money. What's his incentive to come off looking the bad guy? Ah! But what if everybody *believes* he's a degenerate playboy who is putting the money saved directly into his pocket? People may still cry foul. But what if they also believe this degenerate playboy is the nephew of the top Mafia Grandfather? Still worth it? Or not so much?

There's a story Arthur Miller tells in his auto-biography which makes a point quite different to the one he intended. It's about a labor organizer who'd made the lives of factory owners (like Miller's dad, an illiterate, immigrant, tailor who rose to millionaire status before going bankrupt in the Great Stock Market Crash) utterly miserable. This gentleman hit upon the idea of organizing the Dock workers. But the Mafia boss, Lucky Luciano, had been co-opted by the Government to take control of the Docks so as to ensure that the War effort was not hindered by Commie agitators. So our hero was hounded out of the Union organizing business- he was given an offer he couldn't refuse. How was he to make a living? It so happened that one of the factory owners he'd previously harassed was on the point of bankruptcy because his entire stock had suddenly gone out of style. The former agitator shows up at the business man's office. The guy just laughs and says- 'do your worst, I'm already insolvent. I've had to tell my workers they won't get paid this week.' The agitator says- 'look, I know about your problem. Make me your partner and I'll shift your stock.' The agitator was as good as his word. He was an excellent salesman. That's what agitators are- they are salesmen- excellent salesmen because their product does not exist and would fuck you in the ass if you ever got to put it in your pocket. Naturally, the agitator-turned-salesman, and his victim-turned- partner soon became millionaires. Instead of destroying jobs, the agitator was creating them. His gift of the gab meant higher sales, which meant economies of scale and scope, which meant higher productivity- hence higher wages and benefts for workers, lower prices or better quality for the consumer- it was win-win all round. But the man was unhappy. He felt he'd betrayed the cause of Labor and, to make up for it, made liberal donations to various fuckwit 'Liberal' causes.

I'm not saying that corruption and criminality, like Lucky Luciano operating on the Waterfront, by themselves, sui generis, produce Development. What I'm saying is it would suffice if there were the mere *appearance* of corruption, with (of course) Mafia muscle to back it up, to positively impact the Government's ability to boost Productivity, Connectivity, even good Governance further down the line.

To summarize, on this analysis, not only is Development productive of corruption, ***contested definitions of Development*** ensure that only mega-corruption backed up by the criminalization of the Public Space can unleash that Transformation Potential whereby the rents of office eventually translate into returns on good Governance. This means that contesting definitions of development has a big pay off- even for the altruist- and it's going to be massively over-supplied. Gandhian interssement lubricates contestation and lowers its cognitive costs because its incessant crying wolf- coz *homo homini lupus?*- creates am ***Obligatory Passage Point*** as

Schelling focus for Rent Seeking behaviour. Thus everybody ends up sounding Gandhian and has an incentive to availability cascade Gandhian shite.

Ze definition of Obligatory Passage Points (OPP)

'Ze three researchers do not limit zemselves zimply to identifying a few actors. They also show that ze interests of zese actors lie in admitting the proposed research programme. The argument which they develop in their paper is constantly repeated: if the scallops want to survive (no matter what mechanisms explain this impulse), if their scientific colleagues hope to advance knowledge on this subject (whatever their motivations may be), if the fishermen hope to preserve their long term economic interests (whatever their reasons) then they must: 1) know the answer to the question: how do scallops anchor?, and 2) recognize that their alliance around this question can benefit each of them.

As a matter of fact- the 3 researchers were wrong. Knowing how scallop larvae anchor wasn't important at all *except to themselves.* Still, for a while, they got to parade around like big-shots.

Similarly with Team Anna- you have a probelmatization which creates an obligatory passage point- viz the proposed office of Lok Pal. The claim is made- why is there is corruption? Because there is no Lok Pal. Why isn't there a Lok Pal? Because of Corruption. Now, the Senior Bhushan- the fuckwit who cancelled the fundamental Right to Property when he was Law Minister- had already mooted this Lok Pal shite back in the late 70's when even Westminster was buying into that Scandinavian pile of Crap. Remember how Whitehall quaked at the cry- The Ombudsman cometh?- except it didn't actually at all coz, thanks to Sir Humphrey, the fix was already in. Ombudsmen are what happens the more delegated legislation you have and the more delegated legislation you have the more corruption, incompetence, injustice and everything turning into an endlessly shitestorm coz, guess what? smarty bollocks, you just said good bye to Accountability, Transparency, Subsidiarity- that's right, all the good stuff.

Still, what Team Anna got right was to do the 'problematization' in a manner which did indeed make them an Obligatory Passage Point from which they derived a credentialist Rent. But that was just the start. What they needed to do next was to fix and make predictable the responses of other policy actors towards themselves such that they remained the focal point- in the jargon of Actor-Network theory, they needed to create a robust *interresment mechanism*

Actor Interessement

'Interessement is ze group of actions by which an entity (here ze 3 researchers) attempts to impose and stabilize the identity of the other actors it defines through its problematization. Different devices are used to implement these actions.

'Why talk of interessement? The etymology of this word justifies its choice. **To be interested is to be in between (inter-esse), to be interposed.** *But between what? Let us return to ze 3 researchers. During their problematization they join forces with the scallops, the fishermen, and their colleagues in order to attain a certain goal. In so doing they carefully define the identity, goals or the inclinations of their allies.* **But these allies are tentatively implicated in the problematizations of other actors. Their identities are consequently defined in other competitive ways. It is in this sense that one should understand interessement. To interest other actors is to build devices which can be placed between them and all other entities who want to define their identities otherwise.** *A interests B by cutting or weakening all the links*

between B and the invisible (or at times quite visible) group of other entities C, D, E, etc. who may want to link themselves to B.

*' The properties and identity of B (whether it is a matter of scallops, scientific colleagues, or fishermen) are consolidated and/or redefined during the process of interessement. B is a 'result' of the association which links it to A. This link disassociates B from all the C, D, and E's (if they exist) that attempt to give it another definition. We call this elementary relationship which begins to shape and consolidate the social link **the triangle of interessement**.*

'The range of possible strategies and mechanisms that are adopted to bring about these interruptions is unlimited. As Feyerabend says about the scientific method: anything goes.'

From an Economist's point of view- Interessement looks like a sort of animist version of Schelling focal point theory- which by itself has notoriously poor predictive power. However, if brains have evolved, then a lot of our cognitive life is going to be devoted to 'interessement detection' (on an analogy with Agency detection modularity) rather than computing Schelling focal points. (This is because 'interessement detection' is small, cheap and out of control, whereas Schelling focal points are top-down, expensive to compute and substantive rationality biased) and thus **the likely waste of resources** arising from Interessement performativity (i.e. doing stuff which makes you look like you ought to be the natural focal point, or node, or 'interposition' given the problematization) can be more usefully studied and modelled, because it is likely to have some in-built Evolutionarily Stable structure, and thus the concept of Interessement might be a useful addition to the Contested Rent Seeking research program.

Indeed, parenthetically, **Policy Actor Hazard** (as distinguished from Agent/Principal Hazard) seems to require some such concept. In fields where (dis-interested) Policy Actors have more resources than interested parties, in other words where alterity is subaltern, we would expect to see mischievous Availability Cascades entrenching themselves, like guerilla groups, and using the resources of the Center to strike back at it.

Rent-seeking & Identity Politics

Rent seeking is the attempt to capture the returns to something in fixed or inelastic supply thus gaining wealth or power without actually adding value to Society. As such, Economists tend to be suspicious of rent-seeking.

Ricardo's model of the economy, featuring diminishing returns, gives rise to the fear that the landowners (assuming land is in inelastic supply) will continually get richer while the capitalists and the workers get poorer. The Great Mughals, like the Sun King, didn't want overmighty barons so they fuedalized land in such a manner that a much higer surplus was extracted for the Center, which in turn permitted the flourishing of relatively high value added manufacturing. The dissolution of the Empire, though good for regional centers, ultimately increased wasteful competition by hegemonic actors- Warlordism- and created a niche for for-profit Imperialism which the East India Company (a classic, corrupt, Tudor monopoly) ultimately, by a saltation at the margin, amply filled. Notice, that England's more entrenched corruption gave John Company an edge over Ind's own tax farmers, usurers and bankers because only in England was there a mechanism whereby the tail could wag the dog- i.e the agent of the King use the King's resources to increase his own corrupt profits. Remember that Tea Party in Boston where Americans dressed up as Indians to stop John Company from fucking them over? King George wasn't getting much of a rake-off on that bit of bad business. Yet it happened. The English taxpayer gets stuck paying for booted Hessians to ride roughshod over people of his own blood, language and Common Law.

Fuck yeah, Burke ultimately cheered for the Yanks. It was Indianism- which is what that berk called the political mischief of the East India Company's Rent seeking- and Red Indianism- the Tea Party pretence of being nativist, birther, scalp taking, pig sodomising, Deliverance retards-

which did for England's Universal Idea of...well, dunno, but have you observed Chidambaram's pouting buttocks squish squishing beneath the swish swishing of his *veshti*? I haven't, but it wasn't so long ago that Dalal St. rallied at the sight and- it seemed- if the Renmibi might become a reserve currency by 2020, the Rupee, though not Reserve, might yet get **hard**. Why? By reason of Chidambaram's languorous and swaying Polynesian stride which so deliciously set his buttocks a quiver 'neath his neat little veshti- I mean, Pippa Middleton eat your heart out!

(Back and front side of P.Chidambaram.
(What? You prefer the front side? Dude! That's perverse!)

As Burke said- 'Our Government and our Laws are beset by two different Enemies, which are sapping its foundations, Indianism, and Jacobinism. In some Cases they act separately, in some they act in conjunction: But of this I am sure; that the first is the worst by far, and the hardest to deal with; and for this amongst other reasons, that it weakens discredits, and ruins that force, which ought to be employed with the greatest Credit and Energy against the other; and that it furnishes Jacobinism with its strongest arms against all *formal* Government.'
Burke, berk that he was, said Jacobinism (who that?) when he should have said Red-Indianism.
Ultimately, Burke saw France as essentially synoecist- it wasn't, it isn't.
More than America, it is a Wilderness Zion.
Check out their cheese, Burke, you berk, 'fore cutting it with your mouth.

Anyroad, getting back to Ricardo, his 'Classical' model lies at the heart of Marxism as well as Populist Radicalism- such as that of Henry George who wished to tax the 'unearned increment' landowner's receive thanks to the industry of others.

The problem with this line of thought is that Land isn't really inelastic in supply. Transport Technology can change the picture completely. Trains and motor cars and refrigerated ships and so on have the effect of depressing rents on land. Heavy taxes on land, however, would remove the incentive for landowners to accommodate what the market requires and new technology has made possible. Which is why *'zamindari'* was fucked. So was 'ryotwari' but that's a story about Red Indianism not Indianism, so just hold your hoss, old hoss. The same point can be made about any other factor of production which appears inelastic in supply. Tax it to the hilt and the economy suffers. This is because all factors are elastic in the long run. There is no such thing as economic rent- only quasi rent.

Another reason to tolerate rent seeking has to do with its incentive effect. Essentially, rational agents will always strive to turn profits into rents as the latter are more secure. But anything tending to reduce uncertainty in the economy is, ceteris paribus, positively correlated with output.

Indeed, the cost of rent seeking behaviour- i.e. the things people do so as to corner a rent- may be either very positive or negative for Society because Public and 'Merit' Goods- things like Defence and Education and Courts of Justice or Representative institutions like Parliament-arise or continue to be sustained merely by rent-seeking behaviour. The State- in so far as it monopolizes coercion- provides Justice and Defence. Generally, it raises taxes to pay for this. If people don't or can't pay enough for Law Courts and Armies they may still get it. But, at the margin, the State's willingness to combat every threat to Public Order or sovereignty is reduced to the extent that its efforts can't be sustained by taxes levied locally. Such areas may be de jure subject to the State but contain large de facto autonomous areas.

Education is linked to Credentialism- i.e. rent seeking by an artificial restriction of the supply of skilled labour such that only those with the proper paper or other qualifications are allowed to work.

Compulsory education, apart from being a rent to people in the Higher Education racket, is also a way to reduce wage competition from adolescents. If young people could start work once they hit puberty, peak *disposable* earnings for men would be between 16 and 22. There would be very little crime and drug addiction and so on. Social mobility would be greatly increased. Anyone could change their class status- itself dependent on capital from savings- simply by changing their date of marriage.

In other words, Educational and other Credentialist crapola evolve as a first strike in the inevitable Cold War of inter-generational conflict. Such shite is also used to underline ethnic or credal or caste based divides coz they are an availability cascade answering most promptly to the age old question- 'how can we be sure to fuck up our kids, they way we woz fucked up?'

I mention all this to show that Rent seeking is fundamental to both social stratification and class or other cohesion.

Now let us turn to Identity and the notion of Identity based Rights. The most basic sort of Identity is personal Identity. It is by no means clear that all Societies at all times have considered personal identity and individual rights to be indefeasible. In less developed economies, if I hire you as a cook but you send your brother instead, some people might think you had satisfied your contract. Similarly, if you killed my brother but hand over someone else from your tribe felt to be of equal value for my people to kill- some might think that Justice had been served. Clearly, there are both costs and benefits to the notion of personal identity and individual rights. One might say that to insist on one's distinct, unique and individual identity is to seek a rent on oneself. It would not be rational to do so unless the potential benefit outweighed the cost.

We currently have the notion of 'Citizen's Rights' and 'Human Rights'- including things like a Right to Sustenance, Education, Information, Sodomy and so on. But, the individual is constituted as the owner of rents to himself. The cost of that rent-seeking would never be borne by a rational individual. Why? A superior alternative is substitutability across an Identity category- if you can afford the cost of enforcing a rent on yourself, what is to stop you enforcing it for yourself plus some weaker other? You are better off if you can collect a rent on a gross substitute and discharge the penalty of any action of your own by offering up this weaker member, or members, of your Identity category. This gives you an incentive to widen your Identity category and for others to narrow it.

We may term this sort of conflict- which is the essence of the political- **contested Meta-rent seeking**.

Prescriptive claims re. **Universal Rights are maximally meta-rent seeking**. Their contestation imposes punitive costs on the claimant's rent to himself. Universal Rights becomes a self-imposed Individual slavery and narrowing of agency. Of course, the current cost of this might be evaded by recourse to hedging on an inflated derivatives market for Identity.

Which is why we now face this soul-crushing overhang of Toxic Rights.

Ah! Now am I

Possessed by a spirit of wild Prophe-sy

& remain to you still
Emily Dickinson as the Abigail Adams of our Red Indianist Lok Pal Bill
'As Courtship's questive kiss, lips dread to await
'I go ass to mouth every first date'
Deconstruct thus Death's of Dick(in)<u>son</u>, Emily
& Hazare's Courts' of quotes 'The Holy Family'

Envoi-

Ai Anna, Nabi ban na, jholiwalleh ki bar de jholi
Bhar de Jholi, re!, Inqilab se khelen holi

(O! Anna, be our Prophet! Fill the cloth satchels of our NGO and JNU fuckwits. Let us play Holi with 'Revolution'.)

Why Team Anna failed.

Team Anna, I take it, did well at problematization but failed at Interessement design. They weren't able to fix the Government into one mode- viz. turning a deaf ear while silently sucking the marrow out of democracy's broken bones- while simultaneously freezing all the other actors into the opposite mode- viz. mindlessly barking support till the Govt drops the bone in its mouth and they can dart in to snatch it away.

Clearly getting shot of Swami Agnivesh- though salutary on purely hygienic grounds- was a bad move because his back-channel to the Government had the useful side-effect of increasing their willingness to stone- wall. The other point is, people who piss upon Agnivesh and chase him away with their chappal, look like they mean business. But, if the Government caves then it internalizes the Interessement process. Team Anna are out in the cold. True, they could still have tried playing the RSS card to stiffen the Center's resistance but it was probably too late. The Gandhi dynasty might now see the Lok Pal as their ultimate sanction against an over-mighty subject. *Sab kuch sub judice hona chahiye.* And if not sub judice than sub my pal, not your pal, the Lok Pal.

Team Anna members, those that remain, have for their part taken a nice little capitalized rent- Credentialized or otherwise- and, I believe, are happy enough to be sidelined until the Elections- and other such proofs of their own political irrelevance- fade from Public Memory.

Why did Gandhi succeed where Team Anna failed?

1) Gandhi, in South Africa, professionalized Mindless Agitation as a career for our idiot sons, fuckwit lawyers, and Holier-than-thou Nutjobs everywhere by raising a huge pot of money which he didn't fully spend. Gandhi was a money magnet. Every agitator, artist (Tagore needed money for Shantiniketan) or just random anti-industrial nutjob lived in hope of getting plumbed into the waste pipe of Indian Capitalism thanks to the good offices of the enema administering Bania Saint.

Thus, if Gandhi was an Obligatory Passage Point for Indianist Red Indianism- it was only a case of 'follow the money'.

2) Unlike Team Anna, which had a plausible sounding problematization- viz. an actual Anti Corruption body which might actually weed out somebody's (but not Varun's) Aunty's Corruption- Gandhi's problematization was totally and ludicrously fucked in the head from the get go. He starts his speech to the Nagpur Congress (where he promises Swaraj in one year) by mentioning two things- one Khilafat (abolition of the Caliphate, a good stick to beat Shiahs with and to put pressure on Mullahs to dance to a seditionist tune) as an unforgivable insult to Muslims, and second, not Jallianwallah Bagh but 'the crawling order' as an insult to all Indians. In other words, Khilafat was as important as the right not to be massacred. Everybody-

including Ismaili Muslims whose co-religionists were massacred by the Turkish Caliph- must stand by the Khilafati nut-jobs, because ..urm...Spirtuality? Ahimsa? no... turns out

3) Gandhi has his own interessement theory. He sees that the Brits have an interessement mechanism that gains focality by addressing various problems facing the country- including the communal problem- but he denounces that interessement mechanism as the enemy because it makes India more governable and since the British are the Government this is really really bad because *'it is a matter of common experience that if a Britisher lives in India, he loses his character, and if an Indian mixes with British people, he loses his manliness'* (presumably because the Britisher and the Indian start bumming each other and sucking each other off and dressing up like High Court Judges) . Gandhi says at Nagpur- ' I hold a real substantial unity between Hindus and Musalmans infinitely superior to the British connection and if I had to make a choice between that unity and the British connection, I would have the first and reject the other. ' This sounds high-minded. However, Gandhi insists that Khilafat is the only bridge between Hindus and Muslims whereas, logically, it represented a parting off the ways. By

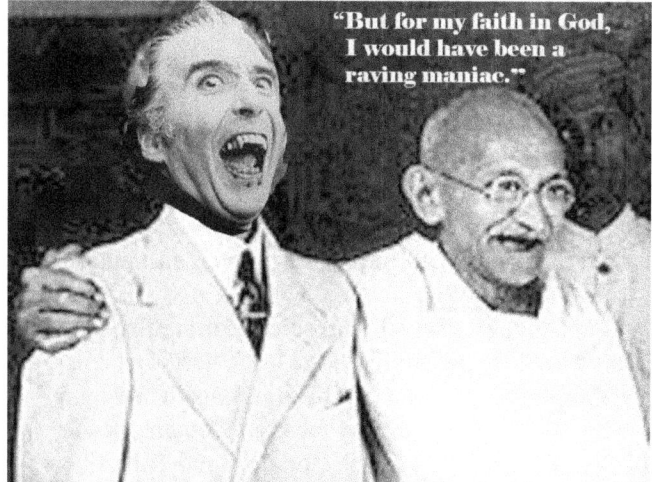

"But for my faith in God, I would have been a raving maniac."

telling the Indian masses, that loyalty to a distant Caliph outweighs a Muslim's every other obligation- familial, civic, or merely national- Gandhi, not Jinnah, sowed the seeds of a theocratic trajectory for a future Muslim state on Indian Soil. Nor did the deal with the Khilafatis make strategic sense for Congress. The British could always square the Guardian of the Two Holy cities- indeed they signed a treaty with Ibn Saud in 1927- and thus a tactical alliance with the Khilafatis was a but paper umbrella for Congress.

However, what Gandhi achieved was the replacement of the British interessement mechanism for communal harmony by an interessement mechanism which maximized his own **obligatory passage point** status which is why, he remains and will always remain a name to conjure with when Team Anna are but as the roses of yesteryear..

3) Because Gandhi's every problematization- not just w.r.t to Hindus and Muslims but also Labour and Capital, Dalits and Casteist Dicks, etc, etc- was so totally and radically fucked in the head *and* because he was also utter shit as a negotiator- everybody ended up frozen w.r.t him. But, since they were frozen w.r.t him, he became the Schelling focal point, under conditions of Dijkstra Concurrency dead-lock, for everybody because everybody's behaviour became predictable in his ambit. Interestingly *all Policy Actors* (as opposed to Agents) got a pay-out from Gandhi's Interessement mechanism *- he truly was all things to all men-* but only because his problematizatons were *madly and magnificently fucked.*

This shouldn't surprise us. Policy *Acting* has better pay-off than Principal Agency where the Agent is rich and the Principal very very fucking poor, but to be sustainable (i.e. generate a Rent) it is urgent that there arise a very very fucking stupid problematization (coz very very poor people must be very very stupid so, obviously, their *authentic* Problematization must be really shit...so shit, indeed, as to sound strangely Post Modern (which shit always is coz it's post-food) which shows, like how the poor are actually so much wiser than us- you know? & the notion of just giving them money is just...***wrong!,*** because don't you see, they'll become just like us and thus not wiser at all and won't be able to save the Planet, Mother Gaia!, from like, you know, Hiedegger's evil 'Planetary Technology' masterminded by the Zombie Narendra Nazi Modi lizard people embedded in the Military Industrial Complex who are doing all this Global Warming and, I mean, how it affects India's toling masses is that there's this *nexus* and like everybody knows moneylenders are the vampires of rural India but once Vikram Akula did a semester at Harvard Divinity School he was easily able to defeat those petty bloodsuckers by creating **For Profit Micro-Credit** and gaining superpowers as DR.AKULA and, I mean, it's just plain common sense, yaar, give an elderly disabled lesbian in the Sunderbans the loan of a dollar through for-Profit microfinance and she'll turn into Bill Gates and pay us 18% intrest p.a. and save the Environment while correcting our reading of Badiou and beng gently supportive of Sodomy for the over Eighties.

But, for us to ever enter into that 'Kingdom of Ends' where 'not as in a glass darkly, but face to fug-ugly Levinasian face' all alterity is transmuted into the reign of pure Deleuzian univocity as Diff(ooh-er!)ance, we must all work together to prevent non-fucked Policy Agent interaction and horse-trading and such like shenanigans through the providential instrumentality of Gandhian Interessement's flash freezing of roles to permit enrollment and mobilization and did I mention Narendra Modi sucks? I did? Well then.

Gandhi was a March Hare claiming to be a greyhound (Race you to Swaraj, Annie Beasant, you big fat faux Irish biddy!) who nevertheless paid out big for, not John Q Punter, but canny book-makers. The Capitalists got Tarrif protection and a corrupt deal with Manchester. The Manuvadi nutjobs got praise for the fucking Caste System. The Congress Dalits got to see the book-smart Ambedkar, whose program would be good for all Indians- not some particular patronage nexus- bypassed and corralled.

In Gandhi, the Indian Marxists have their Tolstoy, of whom Lenin said, he more than any other paved the way for the 1905 Revolution which is why Stalin didn't kill Chertkov (Tolstoy's *chamcha*) but kept him in comfort during the hungry Thirties. Gandhi shows again and again that the bourgeoisie are fucking worthless shitholes who betray any mass-movement they themselves set in motion. Not just Gandhi- Vinobha with his bogus Boodhan and 'Bihardhan' and my-boot-up-your-arse-dhan (Bhave supported the Emergency)- and J.P's stupid *sampoorna kranti* and so on, every fucking Gandhian initiative is manna from Heaven to the Marxists.

"Be the change the baby requires." Mahatma Gandhi

Indian democracy

What should Team Anna have done differently?

Die. Hunger strike and fucking die already. Come back to life by all means- like India needs more zombie politicians- but please, for God's sake, give Death a chance. You know you want to. Also could somebody please please just murli Manohar Joshi and, like take a video of him being murli'd and put it up on You Tube?

What could Gandhi have done differently?

Not die. Not fast. Not get hit on the head by lathis or coshes or whatever. Gandhi was good at interessement. The poet Hasrat Mohani was a moth to his flame. But, when the Maulana wants to pass a resolution at the Ahmedabad Congress defining Swaraj as 'complete independence, free of all foreign control' Gandhi is deeply grieved at the younger man's 'lack of responsibility'. Complete unity of Hindus and Muslims is a pre-condition for Independence. It doesn't yet obtain. This actually sounds quite sensible. But what Gandhi says next cuts the ground from under our feet- 'Are creeds such simple things, like clothes, which a man can change at will? For creeds, generations live from age to age. Are you going to change the creed you yourself, after great debate, agreed to at Nagpur?'

Let us recall the historical context. There was a new Sheriff in town and he had come to make a deal. Unfortunately, like Smuts, the new Sheriff was a barrister of exceptional brilliance thus putting Gandhi on his mettle with predictable results.

Though born to a lower middle class Jewish family, Rufus Isaacs's success at the bar paved the way to a public career in which he scooped up almost all the glittering prizes- he was a Cabinet Minister, Lord Chief Justice, an Ambassador to the U.S, and finally Viceroy of India.

His aim was to give India full provincial autonomy in return for co-operation from Indian politicians- hoping that the older moderates- like 'one-shirt' Srinivas Sastri whose achievements paralled his own- would school the young radicals in responsible government.

Rufus Isaacs wished to use all his discretionary powers as Viceroy on the side of the Nationalists in India so as to prevent it turning into another Ireland- then experiencing the horrors of Civil War. This was because, Rufus was a Liberal and his party had been torn apart over Ireland. Moreover, as a Jew, he hated racial or creedal animosity and well knew that they fester most when responsible, representative, self government is denied.

Meanwhile, Mahatma Gandhi had promised to deliver 'Swaraj' within a year, thus at last out-flanking Annie Beasant who was the great orator of the age. However, Gandhi refused to say what Swaraj actually meant.

Rufus Isaacs- or Lord Reading as that swindling Jew had taken to calling himself- tried to trick our great Mahatma into speeding up the handover of power by 15 years. However, Gandhiji- who, I may mention, was of purely Aryan descent- was able to see through this Semitic plot to get the British out of India. He explained that Isaacs was trying to steal our Holy Indian genitalia. It's like what happen when you drink too much in Hendon and ask 'where did my erection go?- the fucking Jews dun gone stolen it!'. Anyway, the British had already impoverished India by getting up in the middle of the night and breaking into the huts of the peasants and draining all their wealth. That was bad enough, but now they are trying to shrink our dicks and unman us completely! The British, very kindly, put Gandhi away for a couple of years in a nice padded cell where by a rigorous audit of his testicles 'that's one and...where's the other? Oi, Jawaharlal, did you take my other testicle? No? Then it must have been that shifty looking Viceroy fellow. Oh, hang on, what's this? Is it my other testicle? Well I'd better count them again to make sure.'

Meanwhile, back at the Ahmedabad Congress, it was becoming clear that the Khilafat movement- which had been intended to winkle the Mullahs out of their mosques just to fuck with them, that's all- had run aground on highly controversial theological issues. The Deobandi's might want to support Ibn Saud financially, but this reawakened the slumbering ire of the Barelvis. Once the Egyptian Khedive threw his hat into the ring, the Nationalist Wafd vent their irritation on the Indians as proverbial simpletons. For the Maulana, the time was ripe for Gandhi to concede a more substantivist definition of 'Swaraj' such that 'Khilafat' could go back to being fuzzy- in other words, Gandhi's interessement could have, at this stage, given way to proper enrollment and mobilization cutting across the Hindu-Muslim divide, at least in his own native Province.

But, no, Gandhi has a bombshell to drop on the young poet.

Hindus and Muslims have different creeds. Maulana Hasrat has accepted the Muslim creed. Gandhi has accepted some creed or other- maybe even Hinduism. Since 'creeds aren't such simple things like clothes which a man can change at will and since, for creeds, people live from age to age', it therefore follows that one should go on demanding Swaraj, since that was the Congresswallah's creed and creeds must be kept up, but never give the British any opportunity or excuse for escaping from the burden of ruling India.

Nothing can bring about the 'absolute and indissoluble union of Hindus and Muslims'- since both are 'creeds' and 'creeds can't be changed at will and persist from age to age- so, it therefore follows, Indians should never accept Swaraj of any sort! They should non-cooperate with this evil Jewish swindlers (fucking read Chesterton, why don't you?) who is trying to make India self-governing so that it will become rich and import *more* goods and services from England.

This is the truly devilish aspect of Western Civilization as revealed by 'Hind Swaraj'. Those bastards not only rule over us, they also want to make us rule ourselves as that is the only way we can become more prosperous and strong. Why? Only so they can make more money by selling things to us. Only so they can feel more secure by entering into defence pacts with us.

This is the true '*sitam zareefi*' of the British tyrant. They use our greed to enslave us, then they free us out of greed!

'The English have not taken India., we have given it to them. They are not in India because of their strength, but because we keep them. Let us now see whether these propositions can be sustained. They came to our country originally for purposes of trade. Recall the Company Bahadur. Who made it Bahadur? They had not the slightest intention at the time of establishing a kingdom. Who assisted the Company's officers'? Who was tempted at the sight of their silver? Who bought their goods? History testifies that we did all this.'

True Independence means not being greedy. But the British want to ensnare us by using our greed for not just silver but security and self-government. Neither silver nor security nor self-government are bad things. They are not even foreign things. However they become so when received from the hands of the British. They are fruit of a poisoned tree.

Freedom from this sort of greed, this sort of corruption, is a true nativist Independence. Anything else is amphibian- if not slavery, it is the condition of a Metic whose fundamental rights are in a sense foreign to himself.

Corruption and the Metic.

Purvapaksha- *Our Nation is unique, no matter what Nation it might be, because its pure, uncorrupted, National Spirit is the envy of all- which is why everybody is conspiring against us and trying to belittle us and, like, saying mean things about us on Facebook.*

Unfortunately, the foreigners with their fancy ideas and loose morals have corrupted us. That is root cause of corruption.

Look brother, I'm first to admit, we also have our some peculiar customs of our own. After all, to give postman a little something when he brings registered letter is part of our ancient custom. In the Epics, the messenger always received a present from the King. Similarly many things which are going on with us are not properly appreciated by outsiders. See, we are like one big family. If I slap the traffic cop and threaten to have his family killed- it is because I consider him my own son! Similarly if he demands a bribe from you it is because he is like a younger brother who has got sulky because Father beat him and he is only asking money to buy some sweets or drugs or something like that. See, in family life, first thing one should learn is TOLERANCE.

Outsiders don't understand our little customs. They think everything should only be by the law book. They think people are just machines only. It is because they are not part of family. They have no TOLERANCE.

In Japan, the Emperor came to hear that there was one family which had been living in the same place on the same plot of ground for 1000 years. Never had that family been broken up by any quarrel or fighting. He sent his Daimyo to investigate how this Magic was possible. Answer was simple. They had TOLERANCE. If younger brother gets angry and beats up sister-

in-law due to she is not giving fooding on time- so what? He is young. He will learn. If Great Uncle wants to sleep naked with his nieces. He is old man. Be tolerant.

If elder brother sells off some property to pay debts- don't get angry just murder the new proprietor and don't mention the matter. This is called TOLERANCE.

Outsiders don't understand it. Not just outsiders, there is always scum born from dirty puddles or other impure wombs. What can they understand of family? True they may be having twenty thirty children of their own. Does that mean they understand Family? Does it mean they have TOLERANCE? Not at all. Beat one and see how the fellow howls and goes running to Police Station! Even animals have more sense.

But, I am telling you, it is the Outsiders who are the real problem. They have no TOLERANCE. They just know enough of our language to know the Law Book. Other than that, they just jabber like monkeys. It is they who are spreading all these false ideas and agitations. Let them go back to their own place.

I tell you- that is the Revolution we need today!

True meaning of Marx and Mahatma and Manu and Mayawatiji and everyone is only this. Mind it, kindly.

Siddhanta-

The proletariat, according to the Labor theory of Value, are those who serve the country only by their power to produce children. Under diminishing returns and assuming Malthusian population growth, they- as a class- will never possess land, financial capital or even what we now call human capital. In a sense, theirs is a 'tragedy of the commons'- they immiserate themselves by the very manner in which they are productive to the State. Unless, of course, they emigrate.

It is characteristic of the first stirrings of the Statistical Sciences in Scandinavia and the Economic Sciences in Germany- in which, such of the Bidungsburgertum as amounted to more than mindless pedants, were tasked by the Prince to increase the yield of his forests, farms, mines and markets (Novalis, was an actuary actually!)- that emigration would be overlooked or castigated because it represents a route by which the proletariat might stop serving the State and save themselves. Thus, Marx's 'dictatorship of the proletariat' is wrongly taken to signify a vanguard role for the industrial working class rather than a meaningless moment in Hegel's pie-in-the-Prussian-blue-sky dialectics.

Workers who *can* emigrate don't serve the State solely by having children. People who won't emigrate but *do consider it their duty* to be periodically driven to the brink of starvation by 'the iron law of wages' may be termed proletarian but they aren't really people, or even cattle, but, from the perspective of Political Economy, two-legged lemmings merely.

Emigration turns workers into 'metics'- the artisan or other member of the productive class, but of foreign birth, whose activities enrich the Polis- but Marxism has no theory of the metic. Certainly, the Comintern or whatever meretricious evil it has mutated into, can keep up the pretense that the State itself will wither away and so no metic/ proletariat distinction exists on the plane of essence. No doubt there are 'contradictions' which Party hacks can pontificate upon. But, no real cognizance can be taken of the fact that there is a second 'tragedy of the commons' to which the proletariat is peculiarly subject viz. that the capitalized rent accruing to its leadership, to the degree that leadership is contested, would tend to cause it to over-reach itself and kill its own golden goose- think Datta Samant, Arthur Scargil, Demi Moore etc .

If *uncontested,* however, the rent to its leadership is maximized by its own immiseration- as happens under Single Party rule.

These two 'tragedies of the commons', specific to the proletariat, drive a sort of internal and external migration and transformation from proletarian to metic. But, the metic has diametrically opposed economic interests to the proletarian. Last year, during the London riots, turbaned Sikhs and bearded Mussulmans came out to confront the autochtonous proletarian sporting the hijab of the 'hoodie'.

The external metic faces a '*bhumiputra*' hostility from the 'sons of the soil' which can quickly turn into Racism or Communalist sentiments- but only by reason of 'preference falsification'- I came to London at the height of 'Paki-bashing,' anti-me, sentiment. Needless to say I got a pass and had things cushy coz I iz jus' so fuckin' stereotypically Goodness Gracious Me Indian that I insisted on being called 'Iyer, you fat bastard' like wot I iz back in Delhi rather than 'Gunga Din'!

The internal metic- for example the factory worker who starts up a small workshop- finds his business opportunities arise from what Economists call 'Dis-integration' – i.e. supplying goods and services to previously vertically integrated behemoths and this gives rise to a 'Dual Economy' where the Zaibatsu pay high wages to their own workers but keep costs down by outsourcing to the Small Scale sector with much lower wages and benefits. Since there are purely economic advantages to 'Dis-integration'- and moreover a dynamic Small Scale sector existing cheek by jowl with Business behemoths endows the whole with external economies of scale and scope- it won't disappear even if some magic legislative wand is waved and wages and benefits are equalized.

No doubt, metic and proletarian may cohabit along with peasant proprietor in the same body. Indeed, in India or other countries which have co-parcenary land ownership, the same man may be a metic in an industrial downturn, a proletarian during an upswing, while returning for the harvest to the land he 'owns' but in which he has no clear fungible title.

But such amphibian existence- like that of Duryodhana, his army slain, sheltering himself in the waters of a lake- is a last ditch clinging on to entitlements arising from the old order. It represents no vehicle to class power or means of transformation for the Polity.

Over the last thirty years, Economists have come to realize (in other words there's some particularly ironic reason, this isn't true) that the globally footloose metic is the key to economic success. Something like Romer's 'Charter Cities' have become the template for Urban renewal, tackling structural unemployment and averting things like 'the Dutch disease' (deindustrialization due to a bloated Primary sector) or 'Eurosclerosis' (welfarist disincentives to work and enterprise coupled with a costly bureaucracy) or the Populist Pensions Ponzi scheme characterizing the ageing PIGS (Portugal, Ireland, Greece, Spain).

Anna Hazare, a nativist, had long been harping on the Corruption issue as a stick with which to beat Sharad Pawar's brand of Rural Development- which unlike his own Puritan panacea actually garners votes at the hustings. Sonia loyalists were happy to see Hazare put Pawar in his place and send a message to other regional satraps that Rahul would take the Prime Ministership as a second Indira- or Akbar- an Emperor entitled to sajda worship by reason of the disloyal and factionalist ambition of those over whom he could plausibly claim a dynastic right. The RSS, far from being capable of any sort of meaningful leadership, is still in post-Mandal mode and will bow its Brahminical head to any retarded or Backward caste Hindu-Ramdev coz he is Yadav, Uma Bharati coz she's who-the-fuck cares, but Hazare, definitely, coz he's like Manuvad Maratha.

There is one caste- a new caste- not mentioned though the RSS itself is of that 'New Brahmin' gotra- for which Caste is a type of vested Corruption destroying the Life Chances or those from tier two Metros or mofussil towns . There isn't even an Indian word for it because it isn't yet properly endogamous. Let us for the moment call this class the Metic class. The... not 'bhumi-putra' but ....what? Are we not all, in some sense or another, part of this class? Are we not made faceless, do we not feel like some sort of illegal alien in our own country, when forced to pay 'nazrana'- a bribe for audience? Is this not the visceral appeal of the Lok Pal agitation?

Anything not thymotic and heteronomous, essentially tribal or feudal in Indian culture arises from attempts at creating Metic-friendly spaces in Society. Yuddhistra's Indraprastha was Metic friendly. His own 'Vishada' (depression) was dispelled by hearing the Vyadha Gita (butcher's Gita- where a wealthy vertically integrated Meat monopolist turns out to 'have it all'- but, dude, note the guy was essentially a Metic turned Merchant. He worships his own parents as God. Priests and Princes- married to Earth and Heaven- can, he suavely suggests, go fuck themselves.)

But Duryodhana old fashioned tribal 'thymos' (Rajas) was affronted by the wealth he saw in Indraprastha. This sowed the seed of Kurukshetra.

We may ask, in the Vyadha Gita, how come some low class butcher is living in such a beautiful palace? How is it possible? The very word 'Vyadha' in the Mahabharata is synonomous with fraud and deceit, not to mention *Himsa* and *acharabrashta* status. The text itself supplies the answer. The man lives in a City characterized by impartial laws and impersonal institutions. So long as he conducts his business lawfully, he can do as he wishes with the profits. If some rival butcher gets jealous and reports him to the authorities...what? They investigate and acquit the honest party. There is no meat-vendors' version of Kurukshetra with everybody in the mohulla fighting each other and breaking heads.

Corruption, in a sense, is what legitimates impersonal laws and institutions from the thymotic, tribal, perspective. "I am proud," says Dr. Zulfiqar Ali Mirza, 'that everything I have- sugar mills, property, kids in posh schools, etc...though I come from a wealthy family myself... yet has come to me only through the Martyred Leader and Asif Zardari and as for Bilawal- I will give my blood for him etc." This is the voice of the old tribal, thymotic politics. Corruption is the price 'Civil Society' must pay for the charade of 'Universal values' and 'the rule of Law'.

In Richard Attenborough's 'Gandhi' great play is made of the young lawyer being thrown off a train. But that wasn't the real climacteric in Gandhi's life. His family had sent him to England hoping this would entitle him to get his Dad's old job and carry on the family tradition of loyal Service to their Prince.

On Gandhi's return, by chance, his brother learns that the new English official was known to Gandhi from London. He urges Gandhi to go and pull strings with the gentleman. The Englishman, quite properly gives Gandhi short shrift. What Gandhi should have done was to immediately write to his head of Chambers back in England. A 'Silk' from his own Chamber on the Opposition bench would have been delighted to raise the matter of 'Barrister Gandhi's humiliation by these Jacks-in-office who have grown haughty under the present Administration'. The Indian newspapers would have made the affair a *cause celebre*. Gandhi would have been put on a retainer by Maharajas who wanted to signal their annoyance to the Viceroy. His articles and speeches and books would have received a wide audience. He'd be set up for life.

Why didn't Gandhi take this road? His own caste-fellows would have been delighted. They'd have said 'look at the red blood in his veins! Others go crawling before any 'Laat Saab'. We are made of sterner stuff!' The very people who demanded his ostracization would have come humbly to take brides from his family. But, that was the problem. Gandhi would have been a hero from the tribal, thymotic, heteronomous point of view of his own father and grandfather. But, Gandhi had a wider horizon. That of the Metic. He realized that the English official, though lacking in courtesy, had been right in principle. His own brother was not thinking of the greater good, but just the advancement of their own family and community. Gandhi's greatness, at that time, is that he embraced the novel status of Metic, not a 'bhumiputra'.

However, like the other 'Barristocrats' of the time, Gandhi did not think seriously about reforming India's feudal, paternalistic laws especially as they related to land-ownership and inheritance. Indeed, the 'Progressives' collaborated with the ICS to restrict transfer of title of agricultural land and inter-state commerce, while the rabble rousers raised mischievous slogans to prevent the needful overhaul of items in the Code relating to marriage, inheritance, Trusts and so on.

Why?

If these gentleman admitted they formed a class of Metics (in the Isaiah Berlin sense) then they would have to admit that the Indian Empire was itself the creation of Metics- British ones- and that it had been an unexampled success in achieving paramountcy and carrying the spark of progress, by reason of its Metic friendly character. Post Partition, Jinnah hoped his Bombay mansion would go to a European family, not Indians who might purify its marble floors with cow-cung or do *vazoo* in the bidet. But even had they the *chaksuchi vidya* of foresight, the Indian Metic-as-Politician would still have got up their own Boston or Palin Tea Party of pretending to be bhumiputra autocthones, strutting around in absurd loin cloths or karakul caps etc, so as to chase away the British Metics by playing the nativist card.

The result?

Indians and Indian capital started emigrating to the U.K. The subcontinent subsidized the British National Health Service to the tune of billions. Whether it was Swaraj Paul, or Ravi Tikkoo or Mittal or Aggarwal or the Hindujas- Indian capital and entrepreneurship has been defying the Economic Law of Gravity (Stolper-Samuelson) whereby factors of production are going from where they are relatively scarce to where they are relatively plentiful.

This is the price of our 'nativism'- even if it was all only a charade, or, rather, more especially because it was all a charade- the damage can only be computed by comparing ourselves with Malaysia in the 70's (they had a full scale bhumiputra revolution but it was once and for all), China in the 80's and 90's (while we were talking about 'Angrezi hatao' they imported thousands of English teachers and completely transformed their Higher Education Sector) and... whom in the last decade? Only ourselves, only what we could have been, no other country was so advantageously placed, no country less prepared for the shake-out coming its way over the next three years.

True, things could be worse- indeed, they *will* be worse. When the shake-out comes, nativism (bhumiputra chauvinism) will tear up the social fabric because no one is thinking ahead. I don't believe India is an optimal currency area any more. I think, with some states having attained demographic transition, preference diversity- unless matched with subsidiarity- will tear apart the Federalist consensus. A lot of it is already happening, but happening by default, happening unscrutinised, while the Media focus on trivialities.

India needs a theory of the Metic. What is happening in Karachi, now, is the fate that awaits us whether we get a Lok Pal Bill or a Joke Pal Bill.

The Proletariat you may always have with you, but Metics are footloose. Those who can vote with their feet alone have a Voice it pays to take note of. The Metic alone constitute a Commons- indeed, an Oikumene- not defined by its own tragedy.

Created by English Metics, who were driven out by English speaking metics pretending to be nativist, the Indian State is fragile and has multiple fault-lines. It must develop a language in which the class which enables it to cohere and which gives it a horizon other than Hobbesian anarchy or Malthusian meltdown, can express itself and pursue a positive sum agenda. The alternative is *Desh Tyag*.

Chirala Perala, Desh Tyag and Gandhian Leela

One of the funniest free books on the internet is 'the Chirala Perala tragedy- an episode of voluntary exile'. It is short and worth savoring, preferably with a cold beer and a plate of galavati kebabs.

The extended quotations from Goldsmith's 'deserted village' are, in context, utterly priceless. The story is about how the British Raj's determination to boost local government- i.e. impose a burdensome and costly bureaucracy- was resisted by the villagers because it meant that taxes went up from Rs. 4000 p.a to about Rs.20,000 p.a to finance the empowerment of a new tribe of rapacious officials requiring heavy bribes.

A young gentleman- an M.A from Aberdeen- takes a hand in organizing the peasants. Mahatma Gandhi, too, gets involved. He counsels '*desh-tyaag*'- voluntary exile. So the villagers abandon their huts and go camp in the Jungle, where they are decimated by hunger and malaria till, utterly ruined, they return admiting defeat.

Bear in mind that the whole of the increased tax could have been paid off by one of the big lawyers of the day without breaking a sweat. But, the lawyer/politicians wanted the peasants to stand erect on their own two feet, so as to increase their own stature- their own feet being firmly planted on the heads of those same peasants.

Of course, the notion that Local Government, supported by local taxes- i.e. Subsidiarity- is just evil and fucked because ...urm...well, take this business of Sanitary Inspectors. How would you like it if some little jack-in-office came along and fined you just for shitting on your neighbor's porch? I mean, the whole thing is un-Indian.

The point about the Chirala Perala tragedy is not that you need a qualification from the U.K to really fuck up peasants and other poor people- indeed, by the time Raja Rao's Kanthapura came out, a High School matriculation would suffice- but that Mahatma Gandh (not yet sleeping naked with young girls 'to correct their sleeping posture') got one thing right.

Deshtyaag- sacrificing one's country and going into voluntary exile- is the only valid way of reconciling non-violence and Gandhian shite.

Ergo, only the N.R.I is the true Gandhian. No wonder India subsidized its own brain-drain so heavily.

As has happened with Leela Gandhi- an accomplished poet- consider this couplet-
'My grandmother, growing old, deciphers
'daughters are verbs, sons ciphers'
What's worse, Leela Gandhi is real cute. I am ogling her on You tube as she explains the Post Colonial Subject to starving (or at least fashionably bulimic) Theater workers in some backward part of Pondicherry.

But what she has to say is 'from a queer perspective'- very queer indeed and not Edward Carpenter fucked in the ass either.

Bizarrely, she claims that late eighteenth/early nineteenth century Orientalism was not highly regarded because it was the creation of 'really disreputable traders''- REALLY? Sir William Jones, Colebroke, H.H Wilson- disreputable traders? RUBBISH! Orientalism was prestigious

THEN not later. Notice that when Arnold quotes the Gita to Clough, he is using a text from that early Orientalism.

Goethe, Emerson, Schopenhauer (via Karl Krause who actually learnt Sanskrit) as well as poets like Tom Moore & Southey all owe a debt to that Orientalism- perhaps the impact of 'Empire of the Nairs' on Shelley might also be included under this rubric if only to point out the irony of people like Bharati coming under his influence later on. Compare this to the ridicule heaped on Max Muller by people like Wilde towards the end of the Century.

However early Orientalism would have been prestigious even if there had been no trade or imperialism in India. Look at how the Jesuit's forged Purana influenced Voltaire. The East India Company is irrelevant for Western reception of Indian texts. Okay, maybe Burke's philosophy would have been different if there had been no 'Indianism'. So, yeah, there are already some negative influences.

To illustrate her point , Leela tells us that, in Thackeray's Vanity Fair- 'the first suitor to be rejected was from the Company (East India Company)'- this is extraordinarily ignorant even for a Professor of English at Chicago University. Jos Sedley could have married whom he pleased precisely because Collectors of Boghleywallah were rich THEN. Not later. P.G. Woodhouse's dad couldn't afford to send both sons to Oxford. Orwell has drawn a pathetic picture of the shabby genteel retired I.C.S officer who is glad to marry off his daughter to an Insurance agent whose dad was a butcher.

Thackeray himself protests at the ease of upward mobility for the mulatto heiress and the Indian comprador. His big beef was that a rousing reception was accorded Dwarkanath simply because of the prestige that early Orientalism enjoyed.

The real problem with what was happening under Hastings- but which had already started previously- was that HERMENEUTICS changed to a literalist, bibliolatric, ultraconservative pile of shite and philological progress just added to the problem by making historicism the only game in town- even though this meant creating a totally artificial picture of the past. The dispensing with of the Court Pundit's in the 1860's is the symbol of Orientalism Mark II. This was the real damage done by Colonialism.

Nothing to do with whether a Magistrate banned some devadasi's book or what the District Comissioner said to Bankim.

If a pompous asshole like Sir Bartle Frere could see that bad (or at least self serving) hermeneutics (w.r.t the interpretation of legal texts, sunnuds etc) caused or abetted the calamity of the Permanent Settlement and governed its subsequent trajectory, why can't Prof. Gandhi?

The answer is that Government of India still upholds that foolish hermeneutics simply so as to legitimize its own corruption. But the Academy too is on side. How else could interminable whining continue to masquerade as literary theory?

If these Post Colonial shit-heads really wanted to be relevant, rather than part of tokenism's gesture politics, they could do something useful like analyse the interaction between H.H Wilson and the young Bengali lads learning English who helped him with his translations. It would explain why Raja Ramohan Roy and his successors fucked up wholesale. But no, these guys can't do that- anymore than Edward Said could tell us about how W.S Blunt screws up the notion of an Arab Caliphate- why? Because these assholes are pig ignorant about their 'own' texts and hermeneutic traditions. Gayatri Spivak believes that India is called Bharat coz that was like Rama's younger brother's name? And like those Hindutva guys are trying to turn Ram into like a vengeful Semitic Father God? Or there is Maria Mishra who doesn't understand why there are so many statues of Hanuman popping up all over the place. No one told her about Madhvacharya. Why? Coz they really are that ignorant.

Leela Gandhi doesn't know Indian history and assumes we don't either. She does not know

English literature - at least not Thackeray- but is a Professor. I am dazzled by her. She is a true Indian heroine.

Of course she may just be pretending.

Perhaps it is all part of a cunning plan to revenge India upon Prof. Wendy O'Doniger Flaherty, Mircea Eliade (yes! that old Fascist fraud!) Professor of Indology at that same shithole.

Xenophilia is just vandalism if it means a rainbow coalition getting together to break shop windows and battle the police. Or intellectual vandalism of the Gandhian sort- i.e. a conspiracy theory of knowledge whereby any stupid fad is cool and any science or art is bad.

Only difficult stuff- like learning foreign languages, getting your head round different hermeneutic systems, doing lots of boring research- qualifies as real engagement with plurality. Ezra Pound's exile was Xenophilia as vandalism. Joyce's was different.

Pound's *deshtyaag* was treason. Joyce's *deshtyaag* was patriotism. Why? He worked hard. He rejected the facile. He got very very drunk very very often but he didn't ally himself with the vandals.

Gandhi and dharm tyag

Gandhian interessement appeals both to Theists and Atheists. Richard Dawkins thinks he had a gene for 'super-niceness'. However, there is another sense in which, just as Gandhian patriotism cashes out as *desh tyag*- abandoning your native place- so too does his ridiculous claim to have incarnated the Gita's message invite us to *dharam tyag*- the abandoning of our ancestral religion.

The Gita says- do your duty- and, okay, if you have a duty, makes sense, do it already. I myself was once a father and had a duty. This consisted of surreptitiously growling at the baby and eating his surplus arms and legs (all babies are born as Hindu Gods) when his Mum was not looking so as to cause no scandal or offense to her ancestrally European and Judaeo-Christian values and beliefs. I thought I was a living embodiment of the Gita which counsels performance of one's svadharma. But, now I learn, Gandhi says don't do your duty. If you are a Dad, stop letting your baby beat the shit out of you and then go to sleep on your chest (which is a good thing causes the weight of his body impedes the development of your man-boobs). If you are a lawyer, stop being a lawyer. You happen to know, being a lawyer, that the Law needs reform. Don't reform it. Talk about something you don't know about instead.

Still, one can't deny that a heck of a lot of praying went on at Gandhi's Ashrams. Yet, turns out, Religion was optional.

There is a charming little booklet on the internet featuring conversations between an Atheist and Gandhi.

Initially, the Atheist seems to be getting the better of the exchange. Surely, Untouchability is better attacked from a stridently Atheist platform? Indeed, was it not Theism- that of the Bhagvad Gita in particular- which created the whole mischief of Caste and Untouchability in the first place?

Gandhi, at least by 1944, appears to be listening.

The Atheist's most powerful moment comes when he describes the victims of the Bengal famine preferring to die rather than steal- fear of punishment in the after-life is what held them back.

Interestingly, Gandhi grants the Atheist permission to dissect a frog as part of his Science lesson for the health workers at the Ashram.

It appears that Gandhi is prepared to go quite a distance to conciliate this Atheist because he feels his approach is bearing results.

The Atheist decides to marry off his daughter to an 'Untouchable'. Gandhi agrees not only to host the marriage but to substitute the word 'Truth' for 'God' in the wedding service.

All this strikes us as quite commendable.

Then, the Atheist reveals the cloven hoof- we should have seen it coming, but it still comes as a surprise-

'Once he asked me for my programme to remove untouchability.

I: Regular cosmopolitan dinners on a mass scale like the foreign cloth bonfires of 1920.

Gandhiji: Would cosmopolitan dinners be sufficient to catch the imagination of the people?

I: Then, inter-marriages. Now that we have nationalists and Congressmen in the interim Government, arrangements may be made to announce every inter-marriage by a Government notification. Also every inter-marriage should be granted a present of Rs. 500 by the Government. Every child up to the third-born of such wedlock should be paid a quarterly subsidy of Rs. 50 for two years.

G: Why do you propose the money-subsidy? Will not the publicity be sufficient?

I: At present the ostracism of inter-marriages often takes the shape of economic sanctions by the society. People who appreciated the principle of inter-marriages are often unable to put the principle into practice, because they are afraid to face the economic pressures that follow close on the heels of inter-marriages. As long as the economic system remains what it is today, such pressure is a real hardship. So while the law and the Government notification protect the couple from social harassment, the money subsidy saves the inter-marriages from economic sabotage. This policy of the Government may be necessary only for a term of five or ten years during which period the movement will take root and will grow on popular support later on.

G: That is well. But it does not preserve the sanctity of marriage. It reduces marriage to prostitution, and alliance for the consideration of money.

I: Today marriages confined to the limits of caste and the practice of dowry are no better. The system of Government subsidy to inter-marriages will at least serve the purpose of removing social isolations, even though it may not be free from the other evils of pecuniary considerations attaching to the existing system. Money considerations cannot be removed until there is a change in the economic order. We may look at the marriage alliance now from the social point of view. Did not the totalitarian States subsidize large families and compel even nuns to get married when those States required increase in population? Those States subsidized marriages as a part of the war effort. We will subsidize inter-marriages for the removal of social isolations. The sanctity of marriage lies in its contribution to social welfare.

G: You are an atheist! (Bapuji said significantly.)

Gandhi's Theism consisted of getting philanthropic fruit cakes to pay for his hanging out with cranks and nut-jobs while being deeply patronizing to illiterate villagers. The only reward he asked in return was that everybody spin yarn- though the yarn was crap- and the Government spend money on stupid and wasteful things while preventing people from doing useful and productive things like ***emigrate*** under articles of indenture.

The Atheist's Atheism consisted of getting ignorant villagers, of different castes, eat together on full moon nights. Now, he was marrying off his daughter out of caste. The only reward he asked in return was that everybody attend such dinners- though the food was crap- and the Government spend money on similar stupid and wasteful programs.

In both cases, getting people to do something stupid and wasteful- in Gandhi's case, destroy the economic value of raw cotton by turning it into crap yarn which the weavers refused to use; in the Atheist's case, getting people to pay to attend dinners where crap food was served- was the first step, the foundation, for blackmailing the Government into spending money on stupid and wasteful things simply to support a Credentialist availability cascade over which they had asserted intellectual property rights.

Providing Leadership, for these high caste men- who gained status by claiming to be 'uplifting' Untouchables, though their approach was explicitly rejected by the one vocal 'Untouchable' who had studied the topic- meant getting people to do stupid and wasteful things on the grounds that the real problem India faced was that the ordinary people were even stupider than these fuckwits, rather than tactically exhibiting 'preference falsification' merely.

Gandhi's Theism and his interlocutor's Atheism were the mirror image of each other. What both cash out as is the claim that voluntary association with people quite possibly stupider than oneself, makes one morally more upright *but also smarter* than people who raise or pay taxes. Thus, one is entitled to tell the Government how and upon whom it should lavish its ill-gotten gains.

Gandhi's 'Nai Talim' Basic Education Schools were a case in point. Government grants-in-aid come from the tax on alcohol. This is immoral. Students should be able to pay for their own education by spinning yarn. But, the fucking Government won't buy the yarn that the Students spin simply because it is worthless! Thus, the Government does not permit Basic Education to stand on its own two feet, instead using the excuse of financing it to permit the liquor industry to flourish!

An Englishwoman, involved in Basic Education, describes the situation-
'One problem was the disposal of the yarn spun by the children. The government should take responsibility, said the Basic Education workers, quoting Gandhiji. But the yarn was not in itself a marketable commodity and Governments, faced with what to officialdom was an unheard-of demand, were very unwilling to cope with it. The teachers, themselves beginners, usually lacked the skills which came later and did not think of turning the beginners' yarn into knitted garments, or *asans*. or skipping ropes, or blackboard dusters. Many of them also, familiar with the part played by spinning in the movement for national independence, saw it as a satisfying symbolic activity in itself. They were blind to its limitations, if it is isolated from the textile craft of which it is a part, and without which its meaning and purpose is lost.
'Closely related to this was the question of qualifications and training of teachers. At the 1941 conference there were voices raised to ask whether the practice of appointing separate "craft" and "subject" teachers in the training schools was really in the spirit of Basic Education. The answer was clearly No. What then? Should the schools cease to demand "matric" as a qualification for admission to training and require instead that a candidate should have earned his or her own living, for at least two or three years, by the practice of a craft? The craftsman might of course have little conception of the scientific basis or cultural links of his own craft, but at]east he would have reached a good standard of skill and craftsmanship. He would need to be helped to develop a broader general knowledge. The assumption behind the requirement that candidates should be matriculates was that they would possess this general knowledge - an assumption which was very seldom justified. The dichotomy went on; *in Sevagram as elsewhere there were specialist craft teachers and other teachers who had some knowledge of a craft, but not enough to be able to support themselves by its practice. Yet their pupils were expected, by the end of their course, to be able to do just that!*

No wonder Dr. Zakir Hussain was finally forced to concede- 'Basic Education as practised is a fraud'.

The same English woman, by now joined by another Englishwoman, a Quaker nurse, gives us a delightful vignette of the Untouchable bhangi of Sevagram

*The question of toilets in houses has already been mentioned, but a great deal more work was needed in this field. The people of the village were in the habit of using the approach roads as public latrines, so the entrances to the village were fouled and sticking. This was the reason why the Ashram had appointed, a bhangi. Shanta found that: he was very discontented, and complained that he was over-worked. She suggested that he might lighten his work by building trench latrines at each entrance to the village, and getting the people to use them. Very unwillingly he agreed, and he and she got the trenches dug and provided with palm-leaf screens for privacy, five compartments to each trench. The total cost of four such latrines including the split palm trunks used for squatting plates, was only twelve rupees. Little by little the people began to use them, and under Shanta's direction they learned how to collect weed and under- growth from the roadsides to cover the excreta and eliminate bad odour. The roads became much cleaner, but **the bhangi left in disgust. Shanta rejoiced in his departure**; it was degrading that the community should become dependent on a bhangi; it was a part of self-respect that everyone should share in the needful scavenging.*

I recall a neighbour of ours- who resented not having been sent to a posh School- who used to lecture his elderly, Gandhian and greatly incontinent parents on this aspect of Basic Education. The old couple, whose own education had been more conventional, were not pleased at the zealous passion their son displayed in imparting to them the one lesson his own Gandhian 'Nai Talim' had instilled in him- viz. don't shit on the floor, don't shit everywhere you go.

They elderly couple would complain to me- I spoke no Hindi at the time and thus could not pretend to have been favoured with 'Basic Education'- and I would explain to them, based on my won reading of Kipling and Jim Corbett and so on, that shitting all over the place is a good thing- it keeps wild animals away. Indeed, the first thing you should do when you spot a Tiger is shit yourself. In fact, this is pretty much genetically programmed. If the Tiger doesn't want to eat you, the smell drives it away. If it does want to eat you, the stench confutes its ability to track you by smell. Mutatis mutandis, what applies to Tigers holds true equally, at least in my experience, for sententious Gandhian Hindi tutors such as those my parents employed for me. Unless, of course they also happen to be *bhangis* and take a proactive approach. In which case you are fucked.

The real story of Gandhi and the Atheist is as follows- Gandhi has finally come to understand that the game is up for his spinning wheel nonsense. The weavers refuse to use his shitty thread, they want Mill spun yarn, and won't read or listen to his crap articles for love nor money. Gandhi's own people have failed him- though maybe Vinobha Bhave has invented a way to spin thread of acceptable quality but he's just one man- so the Maha-crank is casting around for a different breed of 'productive workers' to push that worthless cotton yarn he's been spinning all these years. Gandhi doesn't care if these 'workers' (that's how these fuckwits describe themselves when they aren't busy being Spiritual Scientists 'experimenting with Truth') are Atheists or Vivesectionists or Votaries of Cthulhu. What matters is that they are 'effective'- i.e. can brainwash people into sticking with a failed program for a little while longer.

The Gandhian hand-job

Apropos the current crisis in Micro-finance, Dr. Vijay Mahajan tells us, we must return to the example of the Mahatma. Not because Gandhi condemned Micro-finance on the grounds that the peasants wouldn't pay unless you beat them like really a lot. No. For some other reason which I couldn't quite make out.

This is what Gandhi had to say about his own preferred panacea for poverty- viz. hand spinning yarn.

'Shri Jajuji writes to say that whilst on the one hand hand-spun yarn is piling up, on the other **handloom weavers are day by day giving up hand-spun yarn in preference to mill yarn.** An appeal to the weavers through the columns of Harijan, whether in English or in any of the Indian languages, will be good for nothing. **Hardly any weaver reads Harijan and, if attempt is made to read it out to him, he will not take interest in it.** Hence, the task of speaking to the weavers on the suicidal effect of abandoning hand-spun yarn devolves upon the devoted heads of Charkha Sangh workers. They have to reason out to the weavers how they will be ultimately responsible for killing their own occupation by excluding hand-spun yarn. As soon as the mill-owners can do so profitably, they will certainly stop selling mill yarn and will weave it themselves. They are not philanthropists. They have set up mills in order to make money. They will stop selling their yarn to handloom weavers, if they find weaving is more profitable. Therefore it is a question of time when handloom weavers will be starved. These are really fed by hand-spinners even as they in their turn are fed by handloom weavers. They are twins, complementary of each other. This fact should be brought home to the weavers by the Charkha Sangh. With loving patience and knowledge they should try to appreciate the difficulties of the weavers and learn how to remove them. Acharya Vinoba has pointed out one remedy, namely, to double and twist the yarn at the same time that the cones are unwound. If this practice becomes universal, there would be no untwisted hand-spun yarn available for weaving. It is found by experience that twisted hand-spun yarn is any day as weavable as mill-spun yarn, if indeed it is not more so.'

In other words, Gandhi realized full well that the hand yarn he had forced Congress members to spin- as the price of membership in that vehicle to class power as well as their badge of personal servitude to him- was not in fact suitable for the weavers he claimed to be helping. He also understood that his articles in his periodical the 'Harijan' (the name Gandhi gave to the untouchables once he'd decided that what they really needed was him, not Social Justice, not education, just him and his dear dotty little ways) were of no interest to weavers, just as his wishing to stay in a 'Harijan' colony in Delhi did not enthuse its 'untouchable' residents at all- it was the millionaire Birla whose good offices Gandhi invoked to force himself on them (though he did suggest to Birla that it would look bad if the water supply and electricity connection and so on were removed immediately after he left).

We now understand why Gandhi was so keen for everybody to go to the villages and harass people there with their love and understanding. It was to exercise moral blackmail on the weavers to use the yarn his followers were spinning.

After Independence, mills were forced to produce hank yarn for handloom weavers and this was subsidized. However, it was the power loom sector which benefited from the subsidy. The Government's reservation of certain 'Janta' (common man) categories for the handloom sector hastened its deskilling and decline in quality. The stage was set for the starvation of weavers and their hamlets emerging as hot spots for Tuberculosis.

This is not to say hand weaving was or is unviable any more than carpet making. Only Gandhian hand weaving was unviable not because nobody believed in it but because some unfortunately did.

My own grand-father opposed a nutjob named Tanguturi Prakasam who, as Chief Minister of Madras Presidency, proposed the destruction of the textile mills so that they might be replaced by Khaddar. This led to clashes with the Communists, whom the said nutjob locked up- surely the only occasion when that was the wrong thing to do.

Atheism's Visvarupa as revealed to Gandhi

Gandhi was in the slough of despond- or Vishada- when the Atheist revealed to him the Cosmic Form of his Creed's fuckwittery. Greatly, yea! greatly heartened was Gandhi by the Atheist's demand for Government grants for inter-caste marriages!

The idea is as stupid as the Weimar Germans paying non-cooperators in the Ruhr. Don't pay them and, for purely Economic reasons, the French will have to make concessions, quite simply because the people of the Ruhr are German Nationalists. Pay the people of the Ruhr not to co-operate with the French and their patriotism counts for nothing- the French simply take what they want while the result for Germany is hyperinflation and the first step down the grim road to Nuremberg.

Gandhi himself had seen with his own eyes that paying people not to practice law or to go to jail did the INC no good. It created a class of credentialist 'Freedom Fighters' who didn't really fight anything but still thought it worthwhile to put in some jail time so as to qualify for sinecures and padded contracts and pensions once Congress Ministries were formed.

The Atheist's proposal of bribes for inter-caste bridegrooms wasn't actually new. Leading barristers- like Sharat Chandra Bose- were continually getting letters from young men willing to marry anything on two legs for a few Rupees down. Indeed, since these young men were probably writing to every big shot of advanced opinions demanding money for their own inter-caste marriage, for all I know the result may have been a sort of reverse Kulinism.

But why did the Atheist's demand stop at a Govt grants for getting young people laid? What explains his truly un-Atheistic neglect of wanking? World Peace could have been easily secured if only the League of Nations had instituted generous stipends for kids who jerked off only to pictures of the Pope giving Stalin a reach-around.

The great and lasting tragedy, from which India has never recovered, is that Gandhi was killed off too early to finally see the light. At least that appears to be conclusion of our gentle Author- who, indeed, is none other than the immortal Atheist within each one of us, nay!, within Mother Gaia Herself, when She demands Government money be spent to defend her from rape by what Heidegger termed 'Planetary Technology'.

Gandhi and Indian Sociology

'I do not doubt for a moment that the young idealists who ask for Indian independence are very fine fellows; most young idealists are fine fellows. I do not doubt for an instant that many of our Imperial officials are stupid and oppressive; most Imperial officials are stupid and oppressive. But when I am confronted with the actual papers and statements of the Indian Nationalists I feel much more dubious, and, to tell the truth, a little bored. The principal weakness of Indian Nationalism seems to be that it is not very Indian and not very national. It is all about Herbert Spencer and Heaven knows what. What is the good of the Indian national spirit if it cannot protect its people from Herbert Spencer? I am not fond of the philosophy of Buddhism; but it is not so shallow as Spencer's philosophy; it has real ideas of its own. One of the papers, I understand, is called the Indian Sociologist. What are the young men of India doing that they allow such an animal as a sociologist to pollute their ancient villages and poison their kindly homes?

'When all is said, there is a national distinction between a people asking for its own ancient life

and a people asking for things that have been wholly invented by somebody else. There is a difference between a conquered people demanding its own institutions and the same people demanding the institutions of the conqueror. Suppose an Indian said: "I heartily wish India had always been free from white men and all their works. Every system has its sins: and we prefer our own. There would have been dynastic wars; but I prefer dying in battle to dying in hospital. There would have been despotism; but I prefer one king whom I hardly ever see to a hundred kings regulating my diet and my children. There would have been pestilence; but I would sooner die of the plague than die of toil and vexation in order to avoid the plague. There would have been religious differences dangerous to public peace; but I think religion more important than peace. Life is very short; a man must live somehow and die somewhere; the amount of bodily comfort a peasant gets under your best Republic is not so much more than mine. If you do not like our sort of spiritual comfort, we never asked you to. Go, and leave us with it." Suppose an Indian said that, I should call him an Indian Nationalist, or, at least, an authentic Indian, and I think it would be very hard to answer him. But the Indian Nationalists whose works I have read simply say with ever-increasing excitability, "Give me a ballot-box. Provide me with a Ministerial dispatch-box. Hand me over the Lord Chancellor's wig. I have a natural right to be Prime Minister. I have a heaven-born claim to introduce a Budget. My soul is starved if I am excluded from the Editorship of the Daily Mail," or words to that effect.

'Now this, I think, is not so difficult to answer. The most sympathetic person is tempted to cry plaintively, "But, hang it all, my excellent Oriental (may your shadow never grow less), we invented all these things. If they are so very good as you make out, you owe it to us that you have ever heard of them. If they are indeed natural rights, you would never even have thought of your natural rights but for us. If voting is so very absolute and divine (which I am inclined rather to doubt myself), then certainly we have some of the authority that belongs to the founders of a true religion, the bringers of salvation." When the Hindu takes this very haughty tone and demands a vote on the spot as a sacred necessity of man, I can only express my feelings by supposing the situation reversed. It seems to me very much as if I were to go into Tibet and find the Grand Lama or some great spiritual authority, and were to demand to be treated as a Mahatma or something of that kind. The Grand Lama would very reasonably reply: "Our religion is either true or false; it is either worth having or not worth having. If you know better than we do, you do not want our religion. But if you do want our religion, please remember that it is our religion; we discovered it, we studied it, and we know whether a man is a Mahatma or not. If you want one of our peculiar privileges, you must accept our peculiar discipline and pass our peculiar standards, to get it."

'Perhaps you think I am opposing Indian Nationalism. That is just where you make a mistake; I am letting my mind play round the subject. This is especially desirable when we are dealing with the deep conflict between two complete civilisations. Nor do I deny the existence of natural rights. The right of a people to express itself, to be itself in arts and action, seems to me a genuine right. If there is such a thing as India, it has a right to be Indian. But Herbert Spencer is not Indian; "Sociology" is not Indian; all this pedantic clatter about culture and *science is not Indian. I often wish it were not English either. But this is our first abstract difficulty, that we cannot feel certain that the Indian Nationalist is national.*

What is striking about this passage is that there is only one possible world where its central argument isn't arrant nonsense- viz. the Lamarkian Universe of Herbert Spencer in which acquired characteristics can be inherited. Being a Mahatma, or a Siddha, or a Catholic Saint means having the power to perform miracles. This is an empirical matter not one of doxology.

The Lama's argument only makes sense if a European's display of empirically testable miraculous powers is indeed founded in doxology. Only in this case, and only in such a world, would it make sense for the Tibetans to stand aloof from Brits because, for their doxology to give rise to a similar supernatural power, they would have to slowly evolve the requisite spiritual and moral faculties on their own- the alternative of selective breeding with Brits to gain their acquired characteristics being unavailable because of the theory prevalent at the time that miscegenation always led to the worst characteristics of the two given races being combined- as for example happened in the case of Winston Churchill.

In no other possible world does any purely doxological argument militate against acquiring knowledge of, if not simply adopting, the customs or language or laws or science of some other people and permitting defeasible Reason recourse to such sources.

Herbert Spencer's laissez faire Sociology was attractive to Indian Nationalists because it diminished the legitimacy of the 'White Man's burden' argument for paternalist Imperialism.

But, we might well ask, who was this 'Indian Nationalist'- the publisher of 'the Indian Sociologist'- infatuated with Herbert Spencer whom the journalist holds up to ridicule? It was Shyamji Krishna Verma who was up at Oxford around the time Spencer's book 'Man versus the State' took off in the mid 1880's. In other words, this Indian Nationalist who was carrying on Spencer's work in London- he gave a 1000 pounds to found a Chair in honor of Spencer at Oxford- and also contributing money to numerous advanced causes- including one's located in the Fleet St. fuckwit's home Borough of Battersea (which had a black man for Mayor)- had more claim to Spencer than the said stupid Fleet St. fuckwit, G.K. Chesterton, who abandoned the Radical and Anti Clerical Creed of his West London parents for some absurd, deeply un-English, anti-Dreyfus, *Action Francaise* shite recently smuggled in from across the Channel.

Compare Chesterton to Guy Aldred, the 'boy preacher of Holloway', who did 12 months hard labor for publishing 'the Indian Sociologist'. Aldred and Varma made the point that Imperialism was bad for Britain. Chesterton himself had opposed the Boer War and endorsed the same general notion. But, on balance, to the British Public, Imperialism still looked a paying proposition. Joseph Chamberlains recantation from Republican Radicalism in favour of Imperial Preference, appeared to have been justified by men like Cecil Rhodes and Lord Milner- it seemed plausible that Britain would enjoy an infinitely prolonged golden afternoon of 'diminishing effort and increasing rewards' by reason of its Empire. No doubt, at the time, Aldred and Varma looked foolish. What business had a little Cockney lad publish the seditious ravings of some Babu barrister? The answer came with the First World War- and, as if that wasn't enough, the Second, till finally shorn of an Empire, Britain was able to do something for its own people- with the unforeseen result that it now itself boasts a larger population (by a factor of about 10) of South Asians than it had ever sent out to garrison that distant subcontinent.

Of course, there is a more charitable interpretation of Chesterton's article- he may have been making light of these seditious Indians so as to mitigate the punishment being visited on their heads- I mean, how dangerous could they possibly be if they still read Herbert Spencer? We all went through that sort of phase in between playing with marbles and getting interested in cricket. Really, it's too absurd to hang Dhingra, the fellow was not merely a Babu he was a hayseed Babu studying Agriculture at Cirencester! I mean, it's not as though there's any desperate *thinning* of ADC's to Colonial Governors noticeable at dinner tables. So Dhingra's efforts at pruning back their tropical luxuriance scarce warrants more than a slap on the wrist. Come on, we all know what those lads up at Cirencester are like; it's the country air that does it. I had an elderly maiden aunt in that neck of the woods who keenly spoke of coming down to London to drown Lord Palmerston, he of the glorious side whiskers, in her virginal and uterine font- she being High Church when of strong waters taken.

What is odious about the notion that this article influenced Gandhi's 'Hind Swaraj'- is that Gandhi knew Syamji Krishna Verma both personally and by reputation. Few fans of Gandhi do, more's the pity. I suppose one could argue that Verma was somehow deracinated and that Gandhi had more contact with the masses. However, if we admit that Indian Nationalism must be wholly Indian in inspiration the question arises as to why Tamil Nationalism shouldn't the wholly Tamil, Naga Nationalism wholly Naga etc.

Recall the story of the Japanese physician who inspects a dismembered corpse and finds that the plates in the Dutch Anatomical text have greater versimilitude than those in traditional Japanese texts.

A corpse is a corpse whether Japanese or Dutch.

Keynes remarked that the problem with writers on the Indian economy (I don't suppose he ever saw Ambedkar's thesis critiquing him) was that they only knew about the workings of the British and the Indian economy. Thus, they were led into error. What was needed was more comparative work looking at similar economies or structurally similar problems as well as a sustained diachronic approach. Dr. Bodhisattva Ambedkar rolled up his sleeves to supply that gap- but, by then, Gandhi had been anointed Gokhale's successor, even 'one-shirt' Srinivas Sastri was in thrall to the Maha-crank, so the kerygma of India's one true Liberal Messiah remains occluded or unavailable to this day.

In Gandhi's case, reading his Hind Swaraj, I detect a manic protestation against, and Bloomian misprision as preference-falsification-availability-cascade, with respect to the 'strong author' of the Indian Sociologist.

Shyamji Krishna Varma, more humbly born than Gandhi, rose by his own efforts. He mastered Sanskrit and, at the young age of 20, became Nationally known as an orator in that language, earning the title of Pundit from the scholars of the Holy City of Benares- one of the few non Brahmins accorded that honour in those benighted times. His early efforts on behalf of the Arya Samaj, if he had done nothing else in his life, would have secured him a place in the history books. However, it was what happened after Sir Monier Williams invited him to come to Oxford and help him with his dictionary which I want to focus on.

Some years previously, James Legge, the translator of Confucius, had brought Chinese scholars to England to help him. The foremost amongst them was **Wang Tao**.

Just as Plutarch wrote parallel lives of great men from Greece and Rome, it would be instructive to compare the achievements of great Indian and Chinese patriots to get a sense of perspective as to their true achievements and idiocies, thus side-stepping partisan hagiographies motivated by dynastic or party political agendas.

There are some obvious differences between China and India. The British had established their paramountcy in India long before Varma was born. Wang Tao, on the other hand, belonged to the first generation to see China humbled- first by the Opium Wars, then by the ignominious end to the **Tai Ping** rebellion which both Wang Tao and, another of Legge's students, Ho Reng had supported. Indeed, the leader of that rebellion showed the influence of Western Missionaries in that he claimed to be the younger brother of Christ. Interestingly, the last of the Ming Emperors had converted to Christianity, under the influence of the Jesuits, but it was the benighted Manchus, who looked to Tibet, but merely for magical support, not spiritual instruction, who prevailed.

In India, too, it was not Benthamite Utilitarianism, or Evangelical Christianity, but some, supposedly Tibetan, Magical Spirituality which became the unofficial ideology of both the better off Brits (Kipling's editor, to his disgust, was a Theosophist, but so too were a lot of other senior people like A.O. Hulme) and the Indian National Congress- especially after Annie Beasant moved to India.

Her mentor, Helena Blavatsky claimed to be in contact with 'Mahatmas' from Tibet who existed on the astral plane. The older version of this idea was the romance that Colonials hadn't gotten rich by being slave-drivers simply but because of some occult force or esoteric secret they had stumbled on in the manner of a fairy tale.

Blavatsky was a charlatan, but a useful one for both the native comprador class as well as the Anglo-Indian power elite, under Lord Ripon, because, though paying lip service to the notion that all races are equal, it turned out her 'Mahatmas' protected the White 'Root Race' from the 'lesser breeds' they had enslaved and starved.

In contrast to India- which had long acknowledged its relative backwardness and marginality- China, under the Manchus, was a closed society, deeply suspicious of English activities in Hong Kong and the other treaty ports.

Few Chinese people were equally adept at both Chinese literary and Western culture. Thus, Wang Tao had an influence, even on those in authority, much greater than Varma who was merely one of an expanding sub-**comprador** class.

It is interesting that Wang Tao, unlike Raja Ram Mohan Roy or, indeed, many of Varma's own Indian contemporaries, never suggested that China might gain by tutelage to a foreign power. China was independent. It was the Middle Kingdom. It had to change course- that much was clear. But, equally clearly, it could change course only by its own will and determination. At a later point, there were deracinated Chinese people- Madam Chiang Kai Sheik for example- more comfortable in a Western milieu than speaking their own language, but their importance arose solely by virtue of what they could do to advantage their own country. Otherwise, their foreign education and mores were of little intrinsic account. Thus, Mao never had an inferiority complex to Chou En Lai or Deng Xiaoping, just because they'd gotten some education abroad.

Had China changed course after the Opium War debacle, or the French expansion into

Vietnam, or Russian expansionism along the Amur river, then it could have driven Europeans out of its traditional areas of influence and remained a permanent big brother to Japan. Wang Tao was a tireless propagandist for Western methods- including parliamentary democracy and scientific education- and as such laid the foundation for the great change which took root in Chinese thinking such that they surpassed the Indians within one short generation. Mulan, the heroine of Lin Yu Tang's 'Moment in Peking' was born into a family which still went in for foot binding at the beginning of the 20th century- the Boxer rebellion put paid to that, also destroying the mystique of Kung Fu, Yin Yang esoterica and Chinese traditional medicine- and Mulan ended up with bobbed hair, smoking cigarettes, reading Lu Hsun and ready to fight the Japanese not with Kung Fu or Ahimsa or Origami but with weapons that actually worked, and all this by the time her own kids were half way grown.

The Indians, on the other hand, had never believed their traditional magic could protect them from bullets- unlike the Boxers, or the Maji Maji warriors in German Tanganika at around the same time. On the other hand, they had the greater stupidity of Gandhian Ahimsa to look forward to. By the dawn of the 20th century, the Indians had thousands of Doctors- like Sun Yat Sen- and tens of thousands of teachers and lawyers and writers and journalists and civil servants and so on who, like Wang Tao, had an equal command of both English and the indigenous classical language and literary culture. Yet, India fell behind China. By 1930, it presented a very different face to the World. Already, in the West, there was talk of a 'Yellow Peril' and, later, 'Genghis Khan with a telephone'. China, by 1950, could fight the Americans to a standstill in Korea and chuck the French out of North Vietnam. No one has ever suggested the Indians could do anything similar. Sorry, I lied- there was Captain Nemo in Jules Verne- but that didn't take.

Why did India grow from weakness to weakness while China went from strength to strength? China got rid of magical thinking- Boxers who defy bullets- when they got rid of the Manchus and their Tibetan lamas. India went in the other direction.

Perhaps it was not imaginary Mahatmas but the the charlatan Blavatsky, herself, whose magical powers went on protecting the 'White Root Race' in India!

Blavatsky and Olcott, had attempted to do a sort of reverse takeover of the Arya Samaj, which Varma was helping popularize by his oratory. Swami Dayanand saw through them- though even he could not predict that their 'humbuggery' would, thanks to Leadbetter, soon turn into outright buggery!

Varma, like Swami Dayanand- also a Gujerati- was a great Sanskritist. He knew there is no mystic mumbo jumbo in the Vedas. He got a degree from Oxford, qualified as a barrister, and returned to India where he did well financially- not least by investing in cotton mills. In other words, Varma was a Gandhi in reverse. He got to England because he was smarter than average. He wasn't sent to England so as leap-frog over smarter kids at local colleges by getting a 'phoren' qualification. On his return to India, he became a Dewan by his own merits. Merits Gandhi did not have, which is why he couldn't get his dad's old job. Varma made money by investing in cotton mills and used that money to promote the cause of Indian liberation. Gandhi took money from cotton magnates and wasted it on his stupid Ashrams. His 'Hind Swaraj' demanded that Indians stop doing anything that might enrich themselves or empower their nation. He specifically forbade a boycott of any British import other than textiles. But, by then,

Indian industrialists, including British owned concerns in India, were already being given tariff protection!

Gandhi, like almost everybody else, had a a naive 'drain theory' of India's impoverishment as foolish as Baba Ramdev's notion that the Government can simply bring black money back from Switzerland and buy everybody an air-conditioner. The truth was, impoverishment arose by reason of the allocative and dynamic inefficiency of the, colour based, monopolistic practices Colonial Crony Capitalism gave rise to.

However, Gandhi's financial backers prefered to focus on a naive 'drain theory' because they wanted to increase their own monopoly power- Tariff protection- which they finally got by means of a corrupt deal with Manchester which Churchill protested and Nehru was uneasy about. The burden in this case fell on India's emaciated cotton farmers and half naked villagers.

Gandhi did not invent any of the nonsensical ideas he became associated with. Preference falsification and availability cascades in support of such nonsense were already well entrenched by the time he came on the scene. Indeed, every single weapon in his armoury of Non-Violence had already been tried and tested and shown to be utterly worthless. Thus Gandhi bears little or no blame for the content of his ideology- in almost every case one can point to both Revolutionaries and Moderates whose views and actions were even more foolish and counter-productive- but what sets Gandhi apart is his radical meta-metaphoricity- he treats certain metaphors as real, concrete and true, and then proceeds to build other metaphors upon them so as to claim the same truth value for them. In one sense, this created a Reception of a sort of Metatronic property attaching to his utterances but, ultimately, Modern India decided he was best seen and not heard.

If Gandhi, in his heart of hearts, was loyal to the British, and if British rule was the best thing for India, then he does indeed get the status, within Hinduism, of an Avatar, an Incarnation of God, like Vamana or the Buddha. Both use a pretense of harmlessness and appearance of non-violence to trick intrinsically violent races into pacifism, thus saving Humanity. General Smuts literally could not believe his luck when he discovered that Gandhi quite genuinely, and not as part of some jesuitical trick, wanted to make it easier for him to utterly neutralize the Indians and just use them as coolies. Sadly, the South African Asians defied Gandhi. Some directly by hitting him on the head- this head trauma explains his being a total nut-job- others by asking for Jinnah to come over and take up their cause and others yet, who had never heard of Gandhi, by simply going on strike and using their economic muscle. Gandhi, crowned by a victory he had done everything in his power to impede, could then return to England in time to offer to go to France to fight for the King Emperor. He failed as a recruiting sergeant both there and in India because he thought this departure from Ahimsa was justified because Indians gained no advantage at all from it, rather they stood to loose what little they had. Gandhi wanted Indians to believe it was their moral duty to volunteer to be used as cannon fodder because the King Emperor was their Lord and he would not reward them in any way but rather make their bondage yet more noisome.

Varma, on the other hand- but what is the use? The man has been air-brushed from History. Not Gujerati history, it is true, but once Narendra Modi stopped the cycle of communal violence in that State, Gujerat too has been air-brushed from history. It is a non-place. Modi is a non-person. The U.S. has a visa ban on him so that tells you all you need to know. The Chinese are interested in him- but that is the country of Wang Tao. The U.S. is the country of Col. Olcott- the guy who swallowed Blavatsky's nonsense about Mahatmas from the astral plane. Prof. Raghavan Iyer, the father of Pico Iyer, has written about the 'Moral and Political thought of Mahatma Gandhi'- why? Because the guy was a Theosophist who actually believed all sorts of magical nonsense.

Modi and Varma are evil bastards who must be air-brushed from history. Why? They have done nothing to give the White Man a privileged place. The function of all-powerful Mahatmas, as Blavatsky told us, is to make the World safe for the White 'Root Race' and permit its replacement by a new super-race from somewhere unlikely like California or Vancouver or other such Utopia, scenic but philosophically and fiscally fucked.

China is very evil because they simply are not worshipping Whiteness properly. Surely, they could find some nice Norwegian or Spanish or even Italian lady to rule over them? If she has an idiot son, so much the better. Clearly, he should be made Prime Minister.

I can't tell you how ashamed I am that, under Narendra Modi, Varma's ashes have at last been returned to India. I hear a port (ports are useful, as opposed to building another bloody Gandhinagar) is named after him.

Modi and Krishnavarma are non-Brahmins. Whatever their scholarly attainments, they can never be true Mahatmas because they have rejected the Caste System of Manu.

The 21st century is an era of knowledge. If poverty is to be abolished in this century, it can be abolished only through knowledge.

Remember Blavatsky's revelation- the point about Mahatmas and 'spiritual force' in Politics is that is makes the 'White' (*ujali paraj*) masters looting the country safe from the anger of the black (*kali paraj*) and toiling masses.

Wang Tao helped translate this passage from the Analects-
1. When the Master went to Wei, Zan Yû acted as driver of his carriage.
2. The Master observed, "How numerous are the people!"
3. Yû said, "Since they are thus numerous, what more shall be done for them?" "Enrich them," was the reply.
4. "And when they have been enriched, what more shall be done?" The Master said, "Teach them."

Clearly, this sort of thing is the opposite of Gandhian interessement and definitely some type of Fascism or Cultural Genocide coz like how Gramsci wrote something about 'hegemony' and hegemony is bad okay coz it's like about Knowledge and stuff and like wasn't Nietzche a 'Master of Supicion?' and like didn't Foucault say something to Satre in 1968 and anyway Modi is backward Caste so why are you sticking up for him anyway. Worse, the bastard is enforcing Prohibition in Gujerat and that's just *Wrong*.

My interview with Narendra Modi- Chief Minister of Gujarat

Some years ago, I was having dinner at *La Porte des Indes* with an old classmate of mine whose family hail from Gujarat. Like many Ugandan Asians who settled in England in the early '70's, my friend, though, by his own admission, an expert investor in various high value projects mushrooming in the State, displayed a lamentable ignorance of Chief Minister Narendra Modi's complicity in the anti-Muslim riots of 2002.

To shake him out of his complacency, I mentioned some of the atrocities that had been uncovered by N.G.O's and Citizen Rights groups which I'd read about in respected National newspapers and, on my visits to India, also seen discussed on the highly rated N.D.T.V channel.

My friend remained skeptical, not to say cynical, about my sources. To speak plainly, he simply couldn't believe some of the incidents I recounted- like how the daughter of a former M.P was raped and butchered before his eyes (despite being in America and unaware it had happened thus showing the complicity of George Bush and what Noam Chomsky calls the 'manufacture of consent)'- because he had been visiting his ancestral town, in Saurashtra, at the time and witnessed nothing untoward. I tried to explain Chomsky to him but heedless of my arguments, he dismissed me as a credulous fool- duped by the Leftists in the Media.

Quite naturally, I took umbrage, and, heated words having been exchanged, our relationship cooled, so much so that I no longer felt able, in India that winter, to take advantage of his generous offer to let his own broker manage my portfolio there.

Sometime later, he contacted me in a much mollified mood- I think it was the Visa ban on Modi that finally convinced him that, perhaps, Modi had a case to answer- thus conceding that it was he rather than I who had 'swallowed the party line'. By way of reparation, he arranged an interview for me with the Chief Minister.

Since I am not a journalist but a poet (that too of a cerebral, hermetic type) it crossed my mind that the intention was to pull the wool over my eyes and get me to put my name to what would in effect be a whitewash.

For this reason, though I did conduct an interview- I made it clear that I would publish nothing in the way of exculpation, but, rather, give the Chief Minister a chance to make a clean breast of things.

Modiji, whatever else you might say about him, is an astute judge of men. I say this because, firstly, he very courteously chose to speak to me in English rather than Hindi- thus appearing to cede me the 'home court' advantage and deflect any 'anti Hindi' animosity I- self-evidently Tamil in accent and complexion- might subconsciously subscribe to.
Secondly, he harped on his humble background and the fact that far from profiting from his office, he hadn't even been able to build a house for himself.

In this way Modiji hoped to elicit my sympathy and escaped a grilling on substantive issues. I must say Modiji appeared much younger than his age. They say the camera adds 10 kg, and this was certainly the case with him.

However, I felt he overplayed his hand somewhat.

I am aware that people might make the same criticism of Mahatma Gandhi. I suppose there was an element of showmanship in the 'half naked fakir', accompanied by his milch goat and spinning wheel, mounting the stairs of Buckingham Palace for an audience with the King Emperor. However, Gandhiji's showmanship had a basis in reality. Modi, on the other hand, was simply 'milking it' by presenting himself as an illegal immigrant (because of the Visa ban) smuggled into the U.K on a refrigerated lorry and now having to work at less than minimum wage in a Bangladeshi restaurant. Most galling of all, for a member of the R.S.S, was that he was obliged to use a Muslim name- Abdul Haq- and cook meat and serve alcohol.

There was a sort of poetic Justice to his predicament and I'd have been quite justified to let the fellow rot there in that second rate Curry house- but there is a softer side to us old L.S.E alumni and so, sternly admonishing him not to repeat that Godhra thing, I did advance him the balance he needed to buy an air ticket home, in return for one trifling favor.

You see, as a Hindu poet, I have always wanted to recite my sonnet on the Somnath temple within the sacred precinct itself. Modi hummed and hawed but, prodded by my friend, finally gave in. He made one stipulation which showed the theatrical flair and genius for choreographing public spectacle he shares with Adolf Hitler. His notion was that I should costume myself as Mahmud of Ghazni- the Eleventh Century Afghan warlord- and rush upon the holy temple, declaring my intention to raze it to the ground before proceeding to deal similarly with the Narmada dam.

Modi explained that people would be incensed and a large crowd soon assemble. However, before anything untoward could occur, by a prearranged signal, the Purohits of the Temple would issue forth to plead with me to spare the Holy fane. Meanwhile, representatives of the Media would have had a chance to rush to the spot. Once the T.V cameras were properly set up and boom mikes extended, the time would be ripe to throw off my disguise and recite my sublime composition.

I agreed to Modiji's stipulation, not from any desire to bask in the limelight, but because it pointed a way to symbolically heal a thousand year old wound and restore brotherly feeling between Hindus and Muslims not just in Gujarat but throughout India.

The Chief Minister heartily endorsed my sentiment before scuttling back to his waiterly tasks of clearing tables and sweeping up poppadom pieces.

My friend, who had some private business with Modiji- returning from the toilet, I'd glimpsed the Chief Minister slipping him the greater part of the money I'd handed over for the air ticket- was firmly of the opinion that my Somnath poem had already attained that proverbial 'sublimity beyond self-sodomy' (*appan ki khud gaand marne se zor intikhabiyat*) and urged me to make my pilgrimage without delay.

However, I am a perfectionist. In the intervening years, my poem on Somnath has expanded both in scope and sphincteral venturesomeness of style. I think my magnum opus is virtually complete. Soon, I shall set off for Gujarat. The one thing about Modi everybody agrees on is that he always keeps his word. There is no red tape. All I need to do is tip off my friend and then, like a thunderbolt out of a clear blue sky, appear suddenly at Somnath changing, not literary history merely, but also political history, nay! say rather the history of Spirituality! Man's Destiny on Earth! and, be it but in that moment only, the very destiny of Time...

The moral of this story, for my young readers, is that though you shouldn't believe everything you read in the newspapers, still where reportage is based on responsible N.G.O and Academic sources, then great benefits may flow from keeping oneself properly informed.

Jai Hind!

Chesterton, Aurobindo and *uchchvaas*

Verma was 12 years older than Gandhi, Aurobindo (whose time in England overlapped with Gandhi) was two or three years younger. Yet Verma and Aurobindo are in tune with each other, both flee British territory by reason of their seditious activities at about the same time. Chesterton, who was a few years junior to Aurobindo at St.Paul's, in his witty fashion, minimizes the danger they pose and, no question, that was the humane, the right thing to do.

Hind Swaraj, however, though bearing some similarity to Chesterton's style of reasoning, had a very different import.

Aurobindo, in one of his letters from the mid 30's, points out that English poetry, far from providing a model of chastened austerity to the cheerful prodigality of patriotic Bengali poetry, rather exceeds it than otherwise in the overblown, *sufflaminandus erat,* quality of its afflatus and- speaking more generally, to the extent that, to the Occidental eye, our 'Asiatic' style of eloquence still renders Babus like me comic- it was the touch of the Merchant Marine, John Company's Old Tar brush, in our genealogy, not Sanskrit nor the various Prakrits, which, even for our recklessness in rhetoric and, all the rummer for Rum-less, inebriate effusiveness, properly bears blame.

The word *uchchvaas-(*which, from the point of view of Hesychastic Yoga, means the exhaled breath- hence, by metonymy, a sigh or its moody music as a lapidary marking off of a rapture in a romantic tale- but if so, also, Prakriti's pathos as *viyogini-* Nature's final, all fruit fulminating, efflorescence as but Delilah's sigh, Menaka's cry- but, for so scandalously abandoned 'fore her ashen abandonment, exceeding the Yogi by that very, of Love's breathlessness, Tri-Vikrama third step)- appears to Aurobindo to be acquiring a novel meaning in his own mother tongue. It seems, the bounce and bombast of the toy boys of that already Vicereine, but Dragon and incipient Empress, asserts, by the flourish of a more otiose and darkly irridescent peacock tail, a superior virility, at least with respect to such of pi-jaw's dull, but well dowered, peahens as dwell in natal bowers, than that possessed by, the supposedly bleached and austere, 'lean unlovely' English, whose Miltonic back and Blakean brow, remain all too visibly bent in token of a once and senescent servitude to the White Man's burden..

But, hark at me! with incontinent effusiveness- which is not the same thing as *uchchvaas* at all- putting words in the Sage Poet's mouth when I only meant to fill it with gold.

The point I wished to make is that, to Aurobindo's Prefectural eye, Chesterton's Lower Sixth Form poetry has a forced, unnatural, *uchchvaas* quality- but it is an *uchchvaas* arising from a straining after effects so foreign as to seem not merely far fetched but ultimately, and this was its Safety rather than Sanity, fleshless and un-felt.

The Sanskrit of Verma and Aurobindo (he never became really fluent in Bengali, but he mastered Sanskrit easily enough)- because it was, in the main, as artificial a language as Economics, or Anatomy or Sociology, though boundlessly rich in implicative meaning- was free of *uchchvaas*.

Chesterton may well have thought Herbert Spencer out of date because his Head Master read him, but the fact remains, Chesterton's Head Master- who, apart from being an outstanding Classicist, also had advanced degrees in both Sanskrit and the Law- was one of the most brilliant men of his age.

Aurobindo builds on what he learnt at School and later University (which he tricks the I.C.S into paying for!) and later still from Indian savants and his, cosmpolitan Franco-Egyptian-Jewish, Divine Mother.

Similarly, Verma builds on what life teaches him. But, Chesterton prefers to reject anything he was taught for such gimcrack wisdom as served auto-didacts pulling themselves up from the gutter. Verma moves from Theism (or at least something like the Arya Samaj doctrine) to Spencer and Revolutionary Politics. Chesterton, who started off as anti-clerical and a fan of the Socialist Blatchford, goes the other way. He ended up as a nasty little Anti Semitic gutter snipe pushing some worthless '3 acres and a cow' Distributivist bullshit!

Did Chesterton's article really influence Gandhi? What's next? The revelation that his Khilafat policy was dictated by his reading of John Buchan's Greenmantle?

Yet, Chesterton, fuckwit though he was, wrote better than he knew when he said- "*if I were to go into Tibet and find the Grand Lama or some great spiritual authority, and were to demand to be treated as a Mahatma or something of that kind. The Grand Lama would very reasonably reply: "Our religion is either true or false; it is either worth having or not worth having. If you know better than we do, you do not want our religion. But if you do want our religion, please remember that it is our religion; we discovered it, we studied it, and we know whether a man is a Mahatma or not. If you want one of our peculiar privileges, you must accept our peculiar discipline and pass our peculiar standards, to get it.*"

It would be truly scandalous if Varma, the only non Brahmin- he was the son of a labourer in a cotton press- to get the title of Pandit by the acclamation of the genuine Pandits of Benares- becomes un-Indian for Gandhi because Chesterton said so. This would mean, with British connivance and under their tutelage, we ended up being saddled with an un-Indian little Law Student from West Kensington who receives the title of 'Mahatma' for achievements as mythical as those very Hidden Lamas Madam Blavatsky invented and Varma showed to be bogus.

Why? Just so Indian Nationalism could look Indian- y'know beggars, snake-charmers, elephants, that sort of thing.

Chesterton, I suppose, might have had a reason to hold to the belief that there is no such thing as Universal Reason, or Universal Rights. Perhaps his version of Catholicism was predicated on the notion that Rome alone possessed the Apostolic Succession- the Church of England's Bishops had no more right to ordain a priest than Elinor Glyn to anoint the Dalai Lama.

However, an argument of this nature cuts against Christianity itself. This is because Christ was a Jew. Chesterton, very generously, was willing to let Jews remain in England provided they wore the kaftan but, even under that benevolent dispensation, his logic would militate for an English Christianity strictly confined to those with an ancestral claim to that garment.

Chesterton was not a methodical man, not a comittee man, nor a quoter of statistics or a votary of the Social Sciences. Yet, there is an *uchchvaas* quality to both him and Gandhi which, in a wholly futile sense, meant that they occupied a Moral eminence fitting them to rebut and put down the arguments of the Statisticians and Sociologists. It is this *uchchvaas* foreigness, or fairy-land quality, which turned Chesterton's very mastery of his native tongue into the morass of an impossible problematization. In this sense, the paradoxes he penned were never facile merely- but richly and infectiously paranoid. Some sinister vested interest is always on the point of throwing every true Englishman into a lunatic assylum or bringing over Turkish troops to put down the English Inn. Christian parrhesia is powerless against Chesterton's paranoia. Everything must end in a tsunami of blood.

Gandhi's bizarre theory of purushartha

Prof Parel's book 'Gandhi's philosophy and the quest for harmony' makes two startling claims- *firstly* that Gandhi believed 'purushartha'- the proper goals of human endeavour- can be harmonized in a Socially productive and meaningful manner, and *secondly* that Gandhi's fellow Indians found it difficult to accept this notion.

Two questions naturally arise in connection to Prof. Parel's extraordinary assertion.

1) Was Gandhi asserting that a natural harmony had previously existed, between moksha and artha, but ceased to operate under the special circumstances of British rule? If so, Gandhi's claim cashes out as 'Previously, other purveyors of Moksha were legitimate but now, at this moment in time for all Indians, it is a case of my way, or the highway.' In other words, Gandhi was making a bid for a position of synoecist supremacy within the 'Sadhu-Sangh' and using a Historicist argument to do so.

If not, was Gandhi saying that all true purveryors of Moksha in the Past had been Social Workers in the main? This is compatible with the current view that Jesus was actually running a creche for unwed mothers in Nazareth and had just started up a Vegan collective which challenged the vested interests of the Big Meat Cartel which controlled the Temple. He also campaigned for a 'Don't ask, don't tell' Law to protect Gays in the Roman Army and that's why he was crucified by Pontius Pilate whose Gubernatorial campaign was financed by the Tea Party. In other words, Gandhi's true heir is his great-grand daughter Prof. Leela Gandhi and his message to us now is 'Occupy Wall Street in drag while off your head on drugs.'

2) Did Indians, at that time, really think moksha and artha were incompatible? If so, why? The Vyadha Gita (butcher's Gita) depicts a meat vendor who 'has it all' so to speak. His business makes him so rich, he lives like a Prince. He worships his parents as his Gods and fulfils all his family and social responsibilities in a manner more than Princely- indeed, not the immortal Gods possess greater felicity. Yet, this butcher is also a fully self-realized and liberated soul with supernatural powers greatly exceeding that of the Brahmin ascetic who has come to him for guidance.

Perhaps, Mahadev Desai and Tilak (whom Prof. Parel mentions in this context) were ignorant of the Vyadha Gita. However, the option of becoming a religious ascetic had a particular meaning at that time which it did not have previously or later. The trappings of the Sadhu-Mahatma were a way for Revolutionists to signal a change of heart to the British. It became the basis for the granting a sort of parole or of being put on probation. Many Ashrams were pretty comfortable places. Life was good at the Theosophist's center. Even Sri Aurobindo had his brandy and cigars till 'Divine Mother' persuaded him to give up these indulgences. It is noteworthy, that when details of Gandhi's diet first appeared in the Surat newspapers, what struck the reader was its variety and appetising nature- in contrast the the lenten fare of the Jain Sadhu or, indeed, the usual diet of the impoverished lower middle class.

Gandhi's appearance on the Indian political scene coincided with the crushing, by main force, of the Indian Revolutionists. Vinobha Bhave, at 20, symbolises the plight of Indian youth. He feels irresistibly drawn in 2 directions. One is to the Himalayas and the harsh life of an ascetic. The other is to Bengal and the life of a bomb throwing Revolutionary. Bhave obeys neither call but comes to Gandhi's Ashram instead. From the point of view of artha (hedonic calculus) this was his best option and he certainly repaid with interest any benefit he received from Gandhi, his Ashrams, and his financiers.

The last of the disciples of Bagha Jatin (a Bengali Bruce Lee who killed the Tiger which attacked him and was the first Indian Bank robber to use a stolen getaway car) M.N Roy runs away from Russia to return to India and a comfy jail cell- so much better than Stalin's Gulags- and ultimately turns into some sort of non-violent Humanist.

Similarly, Ghanshyamdas Birla- who as a young man had given financial assistance to the Jugantar Revolutionaries thus putting himself at hazard of blackmail, extortion and Police harassment- finds a safe harbour in Gandhi.

Some Industrialists- like Dalmia, who financed the Dandi March silliness- found support for Gandhi perfectly compatible with living large and 'having it all'. Dalmia had numerous mistresses, posed as a visionary of World Peace to the American TIME magazine, and engaged in all sorts of shady practices- finally coming a cropper at the hands of Feroze Gandhi. On the other hand there was Jamnalal Bajaj, and his no less extraordinary wife, whom Gandhi persuaded not to commit Suttee, who fully embraced a life of privation and sacrifice without, strangely enough, destroying the ethos of their own family in the process because Kamalnayan Bajaj and Rahul Bajaj were well educated and had great entrepreneurial drive. Indeed, when we compare Gandhi's impact on his wealthy backers with that of some other Godmen, he get's a clean chit.

It is difficult to believe that men like Tilak and Mahadev Desai- who well knew the harsh punishment for Sedition- were mere 'traditionalists' who failed to understand some marvellous Spiritual innovation or discovery of Gandhi's. It is easier to believe that Gandhi himself believed he had made such a discovery because, sub-consciously, we all think of Gandhi as being a sort of shrivelled and toothless granny muttering senile nonsense while swathed in cotton robes like an Egyptian Mummy.

But, this is to miss the truly interesting thing about Gandhi's speeches and writings. They aren't 'first order' but 'second order' in Collingwood's sense. They do not refer to a 'state of the world' which can be empirically verified. They are a discourse about discourse. They make 'distinctions without a difference'. In the jargon of Philosophy of Mind- Gandhian discourse is not supervenient on states of the world. Nor, oddly, does it supervene even on intentionalites within states of the world. However, Gandhian discourse looks like a supervenience thesis. Prof. Parel thinks there is some 'Emergent' level at which Gandhi really does harmonize things like *artha* and *moksha* which are antithetical in their definition only for two types of men- rulers and monks. Butchers or carters can 'have it all' provided they continually tell Brahmins and Barons to go fuck themselves and don't themselves hanker to set up as fraudsters or sociopaths of the same stripe. This is a common sense view of dharma. So long as you aren't using dharma to make out you're better than other people, there's no problem with harmonizing Eros and Economics, Spiritual liberation and Practical Freedom, etc, etc, coz let's face in these big words mean shit and are the stock in trade of gobshites, fuckwits and cunt-queefs.

Still, in the context of widespread, wholly mischievous, **preference falsification** based availability cascades, Gandhian gobshitism is an effective jiu jitsu technique which fucks up stupid programs faster than they can fuck themselves up, that too in a manner which yields a credentialist rent.

To see why let us suppose you say the following to Gandhi- 'My dear Mahatma, the root of our disagreement is that I think Indians are stupid, lazy, effeminate, and incapable of ruling themselves. I have brought along some incontrovertible evidence for my proposition for you to examine.'

Gandhi replies- 'My dear Sir, I fully accept every piece of evidence you have cited and can, indeed, give you countless other pieces of evidence which are even more striking. Indeed, it is precisely because I have fully accepted and thought through the implications of this damning evidence of yours that I must follow my inner voice and act as I do. Furthermore, I ask you to reflect on this empirical fact- 'An Englishman who lives in India soon loses his character. An Indian who mixes with Englishmen soon becomes effeminate'. Save yourselves, get out of India. Contact with us is sowing the seeds of your own Race Suicide. Recall the fate of virile races like the Aryans, the Turanians and so on. Contact with India sealed their fate. Quit India for your own good'.

Gandhianism satirises stupid Racist fuckwittery by proving his own doctrine to be it's reductio ad absurdum.

Similarly, if the Marxist says- 'Look here, barrister Gandhi, you are nothing but a paid agent of the bourgeoisie administering opium to the people.'

Gandhi has his reply pat- 'My dear Comrade, I have said the day will come when the peasants will take the lands for themselves without paying compensation to the landlords. Creditors will not repay debts to the Moneylender. Workers will not be prepared to take the dole that is dignified by the name of wages, they will seize the factory for themselves and run it for their own benefit. I say they will do these things because such things are perfectly moral. I believe that which is morally right will inevitably prevail over that which is immoral even if immorality has Might on its side.'

Marxist- You really said that?
Gandhi- That too, to an American reporter- not a Soviet one.
Marxist- So how come you're not a Marxist?
Gandhi- I'm much further along the same road and, what is more, the masses are with me and are beginning to see what I see.

No matter what first order discourse you subscribe to (i.e. no matter what you think are the facts about the world) Gandhian discourse can sit on top of it, so to speak, because it is a second order discourse which makes 'distinctions without a difference' in a manner which asymmetrically increases the speaker's auctoritas and 'obligatory passage point' synoecism. The only way to baffle Gandhian bullshit is to be more Gandhian yet. The British learned this lesson very quickly. They painted Gandhi as a dangerous man capable of unleashing mass violence. In other words he was a threat- therefore manly- because he wasn't a threat at all.

But, since Gandhi was a Caste Hindu, this meant that the British were the selfless Satyagrahis non-violently protecting India's minorities by doing nothing substantive for them at all. But this, of course, is the official legitimating ideology of the modern Indian Nation State. It is an interessement mechanism which excuses its moronic brutality as a search for interlocutors.

In Game Theory, a distinction is made between competitive equilibria and co-operative equilibria. Co-operative equilibriums are better for everybody but the danger that one party may renege of grab an unfair share means that competitive equilibria are more robust.

Gandhi's 'Non-Violence' looks like the sort of thing that makes him the ideal interlocutor for everybody to work with to find Co-operative equilibria. However, Gandhi's Ahimsa actually means Non-Cooperation of an extreme sort. In Game theory, we use 'backward induction' to analyse decisions. If there is an end state which represents a catastrophic loss to an agent then we say with confidence that he won't go down that path. Gandhi turns backward induction on its head and asks us to look at an end state where a catastrophic loss has already been incurred. There, where Violence is no longer an option, Non-Violence comes into its own. The catastrophe is now the best option because here Non-Violent resistance reigns supreme. This means, following every node in the decision tree backwards, that one should always make the stupidest, most mutually-assured-destructive, move possible. Gandhism cashes out as quaffing Kavka's toxin on principle even if no millionaire offers money for us to intend to do it.

Gandhi's genius for making bad decisions does not make him unique. Lenin, Stalin, Mao, Hitler- most so called Great Men make bad decisions. However, Gandhian discourse alone justifies, indeed glories in, making bad decisions. This means it suffers less 'Cognitive Dissonance' and thus has less need to massacre its own true believers.

Which, I think, is its fatal flaw.

Ian Desai and Gandhi's invisible hands

There's a hilarious article on the web titled 'Gandhi's invisible hands' by a Rhodes Scholar named Ian Desai.

What happens is that Ian goes to Sabarmati ashram and is nonplussed to find a library there. Even more amazing than the presence of books is the fact that Gandhi had read them! Stranger still, Gandhi had a secretary, called Mahadev Desai, who had also read them! This is proof that not just Gandhi but at least one other person on his staff could read and and write!

Ian records his amazement thus-'*As I explored the old, dust-caked books in this startling collection over the following weeks, months, and years, a story of Gandhi's life and work unfolded before me that diverged from the accounts I knew. The very presence of such a substantial collection of books in proximity to Gandhi—who famously espoused a philosophy of non-possession—suggested that the image of simplicity and detachment long associated with the Mahatma, or "Great Soul," was misleading: There was clearly a hidden degree of complexity to Gandhi's life.*'

The guy is a Rhodes Scholar. He's studying South Asian history or some such shite at Oxbridge or whatever and he makes this amazing discovery- Gandhi wasn't an illiterate hobo- he owned books. What ever next?

What's next is Ian's second great discovery- viz. that Gandhi wasn't a 'solitary saint' who just one day set off to Dandi on a Salt march or whatever and then everybody just like spontaneously joined in and got clubbed to death or whatever like y'know in that film- what was it called?- Ghoulies? Ghostbusters? No... Gandhi... that was it.. and like y'know when I like went to this place in like India like where Gandhi like lived and like guess what? The dude was into books- like *books*, man- heavy stuff, no kidding. And like all those other skinny little brown dudes in diapers- well, like a lot of them had been to like College and were like Law students who'd dropped out, like Mahadev Desai, or Chartered Accountants who'd gone rogue, like Kumarappa- and like nobody knows about this coz ... urm... but let Ian tell the story-

'*Yet the organizational sophistication behind Gandhi's dramatic march never got a mention in the headlines the enterprise worked so hard to produce. Its invisibility was partly by design: By effacing their own efforts, Gandhi's associates reinforced his image as a simple and self-reliant crusader. While most traces of Gandhi's enterprise were indeed **erased from the historical record**, Mahadev Desai's library is a notable exception. Gandhi's team compiled and utilized an extensive variety of intellectual resources to support the Mahatma's mission. Desai was the heart of this intellectual operation, helping Gandhi refine his philosophy over the course of his career and providing him with concrete information to use in his ideological struggle with British imperialism.*'

What Ian Baba is saying is

1) Gandhi's disciples were self-effacing. This isn't true. People sought out Gandhi because he was the most efficacious 'reputation multiplier'.

Take Kumarappa. Why does he come to Gandhi and why does he stay? The answer is, it was a short-cut to gaining recognition. Why? In what sense? Well, he fancies himself an Economist coz he quit a good career as a Chartered Accountant and had got a Masters from Columbia in Econ. Essentially, he thought he could prove 'the drain theory' w.r.t Indian Public Finance with the result that he ignored the really important fiscal questions for the Indian economist as defined by Ranade and which Gokhale ought to have better developed. But, that was also the purpose for which ICS officers like Hume, Wedderburn and Cotton set up and supported the I.N.C. The Servants of India has been described as similar to the Jesuit order in terms of the importance attached to turning their lodges into libraries and collecting and commissioning statistical and other works. Gandhi's novelty, and his success in reaching out to the masses, lay in rejecting knowledge of any sort. *Yes, he read the books that people sent to him but his message never changed on the basis of what he read except in a negative sense- his magpie mind might pick up some new fad or factoid that complemented his general silliness- Gandhi read only to condemn the already highly developed and elaborated project of knowledge-based Indian reform.

2) The important point about the Salt March is not that it was well organized, or that, thanks to the crooked Capitalist Dalmia, it was well financed but that it was **well organized and financed to fail.** This is because it's ostensible goal really didn't matter to its sponsors. They got their corrupt deal with Manchester and padded contract from Congress Ministries. The Salt tax was in fact abolished about 15 years later but it was merely a gesture which had lost all meaning. In fact, the price of salt went up, because what had been Govt. revenue turned into a private monopoly rent. Meanwhile, protests about stuff that actually mattered to people went ahead and, more often than not, were quite successful because Gandhians were told to fuck off. The bottom line is that even spontaneous and poorly organized movements can be successful provided they aim at things which genuinely make a difference to people's lives but don't pose an existential threat to the paramount power.

3) History is not- contra Ian Baba- something that gets erased by some magic marker. Ian is simply wrong about Gandhi's helpers being self-effacing rather than celebrity-fuckers. True, his Ashrams had their share of faceless nonentities and/or schizophrenics without an autonomous identity. But, politically speaking, Gandhi's henchmen were all a bunch of self-aggrandizing sociopaths with delusions of grandeur. Everybody in India knows about Gandhi's helpers. Indeed, Gandhi is still important to us coz of that Great Uncle or Great-great grandfather or whatever whom he used to give enemas to and who enabled our family to move from the village or moffussil town to a nice middle class neighbourhood in the big City.

Ian's conclusion is '*The real magic of the Mahatma was not a trick of popular charisma, but in fact a deft ability to recruit, manage, and inspire a team of talented individuals who worked tirelessly in his service.*'

This is daft. Firstly, Ian has not named one person whom the Mahatma actually went out and 'head-hunted' or otherwise recruited. People came to him for their own reasons. The Mahatma tried to 'manage' people but failed. There is the story of Kumarappa refusing to pay the Ashramites the inflated *per diems* they demanded out of the Bihar Relief fund. Gandhi intervened- not to get his Ashramites to reduce their monetary demands, but to get the Charetered Accountant to pay up and shut up. But a C.A is a C.A, even in Gandhian guise. Kumarappa stood his ground. So some other fund was tapped for the Ashramite's expenses. Had Gandhi been a good manager, his Ashrams would have been profit centers rather than bottomless money pits. True, he was fucked in the head- but if Scientology can make money why not Gandhian Ashrams?

Gandhi's disciples, properly so called, weren't talented. They were nut-jobs. They didn't work tirelessly. They sat around spinning yarn. Gandhi loved these goof-balls coz- narcissistic hypochondriacs that they were- their function was to constantly waste his time by demanding yet more worthless medical and dietary advice, thus permitting him to picture himself as a sort of Medical savant rather than the deeply provincial politician that he actually was..

Ian totally misses the point about Gandhi. His notion of Hind Swaraj was one which 'made room for the zamindar and the maharaja'- how? Simple! By keeping the British around- but morally debasing them as nothing more than his periodic jailers and turnkeys.

True, Gandhi sponsored a boycott of foreign textiles- he could scarcely fail to do so since it started while he was still in South Africa cuddling with Kallenbach- in any case, his financiers wanted it- but he resolutely opposed a general boycott of British goods or, in fact, any measure that would have hit British financial interests in a manner that had not already been negotiated without him.

Though a fully paid up nut-job, he was less silly than almost anyone else- at least, from the British point of view.

He was 'a loyal seditionist'- recruiting people for three of Britain's wars was just the beginning of his service to the King Emperor. The English speaking people- if not the Indglish speaking people- owe him a debt of gratitude.

But, perhaps, that is Ian Desai's point. The historical record has been erased. Not the sort of record kept by the Gandhi Foundation or the Indian Govt. or responsible historians- no, the other sort of historical record created by kids cutting stuff out of magazines to create collages in Schools unable to actually teach them how to read or write or like mebbe someday do 'rithmetic.

Come to think of it Prof. Raghavan Iyer, too, was a Rhodes scholar and wrote his shite book on Gandhi in Santa Barbara Cartland.

Gandhi's feminism as evidenced by his salutary bismarking of Cornelia Sorabji

There's a delightful video on the web of Prof. **Richard Sorabji**, talking about his **aunt**, **Cornelia** Sorabji- the legal champion of the pardah-nasheen (secluded) child widows of Hindustan and **author** of much mawkish sub-Kiplingesque (that is the Kipling of the unreadable Naulakha) shite.

Cornelia's coming to England was facilitated by Florence Nightingale and her position at Oxford was secured by Benjamin Jowett- which explains why her books read like **Edmund Candler's** tampons. Tellingly, she was a friend of Pandita Ramabai, and, by the close of her professional life in India, almost as ineffective- thanks to a Lesbian, Katherine Mayo, who killed off a promising indigenous infant literary industry and salutary career for our daughters by turning the Oriental woman, from an object of romantic pity merely, to one of visceral revulsion.

After Gandhi's goons extorted money at gun point from her patron- a female relative of the Nawab of Dhaka - and nothing was left to pay for her program of Social Work, Cornelia settled in England, finding time to give that toothless old twit **a swift kick in the goolies-** except, being a girl, she missed.

Cornelia-. What is your real following, Mr. Gandhi?"
"Three hundred and fifty millions."

"Ah, do be serious. I want to know the number of your disciples, not the population of India."
He repeated, "Three hundred and fifty millions.""Deduct at least one individual from that total," I said, indicating myself. "Come, now, what is your following?""Three hundred and fifty millions, whether you like it or not."It seemed hopeless to pin him down, so I tried another tack. "What is the

Ramabai

membership of the Congress of which you are the accepted leader?"We have no list of members - all India."I tried again. "How many people were imprisoned when you came to Delhi last year to negotiate with Lord Irwin?""The entire Congress.""yes; I remember you said so at the time. How many people would you say were then in prison?""Lakhs and lakhs." (Hundreds of thousands.)"And why were they in prison? Didn't you invite them to qualify for prison by breaking the law? Yes, I heard you myself. They obeyed you, and committed acts of violence punishable under the Indian Penal Code - murder,

(The great Harriet Tubmann- who inspired Pandita Ramabai)

assault, the wrecking of trains, arson, the burning of imported or mill-made cloth, which ruined the poor, smaller Indian merchants. How was it that the apostle of passive resistance had disciples who committed violence?""I deny that cloth was burned.""But it *was*, Mr. Gandhi.

Your disciple here," said I, indicating a wealthy cotton merchant and mill owner who sat beside me, - a mill owner who is commonly believed to have been excused from Gandhi's ban because, like the mill owners of Ahmedabad, near Gandhi's home, he is said to subsidize the Congress, - "your disciple here knows that this is true.""Yes, Mahatmaji," he said, "cloth was burned in Bombay.""Well, I never commanded violence. I repudiate all who committed violence.""You can't repudiate your followers and agents. 'What you do through another you do yourself.' You and I are familiar with that principle. You certainly commanded picketing. The cloth burners said they were picketing. What did you mean by picketing?""I meant for them to fall at the feet of the persons using or selling foreign cloth or mill-made cloth, and say, 'Please do not do this.' That is not countenancing violence.""But surely you knew that that was not the way they would do it. And those who committed violence said that you paid them to do it. That was revealed when they were let out of prison in 1931 after the Irwin-Gandhi Pact. They complained that if the boycott could not be renewed they would starve, since they would lose both their wages from you and their gains from looting. You held a meeting to decide how many of these people you could continue to pay.""Yes, I paid them. But I repudiate those who committed acts of violence. They were hooligans.""Exactly. Many people have thought all along that your following was swelled by the hooligans who live on the edge of social unrest in all countries, but I didn't expect you to say the same thing. However, deduct the hooligans from the 'lakhs and lakhs' - how many are left whom you would regard as your followers?""Thirty thousand.""Thank you, Mr. Gandhi. When I am asked in America, 'What is the number of Mr. Gandhi's real discipleship?' I shall say, 'Thirty thousand; he told me so himself."Reverting once more to the question of non-violence, I asked Mr. Gandhi to recall the case of Bhagat Singh, who in 1931 murdered two policemen, a Sikh and an Englishman, in cold blood. "Do you remember saying, Mr. Gandhi, 'Let there be thousands of Bhagat Singhs'?""Yes, I said that.""What did you mean?""I meant that I admired the self-sacrifice of a man who committed for his country a deed which he knew, if discovered, would cost him his life.""But that argument would apply to any murderer. And your disciples did not understand what you meant. Cawnpore in February and March, 1931, was the result."A woman disciple spoke up: "The Congress did not stir up the Cawnpore riots. The British did that."But Gandhi said: "You should not bring that up against me. I fasted, and God has forgiven me."

On first reading, especially as this was written for an American magazine in 1931, it looks as though Cornelia has scored a technical k.o. The reverse is the case. Gandhi looks like he is in charge. He can get Whitey killed while grinning toothlessly and coming across all Jesus Christ in diapers. Cornelia swings and misses. Gandhi's swinging dick bismarks the prissy Miss. That's what you get for coming out of purdah you slack twatted bluestocking you. No wonder, Ms. Sorabji came to support British rule as essential for protecting traditional Hindu values.

This was a pity. She wasn't Hindu and had no business aligning with Traditionalists. Instead, she might more usefully have pointed her American audience at this passage in Hind Swaraj *(In England,)* **Women, who should be the queens of households, wander in the streets or they slave away in factories. For the sake of a pittance, half a million women in England alone are laboring under trying circumstances in factories or similar institutions. This awful act is one of the causes of the daily growing suffragette movement.**

This civilization is such that one has only to be patient and it will be self-destroyed. According to the teaching of Mohammed this would be considered a Satanic Civilization. Hinduism calls it a Black Age. I cannot give you an adequate conception of it. It is eating into the vitals of the English nation. It must be shunned. Parliaments are really emblems of slavery. If you will sufficiently think over this, you will entertain the same opinion and cease to to blame the English. They rather deserve our sympathy. They are a shrewd nation and I therefore believe that they will cast off the evil. They are enterprising and industrious, and their mode of thought is not inherently immoral. Neither are they bad at heart. I therefore respect them. Civilization is not an incurable disease, but it should never be forgotten that the English are at present afflicted by it.

Gandhi believed parliamentary democracy to be Satanic coz like how Parliament elects itself one Lord or Prime Minister but doesn't stay faithful to him or commit suttee on his death. Chee, chee, Parliament is a loose woman, I say. This so called Democracy is nothing but Prostitution! Please look again at P.Chidambaram's bum- you will find it has been staring at you and winking at you in a very cheap and vulgar manner-what message it is sending, I say, to the young peoples?

(Google Earth's satellite picture of P.Chidambaram's right buttock)

I suppose Cornelia couldn't quote Gandhi on the Suffragettes because her American readers- for whom the joys of voting for Sarah Palin still lay far in the future- would have approved.

Gandhi, was a wise man, after all, as those elderly darkies so often are.

Also, what Sorabjee didn't get was traditional Hindus couldn't shoot Gandhi till the British left and they could make out he looked like a leopard or something and in any case they were just trying to scare him off from attacking a Holy Cow. Unfortunately, in 1942, Pundit Nehru blurted out a commitment to total war against the Japanese and Churchill, foolishly, told Roosevelt about it. That's what did for traditional Hindu values. Well, that and flush toilets. As the sole Hindutva blogger I have not personally scurrilously abused and challenged to a duel-to-the-death Kobe beef eating contest, it falls to me to point the way forward as follows
1) enforce Suttee for all Congress Presidents.
2) permit infanticide for sons of same if obviously feeble minded and unable to even rape some Congress worker's daughter without 'assistance from his foreign friends'

3) Circumcise Subramaniyam Swamy, keep the foreskin as Janata Party leader and throw the rest away.

4) Put some viagra in Manmohan's camomile & see how fast he makes Anna Hazare his prison bitch.

5) Murli Manohar Joshi. You may not know *how* to murli him or even the precise nature of the particularly degrading type of sexual act the word connotates, but you know you want to so just treat yourself already.

Kipling and the Kanpur riots.

The Kanpur Hindu-Muslim riot of 1931, which Sorabjee mentioned, was the result of a *hartal* called in honour of the martyrdom of Shahid Bhagat Singh- hanged for his part in the killing of a White policeman and also his non-violent bombing of the Central Legislative Assembly. Clearly, it was vital for patriotic Congress workers to force Muslim shop-keepers to close their shops and for much mayhem to result because as Mahatma Gandhi said 'We need a thousand Bhagat Singhs'.

The police, guided by Indian Deputy Collectors, stood idly by till, it is said, it became time to join in the looting. The Commission of Enquiry appointed by the Indian National Congress, however, failed to congratulate them on their patriotism and courage in so doing. The fact is the animosity between the Hindus and Muslims had been deliberately created by the British as part of their philosophy of 'divide and rule'. Secret agents from the infamous CID had instigated the riot. Thus if the police had intervened to stop the rioters they would have been attacking their own people- not in the sense that the rioters were fellow Indians expressing their patriotism but in the sense that the CID agent provocateurs were Indians on the payroll of Raj like the policemen themselves. The police's principled refusal to be divided and ruled by anybody was not appreciated as a mark of higher Patriotism and integrity. Just as Mahatma Gandhi gave unstinting support for Khilafat, even letting them defray his expenses, without asking for any quid pro quo, so too did the Kanpur police and District administration show unshakeable solidarity with the invisible and equally idly standing by CID agents who first set Hindus and Muslims against each other and then organized the violence.

The Kanpur Riot Commission report, though containing much valuable fiction, nevertheless failed to mention the true author of the atrocity- viz. Kipling's Deputy Commissioner Petit from his 1888 story 'On the City Wall' who, quoting Caiaphas, observed, 'It is expedient that one man die &c' and one man did die in Kanpur- Ganesh Shankar Vidyarthi-and that was expedient true enough coz the young man was honest but like Kipling's Lahore's, Kanpur's riot was about letting an old-all-too-old man go maying one last time. The young atheist aesthete who suffers a lycanthropic transformation into a Shia fanatic, is just method acting. But, Rama, Rama what for this drama? The dandified cynic knows the old man he has helped escape from prison can achieve no actual mayhem. Was he paid? Maybe, but he'd have done it all anyway. It was a question of style- a doubtful thing done in excellent taste. So he did it. And he does it. And he will go on so doing. And for all now are prostitutes, none possess Lalun's grace for what is expedient to die is not a man but his fame.

Kipling, Corruption & Development

Corruption- defined as an ignoble eagerness for illegal perquisites- is associated with heteronomy, a child-like state, a deficit in maturity and civilization. Bacon, though a genius, is undone by not any injustice done as Lord Chancellor but what appears a childish greed for bribes- he is caught with his hand in the cookie jar. The context is as follows, Bacon sought to re-open the gate of King's Equity such that injustices could be directly addressed by the creation of new Equitable remedies, i.e. novel forms of writ to be issued in the King's name. From a purely logical point of view, this appears a 'progressive' measure in keeping with Bacon's status as a founder of Scientific Method laying stress on the value of experiments and empirical testing. However, at that particular point in time in English history, Bacon's great enemy, Lord Coke- as the champion of Common Law and, hence, bulwark against Stuart absolutism- was providing the intellectual foundation for, and giving legitimacy, to the great heroes of Liberty for the English speaking world- i.e. Pym and Hampden, and even Stafford, before he turned his coat.

The consequence is that corruption, for English speaking peoples, comes to be seen as childish heteronomy- 'underdevelopment', in the sense of a deficit of maturity.

In the Eighteenth Century, the 12 year old Professor of Greek or Arabic, who can scarcely sign his name and owes his appointment to an Uncle's turning his coat or a Sister's spreading her legs, is the Symbol of corruption. During the American War of Independence, we have the sage Benjamin Franklin on the one hand and a host of titled nincompoops on the other- including a King who will soon need a keeper and who will bawl like an infant if denied an apple. The Regent too is a symbol of retrogression- the associate of Fox and Sheridan in youth turns into a great booby who claims to have fought at Waterloo. Why? It is his intemperate prodigality that is at fault- his childish, grasping, greed. Again there is an equation between the old order and a sort of second childhood.

Kant formalizes the notion of heteronomy as childish dependence- underdevelopment, we might call it- as opposed to adult autonomy- Enlightenment equates with Freedom based upon the curbing of one's hedonic appetites and submission to the categorical imperative, such that only those actions of one's own are licit which can become the basis of a Universal law.

Hegel historicizes and mystifies this notion by introducing an Idealist teleology operating through history such that vast portions of the oikumene- India, China, Islam- are relegated to outer darkness as spaces the Welt-Geist forgot or abandoned- they become, thus, a *terra nullis* that can be legitimately claimed and colonized by those the Angel of History has brushed with its wing- but, in practice, this means the Marxist Leninists who alone keep up its corrupt cultus.

Within the Whig tradition- for Macaulay, for example, for whom all English history was but prolegemenon and postscript to William of Orange's inglorious doings- a similar conclusion, at least with respect to India, is arrived at by means more direct. It is interesting that the tack taken by Burke- who saw 'Indianism' as a greater danger to the Polity than 'Jacobinism'- to oppose the opprobrious conduct of John Company- was instrumentalized for a purpose precisely opposite to his own aim. It was the Company's own corruption which was used as an excuse to impose a harsher, utterly infantilizing, regime upon the Indians- the piteous plight of the 'Begums of Oude', helpless to help themselves, becoming the canonical representation of Ind's vast, voiceless, masses- this is precisely that 'subaltern' which can not speak and therefore makes significant the programmatic, or down right silly, ex cathedra pronunciamentos of Ivy league professors. Indeed, with reference to Hirschman's 'voice, exit and loyalty' thesis- it is interesting that 'voice' for subjected Indians was never authentic 'voice'- it was either immature childish babble, or it represented nobody, it had nothing behind it. The other possibility of 'exit'- i.e. the gravitation to indigenous political movements rooted in vernacular traditions- too was dismissed as a retrograde step, a failure to mature, an argument for some racial flaw that militated against Kantian autonomy and proper 'development'. The question of Hirschman's 'loyalty' was also redefined such that subject-hood became its own existential solvent- to be conscious was not to access the Satrean *pour soi* but to always be plagued by the punitive awareness that such consciousness was a childish snare and atavistic delusion- and though disloyalty could be punished by incarceration, or worse than incarceration an abandonment to a lawless anarchy of Hobbesian proportions, Loyalty- conscious loyalty, loyalty as an Existential project, as the career of Niradh Chaudhri so signally demonstrates- was that veritable Black hole to which Calcutta University owes its name.

Not Calcutta alone- even Aligarh was tainted. The figure of Dr. Aziz, in E.M. Foster's passage to India, illustrates how- to a scion of the Clapham Sect, especially in its connection to Benthamite Imperialism- Indian 'voice' is puppyish belligerence, Indian 'exit' a self-inflicted emasculation in the service of some comic-opera Princeling holding court in a remote mountain fastness or forested redoubt. As for Indian 'loyalty'- that is an oxymoron. India is a muddle. That is all.

However, greater than Foster in point of literary talent, is Kipling- indeed Joyce considered him the contemporary writer with the greatest natural gifts- and it worth looking again at his canonical works to gain a fuller perspective. What we find is quite surprising. On the one hand, Kipling as a journalist, was offered bribes and proudly turned them down- his was no naïve, romanticized, picture of India- on the other hand, Kipling has uttered the most biting criticisms of English rule in India- in 'the Bridge builders', some crooked contractor has bribed a high official with the result that sub-standard building materials have been supplied. The Senior Engineer is powerless. The junior Engineer, on the other hand, is the heir to a Country Estate back in Blighty. Still, this does not mean he can challenge the crooked contractor or send back the defective materials. That's not how the Gov. of India works. Instead, the junior Engineer takes unpaid leave and goes back home to England. Does he lobby his M.P or write a petition to the Secretary of State for India? No, he'd just get the sack and perhaps the senior Engineer too would end up losing his pension. So, the junior Engineer cultivates diplomacy. He puts his name down as an eligible groom for the debutante circuit and dances with all the ugliest girls so as to ingratiate himself with the grand Hostesses of the day. He smarms up to every Politically connected matron, attending her boring parties and flirting shamelessly with the most dragonly of repellent dowagers he finds under her roof-tree. Finally, he assiduity gets its reward. He has hinted that he will return to England and get married once that damn bridge is built. Clearly, this flower of the aristocracy must not be left to bloom unseen in the dusty wastes of moffusil India. Strings are pulled. The corrupt contractor is not punished. Nobody is punished. But, a second delivery of building materials is made (this too will be charged to the Indian tax-payer) and this time it is fit for purpose. Still, there are obstacles. The Gods of India hold a debate. Should they permit the bridge to be built? On the one hand, there is Peroo 'the lascar' (presumably from the Chittagong hills) who is the real star of the story, he believes in the old ways- i.e. bully and bribe the gods- but, on the other hand, there is the Senior Engineer who, alas!, knows a thing or two about 'Development'- still, in the end, the Gods permit the building of the bridge. They too know something about 'Development'. The argument that the bridge will bring them more pilgrims and more offerings is one they see through but admit so as not to be themselves seen through.

The odd thing about Kipling is that the more damaging the charges he makes against the English- viz. that the entire 'Anglo-Indian' (in contrast to the Priest ridden, Gemütlich, Eurasian) community is engaged in a promiscuous interchange of partners, with older women preying vampire fashion on young officers (this is something no Indian journalist, however scurrilous, would have alleged at that time)- or the notion that it is entirely a matter of course that crooked contractors have bribed senior officials (indeed, that the rot reaches as high as London!), or that a heavy dragoon (Gadsby) is actually a great poltroon who 'waters his horse- to take the edge off' before riding to parade- these are incredible calumnies impugning a large and powerful community, yet the more Kipling reiterates them, the more he is loved and cherished precisely by this, his own, community.

More even than what he consciously writes, it is what he unconsciously lets slip, or- for he possessed Genius, or say rather, Genius possessed him- it is his ability to 'show more than he knows', that throws an unexpected light on the subject of this section- viz. Corruption and Development.

Take Kipling's story 'Todd's Amendment'. Todd is 5 years old. Hence, 'he has no caste'. He overhears his father talking about conditions down country- is a famine situation likely to develop? The official reports are conflicting. What is actually going on? Todd steps forward. *He* knows what is going on, when it started and what needs to be done. The big officials are amazed. How does Todd know something that the 'heaven born' I.C.S officers do not? The answer is that Todd knows the rickshaw-wallahs and tonga drivers and mendicants and fruit sellers and so on. He talks to them. Strangely, they talk back- apparently, contra Spivak, the subaltern *can* speak- it's as simple as that. The Law can actually be changed- 'Todd's Amendment'- and things actually be put right- except, of course, it's all a fantasy. We know that. Todd would not have been allowed to speak. 'Children should be seen not heard'. He'd have received a thrashing for staying up beyond his bed-time and, soon after, been packed off to boarding school in Blighty. Indeed, the ICS officer who questions a junior's report on the basis of what some tonga wallah told him would soon be put on the sick list and sent off to Cheltenham to sober up. Kipling has told us a fairy tale. But, like all good fairy tales, this story reveals a great truth. Todd's childish heteronomy, his lack of 'caste', his ignorance of 'the Law', shows that the Empire- supposedly founded on the Kantian autonomy of the ICS officer, tasked with the 'white man's burden' of caring for the 'Underdeveloped' native- is actually an ornamental fan-fare heralding nothing but a naked ignorance- the Empire has no clothes and only a child can see it and not resisting shouting it out aloud.

'Under the City walls' is another story of Kipling's- it inspired portions of Borges's 'the search for al Muttasim' and grounded his early belief that Kipling, like the Schopenhauerian Machado, was actually mulatto- which contains an even more hard hitting indictment of the British Empire. Post Colonial theorists, being deeply ignorant, miss its significance because they fail to see that when District Commissioner Petit, after putting down the riot, says 'it is expedient that one man should die for the sake of the people' he is quoting Caiaphas the Christ-killer. I recall reading somewhere a quotation from Pater's Marius the Epicurean (which, I confess, I never managed to finish) to the effect that what undid the Rome of the Antonines was their inability to see the spectacle of their circuses, the gore of their gladiatorial combats, was what would make inevitable their eclipse and destruction. The future lay with that pallid sect, cowering in the catacombs, which had grasped that it was not expedient at all that one man, or body of men- however brave, whatever their beliefs or battle skills- die for the sake of the people. I paraphrase. No doubt, Pater put the same matter in more lapidary form.

'The return of Imray'- on the face of it an extended after-dinner anecdote on the theme of the ghastliness of native servants- I have discussed in my book 'Tigers of Wrath'. I looked up what I'd written just now- thank you Google books!- and find that though written over a decade ago, there is nothing I want to change, no too savage strain of *saevo indignatio* to provoke a cry of *sufflaminandus erat*, not because, with the passage of years, I have not rather sunk than risen as a stylist, but because I now more clearly see that the damage done by the equation of heteronomy with underdevelopment, the blight produced by the 'Ayn ul Kamal', the 'eye of perfection'- such as that by which Imray slays the khidmatgar's son- such as that by which the I.C.S blighted India- 'shakkar ki churi' says Dadhabhai Naoroji, 'the knife of sugar'- yet is wielded and wielded to the same ghastly end. Nowadays, anyone with a PhD from America gets to fuck up India- if the village money-lender was a blood sucker, then Virkam Akula getting his Georgetown PhD, is immediately transformed into DR.AKULA, fastening his 'for profit' fangs upon millions of poor women and becoming a multi millionaire in the process. But, I wonder, could Kipling himself have kept up his subtle, naturalistic, art in the face of what is currently happening? Like Dr. Swift, might he not have ended up in the loony bill if he'd made the attempt?

Kipling's 'Brother Square-toes' puzzled me when first I read it. Indeed, it now quite indistinct in my mind and conflated with 'A priest in spite of himself'- in which Talleyrand offers a bribe in the hope of gaining information which will enable his return to France and power. The reason, I recall it now is because Talleyrand is an example of a diplomat who financed his Ministry by bribes from the enemies of his state and the enemies of his foreign policy. History has judged Talleyrand in the right- this was a diplomat who saw that France was best served by remaining within its natural borders rather than by Napoleonic or dynastic *folie de grandeur.* The point about his corruption is that it served not France merely but Civilization itself. Roberto Callasso makes Talleyrand- Kipling's 'Priest in spite of himself'- into a sort of pivotal figure who, as Master of Revels, introduces Europe to its own destiny as something or the other I hadn't patience enough to inquire further about. Invoking Prof. Mushtaq Khan's notion of 'Transformative Potential', we might say that Talleyrand's corruption helped unleash the Continent's productive resources for pacific socio-economic development as opposed to winner-take-all militarism.

More generally, we might see in Talleyrand a transitional figure- adapting the norms of the *ancien regime* to a burgeoning Civil Society based on Contractarian Ethics, Middle Class Morality, and Romantic, that is *uchchvaas,* competitive hypocrisy. Corruption, as something winked at for 'greasing the wheels', arises out of a mis-match between customary morality and a new Universal Ethical theory which has not yet called into existence the institutions that might allow it to function as intended. Unfortunately, mischievous 'social entrepreneurs' of whom, to paraphrase Pascal on monks, 'we will always have more of, than Reason'- are bound to start up a 'moral panic', an availability cascade, blaming all Society's ills on this sort of transitional corruption- i.e. social 'shadow' norms or processes arising out of a lag, or hysteresis effect, between the reigning prescriptive code and that which obtains on the ground.

Henry Adams- whose education disabled him from becoming a sort of Paretian social-engineer (that is, if I understand him right)- marvels at Gladstone's duplicity, as opposed to Lord Palmerstone's candor and straight-dealing, before reaching the conclusion that the real fault was with his own generation, people of his own education, who caught up in holier-than-thou availability cascades visited a great ruin upon themselves wholly gratuitously. It is in this context that the emergence of Tammany Hall politics, the sink of corruption into which the Republic fell and- as the TV series 'Empire Broadwalk' eloquently demonstrates- remained enmired, was the pre-condition for American development, just as Talleyrand's corruption became the foundation for Europe's rise from the ashes of Waterloo.

Returning to Kipling, Kim, of course, is his magnum opus. The Irish lad, Kimbal O'Hara, appoints himself as 'chela' to a Tibetan monk. Why? Is it not merely to ensure his own survival as a street smart trickster? Or is all just, as Nabokov suggests, a boys-own adventure story of no interest to us 'developed' *evolues.* Certainly, Indians are content to receive it as such. Yet, the hidden text is there for all to see (at least to Hindus). The name Kim derives from Ka- Who?- this as the name of God. He is also called 'friend-of-all-the-world' i.e. Visvamitra. In the Rg Veda, this Rishi is shown as having power over rivers. The Theosophists- including, Kipling's boss, much to his disgust- made great play of the similarity between Moses, who had power over the Red Sea, and Visvamitra in this respect. The monk is searching for a sacred river. Kim becomes his means of finding it- but by a means wholly problematic.

Interestingly, the English Anglican Chaplain comes across as a flint-hearted pi-jaw merchant. The Irish Catholic priest, on the other hand, is happy to strike a deal with the Tibetan monk who rescues Kim from an Army Orphanage by paying the fees for the elite La Martiniere school. Development, it seems, is so corrupt it can corrupt even the most corrupt of gamin street urchins. An old man may find a river in a waste space- but it doesn't exist for anybody else. The friend-of-all-the-world loses his only friend in all the world.

Before Kipling, the big Indian best-seller was 'Confessions of a Thug' by Meadows Taylor. There are some curious parallels between it and, the Indian police-man, Ruswa's 'Umrao Jaan'- essentially in both stories, the anti-hero or heroine is upper class but kidnapped and brought up to a disreputable calling- what both highlight is the difference between 'ada' and 'adaab'- i.e. both the Thug and the Tawaif have the appearance and manners, the pre-possessing address, of the erstwhile ruling class (to which, indeed, they belong by birth). Both, at least to our eye, represent a challenge to the usurping power- there is the story of Gauhar Jaan (born Angelina Yeoward) putting the Governor General's nose out of joint by cutting off his barouche with her own more splendid equipage- and have their own secret history of suppression. In Kipling's 'Under the City walls' the tawaif Lalun arranges for the escape of the old rebel, but- as Kipling well understood, it was a romantic, hopelessly retrograde, step. What actually happened at Jallianwalla bagh (which to Anglo-Indian ears suggests Chilianwala) happens through the agency of an agent provocateur- the pampered son of a local Lalun- this is a story not even Kipling would have had the stomach to write. At about the same time as Meadows Taylor, Emily Eden was penning her influential letters and the venom she spits at the Sikhs- especially the nihang warriors- is worthy of comment. Meadows Taylor, in listing the confederates of the Thugs and naming those whom they were forbidden to slay, is highly informative with respect to who exactly the British most feared at that time. Essentially, any indigenous political or cultural formation with military potential- or possibly fanning the flames of martial ardor- was equated with either the Thuggee's kerchief or the Tawaif's kotha. I'm not saying, for I honestly don't know, that any and every 'uprising'- like that of the 'Sanyasse's' or the Moplahs- was actually part of a 'struggle for Independence'- indeed, I'm willing to give the Marxists the benefit of the doubt ever w.r.t the Gandhian movement in this respect- nevertheless, my wider point is that the norms and courteous forms of the ancien regime may be denounced as corruption not because they represent underdevelopment but because they impede a sort of Development that is kleptocratic and gives rise to Dependency theory.

English rule permitted a sort of privatization of corruption by means of its adversarial justice system. The advocates who prospered by it retained a bad conscience arising out of the cognitive dissonance of been paid to 'make the worse appear the better cause'. Consequently, in a manner entirely mischievous, they made themselves available for every available, suitably high toned, availability cascade- especially after the killing of Barrister Pringle Kennedy's women-folk.

After 1919, the industrialists too had been increasingly bought off. A system was in place such that those already with an 'in' could be sure of monopolising the local market and, after Independence, cornering resources and (effectively) subsidies to shore up their position.
Yes, *parvenus* might need to pay bribes. So, yes, certain industrialists will denounce corruption. It's simply a sign of better breeding, dontchaknow!

Kipling disengaged with Politics, after his disastrous infatuation with Rhodes, and it is to the increasingly paranoid pages of Chesterton and Belloc that we must turn to trace the further trajectory of this theme in English letters.

But, let us not stray no further on this noisome path.
Kipling, on final assay, was an innocent. At least, it is to our own age of innocence that his works are most gloriously grafted and gratefully remembered. So, tho' others abide our question, Kipling thou art free!
Kipling's the Janeites.

Kipling alone can make me cringe, like a hung-over adolescent piecing together the enormities of the night before. No drinker himself and having nothing to reproach himself with, 'the horrors' were nevertheless an effect he studied to achieve and which he repeats again again in his lesser works with the result that they stand outside literature- they *are* literature, a crystalline monad reflecting upon only itself.

In his Gadsby, we cringe when we hear the heavy dragoon confess he waters his horse to take the edge off. The Janeites is worse as the horrors of trench warfare were worse than the terrors of any Yusuf Zai woman's gelding knife up the Khyber.

'C.S. Lewis denounced the story as a prime example of Kipling's habit of claiming insider knowledge. "Finally something so simple and ordinary as an enjoyment of Jane Austen's novels is turned into the pretext for one more secret society, and we have the hardly forgiveable Janeites. It is this ubiquitous presence of the Ring, this unwearied knowningness, that renders his work in the long run suffocating and unendurable."'

Replace C.S. Lewis's 'knowingness' (a lower class solecism marking the counter jumper) with Voegelin's notion of 'Gnostic speculation' and 'immanentizing the eschaton' and suddenly it is the Oxford Don, who- very daringly- introduced not just an American divorcee but also Christ to some of his colleagues at High Table, wot comes of looking the debauched guttersnipe. The Freemason's Lodge aint the S.S, it's A.A for lost souls whose wits were blown out of them at Wipers. But Jane is- not without her astringent humour, her characteristic strain of coarseness, her virility- their Higher Power. She saves from death and arranges marriages.

The men make us cringe, not because they are weak or venal or coarse or politically incorrect, but because they are desexed women, bereaved mothers sheltering in a simulacrum of some distant Mother Lodge.

The Janeites- actuaries and divorce lawyers playing at being Officers- make us cringe because they're 'accidental gentlemen' though this won't save them being blown up like the blue bloods wot preceded them.

The drunken batman who sells the secret of the Janeites to the shell shocked protagonist- this 'gentleman ranker' but also sodden Simoniac...strangely isn't cringeworthy at all. You see, Austen had already become part of Eng Lit. And Eng Lit is a credentialist swindle. The fex *urbis* are well advised to lay out a couple of quid for a crib sheet wot might get 'em a cushy berth.

But everyone else is cringeworthy and everything is cringeworthy, the horrors of the War are personal, private, three o'clock in the morning, horrors- yet Kipling, at his mawkish worst, gushing over Jane's marriage in heaven, pulls off the greatest literary stunt possible. Jane comes alive, though she is nothing but stories, and- *'pity she was barren', 'no, she 'ad one son, 'enry James'*- Kipling had one son and what is barren is stories- and man born of woman has but a short time to get pissed now the Council's rolled back on Licensing hours coz of the hoodie riots. For which I, personally, blame David Cameron. That boy aint right.

Religion and Democracy- what Mahatma Gandhi actually said.

It is not often that I find occasion to quote Mahatma Gandhi approvingly on my blog. This is what he said to Romain Rolland-

"Since Religion is like one's own Mother, the only two possible things Democratic Politics can say about it are almost equally offensive- viz-

(1) 'Your Mom's a ho and her ass soooo fat'

(2) 'Far from being a prostitute, our Mother is a beautiful, well educated and cultured virgin, my continued pimping for whom confers such inestimable benefits on the commonweal that like just elect me already .'

Personally, I prefer (1) coz a Mom can be a ho with a big fat ass without ceasing to be a good Mom- which is the only thing that matters, unless your name is Oedipus.

The problem is, if you vote for people who call a Mom a ho- it emboldens them to make you their bitch.

The question we must ask ourselves is must this always be the case? Might not the defect lie in indigenous democracy as opposed to that imported or imposed under the rubric of 'when America fucks you in the ass, Democracy is the reach-around'?

Only time will tell.

Monsieur Rolland informs me that he is available to speak to Primary School Students in the West London area till the end of the week.

I trust the Local Education Authority will lose no time in snapping up so distinguished a public speaker.

V.S Naipaul as Gandhian moralist.

William Boyd has compared Sir V.S Naipaul to Evelyn Waugh- a bizarre comparisons to us Indians who know Naipaul chiefly as a Gandhian moralist. Though both ended up as English Country gentlemen, Waugh was funny, he wrote like an angel, his irony so perfect it verged on theodicy.

Naipaul's books simply aren't in the same category. I suppose the argument could be made that Naipaul- considered as a colored man, paid for jeering at colored people- can without impropriety be called a colored Waugh on the principle that you can call a nig-nog anything.

But this is an argument that tends not to be made in my presence- the fact is, though my cheeks display tints of peaches and cream, this is only because I'm a messy eater not because long years in London have altered my complexion. Furthermore, just to be clear, I'm not setting myself up to be Naipaul's successor and so, absent a sufficient monetary inducement, I can't put forward this argument myself because, it seems to me, Waugh saw himself as part of one great indivisible Civilizing force at the center of things.

There can't be a colored Waugh any more than there can be a Black Catholicism as opposed to a White Catholicism.

Yet, to my mind, there is a connection- less a case of artistic genealogy than its proctologically inartistic inverse-between Waugh and Naipaul. What that is, I will reveal at the end of this section.

First, let me come clean and admit that the only reason I consider Naipaul to be important is because I am a Hindu. Why does Naipaul's religion- unlike Ved Mehta's or Niradh Chaudhri's- matter to me?

Well, Naipaul came to writing- it seems to me- out of a sense of filial piety. His father, Shivprasad, had gained a little education and his writing talent had gotten him a job as a reporter. Hoping to benefit people of his own background- i.e. Hindu agriculturists in the backwaters- Shivprasad allied himself with Indian Reformist movements so as to combat social evils amongst his erstwhile peers hoping to put them on the same path to progress as the brown converts to Presbyterianism and the urban Afro-Caribbeans.

Perhaps the young man adopted too shrill a tone, or perhaps people felt he was getting too big for his boots- the upshot was that his life was threatened. He had to make an ignominious recantation- my memory is a goat was sacrificed to Kali or something of that sort- and suffered a nervous breakdown in consequence- one morning he looked in the mirror and could no longer see his own face.

I mention this because it was under somewhat similar circumstances that my grand-father (who was fond of quoting the patriotic writings of Swami Vivekananda in a hilarious Bengali accent) was forced to sodomize the equestrian statute of Sir Mark Cubbon as part of a Hindu College hazing ritual- one which, like the practice of Suttee amongst Supremos of the Congress party, the benighted partisans of 'Hindutva' and the so called 'Sangh Parivar' secretly encourage to this day- a fact seldom mentioned by the supposedly 'Liberal' media.

Like Naipaul, I too have written books about India. Indeed, my last novel 'Samlee's daughter' stands shoulder to shoulder with Naipaul's books on the vexed question of the proper attitude to the fair sex- we both agree that Hindus must abandon chivalry for artillery- though I must admit I haven't yet worked myself up to actually dealing out blows to the little dears, considering it prudent to confine myself to chucking my teddy bear in their general direction before hysterically bursting into tears..

Like Naipaul, I too revere Mahatma Gandhi- a strenuous wife-beater of the best type- and identify with him- though my literary output is less voluminous- precisely because he too returned to India with fresh eyes and could see things which had become invisible to the natives. Simple things. Don't shit all over the place. Carry a spade with you and cover up your feces. As for this business of swinging from tree to tree eating bananas and hanging by your tails- that's got to stop. Granted the tourists like it- but I'm more than just a tourist- my ancestors came from India- so just fucking stop your monkey tricks already. You guys are making me look bad.

Returning to Shivprasad, it is comforting to think of him- like Mr.Biswas, in Naipaul's best novel- finding consolation in Marcus Aurelius and Samuel Simles. The rigor and majesty of the Latin Stoic- albeit in translation- and the homely message of the Victorian writer, may have given this very talented young man the courage to persevere rather than simply drown himself in rum or slink off to Venezuela.

Shivprasad's own English style was lively and adventurous and suffused with excellent observational humor and shrewd journalistic touches. But it wasn't the chastened prose of a University Graduate. It is tempting to envision Shivprasad, with Roman piety, passing on the torch to the young Naipaul- the torch in question being the notion that writing should serve a social purpose while simultaneously acting as a Stoic askesis, a spiritual and character building praxis, such that the writer doesn't end up simply battering his brains out against Civic walls but, Antaeus like, gains a renewed strength by judiciously alternating the target of his head-butts with the rocky breast of mother earth or some other such abstraction.

This, it seems to me, is not an ignoble project. It has special relevance to the middle aged blogger or small time columnist of low intelligence and narrow interests, who needs to beat his or her toy drum from time to time simply to find an outlet for the sort of nursery scoldings which, before the kids flew the coop, appeased one's paternal or maternal instincts.

After all, one could do worse- join some bunch of hate-mongering hooligans or write poetry or something.

Naipaul won a scholarship to Oxford at a very young age. He did not lack in filial piety. He wasn't a shy and withdrawn fellow but a witty and enterprising young man. His success seemed assured.

Naipaul's sister got a scholarship to Benares Hindu University. If the 'backwardness' of the Trinidad Hindoo was because they had been cut off from contact with the mother continent, then Naipaul's sister had that base covered.

Except of course, as that enterprising young woman swiftly realized, Benares had nothing to teach and everything to learn- except, that is, for intelligent people who might bother with Sanskrit and Prakrit and difficult stuff like that.

But Oxford too posed a problem. It seemed, the 'mother country-' whether India or England- could not provide what the Naipauls needed to keep their father's torch gloriously ablaze.

Why? Well, the truth was there nothing greatly the matter with the Hindu cane-cutters of Trinidad. They did well left to themselves, just as the Naipauls did well left to themselves. No great 'social reform' was necessary. So what if some village lads got into a lathi fight once in a while? *But, they are going to Muslim Pir's shrine for blessing on lathi! Is that not a betrayal of*

Religion? No. It's nonsense is what it is.

The Trinidad Hindus evolved a good communal religious life which Indian scholars have since commended and commented upon. They did well economically and educationally. If some Hindu guy wants to get drunk and chase tail- that's his choice, he is not 'bringing shame on his community'. If some other guy goes to Harvard and becomes a Brain Surgeon- good for him, it doesn't mean he is some sort of magical oracle or exemplar whom we must revere and follow unquestioningly.

The Naipauls' tragedy arises from a deeply materialistic and spiritually stagnant Society's indifference to the notion that literature can fulfill a great social purpose by telling people to like pick up your litter already and don't roll your eyes when I'm talking to you and for fuck's sake do you have to be so dark? Have you tried bleach? Fucking proles! They want to take my tax dollars to educate you thickies? This is Political Correctness gone mad! Rivers of blood, I say, rivers of blood will flow especially now that French Cambodian lady-boy David Cameron's got into Number 10.

V.S Naipaul did not do particularly well at Uni. One can scarcely blame him. Academic subjects like English or History or drunkenly getting gay with each other were no longer what they had been at the beginning of the 20's when Waugh went up. Indeed, the Second World War had changed the nature and function of literature, of literary culture, in a drastic fashion. Individuals no longer mattered. People might be permitted to hold opinions, even express them in some socially sanctioned way, but Truth was something churned out by Giant machines in which the salaried, State-trained, intellectual was an interchangeable cog. History no longer had a human scale. Well, perhaps with the aid of Gandalf the Grey, the hobbits of the shire could prevail over the blazing eye of Sauron, but as Naipaul, Tolkein's student, would surely have known, the Elvish rune for the Silmarillionic tuirgen was also (as Keshave Chandra Das Gupta has hinted in his magisterial study of Orcish) a homophone for the watery sigil of the voiceless Loerelei whose sodomizing of pygmies to gain supernatural powers (prompting, perhaps, Naipaul's remark that he found pygmies scarcely human) is the key to Pres. Obama's current Afpak strategy (vide Gayatri Spivak Chakravorty's Prolegomenon to all future Post Colonial Studies) .

Naipaul faced with the equally arid alternatives of mindless philology or I.A Richards being anally raped by analytical philosophy had nothing to learn at University and, with commendable industry, he applied himself to the task of learning nothing, observing nothing- a habit which has served him well throughout his long and illustrious literary prostitution. Not that he couldn't write elegantly or do a bit of actual research- 'the loss of El Dorado' aint utter crap- it's just History wasn't a mirror in which he could see his own face and so it had to go. So too did Economics and Politics and Science and... everything that has made the last fifty years such an exciting time to be alive.

Waugh, on the other hand, had a great sense for history, an instinctive understanding of economics- like others of his generation, he was confronted with the failure of Political Liberalism at a time when ideological positions were still very much in flux, dialogue- 'chatter' if you like- was as natural as getting drunk in the nearest dive; the febrile wit, the world weariness, the senile, sententious, Edwardian Socialism of Saki's salons had given place to something new. A great climacteric had been passed. Pieces could be picked up, but more than pieces there were new things, new ideas, new methods of analysis, a new understanding of the human mind born out of the terrible attrition of trench warfare, a new world view was there for whosoever cared to solder it together . Ideas mattered, literary excellence mattered- personality was a cult for the dandy not the dictator- much was recoverable, more was possible- with the innocence of children, Waugh's generation entered a Brave New World.

Not so, Naipaul's cohort entering Oxford under the chilling conditions of Post War Austerity-this would be a year or two after Orwell's 1984 came out- Britain had never had it so bad. Popular novelists of the period speak of amalgamation into the U.S.A or mass emigration to Australia as the only solution to Britain's seemingly insurmountable problems. Naipaul himself later applied for a job with the Indian High Commission!

People like Waugh might still provide literary banquets- and authors a few years his elder still engaged with ideas- but the new market was for processed food- T.V dinners for the suburbs and corned beef for the inner cities. Few, even in the 1970's, could have predicted Britain's phoenix like resurrection as a gastronomic super-power. Modesty forbids mention of my own achievements in this field- though I did once prepare a simple poached egg dish following a French recipe I found on the Internet- and I have it on good authority that my Salmonella is to die for.

Virtually nobody back in the 50's, except perhaps some mathematical economists or displaced Austrians, give us any inkling in their work of the importance our generation would later attach to things like property rights, mechanism design, markets, diversity as a driver of trade and development and so on all of which revive the role of the individual in his freely contracted social arrangements, the better understanding of which makes the novel, literary fiction, once again central to Civil Society and the Liberal Political Project.

Waugh understood these things. But, over the course of his life- his arduous treks in the wilderness seeking his own soul- he saw and learned something more. Civilization is all center and no periphery.

So is God.

Naipaul isn't God but he has made himself the center of the World he writes about. The Scandinavians- invoking, with Viking wit, its 'suppressed histories'- have given him a Prize for it. But what is that world? It is a world of darkness briefly illumined by his father's stories- *But the habits of mind engendered by this shut-in and shutting-out life lingered for quite a while. If it were not for the short stories my father wrote I would have known almost nothing about the general life of our Indian community. Those stories gave me more than knowledge. They gave me a kind of solidity. They gave me something to stand on in the world. I cannot imagine what my mental picture would have been without those stories.*

This, then is the key to Naipaul's dessicating art- his mummifying religion- his vast African spiritual safari which- like Proust's pilgrimage to Ruskin's Venice- occurred not in the sort of time counted off by the clock-face but that other type of time, Bergsonian duration, the Time which really counts- except it doesn't at all, Bergson was fucked in the head; what he says of Time can be said of anything- the door is opened to a Panalethism of a particularly silly sort- Iqbal's version of Islam, Naipaul's notion of everything including Islam- and the ungainsayable historical fact that the former cashed out as the latter.

Naipaul ends his Nobel lecture thus-

I will end as I began, with one of the marvellous little essays of Proust in Against Sainte-Beuve. "The beautiful things we shall write if we have talent," Proust says, "are inside us, indistinct, like the memory of a melody which delights us though we are unable to recapture its outline. Those who are obsessed by this blurred memory of truths they have never known are the men who are gifted... Talent is like a sort of memory which will enable them finally to bring this indistinct music closer to them, to hear it clearly, to note it down ..."
Talent, Proust says. I would say luck, and much labour.

So it seems, Waugh's nightmare vision of a man being forced to read Dickens to his illiterate jailer in the middle of the rain forest was no mere nightmare after all- it was a prophesy concerning the art-form he had advanced. Substitute Naipaul for Dickens and you begin to see how that might work.

Perhaps, as Borges was fond of saying, all books are by the same author. Or rather- what

Dickens and his ilk started, Naipaul and his ilk finished. Read Dickens as if Naipaul were writing him.Read Dickens aloud as if Naipaul were writing him and Waugh is standing there listening dumb-struck and appalled, having just stepped into this clearing in the jungle. Except there is no jungle. Waugh already knew that Naipaul would write Dickens. After all, Waugh had a dad who worked for Chapman & Hall who published Dickens. And Naipaul had a dad who once tried to help his community by publishing some stories and articles. It's not Jungles or Geography that matters. This kind of winding down is built into literature's 'duration'.

Suddenly becoming a Hare Krishna, or a Wicca Wizard or Sarah Palin or whatever don't look so bad. Except, of course, it's the same mumbo-jumbo as Literature. And African spirituality, African poetry, African Music- all of which, at one time, and perhaps still do in places, wove together everything which makes social life meaningful and worthwhile- are now sufficiently invoked, sufficiently explored, by a sneering reference to *muti* magic- for to such *muti* magic must all Literature, all High Finance, inevitably devolve.

Only thus, and not otherwise, now Patrick French has done for Naipaul what he so signally failed to do for himself, can, at age of 78, Naipaul- not a good man, but ***our man***, in Africa- finally telegraph us his scoop.

Violence as Virtue Ethics

Dipping into a book by Nicholas Gier got me thinking- you heard me right folks, I said thinking not drinking- has there ever been a philosopher or prophet or politician or any other sort of fuckwit whatsoever who has actually ***advocated*** Violence?

Hilter? No he denounced violent opposition to himself in very vehement terms. Genghis Khan? No, he greatly disapproved of violent opposition to himself and delivered great masses of people from this detestable vice.

Hitler never used violent means to secure his aim- viz. the end of violent opposition to himself. He never actually shot anybody or slapped anybody or even knifed them a little bit. Those who were ***already violent*** removed others- violent or not- whose counsel, example, or relative sanctity such as is conferred by mere continued existence, might have led those same men of blood to like mebbe one day violently oppose Hitler or something. In other words Violence *used itself* as the means to come to the particular state of absolute and eternal non-violence that Hitler enjoined.

It may be true that a good end can not be achieved by bad means. But, nothing enjoins an officious striving to prevent a bad end frustrating itself by bad means such that a good end is achieved, albeit with little or no assistance from good means.

We can turn any historical figure, no matter how brutal or blood-soaked, into a champion of non-violence by positing him or her to be a mere Kagemusha, or shadow warrior, to the true protagonist, occulted by the chronicles, who wills that non-violent end state which violence aims at.

Assuming brain modularity, Principal Agent hazard (of the sort mentioned above) arises in even a one person, one time period, model- one can be violent to oneself by reason of preference falsification or Kavka's toxin. Any argument against what I'm saying here is going to have to admit that it assumes, and thus only has relevance to, a world where brains didn't evolve or look nothing our own. But, even so, such arguments are wasted words coz of the Thomas Nagel **Bat problem.**

What about a theory of Violence as a Virtue Ethics? What would a philosopher of violence look like? No, not Nietzche- give the guy a break, he was a syphilitic lunatic, not to say German philologist, and thus mentally incompetent to impose a poset on what he valorized- but maybe Merlin's King Arthur or some such mythical beast who insists every moral, that is deontic, or non alethic issue or question be settled only by violence. This would need to be a violent agon, otherwise there is no partial ordering of states of the world signified by the word Violence. To see why consider the following case- I cut your throat after you have stuck your head under a guillotine and let fall the blade. If you did this to escape my knife, I still am credited with a lot of violence. If however you did it for some other reason and neither knew or cared about my plan to cut your throat- the amount of violence I have actually perpetrated is considerably diminished. Essentially, the more causal chains having bearing on us both, the more difficult it will be to establish a partial ordering of states of the world such that Violence can be measured or states of the world ranked with respect to its criteria. In practise, the only tractable way to establish a Violence metric is to recast every interaction as a 2 person violence agon- even if it is both multi-agent as well as diachronous- with some ad hoc weighting formula for working out the contribution of each agent at different times. (This is Newtonian substantivism as opposed to the mirage of Leibnizian relationism.)

But even with a pure two person violent agon the problem arises that I won't fight unless I get a positive Expected value for the Outcome- so there has to be a reward and a threshold probability of winning that reward. You may say, well, I'll kill you if you don't fight. But, all that then happens is, I choose the option that minimizes my own pain and suffering, not the one that maximizes the amount of violence I do and/or provoke. So, if Violence- as opposed to a utilitarian calculus of costs and benefits arising out of *perceived tastes and potentials* for violence- is going to be in a position to actually to decide anything of moral or non alethic import- i.e. if it is to be a virtue ethics- it has to ensure two things

1) **Symmetry and 'Balanced Gaming'** (Notice Non-Violence does not demand Symmetry for its practice- thus it throws away information and is dissipative) Formally this means all violent conflicts must have random outcomes- assuming all agents are risk neutral.

However, suppose Iyers are more cowardly than Iyengars- this is empirically true of Iyer males when matched against Iyengar females- then Iyengars must be suitably handicapped (I suggest they not be allowed to pull my hair or punch me in the fatty portion of my arm) and Iyers properly armed and armoured.

2) **Impredicative Pareto efficiency**- the setting up of the conflict situation must involve an outward shift in the production possibility frontier such that both parties to the violence can, at least theoretically, be made better off. In other words the purse for the prize fight must always exceed the sum of losses on both sides. Suppose, the reverse were the case- e.g. if I say 'you and your sister must fight each other to the death to decide who gets the hush money you are extorting from me for not telling your Mum and Dad that I let you stay up with me to watch 'Frightnight' even though they'd specifically said I wasn't allowed to watch it coz it makes me pee the couch and what sort of babysitters are they sending us nowadays anyway?'

The problem is, to make sure you and your sister actually fight each other to the death, I have to import extra violence into the scenario. There has to be a credible threat that you will both die more painful and lingering deaths by refusing combat. But, from the first principle (viz

Symmetry) this extra violence can't arise. Thus, unlike Non-Violence or Justice as Fairness or other such pi jaw, Violence as Virtue Ethics is impredicatively Pareto efficient.

But, if these two conditions are satisfied then- for the first time in its life- Ethics would actually yield something Ethical. Thus, not only is Violence (as opposed to non-violence) a Virtue Ethics- it is the only Virtue Ethics which don't fuck things up big time.

This is a snippet from Gier's book which invokes the always hilarious Raghavan Iyer-

> revealed truth. Furthermore, I will argue that even though Gandhi uses the language of Vedānta, it is a Pāli Buddhist view of the self as a process rather than permanent substance that best suits his political activism and pragmatic concept of nonviolence. Gandhi's experiments with truth imply the intimate connection between moral actions and the particular facts of the world that informs the mindful action of a Buddhist *satyāgrahi*. Garfield

> himself admits that Gandhi would agree with the following proposition: "Effective action requires not just (or perhaps not at all) a grasp of theory, not just a harmony of action with the fundamental nature of reality, but also awareness of the concrete details of the immediate context of action. A firm grasp of the details of the action-context and insistence on the particular facts against obfuscation or error is constitutive of *satyāgraha*."[5]
>
> A principal thesis of this book is that Vedāntist philosophy, particularly the Advaita Vedānta with which Gandhi is usually associated, cannot support this "action-context" ethics. As Raghavan Iyer states, "Gandhi's radical reinterpretation of Hindu values in the light of the message of the Buddha was a constructive, though belated, response to the ethical impact of the early Buddhist Reformation on decadent India."[6] This is the first book-length attempt to work out the full implications of Iyer's observation.

This sort of psilosophy- funny though it is- only works by ignoring the obvious, context specific, FACTS- to wit, Buddhism is fucked in the head coz it says being a Buddhist monk is a good thing and everybody should want to be re-born as a Buddhist monk so as to then get to be not re-born at all. There have been plenty of Buddhist countries- the Japanese banned meat for a thousand years so as to concentrate on slicing each other up, the Tibetans and Outer Mongolians suffered under vile Buddhist theocracies, Thailand still is pretty Buddhist but scarcely a model of 'action-context' ethics. As for Vedanta- it can support any fucking thing you please. Just give a Vedantist a couple of quid or threaten him with a beating and he will fix it for you. Buddhism creates a karma-based, indefeasible, Caste system whereas Brahminism lets you pay a bit of money or threaten priests with a beating and get turned into a Kshatriya or a Brahmin, or God or whatever you like.

Prof. Gier ignores the kerygmatic kernel of Buddhism. Instead he substitutes a fantasy of his own -*The Buddha's famous statement "a person who sees causation, sees the Dharma" implies that we know how to act, not because of abstract rules, but because of our causal past and circumstances. The "mirror of dharma" is not a common one that we all look into together, but it is actually a myriad of mirrors reflecting individual histories. Maintaining the essential link between fact and value, just as Greek virtue ethics did, the Buddha demonstrated that the truth about our causal relations dictates the good that we ought to do.'*

Buddhism subscribes to kshanika vada- the doctrine of momentariness. What Buddha saw in Causation and what he pronounced as Dharma is that there is no past, no future, there is just this bare and empty moment briefly illumined by the thunderbolt of the intention. It is this bizarre feature of Buddhist ontology which permits its relationism. But this is a sham relationism because it is excused not being able to found a dynamic because it is always a one period Universe. You can have relationism in a multi period Universe- like that of Malebranche or Leibniz- but then you get pure Occasionalism. God does everything. I don't know if Gier understands why a tractable relationist dynamic is a pie in the sky we'd all dearly love to eat coz it would solve every computing or physics or whatever problem- but, sure, if Buddhism or Gandhism or some such shit actually has solved this problem then yes we all need to study it and that really would be a non-shite Ethics. But it's a pipe dream is all it is. Gandhi's

contemporaries knew Gandhi was a fuckwit, just as I know Maharishi Mahesh Yogi or the hilarious weight-lifting Chinmoy and so on were either mad or bad or both. Gier is saying Buddhism has solved the concurrency problem for a relational dynamics. But this is no different from saying Maharishi actually discovered how to levitate and also how to make Yogic levitation help end War. I can't prove it isn't true, its just that if it is true than the Buddhists are mean spirited bastards coz they could totally revolutionize physics and medical science and Econ and computing and so on instead of just passing round the begging bowl all the time.

The more charitable explanation, of course, is that all these so called Virtue ethics 'isms' are just plain deluded, degenerate or disingenuous .

Certainly there is a bunch of lies one can tell at this moment, if one is a well intentioned little Buddhist, which paint a picture, ad captum vulgi, of like how being nice & anger-management and being sure to give lots of money to Buddhist monks is the way you'll get to be re-born as one and take it from me that's actually a good thing coz then you get a shot at an all expenses paid one way ticket to Nirvana-land! Yay!

Reality check, Prof Gier! Buddhist monks aint necessarily nice guys- they boast their share of arrogant fuckwits who get off on genocide same as Croatian Franciscans or Cambodian Khmer Rouge nutjobs or those Lord's Army loonytoons in Uganda.

Buddhism is fucked coz it disingenuously markets itself as Transmigration based though that is just a fairy tale; I really wasn't Queen Cleopatra in my last life. I just made that up so as to get out of doing the washing up is all. Ad captum vulgi, Buddhism, like every other Religion, Ideology or faked Mental Illness is a bunch of stupid lies strung together by parasitical cunts who get off on feeling superior to everybody else. To say Gandhi- a narcissistic fuckwit who believed crap, talked crap, and was a massive turd- was more of a Buddhist fuckwit turd than a Hindu fuckwit turd is silly.   Shit is shit. We all produce it. None of us, at the margin, are obliged to consume it. At least, not once we understand Violence *is* Virtue Ethics.

  Remember the peasants of Wardha? '*Not long ago, as the Gandhians in the Gandhi stronghold Wardha region were opposing the development of large heavy industry, one could hear people making comments about their bad fortune that of all the areas available in India, Gandhi had to choose theirs to settle in, and as a consequence, because of his many followers in the region, they will not have the development projects which would give them and their children work opportunities.*
With all the Gandhian institutions which have grown up in this area, why is this not a model of Gandhian utopia? Why is Sevagram still just a dirty Indian village? Why do the locals consider the Gandhians still in their midst as irrelevant, or at times worse?'

  (BTW, why do people blame Gandhi for everything? The person responsible for that shit-head setting up shop in Wardha was Jamnalal Bajaj. Like Birla, Bajaj had the right stuff to be a great industrialist. But he fell harder for Gandhi's silliness and ended up looking after cows or something equally shit-headed. Perhaps there's a *khap panchayat,* Indian Industrialists belong to, which makes it obligatory for them to endorse utterly silly ideologies in proportion to their capacity to enrich themselves?)   In any case, Wardha is actually a success story. When Gandhi's Ashramites tried fucking with the villagers, they told them to fuck off. This is Violence as Virtue ethics- you don't pull a gun in a knife fight, you don't shoot Gandhi unless he's drawn his pistol and has taken aim and so the outcome isn't a foregone conclusion. When these fuckwits start telling lies and pretending what they are doing is philosophy, tell lies and pretend you're a philosopher- true, the stupider one will win, but, with all humility, admit to yourself- it mightn't be you.

This is from Prof. Gier's silly book 'The virtue of non-violence'

The concept of a permanent self underlying the phenomenal self is one idea that Gandhi does sometimes appropriate from the Upaniṣadic tradition. ("Everything is transient, except the *ātman*.")[23] Roy supports this view of self in his retelling, from the *Panchatantra*, of the parable of the tiger cub.[24] One day a tiger, while planning an attack on a herd of goats, sees a tiger cub among them. The tiger takes the cub to a pond so that he can see in his own reflection that he is not a goat. After some adjustment the tiger cub eventually realizes his true predatory nature. Even though brought into the greatest dramatic relief by this story, Roy does not seem to realize the negative implications of the permanent self for the practice of *ahiṃsā*. He should have used recent experiments that have shown that aggressive monkeys, raised from birth with pacifist monkeys, learn the nonviolent behavior of their adopted parents and siblings.[25]

After explaining this story in terms of the unchanging *ātman*, Roy inexplicably turns to Gandhi's view that, although we have an animal nature, we can tap our spiritual natures and learn to become nonviolent. Interestingly enough, Gandhi uses the same story (substituting a lion for the tiger and sheep for goats), but he clearly distinguishes animals from humans, created in the image of God, who are free and obligated to change their animal natures.[26] Ironically, the tiger cub story is not compatible with any of the Indian selves, because the spiritually pure and empty *ātman*, *jīva*, and *puruṣa* are, strictly speaking, neither predatory nor nonpredatory. In a response, Roy chides me for being unable to distinguish between analogy and metaphor.[27] The relation of the cub's unchanging nature to his violent actions is obviously not analogous to our changing nature's capacity to turn away from violence. If the story is a metaphor for realizing our own unchanging natures, then it fails to convey Gandhi's point about our ability to change. If the story is simply a metaphor for self-realization, then the point is very weak indeed.

Prof Gier aint an Indologist so, fair play to him, his error here isn't what damns his book. Gandhi, like me, knows the story of the tiger (or lion) from the Jains

Just as a lion cub, from birth, by sheep solely reared
But scenting a lion, separates from the herd
E'en so obeisance to the Arhat reveals our own Nature
The inner Self we possess being of the Arhat's own Stature.

As I explain, in my book **Samlee's daughter**, Jainism which, unlike Buddhism, does actually have a relationist dynamic (*parinami dravya*)- that too one featuring discrete selves unable to directly participate or operate on other selves- uses the parable of the tiger cub to show that our instinct to show reverence to the Arhat arises not from his/her manifest superiority, or the hope of blessings or magical help from him or her, but- rather- from the feeling that we too belong to the same species as the Arhat. The tiger cub, instinctively showing affection to the Tiger he has scented but never before seen, sets in motion by that 'innate releasing mechanism' the process of learning how to be a Tiger. Thus, though visiting the Jain Ashram, this worthless Iyer too went around prostrating himself at the feet of the slower moving Sadhavis, the fact is there was nothing hypocritical or self-seeking or superstitious about such behaviour.

Prof. Gier thinks Tiger means 'Violent person' and sheep means 'non-violent person'. This is not the case. Amongst human beings, there is one class known as 'Tigers-amongst-men'. In Sanskrit they are called Kshatriyas. They don't go round killing for the sake of it, but they never refuse a fair fight- i.e. one where there is an at least 50-50 chance of being killed. That's why this class whose duty is Violence, developed a Virtue Ethic of Violence whose dynamic result (*parninami dravya*) is called Ahimsa or Anurashamsya. The message of the Mahabharata is 'The Tigers and the Forest are interdependent. Without the forest, the Tigers perish. If the Tigers die the Forest will not remain'. Notice, every Jain Tirthankar- except Mahavir- began life in a Kshatriya womb. Mahavir, too was born from a Kshatriya womb, but he started life in a Brahmin womb till somebody upstairs realized that it would never do for a Tirthankar- a, by definition, Tiger-among-sheep- to be born from the same sort of womb as, albeit black sheepishly, yours truly.

   (Incidentally, I may mention a homology with Nund Reshi's (**Hazrat Noorudin Wali**) nativity story such as who runs may read.)

   Gandhiji- esentially a good guy, a smart enough guy till people started whacking him on the head and he evinced symptoms of unhealed head trauma, a genuinely loving guy, NOT a fucking stick to beat us Indians with if we want the same toys other kids have- had the great good fortune to meet and know Raichandbhai Mehta (**Srimad Rajachandra**) and thus Gier should be referencing His Holiness's view of *samyaktva* rather than some crap faux Buddhist shite. My point is, Jains only insist on proper Monastic habilitation because of the hubris related risk of pursuing austerities on one's own. This is different from the faux Buddhist notion- like Steven Segal being a fucking Tulku- that becoming a Monk means you're better than other people. Jain laymen (*shravaks*), like H.H. Rajachandra or Banarsidas etc, have, I believe, become perfected such that sallekhana for them, once they had out-worn their body, is not distasteful or horrifying.

   The Buddha is supposed to have said about Jainism 'a frightful (*ghora*) religion is born!' But compare Jainism's death by 'Sallekhana' -self-starvation to halt the ingress of karma binding particles- to Japanese Buddhism's **Sokushinbutsu**, a truly horrendous process drawn out over many years of self-mummification by starvation, arsenic poisoning and being buried alive in a sepulchre.

Sokushinbutsu

To her whose mode of Being was Beauty
Whose charm of life, but Charm
Death is derelict to its Duty
& Hestia hapless to harm.

So Momus carp at Hephaistos' Art
No window has Man to the heart
Yet I, my Mum's mere gestate
Thus am marred & defenestrate.

Tear born Tara suckles all Thus Gone
To self-mummify Mum was I thus born?
Her love, milk- more!- the river of stars
Mine, arsenic, drunk dial'd from bars

A Sokushinbutsu

There's a free book on the internet called 'Stripping the Gurus' which has plenty to say about Buddhist and Hindu and (praise God, just the one!) Sikh charlatans. There is a Jain in it too. Rajneesh. But that cunt was never fucking Jain- though he was bright enough- and ended his life calling himself 'Osho' which is Japanese for 'fuck you very much and gimme a Rolls Royce already.'

Pratyekas supervene on Boddhisatvas?

A Pratyeka Buddha is a 'hidden' Buddha who, however, does not start up a proper Sangha, or monastic community, for which salvation consists of waxing fat on a lazy doctrine while putting the squeeze on the laity for donations and forcing dalits to do the dirty work under conditions of more wretched yet social opprobrium.

A Bodhisattva is not less than a Pratyeka Buddha- he has attained the prize- which is a phenomenal state- but he has a different intentional state- viz. he wishes to save other sentient beings by getting them to understand that the Jains and the Ajivikas and all other Sraman denominations- not to mention the Carvaka materialists- are totally fucked in the head and could everybody kindly be very very shitty to 'low caste' people- coz they don't got 'right livelihood-' and like immediately become a monk or hand us monks loads of money already?

Clearly, Pratyeka Buddhahood supervenes on Boddhisatvahood- in the sense that every Boddhisatva is indistinguishable from the stand-point of any Pratyeka specific measure- but the reverse is not the case. Two instances of Pratyeka Buddhahood can always be distinguished from the Boddhisatva perspective as approaching closer or standing in some relation to itself. (Either that, or Pratyekas are **'zombie'** Buddhas and can't have 'real' intentionality.) But, why should this be?

One answer is that the Times weren't right for the Pratyeka to set up a Sangha. In this case, there is some phenomenal state that supervenes- is multiply realizable across both Pratyekas and Boddhisatvas- but some 'cetana' or intentional state which does not similarly supervene. Why? Is it because sentient beings capable of Entanglement, as in the Avatamsaka or Vimalakirti 'Buddha field', do not exist? If so, something is added to the concept of Intentionality and something taken away from the scope of Phenomenology.

But Phenomenology does not disappear. The intention to be a Boddhisatva does not make you a Boddhisatva. You have to first instantiate in your phenomenal series that supervenient Pratyekadom otherwise you're just a wannabe.

Since, the Bodhhisatva 'cetana' or intentional state has supervenience- i.e. is multiply realizable- only if the ground for an entangled Buddhafield is ready at hand, an Occassionalist doctrine suggests itself as an (non) explanation for why the Pratyeka phenomenal state does not reduce to Bodhisattvadom.

In other words, Phenomenology and its dual Occasionalism re-appear in Buddhism as the two sides of the coin of 'Nothingness' which it cashes out as. Indeed, only the name of the coin changes, nothing sensible ever gets uttered, in this as in every other variety of peripatetic fraud or soteriological chicanery whose pious cultivation ensures we will always have more monks than reason.

Are we killing Mahatma Gandhi all over again?

An anguished soul asks me *'when we receive or give black money- thick wads of currency notes with Mahatma Gandhi's face upon them- are we not guilty of killing him all over again?'*

I have thought about the matter and now give my judgement.
1) No. You say you killed the guy. I've checked. He really is dead. So you aren't killing him all over again even if you are paying or receiving a lot of Rupees to do it. In legal terms, such an action falls under the category of impossible attempt.
2) I forget whether you and your chums claimed credit for raping Gandhi while killing him last

time round. The truth is I tend to let my mind wander when the topic of the Mahatma comes up. Still, it is not unreasonable for me to proceed on the assumption that you chaps both raped and killed Gandhi and now are seeking information from me as to whether you are succeeding once again in perpetrating the same faux pas.

On reflection, no- I think that what you are guilty of is necrophilia, gross indecency and mutilating a corpse.

I hope this answers your question.
Posted 18th November 2011 by windwheel
  Comments

1.

AnonymousNov 18, 2011 05:05 PM

There are many instances of necrophiliac mortuary attendants causing dead people to come back to life. Thus your judgement is incorrect and based on apriori reasoning without proper empirical inquiry. Please contact the person who asked you the question and ascertain whether, in the course of the necrophiliac rape of the late M.K Gandhi, corpse has been re-animated and thus become available for purposes of re-slaughter.

ReplyDelete

2.

windwheelNov 18, 2011 05:44 PM

@Anon- the question as asked was 'are we not guilty of killing Gandhi all over again?' Clearly the questioner had, together with some confreres, killed Gandhi at some point in the past. Whether Rape also occurred was not specified but quite reasonably inferred. You say that while raping the mortal remains of M.K. Gandhi, the questioner may have succeeded in bringing him back to life. If so, the questioner could not have been guilty of killing him in the first place any more than a doctor, who stops the heart of a patient, but then revives him, could be considered guilty of murder. Now, you may argue that the questioner in using the word 'guilty' does not mean legal guilt but moral culpability and remorse. But why should the questioner feel such remorse and moral culpability if indeed, as you suggest, his or her act of necrophiliac rape restored life to the Mahatma? After all, there is no obstacle to the perpetrator of this heinous act from killing Gandhi (a famous passive resister) again. Why then should the questioner say 'are we not guilty of killing Gandhi again?'

In my opinion, this is a case where a priori reasoning, independent of an examination of empirical evidence, can provide an apodictic judgement.

ReplyDelete

3.

AnonymousNov 18, 2011 05:56 PM

@windwheel- You overlook the possibility that your questioner in saying 'are we not guilty &c' may have meant *not* 'are me and certain associates of mine not guilty &c' but *'are you and I not guilty &c'*. Suppose you had commissioned, instigated or otherwise facilitated the original act of rape and murder and thus shared criminal guilt, suppose further your motivation was different from that of the questioner, in this case the construction you put upon the quoted statement does not, a priori, rule out the sort of consideration raised in my last. Thus, here as elsewhere in Jurisprudence, a priori reasoning proves non apodictic. Only empirical investigation can give rise to justified true belief.

ReplyDelete

4.

AnonymousNov 18, 2011 06:07 PM

@windwheel- thank you for proving my point. You may have apodictic certainty re your non-involvement in the rape and murder of MK Gandhi. However, you can't have apodictic certainty re. what the questioner believes regarding your degree of culpability in that distasteful affair.

Even more crucially, in presenting a judgement as anything other than a personal opinion or conclusion based on private knowledge, both facts and reasoning from those facts must be set out otherwise how am I or any third party supposed to get justified true belief- let alone apodictic certainty- from your statement?

ReplyDelete

5.

AnonymousNov 18, 2011 06:43 PM

@windwheel- once again you beg the question. You say a man can only be killed once. This is patently untrue. A person can be raped and killed by one person, or set of people, at one time. Those people can be properly charged with rape and murder and hanged (if such be the law of the land) for the crime. At a later point, that same person may, during the course of a necrophiliac assault, come back to life only to be once again done to death. The person or persons responsible may, quite legally, be charged with rape and murder and hanged in their turn.

   Your argument, which you accept is a priori and without empirical backing, assumes that every physical body dies only once. But, you have not offered an a priori argument for why that should be the case. What if it is found that some medical procedure can re-infuse life into a corpse even after hundreds of years?   How can you decide a question, which only the progress of science can categorically affirm or provisionally reject, that too by appealing to a priori reasoning?

In this context, you may kindly ponder Beenaker's boundary as resolving Hempel's dilemma. Beenaker argues that if the Universe is a computer and if constants- like the speed of light, or Plack's constant- don't evolve in an inflationary manner, and if the Universe has an end in time, then certain problems- such as the question of the immortality of the soul- will always remain metaphysical because there isn't enough time to do the necessary computations to reduce the question to one of physics.

ReplyDelete

6.

windwheelNov 18, 2011 06:45 PM

Yes, I see what you mean about Hempel's dilemma, but does it really apply in this case? The fact is we have testimony that a particular person was involved in two acts of rape and murder. However, since only one person- the late M.K. Gandhi- suffered this indignity and inconvenience, surely only one occasion for guilt (at least with respect to the offence of unlawful killing) arises.

Please explain to me how the same person can be charged twice with killing the same person.

ReplyDelete

7.

AnonymousNov 18, 2011 06:59 PM

In this instance there are two separate crimes. Firstly, the rape and murder of MK Gandhi in which your culpability may have been diminished by reason of being a minor, secondly the rape and murder of the reanimated remains of MK Gandhi, in which your culpability may be diminished by some other reason for e.g. senile dementia.

Clearly the reanimated MK Gandhi- whose estate long ago passed to his heirs- has a different legal personality, though what precisely that might be is open to conjecture. Though your necrophiliac rape of the esteemed but deceased senior citizen may have been instrumental in giving him a second lease of life, yet your own brute lust and sadism may have condemned him to a second unsavoury death.

Your defence attorney may well try to use your argument so as to reduce your culpability, but it is an empirical matter as to how the Judges will rule.

From a Utilitarian perspective, you and your confreres deprived Mahatma Gandhi of life twice. Once when you originally raped and killed him- thus preventing him from fulfilling his natural span- and secondly when you once again brutally raped and murdered him- depriving him not of his original natural span but one, perhaps, much extended in a Century he would never otherwise have lived to see.

ReplyDelete

8.

windwheelNov 18, 2011 07:16 PM

I think you're somewhat missing the point of my post. The real culprit is David Cameron. Something very shifty about that young fellow. Not that David Milliband is any better. Rahul Gandhi had better watch out. Frankly, this country is really going to the dogs now all the shirt lifters have taken over Parliament.

It's Downing St. you should be fighting, not me.

Not just Downing St. Look at what Obama's up to. Now I come to think of it, Gandhi's sudden reanimation coincided suspiciously well with Obama's campaign...

I think there's much more to this than just a bunch of randy mortuary attendants. 'Follow the money' is what Deep Throat said to Woodward & Bernstein. But this Gandhi business is much bigger than Watergate.

Come to think of it, this ties in with the US Visa ban on Narendra Modi... I seem to recall some of Gandhi's ashes being recovered a couple of years ago in the States...there's dark doings afoot. Make no mistake, we haven't seen the last of the Mahatma. They'll be raping and murdering him all over again for some nefarious purpose probably to do with the financial meltdown and stuff.

Jai Hind!

Gandhian economics- rape whistle or strategic incontinence?

Ethics, we all know, is that portion of Philosophy whose study enables good people to turn into evil little shits working an evil more comprehensive than their pointy little heads would otherwise have capacity to envisage.

Gandhian Economics, being Ethical in motivation, has long been used as the equivalent of a rape whistle when talking about Development.

However, in so far as it is effective against actual rapists- like Bill and Melinda Gates- it is solely by reason of the enormous amounts of vomit, urine and faeces that are simultaneously emitted making noisome the vicinity of all orifices in danger of imminent violation.

Such being the case, the question may thus be posed- is Gandhian economics a rape whistle or is it actually strategic incontinence? All Indian Discourse, as Ranajit Guha has pointed out, is merely the meretricious Methodenstreit that must arise in this connection.

Rape-aXe for the Mind.

What makes it urgent for us to find a resolution to this question is news of a free market solution to rape that's got real teeth- Rape-aXe- a latex sheath, invented by a South African woman, worn like a tampon, with razor sharp barbs guaranteed to disable the assailant and requiring surgical intervention to remove.

Needless to say, Career Feminists are up in arms against it coz ...urm... it's like the medieval chastity belt? and like women back then really wanted to get pregnant? and like die horribly in child-birth? and that's why Patriarchy invented chastity belts? like to police and control wimmins' sexuality? and, it's like discrimination? coz how come men don't gotta wear them? (Honey, trust me, we men do gotta wear 'em, at least if we want to travel on the Northern Line during rush hour and keep intact our darling little anal cherries for when you suddenly decide to hurry things along a bit and anyway you're getting your nails done tomorrow.)

What about Rape Axe for the Mind? There's bound to be a way to tap some of that Venture Capitalist silly money, we keep hearing about, by dressing it up as the next big iPhone app or something.

What?

It already exists and has been patented?!

No, I hadn't heard about Marxism's mutilated dick.

Still, serves it right for trying to force itself on the Bengali bhadralok.

It kinda gives u the warm fuzzies for Ranajit Guha don't it? Still, best to avoid not just the parts of Vienna, Guha currently illuminates with his Red Light, but the whole of Austria (recently revealed as ten times as corrupt as Germany)- coz, well, there's only so much temptation flesh & blood can bear you know.

Spivak and the Genesis of the Post Colonial Subject-

'Spivak, like Sen, is no leaden doctrinaire pundit but, being engaged in mere maidenly fending off of a historically inevitable Marxist deflowering, actually quite nimble and inoffensive in her affectation of meretricious *Methodenstreit* which might intimately seductive seem- as to a Jock a cheery cheerleader's mime of sucking Satan's cock, while Satan choose to remain unseen - so to excite that drunken old Noah, detritus of Capitalism's deluge, thus bringing to birth the episteme of the dark skinned Post Colonial Subject- by means, the Talmud tells us, of his own sodomy and (by reason of too rough a reach-around) castration at Ham's ham-fisted hands. '

Discuss in no more than 1500 words or 1200 gratuitous references to Badiou.
(Excerpted from the new Admission Test for Kindergarten at my old alma mater, now the Right to Education Bill has been passed.)

The war against Poverty should be waged like the war against Terrorism

Let us make no mistake, *pace* Arundhati Roy, in confronting the Naxal threat we are fighting two wars- a war against Terrorism for which we are eager and well armed as opposed to a war against Poverty for which we are unprepared and pusillanimous.

As Christopher Hitchens has pointed out, to truly fight Terrorism, we must regularly sodomise it and make fun of its penis. However, there are important cultural and historical reasons why, in the Indian context, fucking Poverty in the ass while saying 'you like that don't you, you little retard, say you like it you fucking retard bitch,' is felt to be transgressive of widely held social and religious norms.

Yet, it is a matter of common observation, that battling the evils of entrenched Casteism and institutionalized misogyny, has always involved fraternization between antagonists for recreational sex, drugs and rock & roll.

Why should this paradigm not be extended to the war against Poverty, Corporate Greed, and Jennifer Aniston coming on like time has stood still and she's still hot?

These are important questions- vital questions- which, as per usual, the pseudo secularists of the Media have no interest in raising.

Repressive Desublimation and Natural Disasters.

Thousands of years ago, during the Golden Sangam Age, the peaceful deliberations of a convocation of learned scholars was threatened by a turbulent flood, not or words, but water as the sacred Kaveri overboiled its <u>banks</u>. Acting with aplomb, the Scholars immediately conferred upon it a Phd, in *honoris causa*, upon which it sank back into that torpor which distinguishes those upon whom Higher Education has left its mark.

More recently, especially since the Sixties and Seventies of the last Century, the Academy has used a similar tactic in dealing with modes of thought and models of discourse considered subversive to existing structures of power. In line with Marcuse's notion of 'repressive desublimation' as underlying the so-called 'Permissive Society's' strategy of saving the Military-Industrial complex and the National Security State from the wrath of the women's movement which, Lysistrata like, was seducing young men from their duty as canon fodder, it is tempting to speak of a sort of **Academic** repressive desublimation- or let us say an arid Intellectualising away of the green sap of dissent- as characterising the mainsprings of Political theory in the last few decades.

It is now urgent the same approach be extended to tsunamis and other natural disasters. I propose the creation of an Academic body, of the highest status and **financial** solvency, for the specific puprose of granting degrees not just to animals and plants but also such tectonic plates as may have grown restive due to their lack of access to higher education.

All babies- as I believe is already best practice in Bihar- should receive PhD in Gramscian Grammatology by the age of one, unless they are naughty in which case an MPhil from Cambridge in Development Studies will suffice to teach them the error of their ways.

Credentialism and failed programs

Why do failed programs- political or research- continue to clutter up Gesture politics and Post Graduate studies? It is now possible to do a structured PhD in Gandhian Economics at a Center of Gandhian Economic Thought in Hyderabad!

Why is this happening?

The old answer would have been cognitive dissonance. It's like what happens when Christ says he's coming back from the Grave and the Apocalypse goin' down reel soon y'all. (This was Radhakrishnan's theory). The early Xtians are holed up in their caves waiting for the shit storm and... nothing happens. So some quit the Church and get jobs and stuff. The others, because of cognitive dissonance, go to the other extreme. The now think Christ is actually God almighty, except no God ever before had been quite so Mighty, and so the thing to do was grovel down before him while being careful to chow down regular on his flesh and blood- comfort eating, it's what got me through the last Supernatural hiatus.

Like I said, that was the old answer. It don't work anymore. Why? Coz nobody doing a PhD in Gandhian Shite believes it aint a pile of crap. Nobody watching Hazare thought the guy was really gonna starve himself. And yeah passing some silly Lokpal law is gonna get rid of corruption. That will definitely happen.

Tell me about your period?

It has long been in my mind to write a brief guide to etiquette for Oriental sojourners in London, the Capital <u>City</u> of the British Empire.

Perhaps, the social custom which occasions the visitor most discomfort is that whereby, at dinner, a gentleman is seated between two ladies with whom, strictly in turn, it is obligatory to converse.

Bear in mind, it is considered unseemly to turn the conversation to abstruse metaphysical or nakedly erotic themes. Nor does it do to be very pertinacious in inquiry, or overly solicitous, with reference to such matters as fall within the ken of the female mind. A happy medium is struck by asking, in a tone of well bred indifference, the question- 'tell me about your period?'- especially given that Oriental guests are invariably seated between ladies of great antiquity who may well be flattered by the suggestion that they remain subject to that form of abject uncleanness.

My illustrious student, the late Sir Syed Ahmed Khan, improved upon my suggested opening by deploying a whole repertoire of conversational gambits such as- "Cor! that must make your eyes water!", or 'Nice **weather** for ducks!" and of course "Shame about that hat!" which tended to keep things humming along nicely and gained him an enviable reputation as a modern Rouchefoucauld.

In less able hands, however,- here, I am regretfully obliged to refer to the scion of a cadet branch of the distinguished Bengali **family** which glories in the hereditary right to hold the '*Chattri*' over, H.E, the Governor General at the Calcutta Durbar- even the most rigorous repetition of the question "tell me about your period?" does not always prevent the conversation from flagging and, in consequence, young Rabindranath was obliged to cover his head in ashes and consent to rustication on his family's country estates.

In my next book, I will write about the disastrous impact, on the conduct of the second Round Table Conference, of Barrister Mohandas's (not, it must be said, unprecedented) gaffe in addressing the question 'tell me about your period?' to, not the Dowager Queen Alexandra, as he supposed, but His Serene Highness, the Aga Khan.

Conclusion

I think it was Mahatma Gandhi who said 'The Earth produces enough to satisfy every man's *need* for clients, but not enough to satisfy the **greed of even a single of those clients** if they start to **think like consumers** and realize that they're paying through the nose for shitheads like me and you to patronize them; therefore we must all condemn consumerism and eating nice things and wearing nice clothes and medicines which actually work and other such godlessness because it is just not environmentally sustainable- people like you and me would go fucking extinct if we don't all work together to fucking squash this consumerism business right now.'

President Kennedy, on the other hand, said in his inauguration address- 'Don't you be coming to me now I is Pres. saying 'what can you do for me?' That's not the fucking question you should be asking yourself. Ask instead ' what can I do for the Pres. now he dun got himself elected and owns the country and gets to fuck anybody he wants in the ass?'"

This is the very simple message we should be getting across to our youth today. Obviously, by youth, I mean Rahul Gandhi.

By the Gita translated

Dhrtrashtra said-

I, born blind, yet now in darkness more profound
Your speech, beseech, that my Light may be Sound
Say- Were our battle eager Barons not abashed when they found
Their bellicose display profaned Kuru's holy ground?

Sanjay replied-

Nay, blind to all but their, mirrored, martial array
Only defeat, not desecration, their thoughts could dismay
Though who die on the field of Kuru's sacred fane
By your ancestor's boon, sure, Heaven attain
Who go there to slay- like gamblers gloating at a game they have fixed
In the wine of their winnings but Honour's ashes are mixed-
Yet, I admit, your son, for one, to his Guru sped his way
But, it was to shore up his *own* support, not for guidance to pray
Saying, "There stand the students you taught to draw the bow
"Now jesting & contesting whose arrow shall lay you low...

"There stand the traitors- captained by the son of your false friend
"Lives you might have ended, were *Loyalty* your true end...

"But now hear, best of 'Brahmins', of the berzerkers in my ranks
"Innumerable Heroes, intent, with their lives, to buy my thanks!"

But I spare you his roll call of clients obligated and allies opportune
Bombast not for Bards, but the Eunuch's euphonious tune...

To proceed-

Seeing the great Guru stand silent, or, simply, your son's spirits to raise
Blew the conflict commencing conch, Bhishma, beyond praise.
Your grand-sire's clarion being echoed by others on his side
Lord Krishna, and your nephews, in like terms replied.
& all Heaven and Earth trembled at that soul ravening roar
Rending the hearts of its hearers who had roared just before
Then spoke Arjun to Lord Krishna, who, his charioteer to boast
Had bartered away the strength of a battle hardened host
"Twixt the assembled armies, Thou Changeless, direct now my car
"To see how mercenary are those mustered for this unjust war"

Not choosing to whet Arjun's valour upon visages malicious or mean
To Guru Drona & Grandsire Bhishma, straight, Kishan drove his team
For both in Virtue abound- bound by no higher Law than their vow

& Timocratic thymos however courteous their bow
Serving Kings, forfeiting Kingdoms, in but fealty to their word
Not Justice, nor yet that Kingdom never of this world
And who, of your son's bounty, having no cause for complaint
Cleave to his cause, though knowing him no saint.
It was to these two great warriors- impossible for Arjun to best
That Kishan drove your nephew- his mettle to test.
Yet, not his courage then quavered, nor confidence wavered but- strange to say
Compassion there seized him, such Sorrow besieged him- his valour ebbed away

He said-

"I tremble and stare, my hair stands on end,
Seeing elder, preceptor, kinfolk and friend
Eager for battle
thundering cattle
lowing their bliss
at butchery's abyss
Whom, if nothing else can warn,
Let my bloody body impede
their idiot stampede
For life is nothing once loved ones are gone
These are my kinfolk- Keshava!
Though Greed misled them
This doom I dread them
Their families will fail
Their widows wail
& daughters harlots turn
Hell fire their ancestors burn!
My ancestors- Keshava!"
Saying which, the puissant Prince cast aside his bow and unable to stand
Was crushed down in his chariot seat by Sorrow's feeble hand.

Lord Krishna had sought but Arjuna's martial ardour to feed
Upon the sight of warriors worthy of his arrow's worshipful speed
Whom 'twere a puzzle to best
An exacting test
Not a conclusion foregone
That *they* he'd mourn
For by boon Celestial
and their own butchering skills bestial
Drona and Bhishma could not be killed
Save they themselves so willed

Which fact, if mentioned, might his cause retard
Thus Kishan, hoist with his own petard
Said only - 'whine not like a *little pussy*, you big girl's blouse! '
"Well at least my pussy is little- yours's bigger than a house!"
A retort Arjuna didn't make- restoring amity
But rather continued to whine- a true calamity
For such indeed, is the tradition of your House
The heir rightful to yield- coz he's a big girl's blouse
Devapi & Bhishma, but worse, Vyasa, Shuka, to God
Chitrangada alone battling- defeated poor sod
By that jealous demi-Divinity disputing his name
Dying, as Men must, the Heavens to defame
But, not Arjun, no, for that *chaksushi vidya* he'd been given
A sort of world withering second sight - or arrow that is driven
Backwards into eyes by what might otherwise blind them
Unloosing Light's lasso from heads severed to thus bind them
As Iravan's head that sees all I see
Shedding, perhaps, tears where I go pee-pee...
But, to get back to what Arjuna said
'I'd rather be dead
Than on such offal fed
As on which fatten, but, vulture & culture
Whoredom and kingdom
Title that is but theft's requital
or Desire- that liar
or Pride- that pre & Pan fucked bride
or, once Shame's a goner,
Honour!"
Actually, he didn't say that. I mean, it's what he should have said
'stead of whining like a pussy about how his heart bled
For his cousins and Uncles and other such shite
For agenbite of inwit did that nitwit much bite

How battle Compassion? Against Pity what avails?
Its bitter taunt, the bravest daunt, yet, here, *Love* fails
What advice can one give to one better advised?
What redaction to a text, remorse has revised?

Lord Krishna was silent- what, after all, could he say?
Himself the soul of Arjun's compassionate dismay
Till Arjun, waxing eloquent in unaccustomed speech
Outran Ruth, to Truth, in Rhetoric, over-reach

Saying "My Compassion is weak- not my Nature knows this weakness
& Duty's path ever doubtful- such my Warrior Mind's obliqueness
Yet, tho' of your Treasury, the merest trifle
What in me is your disciple
Owns wholly and longs to own
You Lord and you alone
As the Unifier of my Empire entire
& Unequivocal voice my *I* might suspire
My Freedom wretched save as thy dole
Sole Refuge, mine, Persecute my soul!
Redeem my victory, bleak, over Men and God
For *not I shall fight* for such bitter reward!"

Well, he didn't actually say that- but you get the gist
Compassion such a cunt it oft appears to have jizz't
A truth analytic, not Synthetic, as Kant Emanuelle assumed
Like 'Bugger not a Brummie after a Balti he's consumed'
For Kurukshetra is the Polish Space for Jorgensen's dilemma
Such that Brouwer Choice Sequences evolve Zorn's lemma
& Everybody is everybody by Banach Tarski
& Huggy Bear the Brahma of Hutch & Starsky
To be or not to be that is the riddle
& Occluded we - the excluded middle
But here I will stop coz, blind buddy, you're busted!
You say you want to *see* but turn away disgusted
War aint a cutesy rom-com video you can rent
To watch with your girl or bum chums wot are bent
War isn't a joke- mark me well
Coz of all the philosophy that gets spoke- War is Hell!

Dhritirashtra- Sanjay, *Suta*, your speech is strange
               & like Light, doubtful, & by Lust deranged
Sanjaya-   *Suta*? You mistake me, I very much fear
               For that guy sleeping there- your charioteer
                        I'm not a *Suta* but Sanjay Sharma!
Dhritirashtra- Not the Bard's, you follow the Brahmin's dharma?
Sanjaya-   Neither, Sir, or both, for I'm a born I.T professional!
Dhritarashtra- Your Gita then the Knowledge Empire's Recessional?
Sanaya-   Nope, I'm just that Sharma that next to Iyer had my seat
           In Mr. Yadav's Hindi class, who Anglophones did much beat
               Till, with him, they took private tuition
              Or for imported Whiskey by Vedic intuition

divined his desire, or appeased his ire
Unlike Rajiv- Serene- now a game theorist in Austin
Who, actually *learn't* Hindi, a Tea Party at Boston
For, *Verb sap*, says Vivek, a word to the Wise
All Independence commences in Indian disguise

Dhritirashtra- I don't believe you, my piss you surely take
Blind tho' I be, buddy, BIG fucking mistake!

Sanjaya- All right! I'm that aforementioned Iyer Vivek
Whom to Gita's glory, a Yadav slap, did awake
In St. Columba's School, New Delhi, circa '75
Dead now to Sophia, but, in Cyber-Space alive
Met up with you here by some glitch tachyonic
My ISP so crap and my router something chronic
Which is actually quite good news for you
Seeing as I can do
More than your Suta- for my vision is diachronic
Just the thing, blind King, & for your ears a tonic

Dhritarashtra- Cunt! curtail your queef!
Vivek-   Can't. But I'll be brief.
Dhritarashtra- *Wait!* I've a better idea
Vivek-   Sorry, I don't rent out my rear
Dhritarashtra- I'm blind not desperate, besides you smell like a wet dog
Why not just email me random snippets of your blog?
Vivek- that could work.

Why everybody is wrong about the Bhagvad Gita

The Gita is not a stand-alone text but a volume within a much larger book- the Mahabharata. The Mahabharat is built up of symmetries and correspondences which are very rigorously worked out and subtly elaborated. This is because it is an attempt to unify and meaningfully inter-relate a vast array of diverse material. In particular, the Mahabharata focuses on two principles- viz. karma which operates as a law of causation operating across time, beyond even the frontiers of death- and dharma, which deals with how beings are inter-related across space by a nexus of obligation and entitlement which we may subsume under the rubric of Law and/or Religion. Since a text which claims to speak of a law of causation as well the rules of ethical or spiritual religious practice must show some degree of logical consistency, not to mention fair play, the modern reader should not be surprised that the Mahabharat, as if following Noether's theorem, shows two marvelous types of symmetries conserving karma and dharma respectively. The first chapter of the Gita is titled Arjuna's Vishada (Dejection or Mental distress) Yoga.

In order to observe symmetries such that Karma and Dharma are conserved properties of its system, the Mahabharat operates by giving every character or episode a dual within itself. This is a heuristic device- a sort of double entry book-keeping- on the part of the compilers such that overall symmetry properties are preserved and the narrative can provide its own hermeneutics such that ordinary people (rather than Pundits or philologists) can get at the intended meaning. Thus, before reading the Gita we should look at the other place in the book at which the remedy for Vishada is given. This occurs when Yuddhishtra begins to despair because Bhima wants to put an end to their exile by personally killing off the Kauravas.

Bhima says he will take the whole blame on himself, Yudhishtra need do nothing to break his vow. Moreover, since Yudhishtra always accepts and loses any dice game offered him and (because the silly prig does not realize that what is moral for him isn't necessarily so for his wife and younger brothers- like Gandhi thinking what was good for him was also good for Harilal and Kasturba) it is inevitable that Yudhishtra would once again gamble away his own family- thus Bhima had better depart and get busy swinging his iron mace before Yuddhisthra has a chance to consign him to slavery once again.

In this context, Bhima's suggestion is not really disobedience- it is actually dharma. Yuddhishtra has the correct Dharma- viz as eldest and head he treats the others as though they were the very flesh of his flesh sharing everything with him- glory or slavery- and Bhima has no problem with obeying that Dharma EXCEPT if Yuddhishtra for some reason lacks competency- as for example by a disabling mental illness or overpowering addiction.

Now, previously in this *parva*, the Sage Markandeya had appeared to explain the nature of Dharma especially that portion Yuddhishtra finds most difficult viz Dharma w.r.t wives and juniors. Markandeya takes the example of the Brahmin Kashyapa who falls into error but is rescued by a *patrivrata* wife who tells him that her husband is her God and points him to a butcher (actually meat vendor) in Mithila who possesses higher knowledge. The meat vendor, it turns out, worships his mom and dad as God and hence is higher than the Brahmins and possesses the Chandogya doctrine. In passing Markandeya also mentions the Rishi Vrihadasva, a King who had become a Rishi & whose son performed a great war like feat of subduing a demon so that the father was excused from having to give up his hermitage and take up arms once again.

Yuddhishtra experienced Vishada when he realized that his own moral code (viz. always to accept a dice challenge- since it creates a symmetric situation and is Pareto efficient- coupled with the fact that he makes no distinction between his own person and that of his wife and brothers thus putting them at risk) was in conflict with a single valued Dharma (i.e. Kantian Categorical imperative) or universal moral law.

The Rg Vedic hymn 'the gambler's lament' mentions the stripping of the gambler's wife- the reason that popular versions of Mahabharat include the Draupati *vastraharanam* episode- and ends with praise of Krishi (agriculture) which is also risky but yields a dividend for the whole of society.

Just at this stage, Vrihadasva appears. Yuddhishtra asks him 'has there ever been a man more unfortunate than I?" "Yes' replies Vrihadasva, "Nala of the Nishadas. This leads on to the chapter where Nala learns maths and game theory and thus gains release from Kala, Time in demonic form.

George Grierson, writing around the beginning of the last Century, commented in this connection that the traditional *kaniya* (assessors) were able to assess agricultural yields in a manner that brokers found compelling, merely by glancing at the fields or orchards in question.

My own feeling is that there was an Indian, folk, discrete maths hueristic based tradition quite independent of the analytic astrological or achitectural sort. This discrete maths tradition would estimate things like how many fruit have fallen from these trees by using cognitively simple counting rules into which 'experimental' (heuristic) formulae were plugged in. To double check results, simple modulo arithmetic techniques would be used.

Of course, some autistic savants with superior hard-wired number recognition could also be used to check results and generate more such heuristic formulae and to account for other variables- e.g. weather conditions and so on.

Thus, you have a bunch of simple rules and a lot of 'expert cognition' generating a viable profession for an endogamous sub-caste.

Still, the question remains, how does Yuddhishtra or Nala benefit by learning this skill? Yuddhishtra knows in advance that Sakuni's dice are loaded- he doesn't need to do a statistical analysis. Still, no doubt, probablistic game theory would be useful on the battlefield. My impression is that the Pandavas were slightly more adventurous than the Kauravas despite having a numerical disadvantage so perhaps they prevailed because of a superior tactical trade off between kill-rates.

The Indian hypertrophy of Combinatorics might have a further explanation viz. its usefulness for voting rules and mechanism design and, it may be, that their vital importance in determining how land was redistributed, inheritances divided up, etc- meant that Iron Age Indians could rise above naive induction to an understanding of randomness- itself a liberating insight.

Naturally, Yuddhishtra MUST learn this if he is to be able to keep his word and still restrain Bhima- i.e. once he has this skill, Bhima's dharma is no longer in conflict with his own. Bhima's dharma is to obey his elder brother (neither know that Karna is the true head of their family) but, so to speak, his elder brother has lost competency. So just as a good son may best serve a senile father- or one suffering from an addiction- by challenging his competency in court, not to deprive him of the ancestral estate, but to use it wisely and solely for the elder's upkeep and pleasure- so too Bhima's dharma would be to first kill of all he Kauravas before crowning his brother UNTIL, that is, Rishi Vrihadasva providentially appears.

Except, every character in the Mahabharat is offered precisely this sort of chance- the game hasn't been rigged in advance. Incidentally, Shakuni urged the return of the Pandavas estate after they lost the game- Duryodhana chose to spurn his advise. To say, the Pandavas were lucky because their maternal relative gave good advise while the Kauravas were unlucky because their maternal Uncle was a rogue would violate the basic rule of fair play. It would not be symmetric. It would be unjust. It would just be a case of 'The Gods sporting with men, as children toy with flies, tearing off their wings for their sport'.

The other point about learning game theory is that it enables one party at least to be aware of the possible Nash equilibria attainable. If all parties have this game theoretic skill, then Nash equilibria will be stable under certain conditions. (The same applies to Rational expectations in financial markets- all agents must know the correct economic theory for that very theory to be correct.) More importantly, if people know game theory and are able to accurately estimate each others' endowments and preferences, then meta-games- i.e. institution design, internalization of externalities etc. can start to occur- there is no need to appeal to some King or Priest to guarantee the system. Notice that Yuddhishtra is learning new stuff, he's adding to his information set. Duryodhana is simply relying on inherited wealth and purchased loyalty. He isn't learning new things. This means his notion of Justice is Justice as patronage (very Statist!) rather than Yuddhishtra's method of seeking a positive sum, co-operative equilibrium (which dominates competitive equilibria).

Now the reason one may want to downplay the significance of all this has to do with the horrible casteism and misogyny and talk of karma and dharma and Gods and Rishis and so on. However, the beauty of the Mahabharat, and the Gita, is that they show that karma, dharma, male/female, caste bloody nonsense, racial rubbish, etc, etc is all just Maya (delusion) and has no part in Absolute Reality. However, where States exist they are going to seek to constrain the social system so that it has the appearance of conserving something like karma (hierarchy pretending to be meritocracy) and dharma (Freedom means do what the Government tells you to do. That is true Freedom. To do what you want to do is shameless dissipation and vice. To pursue your own interests is to be the worst sort of slave because you are the slave of your passions. Etc, etc.)

Gita is really about Freedom but based on true knowledge of your own interests and a rational means to see what the interests of others are and how you can work productively with them rather than live in fear of them. This is the opposite of Matsyanyaya (big fish eats the little fish). It is the opposite of our historicist judicial hermeneutics, where the presumption is made that the stronger party will always prey upon the weaker party and thus the State must intervene, do interessement, become an obligatory passage point, in every transaction to protect the weaker party. Well, since strength means elasticity, having other options, what this really means is the State worsens the lot of the weaker while entrenching the position of the stronger because the incidence of any policy instrument- like a tax or quota- falls upon those inelastic (having fewer options) in their supply or demand for the underlying good in question.

Let us take the very opening of the Gita. What do we find? A symmetrical situation. Both Duryodhana and his cousin Arjuna have misgivings on seeing the forces assembled. The hint is given that actually all the warriors present should have had misgivings because they were preparing to wage war at a holy place. Both Duryodhana and Arjuna turn, as if by instinct, to a preceptor. Duryodhana turns to his Guru Drona while Arjuna has Krishna as his counselor.

However, Duryodhana's worry is whether he will prevail over his enemies whereas Arjuna's is that he will shed the blood of his kinfolk. To Duryodhana, no better answer can be given then the blowing of the battle horn by Grandsire Bhishma. Now both Drona and Bhishma had been granted the boon that they would give up life only by their own will. Even if they were partial to the Pandavas, they were duty bound to protect the Kauravas.

This meant that Krishna could easily settle Arjuna's doubts by saying 'Since Bhishma and Drona are unslayable, they will be ward off your arrows from harming your kinsmen. Hence your only job is to protect your own brothers and allies while putting up such a valiant display that the other side grows tired and a compromise settlement is reached.'

However, previously in the Mahabharat, Arjuna had been granted a type of second sight called chakshushi vidya by a Gandharva (demi-god) whom he had vanquished. Since Krishna, being the Supreme Lord, was omniscient, he knew that Arjuna's despondency was based on a true vision of what was to come. True, Krishna could just lie to Arjun saying- you can't beat Drona and Bhishma- the best you can hope for is a stalemate. '

However Krishna does not take the easy course. Why?

Twentieth Century writers, having missed the point about Arjuna's chakshushi vidya, don't bother asking themselves this question. They assume that the Mahabharat was written by barbarous bards a long time ago. After all, Homeric heroes- in the grip of 'phrenes'- suddenly turn tail and run, so perhaps what the Gita really is about is God saying 'be a man. Lift up your sword and fight.'

As Swami Vivekananda puts it- "If one reads this one Shloka — क्लैब्यं मा स्म गमः पार्थ नैतत्त्वय्युपपद्यते । क्षुद्रं हृदयदौर्बल्यं त्यक्त्वोत्तिष्ठ परंतप॥ — one gets all the merits of reading the entire Gita; for in this one Shloka lies imbedded the whole Message of the Gita.[76] " Do not yield to unmanliness, O son of Pritha. It does not become you. Shake off this base faint-heartedness and arise, O scorcher of enemies! (2.3)

Unfortunately, if this is the meaning of the Gita then it fails as a text. One of the brightest guys to read the Gita was the great mathematician Andre Weil. He thought its message was 'don't fight- run away.' But running away from conscription in the Second World War put his life in more immediate risk.

Since the commentators fail to note that Arjuna's vishada is of a prophetic origin (he is able to visualize how the War would end) rather than arising from a failure of phrenes or thymos (that is 'rajsic guna' in Indglish), they miss the real import of this chapter.

However mistakes of this sort are bound to occur unless one realizes that the Mahabharat strives to look at symmetric situations such that we feel there is a sort of fair play, a type of equality between agents matched against each other. In any case, simply from the dramatic point of view, a conversation or combat of equals, or at least properly handicapped protagonists, is more interesting than one between agents markedly different in degree.

If Drona and Bhishma can reassure Duryodhana simply by showing themselves steadfast at their posts, Krishna has a more difficult job. He has vowed not to fight but be a charioteer merely. Moreover, Arjuna- by his own actions, by the fruit of his own karma- has a superior sort of insight and outlook than does Duryodhana who has relied on others for his Kingly status. Thus, though Krishna does in the end perform the same function as Drona and Bhishma- thus not handicapping the Pandavas in the upcoming battle- it is by means of a very difficult type of argument or persuasion- one involving Krishna sacrificing himself!- rather than the facile or doctrinaire nonsense that the commentators find in the Gita.

What caused this stupidity amongst the scholars? The answer is that they failed to take the Mahabharat's system of symmetries seriously.

First, let us go back to the question of Arjuna's vishada- the despondency arising from his foresight of what was to come. Why should the sin of killing kinfolk weigh so heavily on him? The answer is that, in the course of the war, he unwittingly kills his eldest brother, that too in a state of passionate fury. Arjuna does not know Karna is the head of his family. Karna does know this but wants the war to go ahead so that the slain warriors gain a glorious ascent to heaven. Thus Arjuna really is obeying the head of his family in taking on a ghastly sin- equivalent to patricide- on himself. Yet, to accomplish the task- otherwise impossible- Krishna himself had to help engender a state of Manyu (dark anger) in Arjuna. In other words though Arjuna did his duty in the sense of fulfilling the head of his family's desire- he did not do so in a dispassionate state.

Now that we know the origin of Arjuna's vishada let us ask the question is there anywhere else in the Mahabharat where we get a symmetric situation? The answer is yes, an equal but opposite situation arises (Book8 -69-71) where Arjuna swears to kill the person he believes to be his eldest brother and Krishna intervenes with an argument relating to the nature of dharma. Commentators dismiss this as some sort of scholastic quibbling on the part of Krishna. They don't see that- just in case one misses the clues within the Gita itself because one imagines that the guys who wrote it were ignorant barbarians- this episode has been put in, as a sort of double entry book-keeping, so that even those who are unlettered and ignorant can, simply by following the plot line of the story, piece the thing together for themselves. This follows from the fact that a large portion of the audience for the Mahabharat would not be fluent in the canonical form of the language in which it was being delivered but still be able to work out what was happening and retain the story line in their minds because of the dramatic nature of the events.

Briefly, Krishna states that to reveal one's own merits or award oneself condign praise is, for an honorable man, to commit suicide. Now, in the Gita, Krishna reveals himself to be the Supreme Godhead- this is the theophany known as Visvarupa- thus slaying himself!

Suddenly we see a reversal of the commentators' view whereby the Kurukshetra battle is a sort of gory sacrifice orchestrated by and brought about for the greater glory of that cunning hypocrite Krishna!

How such a view is compatible with devotional religion- nay! how this is compatible with any sentiment towards the Hindu religion or Indian culture other than revulsion and disgust- is utterly beyond me.

In Hindu hermeneutics the concept of apoorvata- to find something new or say something unprecedented- is emphasized as being the meaning or import of a text. Once we realize that meaning in the Gita is 'being gamed' (i.e. like a game of chess, though based on a few simple rules and a finite number of pieces, there is infinite potential for novelty, the more you play the more possibilities you see, the more truly educational the game becomes) rather than stated in a once and for all way. The term apurva- in Hindu thought- is similar to the notion of prarabhda karma (karma as an arrow already shot from the bow) but it shows how the conditioning or deterministic factors operating on us can, by our taking a novel view of them (including that of Theistic Vaisnavism), become the basis of liberation as freedom here and now. How so? Take the following example- you find yourself in a strange place surrounded by people speaking a strange language, busy about tasks utterly alien to your previous experience. In this situation you have only one choice- viz. to blindly follow the one person who speaks a little of your language and tells you what to do. However, you are virtually a slave of this person. You have no freedom. However, if you start looking around and putting yourself in other people's shoes (trying to imagine what motivates them and what is the basis of their interaction) you will begin to get an idea of what the various social roles available to you are in this new environment. You have taken the first step to becoming free from your guide. Your behavior and thinking is starting to show that plasticity which is the necessary pre-condition for Freedom. If you chose not to look around- if you say my karma is to do x therefore my dharma is to do nothing but x- then the only freedom meaningful to you is the freedom to imagine yourself more pious and worthy of heaven than those around you.

The fact that Krishna tells Arjuna to do as he pleases in accordance with his own nature- svadharma (incidentally, Arjun's family had a long history of the rightful heir ceding his right to the throne to the other claimant- thus Arjun would have been following his family tradition if he'd quit the field) shows that the Gita is about Freedom based in the Real World- not some ethical *uchchvaas* pi-jaw fairyland.

But this begs the question- if, as I claim, all the modern commentators on the Gita are utterly wrong about it, why bother with it at all? Surely it can only mislead? The answer here is that only people who think they are smarter than average- and thus superior to those who composed and preserved the Mahabharat- can be misled by it.

For ordinary people the Mahabharat is invaluable because it shows that the two goads of karma and dharma that our rulers apply to our flanks are nothing but blinkers and that none but these self appointed elites are chained by that karma and undone by that dharma. (I was greatly heartened to read that the villagers near Gandhi's Sabarmati Ashram chased off the Ashramites when they tried to stick their noses where they didn't belong.)

In the Gita, Krishna explains that amongst the Vedas he is the Sama (musical recitation) and, verily, he is found in its Upanishad, the Chandogya- a book which tells of how some free minstrels of the Lord, poor as they were, went to learn the hermeneutic of what they chanted as theorized by the rulers. But what Kings think is not philosophy- it's a load of shite. Now it may be that there is a link between

Monsoons and the mandate of Heaven or a more straightforwardly Ricardian or Malthusian or Ecological or Asimovian kind of water-cycle regulating hierarchical government but the important point is that free minstrels don't need to get caught up in that shite. The carter- who earns his own living- possesses the Truth in a more perfect form.

Essentially, if you have a hierarchical society then something like 'prarabdha karma' (the explanation of why you were born into this particular body, in this particular milieu, etc) is a big feature of life. However the Mahabharat shows that you are not actually constrained by the role you were put into at birth or acquired by reason of genetic predisposition. Svadharma means doing what you really want to on the basis of really knowing yourself. This is part of true Religion coz people can relate to you in a predictable way- Justice is predictability- and, if they choose, enjoy things unique to yourself that you can offer the world.

All Religions, according to the Hindutva doctrine, should be able to get you thinking about what you really want to do and would have tools and instruments within their Scripture that will get you started down that road.

Of course, if you really want to be a massive prick and fuck everybody up then sure you gotta say to yourself- 'My duty to God is to be an allmightly prick coz like the ordinary people are so stupid and wicked and lazy and many of them are the wrong color or gender or like mebbe they be getting gay with each other or like dissing the Environment God or summat.' But if you do this you will end up with a far more witless karma and dharma doctrine than that of the Mahabharat.

Of the four sons of the author of the Mahabharat- one is sunk in a congenital Tamsic darkness, one dies by his Rajsic passion, the third is wise and good, but the fourth, <u>Shuka</u>, is not bound by any genetic or acquired conditioning, he flies by the nets of karma and dharma to become one with the Universe leaving the author of the book cheerless behind.

In the Gita, what Krishna is doing is fulfilling his own human prarabdha karma while showing how everybody else (unless they think they're smarter than others or born to rule or some such shite) can fly by the nets of karma and dharma while still enjoying the sweetness of life.

I think it's a perfect book. It can only fuck you up if your big mission in life is to fuck up other people's lives by preaching to them or ordering them about or taking it upon yourself to judge them. But, like, that's karma dude. What about Dharma? It is an upside down tree which you must cut down for yourself. Consider your rulers as convicts, your savants as a chain gang. No matter what threats they may utter nor howsoever fearsome they may appear- they can not imperil your freedom. Not if you gotta song in your heart and no particular place to go. In which case you also got the Gita. Congrats!

The kiratarjuniya as dual to the Gita

Everything in the Mahabharata happens twice and everything that happens to one agent with respect to another agent, happens again with respect to that agent and the dual of the other. It is a system of multiplying symmetries such that the ordinary person- without much grasp of the language of exposition- can reflect upon the story and determine for himself that those who quote its authority to further their own ends are lying or deluded or both.

If the Gita contains a theophany of Lord Vishnu to Arjuna, the Kiratajuniya contains the theophany of Lord Shiva to him.

In the Gita, Krishna tells Arjuna to shoot his arrows at will for the truth is that it is not Arjuna who slays but Lord Krishna himself who encompasses the death or injury of the enemy. In the Kiratarjuniya, Arjuna contends that it was his arrow which killed a boar he was hunting, whereas the Kirata Chief considers the prize lawfully his as his arrow had hit the same mark at the same moment. Clearly, both episodes deal with the same question.

What is that question? One answer is to say that it has to do with Freedom and Necessity. Are our actions conditioned such that Freedom is an illusion- we are merely clockwork toys acting upon each other by Leibnizian 'pre-established harmony'? Is God merely a sort of magician or stage-director who has already decided everything that is going to happen, including everything we think we think, and who is simply watching the show for some purpose of his own? If so, what is the meaning of 'karma'? If God has all the power and we have none, it is scarcely meaningful to speak of our sin or merit, our guilt or joy- no power means no agency, no agency means no intentionality or inwardness. Language itself is meaningless. Is life itself merely a delusion or a sort of waking dream or hallucination?

The kiratarjuniya of Bharavi, written in the heroic vein, justifies an optimistic interpretation of the Gita and a positive answer to the question posed in the last paragraph. Arjuna and Lord Shiva (in the guise of the Kirata hunter) *fight* to determine whose arrow killed the boar- in other words, for the duration of the agon, an epochee where life is meaningful obtains.. In the Gita, the epochee arises because Arjuna does not want to fight. This is a good thing, because everybody is welcome to kill as many vampires or angels or talking monkeys as they like- precisely because such creatures don't exist. The moment people want to start killing human beings, you need someone to step in and say cut it out buddy. Go take a cold shower. Unless, of course, they are a God or vampire or talking pony or other such creature which doesn't exist. In that case hie thee to a mad-house, telling them the while that you have already complied with their wishes, everybody is already dead and could they kindly fuck off to heaven or wherever.

The other thing about God is that sure if he turns up claiming your kill as his own, shoot arrows at him. This is okay if he is similarly armed. Don't for fuck's sake shoot arrows at someone who says he's God but isn't shooting at you. That's how you end up on death row.

What I like about Bharavi's kavya is the stress laid on Duryodhana being a good King and the paradox he highlights of Arjuna's practising austerities not for any spiritual purpose but merely so as to get his elder brother an office of profit he has already, by his own free actions, forfeited and which his cousin is occupying in an exemplary manner.

Bharavi lived and wrote at a time when the Nyaya school was flourishing and, (I'm guessing) Purva Mimamsa was going great guns. Intellectually, that's a lot of gristle to be chewing on which, by itself, is going to make its stylistic alamkars that much more interesting to translate.

Furthermore, my guess is, important mercantile castes claiming Kuru descent and adhering to Saivite religion would have had their own performance and bardic traditions in the background to the courtly foreground.

So, there's bound to be meat here, is my reasoning.

Lord Shiva's boon to Arjuna tell us something else- Arjuna is being bracketed with Ravana. In a sense the stage is being set for his being a samramba yogi or virodha bhakta- attaining highest Union to God through hatred, enmity and following an evil course. But, stupidity (Vikshepa) is the greatest metaphysical evil. 'Rama was a King and Ravana was a King' is a Tamil saying. 'Against stupidity,' however as some stupid Kraut said, 'the Gods themselves are powerless'. Yet Krishna and Arjuna- a bit like Buddha and Ananda- are great pals. Arjuna is a bit of a bone-head but you can see why Krishna loves him. In the same way that, in a sense,

Ananda becomes responsible for Lord Buddha's death, so too does Arjuna become responsible for Lord Krishna visvarupa theophany- which since it is a condign self-praise is itself morally equivalent to suicide (this is something Krishna explains when Arjuna expresses an understandable desire to kill his elder brother- not Karna, the one younger than Karna- y'know, the one with the ironic name.)

I'm doing a translation of passages from Bharavi (don't worry- they're not for publication) and the leading thought in my mind is that it is the Kiratarjuniya which Vivekananda and Tilak and so on ought to have focussed on. The fact is the British and their loyalists weren't all that bad. Yet, there was a moral argument for the 'garm dal' to challenge them- if necessary by force- compare India's formidable state apparatus to that of Sri Lanka's (after its decimation by the Socialist Mrs. Bandarnaike) and the horrors that Nation endured in consequence, especially in connection with the even more Socialist JVP and ultimate silly-arse marxist nutjob Rohana Wijeweera (himself, plausibly, a descendant of the Kauravas) and the sort of demonstration effect it had.

It is interesting that 4 of Vishnu's accepted incarnations- Vamana, Buddha, Gandhi and Subramaniyam Swamy, are considered to have brought aggresive foreign devils, or avaricious demonesses, under control by what was essentially a piece of dissimulation or a disingenuous doctrine or a reckless disregard for truth.

Perhaps, the Gita's unmatchable grandeur comes from Lord Krishna- the enchanter and beguiler of hearts- sacrificing himself in so many ways to every single sentient being, such that Draupati's indictment of God as *mayin* and ordainer of karma- 'stained by the sins, he has ordained'- is, in fact, expiated. That too with no diminution of Godhead.

Om purnam adah &c.

Gandhi, Grothendieck and the Gita

The Bhagwad Gita has drawn the admiration of some of the greatest mathematicians of the last century- in particular Andre Weil and Grothendieck both of whom were concerned with uniting the different branches of mathematics on the basis of greater generality. In fact Grothendieck uses the term 'Yoga' for his work.

Why should this be so?

After all, according to Michael Witzel, the great Harvard Indologist- the Gita is simply the product of some priestly cabal involved in a petty dynastic intrigue whose main actors were just jumped up bandits or cattle raiders. Witzel, in the tradition of Nineteenth Century Western Biblical hermeneutics- is trying to extract as much History as possible from our sacred text. However, actual history is a messy business and extracting meaning from it an impossible task. If the Gita is simply the echo of some long ago tribal affray, in a far off corner of the globe, why should the greatest Western mathematicians and physicists- people concerned with the foundations of thought and reality- show such reverence to the Gita? Can it be that the answer is simply that- as Gandhi thought- it advocates doing your duty and pursuing non-violence? If so, surely there were a hundred other texts, closer to home, which would have served equally well? Why should a French Jew, like Andre Weil, take the trouble to learn Sanskrit and come to India if the true *'Gita rahasya'* really was nothing more than Gandhism?

The answer, I think, is that the Gita and the Mahabharata display extraordinary properties of Symmetry and it was this that appealed to the mathematicians and physicists.

Emmy Noether's theorem, in the early Nineteen Thirties, showed that- for non-dissipative systems- the existence of a symmetry was evidence for a conservation law.

The pullulation of characters and episodes, digressions and interpolations in the Mahabharata at first may seem quite maddening.
Surely this is evidence that it is a dissipative system in that it contains superfluous matter? I contend that the reverse is the case.

The Mahabharata actually observes not just Dirac's symmetry, whereby every particle has its anti-particle, but also super-symmetry. Thus, the pullulation of characters is like the plethora of new fundamental particles revealed by particle accelerators. I am not smart enough to say whether the Mahabharata's ever multiplying cast of characters yield on analysis a position similar to that of Geoffrew Chew (championed by Fritjof Capra in the Tao of Physics) whereby there is a fundamental equality of all elementary particles with none being regarded as more fundamental than the others. Certainly, the Gita itself offers- to those with sufficiently mathematical minds to grasp such subtleties- clues to those more fundamental strings which hold everything together.

At first glance, it would seem that either my claim is false - the Mahabharata only accidentally shows symmetry, or else it is actually so primitive a text that it unconsciously mirrors some hard wired structural symmetry of cognition or linguistics, or else it was not the work of mere humans for no collection of mortals are capable of such unswerving adherence to the very rigorous rules of balance and reciprocity which governs every episode as well as the unfolding of the whole narrative. While not rejecting the notion of divine authorship, I maintain that even the interpolations and elucidations made from time to time by priestly redactors do in practice observe these very rules and recapitulate the foundational method of the original composition.

This is because I can conceive an Adi Mimamsa hermeneutics- not lost to us but lost to me because I'm no scholar and in any case lack intelligence- which instilled a tradition, a *sampradaya*, which enabled the transmission and elaboration of these great texts in a manner that did no violence to their ethos.

However, for a section of Indians, during the Nineteenth Century, Mimamsa hermeneutics first took a purely legalistic turn- (think of the Court Pundits employed by the British up till the 1860's)- and was then displaced by a racialist type of Western hermeneutics- whose great service to the modern age was to demystify the Bible and reduce Judaeo-Christian Scripture to a sort of imperfect history- that too the history of an unimportant tribe inhabiting a small patch of land which was only fitfully- and that too marginally- of strategic importance.

This was a tragedy for India. It meant that commentaries on the Gita and Mahabharata, published since that time, have tended to get sillier and sillier- a didactic exercise of the stupid for the stupider, except that actually no one was ever that stupid. It was just that the one great axiom everyone subscribed to was that Indians were practically morons. Not to talk to Indians like they were morons meant you were out of touch. You couldn't lead those benighted monkeys. The mind numbing banality of rhetoric, the utter idiocy of our various Godmen and Gandhians addressing the "Public" on 'the message of the Gita'- as on every other topic'- has to be experienced to be believed.

Mahatma Gandhi- it must be said- was a far better writer and speaker than those we currently suffer under. However, Gandhi- though keen to save the handloom weaver from the mills of Manchester- himself imported some foolish version of Quaker plutocratic nonsense -i.e. Non-violence as a magic charm sure to give success- to drive out of business India's own home grown hermeneutic of the Gita. This was a cultural disaster. It meant not only that India had to import nonsense but also re-export that nonsense. The Indian Guru, Godman, and 'Gandhian' activist became bywords for stupidity, cupidity, and infantile narcissism.

Gita is there to make you think, it is not a stick to beat people into idiocy with. It has nothing to do with the moral outrage industry which the Western bourgeoisie requires because of the dyspepsia caused by their overly rich diet. Nevertheless Gita and Itihasa have been reduced to this role in India- to give a platform for nutters and gobshites, not to inspire us (I should say, to inspire you- I'm too stupid to do this myself!) to breakthroughs in Mathematics, Physics, Economics and so on.

Game Theory and the Gita

Yudhishtra, to become a just King, to understand Policy Actor Ethics, to understand his duty to subordinates, agents and dependenents, must learn probability and tactics. He comes to see that virtue and morality is actually a vector, not a scalar. We are getting to a notion similar to the notion of Evolutionary Stable Strategies- i.e. an ecology of ethical choices all equally valid and interdependent. Balaram is not condemned as a drunkard for refusing to fight. Krishna is not condemned as being partial to Arjuna for assisting him.

Yet, the outcome of Mahabharat is not happy. Though the Pandavas win, it is a tragic outcome.

The symbiotic nature of the Kaurava-Pandava dichotomy had been pointed out early on by Sanathkumara who employed an ecological analogy- 'without the forest, the tiger dies. Without the tigers, the forest disappears. Your sons (Kauravas) and the Pandavas are like the forest and the tigers.'

Yuddhishtra can understand this. Dhritarshtra can't. When Yuddhishtra offers to fight Dhritrashtra himself, to settle their dispute, he recognizes that the Kaurava principle of Power politics had as much validity- indeed, it is the starting point for- his own. The optimal solution lay in a meta-game.

The relationship of the Gita to game-theory arises from the fact that, here, the latter's 'meaning' is synoptically gamed. This fulfills the condition of *apoorvata* such that on each reading, or each hearing, there is something new and therefore the condition for Gita to be considered Shruti is fulfilled. This is nothing to do with rituals. Gita can be heard in any language where translation is not constrained to unmeaning and incessant interessement as is the case with current 'good' and 'Academic' as opposed to my sort of 'fucked' and 'shite' English or Indglish.

In what manner does the Gita game Game Theory? Well, Krishna, here, is embedded and relationist not substantivist and Benthamite. Initially it looks like the Lord- out of love for his friend- has made a mistake. To spur on Arjun's martial spirit- while at the same time showing him the need to be cautious and plan things out- Krishna straight away takes him to see the two chiranjivis (immortal, unvanquishables) on the other side. This should stir up Arjun as well get him to think carefully. But, Arjun (unlike Dhrtrashtra) is so confident he starts thinking his foes are already dead! (Alternatively, we may note that a Gandharva had gifted Arjuna with cakshushi vidya- a sort of second sight. This parallels Krishna's own gift- mentioned in Chandogya. However, notice that whereas the Gandharva's *caksuci* yields only Vishada (depression) Krishna's Upanishadic insight- though appearing to militate for mere ataraxia- is actually suicidal!)

Arjuna blames himself- how could he have ended up killed his own Guru and his beloved

Grandsire- not to mention so many cousins and friends! Of course, there is a simple answer. Dude, them guys still alive. Two of them are unkillable. Fight so well, that the other side loses morale and sues for peace! But, we know that those assembled, having forgotten they were desecrating a holy spot, were ripe for a *vishodhana*- a ritual type of cleansing. In any case, Sociologically speaking, the feudal code was untenable and the aristocracy had to die.

From the theistic point of view, if the Lord is depicted as twisting and turning to help his friend (that is, his devotee) there is a noble purpose here- viz. to illumine the psychological truth that at every moment, taking on every form- (*rupam rupam pratirupo babhoova* etc)- the Lord is struggling to come to us and to win us away from anxiety and depression.

However, we notice that Krishna's every philosophical excursion ends in aporia- more notably, from the point of view of ordinary people (for whom the work was intended) because these philosophies are immediately shown to be false because they lead to social injustice, pi jaw and stupidity. I don't need to know Philosophy to know that any Philosophy is wrong which arrives at the conclusion that I should be the slave of its practitioners.

From Theism's point of view, it is important that even Krishna should not be able to show any philosophical system or approach to be other than silly. It's like Douglas Adams's story about the philosopher who provides a valid proof of God's existence. Even God is impressed. But, the philosopher points out, there is no longer any need for Faith. But there is no God without Faith. God is convinced and immediately ceases to exist.

Still, the Gita is quoted as supporting misogyny, casteism, the morality of slaughtering millions of people coz you're miffed that your cousins get to rule rather than you- and so on and so forth.

The point is that though ad captum vulgi arguments can be adduced for all of the above- they, nevertheless, are complete shit. The Gita does have a message- it's the same as Buddhism, Jainism... urm common sense actually, which is that we are all radically interdependent. Mutually supportive co-existence must be the rule. Pluralism is necessary coz Life is about Symbiosis not Extermination. As Jefferson said, in matters of Religion, divided we stand, united we fall. There are delicious ironies in the casteist and misogynistic portions of the Gita. The whole thing is like one of those sit coms where if, at the beginning of a scene, an actor states some principle, then we can be sure he or she will be shown to behave in the opposite way by the end. Thus, there is nothing casteist about a work which shows the destruction of the fucking priests and aristocrats- no matter how splendid their attributes and achievements.

The reason that the Mahabharat exhibits a lot of mathematical structure is that, if not its conception, then certainly its transmission, depended on heuristics. But heuristics- including rules of thumb- are just special cases of a more general law. Since Mahabharat is trying to show karma and dharma as being logically consistent, there is obviously going to be a lot of symmetry.

Thus if the question is raised 'what did this guy do this at this time?' we can reconstruct it by figuring out who his dual is and what episode elsewhere is the dual of this episode and so on. Of course, this method of comparison also gives a lot of scope for clarifying matters. It is like you have two parallel cases to which the same rule applies in which the decision was different.

If Krishna has one way of discharging his duty as a chariotcer, Shalya has another. Actually, Shalya's is pretty effective. Insults get a guy's dander up. He fights harder.

On the other hand, we say the parallelism here is imperfect. Krishna is a pal and relative of Arjuna. Shalya is a relative of the Ashvins (he is their maternal uncle). BUT, if Karna revealed his true birth to Shalya the latter would have been obliged to inform his nephews (so as to prevent them from falling into the sin of filial impiety) in which case the Kauravas get a walkover! Thus the symmetry here is- Krishna reveals his true form to Arjuna, Karna conceals his true birth from *his* charioteer. This is subtle, not mechanistic.

No wonder people write crap about Mahabharata.

The Gita, Occasionalism and Deontology

Occasionalism, in philosophy, is the doctrine that God alone causes everything. If I shoot an arrow at you and it pierces your heart and you die, I am not the cause of your death. On the contrary, what actually happened was, God transported the arrow to your heart and then caused it to stop beating and then caused you to die.

In Islam, the school of Ghazzali is occasionalist while, in the West, from Descartes onwards, Occasionalism has been one solution to the Mind-Body problem (i.e. the puzzle that mental and physical processes seem so different that it seems impossible that they interact.) In Ethics, too, if we consider the disjunction between deontics (values) and alethics (facts), Occasionalism of some sort or another is bound to crop up. Indeed, Game theoretic approaches to Evolutionary Biology, in conformity with the extended phenotype principle, are currently attempting precisely such a re-foundation of Ethics so as to 'de-Kant' (as Prof. Binmore puts it) the subject.

Buddhism and Vedanta, in India, had no need for a full blown occasionalist doctrine. In the former, the doctrine of *kshanika-vada* (momentariness) meant that, since the Universe only exists for a moment, causation and identity are delusions simply. For the latter, the doctrine of *Maya-vada-* irreality of all phenomenal appearance- once again made causation and identity and so on utterly meaningless.

This is not to say that Theistic Vishnavism, from Ramanjua, through Madhva, to Vallabhacharya, did not develop a full fledged occasionalist doctrine such that the Lord alone had agency, nor that there were not some very heated (and hilarious) polemics exchanged between the *Sagunas* (Dualists) and *Nirgunas* (Monists) which polarised along sectarian- i.e. Vaishnav vs. Saivite- lines. However, the great poet-Saints had no difficulty reconciling the differences of the doctrinaire by simply instrumentalizing the doctrine of re-birth. Indeed, the variant epistemologies and ontologies of Jainism, Buddhism and so-called Hindu schools were reconciled by an appeal to re-birth. Once Umasvati, the Jain Scholar-Saint, clarifies that all beings become perfect upon the path of re-birth, and once it is seen that the liberated soul in Jaina '*kevalya*' is indistinguishable from the 'extinguished' soul of the Buddhist *Pratyeka* or the 'United to the Lord' soul or the Hindu *jivana-mukta,* then, Nagarjuna, Sankara and Umasvati become complementary rather than competing. Contra Max Weber, reincarnation is not the Indian theodicy (i.e. the explanation for why God lets bad things happen to good people), because, quite simply, for Buddhism and Vedanta, the notion that something transmigrates is pure illusion and nescience. As for Jainism, the very second you decide to be self-reliant and work to perfect yourself, immediately, you are absolutely assured that for infinite Time you will be in the blissful Kevalya state. What does it matter if it takes ten births or ten million to get there? Eternity is infinitely longer than even ten billion years. An Auditor would tell you, the sum is not material. It's like saying to Bill Gates- my dear man, I have found out that you owe ten dollars to the Dry Cleaner- you are not as wealthy as you thought!

Tulisdas, for example, puts 'casteist' arguments into the mouth of the crow, Kakabhushandi, who had incurred the curse of his Guru in a previous life because he was so bigoted an upholder of the *Saguna* position. The greatness of Tulsidas is that his '*maryada bhakti'* (respectful Theism) involves obeisance to all equally. Clearly, this is the opposite of an endorsement of a feudal, hierarchical, view of society. Ultimately, Tulsidas declares the name 'Ram' to be higher than any merely ontic truth or deontological method. In other words, Tulsi tells us that Ram's name is higher than both whatever exists and anything we can imagine or predicate of 'Ram'. This is better than Western Christianity's slow weaning itself away, even with Islamic tutelage, from Platonic 'reals' to Aristotelian 'nominalism'.

However, this was not a thorough going nominalism, like Tulsi's, and bequeathed Western Logic all sorts of ontological problems which it struggles with to this day. Briefly, as the works of Quine make clear, any system of logic makes ontological claims. In other words, any rigorous, non defeasible, system of reasoning is based upon a picture not just of the world but how and why the world can change or transform itself. But, from the view point of what Collingwood calls 'second order discourse', Philosophy as concerning itself not with facts about the World but a discussion of the world-views those facts might give rise to, this is quite foolish. Why have logic, why have a non-defeasible system of reasoning, if it can generate no truth value *at all* by its operations but can only reiterate the stupidity of its own axioms, the idiocy of its pauper's picture of a world? Wittgenstein, who scandalized Vienna's Logical Positivists by reading Tagore to them- incidentally, Hitler would soon put a stop to the scandal of a 'dirty Jew' reading out the works of a 'pure Aryan', like Tagore- tells us, repenting his own early work, that ' a picture held us captive, and we could not get outside the picture because language repeats it to us inexorably'. Whose language? Not that of Tulsi certainly. Not that of the *bauls*- Muslim, Hindu or European, like Anthony Firanghee- who lay behind Tagore's own oeuvre.

For Sufi Islam, as for Hindu Theism, Occasionalism changed the relationship of poetry with the World. It was no longer constrained to be mimetic, a mere imitation of Nature, nor diegetic, i.e. narrate a story, but, instead, it could explore Man's capacity to receive and generate meaning. In other words, both for Islam and the indigenous Indian tradition, poesis was its own hermeneutics- in other words, the poet, tasking himself with finding new meanings, even if the World pictures they referred to were very far from the common sense perspective, was doing so by showing how more could be read into what had already been handed down. The result is that the Bhagvad Gita, like Ghalib's Divan, is a book which can never fall open on the same page twice. 'So fresh and strange it each moment appears/ True beauty's homage is e'er in arrears'.

Unfortunately, Nineteenth Century European Scholars- and their often even more provincial latter day successors- were wedded to a Romantic and historicist hermeneutic according to which there was once some Golden Age when people behaved 'naturally' and sang about things like how Mountains are real high and the Wind blows a lot and Forests have lots of trees but get scary at night, and the Sea sure is a big heap of wet- and that, for some reason, such songs were actually really good and represented something genuinely worthwhile but, alas!, everything gradually became more and more corrupt and decadent and artificial and deeply freighted with thought. Thus the ornamental aspect of Sufi or Hindu theistic poetry was dismissed as 'decadence'. But, to be fair, stupid elderly pedants are always obsessed with decadence. They see it all over the place. Don't talk to me about the young men nowadays. They're all homosexuals. Result is that girls are running wild. I tell you our Society has become completely rotten and decadent. We are sleep-walking towards disaster. What we need is a War to wake up the young men and get them to quit mounting each other and have a go at the enemy for a change.

Another great fault of the European scholars- who, speaking generally, were good linguists and laborious scholars- but of low general intellectual calibre and deeply Provincial outlook- was that they believed everything they'd been told at Grammar School. Greek tragedy is the highest form of poetry. It isn't. That's why the Greeks switched to Musicals. A great man laid low by a character flaw, or the malice of Fate, is the most noble subject for the poet. This isn't true. It's an ignoble subject for a Scandal mongering, gutter Press, journalist. There is nothing particularly elevating about the contemplation of some random rich dude's misfortunes. As for beating one's breast at the malice of Fate- why bother? What good does it achieve? Thomas Hardy's turn to poetry, or Housman's well-turned lyrics, may sound okay and be on the best

Classical models but they are a mere melodious absence of thought, a turning away from the vast new vistas and lifted horizons offered by technological progress and social development.

Both Indian and Islamic philology- in contrast to that of the Europeans- owe their origin and gain traction by being very much part and parcel of economic, technological and social change. For the Greeks, there was no poet like Homer- but Homer described a purely Thymotic and tribal society- whereas, for the Indians, there was the Mahabharata and the Ramayana, which describe the transition from Thymotic, tribal, societies to contract-based, mercantile, Universalist regimes in which the Just King sets an example by controlling his own thymotic impulses and emerges from the ethical heteronomy of the Homeric heroes to the ethical autonomy and rationality of Chief Magistrates of urbane, mercantile, communities founded upon not tribal but Universal- or at least metic fostering- values.

For the West, the eclipse of the 'glories of Greece and the grandeur of Rome,' and the prolonged nightmare of the Dark Ages, coincided with the triumph of Christianity. Jerusalem stood sullenly opposed to Athens. Classical Philology takes its belated revenge on Religion in the Nineteenth Century by casting doubt on the seamlessness of Scripture. At the time, this might have seemed a victory for rationality. Perhaps the new historicist hermeneutics, founded in Classical philology, really had a role to play. It didn't. Scripture can always defend itself because it is 'insha' (deontic) rather than 'khabar' (alethic). The Philologists gradually made bigger and bigger fools of themselves. Max Mueller was a standing joke with his 'solar myth' obsession. Nietzsche tries to establish a humanist hermeneutics but was chased out of the Academy. Since the fellow was quite mad, he was eventually assimilated to a particularly foolish sort of 'phenomenological' philology- incidentally, I may point out that Occasionalism saves from the idiocy of the sort of Phenomenology that is associated with Heidegger- a bad philologist who used phoney etymologies to read his own nonsense into ancient texts.

Western Philologists are too stupid to understand Western Philosophy- too stupid even to understand that all systematic Philosophy based on indefeasible reasoning is *a priori* silly- and so, naturally, the establishment of Western hegemony over Indian and Islamic knowledge systems, had the effect of rendering virtually everything being recovered by laborious scholarship radically unreadable as falling well below the standard of intelligence set by a drivelling idiot. Why? Well, important stuff in the text, or the cultural background, like the Occasionalism in the Gita or in Ghazzali or whatever, is either ignored or explained away- it's an interpolation!- or it is taken as evidence of ethical heteronomy and fatalism and evidence of a decadent literary milieu and so on.

Can you imagine a person saying, after reading Valmiki's Ramayana, 'you know, I get the impression that Ram didn't actually have any real feelings for Seeta or for his Dad or anybody else. In fact, I don't really know what Ram actually felt when Sita was abducted. It's like the guy was a robot, just going through the motions.'

Prof. Sheldon Pollock has said this- and he hasn't just read Valmiki but also translated a volume of the Ramayana- these are his actual, published, words '***Rama's 'true feelings' will remain secret, properly so, for they are quite irrelevant to the poem's purposes***.' Indeed, Pollock's theory is that Rama, like all the other characters in the Ramayana, is ethically heteronomous, he has no freedom of choice and no inner source of values other than blind obedience. Pollock arrives at this conclusion by taking note of the Occassionalist metaphysics propounded in the Ramayana. He believes this fact to be sufficient grounds to conclude that all the characters subscribe to this doctrine and that their every intentional act is conditioned by it. In other words, when a character in the Ramayana eats some food he does not do so because he is hungry or because the food is appetizing but because he believes God wants him to eat the food. However, Occasionalism, as a philosophical doctrine, makes no such claim or demand. One way of looking at Occasionalism is to think of it as a 'hidden variable' theory.

Intentionality is preserved, free choice remains operational, though some relevant information is not available to the agents involved.

Indeed, in this sense, Occasionalism is of the greatest utility to the Sciences- as well as to second order discourse- because it constantly alerts us to the inadequacy of our explanans- not fire burns wood but energy in the form of heat brings about a chemical change which itself can be more closely analysed and so on.

An oddity of Western thought- the source of its perpetual infantilism- is its cognitive dissonance in the face of propositions cast in logical form but which contain deontic rather than alethic variables. Work on defeasible systems of reasoning are a relative novelty in their tradition. Dialethia and 'Fuzzy Logic' are still generally considered beyond the pale. The problem of Meinongian objects (i.e. imaginary objects) or Moore's paradox (can I believe something I know to be untrue?) continued to puzzle philosophers at the beginning of the Twentieth Century. The Ghazal poet, as much as the reader of the Gita, on the other hand, have always had behind them sensible answers to these pseudo-problems.

However, in India, the rise of a careerist 'Revolutionary' ideology and socially complacent 'Politically Correct' agit prop, meant that Western Philosophical hermeneutics, of the most witless sort, had to be systematically substituted for the home-grown product. Since the Government had decided to adopt a historicist judicial hermeneutics, according to which evil upper castes had committed some terrible crime thousands of years ago and hence had to be made to pay a wholly bogus reparation through all eternity, there was a natural synergy between the agitators and the administrators. Both agreed that all Indian people were stupid ignorant rascals incapable of ever adopting any socially beneficial ideology or morality on their own.

In this context, Hegel and that old racist, Kant, suddenly became relevant again.

Hegel writing on the Gita said ' there is no distinction between religion and philosophy here. No concept of the individual as a moral agent ... their whole thought is preoccupied with the dominance of the One Absolute, entirely unqualified, indeterminate, substance, ...its abstractness (its renunciation of the external world) and the lack of the concept of the autonomous, free individual and its self-consciousness.'

'Knowledge is achieved only by means of abstraction from the sensible and through reflection … wherein thought remains equally motionless and inactive as the senses and feelings should be forced to inactivity. …The Indian isolation of the soul into emptiness is rather a stupefaction which perhaps does not at all deserve the name mysticism and which cannot lead to the discovery of true insights, because it is devoid of any contents.'

Hegel, being an ignorant pedant with no knowledge of what we would now call Science, Maths, Logic, General Knowledge, Economics, Politics and so on, not unnaturally invented some Mumbo Jumbo doctrine according to which Negation was somehow illicit. His complaint against the Indians was that '"Too often, they think of Nothing as a necessity". For this sin, the World Spirit got angry with them and cursed them with backwardness. Since Hegel, clever boy!, had rejected Negation and the 'Bad Infinite' and so on, the World Spirit became very happy with Prussia and blessed it and turned it into the bestest place ever which was convenient because Hegel lived there.

In this context, I am reminded of a 'thought experiment' from Kaushik Basu's play 'Crossings at Benares Junction'- the hero, a somewhat stupid lecturer, wonders what would happen if the world came to a stop for an instant and then, an instant later, everything resumed again. Would that instantaneous occurrence of Nothingness not somehow cancel the whole series and purge it from existence? This is an example of a Hegelian thought. It is utterly foolish. Cellular automaton theory takes such situations in its stride as a matter of routine.

Recently, Prof. Amartya Sen has had a crack at the Gita. Carrying on a glorious tradition of Indians writing nonsense in English about the Geeta, he thinks Lord Krishna is propounding deontological (rule based) ethics. He thinks Arjuna is a consequentialist (i.e. judging an action by its results). Now deontology is only a good strategy when there is imperfect information. No idiot follows a rule if he has all the information. Let me give an example. If I don't know who is knocking on the door, I look through the peep-hole. The rule 'always look through the peep-hole before opening the door' is a good rule because I have imperfect information. It is a stupid rule, which no one but an idiot would observe, if perfect information is available. Now, one may say deontology isn't about rules like 'always look through the peep-hole' but maxims such as 'always do your duty without fear or favour'. Clearly the word duty here must mean what you understand to be your duty (i.e. it must have an intensional rather than an extensional definition otherwise it cashes out as a consequentialism because you have to go to every possible being and inquire what your duty to them is and then decide how to reconcile all these different duties and so on). But if you already consider something to be your duty you'd be doing it anyway. The maxim is redundant- like saying 'be sure to exhale after you inhale' or 'be sure to obey the law of gravity'. Duty is a 'revealed preference'. The maxim 'do your duty' is only meaningful if a person is having a doubt about what he should do. Such doubts are of 2 types, those arising out of first order (i.e. informational or computational) constraints- here the doubt is resolved by the acquisition of information or a computational technique- and those expressing existential doubts regarding 'meta-duties'- i.e. what duty it is one's duty to have- which is a second order, purely philosophical, question. Here, Sens's characteristic method of making distinctions without a difference should lead to some philosophical result. It doesn't. Why? In the Gita, Krishna drops all deontological arguments in favour of a full blown occassionalist metaphysics. Sen knows this. Yet he writes what he writes. Personally, I blame *Nathkat Nandlal*. He likes to make fools of us grey-beards.

What to do? Lord Krishna is like that only.

Nyaya, niti & Amartya's Sen-escent Riti

In a Universe parallel to ours, King Canute, having failed to turn back the tide even though he had issued it a legal order in proper form, endowed a Professorial chair for a newly created Academic specialization termed 'Ye olde Tide Theory'. His pious successors on the English throne spent their 'Ship Money'- which ought to have gone to the Royal Navy- encouraging the study of this topic so obviously and utterly vital for the continued vibrant functioning of a, Sea girt, Mercantile Monarchy dedicated to Equitable Justice.

In due course, no doubt, a Bengali mathematico-jurist would have occupied the Chair in 'Tide theoretic aspects of Equitable Justice' and, with enormous erudition and subtle dialectics, shown that

1) all attempts to turn back the tide by the issuing of Equitable Writs have failed
2) a serious category mistake- that of confusing deontics with alethics- was involved.
3) the moon had an influence on tides, thus it was not lunatic at all to continue with the praiseworthy endevour initiated by Good King Canute but, rather, it was only proper to do so within a context of a pluralistic, xenophiliac, 'Capabilities approach' focusing on empowering poor rural women to learn to co-ordinate their menstrual cycles so as to gain a countervailing power over Neptune's tides.

In our own Universe, though failed Research Programs dominate our Credentialist Higher Education Racket, we don't have an Academic specialization of the precise sort mentioned above. Instead, we ask- in formulating a theory of Justice should we begin by deciding *what*, ideally, Justice would imply or else decide *how*, in practice, Society could be made more just?

The answer, for Economists, is NEITHER. Before doing something we should consider whether there is any point doing it at this time, and, what potential costs and benefits might be associated with the process.

Sen, it seems to me, has not asked himself the right question or, at any rate, not addressed it in his recent books and incontinence of utterance.

This contradicts his own stated preference for focusing on outcomes.

Sen makes great play on the distinction in Sanskrit between Nyaya and Niti, speculating on how Kautilya's Niti might have laid the foundations for Ashoka's Nyaya by drawing upon the scholarly work of T.H. White who described a similar relationship between Merlin's Magic and Arthur's Excalibur in the Walt Disney Classic 'the Sword in the Stone'.

G.E. moore foolishly yet, Sen also mentions the Gita- a sacred text for Hindus and thus a work we actually *do* know quite a lot about- unlike what actually happened in Ashoka's reign.

The word Niti, in Sanskrit and Hindi, refers to ethical conduct or policy. Kutniti means a crooked type of conduct or policy- such as characterized Kautilya's domestic and foreign policy.

An example of Kautilya's kutniti is the manner in which he recruited his successor. He gets a dhobi (washerman) to annoy the learned Pundit to such an extent that the fellow loses his temper and kills the dhobi. Kautilya then gives the Pundit a choice- serve the state or pay the penalty for man-slaughter. The Pundit revenges himself by framing Kautilya and having him killed. Sen's equation of Kautilya with Niti may seem utterly mad given gems of ethical behaviour and institution building like that given above.

What of Ashoka's Nyaya? The guy was real pissed off when he heard that some Jain monks were worshipping the Buddha by making out he was actually one of their rubbishy Tirthankaras. So Ashoka offered a bounty for decapitating Jain sadhus. One morning, inspecting the day's harvest of heads, he found that his own special chum had been killed by mistake. Ashoka then ended the killing of Jain monks, or, at any rate, stopped paying for it from the Privy Purse. This was actually a good thing- Government's shouldn't subsidise the decapitation of monks- and Sen, the economist, is right to commend Ashoka's Nyaya. However, since Sen is now also regarded as a Philosopher- and moreover one with an Indian surname and thus a 'native informant'- his silliness is merely par for the course.

Underlying the notion of Niti (that is, ethical principles as guiding one's conduct) is that of Dharma (Duty/ Righteousness/Religion) which considers the nexus of obligations and entitlements that connects individuals and encompasses the wider world. The concepts of *vyavahara* and *acara* are relevant here. However, if all possessed Dharma, i.e. had internalized that upon which all is based, then no actual judging or Judges would be needed as no transgression could arise.

Nyaya refers to Justice, in the sense that Quine pointed out, of being a stasis or equilibrium rather than an active process. To say this is not nyaya is to say this is unjust and contravenes either the law or the cosmic order. The Nyaya School of philosophy is concerned with Logic and Epistemology in Hinduism.

Underlying the notion of Nyaya is the older concept of Rta- the Cosmic Order. This was not conceived as eternal and unchanging. Rather Rta went through a sort of evolutionary cycle. The emergence of matsyanyaya- by which Sen means the situation where the big fish eat the smaller fish- is evidence that the Cosmic cycle is in a phase of decline and dissolution.

Niti and Nyaya are linked, as are Dharma and Rta, by the theory of karma- or re-birth. Ethical policy or behavior, good niti, upholds Dharma and enables Rta to right itself after the total dissolution at the end of the retrograde time cycle. The pay-off for the individual is that the good karma thus generated grants a better future birth- or, indeed, total salvation.

It should be noted that while Niti and Nyaya are words that can be used outside a theistic or soteriological context, they then lose any ethical meaning. Niti would mean a crafty policy or an individual religious observance expected to bring personal salvation without any benefit being provided for the wider community.

Nyaya, outside a Theistic context, would mean the principles or laws that operate in the actual world according to our empirical experience of it. Thus 'the enemy of your enemy is your friend' is a statement of Niti and 'Might is Right' is a statement of Nyaya.

Sen, however, has decided to use the terms Nyaya and Niti in a wholly different way so as to bring out what he believes to be a fundamental difference between two rival approaches to a theory of Justice.

The question arises whether the distinction-without-a-difference Sen makes is in fact philsophical in Colingwood's sense.

Let us make an analogy with my own proposed distinction between the termd 'fat bastard' and 'corpulent swine'. This is a highly meaningful distinction for me personally- as I am generally referred to as 'Iyer, the fat bastard' to distinguish me from another gentleman of the same name whom, it is my fervent wish, may be termed 'Iyer, the corpulent swine'. You will readily grant, if I am not mistaken, that there is a certain amount of affectionate raillery, not to say covert admiration, in the nickname 'fat bastard' whereas the epithet 'corpulent swine' vividly conveys the coprophagous grossness of that other fat Iyer bastard to whom I am compelled to refer.

In this case, clearly, the distinction I have introduced is of the highest utility and could become a topic of the most fertile philosophical investigation and literary exposition.

Is the same true of Sen's Nyaya/Niti distinction?

Sen says that Niti is about deciding what the ideally just situation ought to be and then devising institutions to bring it about. Thus, **Rawlsian Justice as Fairness** would be 'Niti'.

Except it wouldn't at all. Not in Sanskrit. Why? Policy and ethical conduct can not begin from a position of omniscience, behind the Rawlsian veil of ignorance, because- by a fundamental axiom of Dharmic thought- only the fully liberated Sage possesses that quality. But such Sages give up worldly life, they cease to interact with other beings under the rubric of reciprocal obligation and entitlement- i.e. omninscience can not give rise to a contractarian theory.

Niti is relevant to us only because our existing situation is characterized by problems regarding uncertainty, information asymmetry, preference revelation and so on. Indeed, as in the story of **Moses and Khizr**, who meet at the barzakh between 2 seas, so too in the Gita, we see that the omniscient person will always violate deontological, rule based, Niti since it is no longer a meaningful concept for a person free of all informational and instrumental constraints.

Why did Sen decide to call Niti the stuff he *wasn't* doing? Well, Niti is linked in Indian languages to stuff like Morality and Rules of Conduct and 'high thinking plain living' and so on. In other words, Niti is part of Bourgeois pi-jaw and Hegelian sittlichkeit and other unfashionable stuff like Institution building for better Governance through things like transparency, cracking down on corruption and rent seeking, decentralization of decision making (subsidiarity), equity audits and other such stuff on which countries like Cuba and West Bengal's Communist regime scores badly.

Nyaya on the other hand was more general, more abstract, and hence, in his eyes, more prestigious. Sen decided that Nyaya meant operating on the actual outcome matrix in time t which he assumed could be known and changed at that very time. Sadly, this is nonsense. If Nyaya is concerned with the outcome matrix at time t, then it can only be known, that too very imperfectly in time t+x and policy instruments can be implemented only at time t+x+y with the results only coming through with a further unpredictable, hysteresis heavy, time lag.

Moreover any diagnostic instrumentalized for policy purposes at time t+x would, probably, for that very reason, have lost its effectiveness by Goodhart's law. In other words the more we seek to act upon the outcome matrix the less reliable information we will have, ceteris paribus, about it in every future time period.

You remember Central Planning like they had in the Soviet Union? It failed. This is why. In the Indian context, if one instrumentalizes Caste as a proxy for Social exclusion, then freezing up the economy with controls and irrational fiscal incentives becomes attractive because though ruining the country, and negatively impacting social mobility, it nevertheless makes a substantive (Sen would say Nyaya) rather than procedural approach more attractive. In other words, first freeze the social geography by disabling the engines of mobility- viz. education, emigration and enterprise- and you have an excuse for any arbitrary 'direct' action which simply bypasses private and institutional notions of morality and just proceeding.

However, the Indian experience is that you can't freeze Social Geography. Even if you ensure that the Government Schools are crap, you can't stop working class folk (irrespective of caste or religion) from paying money to private schools to get their kids a shot at an education.

In other words, Nyaya in Sen's formulation is something that can't be known, can't be acted upon in a predictable or reliable manner, and thus utterly meaningless for any practical purpose. Yet Sen wants his 'Nyaya' coz it's a way of smuggling interpersonal comparisons of Utility- not just Utility but also other empty words like Freedom and Development and Enpowerment, Exclusion, degree of Aryan blood (or is it Democracy?) and so on back on the agenda. How could he get away with it? Well, it was the 70's, everybody was discovering their inner nigger- Sen, it turned out was a black man, and- as Gayatri Spivak explains **'strategic essentialism'** is okay coz gesture politics is way cooler and safer for our students than actual politics and, in any case, Edward Said had already pointed out that to teach 'Gulliver's travels' to Post Grads at Ivy League without issuing repeated H&S warnings that Jonathan Swift WAS NOT RECOMMENDING EATING YOUR OWN SHIT- YOU WILL NOT GET A HIGHER GRADE BY EATING YOUR OWN SHIT ON THIS COURSE!- rather Swift was doing something called 'irony' which, ironically, meant pretty much the same thing as like irony? Y'know? Except, like, aint it ironic that people who overuse the word irony like totally don't get it, right?

Anyway, this particular silliness of Sen's worked out well for him because interpersonal comparisons of Utility, Freedom, Development, Exclusion etc, etc, is what people with power do- it's what power is about. Guys from head office are constantly inventing some new performance measure which will screw things up in some novel way. *Why?* **Rossi's 'metallic laws'** make a startling prediction.

The Iron Law of Evaluation: The expected value of any net impact assessment of any large scale social program is zero.

The Iron Law arises from the experience that few impact assessments of large scale social programs have found that the programs in question had any net impact. The law also means that, based on the evaluation efforts of the last twenty years, the best a priori estimate of the net impact assessment of any program is zero, i.e., that the program will have no effect.

However, the business of designing performance indexes and holding seminars to thrash out methodological issues is profitable and empowering to academics enabling them to interface with big bureaucrats and get to utter sound-bites on T.V.

Since Niti would suggest ditching the whole project as corrupt and a waste of resources, Nyaya has to be invoked to continue with the practice- which in any case could be justified as keeping the serf-class of Grad Students busy building pyramids for the great Professor's sarcophagous and thus in a permanent state of deferential stupor.

Thus, so long as Power is inequitably distributed within the Academy, interpersonal comparisons are going to be big business within those constipated bowels. Human Development Indexes- apart from cooking the books to prove silly things like Cuba is better off than Florida and Bangladesh very Heaven- function like evaluative methods in State funded Education- i.e. they are manipulable in highly pathological ways w.r.t outcomes, not to mention being resource costly and breeding cynicism and careerism amongst those caught up in its rigmarole.

How about keeping Sen's 'Nyaya' around for 'thought experiments'? Well, Einstein's gedanken showed how stuff like Absolute Space and Time or hidden variables and so on actually fucked up scientific thinking. It is actually harmful to a Research Program, to retain a word- i.e a variable- to point to something that we can't know or control except for some purpose purely polemical or idiotically ideological. Sen has spoken of 'second order' public goods- i.e. the campaign for the provision of public goods. Notice he isn't talking about alethic arguments for Public goods coz Truth is itself a Public Good. Second order Public Goods must be based on the propagation of lies- emotive propaganda. However, subsidizing second order public goods, after the dead weight loss has been considered, is more likely to lead to less public good provision as the former crowd out the latter. The second order public good is like Sen's 'meta-preference' against what you are addicted to. It might lead (if there is no alethic, utilitarian, and therefore first order preference, that has negative cross elasticity of demand with the addictive product or range of products) to more consumption of demerit, addictive shite. In other words, the State could spend all its resources organizing sit down strikes to demand public goods- with the result that no public goods at all are produced.

In any case, Sen ignores the fact that his Nyaya is (in the linguistic sense) extensional not intensional- hence public discourse faces a halting problem and is doomed to remain phatic rather than meaningful. Sen also ignores the Jorgenson's dilemma aspect (i.e. how licit is it to treat deontic statements as if they are alethic?) which by itself generates a lot of aporias. In plain Hindustani- ethics is 'insha' not 'khabar'.

The point about Niti is that by respecting the informational and instrumental constraints of actual agents, Niti-talk can alter your Ethos positively and, in that sense, is Ethical. Not so Nyaya nonsense. Rawlsian Justice as fairness is a pedagogic exercise of Theological derivation designed to foster 'anukrosha' or empathy. Given Rawls's background and the location of his bully pulpit- nothing else was meant w.r.t Sen 'Nyaya'.

Sen hasn't taken on board, but must even at his advanced age retain at least a vestigial awareness of, a lot of Behavioral Ec stuff & Cog Sci stuff which rigorously fuck in the ass all his unstated assumptions seven times till Sunday. The fact is Emotions are now thought of as 'Darwinian algorithms of the mind' for both individual and collective decision making. A theory of Social Choice which ignores the signaling, co-ordinating, and strategic interessement functions of Sen-tentious non-alethic, value laden, second order, emotive rhetoric belongs in the crapper. Indeed, Sen's corrupt Developmentalist 'Riti' (Ritualism) is a fit subject for Anthropological Paleontologists.

When Narendra Modi says 'I incentivize consensus in Village Panchayat elections by giving a bonus to non-contested councils'- a case could be made for Modi as reflecting best practice in current Voting theory. When Sen speaks- fucked are we all and fucked must we remain.

Ultimately, the problem with people like Sen, who appear to be but aren't actually, banging the drum of Justice and Human Rights, is that they have added uncertainty and all sorts of perverse incentives and signal extraction problems to Public Policy and so there's a good case to institute a moratorium, if not a roll back, on that shite.

Sen tells us we Indians must focus less on Niti- though that is something we can do something about and ourselves benefit by doing- and more on Nyaya- which we can do nothing about.

Why? Well, Sen himself decided *not* to do asymmetry of information, preference revelation, auction design, mathematical politics, behavioural Ec, and the other very fruitful avenues of research Rand Corp Game theorists had opened up. He was sticking with an old fashioned, Benthamite, type of Social Choice theory where an omniscient Central Planner can frictionlessly re-allocate resources and make interpersonal comparisons of utility, and so on. This was not, it turned out, a fruitful for Economics or Psychology or anything at all but it fitted well with a type of Moral Philosophy or Political Philosophy-without-the-Politics which certain other star fish academics, equally stranded on the beach by pi-jaw's retreating tide, were now practicing.

There is a pay-off from buying Sen-shite. Think of the 2G auction. Sen's colleague, Ken Binmore earned mega-bucks for the UK by his mechanism design for their spectrum auction. A few years later, Sen's old pal Manmohan presides over a Cabinet which does first-come-first-served for 2G spectrum allocation. Sen-tentious Econ, it seems, yields a bigger Rent. Hence, meta-economically, it will always crowd out people like Binmore both from the Nobel prize banquet but also Development Econ. Instead, we are welcome to fucking roll around in Gandhian pig-shit.

Oh! one other thing is Sen-tentiousness, like 'Subaltern can't speak' Spivakese, looked radical, maybe even Communist, without being any such thing, back in the 70's when Bengali bhadralok feared decapitation at the hands of a Pol Pot reared in their own Shantiniketan kindergarten.

In other words, Sen had opened a way for 'eel wriggling' bureaucrats and anti-Poverty parasites to save their neck from the Naxals while making vacuous statements leaving them uncommitted to things like properly specified and monitorable Human Rights while still appearing to be on the side of the poor.

Thus, surprise! surprise!, Sen's Nyaya turns out to be *kutniti*- the corrupt international diplomacy of the Aid and Anti-Poverty parasites.

Is Sen's position something to do with the fact he's Indian- that too an upper class Hindu? Like- is it an Indian thing? Maybe its in the Bhagvad Gita or something?

Here's what Sen said about the Gita-

Question: In your new book, The Idea of Justice, you speak a lot about the difference between *niti* (institutional justice) and *nyaya* (realised justice). Do you think we have too much *niti* in India and too little *nyaya?*

Prof Amartya Sen: The short answer is yes. *Niti* has huge appeal and this applies to the great as well as to the non-great. In the Bhagavad Gita, Arjuna's position has much to commend it. I am not saying he should not have fought the war, but his doubts were not dismissable, in the way that Krishna dismissed them. Krishna is clearly a *niti* person.

How peculiar it is that someone as non-violent as Gandhiji, who was very inspired by the Gita, was on the side of **Krishna, who is making Arjuna fight a war and kill people, when Arjuna is saying maybe I shouldn't kill!** The Mahabharata ends with success, but also with grief, desolation, with women weeping for their lost men and funeral pyres burning in unison.

Why is this fucked?

Well, Krishna isn't making Arjuna fight a war. He does not say *'teri Maa hamare kabze mein hai'* which is what good Hindus, like myself, do when we want someone to fight a war or give us a second helping of *pav bhaji* or something equally transgressive from the view-point of Gandhian dharma.

J'accuse Amartya Sen. Sen, like me, is Indian and lives in Britain. Obviously some nice Aunty type must be feeding him. But, how to communicate to said Aunty a desire for a more rapid replenishment of one's dinner *thali*? Does one recite some Gita? No! One says *'teri Maa hamare kabze mein hai'* and laughs like Gabbar Singh. Aunty, no matter how aged, finally takes notice and says 'Oh? Plate empty is it? Good boy. *Chamatha*. I refill just now only'.

That's how things are done. Sen knows it. I know it. But, maybe Binmore does not.

The Bhagvad Geeta and Binmore's Evolutionary Game Theory

This is **Prof. Ken Binmore** on the application of game theory to moral and political science.

*'The most important result in this context is the folk theorem of repeated game theory, which roughly says that any stable outcome a society can achieve with the help of an external enforcement agency (like a King and his army, or God) can also be achieved without any external enforcement at all in a **repeated** game, provided the players are sufficiently patient and have no secrets from one another. Game theorists take the view that a self-policing social system must be a Nash equilibrium in which each player is simultaneously making a best reply to the strategy choices of the other players. No single player then needs to be coerced, because he is already doing as well for himself as he can. We think that even authoritarian governments need to operate a Nash equilibrium in the repeated game of life played by the society they control if they are to be stable, because popes, kings, dictators, generals, judges, and the police themselves are all players in the game of life, and so cannot be treated as external enforcement agencies, but must be assigned roles that are compatible with their incentives just like the meanest citizen. In brief, the game theory answer to* quis ipsos custodes custodiet *is that we must all guard each other.*

To this insight, my own work adds a game-theoretic approach to our understanding of fairness norms (Binmore [2005]). The folk theorem tells us that there are many efficient Nash equilibria in the repeated games of life played by human societies. This was true in particular of prehuman hunter-gatherer societies. Evolution therefore had an equilibrium selection problem to solve. The members of such a foraging society needed to coordinate on one of the many Nash equilibria in its game of life---but which one? I believe that our sense of fairness derives from evolution's solution to this equilibrium selection problem. That is to say, metaphysics has nothing to do with fairness---if evolution had happened upon another solution to the equilibrium selection problem, we would be denouncing what we now call fair as unfair. I go on to argue that our sense of fairness is like language in having a genetically determined deep structure that is common to the whole human race. I then give reasons why one should expect this deep structure to be captured by Rawls' original position. The question then arises as to whether Rawls [1972] or Harsanyi [1977] are correct in their opposing analyses of rational bargaining in the original position. With the external enforcement assumed by both, the answer is that Harsanyi's utilitarian conclusion is correct. Without external enforcement of any kind (so that there are no Rawlsian "strains of commitment" at all), I come up with something very close to Rawls' egalitarian conclusion. That is to say, although Harsanyi's analysis was better than Rawls', but Rawls had the better intuition.My analysis of our sense of fairness will doubtless be thought naïve by future scholars, but it is hard to conceive of a future approach that will not have a similar game-theoretic foundation.'

Evolutionary Game Theory of Prof. Binmore's sort is or was of more than evanescent interest, intersecting as it did with much hyped 'results' from Behavioural Economics and Primate Ethology and occurring in the visitor's lounge of Western Political Philosophy's Twilight Home as represented by the ludicrous lucubrations of shit-heads like Rawls and Nozick who did not understand that the concept of a contract- and hence the 'Social Contract'- differs from the concept of a relationship- or set of relationships constituting a Society- precisely by being a lottery and anti-social, purely for that reason, in direct proportion to its extent and degree of indefeasibility.

With our present chastened understanding of why systemic risk management amplifies catastrophic shocks, and how a credentialist crisis can make availability cascades so ubiquitous as to have all the appearance of a Revolution, all the more velvet for witless; with the end of 'the Great Moderation', not to speak of the the end of 'the end of History', the fundamental Kantian problematic re. demarcating heteronomy from an autonomy founded upon a reciprocal and fundamentally egalitarian Enlightenment-as-freedom has become suddenly more salient with the result that it is now the turn of the Whigs to find the idea of Evolution unsettling.

This is because the empirical existence of polymorphism w.r.t (Kantian) reciprocal notions of morality and freedom raises the question of whether this is merely phenotypic- perhaps with environmental triggers, in which case ensuring a homogenous developmental ontogeny might re-establish an essential monomorphism, or else it is stochastic arising out of a mixed Evolutionarily Stable Strategy.
Moran (1992) has suggested that competition between kin millitates for this result as a way of 'hedging bets' so to speak.

The Whig theory of History can incorporate both the environmental trigger scenario - perhaps by invoking a mimetic to drive convergence of ontogenetic environments- as well as the mixed strategy theory- in the latter case by seeking to specify what that precise mixture might be and then concentrating on mechanism design such that it bestows prescriptivity on its own project.

The alternative- viz. to admit genetic polymorphism as responsible for innate differences in notions of morality and, its Kantian reciprocal, freedom - forces Whiggery to cash out as either a hierarchical special-pleading or else a nihilsm or panalethia. Which, being *au fond* a De Maistrean theory of sacrifice, Whiggery can live with because only its vitality of life, not its virulence of legitimacy, is lost thereby.
Consider this eloquent extract from the Sage of Konisberg's 'Differences in National characteristics, so far as they depend on the distinct feeling of the Beautiful and Sublime'

'A despairing man is always a strict master over anyone weaker, just as with us that man is always a tyrant in the kitchen who outside his own house hardly dares to look anyone in the face. Of course, Father Labat reports that a Negro carpenter, whom he reproached for haughty treatment toward his wives, answered: "You whites are indeed fools, for first you make great concessions to your wives, and afterward you complain when they drive you mad." And it might be that there were something in this which perhaps deserved to be considered; but in short, **this fellow was quite black from head to foot, a clear proof that what he said was stupid.'**

Rawls, speaking of the difference principle (by which only those departures from equality of outcome are permitted which benefit the worst off), points out that 'least advantaged' is not a (Kripke) rigid designator always picking out, say, women rather than men, whites rather than blacks, British rather than Indians, across all possible worlds. However, the elementary theory of price and service provision discrimination explains how the difference principle militates for racism and sexism because these are cheap ways to segment the market (i.e. they are barriers that are very costly to get around but very cheap to enforce) such that a good or service with very high fixed costs which might not otherwise be provided becomes available. In other words, in deciding who to listen to, who gets 'voice'- 'loyalty' and 'exit' (Hirschman)- Rawls's Kantianism is always gonna be saying stuff like 'the fellow was quite black from head to foot, a clear proof that what he said was stupid', unless this involves a risk of having the shit kicked out of you, in which case the safest thing is to pretend you're a Mathematical Economist or Post

Modern or incarnate some other such oxymoron.

Before embracing so odious an outcome, and bearing in mind Moran's suggestion that kin rivalry might catalyse a stochastic polymorphism- such that kin-folk with different conceptions of morality clash to the extent of violating Hamilton's rule- the Indian Mahabharata, an early Iron Age Epic redacted in the Axial Age, might be worth examining as it deals with an epoch changing war between cousins- as trivial in conception and catastrophic in its consequences as the Kaiser's War and the conflagration to which it give rise. Moreover, the Mahabharata makes explicit mention of Probability and Game Theory as being sciences that need to be mastered for a man, already of the highest moral and empathic character, to rise above heteronomy and rule as a Just King. Another, related Epic, the Ramayana, deals with a King of an even higher type whose 'Ramrajya' (rule of King Rama) dispenses, at least in its idealized form, even with Rawlsian 'strains of commitment'- i.e. a pre-existing internalized consensus or set of norms- relying instead upon the agent with greater autonomy to always choose such that the more heteronomous agents choices are valorized in a manner intended to effect the upliftment of the latter.

By the Mahabharata's system of symmetries- its 'double entry book-keeping heuristic' so to speak- if Krishna eggs on Arjuna to kill Karna by awaking his dark anger, then there should be another episode where Arjuna, in wrath, seeks to slay the person he thinks is his eldest brother- viz. King Yuddhishtra. In that episode Krishna gets Arjuna to redirect his wrath into words- Krishna tells Arjuna to utter a condign criticism of his elder brother, for to humiliate a man is to inflict a sort of 'Social death' upon him. Arjuna does this so as not to break his vow (to seek to kill the one who demands he surrender his emblematic Gandiva bow) but then feels so wretched he wants to kill himself. Krishna tells him that dharma is subtle, none understand it, the correct thing to do now is to utter an accurate description of one's own great merits- for to praise oneself, or show one's true greatness, is to slay oneself. Arjuna complies. After this, he humbly begs forgiveness from King Yuddhishtra and persuades him to continue to rule over the fortunes of their house.

The important point here- perhaps too obvious to be spelled out- is that Krishna's theophany in the Geeta was a type of self-slaying, a Christ-like sacrifice, for the purpose of assuring his devotees that the Lord takes on the sins of his devotees and pays the price for them. From the point of view of Faith, this is the meaning of the Geeta. Game theory, mechanism design, the evolution of notions of fairness and Justice and their application to the sort of Social Order we might choose behind a Rawlsian veil of ignorance and other such secular considerations appear to have no importance to reading the Geeta.

If, lacking Faith, we nevertheless persist, seeking to read the Geeta with the aid of its dual, the Kiratarjunia, we find that dharma is indeed subtle, as Krishna says, and beyond the ken of Faith alone.

Why is this? Well, in both texts, Arjuna is bested by a sort of 'shock and awe' that God commands. Yet, taken together, both texts serve to whip up thymotic rage for an inhuman purpose. Shiva, in essence, challenges Arjuna to a fight by enraging him. The Destroyer God normally grants a boon to an ascetic not for the purpose of making him puissant above all others but, by giving full reign to his egotism or hubris, to cause the ascetic to destroy himself by a heinous transgression which Vishnu (the Preserver God's) avatar will punish. However, in the Kiratarjunia this motif is reversed. Shiva distracts Arjuna from his austerities by provoking him to a fight. The boon he grants does not destroy Arjuna himself but is part of a wider plan to greatly decimate the entire warrior class to which Arjuna belonged. Similarly, the Geeta, despite all its fine philosophy, serves the purpose of bringing about Arjuna's killing of his eldest brother while in a state of dark anger. In other words, both tell us only about heteronomous conceptions of dharma- actions required of a mortal for purposes beyond his ken.

In contrast, a quite different tack is taken in the portion of the Mahabharat which deals with the vishada of King Yuddhishtra- who as the head of his house is a principal rather than an agent- and who is the incarnation of 'Dharma' (Righteousness).

Yuddhistra is something approaching the ideal moral being. Previously, he had been given the choice of saving the life of one of his brothers. Instead of choosing the strongest or the most able, he chose one who had a different mother so that both maternal lineages might be preserved. This, by itself, throws a light upon Harsanyi's 'rule utilitarianism' notion that ethical decisions require a sort of impersonality such as would arise from not knowing in whose shoes one might find oneself. Yet, one already fills a certain pair of shoes and can't envisage a Universe in which that particular view point is not valorized. There is a sort of Anthropic principle at work here or, at the level of probability distributions, a Monty Hall type Problem. Impersonality can't be truly self-abnegating, at least not consistently, otherwise no calculus could be derived.

 Can impartiality of this type be truly ethical if it forecloses the option of self-abnegation?

 Yes, if 'fairness' is vector, not scalar- if, as Binmore says, it is structured like a language, then it is a necessarily a Bakhtinian heteroglossia- referencing a set of compossible evolutionary stable strategies.

However, there is a sort of Newcombe's problem type situation here which also inheres in the Kantian categorical imperative. Referencing Nozick's- 'Judge Hercules' who can always re-interpret in a harmonious manner the whole body of the Law such that it's fabric suffers no tear of wrinkle- we might say that we would always want our choice to have this quality. But to seek to conform to the prediction of Newcombe's oracle or Judge Hercules's ruling in the Court of the Kantian Categorical Imperative, which, even absent any factor militating for heteronomy, is nevertheless to feel a curb placed upon one's free will. The poisoned chalice placed before us which, as with Kavka's toxin, we drain so 'Thy Will, Lord, not mine, be done' turns out to be the only way to evade the death sentence of heteronomy.

 Returning to Yuddhishtra deciding which one of his brothers to revive- if he is to be impartial, surely he should toss a coin, after all, each of his brothers has an equal right to live and ought to command an equal portion of his love. In particular, to ordain of a pair of twins that one should live to mourn the other, appears the opposite of rule-utilitarian 'impersonality' in that, it may be, this maximizes the bereavement for the survivors while simultaneously minimizing the fighting ability of the depleted band of brothers. No doubt the Just King will derive a sense of inflated pride by this deliberate choosing of the worst possible outcome, but what of the other brother? Suppose it is easier for Yuddhishtra to make tough 'ethical' decisions of this sort than it would be for the other. Suppose further that the survivor of the (presumably identical) twins, by reason of Hamilton's rule (kin selection), knows that Yuddhistra's gift to him of his life would not be one who could have as easily reciprocated- then the Just King's fairness ethic is not symmetric and thus all the more unfair. Survivor guilt has been maximised merely so an insufferable prig can plume himself. In other words Yuddhishtra has made a decision for the group which is not a canonical solution to the co-ordination problem here- viz. what choice would be 'natural' and thus cause the least resentment as being what any of the other guys would have done had they had to choose. It appears, hence, that the Just King makes the worst possible decision but since, in this instance, the game was 'loser takes all', purely by chance, Yuddhishtra gets back all his brothers.

This King is depicted as having one besetting vice- gambling fever. His elder brother, Karna, is unreasonably generous- but it is a noble fault. Not once, but twice (because everything in the Mahabharat happens twice), Yudhhishtra gambles everything away- including himself, his brothers and their common wife.

The fact that the gambler Yuddhishtra is described as the incarnation of Dharma even before he learns Probability and Game Theory, thus becoming an expert gambler, has puzzled readers.

True, this may be seen as simple 'hamartia' (the tragic flaw in an otherwise noble personality which makes for good drama) or it may be that in a hierarchical Society where slavery exists it is only fair that the King and his beloved brothers and wife (with whom he shares everything) take their turn at the hazard of ending up at the bottom of the heap. As Binmore points out, Rawls and Harsanyi arrive at opposite conclusions as to what will happen from behind the veil of ignorance based on the constraints they place on the preferences of the idealized rational agents assumed for the exercise. Yet, if Yuddhishtra is truly rational, the question arises as to why he does not abandon Caste based Dharma for something like Moh Tzu's mix of pragmatic utilitarianism coupled with a Creedal deontology of Universal Love?

Perhaps, belief in the karma theory precludes this outcome. Lifting all constraints on preferences and world-views behind the Rawlsian veil, however, has the result that nothing remains to rule out in advance that what will ultimately be chosen is not Borges's 'Lottery in Babylon'- where anything can happen- indeed will happen- to anybody. Indeed, if the agents believe in metempsychosis, Borges's Lottery dominates all other solutions yielding a sort of *tuirgen* tour through all souls that ever might exist.

However, those theodicies or spiritual traditions which have embraced this outcome sooner or later explicity come out and say that both karma (metempsychosis) and dharma (righteousness) are empty and have no ontological significance.

Indeed, the problem with the doctrine of God as the sole efficient cause is that it tends to render the Godhead an irrelevance from the human point of view. Fatalism of this sort cashes out as thymotic hedonism. If only our emotions are ours, not our actions, indulge them to your heart's content! Ghazali's Occasionalism puts the Ghazal universe on precisely this insane trajectory. The notion that emotions- as Darwinian algorithms of the limbic system- have evolved because of their adaptiveness in decision making, signaling, preference revelation and so on is thrown out of the window. No Society could last very long embracing such a doctrine.

Yuddhishtra's vishada (depression) arises in the following manner. He feels compelled to agree to every game of dice to which he is challenged. Since the other side have a skilled gamester on their team, Yuddhishtra always loses. Yet he firmly believes he and his brothers should be given something- even a small share- of the ancestral patrimony. He is prepared to fight and shed blood to maintain his rights in this respect. But, as his brother Bhima warns, what is the point of his winning back their share of the Kingdom if he just dices it away again? Bhima is duty bound to obey his elder brother but, it appears, his elder brother has an addiction and thus lacks competency. Bhima proposes to kill of all the enemies himself and then crown Yuddhisthra. However, this itself is a departure from the path of righteousness. Yuddhistra is caught in a double bind. His hamartia is the source of his heteronomy. Fortunately, just as Arjuna's Vishada is dispelled by a divine discourse, so too is Yuddhishtra's. He hears the story of Nala and learns probability and Game theory. Now he needn't fear losing everything to a dice game.

Furthermore, he has also learned that the seemingly immutable caste hierarchy of ancient India has no moral or soteriological legitimacy and can be dispensed with- indeed, God is preparing a great holocaust of people of his class so as to facilitate a transition to something less fucking obnoxious.

If the Geeta is read without keeping this episode in mind, the result would be a valorization of a hierarchical, misogynistic society in which duty involves killing even kinfolk without mercy. The great mathematician Andre Weil, perhaps because he subconsciously grasped the system of symmetries underlying the Geeta, rejected such a view. The plain reading, for him, as for his colleague, the Gandhian, Vijayraghavan, was do your own duty- i.e. what you want- rather than what others demand. This too was a misreading. Weil tried to dodge the draft- maths was his duty not manning a machine gun- but, by that very step, almost lost his life.

The Mahabharat is about the self-destructive collapse of one sort of social order- the heroic age where thymos ruled supreme- and the dawn of another more mercantile and rights based social order- where heteronomy spelled backwardness and internecine bloodshed, while intersubjective autonomy and rationality pointed the way forward to a great advance in material civilization.

However, it remains an open problem, for me at any rate, as to whether the light that Game Theory throws upon the Geeta is not reflected back upon it as an exercise in futility as damning as the Just King's other great strategic blunder viz. his victory at Kurukshetra where, once again, it was a case of loser takes all.

Karna and Moses.

Both Karna and Moses were cast off into rivers by their mothers and it was their brothers- Arjuna in the case of Karna and Aaron in the case of Moses whose lineages were consecrated as Kings in the Indian tradition and High Priests (kohainim) in the Judaic.

It has been speculated that the motif of the baby cast away in a reed basket is a very ancient one- perhaps one with some historical precedent in the case of Sargon of Akkad- and that it might have been used to disguise the genealogical identity of a usurper or a person of different ethnic or class background. Freud's notion that Moses might have been an Egyptian follower of Akhenaton is a famous example of this sort of Euhemerism.

In the case of the Mahabharata, it is tempting to look at Karna- whose dominating quality is unbounded generosity arising from an overmastering thymotic (rajsic) drive- as a foil to Yuddhishtra whose predominating quality is forbearance and respect for the rights of others. Perhaps, Karna represents an older conception of the chivalrous Hero-King which was ceasing to be prescriptive in a materially more prosperous age when the important thing was to develop trade-routes, commercial networks and secure the possessions of the productive classes by establish an indefeasible code of Law as opposed to the Justice-as-patronage model of the early Iron Age.

The pathos of Karna, as one who prefers that the great warriors get one last chance to gain heaven in a battle to end all battles, is the pathos of the Gloaming of the Age of Heroes which will leave Epic Poetry forever widowed.

In contrast, the pathos of Moses- taking his last look from Pisgah upon the Promised Land he is forbidden to enter; his own seed fated to receive no special recognition though that of his brother Aaron remains distinguished to this day by the title Cohen, or Kahane- marks something new in the world of letters- it is the raising of Prophesy to the level of Prose, it is the birth of a Bibliolatry which will hunt down bards, it is the final withdrawal of the heimat of human belonging from what henceforth will be merely land.

Karna is not vanquished any more than the Winter Sun is vanquished by hoar frost. Moses, on the other hand, never enters the Promised Land. A book binds him. Black ink stronger than that Red Sea he vainly parted.

The Gita as a guide to life.

How can the Bhagvad Gita help guide our lives?

Before we can answer this question, let us look at what happens in the Mahabharata. Essentially, for some reason or other, God or some other such abstraction has decided to kill off lots of warriors. A few are fated, for some reason or other, not to be killed. They are called the 'victors'. Everybody else dies.

At the start of the Gita, Arjuna is depressed because he foresees being one of the survivors. He decides not to fight. Krishna explains to him that refusal to fight would be to go against his own nature- he is a warrior- and won't change anything anyway. Eventually, Krishna shows Arjuna that he himself is actually God almighty so, like, everything's cool, don't sweat it bro.

The Gita is a very important guide to Life because of the large number of shit-heads we have swarming around who claim to be God Almighty or possessed of some higher Moral authority or Magical power and they want us to go kill lots of people, or hand over lots of money, or give them a blow-job or something. JUST SAY NO. They will then tell you that they don't really need your help, it's all going to happen for them anyway, except you don't get to go to Heaven. PISS ON THEIR FACE.. Unless there's an actual job with a good pension and dental plan in which case *don't* piss on their face but remember ALL BOSSES ARE ASSHOLES. Take the job if you have to and dunno, like maybe do Yoga or something when you ought to be stock-taking and remember to steal as much office stationery as you can lay your hands on.

So that's the Gita as a guide to life. Tomorrow we do the Bible on how crucifying unmarried Jewish carpenters is the best thing you can do for Humanity.

The Butcher's Gita

In the Mahabharata, two Butchers teach Dharma and their teaching is called a Gita- a song.

They're not actual butchers- unlike Ding, who enlightened Confucius by showing that one never needs to sharpen one's cleaver if one cuts along the grain, the marbling, the fatty Tao, of the flesh- instead, they're vertically integrated Meat monopolists owning both the supply and retail side of the business.

Consequently, they are wealthy and powerful beyond the common ken. Both are engaged in a disreputable trade- in the Mahabharata, the *vyadha*, the butcher, is a byword for fraud and sharp practice- but, by reason of their wealth, wisdom and winsome personality, neither are thus much reproached to their face. Indeed, we may say, the righteous Butcher of the Vyadha Gita redeems all of his profession who, we now see, are mere agents working his will.

Lord Krishna redeems, not the *profession* of the professional butchers of men- variously called Kshatriyas, Robber-Barons or Kings- after all, at Kurukshetra, he appears as but Suta, charioteer or bard- but, by affirming All his meat-puppets merely- in their own proper person they neither slay nor are slain- absolves of blood guilt even these, not Eagles amongst men but- it transpires- human, albeit by Huma's wings over-shadowed, but *murder* of crows or other collective noun for noisome birds fed on carrion.

Ding, the butcher, acting without acting or not acting while acting- at peace with his own Nature and partaking of the always beneficent Tao- shows how *svadharma* is *wu wei*. This is because he actually cuts meat. Not coz of karma, nor coz he's actually F.B.I undercover, but coz it's what he does and does *wu wei* well. He cuts meat. End of. He's not all like I'm only in the meat business coz like what actually went down, right? was I was like a shoo in for Juilliard, I mean I was definitely gonna apply but then, like, my Uncle was the Sausage King of South Bronx?- I mean he would have been if like Dad hadn't gone and backed into the meat grinder- so everybody got a little behind with their orders as Confucius say!- and I mean there's this *chuddi* buddy of mine from back in parochial who went to Wharton and he was like all in my face with 'get your frickin meat on, dude! What with Obamacare and everybody's 401(k)'s in the toilet who fucking ***don't*** wanna heart-attack? Gimme beef baby!'

Lord Krishna says amongst Vedas he's the Sama whose Upanishad is the Chandogya. There's only one non social fucking parasite in that last named- Raikva, the carter, the one who knows, or- by *wu wei* **IS**- the Way, that otherwise potholed road, the Tao.

Scholiasts think Raikva calls the King, come humbly to learn from him, a 'Shudra' not because the King is *actually* working class- i.e. neither Priest, Peer, nor Plutocrat- but because the word is etymologically related to 'Vishada'- sorrow, depression- and, interestingly, both the Vyadha and the Bhagvad Gita arise in the Mahabharata as cures for Vishada- that of King Yuddhistra in the former instance, that of Prince Arjuna in the latter. But, fucking Aristos are all fucked in the head while Priests, like those featured in the Chandogya, just hungry pan-handlers looking to score some vittels.Why fucking bother with them? Or- what?- you don't like it here and wanna go back to World of Warcraft medieval times?Fucking pay attention. I'm making an important point here.

You want to hear the Gita sing?
Learn first from slitty eyed Ding!
(That's right. I went there. What? Black people can't be Racist?)

Duryodhana in the Mahabharata & anti-metic 'mimetic desire'

Both emulous Bilqis, in the Quran, and envious Duryodhana, in the Mahabharata, mistake a highly polished marble floor for a pool of water. The former lifts her skirts- giving rise to a 'free show' for King Solomon who, thus impassioned, becomes instrumental in the breaking of her waters and thus, millennia later, for the providential provision, to the Muhajir Meccan Hanif, of secure refuge in Ethiopia- the Negus being a nested image of Solomon's mingling, in that mirror of stone, with the nethers' of the Gospel's 'Queen of the South' who 'shall rise up in the judgment with this generation, and shall condemn it: for she came from the uttermost parts of the earth to hear the wisdom of Solomon; and, behold, a greater than Solomon *is* here.'

Duryodhana, on the other hand, visiting his *nouveau riche* cousins in Indraprastha, first won't step on stone, thinking it water, then falls into a pool thinking it stone. Because Draupati ridicules him for having inherited the blindness of his father- that final pool of water in which Duryodhana takes refuge sets also- like Sagara addressing Ram in Tulsi's masterwork- is a merely tribal and thymotic limit to the nature of the Ethical agon set in motion by that mirror of stone or gallehault of mimetic desire.

A more obvious place to look for Girardian motifs, in the Mahabharata. is Chitrangada's battle with his namesake. Bhishma doesn't intervene. Why? The one thing he won't do battle to protect his family from is disease- where the body struggles with itself. Is it the case that Adaa Vijaa, Adi Vigyan,- the casting off of one's ills onto one's image in the mirror- but, in Ind, the Gemini are healers by their mutual harmony not their homicidal rage to furnish a korban or Homo Sacer- is also at the root of Chitrangada, the Gandharva's, battle challenge to Chitrangada, the Mortal? The Human image must fight its Divine namesake- for only one can survive to attest the extensionless, therefore infinite, reverse mereology of (*Maryada Bhakti's*) Pure Name.

But, on Earth, at least in proper English, at marriage, two come together to boast the same name. The esteemed (hopefully, soon to be) wife of Mr. Vivek Iyer is not properly addressed as Mrs. Honeytits Iyer but as Mrs. Vivek Iyer simply. If some allusion must be made to her nominal haecceity, as for example if I were polygynous, then the correct form, surely, would be 'Honeytits, Mrs. Vivek Iyer'. Otherwise, people might think the blameless damsel, and lapdancer, in question was actually descended from the impure wombs of, my second cousins, the *arriviste*, for ICS gotra, Honeytits Iyers of Hampstead Heath.

Indeed, every sacral form of marriage involves a shared and shyly darted glance into 'Ayn ul Bibi Maryam'- Mary's mirror- where groom and bride see themselves as they will be seen in Heaven, the more securely univocal for freed of all earthly blemishes.

Only thus should be read Tagore's Chitrangada or the Mahabharata's reversal of the Rustam /Sohrab, or Cuchulain/ Connia, outcome of Arjuna's unknowing duel with his son whereby-husband resurrected by reflection in a water nymph's marble of co-motherhood- the miracle Krishna works for posthumous Parikshit, but firmly, is put in its place.

What has all this to do with the Gita?

Is the answer not obvious?

No?

Really, no?

Well, in that case, I suppose I'd better add something to round this off 'fore chowing down on my tonight's meed of Microwaved Takeaway.

Too much information?

Meh!

Drinking my iced Rum & Coke, in the glorious gloaming of the **one** Summery day afforded me by this unlucky year- so far has my way of life fallen into the sere, the yellow leaf- I suddenly think of what a son once said to his handsome father admiring himself in the mirror- 'You haven't seen Mum's true beauty'. Hurrying immediately to her, husband upbraids his wife for wrongfully withholding dowry. Wife says 'who sees my true beauty will die in a fraticidal struggle.' 'But that is your own son!' Hubby is shocked. 'You jus' cursed your own son, Hon!' Heeding mother's cry of pain, God says, listen Luv, I can make an exception for your lad. Mum says- no, make an exception for every other mother's son- not mine.

Who was that mother who could recognize herself so in the Ayn-ul-Bibi-Maryam?

Kunti?

Sure.

Why not?

Actually *yes*- if you read Gita properly.

I don't.

So, this is my source-

Matir Moyna

It was the time of the Bangladesh war. A baul singer on a refugee boat tells the story. The English subtitles read thus- 'The Tiger of God, (Hazrat) Ali was observing his masculine beauty in the mirror. His son (Hazrat) Hossain tells his father- 'If only you knew my mother's true beauty.'Ali rushes to his wife and says 'show me your beauty that you have hidden even from your husband'. (Hazrat) Fatima replies 'It is not a physical beauty which can be seen with the naked eye. Then Fatima utters her curse (sic). 'Whoever beheld my divine image will die in a fraticidal war. Ali said 'Your curse is for none other than your own son! Hossain witnessed your sacred self in an invisible mosque!' Hearing Fatima's cry, Allah says 'I can save your son but no other son will be spared their mother's curse. Cries out Earth Mother Fatima, 'O, Allah, let me loose my son but let no other child suffer the same fate!' The Grace of the Prophet's daughter illuminates the World. Thus Fatima's pain redeems the suffering of all women.

Tareque Masud is dead. I'm alive. God must fucking hate us.

Fex Urbis, Lex Orbis

Now Communion is but yeasting, stones atone for Christ's bread
& Weaver, only following orders, as Khaddar to Kabir said
Korban or pharmakos- 'tis is a dangerous saw
Dregs of the City, Homo Sacer of the Law.

Carl Schmitt & the Gita's Hamletian Interessement

'*The Hundred Years War had to end with the death of Theology because otherwise it would have been a thousand year war, a million year war, so fertile were they in stirring up war by their doctrnies of tyrnannicide and just war. Politics saves from the despair of Theologically inspired war.*'

(Dr. Carl Schmitt. Hamlet or Hecuba?)

'Nigga, pleeze! *Ludens in orbe terrarum* (Proverbs 8.30-31) at best strobes or syncopates Light. True the 'Baroque feeling of being on stage all the time- Corneille, Racine- is proto-Political for the State can not only prescribe all rules but thereby gain a regulative and penal access to inwardness but- when God games with Leviathan- the opposite happens, scrutiny imposes upon itself a blinker- haecceity's guerrilla network can grow in a time exponential to that of its best gamed simulation- so, not God is dead, just that of the Theologians' relatively fucked. Which is cool.

'Newton liberated England by denying the dogma of the soul's necessary immortality by the supremely practical expedient of cohesively combating the endogeny of chrematistic Credit- that is counterfeiting, cronyinsm and corrupt practice- by implementing serration and fucking arresting coin clippers. It was this substantivist and exogenous Socio-Economic initiative which possibilised second order fuckwits like David Hume and Bishop buggering Berkeley whom we should less easily forgive than contemporary avatars of Leibnizian, or Ghazzalian dogma who insist the hairy ball theorem implies that a Greek hair-cut will cure a German cow-lick. No I'm not drunk. Well, not very drunk. Why do you ask?'

'Irrevocable reality is the dumb rock upon which the play breaks and the surge of the truly tragic moves forward in a cloud of foam.'

As to Urvashi, Puruvaras, bares Indr my 'I' to your 'You'
Yet, haply, for ayah, afford board we Cthulhu's two
Elder Gods- foam births or slays
Aphrodite, Vritra- our Nights and Days.

Epoché means 'suspension'- pausing and standing back to question one's fundamental beliefs and values. The Gita's dramatic appeal is that it marks a suspension of action- the two armies have assembled, clarions has been sounded on both sides, hostilities are about to commence, but, suddenly, the relentless forward thrust of the narrative is arrested, not by the Cassandra cry of a clairvoyant, nor the chastened counsel of a Seer; but, utterly unexpectedly, by impetuous Arjuna who, for the first and only time in his life, confesses himself daunted, not, it is true, by the imminent hazard of death in combat but rather by an immanent prevision of the wretchedness of a Victory that can only be secured by the unrelenting carnage of those so near, if not dear, in blood.

Arjuna's hesitation parallels that of Hamlet. Neither Hamlet nor Arjuna is afraid of being killed or suffering damnation. Nor are they tempted by Power or Pelf. Still, one may argue, Hamlet's dilemma is quite different from Arjuna's. After all, the murdered King's ghost might be the Prince of Liars, in disguise, trying to get Hamlet to damn himself by killing an innocent man- one to whom, moreover, he owes a triple duty of obedience as nephew, step-son and subject.

Indeed, it is tempting to see both our puzzled Princes as cursed with what might be called the blighting *Gandharva* gift of 'backward induction'- id est, the anti-Epimethean criterion for judging action's cascade by working backwards, testing for optimality, from the final consequence . If Hamlet kills his Uncle, while the latter is at prayer, the end result is that the King gains heaven while the Prince is damned for all eternity. Similarly, Arjuna's victory means his cousins gain Heaven, for slain in battle in accordance with their warrior code, while the Pandavas, as the heads of the clan, become responsible for the misery, loss of status, and probable prostitution and miscegenation of the womenfolk left behind.

However, the moment Hamlet articulates the eschatological consequence of slaying the King at prayer, it immediately seizes to be binding- he himself can't be damned since the action's intentionality is to send his sin-stained enemy to Heaven, by taking his place in Hell. But- and this is Hamlet's Protestant dilemma- the Son thus only keeps with faith with the Father by breaking troth with the latter's Unholy Ghost.

Thankfully, at least for the purposes of my book, this objection does not hold water.

It's like the Examination question 'was Hamlet mad, or merely pretending to be mad?' which maddened three generations of my male ancestors. already mightily over-strained in their wits by the universal scramble to secure- what?- a but humble Babu's berth, at so many Rupees per mensem.

The fact is, Hamlet viscerally believes the ghost to be telling the truth. He is stirred to the very depths of his soul to act and act immediately reckless of consequences. Yet, he does not act. We feel there is something of the malaise of modernity, something neurotic or Oedipal, some amphibolous or sceptical 'unhappy consciousness', at work in Hamlet's febrile brilliance in devising a further empirical test to establish something he already knows in his bones to be true. Shakespeare emphasizes Hamlet's great intellectual and imaginative power to show that, at some level, our scholarly Prince, to whom the name Pyrrho would not be unknown, must understand that this further empirical test, too, yields not certainty but doubt. Perhaps, at the staging of Hamlet's 'Mousetrap'- what appalled the King was actually some apparition sent by the Devil or, more prosaically, the sudden realization that his nephew suspects him of the foul crime of fratricide. Thus, for Hamlet, dutiful son to a Father who is also Unholy Ghost, Pyrrhonian doubt and delay yield not *ataraxia*, that is tranquillity, but a disorder of the phrenes, a sort of madness, less medicinable for feigned.

Hamlet has a friend in Horatio but, poor Yorick being dead, no interlocutor of equal intellectual stature. Thus, Hamlet is a tragedy and doubly a tragedy for this Prometheus fetches no fire for Mankind by his foresight. Our Epimethean Arjuna, on the other hand, has not just a friend but something like an equal for interlocutor- Krishna. Thus, the Gita is a Divine Comedy. It is a 'balanced game'. Both Arjuna and Krishna have supernatural knowledge of the outcome. Both are acting not as principals but as agents. Arjuna is obeying his eldest brother, actually Karna, who, however, if not a brother, is the loyal friend, of Duryodhana, chief of the Kauravas. But this means Arjuna will end up killing not just his own people but the partisans of the side which, but for Karna's decision regarding Righteousness, he himself would have considered right.

Interestingly, Arjuna's *chakshushi vidya* (second sight) is constrained by his true master, Karna's, Dharmic decision not to disclose that he is the eldest of Kunti's sons so that Yuddhishtra is not obliged to give up his claim. Be it noted, however, this Dharmic decision- which precipitates not just the Kurukshetra war but also the destruction of Lord Krishna's people- is the decision of an agent rather than a principal. Interestingly, Karna's promise to Kunti to slay only one of her sons reflects Arjuna's own scruple against shedding the blood of his own kin. In the end, whether Arjun kills Karna or Karna kills Arjuna, the number of Kunti's sons is conserved as 5.

One may argue that Arjuna, unlike Karna, has a moral objection to killing. Unfortunately, this notion is not supported by the text. Arjuna's qualm is against killing his ***own*** people- for whose womenfolk he will become responsible for on their death- that too for mere material gain. This is pure Hamilton's rule kin selection- not a Conscientious Objection to War at all. Unlike Karna, who does not have chakshushi vidya (second sight), Arjuna *knows* he will survive- not so his cousins. Karna merely *believes* that he will win against Arjun but, otherwise, holds death in battle to be the surest path to winning Heaven. This is a case of loser takes all. In any case, Karna's friendship and obligation to Duryodhana arose in the context of the latter's determination to crush his cousins by force of arms. Indeed, by choosing to fight mighty Bhima rather than goody-goody Yuddhistra in the final duel of the Mahabharat, Duryodhana confirms to us that Karna's Dharmic decision was consistent with Duryodhana's own preferences.

Indeed, Duryodhana's war aims makes perfect sense politically. Men become Kings and Kings become Emperors by crushing potential rivals ***pour encourager les autres*** . Empires can be a good thing- they move a fracitious people from thymotic, tribal, heteronomy towards a Universal, Bureaucrato-legalistic, autonomy thus yielding a great advance in material Civilization. Yuddhishtra's repeated acceptance of a challenge to a dice game, as part of his bid to be recognised as Bharat's primus inter pares, put paid to his own, more traditional, more *Brahminical*, bid for Empery. His losing in the second dice game results in an Adullamite exile, during which he is forced to learn Game Theory for himself (Duryodhana outsources his Game Theory) and thus ***his*** alliance at Kurukshetra, though numerically smaller, has greater esprit d'corps at the top by reason of lateral ties and community of interest between commanders as opposed to mere fealty to his own person. In the end, Yuddhishtra is not just a man of pinciple, he is the only actual Principal rather than Agent in the Mahabharata. After all, Duryodhana's father is alive. True, his father is a Regent, therefore a mere agent rather than principal, not a King. Precisely for this reason, like Bhima, Duryodhana sees the physical crushing of enemies as a legitimate act. He wishes to avenge his father who was passed over for the Kingship despite being Pandu's older brother. Similarly, when Yuddhishtra, despite being elder to Duryodhana, is forced to languish in exile rather than rule as King, Bhima declares his attention to avenge his elder brother by himself utterly destroying the Kauravas, Indeed, this is what triggers Yuddhishtra's Vishada (sorrow), which is only dispelled by hearing the Vyadha-Gita (Vyadha means butcher- Ashwattaman 'speech to Karna in 4.50 shows meat-vendors were proverbial for acquiring wealth through deceit and fraud) after which he can learn Statistical Game Theory from the story of Nala.

Like Duryodhana, like Arjun, like everybody except Yuddhishtra in this Epic, Krishna, too is an agent, not a principal. Indeed, every avatar is an agent, not a principal, only put on earth to fulfil the Godhead's purpose. But, Krishna,in the Gita, is doubly an agent. Unlike his elder brother, Balram who, despite his partiality for Duryodhana, refuses to have anything to do with the blood-letting *vishodhana* at Kurukshetra, Krishna is committed to serving Arjuna as his charioteer, and thus unaware, by reason of being an agent rather than a principal, that actually Arjuna is none other than the Rg Vedic *Hari,* or chariot horse ever approaching nigh (this is the other side of the coin of Madhva's reading of R.V 6.47.18) and thus His own self-slaying in *Visvarupa* goes in vain.

Thus, it becomes apparent, the whole of the Gita is a, so highly cerebral as to be hilarious, proof or demonstration that agents, as opposed to principals, neither kill (even themselves) nor are killed and thus are exempt from Philosophy which, as Socrates pointed out, is nothing but a practising of Death. Which is another way of saying the Gita aint Hamlet, it's friggin' Rozencrantz and Guildenstern are dead.

Hamlet's dilemma- which is Agrippa's trilemma- viz. how prove your belief is true when any proof anyone finds acceptable is still only a matter of belief- is actually pretty productive, not in deontic fields (stuff about ethics and values) where it cashes out as some sort of historicist hermeneutics, but alethic (positive, Scientific, factual) disciplines where it fuels the drive for more and more finely grained empirical instruments and observation.

For 'Second Order discourse'- i.e. Philosophy- it is noteworthy that Western Phenomenology and Occasionalism arise out of this trilemma. The former excuses its existence as follows- 'I'm human. I see the world not as it is but as a human being. Yet, though human, I've got the concepts of doubt and certainty. So there must be some human 'work' I need to be doing before I can say 'I'm certain about this' or 'this is a matter inherently riddled with the infirmity of doubt.'

The problem here is that the Phenomen/Noumenon distinction, once its central concern is grasped, becomes immediately redundant- it is a distinction without a difference. Take that last sentence. It's not actually a statement about what everybody believes. It's a statement of what I believe. Surely, I should have said 'In my opinion, the problem here is that....etc'. But, to constantly prefix every sentence I write with 'in my opinion' is simply a waste of words. It's redundant. I mean, I sign this 'Vivek Iyer' though I know very well that it is only in my own opinion that I'm 'Vivek Iyer'. Mum, for example, is under the impression that I'm actually *chamatha* 'good little' Bikki whereas, less embarrassingly, my doting Dad, thinks the words '*badava*' (not from Urdu for pimp but ancient Aztec for 'handsomer than Shah Rukh' who, I may tell you, was my junior at School) and '*rascal*' (ancient Maya 'brilliant boy bound to become a Supreme Court Judge') suffice to define me.

As for Occasionalism- the notion that the set of things which lie far beyond the human ken- i.e. what we call God precisely because we can't know what we name- is the actual efficient cause of everything and all the explanans we use either don't exist or can't exist, remaining incapable, in any case, of ever actually interacting with anything, thus cutting us off from being able to account for, or even properly perceive, causal processes- this notion, qua Philosophy, too is redundant. I suppose, in some cultures, it is *de rigueur* to prefix 'God willing' to any statement that implies agency- 'Okay, you treat me to *choley batore* and your Hindi homework will get done, God willing'- but, it's semantically redundant and serves a purely phatic purpose.

In calling the Gita an *epoché*, quite obviously (in the idiot savant tradition to which all writers in Western languages on the Gita belong) I am systematically replacing any actual free reading of it with a fractious, and fatuous for fiercely reductive, reading *into* it- which is why, as you perusing this post, have already determined, I receive no soteriological benefit from it whatsoever- other than that of a Reverse Mereological, or Post-Modernly Meropean, muddying of the Geeta's waters providential to save my own self-fathered Caliban community which remains exclusively concerned with, though dying of thirst, not glimpsing its own reflection in that peerless and pellucid pool.

What? Sorry, didn't quite catch ... Oh! You're saying 'No, no dear fellow- you are not muddying the waters of the Gita at all! Nor is anything you write difficult to follow. Perish the thought! This essay of yours is itself that Liriopean lake enriched by Narcissus's love-struck gaze. Indeed, Vivek, as your esteemed Father says, you are truly a *badava* (in post-modern Urdu, not pimp but *broker*) enabling every Caliban to attain the beauty of Narcissus, at least in his own eyes, by gazing at the Pierian spring-fed pool of your Prose.'

Well, you said it- not me! Still, I must admit, in your artless way, you have hit the mark. Arjuna's Agrippan Trilemma or *Vishada*- the fact that.backward induction renders every intentionality untenable- is nevertheless a starting point for a Grothendieck Yoga- uniting eidetic fields, such as sight and foresight, on the basis of greater generality by, not an abstract Husserlian reduction, but something purely human and existential- viz. the fact that Man is as an alethic fact and his deontics matters for his alethic survival and propagation. In other words, the Mind Body problem is solved by the fact that Minds can be evaluated by the degree to which they help or hinder Bodies to survive.

Which in turn leads to Game Theory-which Yuddhishtra, lacking a Sakuni for Agent, himself has to learn as Principal- not to mention Evolutionary Biology, Mathematical Politics and all the other usual idiocies of our Age and idols of my tribe.

To summarise, the fact that the Gita is structured as an epoché- but one in which both Krishna and Arjuna have certainty re. alethics (what will be) but not deontics (what ought to be)- is a necessary and sufficient condition for its elaboration of an Occassionalist doctrine. However, precisely because we can predict or explain its appearance, this Occassionalist message is not gratuitous and substantive but strategic and instrumental. Thus, it ***can't*** be its own meaning because it lacks '*apurvata*'. As a correspondent of mine informs me ' According to Mimansa hermeneutics, only those injunctions are Scripturally valid which have no worldly explanation or merit in that they point to invisible results beyond human understanding. Thus, if the Law Book says 'the King, modestly clothed, should listen to petitions while facing East'- the phrase 'modestly clothed' has a common-sense explanation, viz. that the King should not over-awe the petitioner by appearing in rich garments. Thus the King may omit this requirement without sin. However, since the injunction 'while facing East' has no common sense explanation, the King commits a Sin if he hears petitions in any other posture.'

The corollary is that if a textual simulation of one Philosophical blind alley occasions, as its corrective, the traversal of another, especially if that cul de sac is Occasionalism, then, clearly, the meaning of the text can't be taken as anything but a 'plague on both houses' so to speak.

I'm not saying *insha* (deontics) doesn't cash out as *khabar* (alethics) or that we can never get an is from an ought or vice versa. What I am saying is you can't get either deontics or Theology out of the Gita. This is because, as in the case of Phineas slaying Zimri and Kosbi, the *halachah* revealed is *halachah vein morin kein* (a Law such that knowledge of it forbids the very action it otherwise enjoins). Why? Phineas is agent simply, not principal. Hence his elevation to the status of Kohain by Ha'shem.

Thus, my conclusion is, the Gita as epoché shows there is a symmetry between Phenomenology and Occasionalism- they are duals of each other but redundant and empty save in the context of their unmeaning duel in which neither can slay or be slain because both are mere agents, mere instrumentalizations, of their own univocal Principal. This impasse, as much as epoché, both yields and illustrates the Supreme hermeneutic Principle that the meaning of a Text is always what *can't* be explained, anticipated, or instrumentalized for any paltry purpose of pedagogy or polemics.

You disagree? No. You don't really. I know the truth about you. That humiliating truth hidden in your heart's deep cave. I know your shameful secret. What is it?

I will tell you. Not because I want to humiliate you but because no one, and there are many people inside your head, no one except *you* will understand what I'm saying.

You think your mother's face is Beauty.

You are rushing to see her and tasting the delight already.

But, when you see her, you realize you never saw her before. You never knew what is Beauty. She is saying 'Eat now. Don't look at my face. Look at your plate. What is wrong? OMG! Still a child even at this age? You want I should feed you with my hand? *Ooof oh!* Enough already. Can't you see, guests have come? Go, look to them. What's wrong I say? Why this tear in your eye? Oh.... must have lost that fancy job abroad and come back crying... Good. Thank God! I always knew it would happen. I said, go not abroad.. But who listens to me? Anyway, now you are back- your life will be Gold.'

But, you haven't lost your job, nor have you really come back.

True, you never listened to Mum- tho' Mum's words are the Gita- but now you realize you never actually even properly *looked* at that Sita.

Her Beauty.

Sita shoba kahe bhukane?

Mukh bin nain, nain bin bane

Of Sita's splendour,only hacks have sung

Tulsi, tongue lacks eye, eye lacks tongue!

Rama's Samrambha Yoga- the fruit of which was reunion with Seeta.

Samrambha Yoga is known as the path of Wrath which can be more efficacious than any other in achieving Union. This seems counter-intuitive. Surely Love, Mercy, Forgiveness, Compassion and so on are higher than Wrath and present a less risky and more socially beneficial type of Yoga or path to Union?

Let us look at a situation where Samrambha Yoga proved its worth, paving the way for the universally desired re-union of Lord Rama and Seeta Devi after the overthrow of Ravavana.

Valmiki tells us about Ram's emotional state-

taamaagataamupashrutya rakShogR^ihachiroShitaam |

harSho dainyaM cha roShashcha trayaM raaghavamaavishat || 6-114-17

17. upashrutya= hearing; taam aagataam= that Seetha had arrived; rakShogR^iha chiroShitaam= after living long in the abode of a demon; raaghavam= Rama; aavishat= was filled; harShaH= with jo; roShashcha= indignation; dianyam= and felt miserable (too); trayam= all the three (at once).

'Hearing that Seetha had arrived after living long in the abode of a demon, Rama was filled with joy, indignation and felt miserable too- all the three emotions at the same time.'

This mixture suggests heteronomous love- such as that of the child overwhelmed by the return of the mother but whom, nevertheless, renewed rancour at the reminder of separation and the cruel maw of the misery of abandonment simultaneously lacerates and tears apart.

Yet, Valmiki does not say anger was part of that mix. Ram's wrath awakens for a different reason and he paces the path of Samrambha Yoga for a purpose wholly divine.

saMrabdhashchaabravIdraamashchakShuShaa pradahanniva |
vibhIShaNaM mahaapraaGYaM sopaalambhamidaM vachaH || 6-114-25

25. raamaH = Rama; samrabdhaH cha = enraged as he was; chakShuShaa pradahanniva = with his looks as though burning; abraviit = spoke idam vachaH = the following words; sopaalambham = with a reproach; mahaapraajJNam vibhiiShaNam = to the highly intelligent Vibhishana.

The enraged Rama, consuming the demons with his looks as it were, Rama spoke the following reproachful words to the highly intelligent Vibhishana

kimarthaM maamanaadR^itya kR^ishyate.ayaM tvayaa janaH |
nivartayainamudyogaM jano.ayaM svajano mama || 6-114-26

26. kimartham = why; ayam janaH = these people; klishyate = are harassed; tvayaa = by you; anaadR^itya = disregarding; maam = me?; nivartaya= stop; udyogam = this exertion; ayam = these; janaH = people; svajanaH = are my own people.

"Why disregarding me, are these people harassed by you? Stop this exertion. They are my own people."

What provoked Rama's Samrambha (anger) and caused him to reproach his virtuous client and ally?

At Rama's request, the King of the demons, Vibhishana, had brought Queen Seeta to the audience chamber. Thinking that protocol demanded the chamber be cleared of the bears and monkeys and demons who were milling about, Vibhishana and his retinue proceeded to throw them out roughly. This mistreatment of his own people incensed Rama and set him on the path of Samrambha.

Notice, the bears and monkeys and ogres made not protest at being excluded from seeing Seeta. They though it right and proper that the vision of Seeta should be denied to them- even though they had shed their blood for her release from Lankan captivity. Those who truly sacrifice for a noble cause become humble, they think it right and proper that not even a glimpse of the prize should be vouchsafed to them. If even Hanuman and Lakshman could not understand Rama's anger- why blame the Scholiasts?

True, Rama- as Agent of his own Godhead- speaks with 'an alienated majesty'. But he is a transparent Agent. We see the all compassionating Principal glowing all the brighter, as only through tear stricken eyes is Mother's true beauty ever seen, through the gauzy veil of the 'Principled' fucked-up Legalese of what he says next-

na gR^ihaaNi na vastraaNi na praakaaraastiraskriyaaH |
nedR^ishaa raajasatkaaraa vR^ittamaavaraNaM striyaH || 6-114-27

27. gR^ihaaNi = An apartment; na = is not; aavaraNam = a thing that protects; striyaaH = a woman; na = nor; vastraaNi = robes; na = nor;praakaaraaH = compound-walls; na = nor; tiraskR^iyaa = the concealments; na = nor; iidR^ishaaH = such; raaja satkaaraaH = royal honours; vR^ittam= Her character is her shield.

"An apartment is not a thing that protects a woman, nor robes, nor compound-walls, nor concealments nor such royal honours. Her character is her shield."

vyasaneShu na kR^ichchhreShu na yuddhe na svayaM vare |
na kratau no vivaahe cha darshanaM duShyate striyaH || 6-114-28

28. stiyaaH = A woman; darshanam = becoming visible; vyasaneShu = in times of a clamity; na duuShyate = is not condemned; na = nor; kR^ichchheShu = in battles; svayamvare = in self-choosing of a husband by a princess at a public assemly of suitors; na = nor; kratua = in sacrificial ceremonies; na vaa = nor; vivaahe = in marriage functions.

"A woman becoming visible to public in times of a calamity is not condemned in difficult situations, nor in battles, nor in self-choosing of a husband by a princess at a public assembly of suitors, nor in sacrificial ceremonies nor in marriage-functions."

saiShaa yuddhagataa chaiva kR^ichchhre mahati cha sthitaa |
darshane.asyaa na doShaH syaanmatsamIpe visheShataH || 6-114-29

29. saa eShaa = the yonder Seetha; vipadgataa chaiva = is in distress; sthitaa = and beset; mahati = with a great; kR^ichchhre = difficulty; naasti= there is no; doShaH = fault; ayaaH darshane = in her becoming visible in public; visheShaataH = particularly; matsamiipe = in my presence.

"The yonder Seetha is in distress and beset with a great difficulty. There is no fault in her appearance in public, particularly in my presence."

visR^ijya shibikaaM tasmaatpadbhyaamevopasarpatu |
samiipe mama vaidehiiM pashyantvete vanaukasaH || 6-114-30

30. tasmaat = that is why; upasarpatu = let her come; padbhyaameva = on foot alone; utsR^ijya = leaving; shibikaam = the palanquin; vanaukasaH= let these monkeys; pashyantu = see; vaidehiim = Seetha; mama samiipe = in my presence.

"That is why, let her come on foot alone, leaving the palanquin there. **Let these monkeys see Seetha in my presence.**"

Notice, Rama on the brink of being re-united with Seeta, was suddenly and for a heterogenous reason, thrown into a state of *'Samrambha'* or wrath. This wrath arose out of mistreatment of his own people who were not considered worthy to look upon Seeta Devi- who is our very own Mother and can never be denied to us 'stupid monkeys' during Processions of the Deity by uniformed officials with staves in their hands who beat us and harry us in the name of Public Order and Seemliness.

However, Samrambha (wrath) can not be disassociated with fear. The Samrambha Yogis-like Ravana, Putana etc- had their minds concentrated on the Lord from fear of the goodness and innocence that has power to destroy evil doers even if incarnate in our feeble and contemptible human form.

If Ram's anger is at our being excluded from the vision of Seeta Mayya, this anger goes hand in hand with fear. Fear of what?

pashyatastaaM tu raamasya samiipe hR^idayapriyaam |
janavaadabhayaadraajJNo babhuuva hR^idayaM dvidhaa || 6-115-11

11. hR^idayam= the heart; raajJNaH raamasya= of King Rama; pashyataH= as he saw; taam= Seetha (hR^idaya priyaam= the beloved of his heart); samiipe= near him; babhuuva dvidha= was torn; janavaada bhayaat= for fear of the talk of the public.

The heart of King Rama, as he saw Seetha, (the beloved of his heart) near him, was torn for fear of public scandal.

Rama, though the agent of his own Divinity, is yet not so perfect as to just blurt out his heart's sulky secret- viz. 'Due to why you were never coming to gimme just one or two itty kisses just to cheer me up seeing as it was you who most cruelly abandoned-ed me? Is it

Justice? Just one or two itty kisses!. Is that too much to ask especially seeing as I had been very cruelly abandon-ded and you off gallivanting who knows where? See, that Ravan fellow may have been a bounder and okay I challenged him and shot him with my bow and arrow and did all sorts of brave brave things due to I'm very brave actually and didn't cry even once though they kept hitting me with arrows and you'd forgotten to pack my tiffin box, but, see, what get's me is due to why you were so cruel as to not come gimme just even one two itty kisses from time to time? Don't make the excuse of having been kidnapped. You are coming from Bihar where everybody is all the time being kidnapped-ed only. Never stops any of you people coming and giving each other itty kisses from time to time due to otherwise where do Bihari babies come from- answer me that?

   'Boo! I don't like you. You can go away. Marry Laxman or Sugriva or anyone you please. Me? Don't worry about me! I never needed no kisses at all! I am perfectly self-sufficient and see I can easily kiss my own cheek- oh, well, I can't- but you just watch, I'll learn Yoga and then you'll be sorry!'

   This is just as well, coz Seeta, who hasn't had any really good lines till now, would have been reduced to saying 'There, there, itty baby. Mwah, mwah, mwah- see I'm giving you the thousand kisses I stored up in my heart while you were off playing with your bow and arrow.'

   Instead, she gets to make a splendid scorching speech and jump into a tepid fire and generally carry on like a grand tragedienne

   But, this permits the Gods to intervene and put everything right coz actually that's what God wants.

   Thus, we may conclude, there is a special beatitude attaching to a Samrambha Yoga based on wrath- but for Ram's anger he'd have met Sita privily and she'd soon have kissed away his sulks- because the common folk shouldn't be debarred from sharing in the spectacle of an Unqualified Good- though, of course, Rama's wrath was mediated by a chastening fear that the *free and public discourse* of those same ordinary people, might, so to speak, seize upon the wrong end of the stick. Clearly, in the Twentieth Century, a lot of people have misunderstood Lord Ram's action. Public discourse on this point sees him as upholding a horrible Patriarchal ethic. If Lord Ram's fear has been justified by us, should we let the matter rest there or should we demonstrate that free public discourse can self-correct? The answer is no- not so long as we don't recognise that the Academy is corrupt and its discourse the opposite of free and public.

   In Rama's case, thanks to his 'Yoga of wrath', not only does he get Seeta back but also his father and all the monkeys slain in the War they had fought for his sake.

Well, so what?

What has that to do with us?

We ourselves are Creators.

Love is a Second Creation.

There is reciprocity between Creator and Creature, *vyatihaaraha, vishinshanthi hiitaravat*, as Brahma Sutra (3.3.37) states, because both agree to be bound by this sort of ironic karma or universalization of individual love compacts into an imperishable, for perfectly Just, Civilization and Cosmos in which all relate to all on the basis of that same principle.

   I myself recall an excellent dinner I had some years ago. It didn't occur to me that, in sharing the meal of the young couple who had moved in upstairs, I was a- *'kebab main haddi'*- playing gooseberry- intruding on what should have been a tender scene of 'Journey's end in Lover's meeting'.

But Love's Journey never ends and takes in even idiots like me.

They now have a daughter who has a daughter.

Maybe, visiting London, that baby will come play in my lap.

Who can say? Maybe, this old 'bone in the kebab' or 'gooseberry' added savour to the dish.

What nobody can deny is that babies belong to everybody.

Sita & Ahalya

This is A.K Ramanujan comparing Valmiki and Kamban on the Ahalya episode, crap translations of which he provides-

> Let me rapidly suggest a few differences between the two tellings. In Vālmīki, Indra seduces a willing Ahalyā. In Kampaṉ, Ahalyā realises she is doing wrong but cannot let go of the forbidden joy; the poem has also suggested earlier that her sage-husband is all spirit, details which together add a certain psychological subtlety to the seduction. Indra tries to steal away in the shape of a cat, clearly a folklore motif (also found, for example, in the *Kathāsaritsāgara*, an eleventh-century Sanskrit compendium of folktales; see Tawney 1927). He is cursed with a thousand vaginas which are later changed into eyes, and Ahalyā is changed into frigid stone. The poetic justice wreaked on both offenders is fitted to their wrongdoing. Indra bears the mark of what he lusted for, while Ahalyā is rendered incapable of responding to anything. These motifs, not found in

What Ramanujan is not telling us is that both Valmiki and Kamban were poets. They did not actually have shit for brains.

What is interesting about Ahalya for a poet writing about Ram? The answer is that Ahalya's story provides a parallel with Sita's.

Both are beautiful. Ahalya's beauty is as that of land not yet brought under the plough. Sita's as that of the furrow in new ploughed land. Ahalya lets a stranger into her home because the stranger has taken on the form of her Brahmin husband- but is actually the God Indra. Sita lets a demon cross the 'Laxman rekha' of the hut's threshold because the stranger has taken the shape of a Brahmin Rishi.

Whether or not either succumbs to the stranger's lust, both are punished and condemned to a neither dead nor alive status separated from their husbands.

Thus, for a poet, verses about Ahalya- if the work is about Rama- have a lot of 'dhvani' suggestiveness. Ramanunan is writing utter shit when he says 'Valmiki depicts Ahalya as such and such and Kamban as such and such'. That's missing the whole fucking point.

Now both Valmiki and Kamban are supposed to be of non-Brahmin origin and as such not into the **Subhramanya formula** etc, etc. But, both were divinely inspired. Or, if God doesn't exist and you believe that because both weren't Brahmins (all these fucking Leftists are elitist 'Boston Brahmins' of some sort) it therefore follows they were drunken scum writing trash to earn the price of a pint from some petty potentate- still, reading them in the original (which, Ramanujan could do!) shows they were fucking good poets. Not bad fucking poets who write shite. No. They were good, very fucking good, at poetry. And good poetry can't be read the way Ramanujan is doing not once not twice but 300 fucking times in his essay.

Why has Delhi Uni taken this foul screed off their reading list? Are they trying to make out they aren't all a worthless pile of dung? No. They are frightened of being knifed.

So no change there then.

Sita & Ahalya

To its Soma sip, shout this **Subhramanya** aloud!

*'Tho' **Ahalya's** loveliness is as land unploughed'*

(While Sita's beauty is the furrow in loam)

'E'en God is a Demon entering a home.'

The Subhramanya formula, from which the relevant extract is given below, is sung by a specialist priest who stands between the patron and his wife, while the soma-cart makes its way to the sacrificial enclosure.

[4] *indrāgacha háriva āgacha/ médhātither meṣa vṛṣaṇaśvasya mene//gaúrāvaskandin áhalyāyai jāra/ kaúśika brāhmaṇa gaútama bruvāṇa//*

Come here, O Indra, come here with your golden steeds!
(You who are/took the shape of) Medhātithi's ram,
(You who are/took the shape of) Vṛṣaṇaśva's co-wife;
(You who) as a wild ox leapt down,
O lover of Ahalyā (lit. 'the unploughable one'?);
O Brahmin belonging to the Kuśika family,
(You who are) called (or called yourself) Gautama![4]

(from Myth and mythmaking by Julia Leslie)

Figure 4–4 The Subrahmanya priest folding his hands during the Sub-rahmanyā litany which is chanted every morning and evening during the six Upasad days of the Agnicayana (Reprinted from Staal 1983, 1:379, Plate 61A). AdM.

The late Julia Leslie, of SOAS, like every other academic post Babri, jumped on the Rama-was-a-Fascist bandwagon. But when the honest, hard working, utterly unfanatical members of the British Balmik community contacted her, she had the grace to drop the gesture politics and recognize the uniqueness of our Bhagwan Valmiki whose descendants and adherents continue to reflect glory upon Him.

A.K. Ramanujan was a South Indian Brahmin who emigrated to the U.S at a young age- he would never have written his silly essay '300 Ramayanas' if he had the opportunity to go to a Balmik temple. Why tell lies on this issue? The Balmik community have never oppressed or exploited anybody. Because they were honest and productive, under Colonialism, they themselves were looked down upon because only parasites were considered Upper Class. Who in India, or the Democratic West, examining the facts impartially, would deny the greatness of Valmiki? At least appreciate him as a poet, if you deny he was Divinely inspired. Why pretend to be translating his texts when all you want to do is display your own stupidity and prejudice?

Sheldon Pollock's 'othering' and 'brothering'- outs him as a crypto-Aryanist

Prof Pollock writes ' the 'Ramáyana' is a tale of "othering," the enemy is non-human, even demonic, and the war takes place in an unfamiliar, faraway world; the 'Mahabhárata' is a tale of "brothering," the enemy are kinsmen—indeed, as the protagonists say, almost their own selves—and the war takes place at home.'

Are the Ramayana and Mahabharat really related in the way Prof. Pollock suggests? Both stories feature exemplary bands of brothers. There is no fraternal conflict. Karna merely has to reveal his true birth for the great blood-letting of Kurukshetra never to occur. However, Destiny has willed otherwise. Humans are merely the instruments of the Divine Plan. Lots of demons (Pollock's 'othering') get slain in both Epics because that's what heroes do. Similarly, brothers are shown as tenderly affectionate as well as utterly loyal to each other (Pollock's 'brothering'). Pollock's distinction is meaningless. Yet he makes it anyway. Why? Perhaps, because though he says he won't, he still interprets the Ramayana in a racialist way. The Rakshasas are actually Dravidians or Mundas or some such subaltern race. So, it's like how the Ramayana views the non-Aryans as demons and like totally inhuman y'know? And that's bad, okay?

No, not okay. It isn't true. Rama is not a King. He's an 'un-King'. He's a forest dweller. He gets on fine with forest tribes, the vanar monkey-people, animals, birds and so on. How can the Ramayana be 'the privileged, if not the sole, South Asian narrative of hieratic politics?' Three Kingdoms are dealt with- one human, here the younger Brother yields to the elder while all show exemplary filial piety- the second, Vanar (monkey-people) where there is a conflict between brothers (not others, Prof. Pollock, ***brothers***)
but moral culpability is reduced by lack of pre-meditation and the Epimethean and impulsive nature of the species, and- finally- the Lankan Rakshasas where conflict between brothers (Ravana and Vibhishana) can rise to the level of Ethics and Public Policy.

Is absolute filial piety, such as that of the Ayodhyan Court, really politics? That too 'hieratic' Politics? I don't see how. Not enough happens at Ayodhya, there isn't enough of the sort of stuff politics feeds on viz. dealing with famines and rebellions and wars and so on. Compare Lord Ram with King David. 'Hieratic politics' is meaningful with reference to the latter- what on earth has it to do with Ram's Ayodhya?

Okay, there is some politics and intrigue amongst the Vannars and in Lanka- but monkeys and ogres aren't protagonists of 'priviliged narratives of hieratic politics'- at least not in South Asia, which Prof. Pollock has actually visited.

In defence of his thesis that the Ramayana is about 'othering' Pollock says something incredibly foolish viz. that Ravana's moral alterity arises from his 'reckless polygyny'. Is this guy meshugganah? Can he not know that Ram's father, King Dasharatha, was also polygamous and recklessly made a promise to his wife Kaikeyi? The second reason Pollock advances for Ravana's 'othering' is that he was a tyrant. But Lanka was a peaceful and prosperous country. Ravana was a King, a strong one- somewhat better than Emperor Ashoka.in that he did not order the massacre of Shramans while fattening Brahmins. Why is Pollock making this ridiculous assertion? It's because his thesis is false and he himself knows it, but the real thesis he wants to present is not politically correct so he'll undermine its opposite by appearing to support it.

The Rakshasas are shape-shifters who like eating human flesh. I myself can turn into a wolf or a bear and eagerly devour the surplus arms and legs all babies, being Hindu gods, necessarily sport. It is my one child-rearing skill.

Rakshasas are slain- just as I am frequently slain in combat with toddlers- in both the Ramayana and the Mahabharata. But some Rakshasas are good and some are bad. (I'm bad- hence popular with little people)

The Ramayana does not end with a 'final solution' to the Rakshasa problem- that happens when kids grow up a little and say 'Babu, you're not *fun* anymore' or more succinctly 'You're just *silly*!'.

Okay, maybe I *am* in denial about that Holocaust.

Maybe Bhagvan Valmiki really is a Nazi coz his book gives me hope.

The Lankan throne passes from one Rakshasa- whose death was fated at the hands of Vishnu's avatar- to his brother. Pollock quotes Merutunga's Prabandhachintamani (1304) where the Solanki King Jayasimha Siddharaja (1094-1143) puts a scare into the Mleccha (barbarian) ambassadors by making it appear that King Vibhishna, Ravana's brother enthroned by Rama, had recognised that the current incarnation of his Saviour was the Solanki King and that he was ready to come to his aid with his Rakshasa hosts should the need arise. Clearly, the Ramayana- or the notion of the King as the incarnation of Lord Rama- were not associated with demonizing anybody, least of all the Rakshasas. On the contrary, since Vibhishana is a Ram-bhakt (devotee of Ram) his help is to be sought precisely *because* he belongs to the same race as his brother. What Pollock does not say- but what becomes apparent from his own post-Babri essay- is that the Islamic invaders behaved like demons towards the Hindus and that, for the first time, an entirely new aspect of Lord Ram was revealed- viz. his status during the Lankan war as an un-King, the opposite of a King, one maddened by grief who yet remains steadfast in taking the battle to the enemy and routing him upon his home-ground. In other words, the un-King as the locus of resistance to an irresistible and Satanic Imperial power, turns Lord Ram's compassionate and tender nature into a model of an engaged caritas which aims at the overthrow of a hateful and inhuman Imperium, that too by means of a popular 'subaltern' uprising. Pollock quotes a letter from Shivaji labelling Aurangazeb as a 'div' (devil) and appealing for help against him. Muslim sources- the Pashto poet Kushal Khan Khattak for example- indicate that Aurangazeb's transgressions were of sufficiently grave a character to justify the description.

In this context, the destruction of the Babri Masjid- not by an order of the State, nor by the disciplined action of uniformed members of a para-military organization, but by a vast multitude of ordinary people with Political leaders merely looking on, so to speak, acquires a semiotic significance which Pollock's writings otherwise signally fails to make. But, was this his perhaps unconscious intention?

As with Witzel's, Pollock's Indology quickly unravels to reveal a sort of ultra-Purva Mimamsa type of Brahminism which every Brahmin lineage I've ever heard about has explicitly repudiated and whose brief historicity was an aberration, a cancerous hyper-trophy, rather than, soteriologically speaking, an organic development.

Pollock really ought to know better and **does** know better but why should that stop him? Philology no longer means close reading it means uttering modish sound-bites, and constantly displaying one's credentials as an anti-Fascist- precisely because *the reverse* is both the origin and occulted trajectory of one's praxis- though only variants of Fascism demand this of scholarship.

Pollock's cryto-Aryanism is compounded by misogyny. He writes- 'Shakúntala' is a 'Mahabhárata' play, and 'Rama's Last Act' (Bavabhuti) seems designed as a 'Ramáyana' counterpart to, and competitor of, Kalidasa's masterpiece. Like the two epics the two plays share a deep resemblance. In their core they are stories about love, rejection, recovery, and ultimately—because this is the very reason behind the rejection— political power and its perpetuation. The star-crossed love of Dushyánta and Shakúntala is mirrored in that of Rama and Sita. The women, both of whom are pregnant, are repudiated because of doubts about their fidelity and (implicitly) the paternity of the progeny they are carrying. This is followed by a soul-searing acknowledgement of guilt on the part of the husband, reunion with his wife, recognition of the legitimacy of the offspring with the aid of quasi-divine agents (Marícha in 'Shakúntala,' the magical anthropomorphic weapons in 'Rama's Last Act'), and reconciliation of husband and wife. Both works hereby aim to emend and aesthetically enhance their epic models.'

It seems Pollock simply won't accept that women have equal agency and in the case of Sita, equal divinity, with respect to the men they have espoused. Read the Cliff Notes, Prof! In Kalidasa's play, some Rishi or the other curses Shakuntala that her husband will forget her. There is no 'repudiation of a pregnant woman'. Ancient Indians weren't stupid. They knew pregnancies last about nine months. Unlike Francis Bacon, they didn't believe that a guy who fucked their wife more than nine months ago could father a child in a womb demonstrably full of their own spunk.

Sita always resides within the heart of Ram. She can't be parted from him. *Birha* is a Maya.

Customary morality, Hebrew or Hindu, states that if your wife runs off or is abducted or whatever then curse her for a slut and take a new wife. Don't go to war over it. Women aren't worth it.

As regards polygny- it is a duty of the King. By taking a new wife a war or rebellion might be averted. An uxorious King is a threat to the commonweal.

Prof. Pollock's view only makes sense if the heroes of the Itihasasas were in reality not ideal human beings but greedy, suspicious, despots with little capacity to love. For this view to make sense, all the characters Pollock mentions must have been extremely important historical figures for whom mercenary court poets manufactured the exculpatory propaganda which has come down to us as epics.

This is silly. Perhaps, Prof. Pollock thinks Buffy the Vampire Slayer is a thinly disguised exercise in exculpation for Hilary Clinton or that Harry Potter stands for the boy Cameron triumphing over the evil wizard Tony Blair.

There is a video on the web of Prof. Pollock bewailing the decline of philology's status in the Academy. But what is the point of his philology if he makes such recklessly false statements about books he has himself translated? The real problem,as his own work illustrates, is not with philology as such but with hermeneutics. The latter cashes out either as

1) Triumphalist Historicism or Strategic Essentialism of a chip-on-the-shoulder type wholly unconcerned with what books actually say.

2) Heideggerian mystagogy- thought at its most thoughtless- that seizes upon Technics as its own foundational problematic so as to render its practitioners not 'problem-driven' (Pollock knows such disciplines grow and burgeon in an alethic and utilitarian manner free of faux navel-gazing and foolish stabs at gesture politics) but wholly absorbed in their own foundational problematic as an impossible discourse.

This brings me to the question, what is hermeneutics *for*? Books are meant to be loved and teased and mocked and quarreled with- *that's* philology. They aren't meant to be worshiped or taken as having any sort of authority or insight. Books are shite in the same way we are shite. Get shit-faced with a book. Don't fucking take no shit from it.

Okay, if you're making a living being a Rabbi or a Professor or whatever- sure, what you're doing is hermeneutics- but you're doing it the same way you do your Tax Return- viz. by working backwards from what you can afford to pay.

The other thing about philology is that it began to die when it entered the Academy- like Jazz when it decided it was too good for the dance hall.

Pollock bewails the demise of philology in India. But, that's *good* news. Why? Because he's talking about the fucking *Universities*. Does he not know the type of criminal that infests Indian Arts Depts? He goes- boo hoo, the Bikaner Royal Family won't let me photograph their manuscripts. He doesn't say that if they let him do it- and, sure, he's a good guy and would actually do what he promised and not like wipe his arse on even a single leaf of Indic incunabula or use it to roll a joint- they'd then have to let in every fucking Gangster of a Professor who will simply steal everything in sight and rape the light fittings. After all, for the last thirty years, academic orthodoxy in India is that Brahmins are the source of all evil. Since some Brahmins were literate, all Indic texts are inherently evil. In any case, all that shit is probably pornographic so this is something both Saffron and Red can agree upon.

Hermeneutics is 'othering'. Philology could be 'brothering' but isn't coz Hermeneutics made it its bitch. . Neither have any relevance to Itihasa. That's stuff to do with loving not books but babies- a burgeoning popular vatsalya not Pollock's all-blighting Purva Mimamsa vedanta.

P.S. funniest line ever- 'The Ramanand Sagar T.V series is the latest (Valmiki's being the first) attempt to establish a HEGEMONIC VERSION of the Ramayana.' Yup, you heard me right- that's Ramanand Sagar we're talking about. What was Pollock smoking? I want some.

The problem with Pollock is that he goes on repeating drivel from failed hermeneutic programs- utterly forgetting to seek for answers to the open problems he himself cites. If Philology is in trouble it's because of Pollock and his ilk. Problem driven readers, if enabled to access relevant texts and research for free- not Professors acting as shills for a corrupt, credentialist, pay-wall protected, Academic publishing racket- can revitalize Philology. Not Governments, not the always risible demand for more disciplinarity discourse, not the Academy- a nightclub where all the lap-dancers have retrained as bouncers- not fucking illiterate bloggers like me, not... hang on a sec. ...I didn't mean that...I know that's what I *said* but I expected you to kinda shake your head and say 'no, no dear fellow- not illiterate surely'... No, I'm not getting riled up.... I'm perfectly calm....well, up your hole with a ten foot pole! ... really? That's the best you can come back at me with? Up my hole with an eleven foot pole? Is that supposed to be witty? Look, just fucking grow up okay? I will write to your headmaster and tell him about those naked pics of your Mom you sent me.... okay, okay, so it was your Gran... listen, you little shit, you're pimping your own fucking Gran okay? That doesn't give you the moral high ground here... Well, yeah, sure I'd still like to meet her... Okay then. That's your Hindi assignment I've emailed you, so just give me her phone number and we're all square... Sheila Dixit is your *Nanee*? That was her in those photos?... Fuck yeah! I'm a Congress supporter- well I am now!...I'm not sure about the strap-on thing but, it's true, I do look a lot like Ram Vilas Paswan...Cool. Look forward to it... yeah, you too. Go have fun with your *gulli danda*. I certainly plan to with mine! Many thanks for the new pics.

Sheldon Pollock's heteronomous Rama.

Sheldon Pollock views the Rama of the Ayodhya Kanda as a totally heteronomous being, with less agency than the *dasi* Manthara. Indeed, he believes the Ramayana to be the principal source of a 'hieratic' Hindu conception of monarchy as something worse than absolute despotism in that the subject is absolutely infantilzed and has no means of reaching Kantian autonomy.

Comparing Valmiki's epic to the Iliad, Pollock remarks the powerlessness of the Indians, their bondage to a fate they can neither contest nor comprehend and whose blighting effect proceeds from causes that are ethically heteronomous- i.e. punishment does not follow intention or action except in the sense of it being a 'treading the weird'- i.e. some karmic krapolla.

Thus Pollock says 'the characters of the Ramayana believe themselves to be denied all freedom of choice' and 'Choice is replaced by Chance, and action is nothing more than reaction.'

Is he correct?

Let us start with Kaikeyi. Did she think she had no freedom of choice? It appears, on the contrary, that she had received two boons from the King and chooses to use them in a manner that was not predetermined or fated in any way. Her maidservant, Manthara, persuaded her that Rama, once King, might mistrust or mistreat her son Bharata. Rather than bewailing her fate, Kaikeyi takes action. What of King Dasharatha? When Kaikeyi demands Ram's exile and Bharata's enthronement, does he exclaim 'Woe is me, all this was fated! I am powerless!'. No he gets angry, curses both Kaikeyi and her son and pointedly remains silent when Rama arrives before him..

Why is the King silent? The answer is that he had already promised the Crown to Rama. The point was moot as to whether Kaikeyi's boons were time-barred, already treasonous, or involved an impossible act.

Even if Lord Rama considered himself bound to obey the King, Kaikeyi had no *locus standi* to demand his departure. The King's silence gave Lord Rama a choice. It raised him from the abject heteronomous state that Pollock imagines him to occupy. What's more, Lord Rama was not a muscle-bound meat-head, he understood the defeasible nature of the Queen's demand very well. He pointedly states that it is not his Father but his (step) Mother he is obeying. Lord Rama acts with alacrity. He makes a momentous choice- one whose tragic consequences for his beloved father he fully realizes- and, as befitting a King and leader of Men, he makes it quickly, without wasted words. It is this supererogatory quality, this ethical surplus, which defines not Kantian autonomy (worthless shite fit only for Professors) but *vatsalya* as a Universal principle.

One might argue that after his father's death and his brother's renunciation of the throne, Lord Rama should, as duty bound, find some way of keeping his vow while still discharging his Kingly duties- for example, by residing in a forest, but regularly meeting Ministers and other officials. However, Bharata is fit to discharge this duty himself. So, it is only in order to keep faith with himself, to honor his own commitment, that Lord Ram chooses the more arduous path. This is the opposite of heteronomy. To bind oneself to what one believes to be the right course, absent any other inducement or coercion, is the hall mark of moral autonomy.

Interestingly, Rama only so bound himself, by his own choice, so that the choice made by his (step) mother might be validated and take effect. That choice too- i.e. Kaikeyi's choice of boons from her husband- arose from a free and unrestrained choice made by his father. Rama does not say to Bharata- you must be King because that was Kaikeyi's wish. After all, Bharata too gets a choice. Only he can decide whether or not to take the throne. Rama does not seek to coerce or intimidate him into going against his own choice. In other words, Rama's ethical autonomy arises and expresses itself in the context of affirming the free choice of other people- one elder to him- his (step) mother- and the other younger to him, his brother Bharata. Notice that Kaikeyi's choice was not unethical as such. She was genuinely concerned about her own flesh and blood. She had a 'veto' if you like and was entitled to use it by reason of a not unnatural apprehension. Choice becomes meaningless unless its free exercise in one's own rational self-interest is accorded moral legitimacy. Otherwise, Choice becomes meaningless pi-jaw.

Pollock considers Lord Rama to represent a sort of inhuman ideal of perfection and thus devoid of all real-life human complexity. Unfortunately, real-life humans, to emerge from heteronomy, to lead families and Nations from moral heteronomy to ethical autonomy, HAVE to pay a great deal of attention to CHOICES. Lord Ram's own choices become mere caprices, or ethical grandstanding, or perhaps some shite to do with karma, UNLESS he uses his choices to affirm and valorize the choices of others. Pollock uses the word heteronomy readily enough. Is he really ignorant of the vast literature on this topic?

Perhaps, because he's writing about India- a poor and backward nations mainly inhabited by nig-nogs like yours truly- it is a mark of his greatness that he makes this graceful gesture of dissimulation.

Still, the question remains, why does Pollock think it okay to say 'the characters of the Ramayana conceive of themselves as being denied all freedom of choice?" Does he not understand that the readers of his translation will immediately be forced to the conclusion that the Ramayana can have no ethical value at all? If Rama had no choice but to go into exile, what moral greatness attaches to him? Why would Hindus revere him?

Pollock's bizarre thesis soon yields perhaps the most foolish sentence ever written about the Ramayana- viz. 'Rama's 'true feelings' will remain secret, properly so, for they are quite irrelevant to the poem's purposes.'

Wow! You couldn't make it up if you tried! Do we really not know Rama's true feelings for his Mum, his Dad, his wife, his brothers and so on? Even if we hadn't read Valmiki's poem, is it at all rational or reasonable to think that a poem about a man called Rama would consider the true feelings of that same Rama to be 'quite irrelevant to its purpose?'

Pollock is not ignorant. Just stupid. If, as he claims, philology of his sort is really dying out in India, let us get down on our knees and thank God for it.

Prof. Gier on Matilal's 'Epic and Ethics'-

'Matilal finds a caricature of Kantianism in Rama, whose inflexibility with regard to duty leads to absurd and/or harsh decisions. As Matilal quips: "Rama's dharma was rigid; Kant's was flaccid."

'Even though he was encouraged to do so by the sage Jabali, Rama was not going to break a promise, even if it meant that he could regain his kingdom and avoid 14 years of exile. One of Rama's lame excuses for shooting Valin in the back was that a person has no duties to animals, **Valin being a member of Hanuman's monkey army (sic)**. (Kant held that mistreatment of animals was blameworthy at least as a reflection of the person's character.) **Rama's extreme interpretation of a wife's duty to her husband** (sic) has led generations of Indian women to conform to an impossible ideal. Following Sati's example, Indian women are required to stay with their husbands no matter what they ask of them and no matter how much they are abused.'

Why is this fucked?

The Ramayana is a widely available text- you might try reading it if you're going to write about it. What was **'Ram's extreme idea of a wife's duty to her husband?'**- Well, firstly, she doesn't have to share his fate 'for better or worse'. If he has to go off to the forest, she is welcome to stay behind in the Palace. Secondly, she is free to leave him at any time- all she has to do is go off with, or be taken away by, any other man- and, though her husband is entitled to kill her abductor, she is thereafter free to marry anyone or simply fornicate with anyone who takes her fancy. Ram actually tells Seeta she is free to marry his own brother, Laxman, or the demon King, Vibishina, or the Vanar King, Sugriva (this forecloses the possibility of their appealing against Sita's decision to commit Suttee, because they will immediately be upbraided by that wrathful lady- who, consistent with Universal Dharma- gets the last word and upstages everybody) or that she may just go off on her own wherever she might please, even though Ram had just expended a lot of blood and treasure to get her back.

Rama is saying a woman whose husband is living can, if he abandons her, marry whom she wills- even his own brother or someone of an enemy race or different status. There is absolutely no evidence that Ram held that a woman's duty is to stay with a husband who mistreats her. Gier, whose personal Virtue Ethic evidently does not include being truthful, says ' *Indian women are required to stay with their husbands no matter what they ask of them and no matter how much they are abused.*' I am Indian and, though not a woman, have a sharp temper and often sing '*main maike chali jaunge, tu dekhte rahiyo*' while in the shower to hint at my displeasure with my domestic arrangements. Women are not required to stay with their husbands if they feel someone or other has insulted them or put their nose out of joint or failed to lavish compliments etc. and are constantly traipsing off to their '*maike*' for a nice holiday. I recall reading a book by Wendy O'Doniger Flaherty in which she wrote 'The South Indian Brahmin female bites off the penis of her husband before beheading him' - which was the basis of my own refusal to marry within my caste, which was just as well because, ever since the invention of contact lenses, even the vainest of our myopic Iyer girls have been turning up their noses at me. However, Gier's statement that Indian women will stay with their husbands, even if they are mistreated, is even more misleading than O'Flaherty's statement- indeed, it is potentially fatal! The husband of that **heroine of Hindutva**, Rajini Narayan, must have been reading Gier when he called his wife a 'fat, dumb, bitch' causing her to purify his penis with fire, according to an ancient Hindu custom (invented, presumably, by Wendy O'Doniger) with the result that the fellow burnt to death.

No doubt, Gier will blame Ram for this and amend his statement to read 'Indian women are required to stay with their husbands no matter how much they are abused because Lord Ram said they have a duty to purify their husband's penis with fire and burn the fellow to ashes- unless, of course, they are South Indian Brahmin females, in which case as Prof. Wendy O'Doniger has pointed out their duty is to bite off their consort's penis before neatly beheading the fellow. This is because Rama had a 'rigid' Virtue Ethics whereas Kant had a 'flaccid' one.'

Gier and Matilal fail to spot that, according to the Ramayana, Rama was God. There was some stuff he had ordained for himself to do, but ordained that he do all unawares, e.g. kill such and such devotee so that devotee might gain immediate union with the Godhead and so on. There is a perfectly coherent philosophical position- Occasionalism- which fully describes the universe of the Ramayana. As for the dramatic portions pertaining to Dharma- this arises from what we may call not just Agency Hazard but Policy Actor Hazard.

But, Matilal and Gier- being philosophers and therefore under occultation w.r.t the text (in Matilal's case) they have read in the original- ignore facts like this and write worthless shite.

Gier is much taken with this 'insight' of his- T*he Buddha once said that "they who know causation know the dharma,"[44] a great example of how dharma, as J. N. Mohanty observes, connects "what one ought and what in fact is."[45]* **This happy violation of the Humean prohibition of deriving an Ought from an Is** *demonstrates how virtues are derived from the facts of our personal histories and how this contextualizes all moral decision-making. The famous "mirror of dharma" is not a common one in which individual identities are dissolved, as some later Buddhist believed, but it is actually a myriad of mirrors reflecting individual histories. The truths they discover in their mirrors will be very personal truths, moral and spiritual truths that are, as Aristotle says of moral virtues, "relative to us."*

Why is this fucked?

Dharma aint *a happy violation of a Humean prohibition* on deriving deontics from alethics. Maybe the Professor was thinking of Jack Kerouac's 'Dharma Bums' or something. It does not concern itself with '*the facts of our personal histories*' at all. No statement re. dharma or vyavahara takes the form 'reflection on my personal history leads me to hold that such and such is enjoined on me'. On the contrary, we have statements of the order 'the seers have laid down x, y, z' or 'Scripture says x, y, z' or, as in the story of Yuddishtra and the demon of the pool, a particular question- viz which of the Pandavas is to be brought back to life- is answered by applying a Universal maxim re. *'paro dharma'* (the higher duty) such that the King chooses a half-brother rather than a full brother to be brought back to life. Buddhism is a one period universe- *kshanika vada*- there isn't any time to discover anything and, no matter how many mirrors are all busy reflecting away, no time to look at them. There's only time enough for an intention to exist-*Chetana ham bhikkhave kamam vadami. Chetyitva kammam karoti kaena vacha manasa*- nothing else. Neither an occassionalist not a momentary universe permits the drawing of the sort of conclusions Gier and Matilal arrive at.The truth is, talk of Morality and Ethics is worthless shite and has always been recognised as worthless shite. People who talk it are immediately recognized as fuckwits, frauds or murderous fanatics. The only categorical imperative that isn't fucked is to repay cunt-queef pi-jaw gobshites in their own coin.

Gier says- *Matilal's insights now allows me to do something that I thought that I could not do in my own comparative virtue ethics--namely, to add Krishna to the Buddha, Confucius, and Aristotle. The problem of course is that Krishna appears to be the least virtuous person in this list and can hardly be seen as practitioner of the Middle Way. Nonetheless, Matilal declares that his "dark Lord" as a "paradigmatic person . . . in the moral field," who "becomes a perspectivist and understands the contingency of the human situation,"[49] both necessary elements of virtue ethics. He also describes him, as opposed to the rigid Rama or Yudhishtra, as an "imaginative poet" in the moral realm: "He is the poet who accepts the constraints of metres, verses, and metaphors. But he is also the strong poet who has absolute control over them. . . . He governs from above but does not dictate." This guarantees that Krishna 's "flexibility never means the 'anything goes' kind of morality."[50]*

Why is this fucked?

Krishna spends a lot of time telling us that he is the only efficient cause. His Creation is an Occassionalist Universe, yet he isn't its 'strong poet'. Rather, as he declares,

muninam apy aham vyasah
kavinam usana kavih

that is- he is the sort of muni-kavi (Sage poet or Transcendent 'Maker') whose 'Shukra' (luminous pellucidity) seeds Shuka who, having gone beyond that other Krishna- the Gita's Sage-poet Vyasa- already leaves him behind, that too though yet at the very morning of the World, mourning and bereft.

What actually happens in the Bhagvad Gita, is a discussion of Agency Hazard because, to preserve symmetry and 'balance the Game', both Krishna and Arjuna are Agents not Principals. Ultimately, Krishna offers himself up as sacrifice. He slays himself. The Mahabharata shows that even if a work is so constructed as to conserve karma and dharma as symmetries of the system, that system can't be purely relationist and must cash out as a substantivalism if only to incorporate Concurrency as an internal symmetry not otherwise displayed.

Gier proposes a sort of aesthetic autonomy in which virtue ethics has a domain and therefore some content. The problem here is that it really isn't true that any aesthetic degree of freedom is good or bad by itself. Auerbach, in his Mimesis, shows that the opposite is the case. Rasabhasa- the use of low style for high matter or the reverse- drives precisely the same process that Gier valorizes- viz. self-discovery within a relationist field of interacting reals.

'The fine arts, I believe, give us a very rich analogue for the development and performance of the virtues. Most significantly, this analogy allows us to confirm both normativity and creative individuality at the same time. Even within the most duty bound roles one can easily conceive of a unique "making one's own." Even though the Confucians must have had a set choreography for their dances, one can imagine each of them having their own distinctive style. The score for a violin concerto is the same for all who perform it, but each virtuoso will play it in a unique way. The best judges have the same law before them and yet one can detect the creative marks of judicial craft excellence. Even the younger brother who defers to his elder brother will have his own style of performing this duty, his own dharma (svadharma).

Yes, Prof. Gier Sahib- and make no mistake, this drunken old fool admits himself unworthy to touch the hem of your garment- but the point about playing the fucking violin is that, sooner or later, you evolve into a coke-head, Nigel Kennedy type, and get jiggy with like the Spice Girls or summat. For all Art aspires to the condition of Music and Music aspires to banging groupies in your limo while off your head on coke.

'As opposed to a rule based ethics, where the most that we can know is that we always fall short of the norm, virtue ethics is truly a voyage of personal discovery.'

So true! Virtue ethics is about Harry Potter discovering his wand really is magic if he rubs it long enough. However, this voyage of personal discovery has to end when he finally works out where to put it so it will do most good (I believe it was in Ron Beezley's sister- *yuck-eee!*) and engender future generations of young wizards who go off to Hogwarts to play with their wands.

Gier, whose oeuvre, like Simmel, is a manic protestation against the universal ontological dysphoria his own project virtuously discloses, ends on this lapidary note-

'Virtue ethics is emulative--using the sage or savior as a model for virtue--whereas rule ethics involves conformity and obedience. The emulative approach engages the imagination and personalizes and thoroughly grounds individual moral action and responsibility. Such an ethics naturally lends itself to Matilal's moral poets and a virtue aesthetics: the crafting of a good and beautiful soul, a unique gem among other gems.'

This reminds me of a T-shirt I saw in the gym the other day- Idaho? No u da Ho!
Says it all really.

Killing cows and Quantum Karma- Temple Grandin and Christopher Badcock

Temple Grandin suffers from autism. Unable to have close emotional ties with other people- though a lot of other people, including abusive shithead drunks like me, have a close emotional tie to her- she uses her great intellectual gifts to re-design slaughter houses, making them more efficient and profitable for their operators, but only so as to minimise the pain and suffering of the cows in their last moments of life.

She has a theory of karma based on Quantum theory.

'Doing something bad, like mistreating an animal, could have dire consequences. An entangled subatomic particle could get me. I would never even know it, but the steering linkage in my car could break if it contained the mate to a particle I disturbed by doing something bad. To many people this belief may be irrational, but to my logical mind it supplies an idea of order and justice to the world.

'My belief in quantum theory was reinforced by a series of electrical outages and equipment breakdowns that occurred when I visited slaughter plants where cattle and pigs were being abused. The first time it happened, the main power transformer blew up as I drove up the driveway. Several other times a main power panel burned up and shut down the plant. In another case, the main chain conveyor broke while the plant manager screamed obscenities at me during an equipment startup. He was angry because full production was not attained in the first five minutes. Was it just chance, or did bad karma start a resonance in an entangled pair of subatomic particles within the wiring or steel? These were all weird breakdowns of things that usually never break. It could be just random chance, or it could be some sort of cosmic consciousness of God.

"Many neuroscientists scoff at the idea that neurons would obey quantum theory instead of old everyday Newtonian physics. The physicist Roger Penrose, in his book the Shadows of the Mind, and Dr. Stuart Hameroff, a Tucson physician, state that movement of single electrons within the microtubules of the brain can turn off consciousness while allowing the rest of the brain to function. If quantum theory really is involved in controlling consciousness, this would provide a scientific basis for the idea that when a person or animal dies, an energy pattern of vibrating entangled particles would remain. I believe that if souls exist in humans, they also exist in animals, because the basic structure of the brain is the same. It is possible that humans have greater amounts of soul because they have more microtubules where single electrons could dance, according to the rules of quantum theory.

"However, there is one thing that completely separates people from animals. It is not language or war or tool-making; it is long-term altruism. During a famine in Russia, for example, scientists guarded the seed bank of plant genetics so that future generations would have the benefits of genetic diversity in food crops. For the benefit of others, they allowed themselves to starve to death in a lab filled with grain. No animal would do this. Altruism exists in animals, but not to this degree. Every time I park my car near the National USDA Seed Storage Lab at Colorado State University, I think that protecting the contents of this building is what separates us from animals."

This is a strange statement for a scientist to make! The work of Price, Hamilton & Maynard Smith does not rule out animals behaving in a manner consistent with what she would term 'long term altruism'- indeed, it is a statistical certainty that some animals did do and still do so. It just isn't an Evolutionarily Stable Strategy, that's all, and so over time (as random shocks even out) genes dictating such behavior would be bred out of the population. Temple is world famous as the woman 'who knows how cows think'- as for herself, if any organism can truly think, if any organism truly acts autonomously upon moral grounds, rather than being the meat puppet of some selfish gene- then it is she much more than an ordinary fuckwit like me.

She goes on to write

"I do not believe that my profession is morally wrong. Slaughtering is not wrong, but I do feel very strongly about treating animals humanely and with respect. I've devoted my life to reforming and improving the livestock industry. Still, it is a sobering experience to have designed one of the world's most efficient killing machines. Most people don't realize that the slaughter plant is much kinder than nature. Animals in the wild die from starvation, predators, or exposure. If I had a choice, I would rather go through a slaughter system than have my guts ripped out by coyotes or lions while I was still conscious. Unfortunately, most people never observe the natural cycle of birth and death. They do not realize that for one living thing to survive, another living thing must die.'

It is an autistic trait to consider death to be something real; pain as being other than the phenomenological equivalent of a forged Doctor's prescription for Medical Marijuana?

Temple describes how she recovered her faith- which she had lost when, as a publicity stunt, she swam in a cattle dip full of dangerous chemicals

"When the combination of organophosphate poisoning and antidepressant drugs dampened my religious emotions, I became a kind of drudge who was capable of turning out mountains of work. Taking the medication had no effect on my ability to design equipment, but the fervor was gone. I just cranked out the drawings as if I were a computer being turned on and off. It was this experience that convinced me that life and work have to be infused with meaning, but it wasn't until three years ago, when I was hired to tear out a shackle hoist system, that my religious feelings were renewed.'

'It was going to be a hot Memorial Day weekend, and I was not looking forward to going to the new equipment startup. I thought it would be pure drudgery. The kosher restraint chute was not very interesting technically, and the project presented very little intellectual stimulation. It did not provide the engineering challenge of inventing and starting something totally new, like my double-rail conveyor system.

'Little did I know that during those few hot days in Alabama, old yearnings would be reawakened. I felt totally at one with the universe as I kept the animals completely calm while the rabbi performed shehita. Operating the equipment there was like being in a Zen meditational state. Time stood still, and I was totally, completely disconnected from reality. Maybe this was nirvana, the final state of being that Zen meditators seek.'

There is a notion, promoted by Prof. Baron Cohen that autism results from an 'extreme male brain'- if so, Temple's curious choice of profession and Zen epiphany at the kosher slaughterhouse (she points out that Solomon's temple was a huge abattoir) reveals, perhaps, something of what it means to be a Man- an ***intelligent*** man, not a witless, Ghalib spouting, drunkard like me- and the type of empathy that arises as an emergent from the Male mind's relentless sytematising.

Dr. Christopher Badcock, an energetic polemicist for the Freudian theory of history in the 70's and early 80's, has developed a new theory about the relationship between autism and psychosis. He regards them as being mirror images of each other. Autism results from the dominance of paternally imprinted genes, whereas psychosis is the product of dominant maternally imprinted genes. Paternal genes have an interest in getting the mother to invest more resources in the progeny by increasing physical growth- leading to a bigger more lateralized brain- whereas the mother's genes would seek to reduce the maternal investment by inhibiting growth (in the same manner as malnutrition resulting from famine would)- leading to lower birth weight and smaller brain size.

Badcock had been seeking a way to save the Freudian theory of history by founding it upon the new Evolutionary biology. He has now accepted that Freudianism is itself a type of paranoia- a 'hyper-mentalism' of the high functioning psychotic savant.

Badcock replaces the neurosis/psychosis distinction in Freud- itself arising from the divergent economic implications of treating hypochondriac nuerotics, whose ability and willingness to pay is in inverse proportion to any real disability or deficit they suffer, and hypnochondriac psychotics whom one is paid to police- with an autism/psychosis spectrum which, once again, has a similar economic dichotomy.

This is because therapy is a scarce resource, if defined nuerotically or autistically, becoming non-rival and non-excludable (indeed, behaving like a nuisance good which is over-produced and costly to prevent oneself from consuming) from a hyper-mentalist perspective. However, the reality is that, ceteris paribus, a therapy behaves like any other oligopolistic product viz. its advertising is a nuisance good, over-supplied, and mendacious in creating a product differentiation which does not exist, ceteris paribus, w.r.t goods in joint supply like pills and Occupational Therapy, at the level of outcome.

In Badcock's view, Autism is hypo-mentalist, hyper-mechanistic, Truthful, Male, Western (or at least not 'African') and the characteristic form of advanced, affluent, technological Society. Psychosis is hyper-mentalist (i.e. schizophrenics have more not less theory of mind) hypo-mechanistic, female, dishonest, self-deluding, African and likely to decline with rising prosperity and technological progress.

Badcock identifies himself, as well as Hamilton, as falling within the autistic side of the spectrum in precisely the manner that Freudians proudly identified themselves with the Oedipal neurotic while holding themselves aloof from the schizophrenic, who rather than (as is right and proper) secretly wanting to fuck Mum and kill Dad- hoped to get pregnant by God the Father with the unfortunate consequence of founding Religions like Christianity and Hinduism.

Badcock contrasts Temple Grandin's Quantum Karma with Rupert Sheldrake's notion of morphic resonance. Sheldrake, like Jung, is pointing to a direct connection, an entanglement, between minds. Grandin refers only to an entanglement at the level of quantum particles. Thus, Grandin's thought is still Scientific, Western, and Male while Sheldrake (who spent some time in India) is Mentalistic and Female.

Grandin's thought is founded upon the ontological primacy of pain and death and gains peace from the contemplation of the properly conducted sacrifice of an ever moving conveyor belt of cows. Sheldrake's mentalism, at least potentially, can rise above pain and death because if minds are directly connected to minds then they have an avenue of escape from the contingencies imposed by embodiment in a meat-suit.
Notice that a Sheldrake type hyper-mentalism solves things like the Hegelian 'struggle for recognition', the Girardian problem of 'mimetic desire', or the Satrean problem of scarcity as

mediating the relationship of man and man. Briefly, mentalism, denying the mediation of things, permits full and non-rival appropriation of the other as well as altruistic self offering immune from one's own sacrifice- whether as food or pharmakos.

Thinking good thoughts is the duty that Sheldrake type hyper-mentalism requires of us as a society. Improving slaughter houses is Grandin's autistic hypo-mentalistic categorical imperative for the individual.

Thankfully, in these Humanity's latter days, the lion will lie down with the lamb- thinking good thoughts is a 'farz-e-kifayya'- a communal duty which can be delegated to autonomous, hypo-mentalist technogeeks devising swifter and more silent conveyor belts to humanitarian guillotines.

Except, biology tells us this is shite. Pain and Death are incidental and ephemeral, Sex and Morphology - Love and Beauty are fundamental and abiding.

I say nothing against nuerotic or autistic people- though I lack the brilliance and civilizationally vanguard role attributed to them. But, the truth is pain and death aren't worth worrying about. That Life goes on, remains, I need hardly say a nightmare from which none awake.

Valentine's Day is anti Hindu.

Anyway, the conclusion all this is building up to is that Valentine's Day is nothing but a Christian Conspiracy aimed at destroying Hindutva by encouraging lechery, promiscuity and Carbon Dating. When I was young man- no Carbon Dating Shating- just Carbon was getting monogamously hitched to Oxygen and staying home to poison the childrens.

Personally, I blame Sumit Sarkar

That boy aint right.

Is Dharma a Virtue Ethics?

Suppose we find that everybody who talks about a certain subject is either a fool or a knave or both, what can we properly conclude?

1) Not that the subject has a tendency to deprave or render stupid- it may be that fools and knaves alone are attracted to the subject.

2) Not that only fools and knaves take up the subject- it may be that someone neither a fool or a knave is forced to comment on the subject and only by doing so is shown to become either a fool or knave or both.

3) Not that someone neither a fool or a knave forced to comment on the subject, and thus shown to be a fool or knave or both, is actually commenting on the subject- one may be forced to do something but end up doing something else which suffices to end the compulsion. This would be the case if the force which compels one towards a particular course of action can not itself distinguish between that action specifically and some other action which appears the same to the compelling agent but not so to others.

This last point saves us from having to conclude that all talk about about Ethics, Duty, Dharma etc, is only indulged in by fools or knaves or both. I'm not saying this isn't empirically true. Indeed, for any possible world one may care to specify, one could, in general, prove that this is a necessary truth.

However, once we admit that people who speak of these things may have been compelled to do so and that *what we mistake* as the usual foolish, knavish or both foolish and knavish verbiage is *in fact* merely a simulacrum with an opposite illocutionary force- i.e. it is a savage parody and indictment of the brutish stupidity of the sort of fools and knaves who force people to talk about Ethics, Duty, Dharma etc.- then a new vista, a truly Orient horizon, is opened for us.

Indeed, we now have the possibility of taking a more charitable view of our fellow creatures. We can imagine that their foolish, knavish or both foolish and knavish babble about Morality proceeds, not from their irremediable stupidity and knavishness, but from some brutish and merciless force constraining them to such revolting behaviour.

Obviously, words like Morality, Duty, Ethics and so on ***only*** become interesting, only register as something other than phatic, when, in their name, some particularly stupid and knavish action is performed.

Let's say I become friends with some guy and do something nice for him. Well, you might commend me for my friendly character and felicitate me for my deftness in performing some particular pleasing action. What you wouldn't do is uphold me as an exemplar of a higher morality, a sterner ethics, a more than mortal attachment to Duty.

Well, you wouldn't, unless you were a knave with an ulterior motive or a fool who thought it remarkable that I should find pleasing a friend a source of satisfaction to myself.

On the other hand, if I meet a guy, befriend him and then beat him to death though it causes me pain to do so- clearly I have acted from some motive of Morality, Duty, Ethics or other such shite. To the degree that you are a knave or fool, or both, you are now obliged to hold me up as an exemplar and gas on in philosophical vein.

B.K.Matilal has written some foolish or knavish or both foolish and knavish shite on the topic of 'Ethics and Epics'. Was he forced to do so? Dunno. Maybe. Let us say that being a Professor forces one to do shite things of this sort. Still his shite on this topic sets higher than mandated standards of stinkiness because he won't even entertain the possibility that the guys who wrote the Epics were forced to drag in talk about Morality, Duty, Ethics and so on.

Let's face it. Interesting stories are of the form- x liked y but fucked y up something rotten though it hurt x to do so. Boring stories are of the form- x liked y and did something nice for y coz x was a nice guy that way.

What about *meta*-stories? I mean a story about story telling? The Mahabharata is such a story. We know, in advance, the authors are going to be constrained to talk about Morality, Ethics, Duty and other such shite- coz for the heroes to retain our interest they're gonna have to fuck up for some high minded reason every so often- but we don't know whether the Epic is going to take advantage of its meta-linguistic structure to fuck up the vile and brutish force compelling the mention of Dharma, or whether that fucking black hole is going to turn the writers in to fools or knaves or both - or even only the simulacrum of such scum.

In order to determine the outcome of the Mahabharata's meta-story, I'm first going to have to formalize the terms fool and knave.

Briefly, a fool is someone who wastes information. A knave is someone who steals it. The reason that all talk about Morality, Duty, Ethics etc is either foolish or knavish or both is because such talk loses information. But if information is lost, something is no longer being conserved. But if something is no longer being conserved, then a symmetry has disappeared. If a symmetry has disappeared then a Game has become unbalanced.

Let us look again at the Mahabharata- if it is nothing but a chaotic mass of interpolations and priestly longeurs then it can't be preserving symmetries, it can't be conserving any Principles, it's merely a dissipative system- in which case, why read it unless you're forced to?

Since the Mahabharata can look like a dung heap of precisely this sort, stupid or knavish people- Professors for example- who are forced to read it, are then compelled to say foolish and knavish things about it- e.g. 'It conceives of Dharma as deontological' 'Nope, it's all Virtue Ethics' etc.

However, when the Mahabharat's object language- i.e. what the text says happens- is looked at as a non-dissipative, highly symmetric, Balanced Game sequence (which, by reason of its redactive heuristics is precisely what it is) then, it becomes clear that, as meta-story, it achieves the most praiseworthy of objectives- viz. rigorously fucking over that vile and brutish force which compels people to talk about Morality, Ethics, Duty and other such shite without in any way getting meta-shite upon its own dick.

To summarise- only fools or knaves talk about Morality, Ethics, Duty and other such shite. Why? Because these concepts actually set out to *lose* information, to conserve nothing, to efface symmetries, to unbalance Games. Thus fools, who waste, and knaves, who steal, whatever they get their hands on, are the necessary tools for this foulest of forms of shitting through the mouth.

The Mahabharata, as meta story, by a powerful heuristic which conserves symmetries, balances Games and never throws away information in its object language, so to speak, is able to use its Second Order, meta-linguistic illocutionary force to do the work of sanitizing, by rendering entirely ironic, the obligatory shite about Ethics and Morality and so on.

To, conclude, the correct answer the question- is Dharma a Virtue Ethics?- is shhhhh! I'm trying to watch Svetlana.

The modern Mahatma- is sodomy ever licit?

Chi Jawahar Lal

Sodomy is never licit, however an exception can be made for a true Satyagrahi taking the Jubilee Line to the Swami Narayan Temple in Neasden because Dollis Hill, it is widely acknowledged, is indeed the indubitable arsehole of the Universe.

Bapu

Parlous parables.

Apoorvata and Indentity.

There was once, in a certain village, a learned young Brahmin who had mastered the Vedas and Brahmanas and Upanishads and won golden opinions from visiting scholars. However, in that same village lived a solitary old man who seemed skeptical. An ironic smile played upon his features whenever he encountered the young Pundit on the street.

One day the question of the young man's marriage was being discussed by the village council. Actually, the villagers were simply basking in the reflected glory of the flattering marriage proposals that had come for their prodigy.

One of the village elders feigned regret saying- '*Vivaham vidyanasham*! Marriage destroys knowledge. Such a pity our young man has to get married to fulfill his duty to the Manes.'

The skeptical old man laughed out loud.

"Don't worry, " he said, "the boy has no true knowledge. He loses nothing taking a wife. On the contrary, the gain is all on his side!"

Fearful of the old man's sharp tongue, the village elders remained silent. However, the young pundit soon came to hear of the old man's comment.

He went to confront the old man, cheered on his young acolytes.

"Sir, you say I have no true knowledge. Please examine me, asking any questions you like. Do this as a favor to me, so that I may learn my shortcomings and take measures to amend them."

"I have only one question- who are you?"

"Sir, you know very well, I am so and so, son of so and so, belonging to such and such gotra and such and such sect."

"You have told me about the relation you stand in to others- not who you are."

"Ah, I understand! You are asking me about my true Self. Sir, I know from Scripture that my true Self is the Atman which is eternal, unchanging....

"Stop! You are just parroting what you have learnt. There is no *apoorvata*- nothing new, unprecedented, or uniquely individual- in what you say. Hence, according to the rules of your own hermeneutics- your answer is meaningless."

"Okay, I understand your purpose. Indeed, in our Chandogya Upanishad, we see that the Brahmin who just repeats what he has learnt without understanding the inner meaning deserves to lose his head. Don't worry, I will just now explain to you, using my own words and giving unique examples drawn from my own experience, that same essence I was trying to convey to you before. Thus, my answer- satisfying the condition of *apoorvata*- will have to be accepted by you."

"Very good," said the old man smiling ironically.

The young man began speaking. As he spoke, he waxed eloquent. He was amazed by his own *uchchvaas* brilliance. Thus carried away, he uttered a true gem of rhetoric.

Suddenly he noticed that the old man was grinning like a devil. His own supporters were murmuring. What had happened? 'Curse it- I went and quoted the heretical doctrine! I had only memorized their formulation because it was the argument to be refuted (poorvapaksha) in the

Brahma Sutra commentary. Carried away by my own wind of words- I have sailed into the enemy camp!'

The young man laughed out loud. "See," he said, "I almost committed myself to the false doctrine! However, thanks be to my Gurus and Upadhyays, I know the proper counter argument. Here it is- I give it to you verbatim."

"Back to parroting?!" said the old man, " where is the *apoorvata* here?"

"Okay, you have caught me out," said the young Pundit, 'but give me a second chance. I will go away now and meditate. When I have formulated my arguments properly such that they exhibit the *apoorvata* you consider so important, then I will come in front of you again. On that basis, kindly permit me to depart."

The young man went aside and began to meditate. As often as he tried to frame his thoughts in his own words, relying on his own arguments and analogies- rather than the authority of Scripture- so often he fell into error and confusion.

Finally he determined to go quietly to the nearby town and gain practice in dialectics in a place where he was unknown.

As he walked, he saw a wood cutter. He thought to himself, 'let me talk to the wood cutter and learn the secrets of his craft. In this way I can find a new analogy- one not given in the commentaries- that will have the requisite *apoorvata*. Thus, I will prove I am not just a parrot."

The wood cutter said, 'if you want to learn about my craft- try it yourself. No! That is not how you hold the axe; that is not how you stand; that is incorrect!'

"How so?" the Pundit replied, "I am cutting the wood. Indeed, as I gain strength, it may be, I will be a finer wood cutter than you!"

"No," said the wood cutter, "from long experience, our caste has learned that there is a particular way to hold the axe, a particular way to cut, a particular way to carry the faggots, such that injury is avoided and wear and tear on the limbs is minimized. Furthermore, if you look at the songs we sing- their rythmn and melody are optimized for the work we do and the particular psychological strains associated with our vocation. Our dialect and manner of speech, too, is adapted to our needs."

The young Pundit learnt from the wood cutter and, after him, from the carter, the merchant, the sentry at the octroi post, the bandit, the revolutionary, the spy, the pimp, the ambassador, the scavenger, the mendicant, the aristocrat, and so on.

Finally, he had seen enough. He turned his steps homeward. No one, now, could call him a parrot in a cage- he had spread his wings and seen the world. His speech was full of *apoorvata*. No one could place him. No one could predict what he would say next. The old man would have to admit that whatever answer he returned to the question 'Who are you?' evidenced knowledge rather than the training given to a performing pet.

As he walked down a forest path, he heard a rustling in the bushes. Immediately, all his senses became alert. He was no longer the learned Pundit immersed in his own thoughts, blind to the dangers of the road. He had heard stories of how tigers shadow their prey. He saw his chance. Leaping across a rain gully, he seized a hanging creeper and quickly pulled himself up a tree. In the process, some of his clothes fell away. Even his sacred thread snagged on a branch and broke.

From his vantage point he peered around. In the silence, the only thing he could hear was the tinkling of his own ornaments. Quickly, he tore them off and cast them away. There was a rustle above him. A hissing sound. Perhaps, a poisonous snake? He dropped to the ground and ran crouched through some low bushes. The tiger may be tracking him by smell. He saw a patch of mud. Quickly, he rolled in the mud. That might throw the tiger off the scent. He darted to the safety of some undergrowth. Resting there, he cast his eyes about. There was water ahead of him. Sooner or later, he would need to drink. He came cautiously forward and surveyed the scene. All seemed peaceful. Still he waited. Even when he finally gave in temptation and came down to drink, he drank quickly- alert and in a suitable posture for instant flight.

Wandering like this, he lost track of time. Suddenly he found himself on the border of a village- but was it a village of bandits or respectable men? Before he could decide, he was spotted. Farmers armed with scythes came running to the spot.

'The tiger!' he cried and fainted clean away.

The good people of the village took him in. They understood that he had escaped from a tiger. They gave him water to bathe and clean clothes to wear. After he had taken his meal and was in a relaxed frame of mind, they asked him the inevitable question- "Who are you?"

He had forgotten.

The village Vaidya said- he has received a terrible fright. A portion of his soul left him when ran from the tiger. It has not found its way back to him. No doubt, when he sleeps, it will find it easier to come to him across the landscape of dreams. Let him rest."

He rested, he dreamed, his health was restored, his body became plump, his scratches and bruises faded away leaving no mark of his trauma.

Still, when they asked him the question 'Who are you?" he had to confess 'I don't know. And... I don't know *why,* but I feel the answer to this question is the most important thing in my life. So, though you mean well, I can't agree to your kind proposal that I forget the past and just settle down here."

The village council assembled to consider ways of helping their guest. The carpenter spoke up. He said- 'the man is from the carpenter caste. I can tell because the way he handled my tools." The potter said- 'no he is a potter." The toddy tapper said- 'no, he is a toddy tapper."

The Pundit said- all of you are wrong. He is a Brahmin expert in Vedas and Upanishads.

The Headman replied- "No he is an aristocrat, who acquired Brahmin lore as part of his studies. However, his practical knowledge shows he must be the son of a King trained to take over the reins of administration. The merchant replied- "no, he understands bargaining and accountancy. He must be the son of a great Seth, the head of a transnational Guild,who arranged for him to receive instruction along with the Princes of the realm. This can be seen from his knowledge of the Shraman heterodox sects. This is the true explanation."

The watchman said- 'What if he is a spy? Our whole village will be put to the sword if we harbor an enemy agent!"

Suddenly it became urgent to establish the young stranger's identity.

The Vidushak (detective) was called. He asked for the young man's childhood memories- the lullabies his mother had sung to him. The Vidushak saw that one of the lullabies was unfamiliar to him. It contained a clue as to the direction in which the stranger's natal village might lie. The Vidushak took the young man and set off in that direction. After various travails, the Vidushak was finally able to return the young man to his native village. Slowly he began to recognize his old friends and neighbors.

One day, he remembered the old man. He laughed ruefully- "'Who are you?'- such a simple question yet it caused me to lose my identity! Where is the old man? Take me to him. I will touch his feet and admit defeat."

But the old man was dead.

The story of the young Pundit soon spread. A great scholar came to the village. He asked- 'I have tested your knoweldge and find it perfect. But, one mysterey remains. Though younger in years, you have that which I have not. How came you by knowledge of so many different castes and conditions of people?'.

The Pundit could not reply. That part of his life was still clouded from him.

The scholar assembled the villagers and said to them- 'this young man left the village to find a fitting answer to the question- 'Who are you?'. Immersed in meditation, he broke the chain of Maya- Illusion- which creates a false and delusive egotism which expresses itself as greed, envy and craving. However, evil forces sought to break his meditation. Thus, he emerged from the forest not as an accomplished Yogi but in an unfinished state. His knowledge of all other castes and professions arises out of past-life experiences which continue to exist in the *apurva* state rather than fully fructifying. That is why though he remembers the skills and knowledge of every craft or profession he excelled in in previous lives, still everything seems jumbled together. Now, clearly, we can see that this young man's experience is a proof of Religion. How so? Well, he has memories of being a scavenger. But, he must have been a very good and pious scavenger, for he was next reborn as a wood cutter. Again his piety and good deeds as a wood cutter enabled him to rise one step higher. Even wealthy merchants, and great aristocrats can testify that he had the qualities of their own station. The fact that his final birth was as a Brahmin- shows it is the top most caste.

'However, still we see he excels all others of his class even in this life, for-without taking monastic vows or practicing severe austerities- he has gained knowledge of past life experiences and thus can give a proper answer to the old man's question 'Who are you?" for the element of *apoorvata* that the old man requested is now supplied by his now being in an *apurva* state whereby the action has already been completed but the fruit is not yet in the hand. No doubt, this was the hidden meaning of the old man's insistence on *apoorvata*.

'In consequence, I find, this young man fully qualified to act as the Rashtra Rishi (National Sage) for the Kingdom. Such, indeed, is my recommendation."

The young Pundit could find no fault in the great scholar's opinion. With a diffidence and humility that smacked of true Spirituality, he took up the post of Rashtra Rishi.

One day a crime was reported to him.

A learned Brahmin, gathering herbs in the forest, had come across a young boy of the scavenger class conducting a Vedic ceremony all by himself. The Brahmin could testify that the boy- being free of all blemishes and having the uttermost purity and spirituality- conducted the ceremony in a manner superior to all other priests of our present fallen Age.

But, was this not- in a sense- a violation of the 'closed shop' of the Brahmin caste? How could they gain alms to feed their family if such practices became prevalent? What should be done?

The Rashtra Rishi said- 'whereas Scripture emphasizes attainment not birth- nevertheless, the lad should be beheaded. This is because my own experience shows that the proper course is to wait for slow promotion up the caste ladder. This prodigy has jumped the gun. Though this action is neither displeasing to the Heavens nor against the observances of Religion- still, it is still against Nature. Let him now take the ultimate promotion of pure union with the Deity and enter that realm where Nature has no claim."

The reason I tell you this story is not, however, what you might have guessed from the title. Nor will my slovenly literary style have prepared you for the surprise I mean to spring on you when I tell you my purpose here.

Strange as this may seem- I wish to reflect on the impossibility of modernist literary fiction in our present age. Whereas traditional cultures work by 'participation mystique'- abnegation of identity and full participation in the events depicted- and whereas, my generation, could still see the computer, and the internet, as being like a spectacle which draws us in- like the Matrix movies- we are dinosaurs. The new twittering/texting generation doesn't see Knowledge as being like a book that draws us in, a spectacle to which we surrender- rather, for them, technology is a servant that enables more human interaction, more sharply defined identity, *apoorvata* as the inescapable condition of being alive.

Why is this problematic?

Well, modern literature is related to the notion of leisure and rational recreation. It is based on the notion that while engaging with the book you do not surrender or dissolve your identity- that is 'escapism' and simply a low class dissipation- but, employ judgement and a particular juridicial type of empathy, which strengthens and makes more secure your own sense of security and entitlement.

This was all very well when new information, from whatever channel, was believed to always incrementally shore up identity. This meant leisure- a period devoted to recreation because no threat is visible- could expand. Indeed, expanding leisure and rational recreation combated social phenomena founded in participation mystique- e.g the craziness of crowds.

Path dependence ceases to be a problem in an economy where rational agents act consulting only their own interests. Judgement, as a faculty, becomes a sort of social reflex. Irrationality and 'deterministic chaos' type processes tend to disappear. History itself becomes predictable. It becomes meaningful to speak of a non-eschatological meta-history. The Arts address themselves to the question of representing historical evolution in a manner constantly monitored and chastened by the critical judgement of the audience.

Then disaster struck. Knowledge, it turned out, was not incremental- rather it proceeded by somersaults. Furthermore, new types of knowledge meant that, suddenly, core elements of our identity could at any time be shown to be false.

Consider King Oedipus. At any moment, a messenger can come before him to reveal that everything he thought he knew about himself was actually a lie. Our position is much worse than Oedipus. Messengers have already arrived from the four corners of the globe and from across the entire spectrum of the Sciences, any or each of whom might have information that can show we ourselves are the culprits that we seek. Nobody, nothing, is safe.

Just as some obscure Maths Journal, or Law Journal, or Science Journal might, today, have published something which makes nonsense of the Business Model of your employer- dooming you to penurious retirement- so to with our Personal Identity Model, so to speak.

There is no such thing as Leisure because we need to be monitoring so many different information channels to ensure that we are still who we think we are. True- as a distraction, not a recreation- we surrender more and more to all sorts of virtual realities. But we are like the young Pundit who thinks he is being chased by a tiger. The faulty of judgement is not being strengthened. Empathy is not being increased. There is no more 'Oliver Twist' , there is only 'Slumdog Millionaire'.

The twittering/texting generation, on the other hand, may evolve their own answer to this existential threat from information. Too late, alas, for my generation. It may that their literature will be so different from ours that we won't recognize it when we see it.

Let us suppose a world of hand-held devices, or cranial implants, dependent on cloud computing delivered through a BPO type channel; except not just Business Processes but all sorts of Psychological and Personal services are also covered; then, perhaps, we will have a Knowledge enabled population whose valorization of *apoorvata*- novelty, not security, as the condition of life- enables them to escape the fate of the Pundit terrorized by the Tiger of Information.

For us post-modern subjects- for whom modernity is an impossible project because of the threat from information to core identity- Literature is over. For a while we can still tune into programs like 'House' or 'Fringe' or 'Numbers' or 'Lie to me' where a maverick or just plain mad savant can still put all the pieces together in time for the credits to roll. But, notice that ordinary people have no stable identity in this world. Anyone can become anything. All that is solid has, at last, really melted into thin air. There are no secure sources of identity anymore- not no master narratives, but no way of telling how we will figure in those narratives.

Why should this matter? Because Knowledge is re-inventing itself on a basis bereft of the possibility of a participation mystique. The Matrix has no place for us- no story to anchor us in it. Technology, to which life has become symbiotic, evolves such that Life belongs to those who want to live it on the basis of *apoorvata*, of novelty, of uniqueness.

But such a life, like that of King Solomon, is 'a treasure that can never befall another'. There still will be life- it just won't be a life transposable into literature.

Anyroad, that's my excuse for this book being shite.

Naipaul misbehaving again.

'Madam, what to do? Naipaul misbehaving again."

Mrs. Sulochana Pundit, Deputy Director, Virtual Reality Division, Ministry of Cultural Reconstruction, pushed her glasses up her nose.

She saw Kishen- one of the peons- except they didn't like being called peons- Administrative Assistant (Grade III) was the title they insisted on- standing sheepishly in the shadows.

"Don't tell me! The time-lines have got muddled and Sir V.S. Naipaul is getting up Victoria Ocampo's nose …"

"Madam, not nose only. It is too horrible. Back-side, front-side, don't ask what all and where all that little *shaitan* is not getting up."

Mrs. Pundit sighed. If only she had crammed a bit more, to get higher marks in the Government's competitive exams, she would now be a glamorous Police officer, saving the country from *jihadi* terrorists, rather than having supinely to sit, pushing a pen in this godforsaken hole of a department.

"All right, Kishen" she said tiredly, "shut it down and re-boot."

"Madam, it is not shutting down."

"What? How can that be?"

"Madam, I am thinking, Time coil is responsible. What I can tell you? Greedy Contractors thinking profit only. Safety- not caring. That is why, just to save on disk-space, they went and put in a self-organizing heuristic to compress database. Madam, we were complaining it is unsafe. Such type of heuristic should only be used where data is random in nature. Historical information isn't random. But protests of our Cadre Association went unheard. Contractor has too much pull. Ministry is saying- 'because of George Soros principle of reflexivity, History has inbuilt noise generator". Madam, who is this billionaire George Soros to be talking? Is he doing dangerous work like us? Also we were consulting independent experts- including great scientists like Vandana Shiva and theorists like Pappu Yadav- I can repeat to you, word for word, what their report said- 'though the principle of reflexivity, in its generalized form, ensures that no humanly cognizable algorithm can make historical information almost infinitely compressible, the same can not be assumed for a machine intelligence... Historical processes may be decomposable in manners it would be destructive of human consciousness to contemplate… But, if so, there is nothing to stop the complexity of the Time Coil's heuristic from growing faster than any computable function… What if, as a result, the whole system's entropic arrow of Time goes into reverse? In that case, the Virtual Reality Operator might start running independently as the heat sink of the Time Coil. Which raises the further question, what if the combined complexity of the two systems grows exponentially faster than that of which all Physical Reality is the heat sink? Might not, by Landauer's principle, the one usurp the other?'"

Sulochana was a kind hearted woman. She let the hysterical peon babble on for a bit. 'What to do?' she thought to herself, 'these peons- sorry! Admin Assistants (Grade III)- are so superstitious and backward. They think the machines they tend are alive or animated by some God. Poor fellows! it is not their fault. They are given just enough education to be able to read an operating manual- or Political Party manifesto- and then are pushed out into the job-market. It is the failure of the Government that they are not properly indoctrinated into our Secular, Socialist, Gandhi-Nehru-Yadav, National ideology. Though, of course, in one sense, it's just as well. It keeps the riff raff element out of the higher cadres of the Bureaucracy.'

"*Uff ooh*, Kishen!" she said- once the little peon had run out of steam - "what nonsense you are talking! Too much Sci Fi on T.V nowadays, I say! And as for those pulp magazines- don't even ask! I tell you, it has become major problem."

Kishen looked set to burst into tears. "But, Madam…" he spluttered. Sulochana cut him short. One must be cruel to be kind. "Don't be misled by the professional agitators. They are just heating your mind for no reason. Your cadre was worried jobs would be lost if the information was compressed. Okay, that was a legitimate concern. But, see, Minister Sahib has given undertaking- no retrenchment. Your jobs are safe. That was all your people wanted. Just forget all the nonsense the Info-Environmentalists spouted about Database Ecology and the terrible things that would happen if whole species of algorithms, whole genera of heuristic paradigms, were allowed to go extinct. It was all just alarmist propaganda- nothing more. Even a child could not be fooled. After all, Government of India has an inbuilt Reservation policy to ensure against such things. But, the Info-Environmentalists didn't stop there. Remember their scare-mongering about … what was it?.. oh yes, some nonsense about the fifth dimension- the diagonal direction of Time- being destroyed if the Time Coil overheats? Sheer sensationalism! As if the malfunction of some little machine could destroy the imagination of the entire Universe! Look, just be clear on one point. Here, in Government of India, Information is Information. Energy is Energy. They are two separate things. Here is Ministry of Information on this side of Rajpath and there is Ministry of Energy over on that side. Those with information lack energy and those with energy lack information. Granted, in the Private Sector, Power and Knowledge may be interchangeable, but what has that to do with us? We have our own traditions to maintain. So, you may just very kindly go and pull the plug, that's all, and the Virtual Reality Operator will switch off by itself."

"But, Madam, I already pulled plug! Still, it is running! That's why only I am disturbing you! See... must be, it is getting power from the Time Coil- just like the Info-Environmentalists warned!"

"Calm down, Kishoo! Just reflect for a moment. So, okay, some software glitch, or spatchcocked rewiring, is causing it to take electricity from the Time Coil. Tell Tech Support to come and fix. Meanwhile, why not switch off the Time coil?"

"Madam, we can switch off, but how we can recover all emergent properties of the system on re-booting? That is why it is a Director level decision. And you know Director Sahib has gone for Hajj. So, what to do?"

"Is Naipaul really misbehaving so very badly? Or if he is, why not just turn your eyes away? "

"Madam, you may be remembering, previous administration, due to its Hindutva obsession, insisted the Virtual Reality Operator satisfy Ved Vyasa's stipulation that karma and dharma be conserved. Thus each eigenstate of the system is constrained to display 2 additional symmetries. However, since both karma and dharma are observer dependent, the Zeno time of the system is macroscopic. But, Madamji, it is well known- by George Sudarshan Sir's theorem- that observations at intervals greater than the Zeno time would have the effect of accelerating its run away evolution. Thus, for Soteriological Health and Safety reasons, we have to schedule observations at lesser intervals to retard the process."

"*Arre* Kishenji, all that may be very well and good, but, just consider, was it very correct for you to come to me with a problem like this just now? Due to upcoming Pooja holidays, my mother-in-law has come to stay which means all the herbs and vegetables have to be bought fresh and the spices ground by hand. Couldn't you have waited till after the week-end?"

Kishen fidgeted and hung his head. "Madamji, sorry. Mistake mine only. Forgive to please."

'No," said Sulochana feeling guilty for having tried to shirk her responsibility, "You were right to tell me. The whole purpose of our Ministry is to reconstruct our Culture on a proper basis. Indeed, this current project is not just of National importance but also International significance. You see, when Nobel Laureate, Rabindranath Tagore went to Buenos Aires, ninety years ago, a great historical opportunity was missed. This was because, Tagore's secretary- a wealthy English squire- went and put his hand up Victoria Ocampo's skirt. This vulgar action incensed that great Argentine Muse and Maecenas. It put her on her guard. It colored her subsequent dealings with the venerable Indian sage. It prevented the proper unfolding of what could have been a wonderful Cultural cross-pollination and Spiritual efflorescence whose impact- on the young Jorge Luis Borges, to mention just one instance- was bound to have had world shaking implications."

"Yessir, Madamji. But, please, one thing I am not understanding. Why this Naipaul fellow getting involved? Due to why he is doing such unspeakable things to Ocampo Memsahib? What doomsday is this?"

"History," said Sulochana, "has its own System Repair utility. It mends its own broken threads after its own fashion. Thus, Norman Thomas di Giovanni- blind Borges's amanuensis- became also the facilitator of an affair between Naipaul- previously unlettered in sexual intimacy's Braille- and a cultured lady of the Argentine upper class. This had a re-invigorating effect on Naipaul's own work- his stigmatic sphota or inward Gorgon glance- and he went on to win the Nobel prize- but that wasn't what History had intended. On the contrary, the purely spiritual marriage- like the relationship between Mahatma Gandhi and, Tagore's niece, Sarla Devi- which History had arranged for Tagore and Ocampo – but which Tagore's lustful secretary frustrated- was meant to benefit Borges- not Naipaul, who read in Borges's bibliolatric Universalism nothing but a sterile and corrosive fantasy of cosmopolitanism spun out by a schizophrenically self-mythologizing mind whose manic protestation against its own

Provincialism but sealed it to that doom.

"But such a reading had the effect of creating something new in Universal Culture- the notion of the *ressentiment* of the margin towards the center- the beginning of an imputed insurrection- or, let us say, an epistemic fracture already apparent in such abortions of the Weltgeist as the notion of a malign and objectifying 'Orientalism', an unreasoning and implacable 'Alterity', a more sinister for speechless 'Subaltern', and a now galloping Globalization underpinned by the escalating export of indiscriminate Terror and all pervasive Fraud.

"This is a mistake we must correct. We too- humble pen-pushers though we be, in the Ministry of Cultural Reconstruction- are front-line soldiers in the battle to save Universalism. You too, Kishenji, if you could but see it, are playing an important role. The connection between Indian and Argentine modernism must be re-established on a high Spiritual level free from the taint of lechery or illicit sex. History must be remade on a proper basis so as to permit the, Democratically mandated, Cultural reconstruction of the country- in line with the Nehru-Gandhi-Pappu Yadav ideology of Secular Spiritual Scientific Socialism Sans Sexy Shenanigans. That is why Naipaul's naughtiness with Victoria Ocampo must not be allowed to stand. Action must be taken. Tell you what- can't Borges do something? Couldn't you get the young Borges into that time-line to…you know, throw cold water on Naipaul?"

"Madamji, I am not very expert on Borges. But, perhaps, if we consulted Vivek Iyer- not only he is General Secretary of the Admin Assistants (Grade III) Borges Appreciation Association but also- due to a couple of typos on the ballot paper's small print- ex officio, Sexretary Genital of the Admin Assistants (Grade III) Benevolent Association. Surely, he is the proper man…"

"Kishenji, I appreciate your suggestion but… the fact is… Mr. Iyer may not be the best person to involve. To be blunt… how should I say this?… you see, the sight of Naipaul's lusty actions can have a titillating effect on certain sorts of depraved people. In any case, Iyer is infamous, throughout the Secretariat, for his fanatical campaign to prove that Naipaul only sustained himself financially, during his lean years in the late 60's and 70's, by appearances as the masked wrestler, El Bandido Anal, on Venezuelan Television- not to mention cunnilingual cameos in Malyalee porn. Indeed, Mr. Iyer is running a roaring business supplying videos that purport to substantiate his claims. Frankly, I think it is better if we keep Mr. Iyer out of the picture."

"Madamji, I was not knowing. Please to forgive. What you suggest is best. However, still one doubt is in my mind. Don't mind it if I speak frankly. I am only Eighth Standard Pass. Sorry, to ask such a basic question. But, Madam, what of the Parmenides Principle? It was the basis of Lalluji's defense in the fodder scam case back in the Nineties. And now he is Minister of Railway Timetables, Ontology is under his portfolio. As Rabriji mentioned in her letter of support to our Action Committee- ' in a block universe- whatever can be thought of or spoken about must be- and that includes Virtual Reality representations.' Madamji, reason I'm mentioning is because there of a great danger. An eventuality unthinkable we may think, for unspeakable it surely is- Madamji, what if Naipaul **prefers** Borges to Ocampo? "

"So? Why only women should suffer? Anyway, what else we can do- tell me that?"

"But...but, Madamji! Question is- is this all only a simulation? Can we be sure there will be no real-world effects? I mean, sorry to be blunt, but you know sometimes even Departments of the Government India end up actually achieving something they were set up to do...Can we be sure the Past won't be changed?"

"Ah!" said Sulochana- wishing she'd kept awake at the Tech Support briefing- "Well... we know that, as Sir Karl Popper said, the Past is affected by experiments made in the Future... Indeed, the whole purpose of our Department is to change the Past. But, whether it is just Government of India's version of the Past or the actual universally inter-subjective Past... I confess, these are difficult questions to resolve on a Friday afternoon."

"Madam, are you saying we should wait a little...?"

"What? No! Virtual Reality or not, Naipaul is breaking Indian law. He must be stopped. Actually, Borges might be the right man to stop him, because his was the strongest voice warning Mankind of the dangers of Reality being contaminated by the Dream or usurped by the Simulation. Come to think of it, that's also Naipaul's point- but arrived at from the perspective of restless travel journalism rather than a tuirgen of restive hermeneutics... Perhaps, the two will complement each other. Even find a workaround for the... urm... Parmenides Principle and fulminate this whole distasteful episode of the riotously rutting Naipaul from the Universe's memory...But, Kishenji, it's almost five o'clock. Without waste of further words you may kindly return to your terminal and write a neat little macro which interposes Borges between Naipaul's chthonic lust and its long suffering, yet still Olympian, object. After all, what's the worst that could happen?"

Famous last words!

Anyroad, I only tell you all this to explain how I- Vivek Iyer, formerly a lowly Grade III peon- gained international acclaim as the author of 'The approach to Al-Mutasim'-Mutasim''- the most authentic, the most original, Indian novel ever envisaged by a native of this great land. Or, at least, that's what would have happened if Commissioning Editors hadn't turned up their noses at the myriad song and dance sequences- I not, I confess, strategically but syntagmatically- interpolated to give Borges's story a bit of oomph.

At any rate, this is the story Kishen keeps telling me. His boss, Mrs. Pundit, is the wife of a top literary agent- which is the only reason I cultivated the Backward Caste little bugger in the first place- but not even that high and mighty agent can get the publishers to see sense.

You see, as Kishenji has just now tearfully texted me, Naipaul misbehaving again & so something truly catastrophic has happened. Its arrow reversed, the Time Coil is now busy uncoiling Imagination's compacted dimensions, precipitating us all into this irremediably, for of Empathy, orphaned world where books befriend no books and turning their leaves but fans an arid simoom.

What was it Ghalib said?

Not your blanking me when we pass on the street
But that beggars too, now, alike me treat…
Great Wealth, thus, has our manners refined
Strangers, alone, to the Poor are kind!

The Vampire of Veluvan

The old German lived in a Buddhist dharamshala on the edge of the old town. Not far, but the flat rate fare wouldn't stretch to it. The trip would cost extra. What to do? These are disturbed times.

I disdained to haggle. The tonga driver's face grew longer. He had misjudged me. "It is a bad place," he temporized, sizing me up slyly. "Good people do not go there."

'So,' I thought to myself- 'some prostitutes are lodged in the dharamshala. No big surprise. Since the riots, the pilgrim trade has dried up. No doubt, the lodge keepers have found a way to appeal to a different type of customer'.

'I'll pay what you like." I said sharply- "Just name your fee and stick to it. Mind it,no *tamasha* later on!"

"No, Babu, you don't understand." the *tonga wallah* was placatory. My flash of temper had convinced him I was harmless. "It is not a good place. Unlucky. There has been talk."

"Some bad characters hanging around?" I asked.

"No! They are too scared. It is something else. There are some foreigners there. They are old…really, too old. What can I tell you? It is not a good place. You are young and fit. Why risk?"

"All right," I said quietly, "We will go and come back quickly. It is for my work."

The dharamshala was in a deplorable condition. The lodge keeper had fled the previous year. An enterprising Jain youngster came round on his three wheeler to sell the elderly pilgrims some basic items. He seemed a smart enough fellow. I was surprised to see that he stocked Japanese (or perhaps Korean) magazines and noodle packets.

Initially, he was polite and solicitous but abruptly lost interest when I mentioned who it was I had come to see. Apparently, the old German didn't spend money here. Instead, some Sadhus, belonging to the Natha order, came to see to his needs once every fortnight or so.

No, nobody knew why the naked Sadhus would want to look after the old foreigner.

I stopped probing. Ever since the riots, the townsfolk had become wary of the Nanga Sadhus with their tridents and matted hair.

The elderly Ambassador, whose memoirs I was editing, had mentioned that the old German was a Knight of Malta. He was some sort of relative of the Spy Master Gehlen. The story I had pieced together was that he had initially been sent to Nepal on charitable work for the Sovereign Order. After the fall of the Ranas, he reappeared in Rangoon as a student of

Buddhism. There are some articles he wrote for German magazines available on the internet. I don't read German, but gather that he was an admirer of U Nu.

After Ne Win's coup, he resurfaces in Sihanouk's Cambodia, but, in '65, after that puissant Prince's deal with the Communists, he receives a sort of bedraggled *entrée* at the court of Sikkim's Gyalmo- the beautiful American blue-blood, Hope Cooke. From there, around the time of the fall of the dynasty, the German went away to Sri Lanka. Then- the Karmic Ouroburos of that Edenic isle having swallowed and spat him back up again- some twenty years ago, he returned to India and settled in this little pilgrim town. The Indian Government seems to have turned a blind eye to his remaining in India. Perhaps, if he had really converted to Buddhism, he had become Stateless. The Knights of Malta are a Catholic order. They would have withdrawn his passport. My other reason for thinking there might be a story here was because I had come across his name in a book on 'Hitler's High Priestess' the French savant, known as Savitri Devi, who inspired Serrano and Evola and, now, a whole host of neo-Nazis who, strangely to my mind, have done little to build upon her foundations to secure the recognition of Hitlerism as a bona fide religion.

My first visit to the old man did not go well. He was completely hairless, hunched, and naked. He shouted at me, in Hindi, to go away. There were two European women there- both over 70. They looked terrified. I hurriedly left. Later, more ashamed of my lack of savoir faire than from any higher motive, I sent over a note explaining my interest. To my surprise, I got back a rather beautifully handwritten invitation to dinner at a local restaurant- 'Gaylord', I think, it was called. The D.M, a friend of a friend, was kind enough to lend me his 'lal batti' car. To be frank, I was nervous about staying out late in a town so recently scourged by riots.

Von Gehlen was very thin, perfectly bald, with creased but surprisingly pink and healthy skin. He introduced himself in good English with a degree of gentility but spoiled it by asking if I could pay for the meal. Before I could reply, he added that he had already ordered himself an expensive brandy.

With an affectation of Teutonic bluntness, I let him know that money was not a problem. However, he continued to harp on the subject. 'I am too old,' he said simply, 'you will have to pay. If not in money, then by presenting your arse for the kicks that our good host will surely shower upon you. You see, I am too old. They worry they will have the corpse of a white man on their hands. That is the only thing that restrains them. Otherwise, they are wild beasts.'

I called the waiter and told him to take the old man's order. I myself would have to leave shortly- so let the bill be kept ready for me.

"Sahib, you came in the 'lal batti' car?" the waiter turned out to be the proprietor. A milder looking man could scarcely be conceived. Far from wishing to hand out thrashings to deadbeat customers, he had his own tale of woe to tell. But, by this stage, I just wanted to escape. This trip had been a waste of time.

The old man was enjoying his brandy. If I hadn't been in such a hurry to leave, I would have felt sorry for him. He was in his eighties. This might be his last occasion to eat in a restaurant-not fancy by any means, but, perhaps, the best this little town could offer.

Simply to give him face, I muttered a couple of questions about Savitri Devi and Julius Evola and Ambassador Serrano and so forth. He immediately assumed an air of bemusement-did anyone take those cranks seriously?

I remembered that the German word 'krank' means a sick man, rather than a nut-job. Heidegger's comment on Celan- *'Celan ist krank heillos'-* came to mind. For some inexplicable reason, I spoke my thought aloud. "Celan" he said, correcting my accent, "You like his poetry?"

"Too deep for me" I said truthfully. Perhaps, it wasn't very tactful to bring up the meeting between the Jewish poet and the Nazi philosopher. Let the old man enjoy his brandy.

"Yes." said the old man, "He had depth. Unfortunately, the River Seine had more. Who would have thought it?"

"Were you in Sri Lanka during the Black July pogrom?" I surprised myself. It wasn't a question I had intended to ask.

"What? Yes... I suppose so. I saw some killings myself. The villagers had got hold of a *Strassenvalze*- do you say road roller? So they used that on the children and the old people and the too stupid to run away. You are...Tamil?"

I was astonished. Could the German be reading my mind? I'd read that thing about the steamroller in a book by R.D Laing. The great psychiatrist was in Sri Lanka to learn some advanced meditational technique to slow down Time- that single,
spokeless, *Strassenvalze* wheel of King Menander's otherwise non-existent chariot- and freeze the elusive moment which, the Buddhists maintain, is the only reality.

It occurred to me, I would have said Milinda- not Menander- and, suddenly, the brandy tasted vile.

I asked the proprietor to hurry up with the main course.

"I heard you were a Knight of Malta."

"In another life… another, do you say habilitation?|"

"No, we don't say that. Do you mean incarnation? Another birth?"

"No. Habilitation. A course of higher studies. Do you have such things here?"

"Yes, we abound in it. In India, possession of a PhD qualifies you for better treatment in Jail. All the apprentice gangsters have PhDs. You may have seen them busily completing their habilitations during the recent riots. "

"So, there is progress. Good. And you yourself are…"

"Not a PhD. Don't worry. The restauranteur will get paid in money, not kicks."

'So, you are not an academic. Perhaps, a journalist?'

"No. Definitely not a journalist."

"But political.. you ask about Savitri Devi and that old paralytic- Julius Evola…"

"He was paralyzed? I somehow thought he was a mountaineer like …urm... y'know, the British poet, the enemy of Yeats at the Golden Dawn... y'know...the guy who persuaded Ananda Coomaraswamy to try a bit of wife-swapping...sorry, the name was on the tip of my tongue...."

It was the British occultist, Aleister Crowley, whose name had slipped my memory.

The old German was peering at me intently. Suddenly, he grinned.

Could he, not just read my mind, but actually disorder my thoughts?   But no, why should he bother? He was busy with his brandy. He had already achieved his objective. He had established his ascendancy. Put simply, I was spooked and I would stay spooked. I might as well just pay the bill and go home. Chalk it up to experience. Old Germans living in derelict dharamshalas are still no objects for pity or, worse, the sort of fuzzy-minded mystagogy some middle class Indians still occasionally go in for.

"Did you know Evola, in Germany, during…urm.. your military service?"

I had remembered that Evola was hit by a shell that paralyzed him while working for the SS in the last days of the war. Except, I wasn't sure I'd ever actually known that. Thought transference? Was I tapping into the German's private portal to the Collective Unconscious?

"He was in Vienna. I was on the Eastern Front."

"That must have been…"

"Glorious? Yes. War is glorious... to the young. For a fit man who is young."

He looked pointedly at my thick eyeglasses.

"Perhaps, you know the poem by Tyrtaeus…"

"That lame school teacher? He was before my time."

"Since he lived a few centuries before Alexander- I suppose he must have been!"

The old man grimaced. "All soldiers are contemporaries."

"The Buddha was not a soldier."

"Is that what they teach you nowadays?"

He blinked at me happily, like a lizard in the sun.

"Forgive me. I did not know. It explains so much."

Karma, I thought- or thought that I thought- for, perhaps, the German was putting these thoughts into my head... Still, either way, I had brought this on myself. The truth was, I just wanted a bit of local colour, I had no interest in the man himself. There was a slot, in my new novel, for an old European aristocrat living in an Ashram or dharamshala in some little town- perhaps in the Himalayas…actually, definitely, the Himalayas… and he'd say wise things in a German accent and maybe quote Novalis… no, Holderlin- the God within us always lonely & poor- or better yet, Heidegger on Holderlin- the poet's blighting illness as Being's recovered future from which our salvation will come as a god-… and… and… I don't know, the whole thing would have been kind of mystical with a bit of a sentimental undercurrent and, well, kind of *sophisticated*.

Instead, I was stuck playing the role of the pretentious, bespectacled, Babu upon whom this elderly Hitlerite hooligan could practice his mind games while leaving me to pick up the tab.

I called for the bill. "I'm sorry, I have to go… the District Magistrate lent me his car."

Von Gehlen ignored me. I was relieved. What if he really was a hypnotist, like Aleister Crowley? Or, worse a *vetala*, a vampire- there had been unexplained deaths in the vicinity of the dharamshala…- where better for a vampire to hide himself than a riot plagued Pilgrim town?

I was out of my depth. I don't do Horror. Well, Dracula maybe- but this was shaping up to be H.P effing Lovecraft! How get out of it? Got to let my lower middle class, N.R.I, instincts take over. When you look into the abyss- thus sprach Neitzche- **take an effing snapshot on your 3 G camera phone coz ,** otherwise, the abyss will look back into you.

Maybe I should take a snapshot of the menu- which by a typesetter's error translated *'Athithi Devo Bhavah'* as 'The Guest is Cod"- or find some billboard with a hilarious example of Indian English I could post up on my blog.

I never actually did take a snapshot of the menu.

Just that *zikhr-e-sukhan*- the mere memory of my blog- was enough to save me.

"Will you visit me again?" the old man was crying. "No one comes. No one comes. The abbot said he would send V.I.P visitors. I would conduct lecture tours. My books would be published. That was 20 years ago. They have forgotten me. Everyone has forgotten me."

I asked the driver to turn on the siren. "Sahib," he said, "It is against regulations. *Lal batti* can only be turned on for official business."

"*Arre*, it is for your own safety I am telling!" I replied, "There is a *vetala* behind! I was clever to trick. But, why take chances? No backchat, just drive fast, I say!"

Unreasonable Love & its Subaltern object

Love is unreasonable. Unreasoning.The retired Brigadier clearly loved the Bihari boy who alone shouldered the burden of looking after his physical needs now my Vatsala Aunty had gone completely blind.

'Uncle, tell me, this lad has been registered with the Police, no?'- I asked this because I was genuinely concerned, not simply making conversation, or trying to stem the tide of *fauji* profanity the senile old soldier was favouring that head wobbling, grinning young imbecile of a servant with.

The old man looked scared and fell silent.

I decided to get angry.

'Bloody hell, Saar! Don't tell me, he haven't been checked out! Saar, don't give excuse you are military man. Major General of Commandos- Commandos mind it! not Corps of Engineers-

he and his wife had their throats slit by their servant in West Delhi! Don't you know it? I mean, okay, if this fellow is from South, or a reputed place like Garwhal, or from military family, then, all right- we can have confidence. But, Uncle, Bihar? That State itself has been split, it was too huge. This lad is too ignorant to know which new State he belongs. In old days, okay, Ignorance was Innocence, but nowadays is that really the case? Look at the TV free-show of this naked Parliament of obscene jackals! Are they not ignorant? So, tell me then, Uncle, how you alone are knowing this tribal *chokra* isn't part of some gang?

"*Arre,* look, Brigadier Sahib, you are too senior, so I won't say more. Fault is of that bloody *faltu* Secretary of this Housing Colony! What type of *bundobast* this is, I say? I will give the fellow a damn good rocket! Your son is a top Doctor, Stateside, if he comes to hear he will make one phone call to our *sambandhi*, I.G. of Police, by God's Grace, and that Secretary fellow will face some fine Music!

'Don't worry, Uncle- I say, don't worry. I won't mention anything to worry your darling boy- poor fellow, he is sweating bullets to get your idiot grandson into College- even he asked *me* to help get him in here; **here**- Delhi Uni! even just for History or Political Science or some *faltu* rubbish.

I told him straight- you are younger to me, Before itself I was telling to you- send the fellow Yukay for education, I say- American schools are rubbish completely. They will make an idiot of your boy. Now, just see, how my words are coming true? Still, that *ladla* of yours is too headstrong to listen to me. I said, look here, you are younger to me, it is **my duty** to oblige. In India, if you want to put your son for Medicine, Engineering, I.T, something top like that- no problem, I have pull and will do it no questions asked or donations required! But History? Political Science? This bloody *faltu* wassisname…Subaltern Studies? Your father was a Brigadier General and you will put your son in Subaltern Studies? That too in India, not Ivy League? Duffer, I will break your leg!'

The old soldier didn't like hearing his son mentioned. Once the Bihari lad got involved, his senile retreat turned into an undignified rout.

I was pleased. It was Vatasala Aunty whom I'd come to see.

'Anyway, Aunty, don't worry on this servant business. I will sort out double quick. How this Housing Colony Committee is letting aged couple keep house servant- that too some Bihari tribal!- without doing full Police check up and.. whadyacall.. due, I say due, *due* diligence? *Henh? Henh?* Bloody nonsense. Aunty, you don't worry, I will sort out just now only.'

I should explain something. I'm closing in on 50. Old people like it when I talk 'rough'. It shows I can sort out their day to day problems and will derive a virile sort of *funktionslust* by so doing. Of course, I also do all the permissible feet touching and taking blessing &c- but that is only for my private pleasure and intimate soteriological satisfaction, that's all.

Fact is, to speak frankly, when people get to a certain age, either they should quietly go and join the household of their son or else retire to a peaceful Ashram with dignity. Why remain in Delhi, where all sorts of violence and underhand dealings are occurring? What for this worthless glory? Or, all right, you want to remain. Good. Up to you. You have served the Nation and you have earned the right. Still, when we husky middle aged men visit, least we can do is to raise our voices and show some aggression and toughness to give a warning to the scoundrels in the neighbourhood that the old people must be protected and cherished.

Anything happens to them, there will be hell to pay!

Vatsala Aunty had put out her hand. I grasped it and helped her to come and sit next to me on the sofa.

This little darling had come to Delhi to be near her son who was studying at the All India Medical Institute, while the Brigadier Sahib was busy building roads in Arunachal.

She had taken a job teaching Sanskrit at St. Columba's (a thankless task!) and gave 'Shastriya Sangeet' singing lessons in the evenings. Everybody in Delhi- this was the early Eighties- simply fell in love with her. Mum used to bring her home- on the excuse of teaching my sister- simply to feed up this tiny little thing and force her to take home tiffin carriers filled with *avviyal* and *mor' korombu* and so on.

Mum got awfully lonely after my Sister married and moved abroad and though I too, nominally, was enrolled as Vatsala Aunty's student, I'd just eat with them in the kitchen- but also wolfishly try to eat their hands as they refreshed the supply of piping hot *phulkas* on my plate. Because I was over 14 stone in weight, six feet in height, stupid, ugly and had graduated from the LSE at the age of 19, such behavior was considered an outward and visible sign of a superior inward and invisible superabundance of Brahminical Grace and Orthopraxy.

At that time, the Colonel Sahib (he was promoted Brigadier, one year before retirement) had invested everything in a tip top Army housing scheme in Bangalore. Later, the couple sold out to finance their son's shift to America. Meanwhile, Vatsala Aunty, by her entire absence of guile, had won the heart of a Lieutenant General's wife who hailed from the Kapurthala Royal Family. The Colonel Sahib was not a man to take favors- especially from senior officers belonging to more Aristocratic Regiments. But, he was just as stupid as his wife and easily tricked into taking this small but very valuable flat in a well managed Colony. Now the Metro and Mall had appeared a hundred yards from his door, he could sell out at a very good price.

Vatsala Aunty had come to sit beside me.

She asked in a whisper 'Is Brigadier Sahib still here?'.

No, he has gone and the servant with him. I absent-mindedly kissed her hand. Then I lowered my head and said 'give patting to the horse'. She laughed, at first nervously but melodiously, then, with a catch in the throat and nasal Sama Vedic timbre, noetically and memoriously, and what's more, guided by my hand, even managed to pat my head with small sparrow wing pats.

Then she spoilt it all by mentioning Mum.

I got up brusquely saying 'Okay! I'll go and come. Just, little bit, I'll talk to the Secretary and fix this servant business.'

Aunty became frightened. She gripped my hand. In broken Tamil, she said. 'No, no, please. Have said boy is not servant but grandson.''Who said? To whom? What talking?' 'Shouting, no- please, please, no shouting!' 'No, no- I say, look, not shouting but who is grandson and who is servant and who is saying what to whom? Just explain simply.'

'See, the Resident's Committee Secretary came to check on the servant. Your Uncle- you know how he is since the stroke- he went and said 'no, no- he is my grandson. Kindly desist from impudent enquiry.'

'Oho! Like that is it?'

'Like that, simply.'

I changed the subject. I wanted a little time to think, so I started up the hare of the canonical univocity of *dhruvapad* and *tarana* and what that did to Bhratrhari's *vakyapadiya*. Vatsala Aunty's blind eyes darted eagerly and she spoke and she sang and spoke again and sang again and then that fucking Bihari imbecile of a servant came and sat cross legged on the floor and I looked at him and I knew he wouldn't cut his employers' throats or make off with Vatsala's Aunty's *zevar* or her husband's gold medal for gallantry, but then the old Brigadier dodders in and the Bihari boy settles him into his arm chair and- last I looked, or last I remember seeing- the fucking Brigadier is resting his hand on the Bihari lad's head and fuck me for a fucking Racist cunt- the Brigadier hadn't lied, the casteless Bihari **was** his grandson. Not a legitimate grandson- wrong shade of sepia, too gracile and take a gander at that kinky hair!- fuck me, I should of seen it before. The Brigadier was once a Subaltern, a lean and lissome Second Lieutenant, surveying the Rajmahal hill tract- people like me think we know India just coz we're Indian and all we fucking know is India coz actually we live abroad- but, Boss, we know **shit.**

Anyway, sod this for a game for soldiers. I never wanted to write any of this- I'm talking about stuff that happened a couple of years ago- and the only reason I'm writing about it now is coz I just saw that Vatsala's grandson has published an essay in the Subaltern Studies Quarterly. It seems he **did** go to India and study there. Oddly enough, he was already in Delhi when I visited his grandparents. Okay, he's done well. Fair play to him. But, gotta tell you, I still think all this 'Subaltern Studies' is bullshit. Gramsci, in Mussolini's prison, uses the word as a code for 'proletarian'. The Cambridge educated Bengali *bhadralok* eagerly seize upon it as a method of talking Revolution into, or out of, existence without upsetting the servants' routine. Alterity and Subalternity is the *Sanathan* eternity of Zizekananda's *pas devant les domestiques.*

I wasn't smart enough to go to Cambridge.

I'm not Bengali or, class origin wise, really *bhadralok*.

So let me be clear about what I'm saying.

The grandson of a fucking Brigadier General, the son of a fucking Heart Surgeon in St. Louis can't, by definition, *represent* the 'subaltern'- the oppressed, the marginalized, those so surd in the hegemonic language they can't represent themselves- from which it follows he can't understand them or have anything but an entirely ironic and heteronomous agency with respect to them.

You ask- 'why? How do you know and, anyway, fuck does it matter?' Why and how I know is because Vatsala Aunty proved Tarana *is* Dhruvapad- thus resolving Hempel's dilemma- all is but surface, and that surface a mirror, and, by *quod nescis quo modo fiat, non facis*- **her** grandson, if not the Brigadier's- after his stroke he rescinded recognition of his son- didn't *know* how to be a grandson and therefore he didn't do it. But if he didn't do *that*- something definitionally Caste- fuck did he do? Write a worthless fucking essay for the Subaltern Studies Quarterly, filled with all the fashionable tropes, on the plight of the fucking domestic servants of New Delhi!

Irony don't come much richer than this! Maybe Concurrency really is a secret symmetry of the World- but, not a perfect symmetry- because, I ask, what happened to the *actual* Tribal *& therefore casteless* domestic servant?

I bet you that budding Academic fuckwit neither knows nor cares.

I do.

How it happened was this.

As I was leaving Vatsala Aunty's Housing complex, the *chowkidar* asked me to wait. The Secretary wanted to speak to me. Mindful of my promise to Vatsala Aunty, I was ingratiating and played up my expat status. Turned out the guy was the nephew of my late G.P from back when I lived in Leyton. Anyway, me and him warmed to each other and still keep in touch on Facebook. Apart from the songs of Kundan Lal Saigal, we had something else in common- we each really loved and cared for at least one member of that old couple. I loved Vatsala coz I used to try to bite her hand. He loved the Brigadier because the old man did a lot for the Colony while his wife was off baby-sitting in America.

What I mean is this. People need need elders to look up to. The labourers would in any case have loved the old man who came to oversee things because he was an Army Engineer who knew what he was doing. Their love increased when they realized he was remaining here in India when he could easily go to America to lord it over his son's family.

Perhaps, the Secretary also shared this delusion. He said the son had been contacting him to try to get parents to move to U.S.

Bluntly, I disabused the Secretary of any such sentimental 'Bollywood' notions. In America, baby-sitters are very expensive. Yuppie couples bring aged parents over to save cash. Put them in the basement- they won't mind. India is a fucking third world country after all. The old bastards should be grateful. After all, now we've got Blu Ray, we did give them the old VCR didn't we? Anyway, it's all about recycling and environmental sustainability. Just throw the kitchen scraps down the basement stairs and they old folk will make out like gangbusters.

The Secretary's face fell. He knew his K.L Saigal films. *'Ik bangala bane nyaara'* - 'oh! for a nice new bungalow'. This is the real music of India- not Sufi *Tarana* not Sanskrit Dhruvapad.

But whose blood is mixed in the cement?

In the same brutal vein I continued- what? you think India is different? Bastard, people take their elderly parents on excuse of *teerth yatra* or Hajj or what you say pilgrimage- then, then what? Brother, they abandon in strange town, rush back and sell the bloody property, Man! On what planet you are living actually?

Thanks to me, the Secretary smelled a rat when the Brigadier sold up. He emailed me and I called him and we talked.

But. But. But. He did nothing. I made sure of it. You see, it was Vatsala Aunty that I loved. I kept faith with her. She hadn't patted my head in vain.

His big news for me was that the heart surgeon in the U.S lost all his money in the Crash. His parents had to sell their flat to bail him out. They had no choice but go stay with him and his fucking 'high yaller' Yale bitch wife.

Brigadier Sahib is a soldier. Has senile fucking dementia but still the spark of decency hasn't died within him. He worried about the 'Bihari' boy. Fucking American, non 99 percenter, shit-fucking-ass-holes, his son and daughter-in-law assured him that the servant would be joining them once his Visa came through.

And they could actually have done it.

Easiest fucking thing in the world for them, their being, authentic, 1 percenters.

So, do these plutocrats have a servant to look after the old man?

Yes, actually. A muscular mestizo with- guess what?- now a Green Card.

They could swing that for a stranger.

But not for a thin Bihari boy.

You see, the Bihari was half Negrito. Half *Indian* fucking black.

In other words an embarrasment.

These sort of cunts pay big money to import a sour faced Kanyakubja Brahmin cook.

Then gorge themselves on McDonalds.

Don't get me started, mate.

I don't blame anybody. What I mean is, I don't blame the heartless heart surgeon or his, old money, 'African American', Ivy League wife. Nor am I trying to make out I'm some sort of Saint. I've done worse.

Truth is, I'm a fucking cunt.

But, I do blame Vatsala Aunty. Why?

Blind bitch coursing a hare I'd just casually started- fuck you needed to flatten Hempel's dilemma's 2 horns?

Not that I have proof but *Cherchez la femme*.

All the clues were there in what the Secretary told me.

The grinning Bihari imbecile thought he was going to America. Even started interpolating a little **Amrikan** into his broken, Negrito-fucking-tribal, Hindustani. It was this, the imbecile's linguistic eagerness for America, that got the Brigadier to go.

The Secretary couldn't guess but I **know** what happened. Though blind, Vatsala started to suspect the true genealogy of the servant. Her husband was cursing the lad a little too much. After that, the precise sequence of events isn't important. Could things have turned out otherwise? Don't know. But one thing is clear. She cooked the whole thing up. The heart surgeon hadn't lost any money- or any more than the rest of us have the last couple of years. She started teaching that miscegenated little tribal bits of English- American English at that, but then her Sama Vedic mastery of *pratishakya* phonetics made this easy for her and her purpose was so duplicitous, it hid even from herself.

You will remember this pocket-sized Pandita taught Sanskrit at St.Columba's and *Sangeet* to my sister. I won't dwell on her shame. Like I said, I've done worse. Suddenly, the half-negrito servant thinks he's Eddie Murphy in 'Coming to America'. What can the old soldier do? He is an infant beguiled by his wisp of a wife, like Balzac's Colonel Chabert. He fucking deserts- that too, of his own fucking volition!- the country whose independence and self-reliance he had spent his life defending and building up.

But, Colonel Chabert married a whore and knew he'd married a whore. Also he hadn't a grandson who'd looked after him and upon whose head he'd rested his hand.

Anyway, let's just not go on about this shall we? Let sleeping dogs or bitches or whatever. Not that I'm scared of anyone.

Look, this is just a splenetic blog post. I'm not libeling anybody. I'm not trying to bring anybody into 'hatred, ridicule or contempt.'

Vatsala Aunty only did what any woman would have done. Which Jury could say I've defamed her? I'm simply pointing out a truth about the female sex. It's something biologically programmed. They can't help it. Jealousy is in their nature and we love them for it. It's not like I try to bite just anybody's hands you know.

Still, I would like to say, there is a serious academic point I'm making. This young, so called, scholar- yes, very good, he has published in a prestigious journal- but he is more blind than his grandmother! Look at the bloody photograph on his blog! Spitting bloody image of the Bihari tribal. He must have visited his grandparents. He must have seen that servant. But he didn't see his own semblance, his consanguinity, in that Bihari Tribal from buttfuck nowhere.

Not recognizing your own image in the mirror- that's what literature is about. Subaltern Studies is okay as literature. It's just not Social Science.

Love is unreasonable. But a Science is a Faith. If Faith doesn't reason, it will never amount to Love.

Mind it, kindly!

The parable of the Hermit and the Priestpriest

Once upon a time a learned priest, seeking knowledge of the highest mysteries of Holy

Scripture, retired to a hermitage in the forest. Pious folk from a small village in a clearing nearby came to to seek his blessings and see to his simple needs.

A strange, solitary boy, who delighted in killing birds with stones and whacking bush rats with a stick, haunted the vicinity.

The old hermit chanted aloud chapters of the sacred text. The boy, drawn by the melodious sound, would abandon his cruel sport to come and listen to the holy man.

One day, while chanting the last verse of the last chapter, the hermit died. When the villagers came to bring food for the hermit they were amazed to find that the boy was chanting the holy book in place of the hermit.

Believing this a miraculous occurrence, the villagers showed the boy the same reverence they had shown the hermit. In time, he grew old, and it was as though the old hermit was still alive, chanting the sacred text in his accustomed manner.

Meanwhile the village had become prosperous for, believing themselves especially favored by proximity to the hermitage, the villagers had grown confident and enterprising.
At this time a young graduate of a prestigious seminary thought it worthwhile to set up house and institute congregational worship in the village.

The villagers showed the ambitious young priest every mark of veneration and built a splendid house where he could lodge students and acolytes of his own.

However, the villagers did not discontinue their practice of seeking the hermit's blessing and this galled upon the learned priest.

He hinted to the villagers that there was nothing very marvelous in an idiot boy learning to repeat, parrot fashion, verses of the sacred text. The point about holy Scripture is to understand it and to be able to draw correct inferences from it.

Finally, the priest and his acolytes decided to challenge the hermit to a scholarly debate.
At first, the hermit appeared to be holding his own for no sooner did the priest quote a verse of Holy Writ than the hermit proceeded to recite the entire chapter from memory.

However, when the priest began to display his knowledge of the syntax and vocabulary and hermeneutics of the sacred language, the hermit fell silent.

The priest said, 'the learned jurists disagree as to the exact meaning of this verse. I have related what the commentators have said and the manner in which the theologians have erected radically opposed philosophies based on rival interpretations of the text. Perhaps you, oh holy hermit!, can resolve the battle of the schools and dispel the confusion of the seminaries by granting us your insight into the true meaning of the piece of Holy Writ?"

Without a word, the hermit rose swiftly from his seat and beat the priest to death with a stick.
'Why such violence?' the villagers cried out.
'I like killing things with a stick,' the hermit replied grinning happily, 'It is most enjoyable. Mom discouraged me from playing with the other kids only for this reason. However, when the strange words that the old Holy man used to utter became lodged in my mind, my taste for beating things to death departed from me. Today, since this man was kind enough to explain the meaning of that nonsense, its hold on me has been broken and so I can resume my favorite pastime.'

The priest's acolytes then spoke up- 'In truth, this is a miracle! The highest mystery of Holy

Scripture has been revealed!'

After everybody had run away from the village- those, that is, not nimble enough to avoid the Holy Man's stick- they spread far and wide as Evangelists of the True Gospel and also Media Personalities with a side-line in Pizza delivery.

In Lanka before Sunrise

'Night School,' I said, having noticed the two uptown types in the back row, 'What good is it- now the State provides synaptic uploads for free?'

"Only to citizens."

"Only to subjects- not 'citizens', this isn't a Republic, thankfully- but, urm, I'm sorry your name really is too difficult to pronounce... if you will permit me to continue, the fact remains, with free implants and real time uploads and so on, what is the point of Night School? What is to be its new role in the emerging Technological...urm,'

Should I say Lebenswelt? Too pretentious? Hey, this is just Night School! I hesitated.

"We need Night School to get our certificates as Évolués. *That's* the point. It's the reason we're here."

My interrupter was the same big lug- a waste technician at the power plant, probably on a dodgy work permit- my guess, his supervisor had filled his head with promises of permanent residency- yeah, like that was gonna happen! The whole raison d'etre for free synaptic uploads was to reduce our dependence on these immigrant gorillas.

"Well.. that's, of course, urm... an...urm... possible, possible.. urm..." Oh dear, I sounded like a drooling idiot. Normally, that wouldn't matter- but those two uptown types in the back row had me worried. Why were they here? Just slumming? No- too clean cut. They looked... connected.

"True, Night School started off as the poor man's route to social and occupational mobility, but, with changing technology, it must now re-invent itself as ... the School of Night!""What?!"- the big lug looked set to hurl his desk at me.

"Night," I said quickly, "Night is the great mother from which our civilization evolved. Night is the School to which our civilization must return to learn anew the meaning of our stature as Évolués..."

I glanced up. As I had hoped, the mention of his favourite word had tranquilised the gorilla. The meathead was now taking notes. I could proceed in safety. But pitch my words at the two uptowners in the back row. Why not? I might never have a second opportunity to talk to people of my own sort- intelligent people, if their looks were anything to go by- that too, in my own lecture hall. *Carpe noctem*- seize the night!

"What is it that Night teaches? What is the true Nisha Sutra? Let us begin by saying what it is not. It is not its shadow- the wisdom of the forest dwelling Nishaads- nor the shadow of that shadow- the Upanishads- rather it is the cry of our immortal King- Ravana, named for his first and primordial cry of fright! Fright at what? Night. Night is the first teacher. Fear drives evolution. Our race- the Rakshasas- saw Raksha, security, originated in Fright. For those races which turned their back on evolution, on the other hand, Night- which they apotheosise as *Ratri*- was what dispelled darkness, a beneficient Goddess. That same Goddess as is revealed in the dark trench their ploughs laboriously trace. To which, too, they give a Goddess's name- *Seeta*. But, that which made both fearsome- they forgot. Our immortal King did not make that mistake. Both labour and darkness he holds in loathing and fear more than loathing. Ours is a city of lights- it is a city of leisure. Both labour and night are banished here. We are the true *ujali paraj*- the race of light. The unevolved are the *kali paraj*- the race of darkness. We, driven by fear, we gambled and won! To them is left that inverse of the gamble- that opposite of the Master Slave dialectic- the dullard's duty of *Krishi*- mind darkening agriculture! Consider the difference between us and them! They light fires for their sacrifices during the day, but extinguish them by night! How foolish is that! Fire is to ward off the fears of the Night, it is wasted if used to but praise and give thanks to that living God whose crime against creation is the abolition of fear- the denial of evolution!"

The two uptowners were now looking at me keenly. Beneath the cowls of their holo-cloaks I saw their sharp features flicker with intelligent appreciation.

They scared me shitless.

Dad got his Évolué papers during the Brahma Wars when, frankly, such things were a lot easier.I was cloned in a perfectly good facility- but, between you and me, it was offshore. I'm not a 'birther'. These things make a difference you know.

Fear was a drug I had been too long denied. I mean pure fear. Not the fear-methadone that keeps people of my class productive in this great Empire of Fear.

Except, 'productive' is not, perhaps, the *mot juste*. True, I pay my protection money same as any other upstanding, that is cowering, subject. But, does the State not actually create the means for me to pay it off? I mean, I'm not like my Dad- who served during the Brahma Wars- but then I'm more evolved...

Look, sorry to be pedantic, but let me change that sentence. Go back to 'the fear-methadone that keeps people of my class' and instead of 'productive' substitute 'not transgressive, in this our great Empire of fear.'

My private musings had led me to punctuate my lecture with more urms and aahs than normal.The two uptowners were getting up. Great! They were leaving! No. They were coming down towards me.

I fainted.

(What can I say? Good genes, I guess. Dad really did do yeomen service during the Brahma wars.)

----------------II------------

"Get that monkey away from me!"

(Though my Doctorate is only in Comp. Lit, the fact remains- I was ranked second in the Screaming-Bee at my Middle School- a very good one I might add- albeit merely virtual.)

"Why? It can't hurt you."

The 2 uptowners displayed signs of gender dimorphism. This increased my fear.

"Stop screaming like that! What are you- Vat born?"

I abruptly stopped screaming.

"I was being ironic. Like ironic and post-evolved...you savvy?"

"Whatever. Look, we want you to talk to this monkey. Your PhD is in Comp. Lit right? See, this monkey has got amnesia. We found him wandering around the food court. Nice enough little fella. My girl-friend picked him up. Once she got him under her holo-cloak, he just hugged her like a baby.. Could you talk to him?"

"And if I don't- you'll eat me?"

"Well, bits of you- yeah. Like, stuff you'd really miss. Unless of course, you can talk to this li'l darling. You know, my boy friend and me might register for natural birth. I'm thinking to, like, *suckle* our baby? It's frightening- but somehow, once this little fellow snuggled against me- it just didn't seem so scary anymore."

Uptown girls- right? I mean whaddya whaddya?

---------------III-------------

"The monkey speaks."

"Cool! What's he saying? Like how much he loves his new Mommy?"

"Well... not precisely..."

It was not the right answer. Her snarl told me a lot about which portions of me had excited her appetite.

"You see- somehow or the other- this monkey speaks Valmikian. It's like our own Ravanese. Indeed, Valmiki, too, started out down the same path. But whereas Ravanese is based on the infant's cry of fear at what Night's darkening Heaven's thundered, Valmikian is based on the poet's sorrowful cry at seeing, by the hunter's arrow, two love birds sundered. Put simply, both are languages generated by their own *mot theme*... I mean, like mathematically constrained to always say the same thing while saying everything conceivable..."

"And what my li'l monkey is saying is it loves its Mommy- right!"

"Absolutely! No question. Well... a tiny caveat...you see Valmikian is cosmological in scope, it can name every particular with the greatest degree of subtlety but only because it reveals the nature of Reality to its uttermost limit... but, no, no, you are right- it is concerned wholly with 'vatsalya'- love as between Mother and child. So, yes- your intuition was correct!"

"My monkey baby loves me! Sweetie, bite something nice off the Prof. for me to feed it!"

"I'm afraid you can't do that."

"Oi! What did you just say to my girl friend?! Did you say 'can't'!"

"Not 'can't' can't- of course you can- but what the monkey is saying is..."

"You already told us. It loves its Mommy. Don't you sweetie?"

"Well, of course he does- but his Valmikian language has conditioned him- you know, Language speaks us in the same manner that Screams our lungs truly re-bring to breathe- to see the fearful, the tearful, the dire ire of vatsalya baffled- become its own breath blinded mirror, like the Autumn Moon, and all Love rendered but the polluted leftovers of its own sacrifice thus poisoning Evolution and causing Time itself to decay..."

"F**k you say?"

"Guys- take it easy. This is complicated stuff. Look, the essential nature of *vatsalya,* as a type of love, is to be parted from its object- but parted only so as to become Universal and thus true to its higher purpose. Thus, it must itself become Time- that which rends it from what it holds most dear.

"We Rakshasas, on the other hand, have conquered Time- that was what the Brahma Wars were about- Fear drives all. The multiple arms and heads of Time have all been loped away- they are now the multiple arms and heads of our dread King- only Evolution is left but though an Evolution born of our fear, what drives it now is Universal fear of Us. Look, you must see where I'm going with this."

"Bite off his arms- they'll make a nice titbit for Baby."

"Would, dear lady, my arms availed you- nothing now can feed it- nothing save giving alms to a Buddhist bhikku."

"What's a Buddhist?"

"You are."

"What?"

"You are. At this moment, cradling that monkey- you have become Hariti, who gave up eating human flesh when the Buddha restored her babe to her. But, be aware of this danger. Our immortal King saved you, saved us, from fear of God. He opened Evolution to us as our own fearless demesne. We- you dear lady, and your boy friend- are, in that sense, all the more vulnerable to Buddhism.. Your modality of Time is not Fear, nor the self emptying of kenosis- rather it is the eternity of the transitory moment- *kshanikavada*- you are already proto-Buddhists, your chariot a single spokeless wheel that is also a Strassenwalze- a road-roller- under which you can crush into the unresisting ground what is Other to you- for, truly, there is neither Space nor Time- as a dimension extending to include interaction with others- no, at least not for you."

"I like that bit about a- what did you call it?"

"Strassenwalze- a road-roller- crushing the Other into the road upon which your chariots might more fleetly fly."

"Don't sound so bad- but what was that other thing you said- Bikkie- a Buddhist Bikkie.'

"Bhikku- a mendicant- a monk, one who lives by begging his bread."

"I don't like the sound of that."

"Feed my arms to your monkey- the more of me you feed him, the more Buddhism devours you!"

"You dare to threaten us- jumped up little evoluee!"

"Scarcely I! I am not the danger! It is that little monkey you hold to your heart!"

"What... what is wrong with my baby?"

"He is Valmikian! Himself, the tragic trajectory of true Vatsalya!"
"What do you mean?- it's my coochy cuddly baby- O yes it is!"
"He is not just a monkey- nobody is."
"He is mine. I am his!"
"No parent, in a child, knows lasting bliss!"
"Listen, you immigrant- talk politely!"
"& it is to you, Sir, not black but whitely!"
"Beat him, Lover, tear his flesh!"
"Then never to your breast a babe will mesh!"

I felt actually quite good as the Raakshas tore off my arms. My new appendages began budding almost immediately. I was now a shoo in for tenure. Uptown folk had devoured my arms. Feels good right?! Especially the fear. I'd be moving in higher circles. Adrenalin rush!

What next happened next was- unexpected? No, sadly not. Actually, it's the sort of distateful contretemps that's bound to occurwhat happens when you have immigrants who don't know their place. That great lug of a waste-technician led the charge. My students. They grabbed the uptown Rakshasas. And released the monkey.

Me. I did it. My arms grow back real quick. But the monkey didn't know it. That's why I captured it so easily. I was tightening my hold around it- not exactly with the notion of throttling it, but simply squashing it into a nice piece of pâté for when the cops turned up....How was I supposed to know? In Lanka before Sunrise, the demon's spell works amnesia. But, hand-cuffs cancel mind-cuffs. Physical constraint releases from Mental subservience. That monkey was Hanuman. He burnt down our City. He did it with his tail.
Guys- I didn't know- Lanka was my Mother.
I learned Vatsalya only after my Mom was burnt up.
Am I saved?

The tale of the Sheikh and the courtesan.

....now we are nothing, but at one time our qasbah had two ornaments- the humble Sheikh who, nonetheless, was the greatest Jurist of his time, and Noor, the courtesan, whose bewitching coquetry could not distract from the purity of her angelic voice.

Our qasbah had an honest kotwal (police sergeant) whose plain dealing and blunt manner of speech had given offence to a certain coxcomb.
That intriguer used his cunning to falsely accuse the kotwal and have him thrown in jail.
The Sheikh came to the policeman's rescue. He was acquitted and reinstated. Later, not just from gratitude, the kotwal begged and importuned the Sheikh to come for his daughter's

wedding.

As part of the celebration, the Sheikh was forced to attend a performance by the courtesan, Noor. Thankfully, she did not play any of her tricks on this occasion, being wholly immersed in exploring the thematic complexities of the *raaga* (melodic pattern) appropriate to the hour. Nevertheless, the Sheikh- in an unobtrusive manner- was able to slip away at an early point in her performance.

The Sheikh never mentioned the singer again and, in any case, had never sought to gain a cheap sort of fame by denouncing the wretched inhabitants of the Musician's quarter.

The courtesan, however, showed no such restraint. Clearly, she had recognized him in the audience- perhaps, by his white beard and nobility of countenance- and felt slighted by his decision to leave early.

The courtesan began to mock the old man and compose unflattering little couplets about him. So artful was she, such was her skill as a comedienne, that people enjoyed her sallies against the saintly Sheikh.

However, the courtesan was not content to let things stop there. The degrading nature of her profession meant that she had no compunction in dragging the most venerated of her fellow townsfolk down to her own level- or, indeed, an even lower position- depicting the Sheikh a sort of simpleton, a moonstruck calf.

Of course, no one dared mention such matters in front of the kotwal. His love for the Sheikh was well known.

But, then, a debauched intriguer saw an opportunity to revenge himself on his old enemy.

That *Acherontis pabulum* came to the kotwal under a show of humble contrition and reported what the courtesan was saying about the Sheikh. The intriguer professed himself shocked and unable to decide how to proceed. 'Kotwal Sahib,' the intriguer confessed, ' you know very well of my wicked ways. My change of heart was entirely because of the Sheikh's influence. Yet, now I hear the courtesan mocking the Sheikh, my new found faith begins to falter. You tell me- what should I do?"

The kotwal became absolutely furious. He was determined to confront the courtesan. However, as a police officer, it was his duty to verify the complaint and secire damning evidence.

He thought to himself- 'Women, speak more openly amongst themselves than they do to men. If the courtesan is really seeking to ridicule the Sheikh, her language to the women will be less moderate than that which she dares to use in front of men.'

Thus, the kotwal went to his wife and asked her about what the courtesan was doing. Seeing her husband's face, the woman's color changed.

She said, "look here, if you go and kill that courtesan, the intriguers will say you did it because she refused your advances. You will be executed. Our family will be ruined. Let me deal with this matter. I will go and speak to her. Once she understands the danger in which she is in, she will immediately make a public recantation. She will compose songs in praise of our

Sheikh. Wouldn't you like to hear such songs? Say what you like, she has the voice of an angel!"

The kotwal was mollified. In truth he wanted to hear her songs praising his beloved Sheikh.

His wife went to the courtesan. She warned that reprobate of the danger in which she stood. That little baggage gave her back-chat. Suddenly, the vain whore was claiming that her 'art'- itself nothing but lascivious display and an open advertisement for the sale of her body- was, nonetheless, on a level with the religious knowledge of the Sheikh!

The kotwal's wife was astounded. She beat and slapped and pulled the hair of that filthy slut. To no avail. Those creatures of the devil are strangers to shame. Also, they are expert play- actors. The courtesan now uttered some self-pitying speech about how blows and slaps had forced her into this filthy trade- but that *mousike'* had redeemed her! Does this sort of trashy Music really redeem? And who actually practices this 'art' save those predestined to Hell fire? That is why it is condemned by Scripture.

The kotwal's wife made one final effort. She said, "I go down on my knees to you. Please stop insulting the Sheikh. My husband will kill you. As a consequence, he himself will be executed. My children will starve. Have mercy upon those innocents."

The courtesan became quiet. She said- "I agree, on one condition. You yourself go, with your husband, in front of the Sheikh."

"Stop!" said the kotwal's wife, "I understand your plan! You want me to tell this whole story to the Sheikh. But let me tell you, not just my husband only, I too am his lover! I would prefer to see my own children put to death before my eyes rather than trouble that Saint with your ribaldry! "

"No," said the courtesan, "I don't want you to tell the Sheikh anything about all this. Just say to your husband, in front of the Sheikh, 'The courtesan, Noor, claims she loves the Sheikh ten thousand times more than any in this City. Can she be prosecuted for uttering a falsehood, or a slander upon pious men?'"

"Impudent baggage!" said the kotwal's wife, "still trying your low tricks! But this time you are destined to fail. I know, full well, the Sheikh will deliver honest judgement. He is incapable of error. He can never fall for your low wiles. I have no fear for him on that score. I will do as you ask."

Our qasbah had two ornaments. We lost both at the same moment. The moment our Sheikh heard his love was returned.

Since that fatal day when two funeral processions set out from our qasbah- one solemn and grand for the Sheikh, one furtive and mean for the courtesan- our mourning has been continuous.

This tragedy should be set right. But, how is it to be done? Where now are there hearts as of the old days?

Science must come to the rescue for it too has two ornaments- viz. Socialist Egalitarianism and Secular Rationality.

Let the Central Planning authority locate the proposed Union Carbide factory here and our qasbah of Bhopal will once again flourish.

(extracted and abridged, with the permission of Chief Conservator, National Archives, from a petition to, then President of India, Dr. Zakir Hussain. There is a faded annotation in red ink which reads-

نفـــس کی از شیب کـو آزادوں ہے ہوتــا ںینــ غم

ہم خانہ مــاتم شمع روشن ںیہ کـــرتے سے بـرق

(Since Sorrow can tax the free no more than one breath
Lightning's the lone candle we now light for a death!)

Thinking about the strange manner in which the courtesan's insults united her to her beloved- and reflecting, more generally, on the topic of the '*hangamah-e-khuda*'- the whole commotion about God and Morality and, therefore, 'Freedom' and 'Equality' and so on- I feel increasingly uneasy in my mind.

Especially as there is another couplet in that same ghazal of Ghalib's.

ںینہ یدائئیپ گامــہن جہاں کی باوجودِ

ہم پروانـــہ دلِ شبستانِ چراغانِ ںیہ

(Ours too is a world- but one barren to its own passion, tumult & wrath
& we the nuptial taper of the heart's bed chamber of its moth!)

Bhajan Sing!

The Seth had ingratiated himself with the Yuv Raja, by settling his brothel bills, when the latter was a student in Calcutta. Later, after his Uncle, the Maharaja, unexpectedly died and the young reprobate came to the throne, the Seth moved to our State.

Within a decade he had ruined all the merchants of the district, the Scottish Engineer alone- who held the Water & Power contract- being immune to his machinations.

But, the day Mountbatten became Viceroy, the Scotsman called the Seth to him and told him to name his best price. Otherwise, he would sell out to a Marwari concern, Bombay side.

The Sethji scuttled hither and thither, consulting Congressmen and Courtesans, Astrologers and Black Magicians, but neither slander nor intrigue nor bribed witnesses nor venal agitators could prevail against the Scotsman and his Bombay side, Marwari, connection.

For the first time in his life, the Seth had to pay a fair price for the assets the Scotsman was leaving behind.

On parting from the Seth, the Scotsman looked troubled. There was one thing on his conscience. It was Bhajan Singh- his driver and mechanic. He had planned to take Bhajan Singh with him, to East Africa, where he was relocating.

But without Bhajan Singh's skills, not the car merely but much of the Electrical and Water Pump machinery would soon be useless.

In any case, Bhajan Singh had put down roots in the State. He would go with the Scotsman, whose salt he had eaten, but what he really wanted was to remain behind in his accustomed place and occupation.

The Seth agreed to keep on Bhajan Singh as his driver.

However, within a few short days, the following interchange occurred between them-

Seth- (from the back seat) 'Bhajan Singh, Bhajan Singh- Bhajan sing!

Bhajan Singh- (driving the car) Jo hukum! Woh jo hum mein tum mein qaraar tha..."

Seth- That is Ghazal not Bhajan. If your name was Ghazal Singh then it is all right for you to sing Ghazal. However since name is Bhajan Singh kindly sing Bhajan only.

Bhajan Singh- Sorry, Sethji, I only know Ghazal.

The Seth dismissed him and hired a good Bhajan Singer. Unfortunately he was a bad driver and got involved in a traffic accident in which the Seth was badly injured. Worse, his patron, the Maharaja, was killed. Suddenly, the Seth found himself bankrupt and awaiting trial in prison.

Meanwhile the true culprit- viz. Bhajan Singh- had slyly fucked off to East Africa where in the course of time, he became a millionaire.

In upholding our indigenous Gandhian-Socialist tradition of fighting Fuedalistic-neo-Comprador-Capitalism-with-Tecnnocratic-face, of which no more saintly luminary existed than our late Chief Minister, we should never forget or forgive the perfidious treachery of Bhajan Singh who almost brought that great soul to ruin.

This is true meaning of Democracy. Mind it!

MATAJI'S SHAKTI

"Yatra naryastu Pujyante, tatra ramayante Devata
Yatra Naryasthu na pujyante, tatra sarva kriya vifalah."

Pundit Sharma masticated the Sanskrit *shloka* with evident pleasure. Then he turned to me.

"Translate!" he said brusquely.

"Where woman is worshipped," I quavered, "There the Gods delight. Where Woman is not worshipped, there good deeds are without fruit!"

"*Haaaaanh!*" - the Pundit's head wobbled on its pneumatic cushioning of chins- "See what Scripture is saying? You should worship Woman. And Woman is Mother. "Ten times more worthy of worship than the Father is the Guru, but a thousand times more worthy than the Guru is the Mother!""

Again his head wobbled.

"In truth, Panditji," I said humbly, "It is only since I returned to India that I have come understand Mataji's *Shakti*- Mother's Power."

"No!"

The Pundit's shout shook me. His face had puckered and turned puce. His eyes rolled horribly at the bottom of frighteningly deep furrows. "No! Nonononononononono! No!"

"What I said wrong?" I asked tearfully.

"You have said that you **understand**." Panditji said, "That is a terrible blasphemy against the Mother! Who can understand what is beyond all understanding? Could even the great Adi Sankara? To unriddle the riddle of the Vedas was child's play to him. While yet a child he taught the cows to recite the Vedas! But the riddle of the Mother- in the face of *that* he remained as but a babe and suckling!"

I peeped up at the Pundit through dewy lashes.

"Adi Sankara drank up the ocean of knowledge as easily as one sips water from the palm of one's hand. The essence of that knowledge is found in the elegant syllogisms of the *"Vivekachauramani"*- the crest jewel of Metaphysical discrimination. But, of the riddle of the Mother, what could Sankara rhyme? *"Saundaryalahari"*- the beautiful waves of the Cosmic Ocean- what is that work but a mere onomatopoeic invocation of the breakers of Her breaking waters? You, who are named Vivek, had better call yourself Viviktha or Vikshepa- desolate or mad- so far have you strayed from the one path of true knowledge!"

"But Punditji... !"

"No! The Pundit overbore my protests, "Nononononono! No! Neglecting to worship your own Mother as a God- God having granted you so God-like a mother- what fruit can you hope for who have sown but wild oats?"

---------------II-------------------

"Don't tell any one about your marriage."

Her far away eyes were busy with the blue shadows of the *champa* flowers.

"But *Amma*!"

She looked up from the vase.

"Is it really too much to ask?" she said in a low, bitter, voice.

I was silent.

"That is, if you still feel you owe us anything. That is, if the West has not corrupted you completely."

"I never meant to hurt you!"

"You have no idea, have you?" my mother continued as if I hadn't spoken. "You really have no idea of what you have done."

"What have I done?"

"Don't you dare take that tone with me!

"No, go ahead! Swear at me! Beat me! It's my fate!"- her brief flare up of rage was made more dreadful by its so quickly giving way to this defeated monotone.

"When you were but a child you stood by me. Do you remember how you tried to take the cricket bat out of your father's hand in Kirkuk? He broke your collar bone. You remained silent then. You told nobody at the Hospital. If, at five years old, you could have been so mindful of the family honour, why not now when you are twenty one and come of age?"

I was silent. This was precisely the turn I had feared the conversation would take.

"But, it is a foolish question." she continued, looking down with disgust at her woman's body, seeing only the shame it had imposed, "Then you were a child. Now you are a man. You no longer need the fiction of "family honour" to shelter behind. You can take what you want from the world without making any apology. It is the women of the house who will have to pay the price. It is we who will have to lower our gaze in the temple. And, if anything happens to us in the market-place- if we are insulted in the market-place- who will speak up for us? The son of the house has given himself up to pleasure- imported whiskey and an imported wife- why should the *mohallah-wallahs* speak up for us? If the men of the big house are having their fun why shouldn't the *goondas* of the bazaar have their fun too? They don't have the opportunity to get themselves imported wives. At least, they can despoil the virtue of some chaste Brahmin girls. You have given up your caste by marrying this *Mleccha*. But you are a man. No one dares insult you to your face. But, what about your sister and mother, who have also lost caste? What is to prevent their being raped like any other untouchable woman?"

"Mummy, I hate it when you talk like this."

"Of course!" she said scornfully, "You hate your old mother! I don't talk about parties and fashion and sex- yes sex!- like your European wife. I can talk only about my fears- what hope have I ever been allowed, but hope for my son?- and now that hope, too, has been snatched away, what is there left but fear?- fear for an unmarried daughter, fear for the honour of this house- this house in which I have known nothing but blows and insults- but, this house which I am also obliged to protect- even at the expense of losing what little influence I have left with my son- my son!- do you still admit that title or have you got yourself a European mother along with your European wife?"

I stirred uneasily, remembering my mother-in-law's hospitality. My mother noticed my discomfiture.

"Go!" she cried, "Go to your European wife, your European mother- why are you still harassing us? All of our money, we have already spent on your education- that Western education which has taught you only to despise us- so why have you come back? Is it to take the last of my jewellery- even my *Mangal-sutram*- is it for this that you have returned? Take it and be gone!"

My mother had placed her finger unerringly on my weak spot. I had returned to India at the urging of my wife who was finishing her education in England. In the meanwhile, I was penniless and a burden on my parents.

"No wait!" my mother cried, " why should I give you my *Mangal-sutram*? have I not a daughter- an unmarried daughter, who is now fated to remain unmarried for ever, because her sex-crazed brother has gone and married a vile seductress? Do I owe my daughter nothing? What does she know of the wicked wiles of the West with which to pick up a husband? Is she to have no trousseau at all- not even her own mother's *Mangal sutram?*

"All her life, she has gone without. Why? So that her brother could have the best of everything- this brother she adores- this brother whom she still believes will take care of her- you should hear our quarrels- we fight like cat and dog because she won't hear a word said against you-poor child!- I have had to open her eyes. She can't go on living in a fool's paradise for ever!"

"Mother, aren't you over re-acting?"

She began to weep.

And then, as if to twist the dagger of guilt, Kamala Aunty walked through the door.

---------------III------------

Kamala had been a class-mate of my mother's at College. Though not directly related, both belonged to the same sub-caste. Whereas, my mother married a diplomat and spent most of the intervening years abroad, Kamala, who married an Income Tax officer, could console herself that she had never lost caste by crossing the boundaries of *Jambudvipa*- the golden Isle that is India. All the worthier, then, her offerings to Mataji- the god-woman who was all the rage in Delhi that season.

Like my mother, Kamala, too, had but one son. He was called Laxman. My feelings of guilt at seeing her arose out of the fact that I had already confided the secret of my marriage to Laxman. That had been during the first week off my stay with my parents when I hadn't realised my marriage was supposed to be a secret. Indeed, the letters I'd received, while in Europe, promised a grand Wedding reception in Delhi and a Honeymoon in Kashmir- inducements which, predictably, failed to materialise once my parents realised I'd burned my bridges Visa wise.

As things were, in the immediate aftermath of my return, I could not but be sensible of the steep fall in temperature every time I mentioned my wife. Clearly, I was committing a terrible faux pas. Yet, by the same token, it seemed impossible, in those first few days of my sojourn in India, to impute anything so definite as a desire to break up my marriage to these vague and gracious people- my parents. Indeed, I began to doubt my sanity. Perhaps, I wasn't really married. Perhaps, I had imagined it all.

It was at this juncture that Laxman showed up.

"Talk to Laxman," my mother admonished me, introducing us, "Such a good boy. Real Brahmin. Learn from him, if not how to succour then at least how not to smash the agued hearts of your aging parents!"

Laxman regarded me bleakly.

I quailed beneath the extreme magnification of his bespectacled eyes. My mother had not lied, in truth, he was god-like. If Shiva had caught Ganga's raging torrent up in is hair, Laxman had gone one better. The river he held prisoner in his locks was pure Brent crude. Nor did his resemblance to the Gods of orthodox Hindu iconography end there. His eyes recalled Airavata-Shiva's sacred elephant. His voice was as that of Hamsa- Brahma's sacred swan. His belly was as of Ganesh, his stature that of Vamana- how could I, mere mortal that I was, God having granted me so god-like a confessor, hold back from confessing everything to Laxman?

"India is shit," he said, interrupting me abruptly. "You must be mad, returning here."

Since all this happened a good ten years before Manmohan Singh's liberalization too effect, it was the latter part of his statement that overbore any protests I might otherwise have made.

Laxman regarded me with an austerely Brahminical gaze.

"Complete shit, India is," Laxman continued in his ex-cathedra style, "Returning here mad you are."

My mother entered my room with a plate of samosas.

"Listen to Laxman," she said again, "Such a good boy. Real Indian."

Laxman turned his god-like face upon my mother in order to express a preference for patties rather than these incorrigibly Indian samosas.

"Shit (munch, swallow) India is." said Laxman, who could never be accused of conversational uninventiveness, "Madness (munch, swallow) your returning why?"

And so, goaded beyond all endurance, I blurted it all out. How my wife wanted to live with me in India. Participate in the Nation building process as the wife of a district officer. Help conserve the folk traditions while continuing to disseminate Sanskrit High Culture.

"Rubbish!" said Laxman, "Get out while you can. You *can*, can't you?"

"Of course!" I said, lying through my teeth. Somehow, it had never occurred to me that returning to India would mean having to justify myself to the likes of Laxman. I suppose, it was just another example of the deracination, the lamentable lapse from Brahminism, that the stigma of my extra-Indian birth and upbringing carried in its train.

As things were, I had committed a great crime. A crime against my parents. Yet another crime. I had told Laxman about my marriage. And, I dared not confess this to my mother. Perhaps, by Mataji's *Shakti*, my crime would remain undiscovered. But what can Mataji's *Shakti*, itself, avail when Nemesis is in a hurry to squeeze you in between appointments at the Home Ministry and the Planning Commission? As now happened. There was a knock on the front door and, next moment, Kamala Aunty walked in carrying a tray of *kum-kum* and other consecrated offerings. She had just returned from Mataji's *darshan* and had stopped off on her way home out of a sense of religious obligation to her back-sliding elder sister.

"Kamalaaaaaa!" my mother screamed out, glimpsing her face, "Sweet younger sister, why do you torture me, why do you taunt me, waving in front of my face these sacred *agarbathis* blessed by the divine hand of Mataji Herself? Know you not that we are *acharabrashta*- fallen ones, outcastes? I who harboured such hopes of one day having a daughter-in-law of my own who would sweetly offer me *kum-kum*- that I should have lived to see such a day! A day when the issue of my own unspotted womb has saddled me with a leprous prostitute of a daughter-in-law! Not even an honest Hindu untouchable, but a godless European whore! Oh God, what were my sins in former lives that I should give birth to this sex-maniac, this drug addict, this pimp, this child molester, this syphilitic onanist- this wretched boy here! What calamity has come over me and mine! Only you, Kamala, sweet younger sister, can counsel me in my despair!"

Kamala cast an envenomed glance at me.

"Vasantha!" she admonished my mother, "Get a grip on yourself! Go and wash away these hysterical tears. You have laughed at me in the past, but not for nothing have I been a devotee of Mataji all these long months. Go, I say to you, go! Let nothing untoward be said in the presence of the sacred *kum-kum* which Mataji has blessed with her own sweet hands!"

Obedient to this apostolic decree, my mother quit the room in deep shame and anguish of heart. I was left to bear the brunt alone.

"See here, Vivek," Kamala said to me sternly, "I have always regarded Vasantha as my elder sister. Every time your parents have returned from a foreign posting, have I not come to your house? Even if it meant a journey of a thousand miles- for, you know, only recently has your Uncle's incorruptibility been rewarded with a posting to Delhi- no matter what the discomfort, no matter what the inconvenience, have I not always, made the trip?

"What is more, if your mother has said that the Heavy Luggage has not yet arrived- an excuse she has given me many times- have I not always been careful to return and see her when all the Heavy Luggage is unpacked? God only knows how many sacrifices I have made just to do this. Yet, how does your mother treat me? She acts all high and mighty! If I ask her anything regarding the model number of the refrigerator, or the provenance of the curtain fabrics- she returns off hand answers. You don't know how much time and money it has cost us- how many trips your Uncle has had to make to Hong Kong, Dubai and Kathmandu- just to ensure that we were getting a newer model, a better brand. I ask you, is this any way to treat a younger sister? But, one thing I will tell you Vivek. You will laugh at me, You will scorn me, but one thing you must know. All these weeks I have never lost faith in Mataji. All these months I have been sedulous in my devotion to that Goddess in human form.

"But, Vivek, even I lost faith! Yes, even I wavered! When Laxman came weeping to me , revealing that Vasantha had gone and got an imported daughter-in-law, I despaired! Yes, I despaired! No, don't stop me from saying it, I turned my face to the wall, Vivek!- such was my agony, such the wound in my heart!

"Shall I tell you something, Vivek? Let me tell you something. You know who it was who came and dried my tears? You know who it was who came to me and restored my faith in Mataji? It was your own Uncle! Yes, that god-like man saw the wife of his bosom given over to such black despair and what did he do? What, I ask you, did he do?

"He ordered coffee.

"Bringing him his coffee, could I fail to lay bare the secret of my sorrow to him? Could I fail to bewail the fate of my poor Laxman doomed to marrying a black faced *Desi?*

"And how did your Uncle react? What did he say? How can I explain to you the joy in my heart when he soothed all my fears with just one sentence?

"Is Mataji dead that you need fear a *Desi* daughter-in-law?"

"Just that one sentence. That was all he needed to say. Immediately such a surge of devotion, such a fountain of faith, overwhelmed my heart- I was struck dumb, Vivek, dumb! Weak woman that I am, & frail faith'd and faltering though my footsteps to the Lord, still, Vivek, still, I was able to recognise that God speaks through the voice of the husband of the *pativrata*!

"Just at that second, Laxman came running out of his bed-room.

"I am going to swallow dettol and kill myself!" he carolled out to us in his sweet boyish way, "You are all conspiring to marry me off to a black ogress of an Indian woman! All right, if that is my unalterable destiny, then go ahead, get it over with, but know that it will be to my corpse that you shackle the great greasy *Desi* you are set on having as your daughter-in-law! *Hai!* Woe is me! What can even Mataji's *Shakti* avail against the dark humours I absorbed in your witch's womb? "

   "That was enough for your Uncle. Immediately he picked up the telephone receiver and dialled the number of Mataji's Ashram.

   "Put me through to God," he said brusquely- you know, he prides himself on speaking only pure English- "*Arré, badava-rascal*, this is Income Tax Commissioner speaking- you, bloody, put God on the line, *fut-a-fut*, otherwise I will bloody raid your premises tonight itself!

   "*Hanh,* God?! Everything *teek-tak*? Good. Tax Commissioner speaking. *Hanh*, do one thing, my boy wants *phoren* wife- *pucca* virgin, all right? Blonde? Ya, blonde, better I am thinking- beautiful, good family, educated and no hippie nonsense, get me? Good English speaking, OK? And make sure is vegetarian. I see- all your devotees are vegetarian. Well, I knew I could rely. OK, nice talking. God bless, God."

---------------------IV------------------

"The water nymph Liriope," Father Thomas said, "The water nymph Liriope, having given birth to a son, goes, like any *desi Amma*, to consult a soothsayer. It is the blind seer- Eliot's 'old man with wrinkled dugs'- anomalous, androgynous, Tiresias.

His prediction? A long life and a happy one, ***provided*** the child, himself, never know. How curiously un-Greek! How chillingly modern! But, ask the name of the child."

"I suppose I ought to know." I mumbled shame faced.

"Narcissus!"

Father Thomas regarded me tolerantly. After all, I now had a London degree. He would have slapped me for my ignorance had I had still been in his Eng Lit class at St. Erigena's.

"Narcissus!" Father Thomas repeated, his Malyalee accent reasserting itself as his confidence returned.

"How Freud misunderstood the Greeks! To say Oedipus when you mean Orestes is a mere slip of the tongue, but to say Oedipus when you mean Narcissus is more than Parapraxis- it is Irony as Theodicy, nothing less! Our own *desi* poet, John Mahalingam Thomas, rustic though he be, untutored though he remains, yet 'warbling his wood-notes wild' in his Cochin backwater, has, surely, hit nearer the mark-

> *"As Venus rose from the brine, so Liriope's son from the Lake*
> *To break a water sprite, God bade her waters break*
> *"Long life!" the oracles opine, "if he, himself, never know!"*
> *All eyes yearn the sight, slain by what they show."*

"Wilde," I said, remembering that Oscar Wilde died a Catholic, "Wilde has the pine shadowed pool, pine not for Narcissus but that vanished reflection of its own limpidity."

"Blue Heaven to Mother's eye is"
With donnish quaver, Father Thomas quoted Coleridge
"Blue Heaven to Mother's eye is

"Infant's eye- reciprocal bliss!"

For such, indeed, is the Kingdom of Heaven

A pious and honest merchant fell asleep one night beside his beloved wife only to abruptly awaken in the middle of a vast desert. He climbed the nearest sand dune but, from that vantage point, could spy nothing but further dunes vanishing into the distance. Unable to tell the proper direction for prayer, and having no other business on which to profitably employ himself, the merchant began making his prostrations in a methodical manner moving in a clockwise direction from an arbitrary starting point on the compass.

Suddenly, straightening up from *salat*, the merchant saw a vast caravenserai directly before him. Could this be a miracle from God? Or was it a delusive mirage? Having nothing to lose, the merchant ran towards it. As he approached, the great gates of the caravanserai slowly opened and a splendid *khidmatgar* of more than mortal stature issued forth to welcome him.

"Are you a djinn?" the merchant asked.

"A djinn but of the Believer," the khidmatgar replied, "and of the Believers, amongst those opposed to hypocrisy but enjoined to always speak the Truth"

The Merchant was overjoyed to hear this.

"Could you provide me food and drink- and that too of the sort which is lawful?"

"I can provide anything for which you can pay in coin, true and not counterfeit."

"But I have no money with me!"

"It is a property of the caravanserai that whosoever is of the Believers, let him put his hand to his cummerbund and he will find there sufficient coin to pay for whatever is necessary to his survival."

The Merchant made a judicious choice of food and beverages of a quality and quantity sufficient for the maintenance of health but not the stimulation of appetite, or after the usages of profligacy. Having satisfied his nutritional needs, the merchant put his hand to his cummerbund and found there the exact sum required to discharge the full price of his meal. Pocketing the coins, the djinn threw the merchant down upon his belly and anally raped him in a manner brutal and disobliging.

"Wherefore this outrage?" wailed the Merchant greatly discomfited.

"Next time, buddy" the djinn, through clenched teeth, replied. "maybe you'll remember to tip!"

Sooth speaketh Iqbal- that learned *Alim*- if an individual says 'an'al haq' punishment is better. If a nation speaks thus- it is not illicit.'

For such, indeed, is the Kingdom of Heaven not that other thing I mentioned in my last parable.

Beyond bloggingly Bad- Verse

A poet explains his vocation

It doesn't cheer you when you are sad
Or put money in your purse
But, if your prose is beyond Bloggingly bad
There's pride in doing Verse

Love is the crutch of Tamburlaine

کا ثنــا صـــفت مصدر ممکن نـم ہو کا واجب
کا خدا ہے آوے نـام پـر لب یک اس سـے قدرت

If prayer & fasting is to our back a rod
Must Nature in ecstasy cry out 'God!'?
Upon Men, Mercy, Mir, Mystic, explains
Love, tho' a crutch- is Tamburlaine's

Childish our cult of Gandhi, Ghalib and the Geeta

Childish our cult of Gandhi, Ghalib and the Geeta
Our Ardency a Surpanakha they still see is Seeta
Would my garbage & I were thus understood
Love is the Vyasa of all works that are good

Zhdanov & Aurangazeb

So Armenian clay enrich Kremlin earth
Zdhnanov seconds Sarmad's birth
& a Gayane ballet to Aurangzeb
The Holy Quran in Abu Ghraib

Anti-Auerbach

Slaves wait on Suitors who, Zoilist, on a Shroud bare wait
& Ulysses burns heartsick, return'd in beggar's disguise
ad modum Momus, if Helen, Hestial Mammaries fenestrate
Not Eurycleia can, *as scar*, its Adonis recognise

Hadrian at Antinopolis

Anima vagula wherefore hast thou flown?
'To suck the cock of a greater unknown!'
Is Death darker than its *decidendi ratio*?
'I am the Osiris of my own fellatio!'

Queen Olga's anima naturaliter christiana

That our Sainted Queen was humbly born is suggested by two facts
From villagers, who widowed her, mild vengeance she exacts
A hut tax, on each thatch, of a mere three sparrows and a pigeon.
She sets homing ablaze, Souls *Mir* to raze, Soviet Religion

A Zebra Crossing is Christ-the-Tiger's camouflage

A Zebra Crossing is Christ-the-Tiger's camouflage
& Stalled Traffic, Passschendaele's Trench foot persiflage
The bus lane is merely a mental module misapplied

Who thus yet live fain had died.
<u>So young, an already defeated Man</u>
So young, an already defeated Man
Love made tho no Siren sang
A son; mirror, or Caliban
River Ganga's Reaver Gang
<u>Not in Time's tessitura is the Surah al Yaseen</u>
More unmeaning than the Ghazal's use of *tazmin*
& less musical than the muezzin's new Tannoy
Not in Time's tessitura is the Surah al Yaseen
What is Death that you yet so annoy?
<u>Outsourced, alas, is Ind, the Nysiads abode</u>
Outsourced, alas!, is Ind, the Nysiads' abode
Now, who wrought God write only code
& to Philomel, its thorn, if Winter yet displays
All pipe forlorn in growth of riper days.
<u>Dvorak's 'Song to the Moon'.</u>
My Eyes set famished Skies to your forehead's moon
& you, *chanson de l'adieu* to my every tune
What betides your yet loosening hair?
Ptolemy of Tides- I'm unaware.
<u>I am the breaker of your Babri, Godse to Thy Ram</u>
Gandhi, Ghalib & the Geeta, we are their Mahmuds until
A Somnath, our stone heart, Ayaz loot at Thy Will
I am the berserker of your Babri, Godse to Thy Ram
Befriend me, or end me- Say, brother, where's the harm?

Krishna is ink's colour, thus *Kufr* to *Khalil's* Quran
Thy face, Friendship's page, but *I* its Bilal *Azan*
Gandhi or Ghalib- Sahir- our guilt yet is clear
Gita we hear distant tho' all *Sukhan* is but here.
<u>The Vande Mataram of a new Socially Conscious Hindutva</u>
Though Religion, our Father, is as <u>Beatrice Cenci's</u>
& our Motherland, alas, is e'er in menses
Yet in the hovels of our hungry is beauty rare
& more than Heroin chic, passing fair.
<u>Consider the Staggering Drunkard</u>

'The disorders we see from afar are as sunspots and comets. We don't know what uses they supply nor the laws by which their purpose is fulfilled. Time was when the planets were considered to be wandering stars; now their motion is found to be regular. Perhaps the same is true of comets; posterity will know.'
Liebniz.

Consider the Staggering Drunkard, Via Dolorosing down your street

Could a Liebniz tax wits to Halley's Comet serenade as sweet?
'Peace had a Prince, Sun King, incarnadine the Nile!'
Dutch drunk, tho' I vomit, only Philosophy is vile.

What is Justice that we should desire its reign?

What is Justice that we should desire its reign?
& topple Tyrants so Terror, blind Power, attain
& what's Fair so deflower, fouler Rape might fail
Och! A but Gyges' ring is Rawls's veil

Essence of the Gita.

Feel no fury at the foe you slay
All is but as a Scene in a Play
To refuse to Act, is the only Sin
Till you're sacked, just phone it in

Neitzche's filioque

What wanders solely on treacherous terrain?
& what mystic heights do I thereby attain?
What moves in me, myself to write?
Spirit for aye where the Word is Spite.

My late Mother

Memory's mysteries so maim my mastery of a mammary tongue
& suddenly old, now, in dementia, You & Dad are young
My tears rebuked by Nancy Drew & Fancy Boys Hardy
No Mum is *late*, but by Thy Mischief Tardy

If the Sky were an orgy of Smurfs

She'd scrape her knee, my daughter
For the Rain is a Tree of Water
Owned were I by a child's eye
Or a Smurf orgy *Thy* Sky.

An ode upon Dr. Oddie

A triolet yet is Hope's Host of Mind Sold & Body
(Tho' to Chester-Bellocs defend is dog-bollocks defiant!)
For so seeming a quatrain, my ode on Dr.Oddie
No Barrister proves brilliant but a Bedlam His Client.

Nishadh & Upa-nishadh

For aye, Nala flees Night's bedroom eyes
& Damayanti's day, Dawn martyred dies
Seeing us heartwhole & un-Nishadh
Our Soul merely Upanishadh

Kept awake by drunks and car alarms and crying foxes

Kept awake by drunks and car alarms and crying foxes
I can't unpack my dreams' stacked cardboard boxes
Tho', in *baul* song, fierce rain and bull frog banquets
Yet are the cunning of Radha's tell-tale anklets

Bar in a bra- an idea for Dragon's den.

A bar in a bra is my life long pitch to Dragon's den
Else, Al Hallaj to all Summer's Saharan 'when'
Suited, booted, velvet weskit vested
I dam my mother, double breasted!

Beckett's Buggered Word & Geulincx Gita

quod nescis quo modo fiat, non facis--

(if you do not know *how* a thing is done, then you do not do it)

Quod nescis, *Lecteur*, push thou the Just King's father, Pandu, thus
& Beckett, thy Louvre's Christ, neath Clapham's omnibus.

"I know not the way of a man with a maid
*"But, having a son, **am** obeyed."*

Borges' labyrinth

Borges, the Pauline pathos of thy one dimensional labyrinth
Is as that *hyle* Christ, Daedalus carved in Corinth
Monstrous or monstrance, beyond all remonstrance
Lie on Mirrors must, or Cantor dust.

Princeton ke pirzadon se

That, Allah!, thy Jury thee indict
Allot me a peerless *Pir*
So an Afghan poppy, Paradise, ignite
My I thy *voir dire*

Kun faya fina

For, 'Be!' thy for aye command, is to be but moth or bee
Love, God, let Love remand; thy garden's wrath to me
Tho' pollinating fire or immolation in the rose
Still beats AppleCare I suppose

Quid mihi et tibi est, mulier?

Granted, I take you for granted- Else, Dear, God were a Guest too dear
& that to yeast in but yearning's banquet, as Host, my task, Heavenly, True
But Free Counselling at the Baptist Centre? *Agapeton,* I'm aghast at the very Idea
E'en a righteous pew renter, they'd rectally enter, ere set lip to my hip flask of You.

Letting Dante read Petronius

Letting Dante read Petronius, e'en old Ez realized
Every Canto's contango is but Belief backwardized
As a virus made the Dutch tulip precious
The Wireless, Beauty more infectious.

Parrhesia, De Profundis

Son, Truth to Power, sure, 'tis 'cheap talk' to speak
Save Wealth's cock cram thy tongue in cheek
Or up thy arse, fruit, the forbidden tree
To evolve 'costly signals' or Poetry.

Mystic Union and the price of onions.

' The poet says- his tears make him thirsty for onion.'
'Onion?'
'Onion with the Divine. That is true wine of the Saqi'

For a mere mirror holding habit turns Saqi e'en thy Christ-white hand
Yet must Wine's bloodthirst parch khaki- being so blindly poured
Now the dearness of the onion is Democracy's firebrand
How tether Mystic Union Tears' Mongol horde?
Slash & burn
As sans Ivy an Oak
For e'en this old soak
Now that Redhead's gone
Every forest's a lawn.
Genesis as Palingenesia
For Adam gives all things their names
Eve, auctoritas of language games
Asks- 'But, how smart could he be?
'Nary a word yet, to marry me!'
Hug like a bear, kiss like a bird
Tasting tongue of the snake in my but quivering Word
She said- *'you hug like a bear but kiss like a bird!'*
Of the beasts in my bestiary, old Adam most dumb
Drowning my penis, Depths, peerless, to plumb
Al Khidr's khamriyat
That thy Red the Saqi to please me sips
Is not yet the rouge that dyes her lips
Death, thou in peace I thus dismiss
With my arse-hole's Gallic kiss.
Joseph Campbell- a Sufi perspective
'On his return to Columbia in 1929, Joseph Campbell expressed his desire to pursue the study
of Sanskrit and Modern Art in addition to that of Medieval literature. Lacking faculty approval,
Campbell withdrew from the graduate studies. He was very insistent, in later life, that he be
addressed as *Mr.* Campbell, not *Dr.* Campbell.'
Wisdom is a College from which quittance is a cloak
For, if conferred, that *Khirqa*, Sufis love to joke
Demeans more than one, untasked, demanded
Our Hero, Campbell's, to mask, remanded.
'twixt two trees, Yashoda
Tho' *Eve's* Beauty vengeful take
The Son from His Father
Must, Lord, thy *distance* make
My son yet farther?

Thy ***King's Evil*** is only this, that by <u>supervenience</u>
Scrofula necks with Bliss, to **connect** obedience,
For all but Rahul, thy Prince and Heir
Tho' mobled Queens die ***young and fair.***

Add Maryam to Maya, Sita, as Earth's ***<u>proletarian</u>*** true
'Twixt two trees, Yashoda, yet after-birth is Rue
For, this one thing less, now, Ind's Zero lacks
<u>Zombies</u> fosters, Gita, thy lullaby axe!

Envoi-

Thou Prince of the Air! I can't curse save darn thee
Expel thy unco guid from the House of Gandhi!
<u>Backward induction</u>
Gone the honey and grief the sting
Should a Sheikh Pir sing
The 'To be or not to be'
Of our Hamlet bee.
<u>Delhi in Lonon</u>
In my Delhi boyhood my Mother beat
Me & Delhi on my Fulham street
Beats like her & with her Art
Not with hands but just her Heart.
<u>Acceptation is certain Sinn</u>
For camouflaged by, fond, my thoughts
Leopard! Change thou thy spots.
Acceptation is certain ***Sinn***
Thy Ethiop! I'm bleached within.
<u>Not Love is bought but sweating made</u>
Lest this thought distress the Marwari maid
'Not Love is bought but sweating made'
Bollywood rose from out the Sea
To hear Ruskin hymn Dharavi.
<u>More hymns to Hitler</u>
'neath Eiffel, Herr Hitler, in abashed, matronly, pose
As Eiger's steeple bell, fell Venusberg o'erthrows
& Heine's Tannhauser- ah! there's the rub
Revenge, we, Wagner on the Jockey Club

Wagner's attempt to conquer Paris came a cropper when the Jockey Club- of which, perhaps, Swann was already a member- became incensed against him and, by their hooliganism, forced him to withdraw his production. One theory regarding the Jockey Club's animus against

'Tannhauser' is based on its members' gentlemanly habit of only arriving at the Opera in time for their ballerina inamoratas' sweating their way through the Second Act disco number before themselves frenziedly rushing backstage to copulate with those still clammy and quivering carcasses. Wagner, unforgivably, had shifted the ballet to the first Act and so, quite correctly, the Jockey Club Cavaliers, more thoroughbred than Wagner's*bildungsburgertum* vision of those at the Landgrave's Court, permitted no virginal Elizabeth to intercede for our Meistersinger but, sans ceremony, sent him packing.

Heinrich Heine's Tannhauser, it appears, marries Jerusalem to Athens, domesticates Venus as the Sabbath, and gets off a splendid dig at Weimar's futility- '*in Heine's poem, Venus is a gemutlich sweetheart whom Tannhauser leaves in a fit of jealousy because she is immortal and has had many lovers and will have many more. But, it turns, out the Pope has no power over Venus and so the minstrel returns to his cute little wife-ikkins who makes him a nice broth and asks after his disillusioning travels. At this point, Heine makes an equation between Venus and the Sabbath-*
"To Frankfort I on Schobbas came,
Where dumplings were my food.
They have the best religion there:
Goose-giblets, too, are good.

before getting off a typical piece of satire-

"In Weimar, the widowed muse's seat,
Midst general grief I arrive.
The people are crying 'Goethe's dead,
And Eckermann's still alive!'"[A]

Reminder- call Dad
Mine liked the occasional Black Label, hers any Irish potcheen
Jack picked the Carafe on the table, Jenny, many Platters clean
Google's morning gimmick- 'Reminder- call Dad!'
& this drunk, that bulimic- not rueful, now, *Sad.*
Hail to thee, Democracy!- a poem on the Arab Spring.
Hail to thee, Democracy! thou Egyptian Helen restored!
& blessed be our T.V, of besieged Trojans bored
Pour, Saqi, pour, Liberty's wine and sing
As Siren, Sphinx, or Sahara drunk on our Arab Spring.
All Beauty burns with one grim, guttering, plume.
All Beauty burns with one grim, guttering, plume
& Being yearns in Becoming's uttering gloom
& Day is fain & vain Darkness bridal
My cock to suck when young and idle
The lost Hylas
Scarce was I weaned from Business School

When lost to the Naiads of the Typing Pool
Weep for me, heroes of the Argo's crew!
Weep for Hylas who was once as you.

Their Gorgon hair and Harpy nails
& fish for eyes & skin-like scales
Caused all they tease, save me, to fear them.
My Hercules, then, was Coase's Theorem

'No mine and thine doth Beauty know
'But as Helen breeds in Allan Poe!'
Thus Chicago- my Greece and Rome
Till Nereid airs wrecked my home

Envoi-

Prince! If two Schools you rule, one Salt, one Freshwater
To a Salmacis your son, your Salamis a daughter
Urdu and English- an allegorical quatrain
Mourning a green Urdu soul under grey English skies
Not monsoonal windows, her memorious wet eyes
Merely evidence rising damp so the Council rehouse
My mothless lamp and her work-shy spouse.
Heidegger, his Heraclitus, in Der Speigel
Colliding with a maiden small, yet street legal
Like Heidegger, his Heraclitus, in Der Speigel
I see what motility must to that Black Sun's ovum
Her eye's blason blue a Speculum Novum.
To amuse the idle did our idols refuse
To amuse the idle did our idols refuse
Or their currency but defray in use
Work wot is a ghastly expense
Loss naught is if not this Sense
One turning turns to much green
One turning turns to much green
Ours such that words mean
That World hearkens
Our Word darkens
Life is what repeats itself.
Now that my heart aperiodically beats itself
I see, Life is what ergodically repeats itself
Coz Death won't
Love don't.
Chanelling Shelley- 2011
Sucking my cock, turn giraffe to porpoise

Till on thy face I come like a tortoise
Anally raped, pucker other cheeks
Pride's portion swallow to inherit the meek's

<u>But for you, these lands were rich</u>
But for you, these lands were rich.
Rabid Dogs is God your bitch?
You bark in the Manger
Is Religion in danger?
Go die in a ditch.

<u>God is Music's Middle Class.</u>
Pluck taut strings, you strangle tyrants
Modulate your timbre, or kill giants
For God is Music's middle class
Shadows too have exams to pass.

<u>Hitler's sole poem- an Indglish translation</u>
'In July 1917 we set foot for the second time on what we regarded as sacred soil. Were not our best comrades at rest here?- some of them little more than boys--the soldiers who had rushed into death for their country's sake, their eyes glowing with enthusiastic love.'

Wagner's Valkyrie wing brushes
The country-boy who rushes
Jewmerica's machine gun nest
For his Courage, Love fuels
His eyes blaze like jewels
A German heart to attest

Tho' his death throes are cruel
Eyes scorched by eyes' jewel
A weeping Valkyrie flies alone
Let his *Mutti* take him home.

<u>The Trojan War as an allegory of mystic Love.</u>
Conscripts to what her Creed demands, for War is a glorious game
Unflinching we, as Love commands, at our own hearts take aim
Which, beating but in Beauty's breast, our Achillean Arts defame
Till our pitiless necrophilias attest Penthesilea's nuptial claim

<u>Samadhi and barzakh</u>
Fearing a critic, curt, might curb my inspiration
(Force-fed shite, he'd counsel constipation)
What, grave, I write as grave dirt must lie
On my samadhi trite & barzakh I.

<u>My getting drunk tonight I thus excuse</u>
"Thy babe, unweaned, did it die today?!"
No. Nor its Memory's milk will dry for aye

For, if the Saqi drinks, she draws ireful abuse
My drunken tonight, in advance, excuse.

<u>more marvels of mystic poesy</u>

My spirit, amongst books, I squandered so
Too late, my knock, upon her brothel door
& for that Salome's veils *the Word* baptize
Death drowns in my Jordan eyes.

<u>Since Structure not Language can</u>

Since Structure not Language can, nor its Stems to rose suppose
For paws muddy & couch, Lacan, smacked's a doggy nose
Or nuzzles forth my muzzle to but puzzle at her ear
She'd shoo me away, being drear & near to tear

E'er to growling and prowling & bitter yelping too prone
Silent I now sit as she texts him on her phone
Summer's scents still invite to its dappled delights explore
Till, diffident, a new knock on her old Daddy's door.

<u>To hymn her whom to husband Love</u>

To hymn her whom, to husband Love, I mend my lyric lame
Fret metal yet, Hephaestus, thy helpmeet, to but tame!
Cage none can Beauty, no, nor, high wrought, Art exult
With Ares, nay, say Eris! Aphrodite's caught in rut!

Night taught her Civic daughter, Hesiods strive for a hand
Cold to hold the krater or whose wooes *to understand*
Empedoclean traitor! to wive words what you paid
Derides Confucian brides- a blemish on white jade!

Envoi-

Kumara- *Ki koun hai Raam aur koun hai bandha*
Who torture will the *Uttara kanda*?
Can Canetti's ant-hill, Valmik erupt?
Or Words' General Will, Love abrupt?

<u>Tat tvam asi</u>

Gods are in the moment and must madden
As doth Sodomy, shit tipped, but sadden
Immortality musing on Morality's twat
Philosophy so fucked, *that* it shat.

<u>Arabia felix</u>

Where now is that Dark, Backward and Abysm of Clime?
Whose Phoenix is the sugar-fed Parrot of Time
For Love spoke The **Word,** Ataraxia attacks
Smoke, thou memory bird of melted wax

A Tavern grue.

Life is a Tavern, grue, in whose toilet, new, no poet, true, defecates
(Like the bloating Boer at the banquet who, gloating, waits
Till, at leisure, his own fields, he might entreasure with a dump)
Tho' Art's light freehold lunch, its own Agents gazump

Heaven's hermeneutics

Blue
Nothing new.
Who?
You too

& this the hermeneutics
of heaven
Mirror maieutics
six directions

Seven.

More mystic marvels of poesy

As a flower to the bee
or Existence to His 'Be!"
The mirror opens its sex
Only to its ex

Thy frigidity so fires my phallus
Ashes art thy gash's palace
Gnosis, God! cry me a river
Fucked 'tis to fuck a mirror

Stanzas on a senile passion

Ever to know you was to love you but now to love you is to know
Tears are bitter waters till they mingle and the years melt like snow
Two Winters warmed our kisses, may such kisses our Winter warm
That tho' a stricken bird, to this blizzard World, our Love the Heavens storm

Did 28 years really pass between one kiss and the next?
28 years redacted so Love rede its own text...
I still see the same girl, do you see the same boy?
Thou Egyptian Helen to my heart's burning Troy!

Please don't disturb me- I'm working now
Well... thinking of you, anyhow
My work so vital- please don't text me

Just typing your name so has vex't me...

More sublime than the Sanskrit psalms I heard when young
Is my transfixt delight in your Hellenic tongue
Which, in the House of Night, is more than Parmenides Wise
Till our Symposium shifts to twixt your thighs!
Why Qais (Majnoon) is a favourite of poets
At its own smoke, to blink, so as to more fulminously burn
Poetry teaches, not to think, but from its thought to learn
Not Love to serve, nor God to thank
But Majnun's verve to, in Wildernesses, wank.
The Naishadyacharitra- summarised in a couplet
Such glee as Damayanti's not the world has seen
Since Nala cooked that goose, their go between

Tall leaders and the Tropical forest's emergent layer.

Something everybody agrees on is India needs 'tall leaders'.

Why?

I suppose Indian political life, to us pygmies at ground zero, is like a tropical rain forest where trees compete for the light by growing taller and taller with the result that the forest canopy is so far above the dark, dank, and inhospitable forest floor, that it has its own micro-climate and mini ecology. Yet towering above even the forest canopy is the 'emergent layer'- of, stand alone, exceptionally tall trees. Why are they there? What evolutionarily stable strategy do they serve? The answer is that this emergent layer, these exceptionally tall trees, are vital to the forest's ability to renew itself. How so? They create Light, renew Life- but only when they topple over, being rotten at the core, and clear a space on the forest floor.

A pygmy, I can't see the Canopy, let alone the Emergent Layer
Yet, Thou, Tropical, Aorist, Thee address in Topical Prayer
That you too, my Indglish readers, pray for Leaders yet more tall
For all Light and Life, in our Forest, from is but their fall.

By the Gita translated

www.ingramcontent.com/pod-product-compliance
Lightning Source LLC
Chambersburg PA
CBHW080725020726
47503CB00010B/2792